THE WORLD'S CLASSICS

MR. SCARBOROUGH'S FAMILY

ANTHONY TROLLOPE (1815–82), the son of a failing London barrister, was brought up an awkward and un-happy youth amidst debt and privation. His mother maintained the family by writing, but Anthony's own first novel did not appear until 1847, when he had at length established a successful Civil Service career in the Post Office, from which he retired in 1867. After a slow start, he achieved fame, with 47 novels and some 16 other books, and sales sometimes topping 100,000. He was acclaimed an unsurpassed portraitist of the lives of the professional and landed classes, especially in his peren-nially popular *Chronicles of Barsetshire* (1855–67), and his six brilliant Palliser novels (1864–80). His fascinating *Autobiography* (1883) recounts his successes with an enthusiasm which stems from memories of a miserable youth. Throughout the 1870s he developed new styles of fiction, but was losing critical favour by the time of his death.

GEOFFREY HARVEY is Senior Lecturer in English at the University of Reading, and the author of *The Art of Anthony Trollope*, *The Romantic Tradition in Modern English Poetry*, and *D. H. Lawrence: 'Sons and Lovers': The Critics Debate*. He has edited *The Bertrams* for the World's Classics series.

THE WORLD'S CLASSICS

ANTHONY TROLLOPE

Mr. Scarborough's Family

Edited with an Introduction by
GEOFFREY HARVEY

Oxford New York
OXFORD UNIVERSITY PRESS

Oxford University Press, Walton Street, Oxford OX2 6DP

Oxford New York Toronto
Delhi Bombay Calcutta Madras Karachi
Petaling Jaya Singapore Hong Kong Tokyo
Nairobi Dar es Salaam Cape Town
Melbourne Auckland

and associated companies in
Berlin Ibadan

Oxford is a trade mark of Oxford University Press

Introduction, Note on the Text, Select Bibliography,
Explanatory Notes © Geoffrey Harvey 1989
Chronology © N. J. Hall, 1991

First published 1883
First published by Oxford University Press 1946
First issued as a World's Classics paperback 1989
Reprinted 1992

British Library Cataloguing in Publication Data
Trollope, Anthony, 1815–1882
Mr. Scarborough's family.—(The World's classics).
I. Title II. Harvey, Geoffrey
823'.8[F]
ISBN 0–19–281808–2

Library of Congress Cataloging in Publication Data
Trollope, Anthony, 1815–1882.
Mr. Scarborough's family / Anthony Trollope;
edited with an introduction by Geoffrey Harvey.
p. cm.—(The World's classics)
Bibliography: p.
I. Harvey, Geoffrey, 1943– . II.Title. III. Series.
823'.8—dc19 PR5684.M7 1989 88–21082
ISBN 0–19–281808–2 (pbk.)

Printed in Great Britain by
BPCC Hazells Ltd.
Aylesbury, Bucks.

CONTENTS

INTRODUCTION

In *Mr. Scarborough's Family*, his final major novel, Trollope returned to the subject of the law, which had always held a fascination for him. Although he is still perhaps best known for his chronicles of Barsetshire, or his brilliant Palliser series of novels, he wrote quite as much about the law as he did about the Church, or the world of politics. Eleven of his novels contain trials and the plots of another half dozen hinge on points of law, while the numerous lawyers who crowd the pages of his fiction range from humble rural solicitors to the famous criminal barristers of the Old Bailey, and even the great law officers of the Crown.

Trollope's abiding interest in the law had its obscure origins in his childhood. His father, Thomas Trollope, was a respected Chancery barrister, who eventually lost clients because of his uncertain temper, and threw himself into the futile project of writing an Encyclopaedia Ecclesiastica, as he called it. Indeed, Trollope's father served as the model, in *Ralph the Heir*, for Sir Thomas Underwood, also a Chancery barrister, who is likewise preoccupied with preparing, but never actually writing, a monumental study, in his case of Bacon. For his description of Sir Thomas's chambers in Southampton Buildings, Trollope drew on memories of his father's dingy chambers in Lincoln's Inn, where as a boy he had once spent an entire lonely summer. The quiet, studious environment of the Inns of Court is recalled in several of his legal novels, and also the very different atmosphere of the criminal court, with its alternation of tedium and drama, where Trollope observed with relish the baffling etiquette governing the behaviour of lawyers.

He was also foremost among the Victorian novelists in condemning their chicanery. His animus against his own fictional legal bully, the famous Mr Chaffanbrass, who specializes in defending notorious criminals by destroying the credibility of honest witnesses, is strong even in the novel in which he is introduced, *The Three Clerks*, and later in

Orley Farm Trollope employs Mr Chaffanbrass's successful defence of the guilty Lady Mason to launch an assault on the entire system of advocacy. However, on the whole Trollope was less concerned with the shortcomings of lawyers and the legal form of jury trials than he was with the role of the law in a society which was becoming increasingly urban and commercial, and which was endeavouring to come to terms with the great shift in the balance of power from the landed gentry to the middle class. The question that absorbed not only Trollope, but also his contemporaries—Charles Dickens and Wilkie Collins, for instance, in novels such as *Bleak House* and *The Woman in White*—was whether laws originally framed to support an essentially feudal social structure could accommodate the new claims of a burgeoning commercial and middle-class world. Victorian novelists found the law a rich mine, for not only did its conflict, tragedy, and farce provide the raw material of fiction, but its important function of mediating between the individual and society at large enabled them to employ it in their writing, as a barometer of social change.

As a realistic novelist, who eschewed the sensationalism of some of his contemporaries, Trollope was particularly fascinated by the conflict between legal and moral principles, law and justice. He was especially interested in the moral issues arising out of land law as it related to inheritance, and returned several times in his novels to the law of entail (the settlement of a fixed rule of descent on a landed estate) and the custom of primogeniture (the tradition of bequeathing a property to the eldest son), which was firmly enshrined in law. As the visiting American politician, Trollope's spokesman in *The American Senator* points out, such a system is irrational, unnatural, and unjust. It had remained in place for so long because, as R. D. McMaster has rightly said, it served to secure the power of the landed gentry by ensuring that the great estates were not divided up on their owners' deaths.[1] Of course the sheer weight of tradition also played its part, and Trollope demonstrates in *The Way We Live Now* the tyranny of custom over the conservative imagination when,

[1] See R. D. McMaster, *Trollope and the Law* (Macmillan, 1986), p. 15.

with a heavy heart, Roger Carbury contemplates what he regards as his duty of leaving Carbury Manor to his profligate cousin Sir Felix, the next male heir, knowing that he will dissipate it in gambling at the Beargarden Club. A similar irony arises from the law of entail in *Ralph the Heir*. Distressed that his elder son, Gregory, had had an illegitimate son, old Squire Newton had entailed the property on the male heir in the second generation. Unfortunately for the estate, while Squire Gregory's son is honourable and prudent, the legitimate heir, Ralph Newton, turns out to be irresponsible, and heavily in debt to his breeches-maker.

In *Mr. Scarborough's Family* Trollope gives a strikingly new twist to his earlier complex interweaving of family relationships, inheritance, and the law, when Captain Mountjoy Scarborough, an inveterate gambler and the heir to Tretton Park, which is entailed on the eldest legitimate son, is suddenly declared by his father to be illegitimate. Mr Scarborough loves justice above all, and the origins of his scheme lie in both his moral hatred of the entail and his profound conviction that primogeniture is an example of what he calls 'the gross injustice of the world' (p. 73). His greatest desire has always been to ensure his sons' just treatment at his death, in spite of the law, and he had therefore pursued two parallel strategies. He allowed the income from the estate's highly profitable delf-works to accumulate on behalf of his younger son, Augustus. However, with remarkable foresight, he also kept in his hands the ability to break the entail and make either of his sons his heir at will. He is able to do this because in the past he underwent two separate marriage ceremonies with his complaisant wife, one in Prussia before the birth of his first son, and the second afterwards in Nice. When Mountjoy's debts accumulate to the extent that money-lenders hold post-obits on the estate—huge sums due on Mr Scarborough's death and threatening its very existence—Mr Scarborough produces the second marriage certificate proving Mountjoy's illegitimacy and revels in the discomfiture of the rapacious creditors, as their legal claim falls. Nevertheless, suspicious of his father's true intentions, the new heir, Augustus, repays his brother's creditors the sums that they had originally advanced. This proves to be his undoing, for when he arouses his father's anger by his gleeful anticipation of his death (for throughout the novel Mr Scarborough is dying by slow degrees through several painful operations) his father simply re-establishes the entail by revealing the existence of the original marriage certificate and returns the estate, no longer encumbered by debt, to Mountjoy.

Trollope's outlook had obviously darkened considerably since his altogether sunnier novel, *Ralph the Heir*. In *Mr. Scarborough's Family* the conflict of legal interests is sharper, the tone is sardonic, and the treatment of the story has a surprisingly modern flavour. Whereas in the earlier novel the motive for invoking the power of entail is an old-fashioned concern for the reputation of the family, in *Mr. Scarborough's Family* old Mr Scarborough's rage is directed at what he regards as the immorality of the law itself and he daringly employs Mountjoy's supposed illegitimacy as a device by which to nullify it. Moreover, Tretton Park is not at all like the pretty Hampshire estate that Ralph Newton is to inherit, but a semi-industrialized and urbanized landscape on which the delf-works and the town of Tretton have been built, and as such it represents the modern age with which the law now has to come to terms.

As the embodiment of the abstract ideal of justice, the law matters profoundly to Trollope. He is particularly concerned with its influence on individual lives and in Mountjoy's unusual visit to the old library at Tretton, where he browses among its ancient volumes of history and religious poetry, Trollope tactfully establishes his regret at his loss of its traditional associations, his enlarged understanding of his father's feeling for the property, and his chilling realism about the gambling mania which has brought him to this pass. However, Trollope's imagination is uniquely suited, not only to examining the tangible effects of the law, but also to abstract theorizing. Indeed, his exploration of the moral aspects of the law seems to be most successful when his imagination is free to work with an essentially hypothetical legal issue. In *Orley Farm*, for instance, he examines the relation between law and justice in the case of the forger, Lady Mason, who stands trial and is acquitted on two separate occasions; while in *Ralph the Heir* he teases out the human ironies inherent in the punitive imposition of an entail which pointedly ignores the moral worth of the heir; and in the novel which he wrote immediately before *Mr. Scarborough's Family*, *The Fixed Period*, he tests the extraordinary notion of framing laws making euthanasia compulsory for the aged. Trollope's predilection for the hypothetical clearly continued in his last major novel, with its quite improbable double marriage ceremony, for as R. D. McMaster has pointed out, there were well-tried legal ways of getting round other forms of entail.[2] In this novel, then, unlike some of his earlier fiction, Trollope's interest was not in the traditional squabbling over property between fathers and sons, but in abstract matters of legal and moral principle.

For all that, *Mr. Scarborough's Family* is a novel dominated by its astonishing central character, John Scarborough, a dynamic and heroic figure, who is also a liar and a bully. Contemporary reviewers were puzzled by what they felt to be Trollope's unusual failure of realism in his portrayal of Mr Scarborough and some modern literary critics have added their voices to this view, regarding him as an allegorical figure, and likening him to Mephistopheles, Jonson's Volpone, or the Duke in *Measure for Measure*. However, an important guide to Trollope's intentions, with regard both to his hero and to the nature of the novel he was writing, are the revisions which he made to the manuscript.[3] He transformed the character of Mr Sandover (as Mr Scarborough was called initially) from a casual villain—who, having profited almost accidentally from a false report of his earlier marriage, is exposed towards the end of the book—into a man of powerful intellect who has prosecuted a deeply laid scheme to secure the triumph of his own moral judgement in

[2] See R. D. McMaster, p. 14.
[3] I am indebted for information about the manuscript to Andrew Wright, 'Trollope Revises Trollope', in *Trollope: Centenary Essays*, ed. John Halperin (Macmillan, 1982), pp. 129–32 and Bill Overton, *The Unofficial Trollope* (Brighton, Harvester Press, 1982), pp. 178–9.

defiance of the law. It seems also that Trollope's progressive involvement with the character dictated that Mr Scarborough should be changed from a mere cynical Machiavell into a benevolent though eccentric figure. Consequently references to his philandering were removed, his attitude to his niece, Florence Mountjoy, was altered from utter indifference to deep affection, and an allusion to his doubts about the doctrine of the Trinity was taken out.

However, even the revised Mr Scarborough would not do for the editor of the family periodical, *All the Year Round*, which prided itself on its moral tone, and in which the novel was serialized from May 1882 to June 1883. Trollope died on 6 December 1882, while the serial was coming out, and as P. D. Edwards has noted, in those instalments which appeared after his death small but significant alterations were made to the original manuscript version.[4] When Mr Scarborough's doctor, Mr Merton, reveals his respect for his patient as a man of religious as well as moral principles, the editor removed two references to the dignity of his deathbed and his sure faith in God. As Edwards suggests, it seems most likely that these cuts were made after Trollope's death and without reference to his son. This first conservative reaction to the novel is interesting because it anticipated many readers' uncomfortable feelings about Trollope's own moral and religious judgement of his hero, and also about the way that Mr Scarborough challenges, as he is intended to do, conventional assumptions about the relation between conduct and morality, or law and justice.

In common with many novelists of the period, Trollope reflected the deep division in the mind of a lot of Victorians between a profound respect for tradition and an almost heady faith in individual liberty. Rampant individualism is represented by the romantic Mr Scarborough, a moral rebel whose devious plotting against the law, orchestrated triumphantly from his deathbed, reverberates far beyond Tretton and scandalizes society. However, Trollope avoids the temptations of satire and allegory, with their simple moral

[4] See P. D. Edwards, 'Trollope and *All the Year Round*', *Notes and Queries*, NS 23 (1976), 403–5.

absolutes. Although he is an extraordinary man, John Scarborough is neither an egomaniac, nor a study in morbid psychology, but a passionate, complex man, whose deepest motive is his powerful love for his two unsatisfactory sons. He lives according to his own morality based on freedom, reason, and good nature, which society finds incomprehensible. Hating the irrational tyranny of the law, which mocks him with illusory power, which renders his beloved Tretton Park vulnerable, and which denies him moral freedom, he cherishes an alternative, idealized conception of justice, believing that 'he could do better than the law' (p. 188).

Essentially Mr Scarborough is able to do what the law cannot: foresee the consequences of a property passing to a particular heir and assess his moral worth. What emerges from his extraordinary testing of his sons is a stark contrast between the reckless, domineering Guards officer, Mountjoy, who reveals an innate goodness of heart, and the naked self-interest of his callous, mercenary brother, the lawyer Augustus. While Augustus does not bother to conceal his impatience for his father's death, Mountjoy, in spite of having suffered a severe blow at his father's hands, finds a deepening affection for him during their gloomy encounters. This revelation of the inner moral natures of his sons chimes with Mr Scarborough's instinctive preference for his elder son, and also with his own sense of justice. He reaffirms Mountjoy as his heir and provides with characteristic generosity for the moral outcast, Augustus. As he says at the conclusion of this remarkable endeavour: ' "I have tried them both, as few sons can be tried by their father, and I know them now" ' (p. 538).

Apart from the law, another of Trollope's lifelong interests which influenced the writing of *Mr. Scarborough's Family* was the Jacobean drama, whose plots often revolve around the transfer of property. And in the conflict between the aristocracy and the rising middle class, Trollope discerned an uncomfortable parallel between Jacobean society and his own Victorian world.[5] As in a number of his novels, in *Mr.*

---

[5] For an extended discussion of Trollope's debts to the Jacobean drama, see Geoffrey Harvey, *The Art of Anthony Trollope* (Weidenfeld and Nicolson, 1980), pp. 17–38.

Scarborough's Family there are elements both of design and detail which owe something to his reading in the Jacobean drama.[6] Mr Scarborough's situation exactly mirrors that of Brisac in *The Elder Brother*, by Fletcher and Massinger, who for similar reasons wishes to break an entail in favour of his younger son, while something of Mr Scarborough's physical predicament was suggested to Trollope by Middleton's obsessive figure, Dampit, who throughout *A Trick to Catch the Old One*, lies on his deathbed gloating over his shrewdness and power. Middleton's play also demonstrates the wiles of the landed gentry in defending itself against the ruthless money-lenders, who batten on penniless young heirs, for as in the play, in *Mr. Scarborough's Family* the schemer contrives that the debts should not be paid out of the property. Also, Witgood's three money-lenders are transformed, in the novel, into Mountjoy's trio of pursuing creditors, Tyrrwhit, Juniper and Hart, whose similar disappointment is a source of comic invention.

Trollope's sketch of the predatory Jewish money-lender, Samuel Hart, smacks a little today of anti-semitism, but he is also part of Trollope's debt to dramatic tradition. After tracking the hapless Mountjoy to the gaming-tables of Monte Carlo and then blackmailing his brother with the knowledge of his whereabouts, Hart's defeat comes finally in a marvellously comic but disturbing scene after Mr Scarborough's funeral, when he leads the hunt after Mountjoy from his father's graveside across his own park, until he reaches the refuge of his garden and can slam the gate on his pursuers. Hart is shocked by the Scarboroughs' behaviour, for even money-lenders observe their own code of conduct Trollope informs us, commenting sardonically: 'it was pleasant to see how these commercial gentlemen, all engaged in the natural course of trade, expressed their violent indignation, not so much as to their personal losses, but at the commercial dishonesty generally of which the Scarboroughs, father and son, had been and were about to be guilty' (pp. 584–5).

[6] For a fuller discussion of this aspect of the novel, see Geoffrey Harvey, 'A Parable of Justice: Drama and Rhetoric in *Mr. Scarborough's Family*', *Nineteenth Century Fiction*, 37 (1982), 419–29.

Another important area of *Mr. Scarborough's Family* which owes something to Middleton's play is the story concerning Squire Prosper and his nephew and heir, Harry Annesley. Like Lucre in the play, Mr Prosper wishes to disinherit his nephew, but because he dare not marry is finally compelled to accept a reconciliation. The stupid, entrenched conservatism of Mr Prosper forms a comic contrast to the radicalism of Mr Scarborough. Mr Prosper is appalled by the cheerful vulgarity of the mature brewer's daughter he is courting, who calls him 'deary', and by the equally shameful prospect of his heir taking American citizenship! Trollope's treatment of Squire Prosper's dilemma is integral to the novel's central concerns, for this parallel plot is a comic parody of the main story. Whereas Mr Scarborough's manipulation of the law by means of his powerful intellect is for ends that are rational and moral, Mr Prosper's attempt to break an entail proceeds from a peevish sense of offended dignity because Harry Annesley, his heir, disdains to keep the unspoken bargain of deference in return for an allowance, particularly when it involves having to listen to his uncle's interminable after-dinner sermons.

Mr Prosper's courtship of the redoubtable Matilda Thoroughbung is Trollopian comedy of embarrassment at its richest. Her energetic feminism batters down his feeble pretence of romance, as she bargains strenuously, through her solicitor and then in person, for the right to keep her companion and her ponies. Mr Prosper's horror at her frank exposure of the crude economic realities underlying their proposed marriage is revealed as moral timidity as, after trouncing him in a final, climactic interview, she leaves him paralysed with humiliation. Mr Prosper's use of marriage as a device to break the entail, his neurotic anxiety, his temporary illness and self-pity, are all features of the Scarborough story transposed into a comic key. It is an insulated world in which Mr Prosper, except for occasional moments of introspection, is little more than a figure of fun, on whose comic failure the ironic coincidence of law and justice depends.

As Trollope's debts to the drama suggest, he was working

with fairly traditional materials. The conflict between youth and age, and the problem of the young heir who has to occupy himself somehow until he inherits, are stock situations of Jacobean comedy, and raise issues which Trollope had already examined ironically in *Ralph the Heir* and satirically in *The Way We Live Now*. In tracing the effects of the law of entail on the two heirs, Mountjoy Scarborough and Harry Annesley, Trollope drew on his own early experience, as a young man, of living alone in London. He knew that a family and a career afforded a man a sense of stability and purpose, and was acutely aware of the moral dangers of enforced idleness. Captain Scarborough, who has no wars to fight, no estate to manage, and no wife to steady him, turns for excitement to gambling; while the complacent Harry Annesley, basking in the reflected glory of his role as the heir to Buston Hall, is similarly disinclined to seek a serious occupation. Thus it comes about that Mountjoy and Harry collide outside the Junior United Service Club in Charles Street at two o'clock in the morning, giving rise to Trollope's sarcasm: 'Where Harry had been at that hour need not now be explained, but it may be presumed that he had not been drinking tea with any of his female relatives' (p. 27).

The main stories in *Mr. Scarborough's Family* are linked either by family connections (Harry Annesley's fiancée, Florence Mountjoy, is John Scarborough's niece and the object of the attentions of both Mountjoy and Augustus), or by the law (even Mr Juniper, who is courting the niece of Mr Scarborough's lawyer, asserts that he has a legal claim on Mountjoy). The exception draws attention to itself, when in a remarkable display of kindness, Mr Scarborough, the manipulator of one entail, comes to the aid of Harry Annesley, the victim of a parallel plot, in an effort to counteract Augustus's slander and exonerate him, in Mr Prosper's eyes, of the accusation of having lied about his fight with Mountjoy. However, the main connecting agent for these stories is the lawyer, Mr Grey, who acts for both Mr Scarborough and Mr Prosper. His domestic life in a villa by the Thames in Fulham is quietly suburban, revolving around his spinster daughter, Dolly, his married sister, Mrs Carroll, her feckless husband, and their six strapping girls. His professional experience, however, is dominated by the troublesome Scarborough case, which he brings home to Dolly for advice. Mr Grey is one of Trollope's honourable lawyers of the old school, who believes in the law as 'Holy Writ' (p. 526) and whose old-fashioned idealism clashes with the romantic individualism of his client. Mr Grey is staunch in his defence of entail as symbolizing the authority of the law and when the detested Augustus is discovered to be the true heir, as everyone thinks, Mr Grey works as diligently on his behalf as he had for his brother, devoted only to implementing the law to the letter. However, a very human inconsistency is revealed in Mr Grey's personal dealings which, like Mr Scarborough's, are ruled by the heart rather than by notions of legal form.

In a sense Mr Grey represents the more conservative side of the Victorians: their concern for the maintenance of a decent, ordered society. Trollope plainly admires Mr Grey's integrity and sympathizes with his moral outrage at being twice duped by his client into making a laughing-stock of the very law he reveres. Against Mr Grey's impulse to abandon the Scarborough case altogether are set his long professional connection with the family, and his awareness of Mr Scarborough's great generosity of spirit. Although Mr Scarborough thinks Mr Grey a fool, and Mr Grey regards Mr Scarborough as wicked, each discerns the essential honesty and moral courage of the other, and loves him for it. It is one of the most remarkable relationships in all of Trollope's fiction. Nevertheless, through his experience of the Scarborough case Mr Grey is gradually brought to recognize the fact that the world in which he once felt comfortable has passed away: ' "Old times are changed," he said to himself; "old manners gone" ' (p. 559). It is time for him to retire.

Trollope's fascination with the law also contributes to his art as a story-teller. Although his plotting is much less complex than that of his fellow-novelist, Wilkie Collins, who was also a lawyer, they both felt the need of expert advice on particular points of law, and Trollope was fortunate in being on good terms with several distinguished members of the profession. Where he differs from Collins, however, who drafts his intricate plots with consummate skill, is in his handling of the actual telling of the story which, as Coral Lansbury has pointed out, suggests an approach akin to that of an advocate.[7] As Trollope reveals in his *Autobiography*, to some extent his process of imaginative creation parallels the experience of a good lawyer seeking to understand the deeper motivation of his clients, particularly those whose personality, ideology, or moral views are far removed from his own.[8] And indeed in some respects *Mr. Scarborough's Family* may be thought of as a fictional court, with the author as judge and the reader as jury. We witness Mr Scarborough pleading on behalf of each of his sons, before assuming the role of their judge, and he in turn is brought before the bar of our judgement. Advocacy thus becomes one of Trollope's main narrative methods in this novel, as he employs spokesmen to put the case for and against Mr Scarborough, before he entrusts the verdict to the reader.

Ironically, the burden of prosecution falls on his own lawyer and friend, Mr Grey; but Mr Merton, his physician and secretary during his long final illness, finds himself defending the character of his singular patient. While Mr Grey's despairing complaints at his client's lawlessness are qualified by his naïvety, and by his clinging to an empty legalism, Mr Merton is able in the sick-room to suspend conventional judgement and comes to admire Mr Scarborough's courage and integrity, telling Mountjoy: ' "I think that he has within him a capacity for love, and an unselfishness, which almost atones for his dishonesty" ' (p. 514). And he tentatively acknowledges to Harry Annesley: ' "if you can imagine for yourself a state of things in which neither truth nor morality shall be thought essential, then old Mr Scarborough would be your hero" ' (p. 568). At the conclusion of the novel the author, in his role of judge, offers the reader a balanced summing-up of the Scarborough case:

[7] See Coral Lansbury, *The Reasonable Man: Trollope's Legal Fiction* (Princeton, New Jersey, Princeton University Press, 1981), p. 177.
[8] *An Autobiography* (Oxford University Press, 1953, repr. 1961), p. 200.

He would persevere to injure with a terrible persistency. But yet in every phase of his life he had been actuated by love for others. He had never been selfish, thinking always of others rather than of himself. Supremely indifferent he had been to the opinion of the world around him, but he had never run counter to his own conscience. For the conventionalities of the law he entertained a supreme contempt, but he did wish so to arrange matters with which he was himself concerned as to do what justice demanded. Whether he succeeded in the last year of his life the reader may judge (p. 567).

At first sight it seems that the individual will has been frustrated and that the law has triumphed over natural justice. Indeed, it appears that both Mr Scarborough and Mr Prosper are roundly defeated. At best the issue is left unresolved, for like Mountjoy Scarborough at Tretton Park, Harry Annesley has only a life interest in Buston Hall and no control over the entail. And his honeymoon with Florence in Europe at the conclusion of the novel reminds the reader of the origin of Mr Scarborough's plot all those years before. The novel's stories thus display an ironic circularity which is characteristically Trollopian. However, at least Tretton Park, soon probably to be lost at the gaming-tables of London and Monte Carlo, goes to Mountjoy by a clear act of moral choice, an ironic coincidence of Mr Scarborough's final expression of free will with the arbitrary prescription of the hated law of entail.

What kind of society is it in which Mr Scarborough feels swaddled and Mr Grey comes to regard himself as almost antediluvian? It is plainly one in which the forces of social convention, though under challenge, remain powerful. This is revealed by Trollope's varied treatment of the marriage contract, an area of law which impinges on ordinary life, and which the women of the novel find oppressive. Mr Scarborough dismisses marriage as humbug and mere legal convention; Florence Mountjoy has to battle against her mother's feudal perception of her as almost a chattel of the Tretton Park estate; Miss Thoroughbung strives to mitigate the effect of the marriage contract on her property rights; Mr Grey's impoverished nieces are desperate for dowries in order to attract suitors; while his daughter, Dolly, struggles against the tide of convention to assert her choice of a solitary life. This feeling of oppression is general in the novel and may be seen, for instance, in the way in which meetings and conversations invariably turn into conflicts, battles of wits, importunings, diatribes, or sermons. And this is in turn allied to a disturbing sense of insecurity, as people detect the hitherto stable social and moral foundations beginning to shift; for it is a world in which, for instance, the time-honoured code of the gentleman can no longer be relied upon. Mr Scarborough employs lies as a matter of policy, and in the process finds it expedient to expose his wife's memory to public disgrace; Harry Annesley resorts to a falsehood to cover up his fight with his rival; and although he would not dream of welshing on his gambling debts, Mountjoy Scarborough has no qualms about cheating his creditors of their legitimate profits.

Trollope's subtle probing of such issues is successful because it is rooted firmly in his own experience, which includes the experience of different social milieux. The wonderful immediacy of the world of London—its lawyers' chambers, clubs, railways, and riverside suburbs—derives from Trollope's intimate knowledge not only of the Inns of Court, but of London club life and commuter districts such as Fulham. He also records the cheerful domesticity of Harry Annesley's family home in the Hertfordshire rectory, and the decorous Cheltenham parties where he and Florence meet. However, Trollope extends the novel's scope and places in a wider perspective the peculiarly English problems of Mr Scarborough and Mr Prosper, by including the deadly fatigue of Sir Magnus Mountjoy's diplomatic social treadmill in Brussels, and the contrasting glamour of the gaming and music in Monte Carlo.

Appropriately, gambling features prominently in a novel in which chance appears to rule with a fine impartiality, and in which even games have become deadly serious. As Trollope emphasizes sarcastically, the splendour of the casino at Monte Carlo is funded by human lives, its pleasures punctuated by suicides: 'by whom—out of whose pocket are all these good things provided? . . . He has given his all for the purpose, and has then—blown his brains out. It is one of the disagreeable incidents to which the otherwise extremely pleasant money-making operations of the establishment are liable' (p. 96). And in England those seedy men of the turf, Mr Carroll and Mr Juniper, live straitened lives, relieved only by fitful excitement and bouts of brandy and soda. The gambling scenes in London also ring true. As a young man in London in the 1830s, Trollope became acquainted with this aspect of metropolitan life, and although he never became a gambler, in later years he still enjoyed a nightly rubber of whist at the Garrick. And his understanding of the psychology of gambling informs that depressing scene when Mountjoy Scarborough, barred from his clubs and desperate to play, sits down in a private room with the professional card-player Captain Vignolles, for whom the evening's game, the source of excitement and despair to Mountjoy, is no more than a job.

As might perhaps be expected, Trollope's final major novel, the work of an ageing man in poor health, is shot through with pessimism. In his treatment of the perennial conflict between youth and age, the progress of youth is fraught with frustration and uncertainty, while age is soured by regret, loneliness, and a sense of defeat. Social bonds are weakening, moral values are being eroded, and the new, competitive, legalistic ethos invades even Trollope's own best-loved pursuits of cards and fox-hunting. Although the novel contains some splendidly funny scenes, and flashes of sardonic wit, *Mr. Scarborough's Family* is essentially a dark comedy which, as well as being one of the most intelligent of English legal novels, also offers a penetrating study of Victorian attitudes in the grip of change.

NOTE ON THE TEXT

Trollope began writing *Mr. Scarborough's Family* on 14 March 1881 and completed it on 31 October in the same year. The manuscript—which is in the Taylor Collection at the Firestone Library of Princeton University—like those of most of his novels, is remarkably free from revisions, except for those changes, particularly in the opening chapter, which reveal his decision to reverse the characterization of Mr Scarborough and transform him into a morally challenging figure. Trollope suffered periodic attacks of writer's cramp, and although he wrote approximately half of the manuscript himself, the other half was dictated to his niece, Florence Bland. The novel was first published in serial form in *All the Year Round* between 27 May 1882 and 16 June 1883. This publication was not supervised by Trollope, who died on 6 December 1882, while it was still in progress. Unfortunately the text was bowdlerized by the editor in order to render Mr Scarborough's character less offensive to the readers of this popular family paper. The first edition was published, with the excised passages reinstated, in three volumes (a somewhat outmoded form by this date) by Chatto and Windus in April 1883. It first appeared in World's Classics in 1946, a volume for which the copy-text was the 1883 edition. It was reissued in World's Classics in 1973.

The present edition reproduces the 1973 text with some corrections, restoring the first edition readings for: p. 13, l. 24, p. 100, l. 36, p. 139, l. 5, p. 171, l. 39, p. 402, l. 7, p. 418, l. 8, p. 452, l. 8, p. 504, l. 1, and p. 573, l. 28. Obvious errors in the first edition—which was not corrected by the author—which were subsequently copied in 1946 and 1973, have been amended by: replacing 'was' by 'is', p. 137, l. 3; adding 'of', p. 137, l. 11; introducing a comma, p. 187, l. 38; deleting the question mark, p. 248, l. 28; replacing 'to' by 'for', p. 254, l. 9; replacing the exclamation mark by a question mark, p. 271, l. 8; adding a question mark, p. 528, l. 19;

and replacing 'on' by 'in', p. 540, l. 22. The current spellings of, for instance, 'caviare', 'cotillon', 'Kamschatka', and 'Thibet', have been retained.

SELECT BIBLIOGRAPHY

(Place of publication is London unless otherwise stated.)

Cockshut, A. O. J., *Anthony Trollope: A Critical Study* (Collins, 1955), pp. 229–37.

Edwards, P. D., *Anthony Trollope: His Art and Scope* (Brighton, Harvester Press, 1978), pp. 199–208.

Harvey, Geoffrey, 'A Parable of Justice: Drama and Rhetoric in *Mr. Scarborough's Family*', *Nineteenth Century Fiction*, 37 (1982), 419–29.

Kincaid, James, *The Novels of Anthony Trollope* (Oxford University Press, 1977), pp. 251–6.

Lansbury, Coral, *The Reasonable Man: Trollope's Legal Fiction* (Princeton, New Jersey, Princeton University Press, 1981), pp. 172–82.

McMaster, R. D., *Trollope and the Law* (Macmillan, 1986), pp. 135–54.

Overton, Bill, *The Unofficial Trollope* (Brighton, Harvester Press, 1982), pp. 177–93.

Tracy, Robert, *Trollope's Later Novels* (Berkeley and Los Angeles, University of California Press, 1978), pp. 305–17.

Wright, Andrew, 'Trollope Revises Trollope', in John Halperin (ed.), *Trollope: Centenary Essays* (Macmillan, 1982), pp. 109–33.

—— *Anthony Trollope: Dream and Art* (Macmillan, 1983), pp. 147–54.

A CHRONOLOGY OF ANTHONY TROLLOPE

Virtually all Trollope's fiction after *Framley Parsonage* (1860–1) appeared first in serial form, with book publication usually coming just prior to the final instalment of the serial.

1815   (24 Apr.) Born at 16 Keppel Street, Bloomsbury, the fourth son of Thomas and Frances Trollope.
(Summer ?) Family moves to Harrow-on-the-Hill.

1823   To Harrow School as a day-boy.

1825   To a private school at Sunbury.

1827   To school at Winchester College.

1830   Removed from Winchester and returned to Harrow.

1834   (Apr.) The family flees to Bruges to escape creditors.
(Nov.) Accepts a junior clerkship in the General Post Office, London.

1841   (Sept.) Made Postal Surveyor's Clerk at Banagher, King's County, Ireland.

1843   (mid-Sept.) Begins work on his first novel, *The Macdermots of Ballycloran*.

1844   (11 June) Marries Rose Heseltine.
(Aug.) Transferred to Clonmel, County Tipperary.

1846   (13 Mar.) Son, Henry Merivale Trollope, born.

1847   *The Macdermots of Ballycloran*, published in 3 vols. (Newby).
(27 Sept.) Son, Frederic James Anthony Trollope, born.

1848   *The Kellys and the O'Kellys; or Landlords and Tenants* 3 vols. (Colburn).
(Autumn) Moves to Mallow, County Cork.

1850   *La Vendée; An Historical Romance* 3 vols. (Colburn).
Writes *The Noble Jilt* (A play, published 1923).

1851   (1 Aug.) Sent to south-west of England on special postal mission.

1853   (29 July) Begins *The Warden* (the first of the Barsetshire novels).

(29 Aug.) Moves to Belfast as Acting Surveyor.

1854   (9 Oct.) Appointed Surveyor of Northern District of Ireland.

1855   *The Warden* 1 vol. (Longman).
Writes *The New Zealander*.
(June) Moves to Donnybrook, Ireland.

1857   *Barchester Towers* 3 vols. (Longman).

1858   *The Three Clerks* 3 vols. (Bentley).
Doctor Thorne 3 vols. (Chapman & Hall).
(Jan.) Departs for Egypt on Post Office business.
(Mar.) Visits Holy Land.
(Apr.–May) Returns via Malta, Gibraltar and Spain.
(May–Sept.) Visits Scotland and north of England on postal business.
(16 Nov.) Leaves for the West Indies on postal mission.

1859   *The Bertrams* 3 vols. (Chapman & Hall).
The West Indies and the Spanish Main 1 vol. (Chapman & Hall).
(3 July) Arrives home.
(Nov.) Leaves Ireland; settles at Waltham Cross, Hertfordshire, after being appointed Surveyor of the Eastern District of England.

1860   *Castle Richmond* 3 vols. (Chapman & Hall).
First serialized fiction, *Framley Parsonage*, published in the *Cornhill Magazine*.
(Oct.) Visits, with his wife, his mother and brother in Florence; makes the acquaintance of Kate Field, a 22-year-old American for whom he forms a romantic attachment.

1861   *Framley Parsonage* 3 vols. (Smith, Elder).
Tales of All Countries 1 vol. (Chapman & Hall).
(24 Aug.) Leaves for America to write a travel book.

1862   *Orley Farm* 2 vols. (Chapman & Hall).
North America 2 vols. (Chapman & Hall).
The Struggles of Brown, Jones and Robinson: By One of the Firm 1 vol. (New York, Harper—an American piracy; first English edition 1870, Smith, Elder).
(25 Mar.) Arrives home from America.
(5 Apr.) Elected to the Garrick Club.

1863   *Tales of All Countries*, Second Series, 1 vol. (Chapman &
         Hall).
         Rachel Ray 2 vols. (Chapman & Hall).
         (6 Oct.) Death of his mother, Mrs Frances Trollope.

1864   *The Small House at Allington* 2 vols. (Smith, Elder).
         (12 Apr.) Elected a member of the Athenaeum Club.

1865   *Can You Forgive Her?* 2 vols. (Chapman & Hall).
         Miss Mackenzie 1 vol. (Chapman & Hall).
         Hunting Sketches 1 vol. (Chapman & Hall).

1866   *The Belton Estate* 3 vols. (Chapman & Hall).
         Travelling Sketches 1 vol. (Chapman & Hall).
         Clergymen of the Church of England 1 vol. (Chapman &
         Hall).

1867   *Nina Balatka* 2 vols. (Blackwood).
         The Claverings 2 vols. (Smith, Elder).
         The Last Chronicle of Barset 2 vols. (Smith, Elder).
         Lotta Schmidt and Other Stories 1 vol. (Strahan).
         (1 Sept.) Resigns from the Post Office.
         Assumes editorship of *Saint Pauls Magazine*.

1868   *Linda Tressel* 2 vols. (Blackwood).
         (11 Apr.) Leaves London for the United States on postal
         mission.
         (26 July) Returns from America.
         (Nov.) Stands unsuccessfully as Liberal candidate for
         Beverley, Yorkshire.

1869   *Phineas Finn; the Irish Member* 2 vols. (Virtue & Co).
         He Knew He Was Right 2 vols. (Strahan).
         Did He Steal It? A Comedy in Three Acts (a version of
         The Last Chronicle of Barset, privately printed by Virtue
         & Co).

1870   *The Vicar of Bullhampton* 1 vol. (Bradbury, Evans).
         An Editor's Tales 1 vol. (Strahan)
         The Commentaries of Caesar 1 vol. (Blackwood).
         (Jan.–July) Eased out of *Saint Pauls Magazine*.

1871   *Sir Harry Hotspur of Humblethwaite* 1 vol. (Hurst &
         Blackett).
         Ralph the Heir 3 vols. (Hurst & Blackett).
         (Apr.) Gives up house at Waltham Cross.
         (24 May) Sails to Australia to visit his son.
         (27 July) Arrives at Melbourne.

1872   *The Golden Lion of Granpere* 1 vol. (Tinsley).
(Jan.–Oct.) Travelling in Australia and New Zealand.
(Dec.) Returns via the United states.

1873   *The Eustace Diamonds* 3 vols. (Chapman & Hall).
Australia and New Zealand 2 vols. (Chapman & Hall).
(Apr.) Settles in Montagu Square, London.

1874   *Phineas Redux* 2 vols. (Chapman & Hall).
Lady Anna 2 vols. (Chapman & Hall).
Harry Heathcote of Gangoil. A Tale of Australian Bush Life 1 vol. (Sampson Low).

1875   *The Way We Live Now* 2 vols. (Chapman & Hall).
(1 Mar.) Leaves for Australia via Brindisi, the Suez Canal, and Ceylon.
(4 May) Arrives in Australia.
(Aug.–Oct.) Sailing homewards.
(Oct.) Begins *An Autobiography*.

1876   *The Prime Minister* 4 vols. (Chapman & Hall).

1877   *The American Senator* 3 vols. (Chapman & Hall).
(29 June) Leaves for South Africa.
(11 Dec.) Sails for home.

1878   *South Africa* 2 vols. (Chapman & Hall).
Is He Popenjoy? 3 vols. (Chapman & Hall).
(June–July) Travels to Iceland in the yacht 'Mastiff'.
How the 'Mastiffs' Went to Ireland 1 vol. (privately printed, Virtue & Co).

1879   *An Eye for an Eye* 2 vols. (Chapman & Hall).
Thackeray 1 vol. (Macmillan).
John Candigate 3 vols. (Chapman & Hall).
Cousin Henry 2 vols. (Chapman & Hall).

1880   *The Duke's Children* 3 vols. (Chapman & Hall).
The Life of Cicero 2 vols. (Chapman & Hall).
(July) Settles at South Harting, Sussex, near Petersfield.

1881   *Dr Wortle's School* 2 vols. (Chapman & Hall).
Ayala's Angel 3 vols. (Chapman & Hall).

1882   *Why Frau Frohmann Raised Her Prices; and Other Stories* 1 vol. (Isbister).
The Fixed Period 2 vols. (Blackwood).
Marion Fay 3 vols. (Chapman & Hall).
Lord Palmerston 1 vol. (Isbister).
Kept in the Dark 2 vols. (Chatto & Windus).

(May) Visits Ireland to collect material for a new Irish novel.

(Aug.) Returns to Ireland a second time.

(2 Oct.) Takes rooms for the winter at Garlant's Hotel, Suffolk St., London.

(3 Nov.) Suffers paralytic stroke.

(6 Dec.) Dies in nursing home, 34 Welbeck St., London.

1883   *Mr. Scarborough's Family* 3 vols. (Chatto & Windus).
        The Landleaguers (unfinished) 3 vols. (Chatto & Windus).
        An Autobiography 2 vols. (Blackwood).

1884   *An Old Man's Love* 2 vols. (Blackwood).

1923   *The Noble Jilt* 1 vol. (Constable).

1927   *London Tradesmen* 1 vol. (Elkin Mathews and Marrat).

1972   *The New Zealander* 1 vol. (Oxford University Press).

MR. SCARBOROUGH'S FAMILY

CONTENTS

CONTENTS

Chapter I

MR. SCARBOROUGH

IT will be necessary, for the purpose of my story, that I shall go back more than once from the point at which it begins, so that I may explain with the least amount of awkwardness the things as they occurred which led up to the incidents that I am about to tell; and I may as well say that these first four chapters of the book—though they may be thought to be the most interesting of them all by those who look to incidents for their interest in a tale—are in this way only preliminary.

The world has not yet forgotten the intensity of the feeling which existed when old Mr. Scarborough declared that his well-known eldest son was not legitimate. Mr. Scarborough himself had not been well known in early life. He had been the only son of a squire in Staffordshire, over whose grounds a town had been built and pottery works established. In this way a property which had not originally been extensive, had been greatly increased in value, and Mr. Scarborough, when he came into possession, had found himself to be a rich man. He had then gone abroad, and had there married an English lady. After the lapse of some years he had returned to Tretton Park, as his place was named, and there had lost his wife. He had come back with two sons, Mountjoy and Augustus; and there, at Tretton, he had lived, spending, however, a considerable portion of each year in chambers in the Albany.* He was a man, who, through many years, had had his own circle of friends, but as I have said before, he was not much known in the world. He was luxurious and self-indulgent, and altogether indifferent to the opinion of those around him. But he was affectionate to his children, and anxious above all things for their welfare, or rather happiness. Some marvellous stories were told as to his income, which arose chiefly from the Tretton delf-works*and from the town of Tretton, which had been built chiefly on his very park, in consequence of the nature of the clay and the quality of the water. As a fact the original four thousand a year, to which his father had been born, had grown to twenty thousand by the nature of the operations which had taken place. But the whole of this, whether four thousand or twenty thousand, was strictly entailed, and Mr. Scarborough had been very anxious, since his second son was born, to create for him also something which might amount to opulence. But they who knew him best knew that of all things he hated most the entail.*

The boys were both educated at Eton, and the elder went into the Guards, having been allowed an intermediate year in order to learn languages on the Continent. He had then become a cornet*in the Coldstreams, and had, from that time, lived a life of reckless expenditure. His brother Augustus had in the meantime gone to Cambridge, and become a barrister. He had been called but two years when the story was made known of his father's singular assertion. As from that time it became unnecessary for him to practise his profession, no more was heard of him as a lawyer. But they who had known the young man in the chambers of that great luminary, Mr. Rugby, declared that a very eminent advocate was now spoilt by a freak of fortune.

Of his brother Mountjoy,—or Captain Scarborough as he came to be known at an early period of his life,—the stories which were told in the world at large were much too remarkable to be altogether true. But it was only too true that he lived as though the wealth at his command were without limit. For some few years his father bore with him patiently, doubling his allowance, and paying his bills for him again and again. He made up his mind,—with many regrets,—that enough had been done for his younger son, who would surely by his intellect be able to do much for himself. But then it became necessary to encroach on the funds already put by, and at last there came the final blow, when he discovered that Captain Scarborough had raised large sums on post-obits*from the Jews. The Jews simply requested the father to pay the money or some portion of it, which if at once paid would satisfy them, explaining to him that otherwise the whole property would at his death fall into their hands. It need not here be explained how, through one sad year, these negotiations were prolonged; but at last there came a time in which Mr. Scarborough, sitting in his chambers in the Albany, boldly declared his purpose. He sent for his own lawyer, Mr. Grey, and greatly astonished that gentleman by declaring to him that Captain Scarborough was illegitimate.

At first Mr. Grey refused altogether to believe the assertion made to him. He had been very conversant with the affairs of the family, and had even dealt with marriage settlements on behalf of the lady in question. He knew Mr. Scarborough well,—or rather had not known him,—but had heard much of him, and therefore suspected him. Mr. Grey was a thoroughly respectable man, and Mr. Scarborough, though upright and honourable in many dealings, had not been thoroughly respectable. He had lived with his wife, off and on as people say. Though he had saved much of his money for the purpose above described, he had also spent much of it in a manner which did not approve itself to Mr. Grey. Mr. Grey had thoroughly disliked the eldest son, and had in fact been afraid of him. The captain, in the few interviews that had been necessary between them, had attempted to domineer over the lawyer, till there had at last sprung up a quarrel, in which, to tell the truth, the father took the part of the son. Mr. Grey

had for a while been so offended as to find it necessary to desire Mr. Scarborough to employ another
lawyer. He had not, however, done so, and the
breach had never become absolute. In these circumstances Mr. Scarborough had sent for Mr. Grey to
come to him at the Albany, and had there, from his
bed, declared that his eldest son was illegitimate.
Mr. Grey had at first refused to accept the assertion
as being worth anything, and had by no means confined himself to polite language in expressing his
belief. 'I would much rather have nothing to do with
it,' he had said when Mr. Scarborough insisted on
the truth of his statement.

'But the evidence is all here,' said Mr. Scarborough, laying his hand on a small bundle of papers.
'The difficulty would have been, and the danger, in
causing Mountjoy to have been accepted in his
brother's place. There can be no doubt that I was
not married till after Mountjoy was born.'

Mr. Grey's curiosity was roused, and he began to
ask questions. Why, in the first place, had Mr. Scarborough behaved so dishonestly? Why had he originally not married his wife? And then, why had he
married her? If, as he said, the proofs were so easy,
how had he dared to act so directly in opposition to
the laws of his country? Why, indeed, had he been
through the whole of his life so bad a man,—so bad
to the woman who had borne his name, so bad to the
son whom he called illegitimate, and so bad also to
the other son whom he now intended to restore to
his position, solely with the view of defrauding the
captain's creditors?

In answer to this Mr. Scarborough, though he was
suffering much at the time,—so much as to be considered near to his death,—had replied with the most
perfect good-humour. He had done very well, he
thought, by his wife, whom he had married after she
had consented to live with him on other terms. He
had done very well by his elder son, for whom he had

intended the entire property. He had done well by
his second son, for whom he had saved his money.
It was now his first duty to save the property. He
regarded himself as being altogether unselfish and
virtuous from his point of view.

When Mr. Grey had spoken about the laws of
his country he had simply smiled, though he was
expecting a grievous operation on the following day.
As for marriage, he had no great respect for it, except as a mode of enabling men and women to live
together comfortably. As for the 'outraged laws of
his country,' of which Mr. Grey spoke so much, he
did not care a straw for such outrages—nor, indeed,
for the expressed opinion of mankind as to his conduct. He was very soon about to leave the world,
and meant to do the best he could for his son Augustus. The other son was past all hope. He was hardly
angry with his eldest son, who had undoubtedly given
him cause for just anger. His apparent motives in
telling the truth about him at last were rather those
of defrauding the Jews, who had expressed themselves to him with brutal audacity, than that of
punishing the one son or doing justice to the other;
but even of them he spoke with a cynical good-
humour, triumphing in his idea of thoroughly getting
the better of them.

'I am consoled, Mr. Grey,' he said, 'when I think
how probably it might all have been discovered after
my death. I should have destroyed all these,' and he
laid his hands upon the papers, 'but still there might
have been discovery.'

Mr. Grey could not but think that during the last
twenty-four years,—the period which had elapsed
since the birth of the younger son,—no idea of such
a truth had occurred to himself.

He did at last consent to take the papers in his
hands, and to read them through with care. He took
them away with that promise, and with an assurance that he would bring them back on the day but

one following,—should Mr. Scarborough then be alive.

Mr. Scarborough, who seemed at that moment to have much life in him, insisted on this proviso.

'The surgeon is to be here tomorrow, you know, and his coming may mean a great deal. You will have the papers, which are quite clear, and will know what to do. I shall see Mountjoy myself this evening. I suppose he will have the grace to come, as he does not know what he is coming for.'

Then the father smiled again, and the lawyer went.

Mr. Scarborough, though he was very strong of heart, did have some misgivings as the time came at which he was to see his son. The communication which he had to make was certainly one of vital importance. His son had some time since instigated him to come to terms with the 'family creditors,' as the captain boldly called them.

'Seeing that I never owed a shilling in my life, or my father before me, it is odd that I should have family creditors,' the father had answered.

'The property has, then, at any rate,' the son had said with a scowl.

But that was now twelve months since, before mankind and the Jews among them had heard of Mr. Scarborough's illness. Now there could be no question of dealing on favourable terms with these gentlemen. Mr. Scarborough was therefore aware that the evil thing which he was about to say to his son would have lost its extreme bitterness. It did not occur to him that, in making such a revelation as to his son's mother, he would inflict any great grief on his son's heart. To be illegitimate would be, he thought, nothing unless illegitimacy carried with it loss of property. He hardly gave weight enough to the feeling that the eldest son was the eldest son, and too little to the triumph which was present to his own mind in saving the property for one of the family. Augustus was but the captain's brother, but he was the old squire's son. The two brothers had hitherto lived together on fairly good terms, for the younger had been able to lend money to the elder, and the elder had found his brother neither severe nor exacting. How it might be between them when their relations with each other should be altogether changed, Mr. Scarborough did not trouble himself to enquire. The captain by his own reckless folly had lost his money, —had lost all that fortune would have given him as his father's eldest son. After having done so, what could it matter to him whether he were legitimate or illegitimate? His brother, as possessor of Tretton Park, would be able to do much more for him than could be expected from a professional man working for his bread.

Mr. Scarborough had looked at the matter all round for the space of two years, and during the latter year had slowly resolved on his line of action. He had had no scruple in passing off his eldest-born as legitimate, and now would have none in declaring the truth to the world. What scruple need he have, seeing that he was so soon about to leave the world?

As to what took place at that interview between the father and the son very much was said among the clubs, and in societies to which Captain Mountjoy Scarborough was well known; but very little of absolute truth was ever revealed. It was known that Captain Scarborough left the room under the combined authority of apothecaries and servants, and that the old man had fainted from the effects of the interview. He had undoubtedly told the son the simple facts as he had declared them to Mr. Grey, but had thought it to be unnecessary to confirm his statement by any proof. Indeed, the proofs, such as they were,—the written testimony that is,—were at that moment in the hands of Mr. Grey, and to Mr. Grey the father had at last referred the son. But the son had absolutely refused to believe for a moment

in the story, and had declared that his father and Mr.
Grey had conspired together to rob him of his inheritance and good name. The interview was at last
over, and Mr. Scarborough at one moment fainting,
and in the next suffering the extremest agony, was
left alone with his thoughts.

Captain Scarborough, when he left his father's
room, and found himself going out from the Albany
into Piccadilly, was an infuriated but at the same
time a most wretched man. He did believe that a
conspiracy had been hatched, and he was resolved to
do his best to defeat it, let the effect be what it might
on the property; but yet there was a strong feeling
in his breast that the fraud would be successful. No
man could possibly be environed by worse circumstances as to his own condition. He owed he knew
not what amount of money to several creditors: but
then he owed, which troubled him more, gambling
debts, which he could only pay by his brother's assistance. And now, as he thought of it, he felt convinced that his brother must be joined with his father
and the lawyer in this conspiracy. He felt, also, that
he could meet neither Mr. Grey nor his brother without personally attacking them. All the world might
perish, but he, with his last breath, would declare
himself to be Captain Mountjoy Scarborough, of
Tretton Park; and though he knew at the moment
that he must perish,—as regarded social life among
his comrades,—unless he could raise five hundred
pounds from his brother, yet he felt that, were he to
meet his brother, he could not but fly at his throat
and accuse him of the basest villainy.

At that moment, at the corner of Bond Street, he
did meet his brother.

'What is this?' said he fiercely.

'What is what?' said Augustus, without any fierce-
ness. 'What is up now?'

'I have just come from my father.'

'And how is the governor? If I were he I should

be in a most awful funk. I should hardly be able to think of anything but that man who is to come to-morrow with his knives. But he takes it all as cool as a cucumber.'

There was something in this which at once shook, though it did not remove, the captain's belief, and he said something as to the property. Then there came questions and answers, in which the captain did not reveal the story which had been told to him, but the barrister did assert that he had as yet heard nothing as to anything of importance. As to Tretton, the captain believed his brother's manner rather than his words. In fact, the barrister had heard nothing as yet of what was to be done on his behalf.

The interview ended in the two men going and dining at a club, where the captain told the whole story of his father's imagined iniquity.

Augustus received the tale almost in silence. In reply to his brother's authoritative domineering speeches he said nothing. To him it was all new, but to him, also, it seemed certainly to be untrue. He did not at all bring himself to believe that Mr. Grey was in the conspiracy, but he had no scruple of paternal regard to make him feel that his father would not concoct such a scheme simply because he was his father. It would be a saving of the spoil from the Amalekites,* and of this idea he did give a hardly expressed hint to his brother.

'By George!' said the captain, 'nothing of the kind shall be done with my consent.'

'Why, no,' the barrister had answered, 'I suppose that neither your consent nor mine is to be asked; and it seems as though it was a farce ordered to be played over the poor governor's grave. He has pre-pared a romance, as to the truth or falsehood of which neither you nor I can possibly be called as witnesses.'

It was clear to the captain that his brother had thought that the plot had been prepared by their father in anticipation of his own death. Nevertheless, by the younger brother's assistance, the much needed sum of money was found for the supply of the elder's immediate wants.

The next day was the day of terror, and nothing more was heard, either then or for the following week, of the old gentleman's scheme. In two days it was understood that his death might be hourly expected, but on the third it was thought that he might 'pull through,' as his younger son filially expressed himself. He was constantly with his father, but not a word passed his lips as to the property. The elder son kept himself gloomily apart, and, indeed, during a part of the next week was out of London. Augustus Scarborough did call on Mr. Grey, but only learned from him that it was, at any rate, true that the story had been told by his father. Mr. Grey refused to make any further communication, simply saying that he would as yet express no opinion.

'For myself,' said Augustus, as he left the attorney's chambers, 'I can only profess myself so much astonished as to have no opinion. I suppose I must simply wait and see what Fortune intends to do with me.'

At the end of a fortnight Mr. Scarborough had so far recovered his strength as to be able to be moved down to Tretton, and thither he went. It was not many days after that 'the world' was first informed that Captain Scarborough was not his father's heir. 'The world' received the information with a great deal of expressed surprise and inward satisfaction,—satisfaction that the money-lenders should be done out of their money; that a professed gambler like Captain Scarborough should suddenly become an illegitimate nobody; and, more interesting still, that a very wealthy and well-conditioned, if not actually respectable, squire, should have proved himself to be a most brazen-faced rascal. All of these were matters which gave extreme delight to the

world at large. At first there came little paragraphs
without any name, and then, some hours afterwards,
the names became known to the quidnuncs,* and in a
short space of time were in possession of the very
gentry who found themselves defrauded in this singular manner.

It is not necessary here that I should recapitulate
all the circumstances of the original fraud, for a gross
fraud had been perpetrated. After the perpetration
of that fraud papers had been prepared by Mr. Scarborough himself with a great deal of ingenuity, and
the matter had been so arranged that but for his own
declaration his eldest son would undoubtedly have
inherited the property. Now there was no measure
to the clamour and the uproar raised by the money-
lenders. Mr. Grey's outer office was besieged, but
his clerk simply stated that the facts would be proved
on Mr. Scarborough's death as clearly as it might be
possible to prove them. The curses uttered against
the old squire were bitter and deep, but during this
time he was still supposed to be lying at death's door,
and did not in truth himself expect to live many days.
The creditors, of course, believed that the story was
a fiction. None of them were enabled to see Captain
Scarborough, who, after a short period, disappeared
altogether from the scene. But they were, one and
all, convinced that the matter had been arranged between him and his father.

There was one from whom better things were
expected than to advance money on post-obits to a
gambler at a rate by which he was to be repaid one
hundred pounds for every forty pounds, on the death
of a gentleman who was then supposed to be dying.
For it was proved afterwards that this Mr. Tyrrwhit
had made most minute inquiries among the old
squire's servants as to the state of their master's
health. He had supplied forty thousand pounds, for
which he was to receive one hundred thousand pounds
when the squire died, alleging that he should have

difficulty in recovering the money. But he had collected the sum so advanced on better terms among his friends, and had become conspicuously odious in the matter.

In about a month's time it was generally believed that Mr. Scarborough had so managed matters that his scheme would be successful. A struggle was made to bring the matter at once into the law courts, but the attempt for the moment failed. It was said that the squire down at Tretton was too ill, but that proceedings would be taken as soon as he was able to bear them. Rumours were afloat that he would be taken into custody, and it was even asserted that two policemen were in the house at Tretton. But it was soon known that no policemen were there, and that the squire was free to go whither he would, or rather whither he could. In fact, though the will to punish him, and even to arrest him, was there, no one had the power to do him an injury.

It was then declared that he had in no sense broken the law,—that no evil act of his could be proved,— that though he had wished his eldest son to inherit the property wrongfully he had only wished it; and that he had now simply put his wishes into unison with the law, and had undone the evil which he had hitherto only contemplated. Indeed the world at large rather sympathised with the squire when Mr. Tyrrwhit's dealings became known, for it was supposed by many that Mr. Tyrrwhit was to have become the sole owner of Tretton.

But the creditors were still loud, and still envenomed. They and their emissaries hung about Tretton and demanded to know where was the captain. Of the captain's whereabouts his father knew nothing, not even whether he was still alive; for the captain had actually disappeared from the world, and his creditors could obtain no tidings respecting him. At this period, and for long afterwards, they imagined that he and his father were in league together, and were determined to try at law the question as to the legitimacy of his birth as soon as the old squire should be dead. But the old squire did not die. Though his life was supposed to be most precarious he still continued to live, and became even stronger. But he remained shut up at Tretton, and utterly refused to see any emissary of any creditor. To give Mr. Tyrrwhit his due it must be acknowledged that he personally sent no emissaries, having contented himself with putting the business into the hands of a very sharp attorney. But there were emissaries from others, who after a while were excluded altogether from the Park.

Here Mr. Scarborough continued to live, coming out on to the lawn in his easy chair, and there smoking his cigar and reading his French novel through the hot July days. To tell the truth he cared very little for the emissaries, excepting so far as they had been allowed to interfere with his own personal comfort. In these days he had down with him two or three friends from London, who were good enough to make up for him a whist-table in the country; but he found the chief interest in his life in the occasional visits of his youger son.

'I look upon Mountjoy as utterly gone,' he said.

'But he has utterly gone,' his other son replied.

'As to that I care nothing. I do not believe that a man can be murdered without leaving a trace of his murder. A man cannot even throw himself overboard without being missed. I know nothing of his whereabouts,—nothing at all. But I must say that his absence is a relief to me. The only comfort left to me in this world is in your presence, and in those material good things which I am still able to enjoy.'

This assertion as to his ignorance about his eldest son the squire repeated again and again to his chosen heir, feeling it was only probable that Augustus might participate in the belief which he knew to be only too common. There was no doubt an idea

prevalent that the squire and the captain were in
league together to cheat the creditors, and that the
squire, who in these days received much undeserved
credit for Machiavellian*astuteness, knew more than
anyone else respecting his eldest son's affairs. But, in
truth, he at first knew nothing, and in making these
assurances to his younger son was altogether wasting
his breath, for his younger son knew everything.

Chapter II

FLORENCE MOUNTJOY

MR. SCARBOROUGH had a niece, one Florence
Mountjoy, to whom it had been intended that
Captain Scarborough should be married. There had
been no considerations of money when the intention
had been first formed, for the lady was possessed of
no more than ten thousand pounds, which would have
been as nothing to the prospects of the captain when
the idea was first entertained. But Mr. Scarborough
was fond of people who belonged to him. In this way
he had been much attached to his late brother-in-law,
General Mountjoy, and had perceived that his niece
was beautiful and graceful, and was in every way
desirable as one who might be made in part thus to
belong to himself. Florence herself, when the idea
of the marriage was first suggested to her by her
mother, was only eighteen, and received it with awe
rather than with pleasure or abhorrence. To her her
cousin Mountjoy had always been a most magnificent personage. He was only seven years her senior,
but he had early in life assumed the manners as he
had also done the vices of mature age, and loomed
large in the girl's eyes as a man of undoubted wealth
and fashion. At that period, three years antecedent
to his father's declaration, he had no doubt been much
in debt, but his debts had not been generally known,

and his father had still thought that a marriage with his cousin might serve to settle him,—to use the phrase which was common with himself. From that day to this the courtship had gone on, and the squire had taught himself to believe that the two cousins were all but engaged to each other. He had so considered it at any rate for two years, till during the last final year he had resolved to throw the captain overboard. And even during this year there had been periods of hope, for he had not finally made up his mind till but a short time before he had put it in practice. No doubt he was fond of his niece in accordance with his own capability for fondness. He would caress her and stroke her hair, and took delight in having her near to him. And of true love for such a girl his heart was quite capable. He was a good-natured, fearless, but not a selfish man, to whom the fate in life of this poor girl was a matter of real concern.

And his eldest son, who was by no means good-natured, had something of the same nature. He did love truly after his own fashion of loving. He would have married his cousin at any moment with or without her ten thousand pounds—for of all human beings he was the most reckless. And yet in his breast was present a feeling of honour of which his father knew nothing. When it was explained to him that his mother's fair name was to be aspersed—a mother whom he could but faintly remember, the threat did bring with it its own peculiar agony. But of this the squire neither felt nor knew anything. The lady had been long dead, and could be none the better or the worse for aught that could be said of her. To the captain it was not so, and it was preferable to him to believe his father to be dishonest than his mother. He at any rate was in truth in love with his cousin Florence, and when the story was told to him, one of its first effects was the bearing which it would have upon her mind.

It has been said that within two or three days after the communication, he had left London. He had done so in order that he might at once go down to Cheltenham, and see his cousin. There Miss Mountjoy lived with her mother.

The time had been when Florence Mountjoy had been proud of her cousin; and, to tell the truth of her feelings, though she had never loved him, she had almost done so. Rumours had made their way through even to her condition of life, and she in her innocence had gradually been taught to believe that Captain Scarborough was not a man whom she could be safe in loving. And there had, perhaps, come another as to whom her feelings were different. She had no doubt at first thought that she would be willing to become her cousin's wife, but she had never said as much herself. And now both her heart and mind were set against him.

Captain Scarborough, as he went down to Cheltenham, turned the matter over in his mind, thinking within himself how best he might carry out his project. His intention was to obtain from his cousin an assurance of her love, and a promise that it should not be shaken by any stories which his father might tell respecting him. For this purpose he must make known to her the story his father had told him, and his own absolute disbelief in it. Much else must be confided to her. He must acknowledge in part his own debts, and must explain that his father had taken this course in order to defraud the creditors. All this would be very difficult; but he must trust in her innocence and generosity. He thought that the condition of his affairs might be so represented that the story should tend rather to win her heart towards him than to turn it away. Her mother had hitherto always been in his favour, and he had in fact been received almost as an Apollo* in the house at Cheltenham.

'Florence,' he said, 'I must see you alone for a

few minutes. I know that your mother will trust you with me.'

This was spoken immediately on his arrival, and Mrs. Mountjoy at once left the room. She had been taught to believe that it was her daughter's duty to marry her cousin; and though she knew that the captain had done much to embarrass the property, she thought that this would be the surest way to settle him. The heir of Tretton Park was, in her estimation, so great a man that very much was to be endured at his hands.

The meeting between the two cousins was very long, and when Mrs. Mountjoy at last returned unannounced to the room, she found her daughter in tears.

'Oh, Florence, what is the matter?' asked her mother.

The poor girl said nothing, but still continued to weep, while the captain stood by, looking as black as a thunder-cloud.

'What is it, Mountjoy?' said Mrs. Mountjoy, turning to him.

'I have told Florence some of my troubles,' said he, 'and they seem to have changed her mind towards me.'

There was something in this which was detestable to Florence—an unfairness, a dishonesty in putting off upon his trouble that absence of love which she had at last been driven by his vows to confess. She knew that it was not because of his present trouble, which she understood to be terrible, but which she could not in truth comprehend. He had blurted it all out roughly—the story as told by his father of his mother's dishonour, of his own insignificance in the world, of the threatened loss of the property, of the heaviness of his debts, and added his conviction that his father had invented it all, and was, in fact, a thorough rascal. The full story of his debts he kept back, not with any predetermined falseness, but

because it is so difficult for a man to own that he has
absolutely ruined himself by his own folly. It was
not wonderful that the girl should not have understood such a story as had then been told her. Why
was he defending his mother? Why was he accusing
his father? The accusations against her uncle whom
she did know were more fearful to her than these
mysterious charges against her aunt whom she did
not know, from which her son defended her. But
then he had spoken passionately of his own love, and
she had understood that. He had besought her to
confess that she loved him, and then she had at once
become stubborn. There was something in the word
'confess' which grated against her feelings. It seemed
to imply a conviction on his part that she did love
him. She had never told him so, and was now sure
that it was not so. When he had pressed her she
could only weep. But in her weeping she never for a
moment yielded. She never uttered a single word
on which he could be enabled to build a hope. Then
he had become blacker and still blacker, fiercer and
still fiercer, more and more earnest in his purpose,
till at last he asked her whom it was that she loved,
as she could not love him. He knew well whom it
was that he suspected—and she knew also. But he
had no right to demand any statement from her on
that head. She did not think that the man loved her;
nor did she know what to say or to think of her own
feelings. Were he, the other man, to come to her,
she would only bid him go away; but why she should
so bid him she had hardly known. But now this dark
frowning captain, with his big moustache and his
military look, and his general aspect of invincible
power threatened the other man.

'He came to Tretton as my friend,' he said, 'and
by Heaven if he stands in my way, if he dare to cross
between you and me, he shall answer it with his life.'

The name had not been mentioned; but this had
been very terrible to Florence, and she could only weep.

He went away, refusing to stay to dinner, but said that on the following afternoon he would again return. In the street of the town he met one of his creditors, who had discovered his journey to Cheltenham, and had followed him.

'Oh! Captain Mountjoy, what is all dis that they are talking about in London?'

'What are they talking about?'

'De inheritance!' said the man, who was a veritable Jew, looking up anxiously in his face.

The man had his acceptance for a very large sum of money, with an assurance that it should be paid on his father's death, for which he had given him about two thousand pounds in cash.

'You must ask my father.'

'But is it true?'

'You must ask my father. Upon my word, I can tell you nothing else. He has concocted a tale of which I for one do not believe a word. I never heard of the story till he condescended to tell it me the other day. Whether it be true or whether it be false, you and I, Mr. Hart, are in the same boat.'

'But you have had de money.'

'And you have got the bill. You can't do anything by coming after me. My father seems to have contrived a very clever plan by which he can rob you; but he will rob me at the same time. You may believe me or not as you please; but that you will find to be the truth.'

Then Mr. Hart left him, but certainly did not believe a word the captain had said to him.

To her mother Florence would only disclose her persistent intention of not marrying her cousin. Mrs. Mountjoy, over whose spirit the glamour of the captain's prestige was still potent, said much in his favour. Everybody had always intended the marriage, and it would be the setting right of everything. The captain, no doubt, owed a large sum of money, but that would be paid by Florence's fortune.

So little did the poor lady know of the captain's condition. When she had been told that there had been a great quarrel between the captain and his father, she declared that the marriage would set that all right.

'But, mamma, Captain Scarborough is not to have the property at all.'

Then Mrs. Mountjoy, believing thoroughly in entails, had declared that all Heaven could not prevent it.

'But that makes no difference,' said the daughter. 'If I—I—I loved him I would marry him so much the more if he had nothing.'

Then Mrs. Mountjoy declared that she could not understand it at all.

On the next day Captain Scarborough came, according to his promise, but nothing that he could say would induce Florence to come into his presence. Her mother declared that she was so ill that it would be wicked to disturb her.

Chapter III

HARRY ANNESLEY

TOGETHER with Augustus Scarborough at Cambridge had been one Harry Annesley, and he it was to whom the captain in his wrath had sworn to put an end if he should come between him and his love. Harry Annesley had been introduced to the captain by his brother, and an intimacy had grown up between them. He had brought him to Tretton Park when Florence was there, and Harry had since made his own way to Cheltenham, and had endeavoured to plead his own cause after his own fashion. This he had done after the good old English plan which is said to be somewhat loutish, but is not without its efficacy. He had looked at her and danced with her, and done the best with his gloves and his cravat, and had let her see by twenty unmistakable signs that in order to be perfectly happy he must be near her. Her gloves, and her flowers, and her other little properties were sweeter to him than any scents, and were more valuable in his eyes than precious stones. But he had never as yet actually asked her to love him. But she was so quick a linguist that she had understood down to the last letter what all these tokens had meant. Her cousin, Captain Scarborough, was to her magnificent, powerful, but terrible withal. She had asked herself a thousand times whether it would be possible for her to love him and to become his wife. She had never quite given even to herself an answer to this question till she had suddenly found herself enabled to do so by his over confidence in asking her to confess that she loved him. She had never acknowledged anything, even to herself, as to Harry Annesley. She had never told herself that it would be possible that he should ask her any such question. She had a wild, dreamy, fearful feeling that, although it would be possible to her to refuse her cousin, it would be impossible that she should marry any other while he should still be desirous of making her his wife. And now Captain Scarborough had threatened Harry Annesley, not indeed by name, but still clearly enough. Any dream of her own in that direction must be a vain dream.

As Harry Annesley is going to be, what is generally called, the hero of this story, it is necessary that something should be said of the particulars of his life and existence up to this period. There will be found to be nothing very heroic about him. He is a young man with more than a fair allowance of a young man's folly—it may also be said of a young man's weakness. But I myself am inclined to think that there was but little of a young man's selfishness, with nothing of falseness or dishonesty; and I am therefore tempted to tell his story.

He was the son of a clergyman, and the eldest of a large family of children. But as he was the acknowledged heir to his mother's brother, who was the squire of the parish of which his father was rector, it was not thought necessary that he should follow any profession. This uncle was the squire of Buston, and was, after all, not a rich man himself. His whole property did not exceed two thousand a year, an income which fifty years since was supposed to be sufficient for the moderate wants of a moderate country gentleman; but though Buston be not very far removed from the centre of everything, being in Hertfordshire and not more than forty miles from London, Mr. Prosper lived so retired a life, and was so far removed from the ways of men, that he apparently did not know but that his heir was as completely entitled to lead an idle life as though he were son of a duke or a brewer. It must not, however, be imagined that Mr. Prosper was especially attached to his nephew. When the boy left the Charterhouse,* where his uncle had paid his school-bills, he was sent to Cambridge with an allowance of two hundred and fifty pounds a year, and that allowance was still continued to him with an assurance that under no circumstances could it ever be increased. At college he had been successful, and left Cambridge with a college fellowship. He therefore left it with one hundred and seventy-five pounds added to his income, and was considered by all those at Buston Rectory to be a rich young man. But Harry did not find that his combined income amounted to riches amidst a world of idleness. At Buston he was constantly told by his uncle of the necessity of economy. Indeed, Mr. Prosper, who was a sickly little man about fifty years of age, always spoke of himself as though he intended to live for another half century. He rarely walked across the park to the rectory, and once a week, on Sundays, entertained the rectory family. A sad occasion it generally was to the elder of the rectory children,

who were thus doomed to abandon the loud pleasan-
tries of their own home for the sober Sunday solem-
nities of the Hall. It was not that the squire of Buston
was peculiarly a religious man, or that the rector was
the reverse; but the parson was joyous, whereas the
other was solemn. The squire who never went to
church because he was supposed to be ill, made up for
the deficiency by his devotional tendencies when the
children were at the Hall. He read through a sermon
after dinner, unintelligibly and even inaudibly. At
this his brother-in-law, who had an evening service
in his own church, of course never was present; but
Mrs. Annesley and the girls were there, and the
younger children. But Harry Annesley had absolutely declined, and his uncle having found out that
he never attended the church service although he
always left the Hall with his father, made this a
ground for a quarrel. It at last came to pass that
Mr. Prosper, who was jealous and irritable, would
hardly speak to his nephew; but the two hundred and
fifty pounds went on with many bickerings on the
subject between the parson and the squire. Once
when the squire spoke of discontinuing it, Harry's
father reminded him that the young man had been
brought up in absolute idleness in conformity with
his uncle's desire. This the squire denied in strong
language; but Harry had not hitherto run loudly in
debt, nor kicked over the traces very outrageously,
and as he absolutely must be the heir, the allowance
was permitted to go on.

There was one lady who conceived all manner of
bad things as to Harry Annesley, because, as she
alleged, of the want of a profession and of any fixed
income. Mrs. Mountjoy, Florence's mother, was this
lady. Florence herself had read every word in Harry's
language, not knowing, indeed, that she had read
anything, but still never having missed a single letter.
Mrs. Mountjoy also had read a good deal, though
not all, and dreaded the appearance of Harry as a

declared lover. In her eyes Captain Scarborough was
a very handsome, very powerful, and very grand
personage; but she feared that Florence was being
induced to refuse her allegiance to this sovereign by
the interference of her other very indifferent suitor.
What would be Buston and two thousand a year, as
compared with all the glories and limitless income of
the great Tretton property? Captain Scarborough
with his moustachios and magnificence was just the
man who would be sure to become a peer. She had
always heard the income fixed at thirty thousand a
year. What would a few debts signify to thirty
thousand a year? Such had been her thoughts up to
the period of Captain Scarborough's visit, when he
had come to Cheltenham, and had renewed his demand for Florence's hand somewhat roughly. He had
spoken ambiguous words, dreadful words, declaring
that an internecine quarrel had taken place between
him and his father; but these words, though they had
been very dreadful, had been altogether misunderstood by Mrs. Mountjoy. The property she knew to
be entailed, and she knew that when a property was
entailed the present owner of it had nothing to do
with its future disposition. Captain Scarborough at
any rate was anxious for the marriage, and Mrs.
Mountjoy was inclined to accept him, encumbered as
he now was with his father's wrath, in preference to
poor Harry Annesley.

In June Harry came up to London, and there
learned at his club the singular story in regard to old
Mr. Scarborough and his son. Mr. Scarborough had
declared his son to be illegitimate, and all the world
knew now that he was utterly penniless and hopelessly in debt. That he had been greatly embarrassed
Harry had known for many months, and added to
that was now the fact, very generally believed, that
he was not and never had been the heir to Tretton
Park. All that still increasing property about Tretton, on which so many hopes had been founded,

would belong to his brother. Harry, as he heard the tale, immediately connected it with Florence. He had, of course, known that the captain was a suitor to the girl's hand, and there had been a time when he thought that his own hopes were consequently vain. Gradually the conviction dawned upon him that Florence did not love the grand warrior, that she was afraid of him rather, and awe-struck. It would be terrible now were she brought to marry him by this feeling of awe. Then he learned that the warrior had gone down to Cheltenham, and in the restlessness of his spirit he pursued him. When he reached Cheltenham the warrior had already gone.

'The property is certainly entailed,' said Mrs. Mountjoy. He had called at once at the house and saw the mother, but Florence was discreetly sent away to her own room when the dangerous young man was admitted.

'He is not Mr. Scarborough's eldest son at all,' said Harry; 'that is, in the eye of the law.' Then he had to undertake that task, very difficult for a young man, of explaining to her all the circumstances of the case.

But there was something in them so dreadful to the lady's imagination that he failed for a long time to make her comprehend it. 'Do you mean to say that Mr. Scarborough was not married to his own wife?'

'Not at first.'

'And that he knew it?'

'No doubt he knew it. He confesses as much himself.'

'What a very wicked man he must be,' said Mrs. Mountjoy. Harry could only shrug his shoulder. 'And he meant to rob Augustus all through?' Harry again shrugged his shoulder. 'Is it not much more probable that if he could be so very wicked he would be willing to deny his eldest son in order to save paying the debts?'

Harry could only declare the facts were as he told

them, or at least that all London believed them to be so, that at any rate Captain Mountjoy had gambled so recklessly as to put himself for ever and ever out of reach of a shilling of the property, and that it was clearly the duty of Mrs. Mountjoy, as Florence's mother, not to accept him as a suitor.

It was only by slow degrees that the conversation had arrived at this pass. Harry had never as yet declared his own love either to the mother or daughter, and now appeared simply as a narrator of this terrible story. But at this point it did appear to him that he must introduce himself in another guise.

'The fact is, Mrs. Mountjoy,' he said, starting to his feet, 'that I am in love with your daughter myself.'

'And therefore you have come here to vilify Captain Scarborough.'

'I have come,' said he, 'at any rate to tell the truth. If it be as I say, you cannot think it right that he should marry your daughter. I say nothing of myself, but that at any rate cannot be.'

'It is no business of yours, Mr. Annesley.'

'Except that I would fain think that her business should be mine.'

But he could not prevail with Mrs. Mountjoy, either on this day or on the next, to allow him to see Florence, and at last was obliged to leave Cheltenham without having done so.

Chapter IV

CAPTAIN SCARBOROUGH'S DISAPPEARANCE

A FEW days after the visits to Cheltenham, described in the last chapters, Harry Annesley, coming down a passage by the side of the Junior United Service Club* into Charles Street, suddenly met Captain Scarborough at two o'clock in the morning. Where Harry had been at that hour need not now be explained, but it may be presumed that he had not been drinking tea with any of his female relatives.

Captain Scarborough had just come out of some neighbouring club, where he had certainly been playing, and where, to all appearances, he had been drinking also. That there should have been no policemen in the street was not remarkable, but there was no one else there present to give any account of what took place during the five minutes in which the two men remained together. Harry, who was at the moment surprised by the encounter, would have passed the captain by without notice, had he been allowed to do so; but this the captain perceived, and stopped him suddenly, taking him roughly by the collar of his coat. This Harry naturally resented, and before a word of intelligible explanation had been given, the two young men had quarrelled.

Captain Scarborough had received a long letter from Mrs. Mountjoy, praying for an explanation of circumstances which could not be explained, and stating over and over again that all her information had come from Harry Annesley.

The captain now called him an interfering, meddlesome idiot, and shook him violently while holding him in his grasp. This was a usage which Harry was not the man to endure, and there soon arose a scuffle, in which blows had passed between them. The captain stuck to his prey, shaking him again and again in his drunken wrath, till Harry, roused to a passion almost equal to that of his opponent, flung him at last against the corner of the club railings, and there left his foe sprawling upon the ground, having struck his head violently against the ground as he fell. Harry passed on to his own bed, indifferent, as it was afterwards said, to the fate of his antagonist. All this occupied probably five minutes in the doing, but was seen by no human eye.

As the occurrence of that night was subsequently made the ground for heavy accusation against Harry Annesley, it has been told here with sufficient minuteness to show what might be said in justification or in condemnation of his conduct,—to show what might be said if the truth were spoken. For, indeed, in the discussions which arose on the subject, much was said which was not true. When he had retired from the scuffle on that night, Harry had certainly not dreamed that any serious damage had been done to the man who had certainly been altogether to blame in his provocation of the quarrel. Had he kept his temper and feelings completely under control, and knocked down Captain Scarborough only in self-defence; had he not allowed himself to be roused to wrath by treatment which could not but give rise to wrath in a young man's bosom; no doubt, when his foe lay at his feet, he would have stooped to pick him up, and have tended his wounds. But such was not Harry's character,—nor that of any of the young men with whom I have been acquainted. Such, however, was the conduct apparently expected from him by many, when the circumstances of those five minutes were brought to the light. But, on the other hand, had passion not completely got the better of him, had he not at the moment considered the attack made upon him to amount to misconduct so gross as to supersede all necessity for gentle usage on his own part, he would hardly have left the man to live or die as chance would have it. Boiling with passion, he went his way, and did leave the man on the pavement, not caring much, or rather, not thinking much, whether his victim might live or die.

On the next day Harry Annesley left London, and went down to Buston, having heard no word further about the captain. He did not start till late in the afternoon, and during the day took some trouble to make himself conspicuous about the town; but he heard nothing of Captain Scarborough. Twice he walked along Charles Street, and looked at the spot on which he had stood on the night before in what might have been deadly conflict. Then he told himself that he had not been in the least wounded, that the ferocious maddened man had attempted to do no more than shake him, that his coat had suffered and not himself, and that in return he had certainly struck the captain with all his violence. There were probably some regrets, but he said not a word on the subject to anyone, and so he left London.

For three or four days nothing was heard of the captain, nor was anything said about him. He had lodgings in town, at which he was no doubt missed, but he also had quarters at the barracks, at which he did not often sleep, but to which it was thought possible on the next morning that he might have betaken himself. Before the evening of that day had come, he had no doubt been missed, but in the world at large no special mention was made of his absence for some time. Then, among the haunts which he was known to frequent, questions began to be asked as to his whereabouts, and to be answered by doubtful assertions that nothing had been seen or heard of him for the last sixty or seventy hours.

It must be remembered that at this time Captain Scarborough was still the subject of universal remark because of the story told as to his birth. His father had declared him to be illegitimate, and had thereby robbed all his creditors. Captain Scarborough was a man quite remarkable enough to ensure universal attention for such a tale as this; but now, added to his illegitimacy was his disappearance. There was at first no idea that he had been murdered. It became quickly known to all the world that he had, on the night in question, lost a large sum of money at a whist club which he frequented, and, in accordance with the custom of the club, had not paid the money on the spot.

The fatal Monday had come round, and the money

undoubtedly was not paid. Then he was declared a defaulter, and in due process of time his name was struck off the club books with some serious increase of the ignominy hitherto sustained.

During the last fortnight or more Captain Scarborough's name had been subjected to many remarks and to much disgrace. But this non-payment of the money lost at whist was considered to be the turning-point. A man might be declared illegitimate, and might in consequence of that or any other circumstance defraud all his creditors. A man might conspire with his father with the object of doing this fraudulently, as Captain Scarborough was no doubt thought to have done by most of his acquaintances. All this he might do and not become so degraded but that his friends would talk to him and play cards with him. But to have sat down to a whist-table and not be able to pay the stakes was held to be so foul a disgrace that men did not wonder that he should have disappeared.

Such was the cause alleged for the captain's disappearance among his intimate friends; but by degrees more than his intimate friends came to talk of it. In a short time his name was in all the newspapers, and there was not a constable in London whose mind was not greatly exercised on the matter. All Scotland Yard*and the police-officers were busy. Mr. Grey, in Lincoln's Inn* was much troubled on the matter. By degrees facts had made themselves clear to his mind, and he had become aware that the captain had been born before his client's marriage. He was ineffably shocked at the old squire's villainy in the matter, but declared to all to whom he spoke openly on the subject that he did not see how the sinner could be punished. He never thought that the father and son were in a conspiracy together. Nor had he believed that they had arranged the young man's disappearance in order the more thoroughly to defraud the creditors. They could not at any rate harm a man of whose whereabouts they were unaware, and who, for all they knew, might be dead. But the reader is already aware that this surmise on the part of Mr. Grey was unfounded.

The captain had been absent for three weeks when Augustus Scarborough went down for a second time to Tretton Park, in order to discuss the matter with his father.

Augustus had, with much equanimity and a steady fixed purpose, settled himself down to the position as eldest son. He pretended no anger to his father for the injury he intended, and was only anxious that his own rights should be confirmed. In this he found that no great difficulty stood in his way. The creditors would contest his rights when his father should die; but for such contest he would be prepared. He had no doubt as to his own position, but thought that it would be safer and that it would also probably be cheaper to purchase the acquiescence of all claimants than to encounter the expense of a prolonged trial, to which there might be more than one appeal, and of which the end after all would be doubtful.

No very great sum of money would probably be required. No very great sum would at any rate be offered. But such an arrangement would certainly be easier if his brother were not present to be confronted with the men whom he had duped.

The squire was still ill down at Tretton, but not so ill but that he had his wits about him in all their clearness. Some said that he was not ill at all, but that in the present state of affairs the retirement suited him. But the nature of the operation which he had undergone was known to many who would not have him harassed in his present condition. In truth he had only to refuse admission to all visitors, and to take care that his commands were carried out in order to avoid disagreeable intrusions.

'Do you mean to say that a man can do such a thing as this and that no one can touch him for it?'

This was an exclamation made by Mr. Tyrrwhit to his lawyer in a tone of aggrieved disgust.

'He hasn't done anything,' said the lawyer. 'He only thought of doing something, and has since repented. You cannot arrest a man because he had contemplated the picking of your pocket, especially when he has shown that he is resolved not to pick it.'

'As far as I can learn, nothing has been heard about him as yet,' said the son to the father.

'Those limbs weren't his that were picked out of the Thames near Blackfriars Bridge?'

'They belonged to a poor cripple who was murdered two months since.'

'And that body that was found down among the Yorkshire hills?'

'He was a pedlar. There is nothing to induce a belief that Mountjoy has killed himself or been killed. In the former case his dead body would be found or his live body would be missing. For the second there is no imaginable cause for suspicion.'

'Then where the devil is he?' said the anxious father.

'Ah! that's the difficulty. But I can imagine no position in which a man might be more tempted to hide himself. He is disgraced on every side, and could hardly show his face in London after the money he has lost. You would not have paid his gambling debts?'

'Certainly not,' said the father. 'There must be an end to all things.'

'Nor could I. Within the last month past he has drawn from me every shilling that I have had at my immediate command.'

'Why did you give 'em to him?'

'It would be difficult to explain all the reasons. He was then my elder brother, and it suited me to have him somewhat under my hand. At any rate I did do so, and am unable for the present to do more.

Looking round about, I do not see where it was possible for him to raise a sovereign as soon as it was once known that he was nobody.'

'What will become of him?' said the father. 'I don't like the idea of his being starved. He can't live without something to live upon.'

'God tempers the wind to the shorn lamb,' said the son. 'For lambs such as he there always seems to be pasture provided of one sort or another.'

'You would not like to have to trust to such pastures,' said the father.

'Nor should I like to be hanged; but I should have to be hanged if I had committed murder. Think of the chances which he has had, and the way in which he has misused them. Although illegitimate he was to have had the whole property, of which not a shilling belongs to him; and he has not lost it because it was not his own, but has simply gambled it away among the Jews. What can happen to a man in such a condition better than to turn up as a hunter among the Rocky Mountains, or as a gold-digger in Australia? In this last adventure he seems to have plunged horribly, and to have lost over three thousand pounds. You wouldn't have paid that for him?'

'Not again—certainly not again.'

'Then what could he do better than disappear? I suppose I shall have to make him an allowance some of these days, and if he can live and keep himself dark I will do so.'

There was in this a tacit allusion to his father's speedy death which was grim enough; but the father passed it by without any expression of displeasure. He certainly owed much to his younger son, and was willing to pay it by quiescence. Let them both forbear. Such was the language which he held to himself in thinking of his younger son. Augustus was certainly behaving well to him. Not a word of rebuke had passed his lips as to the infamous attempt at spoliation which had been made. The old squire felt grateful for his younger son's conduct, but yet in his heart of hearts he preferred the elder.

'He has denuded me of every penny,' said Augustus, 'and I must ask you to refund me something of what has gone.'

'He has kept me very bare. A man with so great a propensity for getting rid of money, I think no father ever before had to endure.'

'You have had the last of it.'

'I do not know that. If I live, and he lets me know his whereabouts, I cannot leave him penniless. I do feel that a great injustice has been done him.'

'I don't exactly see it,' said Augustus.

'Because you're too hard-hearted to put yourself in another man's place. He was my eldest son.'

'He thought that he was.'

'And should have remained so had there been a hope for him,' said the squire, roused to temporary anger. Augustus only shrugged his shoulders. 'But there is no good talking about it.'

'Not the least in the world. Mr. Grey, I suppose, knows the truth at last. I shall have to get three or four thousand pounds from you, or I too must resort to the Jews. I shall do it at any rate under better circumstances than my brother.'

Some arrangement was at last made which was satisfactory to the son, and which we must presume that the father found to be endurable. Then the son took his leave, and went back to London with the understood intention of pushing the enquiries as to his brother's existence and whereabouts.

The sudden and complete disappearance of Captain Scarborough struck Mrs. Mountjoy with the deepest awe. It was not at first borne in upon her to believe that Captain Mountjoy Scarborough, an officer in the Coldstreams, and the acknowledged heir to the Tretton property, had vanished away as a stray street-sweeper might do, or some milliner's lowest workwoman. But at last there were advertisements in all the newspapers and placards on all the walls, and Mrs. Mountjoy did understand that the captain was gone. She could as yet hardly believe that he was no longer heir to Tretton; and in such short discussions with Florence as were necessary on the subject, she preferred to express no opinion whatever as to his conduct. But she would by no means give way when urged to acknowledge that no marriage between Florence and the captain was any longer to be regarded as possible. While the captain was away the matter should be left as if in abeyance; but this by no means suited the young lady's views. Mrs. Mountjoy was not a reticent woman, and had no doubt been too free in whispering among her friends something of her daughter's position. This Florence had resented; but it had still been done, and in Cheltenham generally she was regarded as an engaged young lady. It had been in vain that she had denied that it was so. Her mother's word on such a subject was supposed to be more credible than her own; and now this man with whom she was believed to be so closely connected, had disappeared from the world among the most disreputable circumstances. But when she explained the difficulty to her mother, her mother bade her hold her tongue for the present, and seemed to hold out a hope that the captain might at last be restored to his old position.

'Let them restore him ever so much, he would never be anything to me, mamma.' Then Mrs. Mountjoy would only shake her head and purse her lips.

On the evening of the day after the fracas in the street, Harry Annesley went down to Buston, and there remained for the next two or three days, holding his tongue absolutely as to the adventure of that night. There was no one at Buston to whom he would probably have made known the circumstances. But there was clinging to it a certain flavour of disreputable conduct on his own part which sealed his

lips altogether. The louder and more frequent the
tidings which reached his ears as to the captain's
departure, the more strongly did he feel that duty
required him to tell what he knew upon the matter.
Many thoughts and many fears encompassed him.
At first was the idea that he had killed the man by the
violence of his blow, or that his death had been
caused by his fall. Then it occurred to him that it
was impossible that Scarborough should have been
killed, and that no account should be given as to the
finding of the body. At last he persuaded himself
that he could not have killed the man, but he was
assured at the same time that the disappearance
must in some sort have been occasioned by what then
took place. And it could not but be that the captain,
if alive, should be aware of the nature of the struggle
which had taken place. He heard chiefly from the
newspapers the full record of the captain's illegitimacy; he heard of his condition with the creditors; he
heard of those gambling debts which were left unpaid at the club. He saw it also stated and repeated
that these were the grounds for the man's disappearance. It was quite credible that the man should disappear, or endeavour to disappear, under such a
cloud of difficulties. It did not require that he and
his violence should be adduced as an extra cause.
Indeed, had the man been minded to vanish before
the encounter, he might in all human probability have
been deterred by the circumstances of the quarrel.
It gave no extra reason for his disappearance, and
could in no wise be counted with it were he to tell
the whole story in Scotland Yard. He had been
grossly misused on the occasion, and had escaped
from such misusage by the only means in his power.
But still he felt that had he told the story, people far
and wide would have connected his name with the
man's absence, and, worse again, that Florence's
name would have become entangled with it also.
For the first day or two he had from hour to hour

abstained from telling all that he knew, and then, when the day or two were passed, and when a week had run by—when a fortnight had been allowed to go —it was impossible for him not to hold his tongue.

He became nervous, unhappy, and irritated down at Buston, with his father and mother, and sisters, but more especially with his uncle. Previous to this his uncle for a couple of months had declined to see him; now he was sent for to the Hall, and interrogated daily on this special subject. Mr. Prosper was aware that his nephew had been intimate with Augustus Scarborough, and that he might therefore be presumed to know much about the family. Mr. Prosper took the keenest interest in the illegitimacy and the impecuniosity and final disappearance of the captain, and no doubt did, in his cross-examinations, discover the fact that Harry was unwilling to answer his questions. He found out for the first time that Harry was acquainted with the captain, and also contrived to extract from him the name of Miss Mountjoy. But he could learn nothing else, beyond Harry's unwillingness to talk upon the subject, which was in itself much. It must be understood that Harry was not specially reverential in these communications. Indeed, he gave his uncle to understand that he regarded his questions as impertinent, and at last declared his intention of not coming to the Hall any more for the present. Then Mr. Prosper whispered to his sister that he was quite sure that Harry Annesley knew more than he chose to say as to Captain Scarborough's whereabouts.

'My dear Peter,' said Mrs. Annesley, 'I really think that you are doing poor Harry an injustice.'

Mrs. Annesley was always on the guard to maintain something like an affectionate intercourse between her own family and the squire.

'My dear Anne, you do not see into a millstone*as far as I do. You never did.'

'But, Peter, you really shouldn't say such things of

Harry. When all the police-officers are looking about themselves to catch up anything in their way, they would catch him up at a moment's notice if they heard that a magistrate of the county had expressed such an opinion.'

'Why don't he tell me?' said Mr. Prosper.

'There's nothing to tell.'

'Ah! that's your opinion; because you can't see into a millstone. I tell you that Harry knows more about this Captain Scarborough than anyone else. They were very intimate together.'

'Harry only just knew him.'

'Well, you'll see. I tell you that Harry's name will become mixed up with Captain Scarborough's, and I hope that it will be in no discreditable manner. I hope so, that's all.' Harry in the meantime had returned to London in order to escape his uncle, and to be on the spot to learn anything that might come in his way as to the now acknowledged mystery respecting the captain.

Such was the state of things at the commencement of the period to which my story refers.

Chapter V

AUGUSTUS SCARBOROUGH

HARRY ANNESLEY, when he found himself in London could not for a moment shake off that feeling of nervous anxiety as to the fate of Mountjoy Scarborough which had seized hold of him. In every newspaper which he took in his hand he looked first for the paragraph respecting the fate of the missing man, which the paper was sure to contain in one of its columns. It was his habit during these few days to breakfast at a club, and he could not abstain from speaking to his neighbours about the wonderful Scarborough incident. Every man was at this time will-

ing to speak on the subject, and Harry's interest
might not have seemed to be peculiar; but it became
known that he had been acquainted with the missing
man, and Harry in conversation said much more than
it would have been prudent for him to do on the
understanding that he wished to remain unconnected
with the story. Men asked him questions as though
he were likely to know; and he would answer them
asserting that he knew nothing; but still leaving an
impression behind that he did know more than he
chose to avow. Many enquiries were made daily at
this time in Scotland Yard as to the captain. These,
no doubt, chiefly came from the creditors and their
allies. But Harry Annesley became known among
those who asked for information as Henry Annesley,
Esq., late of St. John's College, Cambridge; and even
the police were taught to think that there was something noticeable in the interest which he displayed.

On the fourth day after his arrival in London, just
at that time of the year when everybody was supposed to be leaving town, and when faded members
of Parliament, who allowed themselves to be retained
for the purpose of final divisions, were cursing their
fate amidst the heats of August, Harry accepted an
invitation to dine with Augustus Scarborough at his
chambers in the Temple.* He understood when he
accepted the invitation that no one else was to be
there, and must have been aware that it was the intention of the heir of Tretton to talk to him respecting his brother. He had not seen Scarborough since
he had been up in town, and had not been desirous
of seeing him; but when the invitation came, he had
told himself that it would be better that he should
accept it, and that he would allow his host to say
what he pleased to say on the subject, he himself
remaining reticent. But poor Harry little knew the
difficulty of reticence when the heart is full. He had
intended to be very reticent when he came up to
London, and had in fact done nothing but talk about

the missing man, as to whom he had declared that
he would altogether hold his tongue.

The reader must here be pleased to remember that
Augustus Scarborough was perfectly well aware of
what had befallen his brother, and must therefore
have known, among other things, of the quarrel which
had taken place in the streets. He knew therefore
that Harry was concealing his knowledge, and could
make a fair guess at the state of the poor fellow's
mind.

'He will guess,' he had said to himself, 'that he
did not leave him for dead on the ground, or the body
would be there to tell the tale. But he must be
ashamed of the part which he took in the street-fight,
and be anxious to conceal it. No doubt Mountjoy
was the first offender, but something has occurred
which Annesley is unwilling should make its way
either to his uncle's ears, or to his father's, or to
mine, or to the squire's—or to those of Florence.'

It was thus that Augustus Scarborough reasoned
with himself when he asked Harry Annesley to dine
with him.

It was not supposed by any of his friends that
Augustus Scarborough would continue to live in the
moderate chambers which he now occupied in the
Temple; but he had as yet made no sign of a desire
to leave them. They were up two pair of stairs, and
were not great in size; but they were comfortable
enough, and even luxurious as a bachelor's abode.

'I've asked you to come alone,' said Augustus,
'because there is such a crowd of things to be talked
of about poor Mountjoy which are not exactly fitted
for the common ear.'

'Yes, indeed,' said Harry, who did not, however,
quite understand why it would be necessary that the
heir should discuss with him the affairs of his unfortunate brother. There had, no doubt, been a certain degree of intimacy between them, but nothing
which made it essential that the captain's difficulties

should be exposed to him. The matter which touched
him most closely, was the love which both the men
had borne to Florence Mountjoy; but Harry did not
expect that any allusion to Florence would be made
on the present occasion.

'Did you ever hear of such a mess?' said Augustus.

'No, indeed. It is not only that he has disappeared——'

'That is as nothing when compared with all the
other incidents of this romantic tale. Indeed it is the
only natural thing in it. Given all the other circumstances, I should have foretold his disappearance as
a thing certain to occur. Why shouldn't such a man
disappear, if he can?'

'But how has he done it?' replied Harry. 'Where
has he gone to? At this moment where is he?'

'Ah! if you will answer all those questions, and
give your information in Scotland Yard, the creditors, no doubt, will make up a handsome purse for
you. Not that they will ever get a shilling from him,
though he were to be seen walking down St. James's
Street tomorrow. But they are a sanguine gentry,
these holders of bills, and I really believe that if they
could see him they would embrace him with the
warmest affection. In the meantime let us have some
dinner, and we will talk about poor Mountjoy when
we have got rid of young Pitcher. Young Pitcher is
my laundress's son, to the use of whose services I
have been promoted since I have been known to be
the heir of Tretton.'

Then they sat down and dined, and Augustus
Scarborough made himself agreeable. The small
dinner was excellent of its kind, and the wine was
all that it ought to be. During dinner not a word
was said as to Mountjoy, nor as to the affairs of the
estate. Augustus, who was old for his age, and had
already practised himself much in London life, knew
well how to make himself agreeable. There was
plenty to be said while young Pitcher was passing

in and out of the room, so that there appeared no awkward intervals of silence while one course succeeded the other. The weather was very hot, the grouse were very tempting, everybody was very dull, and Members of Parliament more stupid than anybody else; but a good time was coming. Would Harry come down to Tretton and see the old governor? There was not much to offer him in the way of recreation, but, when September came, the partridges would abound. Harry gave a half promise that he would go to Tretton for a week, and Augustus Scarborough expressed himself as much gratified. Harry at the moment thought of no reason why he should not go to Tretton, and thus committed himself to the promise; but he afterwards felt that Tretton was of all places the last which he ought just at present to visit.

At last Pitcher and the cheese were gone, and young Scarborough produced his cigars.

'I want to smoke directly I've done eating,' he said. 'Drinking goes with smoking as well as it does with eating, so there need be no stop for that. Now tell me, Annesley, what it is that you think about Mountjoy?'

There was an abruptness in the question which for the moment struck Harry dumb. How was he to say what he thought about Mountjoy Scarborough, even though he should have no feeling to prevent him from expressing the truth? He knew, or thought that he knew, Mountjoy Scarborough to be a thorough blackguard; one whom no sense of honesty kept from spending money, and who was now a party to robbing his creditors without the slightest compunction,—for it was in Harry's mind that Mountjoy and his father were in league together to save the property by rescuing it from the hands of the Jews. He would have thought the same as to the old squire,—only that the old squire had not interfered with him in reference to Florence Mountjoy.

And then there was present to his mind the brutal attack which had been made on himself in the street. According to his views Mountjoy Scarborough was certainly a blackguard; but he did not feel inclined quite to say so to the brother, nor was he perfectly certain as to his host's honesty. It might be that the three Scarboroughs were all in a league together; and if so, he had done very wrong, as he then remembered, to say that he would go down to Tretton. When, therefore, he was asked the question he could only hold his tongue.

'I suppose you have some scruple in speaking, because he's my brother. You may drop that altogether.'

'I think that his career has been what the novel readers would call romantic; but what I, who am not one of them, should describe as unfortunate.'

'Well, yes; taking it altogether it has been unfortunate. I am not a soft-hearted fellow, but I am driven to pity him. The worst of it is that had not my father been induced at last to tell the truth, from most dishonest causes, he would not have been a bit better off than he is. I doubt whether he could have raised another couple of thousand on the day when he went. If he had done so then, and again more and more, to any amount you choose to think of, it would have been the same with him.'

'I suppose so.'

'His lust for gambling was a bottomless quicksand which no possible amount of winning could ever have satiated. Let him enter his club with five thousand pounds at his banker's, and no misfortune could touch him. He being such as he is, or alas! for aught we know, such as he was,—the escape which the property has had cannot but be regarded as very fortunate. I don't care to talk much of myself in particular, though no wrong can have been done to a man more infinite than that which my father contrived for me.'

'I cannot understand your father,' said Harry. In truth there was something in Scarborough's manner in speaking of his father which almost produced belief in Harry's mind. He began to doubt whether Augustus was in the conspiracy.

'No; I should say not. It is hard to understand that an English gentleman should have the courage to conceive such a plot, and the wit to carry it out. If Mountjoy had run only decently straight, or not more than indecently crooked, I should have been a younger brother, practising law in the Temple to the end of my days. The story of Esau and of Jacob* is as nothing to it. But that is not the most remarkable circumstance. My father, for purposes of his own, which include the absolute throwing over of Mountjoy's creditors, changes his plan, and is pleased to restore to me that of which he had resolved to rob me. What father would dare to look in the face the son whom he had thus resolved to defraud? My father tells me the story with a gentle chuckle, showing almost as much indifference to Mountjoy's ruin as to my recovered prosperity! He has not a blush when he reveals it all. He has not a word to say, or, as far as I can see, a thought as to the world's opinion. No doubt he is supposed to be dying. I do presume that three or four months will see the end of him. In the meantime he takes it all as quietly as though he had simply lent a five-pound note to Mountjoy out of my pocket.'

'You, at any rate, will get your property?'

'Oh, yes; and that, no doubt, is his argument when he sees me. He is delighted to have me down at Tretton; and, to tell the truth, I do not feel the slightest animosity towards him. But, as I look at him, I think him to be the most remarkable old gentleman that the world has ever produced. He is quite unconscious that I have any ground of complaint against him.'

'He has probably thought that the circumstances

of your brother's birth should not militate against his prospects.'

'But the law, my dear fellow,' said Scarborough, getting up from his chair and standing with his cigar between his finger and thumb, 'the law thinks otherwise. The making of all right and wrong in this world depends on the law. The half-crown in my pocket is merely mine because of the law. He did choose to marry my mother before I was born, but did not choose to go through that ceremony before my brother's time. That may be a trifle to you, or to my moral feeling, may be a trifle; but because of that trifle all Tretton will be my property, and his attempt to rob me of it was just the same as though he should break into a bank and steal what he found there. He knows that just as well as I do; but to suit his own purposes he did it.'

There was something in the way in which the young man spoke both of his father and his mother which made Harry's flesh creep. He could not but think of his own father, and his own mother, and of his feelings in regard to them. But here this man was talking of the misdoings of the one parent and the other with the most perfect *sang froid*. 'Of course I understand all that,' said Harry.

'There is a manner of doing evil so easy and indifferent as absolutely to quell the general feeling respecting it. A man shall tell you that he has committed a murder in a tone so careless as to make you feel that a murder is nothing. I don't suppose my father can be punished for his attempt to rob me of twenty thousand a year, and therefore he talks to me about it as though it were a good joke. Not only that, but he expects me to receive it in the same way. Upon the whole he prevails. I find myself not in the least angry with him, and rather obliged to him than otherwise for allowing me to be his eldest son.'

'What must Mountjoy's feelings be?' said Harry.

'Exactly. What must be Mountjoy's feelings?

There is no need to consider my father's, but poor Mountjoy's! I don't suppose that he can be dead.'

'I should think not.'

'While a man is alive he can carry himself off, but when a fellow is dead, it requires at least one, or probably two, to carry him. Men do not wish to undertake such a work secretly unless they've been concerned in the murder; and then there will have been a noise which must have been heard, or blood which must have been seen, and the body will at last be forthcoming, or some sign of its destruction. I do not think he can be dead.'

'I should hope not,' said Harry rather tamely, and feeling that he was guilty of a falsehood by the manner in which he expressed his hope.

'When was it you saw him last?' Scarborough asked the question with an abruptness which was pre-determined, but which did not quite take Harry aback.

'About three months since—in London,' said Harry, going back in his memory to the last meeting, which had occurred before the squire had declared his purpose.

'Ah! you haven't seen him then since he knew that he was nobody?' This he asked in an indifferent tone, being anxious not to discover his purpose, but in doing so he gave Harry great credit for his readiness of mind.

'I have not seen him since he heard the news which must have astonished him more than anyone else.'

'I wonder,' said Augustus, 'how Florence Mountjoy has borne it.'

'Neither have I seen her. I have been at Cheltenham, but was not allowed to see her.' This he said with an assertion to himself that though he had lied as to one particular he would not lie as to any other.

'I suppose she must have been much cut up by it all. I have half a mind to declare to myself that she shall still have an opportunity of becoming the mistress of Tretton. She was always afraid of Mountjoy; but I do not know that she ever loved him. She had become so used to the idea of marrying him that she would have given herself up in mere obedience. I too think that she might do as a wife, and I shall certainly make a better husband than Mountjoy would have done.'

'Miss Mountjoy will certainly do as a wife for anyone who may be lucky enough to get her,' said Harry with a certain tone of magnificence which at the moment he felt to be overstrained and ridiculous.

'Oh, yes; one has got to get her as you call it, of course. You mean to say that you are supposed to be in the running. That is your own look-out. I can only allege on my own behalf, that it has always been considered to be an old family arrangement that Florence Mountjoy shall marry the heir to Tretton Park. I am in that position now, and I only throw it out as a hint that I may feel disposed to follow out the family arrangement. Of course if other things come in the way there will be an end of it. Come in.'

This last invitation was given in consequence of a knock at the door. The door was opened, and there entered a policeman in plain clothes* named Prodgers, who seemed from his manner to be well acquainted with Augustus Scarborough.

The police for some time past had been very busy on the track of Mountjoy Scarborough, but had not hitherto succeeded in obtaining any information. Such activity as had been displayed cannot be procured without expense, and it had been understood in this case that old Mr. Scarborough had refused to furnish the means. Something he had supplied at first, but had latterly declined even to subscribe to a fund. He was not at all desirous, he said, that his son should be brought back to the world, particularly as he had made it evident by his disappearance that he was anxious to keep out of the way. 'Why should I pay the fellows? It's no business of mine,' he had said to his son. And from that moment he had declined to do more than make up the first subscription which had been suggested to him. But the police had been kept very busy, and it was known that the funds had been supplied chiefly by Mr. Tyrrwhit. He was a resolute and persistent man, and was determined to 'run down' Mountjoy Scarborough, as he called it, if money would enable him to do so. It was he who had appealed to the squire for assistance in this object, and to him the squire had expressed his opinion that, as his son did not seem anxious to be brought back, he should not interfere in the matter.

'Well, Prodgers, what news have you today?' asked Augustus.

'There is a man a-wandering about down in Skye, just here and there, with nothing in particular to say for himself.'

'What sort of a looking fellow is he?'

'Well, he's light, and don't come up to the captain's marks; but there's no knowing what disguises a fellow will put on. I don't think he's got the captain's legs, and a man can't change his legs.'

'Captain Scarborough would not remain loitering about in Skye, where he would be known by half the autumn tourists who saw him.'

'That's just what I was saying to Wilkinson,' said Prodgers. 'Wilkinson seems to think that a man may be anybody as long as nobody knows who he is. "That ain't the captain," said I.'

'I'm afraid he's got out of England,' said the captain's brother.

'There's no place where he can be run down like New York, or Paris, or Melbourne, and it's them they mostly go to. We've wired 'em all three, and a dozen other places of the kind. We catches 'em mostly if they go abroad; but when they remains at home they're uncommon troublesome. There was a man wandering about in County Donegal. We call

Ireland at home, because we've so much to do with
their police since the Land League*came up; but this
chap was only an artist who couldn't pay his bill.
What do you think about it, Mr. Annesley?' said the
policeman, turning short round upon Harry, and
addressing him a question. Why should the policeman even have known his name?

'Who? I? I don't think about it at all. I have no
means of thinking about it.'

'Because you have been so busy down there at
the Yard. I thought that, as you was asking so
many questions, you was, perhaps, interested in the
matter.'

'My friend Mr. Annesley,' said Augustus, 'was
acquainted with Captain Scarborough, as he is with
me.'

'It did seem as though he was more than usually
interested, all the same,' said the policeman.

'I am more than usually interested,' replied Harry;
'but I do not know that I am going to give you my
reason. As to his present existence, I know absolutely nothing.'

'I dare say not. If you'd any information as was
reliable, I dare say as it would be forthcoming. Well,
Mr. Scarborough, you may be sure of this; if we can
get upon his trail we'll do so, and I think we shall.
There isn't a port that hasn't been watched from two
days after his disappearance, and there isn't a port as
won't be watched as soon as any English steamer
touches 'em. We've got our eyes out, and we means
to use 'em. Good night, Mr. Scarborough; good-
night, Mr. Annesley,' and he bobbed his head to our
friend Harry. 'You say as there is a reason as is unknown. Perhaps it won't be unknown always. Good-
night, gentlemen.' Then Constable Prodgers left
the room.

Harry had been disconcerted by the policeman's
remarks, and showed that it was so as soon as he was
alone with Augustus Scarborough.

'I'm afraid you think the man intended to be impertinent,' said Augustus.

'No doubt he did, but such men are allowed to be impertinent.'

'He sees an enemy, of course, in everyone who pretends to know more than he knows himself—or, indeed, in everyone who does not. You said something about having a reason of your own, and he at once connected you with Mountjoy's disappearance. Such creatures are necessary, but from the little I've seen of them I do not think that they make the best companions in the world. I shall leave Mr. Prodgers to carry on his business to the man who employs him —namely, Mr. Tyrrwhit—and I advise you to do the same.'

Soon after that Harry Annesley took his leave, but he could not divest himself of an opinion that both the policeman and his host had thought that he had some knowledge respecting the missing man. Augustus Scarborough had said no word to that effect, but there had been a something in his manner which had excited suspicion in Harry's mind. And then Augustus had declared his purpose of offering his hand and fortune to Florence Mountjoy. He to be suitor to Florence—he, so soon after Mountjoy had been banished from the scene? And why should he have been told of it?—he, of whose love for the girl he could not but think that Augustus Scarborough had been aware. Then, much perturbed in his mind, he resolved, as he returned to his lodgings, that he would go down to Cheltenham on the following day.

Chapter VI

HARRY ANNESLEY TELLS HIS SECRET

HARRY hurried down to Cheltenham, hardly knowing what he was going to do or say when he got there. He went to the hotel and dined alone.

'What's all this that's up about Captain Mountjoy?' said a stranger, coming and whispering to him at his table.

The stranger was almost a stranger, but Harry did know his name. It was Mr. Baskerville, the hunting man. Mr. Baskerville was not rich, and not especially popular, and had no special amusement but that of riding two nags in the winter along the roads of Cheltenham in the direction which the hounds took. It was still summer, and the nags who had been made to do their work in London were picking up a little strength in idleness, or as Mr. Baskerville called it, getting into condition. In the meantime Mr. Baskerville amused himself as well as he could by lying in bed or playing lawn-tennis. He sometimes dined at the hotel in order that the club might think that he was entertained at friends' houses; but the two places were nearly the same to him, as he could achieve a dinner and half-a-pint of wine for five or six shillings at each of them. A more empty existence, or, one would be inclined to say, less pleasurable, no one could pass; but he had always a decent coat on his back and a smile on his face, and five shillings in his pocket with which to pay for his dinner. His asking what was up about Scarborough showed, at any rate, that he was very backward in the world's news.

'I believe he has vanished,' said Harry.

'Oh, yes, of course he's vanished. Everybody knows that; he vanished ever so long ago. But where is he?'

'If you can tell them at Scotland Yard they will be obliged to you.'

'I suppose it is true that the police are after him? Dear me! Forty thousand a year! This is a very queer story about the property, isn't it?'

'I don't know the story exactly, and therefore can hardly say whether it is queer or not.'

'But about the younger son? People say that the father has contrived that the younger son shall have the money. What I hear is that the whole property is to be divided, and that the captain is to have half, on condition that he keeps out of the way. But I am sure that you know more about it. You used to be intimate with both the brothers. I have seen you down here with the captain. Where is he?' And again he whispered into Harry's ear. But he could not have selected any subject more distasteful, and, therefore, Harry repulsed Mr. Baskerville not in the most courteous manner.

'Hang it! what airs that fellow gives himself,' he said to another friend of the same kidney; 'that's young Annesley, the son of a twopenny-halfpenny parson down in Hertfordshire. The ways these fellows put on now are unbearable. He hasn't got a horse to ride, but to hear him talk you'd think he was mounted three days a week.'

'He's heir to old Prosper, of Buston Hall.'

'How's that? But is he? I never heard that before. What's Buston Hall worth?' Then Mr. Baskerville made up his mind to be doubly civil to Harry Annesley the next time he saw him.

Harry had to consider on that night in what manner he would endeavour to see Florence Mountjoy on the next day. He was thoroughly discontented with himself as he walked about the streets of Cheltenham. He had now not only allowed the disappearance of Scarborough to pass by without stating when and where and how he had last seen him, but had directly lied on the subject. He had told the man's brother that he had not seen him for some weeks previous, whereas to have concealed his knowledge on such a subject was in itself held to be abominable. He was ashamed of himself, and the more so because there was no one to whom he could talk openly on the matter. And it seemed to him as though all whom he met questioned him as to the man's disappearance, as if they suspected him. What was the man to him, or the man's guilt, or his father, that he should be made miserable? The man's attack upon him had been ferocious in its nature—so brutal, that when he had escaped from Mountjoy Scarborough's clutches there was nothing for him but to leave him lying in the street where, in his drunkenness, he had fallen. And now, in consequence of this, misery had fallen upon himself. Even this empty-headed fellow Baskerville, a man the poverty of whose character Harry perfectly understood, had questioned him about Mountjoy Scarborough. It could not, he thought, be possible that Baskerville could have had any reasons for suspicion, and yet the very sound of the enquiry stuck in his ears.

On the next morning at eleven o'clock he knocked at Mrs. Mountjoy's house in Montpellier Place, and asked for the elder lady. Mrs. Mountjoy was out, and Harry at once enquired for Florence. The servant at first seemed to hesitate, but at last showed Harry into the dining-room. There he waited five · minutes, which seemed to him to be half-an-hour, and then Florence came to him.

'Your mother is not at home?' he said, putting out his hand.

'No, Mr. Annesley, but I think she will be back soon. Will you wait for her?'

'I do not know whether I am not glad that she should be out. Florence, I have something that I must tell you.'

'Something that you must tell me!'

He had called her Florence once before, on a happy afternoon which he well remembered, but he was not thinking of that now. Her name, which was always in his mind, had come to him naturally, as though he had no time to pick and choose about names in the importance of the communication which he had to make.

'Yes; I don't believe that you were ever really engaged to your cousin Mountjoy.'

'No, I never was,' she answered briskly. Harry Annesley was certainly a handsome man, but no young man living ever thought less of his own beauty. He had fair wavy hair, which he was always submitting to some barber, very much to the unexpressed disgust of poor Florence; because to her eyes the longer the hair grew the more beautiful was the wearer of it. His forehead, and eyes, and nose, were all perfect in their form.

> Hyperion's curls; the front of Jove himself;
> An eye like Mars, to threaten and command.[*]

There was a peculiar brightness in his eye which would have seemed to denote something absolutely great in his character, had it not been for the wavering indecision of his mouth. There was, as it were, a vacillation in his lips which took away from the manliness of his physiognomy. Florence, who regarded his face as almost divine, was yet conscious of some weakness about his mouth which she did not know how to interpret. But yet, without knowing why it was so, she was accustomed to expect from him doubtful words, half expressed words, which would not declare to her his perfected thoughts as she would have them declared. He was six feet high, neither broad, nor narrow, nor fat, nor thin; and a very Apollo in Florence's eye. To the elders who knew him, the quintessence of his beauty lay in the fact that he was altogether unconscious of it. He was a man who counted nothing on his personal appearance for the performance of those deeds which he was most anxious to achieve. The one achievement now essentially necessary to his happiness was the possession of Florence Mountjoy; but it certainly never occurred to him that he was more likely to obtain this because he was six feet high, or because his hair waved becomingly.

'I have supposed so,' he said, in answer to her last assertion.

'You ought to have known it for certain. I mean to say that had I ever been engaged to my cousin, I should have been miserable at such a moment as this. I never should have given him up because of the gross injustice done to him about the property. But his disappearance in this dreadful way would, I think, have killed me. As it is, I can think of nothing else, because he is my cousin.'

'It is very dreadful,' said Harry. 'Have you any idea what can have happened to him?'

'Not in the least. Have you?'

'None at all. But——'

'But what?'

'I was the last person who saw him.'

'You saw him last!'

'At least I know no one who saw him after me.'

'Have you told them?'

'I have told no one but you. I have come down here to Cheltenham on purpose to tell you.'

'Why me?' she said, as though struck with fear at such an assertion on his part.

'I must tell someone, and I have not known whom else to tell. His father appears not at all anxious about him. His brother I do not altogether trust. Were I to go to these men who are only looking after their money, I should be communicating with his enemies. Your mother already regards me as his enemy. If I told the police I should simply be brought into a court of justice, where I should be compelled to mention your name.'

'Why mine?'

'I must begin the story from the beginning. One

night I was coming home in London very late, about
two o'clock, when whom should I meet in the street
suddenly but Mountjoy Scarborough. It came out
afterwards that he had then been gambling; but when
he encountered me he was intoxicated. He took me
suddenly by the collar and shook me violently, and
did his best to maltreat me. What words were spoken
I cannot remember; but his conduct to me was as
that of a savage beast. I struggled with him in the
street, as a man would struggle who is attacked by a
wild dog. I think that he did not explain the cause of
his hatred, though, of course, my memory as to what
took place at that moment is disturbed and imperfect;
but I did know in my heart why it was that he had
quarrelled with me.'

'Why was it?' Florence asked.

'Because he thought that I had ventured to love
you.'

'No, no,' cried Florence; 'he could not have thought
that.'

'He did think so, and he was right enough. If I
have never said so before, I am bound at any rate to
say it now.' He paused for a moment, but she made
him no answer. 'In the struggle between us he fell
on the pavement against the rail,—and then I left
him.'

'Well?'

'He has never been heard of since. On the following day, in the afternoon, I left London for Buston;
but nothing had been then heard of his disappearance.
I neither knew of it nor suspected it. The question is,
when others were searching for him, was I bound to
go to the police and declare what I had suffered from
him that night? Why should I connect his going
with the outrage which I had suffered?'

'But why not tell it all?'

'I should have been asked why he had quarrelled
with me. Ought I to have said that I did not know?
Ought I to have pretended that there was no cause?

I did know, and there was a cause. It was because he thought that I might prevail with you now that he was a beggar, disowned by his own father.'

'I would never have given him up for that,' said Florence.

'But do you not see that your name would have been brought in,—that I should have had to speak of you as though I thought it possible that you loved me?' Then he paused, and Florence sat silent. But another thought struck him now. It occurred to him that under the plea put forward he would appear to seek shelter from his silence as to her name. He was aware how anxious he was on his own behalf not to mention the occurrence in the street, and it seemed that he was attempting to escape under the pretence of a fear that her name would be dragged in. 'But independently of that I do not see why I should be subjected to the annoyance of letting it be known that I was thus attacked in the streets. And the time has now gone by. It did not occur to me when first he was missed that the matter would have been of such importance. Now it is too late.'

'I suppose that you ought to have told his father.'

'I think that I ought to have done so. But at any rate I have come to explain it all to you. It was necessary that I should tell someone. There seems to be no reason to suspect that the man has been killed.'

'Oh, I hope not; I hope not that.'

'He has been spirited away—out of the way of his creditors. For myself I think that it has all been done with his father's connivance. Whether his brother be in the secret or not I cannot tell, but I suspect he is. There seems to be no doubt that Captain Scarborough himself has run so overhead into debt as to make the payment of his creditors impossible by anything short of the immediate surrender of the whole property. Some month or two since they all thought that the squire was dying, and that there would be nothing to do but to sell the property which would then be Mountjoy's, and pay themselves. Against this the dying man has rebelled, and has come, as it were, out of the grave to disinherit the son who has already contrived to disinherit himself. It is all an effort to save Tretton.'

'But it is dishonest,' said Florence.

'No doubt about it. Looking at it any way it is dishonest. Either the inheritance must belong to Mountjoy still, or it could not have been his when he was allowed to borrow money upon it.'

'I cannot understand it. I thought it was entailed upon him. Of course it is nothing to me. It never could have been anything.'

'But now the creditors declare that they have been cheated, and assert that Mountjoy is being kept out of the way to aid old Mr. Scarborough in the fraud. I cannot but say that I think it is so. But why he should have attacked me just at the moment of his going, or why rather he should have gone immediately after he had attacked me, I cannot say. I have no concern whatever with him or his money, though I hope,—I hope that I may always have much with you. Oh, Florence, you surely have known what has been within my heart.'

To this appeal she made no response, but sat a while considering what she would say respecting Mountjoy Scarborough and his affairs.

'Am I to keep all this a secret?' she asked him at last.

'You shall consider that for yourself. I have not exacted from you any silence on the matter. You may tell whom you please, and I shall not consider that I have any ground of complaint against you. Of course for my own sake I do not wish it to be told. A great injury was done me, and I do not desire to be dragged into this which would be another injury. I suspect that Augustus Scarborough knows more than he pretends, and I do not wish to be brought into the mess by his cunning. Whether you will tell your mother you must judge yourself.'

'I shall tell nobody unless you bid me.' At that moment the door of the room was opened, and Mrs. Mountjoy entered with a frown upon her brow. She had not yet given up all hope that Mountjoy might return, and that the affairs of Tretton might be made to straighten themselves.

'Mamma, Mr. Annesley is here.'

'So I perceive, my dear.'

'I have come to your daughter, to tell her how dearly I love her,' said Harry boldly.

'Mr. Annesley, you should have come to me before speaking to my daughter.'

'Then I shouldn't have seen her at all.'

'You should have left that as it might be. It is not at all a proper thing that a young gentleman should come and address a young lady in this way behind her only parent's back.'

'I asked for you, and I did not know that you would not be at home.'

'You should have gone away at once,—at once. You know how terribly the family is cut up by this great misfortune to our cousin Mountjoy. Mountjoy Scarborough has been long engaged to Florence.'

'No, mamma; no, never.'

'At any rate, Mr. Annesley knows all about it. And that knowledge ought to have kept him away at the present moment. I must beg him to leave us now.'

Then Harry took his hat and departed; but he had great consolation in feeling that Florence had not repudiated his love, which she certainly would have done had she not loved him in return. She had spoken no word of absolute encouragement, but there had been much more of encouragement than of repudiation in her manner.

Chapter VII

HARRY ANNESLEY GOES TO TRETTON

HARRY had promised to go down to Tretton, and, when the time came, Augustus Scarborough did not allow him to escape from the visit. He explained to him that in his father's state of health there would be no company to entertain him; that there was only a maiden sister of his father's staying in the house, and that he intended to take down into the country with him one Septimus Jones, who occupied chambers on the same floor with him in London, and whom Annesley knew to be young Scarborough's most intimate friend. 'There will be a little shooting,' he said, 'and I have bought two or three horses, which you and Jones can ride. Cannock Chase is one of the prettiest parts of England, and as you care for scenery you can get some amusement out of that. You'll see my father, and hear no doubt what he has got to say for himself. He is not in the least reticent in speaking about my brother's affairs.'

There was a good deal in this which was not agreeable. Miss Scarborough was sister to Mrs. Mountjoy as well as to the squire, and had been one of the family party most anxious to assure the marriage of Florence and the captain. The late General Mountjoy had been supposed to be a great man in his way, but had died before Tretton had become as valuable as it was now. Hence the eldest son had been christened with his name, and much of the Mountjoy prestige still clung to the family. But Harry did not care much about the family, except as far as Florence was concerned. And then he had not been on peculiarly friendly terms with Septimus Jones, who had always been submissive to Augustus; and, now that Augustus was a rich man, and could afford to buy horses, was likely to be more submissive than ever.

He went down to Tretton alone early in September, and when he reached the house he found that the two young men were out shooting. He asked for his own room, but was instead immediately taken to the old squire, whom he found lying on a couch in a small dressing-room, while his sister, who had been reading to him, was by his side. After the usual greetings Harry made some awkward apology as to his intrusion at the sick man's bedside.

'Why! I ordered them to bring you in here,' said the squire; 'you can't very well call that intrusion. I have no idea of being shut up from the world before they nail me down in my coffin.'

'That will be a long time first, we all hope,' said his sister.

'Bother! you hope it, but I don't know that anyone else does; I don't for one. And if I did, what's the good of hoping? I have a couple of diseases, either of which is enough to kill a horse.' Then he mentioned his special maladies in a manner which made Harry shrink. 'What are they talking about in London just at present?' he asked.

'Just the old set of subjects,' said Harry.

'I suppose they have got tired of me and my iniquities?' Harry could only smile and shake his head. 'There has been such a complication of romances that one expects the story to run a little more than the ordinary nine days.'

'Men still do talk about Mountjoy.'

'And what are they saying? Augustus declares that you are especially interested on the subject.'

'I don't know why I should be,' said Harry.

'Nor I either. When a fellow becomes no longer of any service to either man, woman, or beast, I do not know why any should take an interest in him. I suppose you didn't lend him money?'

'I was not likely to do that, sir.'

'Then I cannot conceive how it can interest you whether he be in London or Kamschatka.* It does not

interest me the least in the world. Were he to turn
up here, it would be a trouble; and yet they expect
me to subscribe largely to a fund for finding him.
What good could he do me if he were found?'

'Oh! John, he is your son,' said Miss Scarborough.

'And would be just as good a son as Augustus,
only that he has turned out uncommonly badly. I have
not the slightest feeling in the world as to his birth,
and so I think I showed pretty plainly. But nothing
could stop him in his course, and therefore I told the
truth, that's all.'

In answer to this, Harry found it quite impossible
to say a word; but got away to his bed-room and
dressed for dinner as quickly as possible. While he
was still thus employed, Augustus came into the
room still dressed in his shooting clothes.

'So you've seen my father,' he said.

'Yes; I saw him.'

'And what did he say to you about Mountjoy?'

'Little or nothing that signifies. He seems to think
it unreasonable that he should be asked to pay for
finding him, seeing that the creditors expect to get
the advantage of his presence when found.'

'He is about right there.'

'Oh, yes; but still he is his father. It may be that
it would be expected that he should interest himself
in finding him.'

'Upon my word I don't agree with you. If a thousand a year could be paid to keep Mountjoy out of the
way, I think it would be well expended.'

'But you were acting with the police.'

'Oh, the police! What do the police know about
it? Of course I talk it all over with them. They have
not the smallest idea where the man is, and do not
know how to go to work to discover him. I don't say
that my father is judicious in his brazen-faced opposition to all enquiry. He should pretend to be a little
anxious,—as I do. Not that there would be any use
now in pretending to keep up appearances. He has

declared himself utterly indifferent to the law, and has defied the world. Never mind, old fellow, we shall eat the more dinner, only I must go and prepare myself for it.'

At dinner Harry found only Septimus Jones, Augustus Scarborough, and his aunt. Miss Scarborough said a good deal about her brother, and declared him to be much better.

'Of course you know, Augustus, that Sir William Brodrick was down here for two days.'

'Only fancy,' replied he, 'what one has to pay for two days of Sir William Brodrick in the country.'

'What can it matter?' said the generous spinster.

'It matters exactly so many hundred pounds; but no one will begrudge it if he does so many hundred pounds' worth of good.'

'It will show, at any rate, that we have had the best advice,' said the lady.

'Yes, it will show; that is exactly what people care about. What did Sir William say?'

Then during the first half of dinner a prolonged reference was made to Mr. Scarborough's maladies, and to Sir William's opinion concerning them. Sir William had declared that Mr. Scarborough's constitution was the most wonderful thing that he had ever met in his experience. In spite of the fact that Mr. Scarborough's body was one mass of cuts and bruises, and faulty places, and that nothing would keep him going except the wearing of machinery which he was unwilling to wear; yet the facilities for much personal enjoyment were left to him, and Sir William declared that if he would only do exactly as he were told, he might live for the next five years.

'But everybody knows that he won't do anything that he is told,' said Augustus in a tone of voice which by no means expressed extreme sorrow.

From his father he led the conversation to the partridges, and declared his conviction that with a little trouble and some expense, a very good head of game might be got up at Tretton.

'I suppose it wouldn't cost much,' said Jones, who beyond ten shillings to a gamekeeper never paid six-pence for whatever shooting came in his way.

'I don't know what you call much,' said Augustus, 'but I think it may be done for three or four hundred a year. I should like to calculate how many thousand partridges at that rate Sir William has taken back in his pocket.'

'What does it matter?' asked Miss Scarborough.

'Only as a speculation. Of course my father, while he lives, is justified in giving his whole income to doctors if he likes it; but one gets into a manner of speaking about him as though he had done a good deal with his money in which he was not justi-fied.'

'Don't talk in that way, Augustus.'

'My dear aunt, I am not at all inclined to be more open-mouthed than he is. Only reflect what it was that he was disposed to do to me, and the good-humour with which I have borne it!'

'I think I should hold my tongue about it,' said Harry Annesley.

'And I think that in my place you would do no such thing. To your nature it would be almost im-possible to hold your tongue. Your sense of justice would be so affronted that you would feel yourself compelled to discuss the injury done to you with all your intimate friends. But with your father your quarrel would be eternal. I make nothing of it, and indeed if he pertinaciously held his tongue on the subject, so should I.'

'But because he talks,' said Harry, 'why should you?'

'Why should he not?' said Septimus Jones. 'Upon my word, I don't see the justice of it.'

'I am not speaking of justice, but of feeling.'

'Upon my word, I wish you would hold your

tongues about it; at any rate till my back is turned,' said the old lady.

Then Augustus finished the conversation.

'I am determined to treat it all as though it were a joke, and, as a joke, one to be spoken of lightly. It was a strong measure, certainly, this attempt to rob me of twenty or thirty thousand pounds a year. But it was done in favour of my brother, and therefore let it pass. I am at a loss to conceive what my father has done with his money. He hasn't given Mountjoy, at any rate, more than a half of his income for the last five or six years, and his own personal expenses are very small. Yet he tells me that he has the greatest difficulty in raising a thousand pounds, and positively refuses in his present difficulties to add above five hundred a year to my former allowance. No father, who had thoroughly done his duty by his son, could speak in a more fixed and austere manner. And yet he knows that every shilling will be mine as soon as he goes.' The servant who was waiting upon them had been in and out of the room while this was said, and must have heard much of it. But to that Augustus seemed to be quite indifferent. And, indeed, the whole family story was known to every servant in the house. It is true that gentlemen and ladies who have servants do not usually wish to talk about their private matters before all the household, even though the private matters may be known; but this household was unlike all others in that respect. There was not a housemaid about the rooms, or a groom in the stables, who did not know how terrible a reprobate their master had been.

'You will see your father before you go to bed?' Miss Scarborough said to her nephew as she left the room.

'Certainly, if he will send to say that he wishes it.'

'He does wish it, most anxiously.'

'I believe that to be your imagination. At any rate I will come,—say in an hour's time. He would be just as pleased to see Harry Annesley for the matter of that, or Mr. Grey, or the inspector of police. Any one whom he could shock, or pretend to shock by the peculiarity of his opinions, would do as well.' By that time, however, Miss Scarborough had left the room.

Then the three men sat and talked, and discussed the affairs of the family generally. New leases had just been granted for adding manufactories to the town of Tretton; and as far as outward marks of prosperity went, all was prosperous. 'I expect to have a water-mill on the lawn before long,' said Augustus. 'These mechanics*have it all their own way. If they were to come and tell me that they intended to put up a windmill in my bedroom tomorrow morning, I could only take off my hat to them. When a man offers you five per cent. where you've only had four, he is instantly your lord and master. It doesn't signify how vulgar he is or how insolent, or how exacting. Associations of the tenderest kind must all give way to trade. But the shooting which lies to the north and west of us is, I think, safe for the present. I suppose I must go and see what my father wants or I shall be held to have neglected my duty to my affectionate parent.'

'Capital fellow, Augustus Scarborough,' said Jones as soon as their host had left them.

'I was at Cambridge with him, and he was popular there.'

'He'll be more popular now that he's the heir to Tretton. I don't know any fellow that I can get along better with than Scarborough. I think you were a little hard upon him about his father, you know.'

'In his position he ought to hold his tongue.'

'It's the strangest thing that has turned up in the whole course of my experience. You see, if he didn't talk about it people wouldn't quite understand what it was that his father had done. It's only matter of report now, and the creditors, no doubt, do believe that when old Scarborough goes off the hooks they will be able to walk in and take possession. Augustus has got to make the world think that he is the heir, and that will go a long way. You may be sure he doesn't talk as he does without having a reason for it. He's the last man I know to do anything without a reason.'

The evening dragged along very slowly while Jones continued to tell all that he knew of his friend's character. But Augustus Scarborough did not return, and soon after ten o'clock, when Harry Annesley could smoke no more cigars, and declared that he had no wish to begin upon brandy and water after his wine, he went to his bed.

Chapter VIII

HARRY ANNESLEY TAKES A WALK

'THERE was the deuce to pay with my father last night after I went to him,' said Scarborough to Harry next morning. 'He now and then suffers agonies of pain, and it is the most difficult thing in the world to get him right again. But anything equal to his courage I never before met.'

'How is he this morning?'

'Very weak, and unable to exert himself. But I cannot say that he is otherwise much the worse. You won't see him this morning; but to-morrow you will, or next day. Don't you be shy about going to him when he sends for you. He likes to show the world that he can bear his sufferings with a light heart, and is ready to die to-morrow without a pang or a regret. Who was the fellow who sent for a fellow to let him see how a Christian could die?* I can fancy my father doing the same thing, only there would be nothing about Christianity in the message. He will bid you come and see a pagan depart in peace, and would be very unhappy if he thought that your dinner would be disturbed by the ceremony. Now come down to breakfast, and then we'll go out shooting.'

For three days Harry remained at Tretton, and ate and drank, and shot and rode always in young Scarborough's company. During this time he did not see the old squire, and understood from Miss Scarborough's absence that he was still suffering from his late attack. The visit was to be prolonged for one other day, and he was told that on that day the squire would send for him.

'I'm sick of these eternal partridges,' said Augustus. 'No man should ever shoot partridges two days running. Jones can go out by himself. He won't have to tip the gamekeeper any more for an additional day, and so it will be all gain to him. You'll see my father in the afternoon after lunch, and we will go and take a walk now.'

Harry started for his walk, and his companion immediately began again about the property. 'I'm beginning to think,' said he, 'that it's nearly all up with the governor. These attacks come upon him worse and worse, and always leave him absolutely prostrate. Then he will do nothing to prevent them. To assure himself a week of life, he will not endure an hour of discomfort. It is plucky, you know.'

'He is in all respects as brave a man as I have known.'

'He sets God and man at absolute defiance, and always does it with the most profound courtesy. He was very much troubled about you yesterday.'

'What has he to say of me?'

'Nothing in the least uncivil; but he has an idea in his head which nothing on earth will put out of it, and in which, but for your own word, I should be inclined to agree.' Harry when this was said stood still on the mountain-side, and looked full into his companion's face. He felt at the moment that the idea had some reference to Mountjoy Scarborough and his disappearance. They were together on the heathy, unenclosed ground of Cannock Chase, and had already walked some ten or twelve miles. 'He thinks you know where Mountjoy is.'

'Why should I know?'

'Or at any rate that you have seen him since any of us. He professes not to care a straw for Mountjoy or his whereabouts, and declares himself under obligation to those who have contrived his departure. Nevertheless he is curious.'

'What have I to do with Mountjoy Scarborough?'

'That's just the question. What have you to do with him? He suggests that there have been words between you as to Florence, which have caused Mountjoy to vanish. I don't profess to explain anything beyond that—nor indeed do I profess to agree with my father. But the odd thing is that Prodgers, the policeman, has the same thing running in his head.'

'Because I have shown some anxiety about your brother in Scotland Yard.'

'No doubt; Prodgers says that you've shown more anxiety than was to be expected from a mere acquaintance. I quite acknowledge that Prodgers is as thick-headed an idiot as you shall catch on a summer's day; but that's his opinion. For myself I know your word too well to doubt it.' Harry walked on in silence, thinking, or trying to think, what, at the spur of the moment, he had better do. He was minded to speak out the whole truth, and declare to himself that it was nothing to him what Augustus Scarborough might say or think. And there was present to him a feeling that his companion was dealing unfairly with him, and was endeavouring in some way to trap him and lead him into a difficulty. But he had made up his mind, as it were, not to know anything of Mountjoy Scarborough, and to let those five minutes in the street be as though they had never been. He had been brutally attacked, and had thought it best to say nothing on the subject. He would not allow his secret, such as it was, to be wormed out of him. Scarborough was endeavouring to extort from him that which he had resolved to conceal; and he determined at last that he would not become a puppet in his hands. 'I don't see why you should care a straw about it,' said Scarborough.

'Nor do I.'

'At any rate you repeat your denial. It will be well that I should let my father know that he is mistaken, and also that ass Prodgers. Of course with my father it is sheer curiosity. Indeed, if he thought that you were keeping Mountjoy under lock and key, he would only admire your dexterity in so preserving him. Any bold line of action that is contrary to the law recommends itself to his approbation. But Prodgers has a lurking idea that he should like to arrest you.'

'What for?'

'Simply because he thinks you know something that he doesn't know. As he's a detective, that, in his mind, is quite enough for arresting any man. I may as well give him my assurance then that he is mistaken.'

'Why should your assurance go for more than mine? Give him nothing of the kind.'

'I may give him at any rate my assurance that I believe your word.'

'If you do believe it you can do so.'

'But you repeat your assertion that you saw nothing of Mountjoy just before his disappearance?'

'This is an amount of cross-questioning which I do not take in good part, and to which I will not submit.' Here Scarborough affected to laugh loudly. 'I know nothing of your brother, and care almost as little. He has professed to admire a young lady to whom I am not indifferent, and has, I believe, expressed a wish to make her his wife. He is also her cousin, and the lady in question has no doubt been much interested about him. It is natural that she should be so.'

'Quite natural,—seeing that she has been engaged to him for twelve months.'

'Of that I know nothing. But my interest about your brother has been because of her. You can explain all this about your brother if you please, or can let it alone. But for myself I decline to answer any more questions. If Prodgers thinks he can arrest me, let him come and try.'

'The idea of you flying into a passion because I have endeavoured to explain it all to you! At any rate I have your absolute denial, and that will enable me to deal both with my father and with Prodgers.' To this Harry made no answer, and the two young men walked back to Tretton together without any more words between them.

When Harry had been in the house about half-an-hour, and had already eaten his lunch somewhat sulkily, a message came to him from Miss Scarborough requiring his presence. He went to her, and was told by her that Mr. Scarborough would now see him. He was aware that Mr. Scarborough never saw Septimus Jones, and that there was something peculiar in the sending of this message to him. Why should the man who was supposed to have but a few weeks to live be so anxious to see one who was comparatively a stranger to him?

'I am so glad you have come in before dinner, Mr. Annesley, because my brother is so anxious to see you, and I'm afraid you'll go too early in the morning.' Then he followed her, and again found Mr. Scarborough on a couch in the same room to which he had been first introduced.

'I've had a sharp bout of it since I saw you,' said the sick man.

'So we heard, sir.'

'There is no saying how many or rather how few bouts of this kind it will take to polish me off. But I think I am entitled to some little respite now. The apothecary from Tretton was here this morning, and I believe has done me just as much good as Sir William Brodrick. His charge will be ten shillings, while Sir William demanded three hundred pounds. But it would be mean to go out with no one but the Tretton apothecary to look after one.'

'I suppose Sir William's knowledge has been of some service.'

'His dexterity with his knife has been of more. So you and Augustus have been quarrelling about Mountjoy?'

'Not that I know of.'

'He says so; and I believe his word on such a subject sooner than yours. You are likely to quarrel without knowing it, and he is not. He thinks that you know what has become of Mountjoy.'

'Does he? Why should he think so when I have told him that I know nothing? I tell you that I know absolutely nothing. I am ignorant whether he is dead or alive.'

'He is not dead,' said the father.

'I suppose not; but I know nothing about him. Why your second son——'

'You mean my eldest according to law—or rather my only son.'

'Why Augustus Scarborough,' continued Harry Annesley, 'should take upon himself to suspect that I know aught of his brother I cannot say. He has some cock-and-bull story about a policeman whom he professes to believe to be ignorant of his own business. This policeman, he says, is anxious to arrest me.'

'To make you give evidence before a magistrate,' said the squire.

'He did not dare to tell me that he suspected me himself.'

'There—I knew you had quarrelled.'

'I deny it altogether. I have not quarrelled with

Augustus Scarborough. He is welcome to his suspicions if he chooses to entertain them. I should have liked him better if he had not brought me down to Tretton, so as to extract from me whatever he can. I shall be more guarded in future in speaking of Mountjoy Scarborough; but to you I give my positive assurance, which I do not doubt you will believe, that I know nothing respecting him.' An honest indignation gleamed in his eyes as he spoke; but still there were the signs of that vacillation about his mouth which Florence had been able to read, but not to interpret.

'Yes,' said the squire after a pause, 'I believe you. You haven't that kind of ingenuity which enables a man to tell a lie and stick to it. I have. It's a very great gift, if a man be enabled to restrain his appetite for lying.' Harry could only smile when he heard the squire's confession. 'Only think how I have lied about Mountjoy; and how successful my lies might have been, but for his own folly.'

'People do judge you a little harshly now,' said Harry.

'What's the odds? I care nothing for their judgment. I endeavoured to do justice to my own child, and very nearly did it. I was very nearly successful in rectifying the gross injustice of the world. Why should a little delay in a ceremony in which he had no voice have robbed him of his possessions? I determined that he should have Tretton, and I determined also to make it up to Augustus by denying myself the use of my own wealth. Things have gone wrongly, not by my own folly. I could not prevent the mad career which Mountjoy has run; but do you think that I am ashamed, because the world knows what I have done? Do you suppose that my deathbed will be embittered by the remembrance that I have been a liar? Not in the least. I have done the best I could for my two sons; and in doing it have denied myself many advantages. How many a man would have spent his money on himself, thinking nothing of his boys, and then have gone to his grave with all the dignity of a steady Christian father. Of the two men I prefer myself; but I know that I have been a liar.'

What was Harry Annesley to say in answer to such an address as this? There was the man stretched on his bed before him, haggard, unshaved, pale, and grizzly, with a fire in his eyes, but weakness in his voice—bold, defiant, self-satisfied, and yet not selfish. He had lived through his life with the one strong resolution of setting the law at defiance in reference to the distribution of his property; but chiefly because he had thought the law to be unjust. Then, when the accident of his eldest son's extravagance had fallen upon him, he had endeavoured to save his second son, and had thought, without the slightest remorse, of the loss which was to fall on the creditors. He had done all this in such a manner, that, as far as Harry knew, the law could not touch him, though all the world was aware of his iniquity. And now he lay boasting of what he had done. It was necessary that Harry should say something as he rose from his seat, and he lamely expressed a wish that Mr. Scarborough might quickly recover. 'No, my dear fellow,' said the squire; 'men do not recover when they are brought to such straits as I am in. Nor do I wish it. Were I to live, Augustus would feel the second injustice to be quite intolerable. His mind is lost in amazement at what I had contemplated. And he feels that the matter can only be set right between him and Fortune by my dying at once. If he were to understand that I were going to live ten years longer, I think that he would either commit a murder or lose his senses.'

'But there is enough for both of you,' said Harry.

'There is no such word in the language as enough. An estate can have but one owner here. I do not blame him in the least. Why should he desire to spare a father's rights, when that father showed himself so willing to sacrifice his? Goodbye, Annesley,

I am sorry you are going, for I like to have some honest fellow to talk to. You are not to suppose that because I have done this thing I am indifferent of what men shall say of me. I wish them to think me good, though I have chosen to run counter to the prejudices of the world.'

Then Harry escaped from the room, and spent the remaining evening with Augustus Scarborough and Septimus Jones. The conversation was devoted chiefly to the partridges and horses; and was carried on by Septimus with severity towards Harry, and by Scarborough with an extreme civility which was the more galling of the two.

Chapter IX

AUGUSTUS HAS HIS OWN DOUBTS

'THAT'S an impertinent young puppy,' said Septimus Jones, as soon as the fly which was to carry Harry Annesley to the station had left the hall-door on the following morning. It may be presumed that Mr. Jones would not thus have expressed himself, unless his friend Augustus Scarborough had dropped certain words in conversation in regard to Harry to the same effect. And it may be presumed also that Augustus would not have dropped such words without a purpose of letting his friend know that Harry was to be abused. Augustus Scarborough had made up his mind, looking at the matter all round, that more was to be got by abusing Harry than by praising him.

'The young man has a good opinion of himself, certainly.'

'He thinks himself to be a deal better than anybody else,' continued Jones, 'whereas I for one don't see it. And he has a way with him of pretending to be quite equal to his companions, let them be who they may, which to me is odious. He was down upon

you and down upon your father. Of course your
father has made a most fraudulent attempt; but what
is it to him?' The other young man made no answer,
but only smiled. The opinion expressed by Mr.
Jones as to Harry Annesley had only been a reflex
of that felt by Augustus Scarborough. But the reflex,
as is always the case when the looking-glass is true,
was correct.

Scarborough had known Harry Annesley for a
long time, as time is counted in early youth, and had
by degrees learned to hate him thoroughly. He was
a little the elder, and had at first thought to domineer
over his friend. But the friend had resisted, and had
struggled manfully to achieve what he considered an
equality in friendship. 'Now, Scarborough, you may
as well take it once for all that I am not going to be
talked down. If you want to talk a fellow down you
can go to Walker, or Brown, or Green. Then when
you are tired of the occupation you can come back to
me.' It was thus that Annesley had been wont to
address his friend. But his friend had been anxious
to talk down this special young man for special purposes, and had been conscious of some weakness in
the other's character which he thought entitled him
to do so. But the weakness was not of that nature,
and he had failed. Then had come the rivalry between Mountjoy and Harry, which had seemed to
Augustus to be the extreme of impudence. From of
old he had been taught to regard his brother Mountjoy as the first of young men, among commoners;
the first in prospects and the first in rank; and to him
Florence Mountjoy had been allotted as a bride. How
he had himself learned first to envy and then to covet
this allotted bride need not here be told. But by
degrees it had come to pass that Augustus had determined that his spendthrift brother should fall under
his own power, and that the bride should be the
reward. How it was that two brothers, so different
in characters, and yet so alike in their selfishness,

should have come to love the same girl with a true
intensity of purpose, and that Harry Annesley, whose
character was essentially different, and who was in
no degree selfish, should have loved her also, must
be left to explain itself as the girl's character shall
be developed. But Florence Mountjoy had now for
many months been the cause of bitter dislike against
poor Harry in the mind of Augustus Scarborough.
He understood, much more clearly than his brother
had done, who it was that the girl really preferred.
He was ever conscious, too, of his own superiority—
falsely conscious—and did feel that if Harry's character were really known, no girl would in truth prefer
him. He could not quite see Harry with Florence's
eyes, nor could he see himself with any other eyes
but his own. Then had come the meeting between
Mountjoy and Harry Annesley in the street, of which
he had only such garbled account as Mountjoy himself had given him within half-an-hour afterwards.
From that story, told in the words of a drunken man
—a man drunk, and bruised, and bloody, who clearly
did not understand in one minute the words spoken in
the last—Augustus did learn that there had been some
great row between his brother and Harry Annesley.
Then Mountjoy had disappeared—had disappeared,
as the reader will have understood, with his brother's
co-operation—and Harry had not come forward when
enquiries were made, to declare what he knew of the
occurrences of that night. Augustus had narrowly
watched his conduct, in order at first that he might
learn in what condition his brother had been left in
the street, but afterwards with the purpose of ascer-
taining why it was that Harry had been so reticent.
Then he had allured Harry on to a direct lie, and soon
perceived that he could afterwards use the secret for
his own purpose.

'I think we shall have to see what that young
man's about, you know,' he said afterwards to Septimus Jones.

'Yes, yes, certainly,' said Septimus; but Septimus did not quite understand why it was that they should have to see what the young man was about.

'Between you and me, I think he means to interfere with me, and I do not mean to stand his interference.'

'I should think not.'

'He must go back to Buston among the Bustonians, or he and I will have a stand-up fight of it. I rather like a stand-up fight.'

'Just so. When a fellow's so bumptious as that he ought to be licked.'

'He has lied about Mountjoy,' said Augustus. Then Jones waited to be told how it was that Harry had lied. He was aware that there was some secret unknown to him, and was anxious to be informed. Was Harry aware of Mountjoy's hiding-place, and if so, how had he learned it? Why was it that Harry should be acquainted with that which was dark to all the world besides? Jones was of opinion that the squire knew all about it, and thought it not improbable that the squire and Augustus had the secret in their joint keeping. But if so, how should Harry Annesley know anything about it? 'He has lied like the very deuce,' continued Augustus after a pause.

'Has he, now?'

'And I don't mean to spare him.'

'I should think not.' Then there was a pause, at the end of which Jones found himself driven to ask a question: 'How has he lied?' Augustus smiled and shook his head, from which the other man gathered that he was not now to be told the nature of the lie in question. 'A fellow that lies like that,' said Jones, 'is not to be endured.'

'I do not mean to endure him. You have heard of a young lady named Miss Mountjoy, a cousin of ours?'

'Mountjoy's Miss Mountjoy?' suggested Jones.

'Yes; Mountjoy's Miss Mountjoy. That of course

is over. Mountjoy has brought himself to such a pass that he is not entitled to have a Miss Mountjoy any longer. It seems the proper thing that she shall pass with the rest of the family property to the true heir.'

'You marry her!'

'We need not talk about that just at present. I don't know that I've made up my mind. At any rate I do not intend that Harry Annesley shall have her.'

'I should think not.'

'He's a pestilential cur, who has got himself introduced into the family, and the sooner we get quit of him the better. I should think the young lady would hardly fancy him, when she knows that he has lied with the object of getting her former lover out of the way.'

'By Jove, no, I should think not!'

'And when the world comes to understand that Harry Annesley, in the midst of all these enquiries, knows all about poor Mountjoy—was the last to see him in London—and has never come forward to say a word about him, then I think the world will be a little hard upon the immaculate Harry Annesley. His own uncle has quarrelled with him already.'

'What uncle?'

'The gentleman down in Hertfordshire, on the strength of whose acres Master Harry is flaunting it about in idleness. I have my eyes open and can see as well as another. When Harry lectures me about my father and my father about me, one would suppose that there's not a hole in his own coat.* I think he'll find that the garment is not altogether water-tight.' Then Augustus, finding that he had told as much as was needful to Septimus Jones, left his friend and went about his family business.

On the next morning Septimus Jones took his departure, and on the day following Augustus followed him. 'So you're off,' his father said to him when he came to make his adieux.

'Well, yes; I suppose so. A man has got so many

things to look after which he can't attend to down here.'

'I don't know what they are, but you understand it all. I'm not going to ask you to stay. Does it ever occur to you that you may never see me again?'

'What a question!'

'It's one that requires an answer, at any rate.'

'It does occur to me; but not at all as probable.'

'Why not probable?'

'Because there's a telegraph wire from Tretton to London, and because the journey down here is very short. It also occurs to me to think so from what has been said by Sir William Brodrick. Of course any man may die suddenly.'

'Especially when the surgeons have been at him.'

'You have your sister with you, sir, and she will be of more comfort to you than I can. Your condition is in some respects an advantage to you. These creditors of Mountjoy can't force their way in upon you.'

'You are wrong there.'

'They have not done so.'

'Nor should they, though I were as strong as you. What are Mountjoy's creditors to me? They have not a scrap of my handwriting in their possession. There is not one who can say that he has even a verbal promise from me. They never came to me when they wanted to lend him money at fifty per cent. Did they ever hear me say that he was my heir?'

'Perhaps not.'

'Not one has ever heard it. It was not to them I lied, but to you and Grey. The creditors! What do I care for them, though they be all ruined?'

'Not in the least.'

'Why do you talk to me about the creditors? You, at any rate, know the truth.'

Then Augustus quitted the room, leaving his father in a passion. But, as a fact, he was by no means assured as to the truth. He supposed that he was the heir, but might it not be possible that his father had contrived all this so as to save the property from Mountjoy and that greedy pack of money-lenders? Grey must surely know the truth. But why should not Grey be deceived on the second event as well as on the first? There was no limit, Augustus sometimes thought, to his father's cleverness. This idea had occurred to him within the last week, and his mind was tormented with reflecting what might yet be his condition. But of one thing he was sure, that his father and Mountjoy were not in league together. Mountjoy at any rate believed himself to have been disinherited. Mountjoy conceived that his only chance of obtaining money arose from his brother. The circumstances of Mountjoy's absence were at any rate unknown to his father.

Chapter X

SIR MAGNUS MOUNTJOY

IT was the peculiarity of Florence Mountjoy that she did not expect other people to be as good as herself. It was not that she erected for herself a high standard, and had then told herself that she had no right to demand from others one so exalted. She had erected nothing. Nor did she know that she attempted to live by grand rules. She had no idea that she was better than anybody else; but it came to her naturally, as the result of what had gone before, to be unselfish, generous, trusting, and pure. These may be regarded as feminine virtues, and may be said to be sometimes tarnished by faults which are equally feminine. Unselfishness may become want of character; generosity essentially unjust; confidence may be weak, and purity insipid. Here it was that the strength of Florence Mountjoy asserted itself.

She knew well what was due to herself, though she would not claim it. She could trust to another, but in silence be quite sure of herself. Though pure herself, she was rarely shocked by the ways of others. And she was as true as a man pretends to be.

In figure, form, and face she never demanded immediate homage by the sudden flash of her beauty. But when her spell had once fallen on a man's spirit it was not often that he could escape from it quickly. When she spoke a peculiar melody struck the hearer's ears. Her voice was soft and low and sweet, and full at all times of harmonious words; but when she laughed it was like soft winds playing among countless silver bells. There was something in her touch which to men was almost divine. Of this she was all unconscious, but was as chary with her fingers as though it seemed that she could ill spare her divinity.

In height she was a little above the common, but it was by the grace of her movements that the world was compelled to observe her figure. There are women whose grace is so remarkable as to demand the attention of all. But then it is known of them, and momentarily seen, that their grace is peculiar. They have studied their graces, and the result is there only too evident. But Florence seemed to have studied nothing. The beholder felt that she must have been as graceful when playing with her doll in the nursery. And it was the same with her beauty. There was no peculiarity of chiselled features. Had you taken her face and measured it by certain rules, you would have found that her mouth was too large and her nose irregular. Of her teeth she showed but little, and in her complexion there was none of that pellucid clearness in which men ordinarily delight. But her eyes were more than ordinarily bright, and when she laughed there seemed to stream from them some heavenly delight. When she did laugh it was as though some spring had been opened from which ran for the time a stream of sweetest intimacy. For the time you would then fancy that you had been let into the inner life of this girl, and would be proud of yourself that so much should have been granted you. You would feel that there was something also in yourself in that this should have been permitted. Her hair and eyebrows were dark brown, of the hue most common to men and women, and had in them nothing that was peculiar; but her hair was soft and smooth, and ever well dressed, and never redolent of peculiar odours. It was simply Florence Mountjoy's hair, and that made it perfect in the eyes of her male friends generally.

'She's not such a wonderful beauty, after all,' once said of her a gentleman, to whom it may be presumed that she had not taken the trouble to be peculiarly attractive. 'No,' said another; 'no. But, by George! I shouldn't like to have the altering of her.' It was thus that men generally felt in regard to Florence Mountjoy. When they came to reckon her up they did not see how any change was to be made for the better.

To Florence, as to most other girls, the question of her future life had been a great trouble. Whom should she marry? And whom should she decline to marry! To a girl, when it is proposed to her suddenly to change everything in life, to go altogether away and place herself under the custody of a new master, to find for herself a new home, new pursuits, new aspirations, and a strange companion, the change must be so complete as almost to frighten her by its awfulness. And yet it has to be always thought of, and generally done. But this change had been presented to Florence in a manner more than ordinarily burdensome. Early in life, when naturally she would not have begun to think seriously of marriage, she had been told rather than asked to give herself to her cousin Mountjoy. She was too firm of character to accede at once,—to deliver herself over body and soul to the tender mercies of one in truth unknown.

But she had been unable to interpose any reason
that was valid, and had contented herself by demanding time. Since that there had been moments in
which she had almost yielded. Mountjoy Scarborough had been so represented to her that she had
considered it to be almost a duty to yield. More than
once the word had been all but spoken; but the word
had been never spoken. She had been subjected to
what might be called cruel pressure. In season and
out of season her mother had represented as a duty
this marriage with her cousin. Why should she not
marry her cousin? It must be understood that these
questions had been asked before any of the terrible
facts of Captain Scarborough's life had been made
known to her. Because, it may be said, she did not
love him. But in these days she had loved no man,
and was inclined to think so little of herself as to
make her want of love no necessary bar to the accom-
plishment of the wish of others. By degrees she was
spoken of among their acquaintances as the promised
bride of Mountjoy Scarborough, and though she
ever denied the imputation, there came over her girl's
heart the feeling—very sad and very solemn, but still
all but accepted—that so it must be. Then Harry
Annesley had crossed her path, and the question had
been at last nearly answered, and the doubts nearly
decided. She did not quite know at first that she
loved Harry Annesley, but was almost sure that it
was impossible for her to become the wife of Mountjoy Scarborough.

Then there came nearly twelve months of most
painful uncertainty in her life. It is very hard for a
young girl to have to be firm with her mother in
declining a proposed marriage, when all the circumstances of the connection are recommended to her as
being peculiarly alluring. And there was nothing in
the personal manners of her cousin which seemed to
justify her in declaring her abhorrence. He was a
dark, handsome, military-looking man, whose chief

sin it was in the eyes of his cousin that he seemed to demand from her affection, worship, and obedience. She did not analyse his character, but she felt it. And when it came to pass that tidings of his debts at last reached her, she felt that she was glad of an excuse, though she knew that the excuse would not have prevailed with her had she liked him. Then came his debts, and with the knowledge of them a keener perception of his imperiousness. She could consent to become the wife of the man who had squandered his property and wasted his estate; but not of one who before his marriage demanded of her that submission which, as she thought, should be given by her freely after her marriage. Harry Annesley glided into her heart after a manner very different from this. She knew that he adored her, but yet he did not hasten to tell her so. She knew that she loved him, but she doubted whether a time would ever come in which she could confess it. It was not till he had come to acknowledge the trouble to which Mountjoy had subjected him that he had ever ventured to speak plainly of his own passion, and even then he had not asked for a reply. She was still free as she thought of all this, but she did at last tell herself that, let her mother say what she would, she certainly never would stand at the altar with her cousin Mountjoy.

Even now when the captain had been declared not to be his father's heir, and when all the world knew that he had disappeared from the face of the earth, Mrs. Mountjoy did not altogether give him up. She partly disbelieved her brother, and partly thought that circumstances could not be as bad as they were described. To her feminine mind—to her, living not in the world of London, but in the very moderate fashion of Cheltenham—it seemed to be impossible that an entail should be thus blighted in the bud. Why was an entail called an entail unless it were ineradicable,—a decision of fate rather than of man

and of law? And to her eyes Mountjoy Scarborough
was so commanding that all things must at last be
compelled to go as he would have them. And to tell
the truth, there had lately come to Mrs. Mountjoy a
word of comfort, which might be necessary if the
world should be absolutely upset in accordance with
the wicked skill of her brother, which even in that
case might make crooked things smooth. Augustus,
whom she had regarded always as quite a Mountjoy,
because of his talent, and appearance, and habit of
command, had whispered to her a word. Why should
not Florence be transferred with the remainder of the
property? There was something to Mrs. Mountjoy's
feelings base in the idea at the first blush of it. She
did not like to be untrue to her gallant nephew. But
as she came to turn it in her mind, there were certain
circumstances which recommended the change to her
—should the change be necessary. Florence certainly
had expressed an unintelligible objection to the elder
brother. Why should not the younger be more successful? Mrs. Mountjoy's heart had begun to droop
within her, as she had thought that her girl would
prove deaf to the voice of the charmer. Another
charmer had come, most objectionable in her sight,
but to him no word of absolute encouragement had,
as she thought, been yet spoken. Augustus had already obtained for himself among his friends the
character of an eloquent young lawyer. Let him
come and try his eloquence on his cousin,—only let
it first be ascertained, as an assured fact, and beyond
the possibility of all retrogression, that the squire's
villainy was certain.

'I think, my love,' she said to her daughter one
day, 'that under the immediate circumstances of the
family, we should retire for a while into private life.'
This occurred on the very day on which Septimus
Jones had been vaguely informed of the iniquitous
falsehood of Harry Annesley.

'Good gracious, mamma! is not our life always

private?' She had understood it all—that the private life was intended altogether to exclude Harry, but was to be made open to the manœuvres of her cousin, such as they might be.

'Not in the sense in which I mean. Your poor uncle is dying.'

'We hear that Sir William says that he is better.'

'I fear nevertheless that he is dying,—though it may perhaps take a long time. And then poor Mountjoy has disappeared. I think that we should see no one till the mystery about Mountjoy has been cleared up. And then the story is so very discreditable.'

'I do not see that that is an affair of ours,' said Florence, who had no desire to be shut up just at the present moment.

'We cannot help ourselves. This making his eldest son out to be—oh, something so very different! —is too horrible to be thought of. I am told that nobody knows the truth.'

'We at any rate are not implicated in that.'

'But we are. He at any rate is my brother, and Mountjoy is my nephew,—or at any rate was. Poor Augustus is thrown into terrible difficulties.'

'I am told that he is greatly pleased at finding that Tretton is to belong to him.'

'Who tells you that? You have no right to believe anything about such near relatives from anyone. Whoever told you so has been very wicked.' Mrs. Mountjoy no doubt thought that this wicked communication had been made by Harry Annesley. 'Augustus has always proved himself to be affectionate and respectful to his elder brother, that is, to his brother who is—is older than himself,' added Mrs. Mountjoy, feeling that there was a difficulty in expressing herself as to the presumed condition of the two Scarboroughs. 'Of course he would rather be owner of Tretton than let anyone else have it, if you mean that. The honour of the family is very much to him.'

'I do not know that the family can have any honour left,' said Florence severely.

'My dear, you have no right to say that. The Scarboroughs have always held their heads very high in Staffordshire, and more so of late than ever. I don't mean quite of late, but since Tretton became of so much importance. Now, I'll tell you what I think we had better do. We'll go and spend six weeks with your uncle at Brussels. He has always been pressing us to come.'

'Oh, mamma, he does not want us.'

'How can you say that? How do you know?'

'I am sure Sir Magnus will not care for our coming now. Besides, how could that be retiring into private life? Sir Magnus, as ambassador, has his house always full of company.'

'My dear, he is not ambassador. He is minister plenipotentiary.* It is not quite the same thing. And then he is our nearest relative—our nearest, at least, since my own brother has made this great separation, of course. We cannot go to him to be out of the way of himself.'

'Why do you want to go anywhere, mamma? Why not stay at home?' But Florence pleaded in vain, as her mother had already made up her mind. Before that day was over she succeeded in making her daughter understand that she was to be taken to Brussels as soon as an answer could be received from Sir Magnus and the necessary additions could be made to their joint wardrobe.

Sir Magnus Mountjoy, the late general's elder brother, had been for the last four or five years the English Minister at Brussels. He had been minister somewhere for a very long time, so that the memory of man hardly ran back beyond it, and was said to have gained for himself very extensive popularity. It had always been a point with successive governments to see that poor Sir Magnus got something, and Sir Magnus had never been left altogether in the

cold. He was not a man who would have been left
out in the cold in silence, and perhaps the feeling that
such was the case had been as efficacious on his behalf
as his well-attested popularity. At any rate poor Sir
Magnus had always been well placed, and was now
working out his last year or two before the blessed
achievement of his pursuit should have been reached.
Sir Magnus had a wife of whom it was said at home
that she was almost as popular as her husband, but
the opinion of the world at Brussels on this subject
was a good deal divided. There were those who
declared that Lady Mountjoy was of all women the
most overbearing and impertinent. But they were
generally English residents at Brussels,* who had
come to live there as a place at which education for
their children would be cheaper than at home. Of
these Lady Mountjoy had been heard to declare that
she saw no reason why because she was the minister's
wife she should be expected to entertain all the second-
class world of London. This of course must be understood with a good deal of allowance, as the English
world at Brussels was much too large to expect to be
so received; but there were certain ladies living on
the confines of high society, who thought that they
had a right to be admitted, and who grievously resented their exclusion. It cannot therefore be said
that Lady Mountjoy was popular; but she was large
in figure, and painted well, and wore her diamonds
with an air which her peculiar favourites declared to
be majestic. You could not see her going along the
boulevards in her carriage without being aware that
a special personage was passing. Upon the whole it
may be said that she performed well her special rôle
in life. Of Sir Magnus it was hinted that he was
afraid of his wife; but in truth he desired it to be
understood that all the disagreeable things done at
the Embassy were done by Lady Mountjoy and not
by him. He did not refuse leave to the ladies to drop
their cards at his hall-door. He could ask a few men

to his table without referring the matter to his wife; but everyone would understand that the asking of ladies was based on a different footing. He knew well that as a rule it was not fitting that he should ask a married man without his wife; but there are occasions on which an excuse can be given, and upon the whole the men liked it. He was a stout, tall, portly old gentleman, sixty years of age, but looking somewhat older, whom it was a difficulty to place on horseback, but who, when there, looked remarkably well. He rarely rose to a trot during his two hours of exercise, which to the two attachés who were told off for the duty of accompanying him, was the hardest part of their allotted work. But other gentlemen would lay themselves out to meet Sir Magnus and to ride with him, and in this way he achieved that character for popularity which had been a better aid to him in life than all the diplomatic skill which he possessed.

'What do you think?' said he, walking off with Mrs. Mountjoy's letter into his wife's room.

'I don't think anything, my dear.'

'You never do.' Lady Mountjoy, who had not yet undergone her painting, looked cross and ill-natured. 'At any rate Sarah and her daughter are proposing to come here.'

'Good gracious! At once?'

'Yes, at once. Of course, I've asked them over and over again, and something was said about this autumn, when we had come back from Pimperingen.'

'Why did you not tell me?'

'Bother! I did tell you. This kind of thing always turns up at last. She's a very good kind of woman, and the daughter is all that she ought to be.'

'Of course she'll be flirting with Anderson.' Anderson was one of the two mounted attachés.

'Anderson will know how to look after himself,' said Sir Magnus. 'At any rate they must come.

They have never troubled us before, and we ought
to put up with them once.'

'But, my dear, what is all this about her brother?'

'She won't bring her brother with her.'

'How can you be sure of that?' said the anxious lady.

'He is dying, and can't be moved.'

'But that son of his,—Mountjoy. It's altogether
a most distressing story. He turns out to be nobody
after all, and now he has disappeared, and the papers
for an entire month were full of him. What would
you do if he were to turn up here? The girl was
engaged to him, you know, and has only thrown him
off since his own father declared that he was not
legitimate. There never was such a mess about anything since London first began.'

Then Sir Magnus declared that, let Mountjoy
Scarborough and his father have misbehaved as they
might, Mr. Scarborough's sister must be received
at Brussels. There was a little family difficulty. Sir
Magnus had borrowed three thousand pounds from
the general which had been settled on the general's
widow, and the interest was not always paid with
extreme punctuality. To give Mrs. Mountjoy her
due, it must be said that this had not entered into her
consideration when she had written to her brother-
in-law; but it was a burden to Sir Magnus, and had
always tended to produce from him a reiteration of
those invitations, which Mrs. Mountjoy had taken
as an expression of brotherly love. Her own income
was always sufficient for her wants, and the hundred
and fifty pounds coming from Sir Magnus had not
troubled her much. 'Well, my dear, if it must be it
must,—only what I'm to do with her I do not know.'

'Take her about in the carriage,' said Sir Magnus,
who was beginning to be a little angry with this
interference.

'And the daughter? Daughters are twice more
troublesome than their mothers.'

'Pass her over to Miss Abbot. And for goodness

sake don't make so much trouble about things which
need not be troublesome.' Then Sir Magnus left his
wife to ring for her chambermaid and go on with her
painting, while he himself undertook the unwonted
task of writing an affectionate letter to his sister-in-
law. It should be here explained that Sir Magnus
had no children of his own, and that Miss Abbot was
the lady who was bound to smile and say pretty
things on all occasions to Lady Mountjoy for the
moderate remuneration of two hundred a year and
her maintenance.

The letter which Sir Magnus wrote was as follows:

'MY DEAR SARAH,

'Lady Mountjoy bids me say that we shall be
delighted to receive you and my niece at the British
Ministry on the first of October, and hope that you
will stay with us till the end of the month.—Believe
me, most affectionately yours,

'MAGNUS MOUNTJOY.'

'I have a most kind letter from Sir Magnus,' said
Mrs. Mountjoy to her daughter.

'What does he say?'

'That he will be delighted to receive us on the
first of October. I did say that we should be ready
to start in about a week's time, because I know that
he gets home from his autumn holiday by the middle
of September. But I have no doubt he has his house
full till the time he has named.'

'Do you know her, mamma?' asked Florence.

'I did see her once; but I cannot say that I know
her. She used to be a very handsome woman, and
looks to be quite good-natured; but Sir Magnus has
always lived abroad, and except when he came home
about your poor father's death I have seen very little
of him.'

'I never saw him but that once,' said Florence.

And so it was settled that she and her mother
were to spend a month at Brussels.

Chapter XI

MONTE CARLO

TOWARDS the end of September, while the weather was so hot as to keep away from the south of France all but very determined travellers, an English gentleman, not very beautiful in his outward appearance, was sauntering about the great hall of the gambling-house at Monte Carlo,* in the kingdom or principality of Monaco, the only gambling-house now left in Europe in which idle men of a speculative nature may yet solace their hours with some excitement. Nor is the amusement denied to idle ladies, as might be seen by two or three highly-dressed habituées, who at this moment were depositing their shawls and parasols with the porters. The clock was on the stroke of eleven, when the gambling-room would be open, and the amusement was too rich in its nature to allow of the loss of even a few minutes. But this gentleman was not an habitué, nor was he known even by name to any of the small crowd that was then assembled. But it was known to many of them that he had had a great 'turn of luck' on the preceding day, and had walked off from the 'rouge-et-noir'* table with four or five hundred pounds.

The weather was still so hot that but few Englishmen were there, and the play had not as yet begun to run high. There were only two or three,—men who cannot keep their hands from ruin when ruin is open to them. To them heat and cold, the dog-star or twenty degrees below zero, make no difference while the croupier is there with his rouleaux before him, capable of turning up the card. They know that the chance is against them—one in twenty, let us say— and that in the long run one in twenty is as good as two to one to effect their ruin. For a day they may stand against one in twenty, as this man had done.

For two or three days, for a week, they may possibly
do so; but they know that the doom must come at
last,—as it does come invariably,—and they go on.
But our friend, the Englishman who had won the
money, was not such a one as these, at any rate in
regard to Monaco. Yesterday had been his first appearance, and he had broken ground there with great
success. He was an ill-looking person, poorly clad—
what, in common parlance, we call seedy. He had
not a scrap of beard on his face, and though swarthy
and dark as to his countenance, was light as to his
hair, which hung in quantities down his back. He
was dressed from head to foot in a suit of cross-barred
light-coloured tweed, of which he wore the coat but-
toned tight over his chest, as though to hide some
deficiency of linen. The gentleman was altogether
a disreputable-looking personage, and they who had
seen him win his money,—Frenchmen and Italians
for the most part,—had declared among themselves
that his luck had been most miraculous. It was observed that he had a companion with him, who stuck
close to his elbow, and it was asserted that this companion continually urged him to leave the room. But
as long as the croupier remained at the table, he
remained, and continued to play through the day with
almost invariable luck. It was surmised among the
gamblers there that he had not entered the room with
above twenty or thirty pieces*in his pocket, and that
he had taken away with him, when the place was
closed, six hundred napoleons.* 'Look there; he has
come again to give it all back to Madame Blanc,* with
interest,' said a Frenchman to an Italian.

'Yes; and he will end by blowing his brains out
within a week. He is just the man to do it.'

'These Englishmen always rush at their fate like
mad bulls,' said the Frenchman. 'They get less distraction for their money than anyone.'

'Che va piano va sano,'*said the Italian, jingling
the four napoleons in his pocket which had been six

on yesterday morning. Then they sauntered up to the Englishman, and both of them touched their hats to him. The Englishman just acknowledged the compliment, and walked off with his companion, who was still whispering something into his ear.

'It is a gendarme who is with him, I think,' said the Frenchman, 'only the man does not walk erect.'

Who does not know the outside hall of the magnificent gambling-house at Monte Carlo, with all the golden splendour of its music-room* within? Who does not know the lofty roof and lounging seats, with all its luxuries of liveried servants, its wealth of newspapers, and every appanage of costly comfort which can be added to it? And its music within,—who does not know that there are to be heard sounds in a greater perfection of orchestral melody than are to be procured by money and trouble combined in the great capitals of Europe? Think of the trouble endured by those unhappy fathers of families who indulge their wives and daughters at the Philharmonic* and St. James's Hall!* Think of the horrors of our theatres, with their hot gas, and narrow passages, and difficulties of entrance, and almost impossibility of escape! And for all this money has to be paid—high prices —and the day has to be fixed long beforehand, so that the tickets may be secured, and the daily feast —papa's too often solitary enjoyment—has to be turned into a painful early fast. And when at last the thing has been done, and the torment endured, the sounds heard have not always been good of their kind, for the money has not sufficed to purchase the aid of a crowd of the best musicians. But at Monte Carlo you walk in with your wife in her morning costume, and seating yourself luxuriously in one of those soft stalls which are there prepared for you, you give yourself up with perfect ease to absolute enjoyment. For two hours the concert lasts, and all around is perfection and gilding. There is nothing to annoy the most fastidious taste. You have not heated yourself with fighting your way up crowded stairs; no box-keeper has asked you for a shilling; no linkboy*has dunned you because he has stood useless for a moment at the door of your carriage; no panic has seized you and still oppresses you because of the narrow dimensions in which you have to seat yourself for the next three hours. There are no twenty minutes during which you are doomed to sit in miserable expectation. Exactly at the hour named the music begins, and for two hours it is your own fault if you be not happy. A railway carriage has brought you to steps leading up to the garden in which these princely halls are built, and when the music is over will again take you home. Nothing can be more perfect than the concert-room at Monte Carlo, and nothing more charming; and for all this there is nothing whatever to pay.

But by whom—out of whose pocket are all these good things provided? They tell you at Monte Carlo that from time to time are to be seen men walking off in the dark of the night, or the gloom of the evening, or for the matter of that in the broad light of day, if the stern necessity of the hour require it, with a burden among them, to be deposited where it may not be seen or heard of any more. They are carrying away 'all that mortal remains"*of one of the gentlemen who have paid for your musical entertainment. He has given his all for the purpose, and has then— blown his brains out. It is one of the disagreeable incidents to which the otherwise extremely pleasant money-making operations of the establishment are liable. Such accidents will happen. A gambling-house, the keeper of which is able to maintain the royal expense of the neighbouring court out of his winnings, and also to keep open for those who are not ashamed to accept it—gratis, all for love—a con-cert-room brilliant with gold, filled with the best performers whom the world can furnish, and comfortable beyond all opera-houses known to men, must be liable to a few such misfortunes. Who is not ashamed to accept it, I have said, having lately been there and thoroughly enjoyed myself! But I did not put myself in the way of having to cut my throat, on which account I felt, as I came out, that I had been somewhat shabby. I was ashamed in that I had not put a few napoleons down on the table. Conscience had prevented me, and a wish to keep my money! But should not conscience have kept me away from all that happiness for which I had not paid? I had not thought of it before I went to Monte Carlo, but I am inclined now to advise others to stay away, or else to put down half-a-napoleon at any rate as the price of a ticket. The place is not overcrowded, because the conscience of many is keener than was mine.

We ought to be grateful to the august sovereign of Monaco in that he enabled an enterprising individual to keep open for us in so brilliant a fashion the last public gambling-house in Europe. The principality is but large enough to contain the court of the sovereign which is held in the little town of Monaco, and the establishment of the last of legitimate gamblers which is maintained at Monte Carlo. If the report of the world does not malign the prince he lives, as does the gambler, out of the spoil taken from the gamblers. He is to be seen in his royal carriage going forth with his royal consort,—and very royal he looks! His little teacup of a kingdom, or rather a roll of French bread, for it is crusty and picturesque, —is now surrounded by France. There is Nice away to the west, and Mentone to the east, and the whole kingdom lies within the compass of a walk. Mentone, in France, at any rate is within five miles of the monarch's residence. How happy it is that there should be so blessed a spot left in tranquillity on the earth's surface!

But on the present occasion Monte Carlo was not in all its grandeur, because of the heat of the weather. Another month, and English lords, and English

Members of Parliament, and English barristers would be there,—all men for instance who could afford to be indifferent as to their character for a month,—and the place would be quite alive with music, cards, and dice. At present men of business only flocked to its halls, eagerly intent on making money, though, alas! almost all doomed to lose it. But our one friend with the long light locks was impatient for the fray. The gambling-room had now been opened, and the servants of the table, less impatient than he, were slowly arranging their money and their cards. Our friend had taken his seat, and was already resolving, with his eyes fixed on the table, where he would make his first plunge. In his right hand was a bag of gold, and under his left hand were hidden the twelve napoleons with which he intended to commence. Yesterday he had gone through his day's work by twelve, though on one or two occasions he had plunged deeply. It had seemed to this man as though a new heaven had been open to him, as of late he had seen little of luck in this world. The surmises made as to the low state of his funds when he entered the room had been partly true; but time had been when he was able to gamble in a more costly fashion even than here, and to play among those who had taken his winnings and losings simply as a matter of course.

And now the game had begun, and the twelve napoleons were duly deposited. Again he won his stake, an omen for the day, and was exultant. A second twelve, and a third was put down, and on each occasion he won. In the silly imagination of his heart he declared to himself that the calculation of all chances was as nothing against his run of luck. Here was the spot on which it was destined that he should redeem all the injury which fortune had done him. And in truth this man had been misused by fortune. His companion whispered in his ear, but he heard not a word of it. He increased the twelve to fifteen, and again won. As he looked round there was a halo of triumph which seemed to illumine his face. He had chained Chance to his chariot-wheel,* and would persevere now that the good time had come. What did he care for the creature at his elbow? He thought of all the good things which money could again purchase for him as he carefully fingered the gold for the next stake. He had been rich, though he was now poor; though how could a man be accounted poor who had an endless sum of six hundred napoleons in his pocket, a sum which was, in truth, endless, while it could be so rapidly recruited in this fashion? The next stake he also won, but as he raked all the pieces which the croupier pushed towards him, his mind had become intent on another sphere and on other persons. Let him win what he might, his old haunts were now closed against him. What good would money do him, living such a life as he must now be compelled to pass? As he thought of this the five-and-twenty napoleons on the table were taken away from him almost without consciousness on his part.

At that moment there came a voice in his ear, not the voice of his attending friend, but one of which he accurately knew the lisping fiendish sound, 'Ah, Captain Scarborough, I thought it vas posshible you might be here. Dis ish a very nice place.' Our friend looked round and glared at the man, and felt that it was impossible that his occupation should be continued under his eyes. 'Yesh; it was likely. How do you like Monte Carlo? You have plenty of money— plenty!' The man was small, and oily, and black-haired, and beaky nosed, with a perpetual smile on his face, unless when on special occasions he would be moved to the expression of deep anger. Of the modern Hebrews a most complete Hebrew; but a man of purpose who never did things by halves, who could count upon good courage within, and who never allowed himself to be foiled by misadventure. He was one who, beginning with nothing, was determined to die a rich man, and was likely to achieve his purpose.

Now there was no gleam of anger on his face, but a look of invincible good humour, which was not, however, quite good humour when you came to examine it closely.

'Oh! that is you, is it, Mr. Hart?'

'Yesh; it is me. I have followed you. Oh, I have had quite a pleasant tour following you. But ven I got my noshe once on to the schent, then I was sure it was Monte Carlo. And it is Monte Carlo; eh! Captain Scarborough?'

'Yes; of course it is Monte Carlo. That is to say, Monte Carlo is the place where we are now. I don't know what you mean by running on in that way.' Then he drew back from the table, Mr. Hart following close behind him, and his attendant at a further distance behind him. As he went he remembered that he had slightly increased the six hundred napoleons of yesterday, and that the money was still in his own possession. Not all the Jews in London could touch the money while he kept it in his pocket.

'Who ish dat man there?' asked Mr. Hart.

'What can that be to you?'

'He seems to follow you pretty close.'

'Not so close as you do, by George; and perhaps he has something to get by it, which you haven't.'

'Come, come, come! If he have more to get than I, he mush be pretty deep. There is Mishter Tyrrwhit. No one have more to get than I, only Mishter Tyrrwhit. Vy, Captain Scarborough, the little game you wash playing there, which wash a very pretty little game, is as nothing to my game wish you. When you see the money down, on the table there, it seems to be mush, because the gold glitters; but it is as noting to my little game where the gold does not glitter, because it is pen and ink. A pen and ink soon writes ten thousand pounds. But you think mush of it when you win two hundred pounds at roulette.'

'I think nothing of it,' said our friend Captain Scarborough.

'And it goes into your pocket to give champagne to the ladies instead of paying your debts to the poor fellows who have supplied you for so long with all de money.'

All this occurred in the gambling-house at a distance from the table, but within hearing of that attendant who still followed the player. These moments were moments of misery to the captain in spite of the bank-notes for six hundred napoleons which were still in his breast coat pocket. And they were not made lighter by the fact that all the words spoken by the Jew were overheard by the man who was supposed to be there in the capacity of his servant. But the man, as it seemed, had a mission to fulfil, and was the captain's master as well as servant. 'Mr. Hart,' said Captain Scarborough, repressing the loudness of his words as far as his rage would admit him; but still speaking so as to attract the attention of some of those round him, 'I do not know what good you propose to yourself by following me in this manner. You have my bonds, which are not even payable till my father's death.'

'Ah! there you are very much mistaken.'

'And are then only payable out of the property to which I believed myself to be heir when the money was borrowed.'

'You are still de heir—de heir to Tretton. There is not a shadow of a doubt as to that.'

'I hope when the time comes,' said the captain, 'you'll be able to prove your words.'

'Of course we shall prove dem. Why not? Your father and your brother are very clever shentlemen, I think, but they will not be more clever than Mishter Samuel Hart. Mr. Tyrrwhit also is a clever man. Perhaps he understands your father's way of doing business. Perhaps it is all right with Mr. Tyrrwhit. It shall be all right with me too, I swear it. When will you come back to London, Captain Scarborough?'

Then there came an angry dispute in the gambling-room, during which Mr. Hart by no means strove to repress his voice. Captain Scarborough asserted his rights as a free agent, declaring himself capable, as far as the law was concerned, of going wherever he pleased without reference to Mr. Hart; and told that gentleman that any interference on his part would be regarded as an impertinence.

'But my money—my money, which you must pay this minute, if I please to demand it.'

'You did not lend me five-and-twenty thousand pounds without security.'

'It is forty-five—now, at this moment.'

'Take it, get it; go and put it in your pocket. You have a lot of writings; turn them into cash at once. Take them to any other Jew in London and sell them. See if you can get your five-and-twenty thousand pounds for them—or twenty-five thousand shillings. You certainly cannot get five-and-twenty pence for them here, though you had all the police of this royal kingdom to support you. My father says that the bonds I gave you are not worth the paper on which they were written. If you are cheated, so have I been. If he has robbed you, so has he me. But I have not robbed you, and you can do nothing to me.'

'I vill stick to you like beesvax,' said Mr. Hart, while the look of good humour left his countenance for a moment. 'Like beesvax! You shall not escape me again.'

'You will have to follow me to Constantinople, then.'

'I vill follow you to the devil.'

'You are likely to go before me there. But for the present I am off to Constantinople, from whence I intend to make an extended tour to Mount Caucasus, and then into Thibet. I shall be very glad of your company, but cannot offer to pay the bill. When you and your companions have settled yourselves comfortably at Tretton, I shall be happy to come and see you there. You will have to settle the matter first with my younger brother, if I may make bold to call that well-born gentleman my brother at all. I wish you a good morning, Mr. Hart.' Upon that he walked out into the hall and thence down the steps into the garden in front of the establishment, his own attendant following him.

Mr. Hart also followed him, but did not immediately seek to renew the conversation. If he meant to show any sign of keeping his threat and of sticking to the captain like beeswax, he must show his purpose at once. The captain for a time walked round the little enclosure in earnest conversation with the attendant, and Mr. Hart stood on the steps watching them. Play was over, at any rate for that day, as far as the captain was concerned.

'Now, Captain Scarborough, don't you think you've been very rash?' said the attendant.

'I think I've got six hundred and fifty napoleons in my pocket, instead of waiting to get them in driblets from my brother.'

'But if he knew that you had come here, he would withdraw them altogether. Of course, he will know now. That man will be sure to tell him. He will let all London know. Of course, it would be so when you came to a place of such common resort as Monte Carlo.'

'Common resort! Do you believe he came here as to a place of common resort? Do you think that he had not tracked me out, and would not have done so whether I had gone to Melbourne, or New York, or St. Petersburg? But the wonder is that he should spend his money in such a vain pursuit.'

'Ah, captain, you do not know what is vain and what is not. It is your brother's pleasure that you should be kept in the dark for a time.'

'Hang my brother's pleasure! Why am I to follow my brother's pleasure?'

'Because he will allow you an income. He will keep a coat on your back and a hat on your head,

and supply meat and wine for your needs.' Here
Captain Scarborough jingled the loose napoleons in
his trousers' pocket. 'Oh, yes, that is all very well,
but it will not last for ever. Indeed, it will not last
for a week unless you leave Monte Carlo.'

'I shall leave it this afternoon by the train for
Genoa.'

'And where shall you go then?'

'You heard me suggest to Mr. Hart to the devil
—or else to Constantinople, and after that to Thibet.
I suppose I shall still enjoy the pleasure of your
company!'

'Mr. Augustus wishes that I should remain with
you, and, as you yourself say, perhaps it will be best.'

Chapter XII

HARRY ANNESLEY'S SUCCESS

HARRY ANNESLEY, a day or two after he had
left Tretton, went down to Cheltenham; for he
had received an invitation to a dance there, and with
the invitation an intimation that Florence Mountjoy
was to be at the dance. If I were to declare that the
dance had been given and Florence asked to it merely
as an act of friendship to Harry, it would perhaps be
thought that modern friendship is seldom carried to
so great a length. But it was undoubtedly the fact
that Mrs. Armitage, who gave the dance, was a great
friend and admirer of Harry's, and that Mr. Armitage was an especial chum. Let not, however, any
reader suppose that Florence was in the secret. Mrs.
Armitage had thought it best to keep her in the dark
as to the person asked to meet her. 'As to my going
to Montpellier Place,'*Harry had once said to Mrs.
Armitage, 'I might as well knock at a prison-door.'
Mrs. Mountjoy lived at Montpellier Place.

'I think we could perhaps manage that for you,' Mrs. Armitage had replied, and she had managed it.

'Is she coming?' Harry said to Mrs. Armitage in an anxious whisper as he entered the room.

'She has been here this half-hour—if you had taken the trouble to leave your cigars and come and meet her.'

'She has not gone?' said Harry, almost awestruck at the idea.

'No; she is sitting like Patience on a monument, smiling at grief,* in the room inside. She has got horrible news to tell you.'

'Oh, heavens! What news?'

'I suppose she will tell you, though she has not been communicative to me in regard to your Royal Highness. The news is simply that her mother is going to take her to Brussels, and that she is to live for a while amidst the ambassadorial splendours with Sir Magnus and his wife.'

By retiring from the world Mrs. Mountjoy had not intended to include such slight social relaxations as Mrs. Armitage's party, for Harry, on turning round, encountered her talking to another Cheltenham lady. He greeted her with his pleasantest smile, to which Mrs. Mountjoy did not respond quite so sweetly. She had ever greatly feared Harry Annesley, and had today heard a story very much, as she thought, to his discredit. 'Is your daughter here?' asked Harry, with well-trained hypocrisy. Mrs. Mountjoy could not but acknowledge that her daughter was in the room, and then Harry passed on in pursuit of his quarry.

'Oh! Mr. Annesley, when did you come to Cheltenham?'

'As soon as I heard that Mrs. Armitage was going to have a party, I began to think of coming immediately.' Then an idea for the first time shot through Florence's mind, that her friend Mrs. Armitage was a woman fond of intrigue. 'What dance have you disengaged? I have something that I must tell you to-night. You don't mean to say that you will not give me one dance?' This was merely a lover's anxious doubt on his part, because Florence had not at once replied to him. 'I am told that you are going away to Brussels.'

'Mamma is going on a visit to her brother-in-law.'

'And you with her?'

'Of course I shall go with mamma.'

All this had been said apart, while a fair-haired lackadaisical young gentleman was standing twiddling his thumbs waiting to dance with Florence. At last the little book from her waist was brought forth, and Harry's name was duly inscribed. The next dance was a quadrille, and he saw that the space after that was also vacant; so he boldly wrote down his name for both. I almost think that Florence must have suspected that Harry Annesley was to be there that night, or why should the two places have been kept vacant?

'And now what is this,' he began, 'about your going to Brussels?'

'Mamma's brother is minister there, and we are just going on a visit.'

'But why now? I am sure there is some especïal cause.' Florence would not say that there was no especial cause, so she could only repeat her assertion that they certainly were going to Brussels. She herself was well aware that she was to be taken out of Harry's way, and that something was expected to occur during this short month of her absence which might be detrimental to him—and to her also. But this she could not tell, nor did she like to say that the plea given by her mother was the general state of the Scarborough affairs. She did not wish to declare to this lover that that other lover was as nothing to her. 'And how long are you to be away?' asked Harry.

'We shall be a month with Sir Magnus; but

mamma is talking of going on afterwards to the Italian lakes.'

'Good Heavens! you will not be back, I suppose, till ever so much after Christmas?'

'I cannot tell. Nothing as yet has been settled. I do not know that I ought to tell you anything about it.' Harry at this moment looked up and caught the eye of Mrs. Mountjoy, as she was standing in the doorway opposite. Mrs. Mountjoy certainly looked as though no special communication as to Florence's future movements ought to be made to Harry Annesley.

Then, however, it came to his turn to dance, and he had a moment allowed him to collect his thoughts. By nothing that he could do or say could he prevent her going, and he could only use the present moment to the best purpose in his power. He bethought himself then that he had never received from her a word of encouragement, and that such word, if ever it be spoken, should be forthcoming that night. What might not happen to a girl who was passing the balmy Christmas months amidst the sweet shadows of an Italian lake? Harry's ideas of an Italian lake were in truth at present somewhat vague. But future months were, to his thinking, interminable; the present moment only was his own. The dance was now finished. 'Come and take a walk,' said Harry.

'I think I will go to mamma.' Florence had seen her mother's eye fixed upon her.

'Oh! come, that won't do at all,' said Harry, who had already got her hand within his arm. 'A fellow is always entitled to five minutes, and then I am down for the next waltz.'

'Oh no!'

'But I am, and you can't get out of it now. Oh! Florence, will you answer me a question—one question? I asked it you before, and you did not vouchsafe me any answer.'

'You asked me no question,' said Florence, who

remembered to the last syllable every word that had been said to her on that occasion.

'Did I not? I am sure you knew what it was that I intended to ask.' Florence could not but think that this was quite another thing. 'Oh! Florence, can you love me?' Had she given her ears for it, she could not have told him the truth then, on the spur of the moment. Her mother's eye was, she knew, watching her through the doorway, all the way across from the other room. And yet, had her mother asked her, she would have answered boldly that she did love Harry Annesley, and intended to love him for ever and ever with all her heart. And she would have gone further if cross-questioned, and have declared that she regarded him already as her lord and master. But now she had not a word to say to him. All she knew was that he had now pledged himself to her, and that she intended to keep him to his pledge. 'May I not have one word,' he said; 'one word?'

What could he want with a word more? thought Florence. Her silence now was as good as any speech. But as he did want more, she would, after her own way, reply to him. So there came upon his arm the slightest possible sense of pressure from those sweet fingers, and Harry Annesley was on a sudden carried up among azure-tinted clouds into the furthest heaven of happiness. After a moment he stood still, and passed his fingers through his hair and waved his head as a god might do. She had now made to him a solemn promise than which no words could be more binding. 'Oh! Florence,' he exclaimed, 'I must have you alone with me for one moment.' For what could he want her alone for any moment? thought Florence. There was her mother still looking at them; but for her Harry did not care one straw. Nor did he hate those bright Italian lakes with nearly so strong a feeling of abhorrence. 'Florence, you are now all my own.' There came another slightest pressure; slight, but so eloquent from those fingers.

'I hate dancing. How is a fellow to dance now? I shall run against everybody. I can see no one. I should be sure to make a fool of myself. No, I don't want to dance even with you. No, certainly not! Let you dance with somebody else, and you engaged to me! Well, if I must, of course I must. I declare, Florence, you have not spoken a single word to me, though there is so much that you must have to say. What have you got to say? What a question to ask! You must tell me. Oh, you know what you have got to tell me! The sound of it will be the sweetest music that a man can possibly hear.'

'You know it all, Harry,' she whispered.

'But I want to hear it. Oh! Florence, Florence, I do not think you can understand how completely I am beyond myself with joy. I cannot dance again, and will not. Oh! my wife, my wife.'

'Hush!' said Florence, afraid that the very walls might hear the sounds of Harry's words.

'What does it signify though all the world knew it?'

'Oh yes!'

'That I should have been so fortunate! That is what I cannot understand. Poor Mountjoy! I do feel for him. That he should have had the start of me so long, and have done nothing!'

'Nothing,' whispered Florence.

'And I have done everything. I am so proud of myself that I think I must look almost like a hero.'

They had now got to the extremity of the room near an open window, and Florence found that she was able to say one word. 'You are my hero.' The sound of this nearly drove him mad with joy. He forgot all his troubles—Prodgers, the policeman, Augustus Scarborough, and that fellow whom he hated so much, Septimus Jones. What were they all to him now! He had set his mind upon one thing of value, and he had got it. Florence had promised to be his, and he was sure that she would never break

her word to him. But he felt that for the full enjoyment of his triumph he must be alone somewhere
with Florence for five minutes. He had not actually
explained to himself why, but he knew that he wished
to be alone with her. At present there was no prospect of any such five minutes; but he must say something in preparation of some future five minutes at
a time to come. Perhaps it might be tomorrow,
though he did not at present see how that might be
possible, for Mrs. Mountjoy, he knew, would shut
her door against him. And Mrs. Mountjoy was
already prowling round the room after her daughter.
Harry saw her as he got Florence to an opposite door,
and there for the moment escaped with her. 'And
now,' he said, 'how am I to manage to see you before
you go to Brussels?'

'I do not know that you can see me.'

'Do you mean that you are to be shut up, and that
I am not to be allowed to approach you?'

'I do mean it. Mamma is, of course, attached to
her nephew.'

'What! after all that has passed?'

'Why not? Is he to blame for what his father has
done?' Harry felt that he could not press the case
against Captain Scarborough without some want of
generosity. And though he had told Florence once
about that dreadful midnight meeting, he could say
nothing further on that subject. 'Of course mamma
thinks that I am foolish.'

'But why?' he asked.

'Because she doesn't see with my eyes, Harry.
We need not say anything more about it at present.
It is so; and therefore I am to go to Brussels. You
have made this opportunity for yourself before I start.
Perhaps I have been foolish to be taken off my guard.'

'Don't say that, Florence.'

'I shall think so, unless you can be discreet.
Harry, you will have to wait. You will remember
that we must wait; but I shall not change.'

'Nor I; nor I.'

'I think not, because I trust you. Here is mamma, and now I must leave you. But I shall tell mamma everything before I go to bed.'

Then Mrs. Mountjoy came up, and took Florence away with a few words of most disdainful greeting to Harry Annesley.

When Florence had gone Harry felt that as the sun and the moon and the stars had all set, and as absolute darkness reigned through the rooms, he might as well escape into the street where there was no one but the police to watch him, as he threw his hat up into the air in his exultation. But before he did so he had to pass by Mrs. Armitage and thank her for all her kindness; for he was aware how much she had done for him in his present circumstances.

'Oh! Mrs. Armitage, I am so obliged to you; no fellow was ever so obliged to a friend before.'

'How has it gone off? For Mrs. Mountjoy has taken Florence home.'

'Oh! yes, she has taken her away. But she hasn't shut the stable-door till the steed has been stolen.'

'Oh! the steed has been stolen?'

'Yes, I think so; I do think so.'

'And that poor man who has disappeared is nowhere.'

'Men who disappear never are anywhere. But I do flatter myself that if he had held his ground and kept his property, the result would have been the same.'

'I dare say.'

'Don't suppose, Mrs. Armitage, that I am taking any pride to myself. Why on earth Florence should have taken a fancy to such a fellow as I am, I cannot imagine.'

'Oh! no; not in the least.'

'It's all very well for you to laugh, Mrs. Armitage, but as I have thought of it all, I have sometimes been in despair.'

'But now you are not in despair.'

'No, indeed; just now I am triumphant. I have thought so often that I was a fool to love her, because everything was so much against me.'

'I have wondered that you continued. It always seemed to me that there wasn't a ghost of a chance for you. Mr. Armitage bade me give it all up, because he was sure you would never do 'any good.'

'I don't care how much you laugh at me, Mrs. Armitage. Let those laugh who win.'

Then he rushed out into the Paragon,* and absolutely did throw his hat up in the air in his triumph.

Chapter XIII

MRS. MOUNTJOY'S ANGER

FLORENCE, as she went home in the fly with her mother after the party at which Harry had spoken to her so openly, did not find the little journey very happy. Mrs. Mountjoy was a woman endowed with a strong power of wishing rather than of willing, of desiring rather than of contriving; but she was one who could make herself very unpleasant when she was thwarted. Her daughter was now at last fully determined that if she ever married anybody, that person should be Harry Annesley. Having once pressed his arm in token of assent, she had as it were given herself away to him, so that no reasoning, no expostulations could, she thought, change her purpose; and she had much more power of bringing about her purposed design than had her mother. But her mother could be obstinate and self-willed, and would for the time make herself disagreeable. Florence had assured her lover that everything should be told her mother that night before she went to bed. But Mrs. Mountjoy did not wait to be simply told. No sooner were they seated in the fly together than she began to make her enquiries. 'What has that man been saying to you?' she demanded.

Florence was at once offended by hearing her lover so spoken of, and could not simply tell the story of Harry's successful courtship, as she had intended. 'Mamma,' she said, 'why do you speak of him like that?'

'Because he is a scamp.'

'No, he is no scamp. It is very unkind of you to speak in such terms of one who you know is very dear to me.'

'I do not know it. He ought not to be dear to you at all. You have been for years intended for another purpose.' This was intolerable to Florence,—this idea that she should have been considered as capable of being intended for the purposes of other people. And a resolution at once was formed in her mind that she would let her mother know that such intentions were futile. But for the moment she sat silent. A journey home at twelve o'clock at night in a fly was not the time for the expression of her resolution. 'I say he's a scamp,' said Mrs. Mountjoy. 'During all these enquiries that have been made after your cousin, he has known all about it.'

'He has not known all about it,' said Florence.

'You contradict me in a very impertinent manner, and cannot be acquainted with the circumstances. The last person who saw your cousin in London was Mr. Henry Annesley, and yet he has not said a word about it, while search was being made on all sides. And he saw him under circumstances most suspicious in their nature; so suspicious as to have made the police arrest him if they were aware of them. He had at that moment grossly ill-treated Captain Scarborough.'

'No, mamma; no, it was not so.'

'How do you know? How can you tell?'

'I do know; and I can tell. The ill-usage had come from the other side.'

'Then you, too, have known the secret, and have said nothing about it? You, too, have been aware of the violence which took place at that midnight meeting? You have been aware of what befell your cousin, the man to whom you were all but engaged? And you have held your tongue at the instigation, no doubt, of Mr. Henry Annesley. Oh! Florence, you also will find yourself in the hands of the policeman.' At this moment the fly drew up at the door of the house in Montpellier Place, and the two ladies had to get out and walk up the steps into the hall, where they were congratulated on their early return from the party by the lady's-maid.

'Mamma, I will go to bed,' said Florence as soon as she reached her mother's room.

'I think you had better, my dear, though Heaven knows what disturbances there may be during the night.' By this Mrs. Mountjoy had intended to imply that Prodgers, the policeman, might probably lose not a moment more before he would at once proceed to arrest Miss Mountjoy for the steps she had taken in regard to the disappearance of Captain Scarborough. She had heard from Harry Annesley the fact that he had been brutally attacked by the captain in the middle of the night in the streets of London; and for this, in accordance with her mother's theory, she was to be dragged out of bed by a constable, and that probably before the next morning should have come. There was something in this so ludicrous as regarded the truth of the story, and yet so cruel as coming from her mother, that Florence hardly knew whether to cry or laugh as she laid her head upon the pillow.

But in the morning, as she was thinking that the facts of her own position had still to be explained to her mother,—that it would be necessary that she should declare her purpose and the impossibility of change now that she had once pledged herself to her lover,—Mrs. Mountjoy came into the room, and stood at her bedside with that appearance of ghostly displeasure which always belongs to an angry old lady in a night-cap.

'Well, mamma.'

'Florence, there must be an understanding between us.'

'I hope so. I thought there always had been. I am sure, mamma, you have known that I have never liked Captain Scarborough so as to become his wife, and I think you have known that I have liked Harry Annesley.'

'Likings are all fiddlesticks.'

'No, mamma; or if you object to the word, I will say love. You have known that I have not loved my cousin, and that I have loved this other man. That is not nonsense; that at any rate is a stern reality, if there be anything real in the world.'

'Stern! You may well call it stern.'

'I mean unbending, strong, not to be overcome by outside circumstances. If Mr. Annesley had not spoken to me as he did last night—could never have so spoken to me—I should have been a miserable girl, but my love for him would have been just as stern. I should have remained and thought of it, and have been unhappy through my whole life. But he has spoken, and I am exultant. That is what I mean by stern. All that is most important, at any rate to me.'

'I am here now to tell you that it is impossible.'

'Very well, mamma. Then things must go on, and we must bide our time.'

'It is proper that I should tell you that he has disgraced himself.'

'Never! I will not admit it. You do not know the circumstances,' exclaimed Florence.

'It is most impertinent in you to pretend that you know them better than I do,' said her mother indignantly.

'The story was told to me by himself.'

'Yes; and therefore told untruly.'

'I grieve that you should think so of him, mamma; but I cannot help it. Where you have got your information from I cannot tell. But that mine has been accurately told to me I feel certain.'

'At any rate my duty is to look after you, and to keep you from harm. I can only do my duty to the best of my ability. Mr. Annesley is to my thinking a most objectionable young man, and he will, I believe, be in the hands of the police before long. Evidence will have to be given in which your name will unfortunately be mentioned.'

'Why my name?'

'It is not probable that he will keep it secret when cross-questioned as to his having divulged the story to someone. He will declare that he has told it to you. When that time shall come, it will be well that we should be out of the country. I propose to start from here on this day week.'

'Uncle Magnus will not be able to have us then.'

'We must loiter away our time on the road. I look upon it as quite imperative that we shall both be out of England within eight days' time of this.'

'But where will you go?'

'Never mind. I do not know that I have as yet quite made up my mind. But you may understand that we shall start from Cheltenham this day week. Baker will go with us, and I shall leave the other two servants in charge of the house. I cannot tell you anything further as yet,—except that I will never consent to your marriage with Mr. Henry Annesley. You had better know that for certain, and then there will be less cause for unhappiness between us.' So saying, the angry ghost with the night-cap on stalked out of the room.

It need hardly be explained that Mrs. Mountjoy's information respecting the scene in London had come to her from Augustus Scarborough. When he told her that Annesley had been the last in London to see his brother Mountjoy, and had described the nature of the scene that had occurred between them, he had no doubt forgotten that he himself had subsequently seen his brother. In the story, as he had told it, there was no need to mention himself,—no necessity for such a character in making up the tragedy of that night. No doubt, according to his idea, the two had been alone together. Harry had struck the blow by which his brother had been injured, and had then left him in the street. Mountjoy had subsequently disappeared, and Harry had told to no one that such an encounter had taken place. This had been the meaning of Augustus Scarborough when he informed his aunt that Harry had been the last who had seen Mountjoy before his disappearance. To Mrs. Mountjoy the fact had been most injurious to Harry's character. Harry had wilfully kept the secret while all the world was at work looking for Mountjoy Scarborough; and, as far as Mrs. Mountjoy could understand, it might well be that Harry had struck the fatal blow that had sent her nephew to his long account. All the impossibilities in the case had not dawned upon her. It had not occurred to her that Mountjoy could not have been killed and his body made away without some great effort, in the performance of which the 'scamp' would hardly have risked his life or his character. But the scamp was certainly a scamp, even though he might not be a murderer, or he would have revealed the secret. In fact, Mrs. Mountjoy believed in the matter exactly what Augustus had intended, and so believing had resolved that her daughter should suffer any purgatory rather than become Harry's wife.

But her daughter made her resolutions exactly in the contrary direction. She in truth did know what had been done that night, while her mother was in ignorance. The extent of her mother's ignorance she understood, but she did not at all know where her mother had got her information. She felt that

Harry's secret was in hands other than he had intended; and that someone must have spoken of the scene. It occurred to Florence at the moment that this must come from Mountjoy himself, whom she believed—and rightly believed—to have been the only second person present on the occasion. And if he had told it to anyone, then must that 'anyone' know where and how he had disappeared. And the information must have been given to her mother solely with the view of damaging Harry's character, and of preventing Harry's marriage.

Thinking of all this, Florence felt that a premeditated and foul attempt,—for as she turned it in her mind the attempt seemed to be very foul,—was being made to injure Harry. A false accusation was brought against him, and was grounded on a misrepresentation of the truth in such a manner as to subvert it altogether, to Harry's injury. It should have no effect upon her. To this determination she came at once, and declared to herself solemnly that she would be true to it. An attempt was made to undermine him in her estimation; but they who made it had not known her character. She was sure of herself now, within her own bosom, that she was bound in a peculiar way to be more than ordinarily true to Harry Annesley. In such an emergency she ought to do for Harry Annesley more than a girl in common circumstances would be justified in doing for her lover. Harry was maligned, ill-used, and slandered. Her mother had been induced to call him a scamp, and to give as her reason for doing so an account of a transaction which was altogether false, though she no doubt had believed it to be true. As she thought of all this, she resolved that it was her duty to write to her lover, and tell him the story as she had heard it. It might be most necessary that he should know the truth. She would write her letter and post it,— so that it should be altogether beyond her mother's control,—and then would tell her mother ·that she had written it. She at first thought that she would keep a copy of the letter and show it to her mother. But when it was written,—those first words intended for a lover's eyes which had ever been produced by her pen,—she found that she could not subject those very words to her mother's hard judgment.

Her letter was as follows:

'DEAR HARRY,—You will be much surprised at receiving a letter from me so soon after our meeting last night. But I warn you that you must not take it amiss. I should not write now were it not that I think it may be for your interest that I should do so. I do not write to say a word about my love, of which I think you may be assured without any letter. I told mamma last night what had occurred between us, and she of course was very angry. You will understand that, knowing how anxious she has been on behalf of my cousin Mountjoy. She has always taken his part, and I think it does mamma great honour not to throw him over now that he is in trouble. I should never have thrown him over in his trouble, had I ever cared for him in that way. I tell you that fairly, Master Harry.

'But mamma, in speaking against you, which she was bound to do in supporting poor Mountjoy, declared that you were the last person who had seen my cousin before his disappearance, and she knew that there had been some violent struggle between you. Indeed, she knew all the truth as to that night, except that the attack had been made by Mountjoy on you. She turned the story all round, declaring that you had attacked him—which, as you perceive, gives a totally different appearance to the whole matter. Somebody had told her, though who it may have been I cannot guess; but somebody has been endeavouring to do you all the mischief he can in the matter, and has made mamma think evil of you. She says that after attacking him, and brutally ill-using him, you had left him in the street, and had subsequently denied all knowledge of having seen him. You will perceive that somebody has been at work inventing a story to do you a mischief, and I think it right that I should tell you.

'But you must never believe that I shall believe anything to your discredit. It would be to my discredit now. I know that you are good, and true, and noble, and that you would not do anything so foul as this. It is because I know this that I have loved you, and shall always love you. Let mamma and others say what they will, you are now to me all the world. Oh! Harry, Harry, when I think of it, how serious it seems to me, and yet how joyful! I exult in you, and will do so, let them say what they may against you. You will be sure of that always. Will you not be sure of it?

'But you must not write me a line in answer, not even to give me your assurance. That must come when we shall meet at length,—say after a dozen years or so. I shall tell mamma of this letter, which circumstances seem to demand, and shall assure her that you will write no answer to it.

'Oh! Harry, you will understand all that I might say of my feelings, in regard to you.—Your own,
'FLORENCE.'

This letter, when she had written it and copied it fair and posted the copy in the pillar-box close by, she found that she could not in any way show absolutely to her mother. In spite of all her efforts it had become a love-letter. And what genuine love-letter can a girl show even to her mother? But she at once told her of what she had done. 'Mamma, I have written a letter to Harry Annesley.'

'You have?'

'Yes, mamma; I have thought it right to tell him what you had heard about that night.'

'And you have done this without my permission, —without even telling me what you were going to do?'

'If I had asked you, you would have told me not.'

'Of course I should have told you not. Good gracious! has it come to this, that you correspond with a young gentleman without my leave, and when you know that I would not have given it?'

'Mamma, in this instance it was necessary.'

'Who was to judge of that?'

'If he is to be my husband——'

'But he is not to be your husband. You are never to speak to him again. You shall never be allowed to meet him; you shall be taken abroad, and there you shall remain, and he shall hear nothing about you. If he attempts to correspond with you——'

'He will not.'

'How do you know?'

'I have told him not to write.'

'Told him, indeed! Much he will mind such telling! I shall give your Uncle Magnus a full account of it all, and ask for his advice. He is a man in a high position, and perhaps you may think fit to obey him, although you utterly refuse to be guided in any way by your mother.' Then the conversation for the moment came to an end. But Florence, as she left her mother, assured herself that she could not promise any close obedience in any such matters to Sir Magnus.

Chapter XIV

THEY ARRIVE IN BRUSSELS

FOR some weeks after the party at Mrs. Armitage's house, and the subsequent explanations with her mother, Florence was made to suffer many things. First came the one week before they started, which was, perhaps, the worst of all. This was specially

embittered by the fact that Mrs. Mountjoy absolutely
refused to divulge her plans as they were made. There
was still a fortnight before she could be received at
Brussels, and as to that fortnight she would tell
nothing. Her knowledge of human nature probably
went so far as to teach her that she could thus most
torment her daughter. It was not that she wished to
torment her in a revengeful spirit. She was quite sure
within her own bosom that she did all in love. She
was devoted to her daughter. But she was thwarted;
and therefore told herself that she could best further
the girl's interests by tormenting her. It was not
meditated revenge; but that revenge which springs
up without any meditation, and is often therefore the
most bitter. 'I must bring her nose to the grindstone,'
was the manner in which she would have probably
expressed her thoughts to herself. Consequently
Florence's nose was brought to the grindstone; and
the operation made her miserable. She would not,
however, complain when she had discovered what her
mother was doing. She asked such questions as appeared to be natural, and put up with replies which
purposely withheld all information. 'Mamma, have
you not settled on what day we shall start?' 'No, my
dear.' 'Mamma, where are we going?' 'I cannot tell
you as yet; I am by no means sure myself.' 'I shall be
glad to know, mamma, what I am to pack up for use
on the journey.' 'Just the same as you would do on
any journey.' Then Florence held her tongue, and
consoled herself with thinking of Harry Annesley.

At last the day came, and she knew that she was
to be taken to Boulogne. Before this time she had
received one letter from Harry, full of love, full of
thanks, just what a lover's letter ought to have been;
but yet she was disturbed by it. It had been delivered
to herself in the usual way, and she might have concealed the receipt of it from her mother, because the
servants in the house were all on her side. But this
would not be in accordance with the conduct which

she had arranged for herself, and she told her mother. 'It is just an acknowledgment of mine to him. It was to have been expected, but I regret it.'

'I do not ask to see it,' said Mrs. Mountjoy angrily.

'I could not show it you, mamma, though I think it right to tell you of it.'

'I do not ask to see it, I tell you. I never wish to hear his name again from your tongue. But I knew how it would be,—of course. I cannot allow this kind of thing to go on. It must be prevented.'

'It will not go on, mamma.'

'But it has gone on. You tell me that he has already written. Do you think it proper that you should correspond with a young man of whom I do not approve?' Florence endeavoured to reflect whether she did think it proper or not. She thought it quite proper that she should love Harry Annesley with all her heart; but was not quite sure as to the correspondence. 'At any rate, you must understand,' continued Mrs. Mountjoy, 'that I will not permit it. All letters, while we are abroad, must be brought me; and if any come from him they shall be sent back to him. I do not wish to open his letters; but you cannot be allowed to receive them. When we are at Brussels, I shall consult your uncle upon the subject. I am very sorry, Florence, that there should be this cause of quarrel between us; but it is your doing.'

'Oh! mamma, why should you be so hard?'

'I am hard, because I will not allow you to accept a young man, who has, I believe, behaved very badly, and who has got nothing of his own.'

'He is his uncle's heir.'

'We know what that may come to. Mountjoy was his father's heir; and nothing could be entailed more strictly than Tretton. We know what entails have come to there. Mr. Prosper will find some way of escaping from it. Entails go for nothing now; and I hear that he thinks so badly of his nephew that he has already quarrelled with him. And he is quite a young man himself. I cannot think how you can be so foolish; you, who declare that you are throwing your cousin over because he is no longer to have all his father's property.'

'Oh! mamma, that is not true.'

'Very well, my dear.'

'I never allowed it to be said in my name, that I was engaged to my cousin Mountjoy.'

'Very well; I will never allow it to be said in my name, that with my consent you are engaged to Mr. Henry Annesley.'

Six or seven days after this they were settled together most uncomfortably in an hotel at Boulogne. Mrs. Mountjoy had gone there because there was no other retreat to which she could take her daughter, and because she had resolved to remove her from beyond the sphere of Harry Annesley's presence. She had at first thought of Ostend; but it had seemed to her that Ostend was within the kingdom reigned over by Sir Magnus; and that there would be some impropriety in removing from thence to the capital in which Sir Magnus was reigning. It was as though you were to sojourn for three days at the park-gates before you were entertained at the mansion. Therefore they stayed at Boulogne, and Mrs. Mountjoy tried the bathing, cold as the water was with equinoctial gales, in order that there might be the appearance of a reason for her being at Boulogne. And for company's sake, in the hope of maintaining some fellowship with her mother, Florence bathed also. 'Mamma, he has not written again,' said Florence, coming up one day from the strand.

'I suppose that you are impatient.'

'Why should there be a quarrel between us? I am not impatient. If you would only believe me, it would be so much more happy for both of us. You always used to believe me.'

'That was before you knew Mr. Henry Annesley.'

There was something in this very aggravating,—

something specially intended to excite angry feelings; but Florence determined to forbear. 'I think you may believe me, mamma. I am your own daughter, and I shall not deceive you. I do consider myself engaged to Mr. Annesley.'

'You need not tell me that.'

'But while I am living with you I will promise not to receive letters from him without your leave. If any should come I will bring it to you unopened, so that you may deal with it as though it had been delivered to yourself. I care nothing about my uncle as to this affair. What he may say cannot affect me; but what you say does affect me very much. I will promise neither to write nor to hear from Mr. Annesley for three months. Will not that satisfy you?' Mrs. Mountjoy would not say that it did satisfy her; but she somewhat mitigated her treatment of her daughter, till they arrived together at Sir Magnus's mansion.

They were shown through a great hall by three lacqueys into an inner vestibule, where they encountered the great man himself. He was just then preparing to be put on to his horse, and Lady Mountjoy had already gone forth in her carriage for her daily airing, with the object, in truth, of avoiding the new-comers.

'My dear Sarah,' said Sir Magnus, 'I hope I have the pleasure of seeing you and my niece very well. Let me see, your name is——'

'My name is Florence,' said the young lady so interrogated.

'Ah! yes; to be sure. I shall forget my own name soon. If anyone was to call me Magnus without the Sir, I shouldn't know whom they meant.' Then he looked his niece in the face, and it occurred to him that Anderson might not improbably desire to flirt with her. Anderson was the riding attaché, who always accompanied him on horseback, and of whom Lady Mountjoy had predicted that he would be sure to flirt with the minister's niece. At that moment

Anderson himself came in, and some ceremony of introduction took place. Anderson was a fair-haired, good-looking young man, with that thorough look of self-satisfaction and conceit which attachés are much more wont to exhibit than to deserve. For the work of an attaché at Brussels is not of a nature to bring forth the highest order of intellect; but the occupations are of a nature to make a young man feel that he is not like other young men.

'I am so sorry that Lady Mountjoy has just gone out. She did not expect you till the later train. You have been staying at Boulogne. What on earth made you stay at Boulogne?'

'Bathing,' said Mrs. Mountjoy in a low voice.

'Ah! yes; I suppose so. Why did you not come to Ostend? There is better bathing there, and I could have done something for you. What! The horses ready, are they? I must go out and show myself or otherwise they'll all think that I am dead. If I were absent from the boulevard at this time of day, I should be put into the newspapers. Where is Mrs. Richards?' Then the two guests with their own special Baker were made over to the ministerial housekeeper, and Sir Magnus went forth upon his ride.

'She's a pretty girl, that niece of mine,' said Sir Magnus.

'Uncommonly pretty,' said the attaché.

'But I believe she is engaged to someone. I quite forget who; but I know there is some aspirant. Therefore you had better keep your toe in your pump, young man.'

'I don't know that I shall keep my toe in my pump because there is another aspirant,' said Anderson. 'You rather whet my ardour, sir, to new exploits. In such circumstances, one is inclined to think that the aspirant must look after himself. Not that I conceive for a moment that Miss Mountjoy should ever look after me.'

When Mrs. Mountjoy came down to the drawing-room there seemed to be quite 'a party' collected to enjoy the hospitality of Sir Magnus, but there were not in truth many more than the usual number at the board. There were Lady Mountjoy, and Miss Abbott, and Mr. Anderson and Mr. Montgomery Arbuthnot, the two attachés. Mr. Montgomery Arbuthnot was especially proud of his name, but was otherwise rather a humble young man as an attaché, having as yet been only three months with Sir Magnus, and desirous of perfecting himself in Foreign Office manners under the tuition of Mr. Anderson. Mr. Blow, the Secretary of Legation,* was not there. He was a married man of austere manners, who, to tell the truth, looked down from a considerable height as regarded Foreign Office knowledge upon his chief. It was Mr. Blow who did the 'grinding' on behalf of the Belgian Legation, and who sometimes did not hesitate to let it be known that such was the fact. Neither he nor Mrs. Blow were popular at the embassy; or it may perhaps be said with more truth that the embassy was not popular with Mr. and Mrs. Blow. It may be stated also that there was a clerk attached to the establishment, Mr. Bunderdown, who had been there for some years, and who was good-naturedly regarded by the English inhabitants as a third attaché. Mr. Montgomery Arbuthnot did his best to let it be understood that this was a mistake. In the small affairs of the legation, which no doubt did not go beyond the legation, Mr. Bunderdown generally sided with Mr. Blow. Mr. Montgomery Arbuthnot was recognised as a second mounted attaché, though his attendance on the boulevard was not as constant as that of Mr. Anderson, in consequence probably of the fact that he had not a horse of his own. But there were others also present. There was Sir Thomas Tresham, with his wife, who had been sent over to inquire into the iron trade of Belgium. He was a learned free-trader,* who could not be got to agree with the old familiar views

of Sir Magnus,—who thought that the more iron
that was produced in Belgium the less would be forthcoming from England. But Sir Thomas knew better;
and as Sir Magnus was quite unable to hold his own
with the political economist, he gave him many dinners, and was civil to his wife. Sir Thomas no doubt
felt that in doing so Sir Magnus did all that could be
expected from him. Lady Tresham was a quiet little
woman, who could endure to be patronised by Lady
Mountjoy without annoyance. And there was M.
Grascour, from the Belgian Foreign Office, who spoke
English so much better than the other gentlemen
present, that a stranger might have supposed him to
be a schoolmaster, whose mission it was to instruct
the English Embassy in their own language.

'Oh! Mrs. Mountjoy, I am so ashamed of myself!'
said Lady Mountjoy, as she waddled into the room
two minutes after the guests had been assembled.
She had a way of waddling that was quite her own,
and which they who knew her best declared that she
had adopted in lieu of other graces of manner. She
puffed a little also, and did contrive to attract peculiar
attention. 'But I have to be in my carriage every
day at the same hour. I don't know what would be
thought of us if we were absent.' Then she turned
with a puff and a waddle to Miss Abbott. 'Dear
Lady Tresham was with us.' Mrs. Mountjoy murmured something as to her satisfaction at not having
delayed the carriage-party, and bethought herself
how exactly similar had been the excuse made by Sir
Magnus himself. Then Lady Mountjoy gave another
little puff, and assured Florence that she hoped she
would find Brussels sufficiently gay,—'not that we
pretend at all to equal Paris.'

'We live at Cheltenham,' said Florence, 'and that
is not at all like Paris. Indeed, I never slept but two
nights at Paris in my life.'

'Then we shall do very well at Brussels.'

After this she waddled off again, and was stopped

in her waddling by Sir Magnus, who sternly desired
her to prepare for the august ceremony of going in to
dinner. The one period of real importance at the
English Embassy was, no doubt, the daily dinner-
hour.

Florence found herself seated between Mr. Anderson, who had taken her in, and M. Grascour, who had
performed the same ceremony for her ladyship. 'I am
sure you will like this little capital very much,' said
M. Grascour. 'It is as much nicer than Paris, as it is
smaller and less pretentious.' Florence could only
assent. 'You will soon be able to learn something of
us; but in Paris you must be to the manner born, or
half a lifetime will not suffice.'

'We'll put you up to the time of day,' said Mr.
Anderson, who did not choose, as he said afterwards,
that this tid-bit should be taken out of his mouth.

'I dare say that all that I shall want will come
naturally without any putting up.'

'You won't find it amiss to know a little of what's
what. You have not got a riding-horse here?'

'Oh no!' said Florence.

'I was going on to say that I can manage to secure
one for you. Billibong has got an excellent horse,
that carried the Princess of Styria* last year.' Mr.
Anderson was supposed to be peculiarly up to everything concerning horses.

'But I have not got a habit. That is a much more
serious affair.'

'Well, yes. Billibong does not keep habits. I wish
he did. But we can manage that too. There does live
a habit-maker in Brussels.'

'Ladies' habits certainly are made in Brussels,'
said M. Grascour. 'But if Miss Mountjoy does not
choose to trust herself to a Belgian tailor, there is the
railway open to her. An English habit can be sent.'

'Dear Lady Centaur had one sent to her only last
year when she was staying here,' said Lady Mountjoy
across her neighbour, with two little puffs.

'I shall not at all want the habit,' said Florence, 'not having the horse, and indeed, never being accustomed to ride at all.'

'Do tell me what it is that you do do,' said Mr. Anderson with a convenient whisper when he found that M. Grascour had fallen into conversation with her ladyship. 'Lawn-tennis?'

'I do play at lawn-tennis, though I am not wedded to it.'

'Billiards? I know you play billiards.'

'I never struck a ball in my life.'

'Goodness gracious, how odd! Don't you ever amuse yourself at all? Are they so very devotional down at Cheltenham?'

'I suppose we are stupid. I don't know that I ever do especially amuse myself.'

'We must teach you,—we really must teach you. I think I may boast of myself that I am a good instructor in that line. Will you promise to put yourself into my hands?'

'You would find me a most unpromising pupil.'

'Not in the least. I will undertake that when you leave this you shall be *au fait* in everything. Leap-frog is not too heavy for me and spilikins* not too light. I am up to them all, from backgammon* to a cotillon,—not but what I prefer the cotillon* for my own taste.'

'Or leap-frog, perhaps,' suggested Florence.

'Well, yes; leap-frog used to be a good game at Gother School,* and I don't see why we shouldn't have it back again. Ladies of course must have a costume on purpose. But I am fond of anything that requires a costume. Don't you like everything out of the common way? I do.' Florence assured him that their tastes were wholly dissimilar, as she liked everything in the common way. 'That's what I call an uncommonly pretty girl,' he said afterwards to M. Grascour, while Sir Magnus was talking to Sir Thomas. 'What an eye!'

'Yes, indeed; she is very lovely.'

'My word, you may say that! And such a turn of the shoulders! I don't say which are best-looking as a rule, English or Belgians, but there are very few of either to come up to her.'

'Anderson, can you tell us how many tons of steel rails they turn out at Liège every week? Sir Thomas asks me just as though it were the simplest question in the world.'

'Forty million,' said Anderson,—'more or less.'

'Twenty thousand would perhaps be nearer the mark,' said M. Grascour; 'but I will send him the exact amount tomorrow.'

Chapter XV

MR. ANDERSON'S LOVE

LADY MOUNTJOY had certainly prophesied the truth when she said that Mr. Anderson would devote himself to Florence. The first week in Brussels passed by quietly enough. A young man can hardly declare his passion within a week, and Mr. Anderson's ways in that particular were well known. A certain amount of license was usually given to him, both by Sir Magnus and Lady Mountjoy, and when he would become remarkable by the rapidity of his changes, the only adverse criticism would come generally from Mr. Blow. 'Another peerless Bird of Paradise,' Mr. Blow would say. 'If the birds were less numerous, Anderson might perhaps do something.' But at the end of the week, on this occasion, even Sir Magnus perceived that Anderson was about to make himself peculiar. 'By George!' he said one morning, when Sir Magnus had just left the outer office, which he had entered with the object of giving some instruction as to the day's ride, 'take her altogether, I never saw a girl so fit as Miss Mountjoy.' There was something very remarkable in this speech, as, according to his usual habit of life, Anderson would certainly have called her Florence, whereas his present appellation showed an unwonted respect.

'What do you mean when you say a young lady is fit?' said Mr. Blow.

'I mean that she is right all round; which is a great deal more than can be said of most of them.'

'The divine Florence——' began Mr. Montgomery Arbuthnot, struggling to say something funny.

'Young man, you had better hold your tongue, and not talk of young ladies in that language.'

'I do believe that he is going to fall in love,' said Mr. Blow.

'I say that Miss Mountjoy is the fittest girl I have seen for many a day; and when a young puppy calls her the divine Florence he does not know what he is about.'

'Why didn't you blow Mr. Blow up when he called her a Bird of Paradise?' said Montgomery Arbuthnot. 'Divine Florence is not half so disrespectful of a young lady as Bird of Paradise. Divine Florence means divine Florence, but Bird of Paradise is chaff.'

'Mr. Blow, as a married man,' said Anderson, 'has a certain freedom allowed him. If he uses it in bad taste, the evil falls back upon his own head. Now, if you please, we'll change the conversation.'

From this it will be seen that Mr. Anderson had really fallen in love with Miss Mountjoy.

But though the week had passed in a harmless way to Sir Magnus and Lady Mountjoy,—in a harmless way to them as regarded their niece and their attaché, —a certain amount of annoyance had no doubt been felt by Florence herself. Though Mr. Anderson's expressions of admiration had been more subdued than usual, though he had endeavoured to whisper his love rather than to talk it out loud, still the admiration had been both visible and audible; and especially so to Florence herself. It was nothing to Sir Magnus with whom his attaché flirted. Anderson was the younger son of a baronet, who had a sickly elder brother, and some fortune of his own. If he chose to marry the girl, that would be well for her, and if not, it would be quite well that the young people should amuse themselves. He expected Anderson to help to put him on his horse, and to ride with him at the appointed hour. He, in return, gave Anderson his dinner and as much wine as he chose to drink. They were both satisfied with each other, and Sir Magnus did not choose to interfere with the young man's amusements. But Florence did not like being the subject of a young man's love-making, and complained to her mother.

Now it had come to pass that not a word had been said as to Harry Annesley since the mother and daughter had reached Brussels. Mrs. Mountjoy had declared that she would consult her brother-in-law in that difficulty, but no such consultation had as yet taken place. Indeed, Florence would not have found her sojourn at Brussels to be unpleasant were it not for Mr. Anderson's unpalatable little whispers. She had taken them as jokes as long as she had been able to do so, but was now at last driven to perceive that other people would not do so. 'Mamma,' she said, 'don't you think that Mr. Anderson is an odious young man?'

'No, my dear; by no means. What is there odious about him? He is very lively; he is the second son of Sir Gregory Anderson, and has very comfortable means of his own.'

'Oh! mamma, what does that signify?'

'Well, my dear, it does signify. In the first place, he is a gentleman; and in the next, has a right to make himself attentive to any young lady in your position. I don't say anything more. I am not particularly wedded to Mr. Anderson. If he were to come to me, and ask for my permission to address you, I should simply refer him to yourself, by which I should mean to imply that if he could contrive to recommend himself to you I should not refuse my sanction.'

Then the subject for that moment dropped, but Florence was astonished to find that her mother could talk about it, not only without reference to Harry Annesley, but also without an apparent thought of Mountjoy Scarborough; and it was distressing to her to think that her mother should pretend to feel that she, her own daughter, should be free to receive the advances of another suitor. As she reflected, it came across her mind that Harry was so odious that her mother would have been willing to accept on her behalf any suitor who presented himself, even though her daughter, in accepting him, should have proved herself to be heartless. Any alternative would have been better to her mother than that choice to which Florence had determined to devote her whole life.

'Mamma,' she said, going back to the subject on the next day, 'if I am to stay here for three weeks longer——'

'Yes, my dear, you are to stay here for three weeks longer.'

'Then somebody must say something to Mr. Anderson.'

'I do not see who can say it but yourself. As far as I can see, he has not misbehaved.'

'I wish you would speak to my uncle.'

'What am I to tell him?'

'That I am engaged.'

'He would ask me to whom, and I cannot tell him. I should then be driven to put the whole case in his hands, and to ask his advice. You do not suppose that I am going to say that you are engaged to marry that odious young man. All the world knows how atrociously badly he has behaved to your own cousin. He left him lying for dead in the street, by a blow from his own hand, and though from that day to this nothing has been heard of Mountjoy, nothing is

known to the police of what may have been his fate;
—even stranger, he may have perished under the
usage which he received, yet Mr. Annesley has not
thought it right to say a word of what had occurred.
He has not dared even to tell an inspector of police the
events of that night. And the young man was your
own cousin, to whom you were known to have been
promised for the last two years.'

'No, no!' said Florence.

'I say that it was so. You were promised to your
cousin, Mountjoy Scarborough.'

'Not with my own consent.'

'All your friends,—your natural friends,—knew
that it was to be so. And now you expect me to take
by the hand this young man who has almost been his
murderer.'

'No, mamma, it is not true. You do not know
the circumstances, and you assert things which are
directly at variance with the truth.'

'From whom do you get your information? From
the young man himself. Is that likely to be true?
What would Sir Magnus say as to that were I to tell
him?'

'I do not know what he would say, but I do know
what is the truth. And can you think it possible that
I should now be willing to accept this foolish young
man in order thus to put an end to my embarrass-
ments?' Then she left her mother's room, and, retreating to her own, sat for a couple of hours thinking,
partly in anger and partly in grief, of the troubles of
her situation. Her mother had now in truth frightened
her as to Harry's position. She did begin to see what
men might say of him, and the way in which they
might speak of his silence, though she was resolved
to be as true to him in her faith as ever. Some exertion of spirit would indeed be necessary. She was
beginning to understand in what way the outside
world might talk of Harry Annesley, of the man to
whom she had given herself and her whole heart.

Then her mother was right. And as she thought of it, she began to justify her mother. It was natural that her mother should believe the story which had been told to her, let it have come from where it might. There was in her mind some suspicion of the truth. She acknowledged a great animosity to her cousin Augustus, and regarded him as one of the causes of her unhappiness. But she knew nothing of the real facts; she did not even suspect that Augustus had seen his brother after Harry had dealt with him, or that he was responsible for his brother's absence. But she knew that she disliked him, and in some way she connected his name with Harry's misfortune.

Of one thing she was quite certain. Let them—the Mountjoys, and Prospers, and the rest of the world —think and say what they would of Harry, she would be true to him. She could understand that his character might be made to suffer, but it should not suffer in her estimation. Or rather let it suffer so, that should not affect her love and her truth. She did not say this to herself. By saying it even to herself she would have committed some default of truth. She did not whisper it even to her own heart. But within her heart there was a feeling that, let Harry be right or wrong in what he had done, even let it be proved, to the satisfaction of all the world, that he had sinned grievously when he had left the man stunned and bleeding on the pavement,—for to such details her mother's story had gone,—still to her he should be braver, more noble, more manly, more worthy of being loved, than was any other man. She, perceiving the difficulties that were in store for her, and looking forward to the misfortune under which Harry might be placed, declared to herself that he should at least have one friend who would be true to him.

'Miss Mountjoy, I have come to you with a message from your aunt.' This was said, three or four days after the conversation between Florence and her mother, by Mr. Anderson, who had contrived to follow the young lady into a small drawing-room after luncheon. What was the nature of the message it was not necessary for us to know. We may be sure that it had been manufactured by Mr. Anderson for the occasion. He had looked about and spied, and had discovered that Miss Mountjoy was alone in the little room. And in thus spying we consider him to have been perfectly justified. His business at the moment was that of making love, a business which is allowed to override all other considerations. Even the making of an office copy of a report made by Mr. Blow for the signature of Sir Magnus, might, according to our view of life, have been properly laid aside for such a purpose. When a young man has it in him to make love to a young lady, and is earnest in his intention, no duty, however paramount, should be held as a restraint. Such was Mr. Anderson's intention at the present moment, and therefore we think that he was justified in concocting a message from Lady Mountjoy. The business of love-making warrants any concoction to which the lover may resort. 'But oh! Miss Mountjoy, I am so glad to have a moment in which I can find you alone.' It must be understood that the amorous young gentleman had not yet been acquainted with the young lady for quite a fortnight.

'I was just about to go upstairs to my mother,' said Florence, rising to leave the room.

'Oh, bother your mother! I beg her pardon and yours. I really didn't mean it. There is such a lot of chaff going on in that outer room, that a fellow falls into the way of it whether he likes it or no.'

'My mother won't mind it at all; but I really must go.'

'Oh no! I am sure you can wait for five minutes. I don't want to keep you for more than five minutes. But it is so hard for a fellow to get an opportunity to say a few words.'

'What words can you want to say to me, Mr.

Anderson?' This she said with a look of great surprise, as though utterly unable to imagine what was
to follow.

'Well, I did hope that you might have some idea
of what my feelings are.'

'Not in the least.'

'Haven't you, now? I suppose I am bound to believe you, though I doubt whether I quite do. Pray
excuse me for saying this, but it is best to be open.'
Florence felt that he ought to be excused for doubting
her, as she did know very well what was coming.
'I—I—— Come, then; I love you. If I were to go
on beating about the bush for twelve months, I could
only come to the same conclusion.'

'Perhaps you might then have considered it better.'

'Not in the least. Fancy considering such a thing
as that for twelve months before you speak of it! I
couldn't do it,—not for twelve days.'

'So I perceive, Mr. Anderson.'

'Well, isn't it best to speak the truth when you're
quite sure of it? If I were to remain dumb for three
months, how should I know but what someone else
might come in the way?'

'But you can't expect that I should be so sudden?'

'That's just where it is. Of course I don't. And
yet girls have to be sudden too.'

'Have they?'

'They're expected to be ready with their answer
as soon as they're asked. I don't say this by way of
impertinence, but merely to show that I have some
justification. Of course if you like to say that you
must take a week to think of it, I am prepared for
that. Only let me tell my own story first.'

'You shall tell your own story, Mr. Anderson;
but I am afraid it can be to no purpose.'

'Don't say that,—pray don't say that,—but do let
me tell it.' Then he paused, but as she remained
silent, after a moment he resumed the eloquence of
his appeal. 'By George, Miss Mountjoy, I have been

so struck of a heap that I do not know whether I am standing on my head or my heels. You have knocked me so completely off my pins that I am not at all like the same person. Sir Magnus himself says he never saw such a difference. I only say that to show that I am quite in earnest. Now I am not quite like a fellow that has no business to fall in love with a girl. I have four hundred a year besides my place in the Foreign Office. And then, of course, there are chances.' In this he alluded to his brother's failing health, of which he could not explain the details to Miss Mountjoy on the present occasion. 'I don't mean to say that this is very splendid, or that it is half what I should like to lay at your feet. But a competence is comfortable.'

'Money has nothing to do with it, Mr. Anderson.'

'What then? Perhaps it is that you don't like a fellow. What girls generally do like is devotion, and, by George! you'd have that. The very ground that you tread upon is sweet to me. For beauty—I don't know how it is, but to my taste there is no one I ever saw at all like you. You fit me—well, as though you were made for me. I know that another fellow might say it a deal better, but no one more truly. Miss Mountjoy, I love you with all my heart, and I want you to be my wife. Now you've got it.'

He had not pleaded his cause badly, and so Florence felt. That he had pleaded it hopelessly was a matter of course. But he had given rise to feelings of gentle regard rather than of anger. He had been honest, and had contrived to make her believe him. He did not come up to her ideal of what a lover should be, but he was nearer to it than Mountjoy Scarborough. He had touched her so closely that she determined at once to tell him the truth, thinking that she might best in this way put an end to his passion for ever. 'Mr. Anderson,' she said, 'though I have known it to be vain, I have thought it best to listen to you, because you asked it.'

'I am sure I am awfully obliged to you.'

'And I ought to thank you for the kind feeling you have expressed to me. Indeed, I do thank you. I believe every word you have said. It is better to show my confidence in your truth than to pretend to the humility of thinking you untrue.'

'It is true; it is true,—every word of it.'

'But I am engaged.' Then it was sad to see the thorough change which came over the young man's face. 'Of course a girl does not talk of her own little affairs to strangers, or I would let you have known this before, so as to have prevented it. But in truth I am engaged.'

'Does Sir Magnus know it, or Lady Mountjoy?'

'I should think not.'

'Does your mother?'

'Now you are taking advantage of my confidence and pressing your questions too closely. But my mother does know of it. I will tell you more,—she does not approve of it. But it is fixed in heaven itself. It may well be that I shall never be able to marry the gentleman to whom I allude, but most certainly I shall marry no one else. I have told you this because it seems to be necessary to your welfare, so that you may get over this passing feeling.'

'It is no passing feeling,' said Anderson with some tragic grandeur.

'At any rate, you have now my story, and remember, that it is trusted to you as a gentleman. I have told it you for a purpose.' Then she walked out of the room, leaving the poor young man in temporary despair.

Chapter XVI

MR. AND MISS GREY

IT was now the middle of October, and it may be said that from the time in which old Mr. Scarborough had declared his intention of showing that the elder of his two sons had no right to the property, Mr. Grey, the lawyer, had been so occupied with the Scarborough affairs as to have had left him hardly a moment for other considerations. He had a partner, who, during these four months, had in fact carried on the business. One difficulty had grown out of another till Mr. Grey's whole time had been occupied, and all his thoughts had been filled with Mr. Scarborough, which is a matter of much greater moment to a man than the loss of his time. The question of Mountjoy Scarborough's position had been first submitted to him in June. October had now been reached, and Mr. Grey had been out of town only for a fortnight, during which fortnight he had been occupied entirely in unravelling the mystery. He had at first refused altogether to have anything to do with the unravelling, and had desired that some other lawyer might be employed. But it had gradually come to pass that he had entered heart and soul into the case, and, with many execrations on his own part against Mr. Scarborough, could find a real interest in nothing else. He had begun his investigations with a thorough wish to discover that Mountjoy Scarborough was in truth the heir. Though he had never loved the young man, and, as he went on with his investigations, became aware that the whole property would go to the creditors should he succeed in proving that Mountjoy was the heir, yet for the sake of abstract honesty he was most anxious that it should be so. And he could not bear to think that he and other lawyers had been taken in by the wily

craft of such a man as the squire of Tretton. It went
thoroughly against the grain with him to have to
acknowledge that the estate would become the property of Augustus. But it was so, and he did acknowledge it. It was proved to him that, in spite of all the
evidence which he had hitherto seen in the matter,
the squire had not married his wife until after the
birth of his eldest son. He did acknowledge it, and
he said bravely that it must be so. Then there came
down upon him a crowd of enemies in the guise of
baffled creditors, all of whom believed, or professed
to believe, that he, Mr. Grey, was in league with the
squire to rob them of their rights. If it could be
proved that Mountjoy had no claim to the property,
then would it go nominally to Augustus, who, according to their own showing, was also one of the confederates, and the property could thus, they said, be
divided. Very shortly the squire would be dead, and
then the confederates would get everything, to the
utter exclusion of poor Mr. Tyrrwhit, and poor Mr.
Samuel Hart, and all the other poor creditors who
would thus be denuded, defrauded, and robbed by a
lawyer's trick. It was in this spirit that Mr. Grey
was attacked by Mr. Tyrrwhit and the others; and
Mr. Grey found it very hard to bear.

And then there was another matter which was also
very grievous to him. If it were as he now stated;
if the squire had been guilty of this fraud; to what
punishment would he be subjected? Mountjoy was
declared to have been innocent. Mr. Tyrrwhit, as he
put the case to his own lawyers, laughed bitterly as
he made this suggestion. And Augustus was, of
course, innocent. Then there was renewed laughter.
And Mr. Grey! Mr. Grey had, of course, been innocent. Then the laughter was very loud. Was it to
be believed that anybody could be taken in by such a
story as this. There was he, Mr. Tyrrwhit; he had
ever been known as a sharp fellow; and Mr. Samuel
Hart, who was now away on his travels; and the

others,—they were all of them sharp fellows. Was it to be believed, that such a set of gentlemen, so keenly alive to their own interest, should be made the victims of such a trick as this? Not if they knew it! Not if Mr. Tyrrwhit knew it!

It was in this shape that the matter reached Mr. Grey's ears; and then it was asked, if it were so, what would be the punishment to which they would be subjected who had defrauded Mr. Tyrrwhit of his just claim? Mr. Tyrrwhit, who on one occasion made his way into Mr. Grey's presence, wished to get an answer to that question from Mr. Grey. 'The man is dying,' said Mr. Grey solemnly.

'Dying! He is not more likely to die than you are, from all I hear.' At this time rumours of Mr. Scarborough's improved health had reached the creditors in London. Mr. Tyrrwhit had begun to believe that Mr. Scarborough's dangerous condition had been part of the hoax; that there had been no surgeon's knives, no terrible operations, no moment of almost certain death. 'I don't believe he's been ill at all,' said Mr. Tyrrwhit.

'I cannot help your belief,' said Mr. Grey.

'But because a man doesn't die and recovers, is he on that account to be allowed to cheat people as he has cheated me, with impunity?'

'I am not going to defend Mr. Scarborough; but he has not in fact cheated you.'

'Who has? Come; do you mean to tell me that if this goes on I shall not have been defrauded of a hundred thousand pounds?'

'Did you ever see Mr. Scarborough on this matter?'

'No; it was not necessary.'

'Or have you got his writing to any document? Have you anything to show that he knew what his son was doing when he borrowed money of you? Is it not perfectly clear that he knew nothing about it?'

'Of course he knew nothing about it,—then; at

that time. It was afterwards that his fraud began.
When he found that the estate was in jeopardy, then
the falsehood was concocted.'

'Ah, there, Mr. Tyrrwhit, I can only say that I
disagree with you. I must express my opinion that
if you endeavour to recover your money on that plea
you will be beaten. If you can prove fraud of that
kind, no doubt you can punish those who have been
guilty of it,—me among the number.'

'I say nothing of that,' said Mr. Tyrrwhit.

'But if you have been led into your present difficulty by an illegal attempt on the part of my client to
prove an illegitimate son to have been legitimate, and
then to have changed his mind for certain purposes, I
do not see how you are to punish him. The act will
have been attempted and not completed. And it will
have been an act concerning his son, and not concerning you.'

'Not concerning me?' shrieked Mr. Tyrrwhit.

'Certainly not, legally. You are not in a position
to prove that he knew that his son was borrowing
money from you on the credit of the estate. As a fact,
he certainly did not know it.'

'We shall see about that,' said Mr. Tyrrwhit.

'Then you must see about it, but not with my aid.
As a fact, I am telling you all that I know about it.
If I could I would prove Mountjoy Scarborough to be
his father's heir tomorrow. Indeed, I am altogether
on your side in the matter,—if you would believe it.'
Here Mr. Tyrrwhit again laughed. 'But you will
not believe it, and I do not ask you to do so. As it is,
we must be opposed to each other.'

'Where is the young man?' asked Mr. Tyrrwhit.

'Ah! that is a question I am not bound to answer,
even if I knew. It is a matter on which I say nothing.
You have lent him money at an exorbitant rate of
interest.'

'It is not true.'

'At any rate it seems so to me; and it is out of the

question that I should assist you in recovering it. You did it at your own peril, and not on my advice. Good-morning, Mr. Tyrrwhit.' Then Mr. Tyrrwhit went on his way, not without sundry threats as to the whole Scarborough family.

It was very hard upon Mr. Grey, because he certainly was an honest man, and had taken up the matter simply with a view of learning the truth. It had been whispered to him within the last day or two that Mountjoy Scarborough had lately been seen alive, and gambling with reckless prodigality at Monte Carlo. It had only been told to him as probably true; but he certainly believed it. But he knew nothing of the details of his disappearance, and had not been much surprised, as he had never believed that the young man had been murdered or had made away with himself. But he had heard before that of the quarrel in the street between him and Harry Annesley. And the story had been told to him so as to fall with great discredit on Harry Annesley's head. According to that story, Henry Annesley had struck his foe during the night, and left him for dead upon the pavement. Then Mountjoy Scarborough had been missing, and Henry Annesley had told no one of the quarrel. There had been some girl in question. So much and no more Mr. Grey had heard, and was, of course, inclined to think that Harry Annesley must have behaved very badly. But of the mode of Mountjoy's subsequent escape he had heard nothing.

Mr. Grey at this time was living down at Fulham in a small old-fashioned house which overlooked the river, and was called the Manor House. He would have said that it was his custom to go home every day by an omnibus, but he did in truth almost always remain at his office so late as to make it necessary that he should return by a cab. He was a man fairly well to do in the world, as he had no one depending on him but one daughter;—no one, that is to say, whom he was obliged to support. But he had a married sister with a scapegrace husband and six daughters, whom, in fact, he did support. Mrs. Carroll, with the kindest intentions in the world, had come and lived near him. She had taken a genteel new house in Bolsover Terrace, on the Fulham Road, about a quarter of a mile from her brother. Mr. Grey lived in the old Manor House, a small uncomfortable place, which had a nook of its own, close upon the water, and with a lovely little lawn. It was certainly most uncomfortable as a gentleman's residence, but no consideration would induce Mr. Grey to sell it. There were but two sitting-rooms in it, and one was for the most part uninhabited. The upstairs drawing-room was furnished, but anyone with half an eye could see that it was never used. A stray 'caller' might be shown up there, but callers of that class were very uncommon in Mr. Grey's establishment. With his own domestic arrangements Mr. Grey would have been quite contented, had it not been for Mrs. Carroll. It was now some years since he had declared that though Mr. Carroll,—or Captain Carroll as he had then been called,—was an improvident, worthless, drunken Irishman, he would never see his sister want. The consequence was that Carroll had come with his wife and six daughters, and taken a house close to him. There are such 'whips and scorns'* in the world to which a man shall be so subject as to have the whole tenor of his life changed by them. The hero bears them heroically, making no complaints to those around him. The common man shrinks, and squeals, and cringes, so that he is known to those around him as one specially persecuted. In this respect Mr. Grey was a grand hero. When he spoke to his friends of Mrs. Carroll, his friends were taught to believe that his outside arrangements with his sister were perfectly comfortable. No doubt there did creep out among those who were most intimate with him a knowledge that Mr. Carroll,—for the captain had in truth never been more than a lieutenant, and had now long since sold out,—was impecunious, and a trouble rather than otherwise. But I doubt whether there was a single inhabitant of the neighbourhood of Fulham who was aware that Mrs. Carroll and the Misses Carroll cost Mr. Grey on an average above six hundred a year.

There was one in Mr. Grey's family to whom he was so attached that he would, to oblige her, have thrown over the whole Carroll family; but of this that one person would not hear. She hated the whole Carroll family with an almost unholy hatred of which she herself was endeavouring to repent daily, but in vain. She could not do other than hate them; but she could do other than allow her father to withdraw his fostering protection,—for this one person was Mr. Grey's only daughter and his one close domestic associate. Miss Dorothy Grey was known well to all the neighbourhood, and was both feared and revered. As we shall have much to do with her in the telling of our story, it may be well to make her stand plainly before the reader's eyes. In the first place it must be understood that she was motherless, brotherless, and sisterless. She had been Mr. Grey's only child, and her mother had been dead for fifteen or sixteen years. She was now about thirty years of age, but was generally regarded as ranging somewhere between forty and fifty. 'If she isn't nearer fifty than forty, I'll eat my old shoes,' said a lady in the neighbourhood to a gentleman. 'I've known her these twenty years, and she's not altered in the least.' As Dolly Grey had been only ten twenty years ago, the lady must have been wrong. But it is singular how a person's memory of things may be created out of their present appearances. Dorothy herself had apparently no desire to set right this erroneous opinion which the neighbourhood entertained respecting her. She did not seem to care whether she was supposed to be thirty, or forty, or fifty. Of youth, as a means of getting lovers, she entertained a profound

contempt. That no lover would ever come she was
assured, and would not at all have known what to
do with one had he come. The only man for whom
she had ever felt the slightest regard was her father.
For some women about she did entertain a passion-
less, well-regulated affection, but they were generally
the poor, the afflicted, or the aged. It was, however,
always necessary that the person so signalised should
be submissive. Now Mrs. Carroll, Mr. Grey's
sister, had long since shown that she was not submissive enough, nor were the girls, the eldest of
whom was a pert, ugly, well-grown minx, now about
eighteen years old. The second sister, who was
seventeen, was supposed to be a beauty; but which
of the two was the more odious in the eyes of their
cousin it would be impossible to say.

Miss Dorothy Grey was Dolly only to her father.
Had anyone else so ventured to call her, she would
have started up at once, the outraged aged female of
fifty. Even her aunt, who was trouble enough to her,
felt that it could not be so. Her uncle tried it once,
and she declined to come into his presence for a
month; letting it be fully understood that she had
been insulted.

And yet she was not, according to my idea, by any
means an ill-favoured young woman. It is true that
she wore spectacles; and, as she always desired to
have her eyes about with her, she never put them off
when out of bed. But how many German girls do
the like, and are not accounted for that reason to be
plain? She was tall and well made, we may almost
say robust. She had the full use of all her limbs, and
was never ashamed of using them. I think she was
wrong when she would be seen to wheel the barrow
about the garden, and that her hands must have
suffered in her attempts to live down the conventional absurdities of the world. It is true that she
did wear gloves during her gardening, but she wore
them only in obedience to her father's request. She

had bright eyes, somewhat far apart, and well-made, wholesome, regular features. Her nose was large, and her mouth was large; but they were singularly intelligent, and full of humour when she was pleased in conversation. As to her hair, she was too indifferent to enable one to say that it was attractive; but it was smoothed twice a day, was very copious, and always very clean. Indeed, for cleanliness from head to foot she was a model. 'She is very clean, but then it's second to nothing to her,' had said a sarcastic old lady, who had meant to imply that Miss Dorothy Grey was not constant at church. But the sarcastic old lady had known nothing about it. Dorothy Grey never stayed away from morning church unless her presence were desired by her father, and for once or twice that she might do so, she would take her father with her three or four times,—against the grain with him, it must be acknowledged.

But the most singular attribute of the lady's appearance has still to be mentioned. She always wore a slouch hat,* which from motives of propriety she called her bonnet, which gave her a singular appearance, as though it had been put on to thatch her entirely from the weather. It was made generally of black straw, and was round, equal at all points of the circle, and was fastened with broad brown ribbons. It was supposed in the neighbourhood to be completely weather-tight. The unimaginative nature of Fulham did not allow the Fulham mind to gather in the fact that, at the same time, she might possess two or three such hats. But they were undoubtedly precisely similar, and she would wear them in London with exactly the same indifference as in the comparatively rural neighbourhood of her own residence. She would in truth go up and down in the omnibus, and would do so alone without the slightest regard to the opinion of any of her neighbours. The Carroll girls would laugh at her behind her back, but no

Carroll girl had been seen ever to smile before her face, instigated to do so by their cousin's vagaries.

But I have not yet mentioned that attribute of Miss Grey's which is perhaps the most essential in her character. It is necessary at any rate that they should know it who wish to understand her nature. When it had once been brought home to her that duty required her to do this thing or the other, or to say this word or another, the thing would be done or the word said let the result be what it might. Even to the displeasure of her father, the word was said or the thing was done. Such a one was Dolly Grey.

Chapter XVII

MR. GREY DINES AT HOME

MR. GREY returned home in a cab on the day of Mr. Tyrrwhit's visit, not in the happiest humour. Though he had got the best of Mr. Tyrrwhit in the conversation, still, the meeting, which had been protracted, had annoyed him. Mr. Tyrrwhit had made accusations against himself personally which he knew to be false, but which, having been covered up, and not expressed exactly, he had been unable to refute. A man shall tell you you are a thief and a scoundrel in such a manner as to make it impossible for you to take him by the throat. 'You, of course, are not a thief and a scoundrel,' he shall say to you, but shall say it in such a tone of voice as to make you understand that he conceives you to be both. We all know the parliamentary mode of giving an opponent the lie so as to make it impossible that the Speaker* shall interfere. Mr. Tyrrwhit had treated Mr. Grey in the same fashion, and as Mr. Grey was irritable, thin-skinned, and irascible, and as he would brood over things of which it was quite unnecessary that a lawyer should take any cognisance, he went back home an unhappy man. Indeed, the whole Scarborough affair had been from first to last a great trouble to him. The work which he was now performing could not, he imagined, be put into his bill. To that he was supremely indifferent, but his younger partner thought it a little hard that all the other work of the firm should be thrown on his shoulders during the period which naturally would have been his holidays, and he did make his feelings intelligible to Mr. Grey. Mr. Grey, who was essentially a just man, saw that his partner was right, and made offers, but he would not accede to the only proposition which his partner made. 'Let him go and look for a lawyer elsewhere,' said his partner. They both of them knew that Mr. Scarborough had been thoroughly dishonest, but he had been an old client. His father before him had been a client of Mr. Grey's father. It was not in accordance with Mr. Grey's theory to treat the old man after this fashion. And he had taken intense interest in the matter. He had, first of all, been sure that Mountjoy Scarborough was the heir, and though Mountjoy Scarborough was not at all to his taste, he had been prepared to fight for him. He had now assured himself, after most laborious enquiry, that Augustus Scarborough was the heir, and although in the course of the business he had come to hate the cautious money-loving Augustus twice worse than the gambling spendthrift Mountjoy, still, in the cause of honesty, and truth, and justice, he fought for Augustus against the world at large, and against even the band of creditors, till the world at large and the band of creditors began to think that he was leagued with Augustus,—so as to be one of those who would make large sums of money out of the irregularity of the affair. This made him cross, and put him into a very bad humour as he went back to Fulham.

One thing must be told of Mr. Grey which was

very much to his discredit, and which, if generally
known, would have caused his clients to think him
to be unfit to be the recipient of their family secrets.
He told all the secrets to Dolly. He was a man who
could not possibly be induced to leave his business
behind him at his office. It made the chief subject of
conversation when he was at home. He would even
call Dolly into his bedroom late at night, bringing her
out of bed for the occasion, to discuss with her some
point of legal strategy,—of legal but still honest
strategy which had just occurred to him. Maybe he
had not quite seen his way as to the honesty, and
wanted Dolly's opinion on the subject. Dolly would
come in in her dressing-gown, and, sitting on his
bed, would discuss the matter with him as advocate
against the devil. Sometimes she would be convinced; more frequently she would hold her own.
But the points which were discussed in that way,
and the strength of argumentation which was used
on either side, would have surprised the clients, and
the partner, and the clerks, and the eloquent barrister
who was occasionally employed to support this side
or the other. The eloquent barrister, or it might be
the client himself, startled sometimes at the amount
of enthusiasm which Mr. Grey would throw into his
argument, would little dream that the very words
had come from the young lady in her dressing-gown.
To tell the truth, Miss Grey thoroughly liked these
discussions, whether held on the lawn, or in the
dining-room armchairs, or during the silent hours of
the night. They formed, indeed, the very salt of her
life. She felt herself to be the Conscience of the firm.
Her father was the Reason. And the partner, in her
own phraseology, was the—Devil. For it must be
understood that Dolly Grey had a spice of fun about
her of which her father had the full advantage. She
would not have called her father's partner the 'Devil'
to any other ear but her father's. And that her father
knew, understanding also the spirit in which the

sobriquet had been applied. He did not think that his partner was worse than another man, nor did he think that his daughter so thought. The partner, whose name was Barry, was a man of average honesty, who would occasionally be surprised at the searching justness with which Mr. Grey would look into a matter after it had been already debated for a day or two in the office. But Mr. Barry, though he had the pleasure of Miss Grey's acquaintance, had no idea of the nature of the duties which she performed in the firm.

'I'm nearly broken-hearted about this abominable business,' said Mr. Grey, as he went upstairs to his dressing-room. The normal hour for dinner was half-past six. He had arrived on this occasion at half-past seven, and had paid a shilling extra to the cabman to drive him quick. The man, having a lame horse, had come very slowly, fidgeting Mr. Grey into additional temporary discomfort. He had got his additional shilling, and Mr. Grey had only got the additional discomfort. 'I declare I think he is the wickedest old man the world ever produced.' This he said as Dolly followed him upstairs; but Dolly, wiser than her father, would say nothing about the wicked old man in the servants' hearing.

In five minutes Mr. Grey came down 'dressed,'— by the use of which word was implied the fact that he had shaken his neckcloth, washed his hands and face, and put on his slippers. It was understood in the household that though half-past six was the hour named for dinner, half-past seven was a much more probable time. Mr. Grey pertinaciously refused to have it changed. '*Stare super vias antiquas*,'*he had stoutly said when the proposition had been made to him,—by which he had intended to imply that as during the last twenty years he had been compelled to dine at half-past six instead of six, he did not mean to be driven any further in the same direction. Consequently his cook was compelled to prepare his dinner in such a manner that it might be eaten at one hour or the other, as chance would have it.

The dinner passed without much conversation other than that incidental to Mr. Grey's wants and comforts. His daughter knew that he had been at the office for eight hours, and knew also that he was not a young man. Every kind of little cosseting was therefore applied to him. There was a pheasant for dinner, and it was essentially necessary in Dolly's opinion that he should have first the wing quite hot and then the leg, also hot, and that the bread-sauce should be quite hot on the two occasions. For herself, if she had had an old crow for dinner it would have been the same thing. Tea and bread-and-butter were her luxuries, and her tea and bread-and-butter had been enjoyed three hours ago.

'I declare I think that after all the leg is the better joint of the two.'

'Then why don't you have the two legs?'

'There would be a savour of greediness in that, though I know that the leg will go down,—and I shouldn't then be able to draw the comparison. I like to have them both, and I like always to be able to assert my opinion that the leg is the better joint. Now, how about the apple-pudding? You said I should have an apple-pudding.' From which it appeared that Mr. Grey was not superior to having the dinner discussed in his presence at the breakfast-table. The apple-pudding came and was apparently enjoyed. A large portion of it was put between two plates. 'That's for Mrs. Grimes,' suggested Mr. Grey. 'I am not quite sure that Mrs. Grimes is worthy of it.' 'If you knew what it was to be left without a shilling of your husband's wages you'd think yourself worthy.'

When the conversation about the pudding was over Mr. Grey ate his cheese, and then sat quite still in his armchair over the fire while the things were being taken away.

'I declare I think he is the wickedest man the world has ever produced,' said Mr. Grey as soon as the door was shut, thus showing by the repetition of the words he had before used that his mind had been intent on Mr. Scarborough rather than on the pheasant.

'Why don't you have done with them?'

'That's all very well; but you wouldn't have done with them if you had known them all your life.'

'I wouldn't spend my time and energies in whitewashing any rascal,' said Dolly with vigour.

'You don't know what you'd do. And a man isn't to be left in the lurch altogether because he's a rascal. Would you have a murderer hanged without someone to stand up for him?'

'Yes, I would,' said Dolly thoughtlessly.

'And he mightn't have been a murderer after all; or not legally so, which, as far as the law goes, is the same thing.'

But this special question had been often discussed between them, and Mr. Grey and Dolly did not intend to be carried away by it on the present occasion. 'I know all about that,' she said; 'but this isn't a case of life and death. The old man is only anxious to save his property, and throws upon you all the burden of doing it. He never agrees with you as to anything you say.'

'As to legal points he does.'

'But he always keeps you in hot water, and puts forward so much villainy that I would have nothing further to do with him. He has been so crafty that you hardly know now which is in truth the heir.'

'Oh! yes, I do,' said the lawyer. 'I know very well, and am very sorry that it should be so. And I cannot but feel for the rascal because the dishonest effort was made on behalf of his own son.'

'Why was it necessary?' said Dolly, with sparks flying from her eye. 'Throughout from the beginning he has been bad. Why was the woman not his wife?'

'Ah! why indeed? But had his sin consisted only in that, I should not have dreamed of refusing my assistance as a family lawyer. All that would have gone for nothing then.'

'When evil creeps in,' said Dolly sententiously, 'you cannot put it right afterwards.'

'Never mind about that. We shall never get to the end if you go back to Adam and Eve.'

'People don't go back often enough.'

'Bother!' said Mr. Grey, finishing his second and last glass of port-wine. 'Do keep yourself in some degree to the question in dispute. In advising an attorney of today as to how he is to treat a client, you can't do any good by going back to Adam and Eve. Augustus is the heir, and I am bound to protect the property for him from these money-lending harpies. The moment the breath is out of the old man's body, they will settle down upon it if we leave them an inch of ground on which to stand. Every detail of his marriage must be made as clear as daylight; and that must be done in the teeth of former false statements.'

'As far as I can see the money-lending harpies are the honestest lot of people concerned.'

'The law is not on their side. They have got no right. The estate, as a fact, will belong to Augustus the moment his father dies. Mr. Scarborough endeavoured to do what he could for him whom he regarded as his eldest son. It was very wicked. He was adding a second and a worse crime to the first. He was flying in the face of the laws of his country. But he was successful; and he threw dust into my eyes, because he wanted to save the property for the boy. And he endeavoured to make it up to his second son, by saving for him a second property. He was not selfish; and I cannot but feel for him.'

'But you say he is the wickedest man the world ever produced.'

'Because he boasts of it all, and cannot be got in

any way to repent. He gives me my instructions as though from first to last he had been a highly honourable man, and only laughs at me when I object. And yet he must know that he may die any day. He only wishes to have this matter set straight so that he may die. I could forgive him altogether if he would but once say that he was sorry for what he'd done. But he has completely the air of the fine old head of a family who thinks he is to be put into marble the moment the breath is out of his body, and that he richly deserves the marble he is to be put into.'

'That is a question between him and his God,' said Dolly.

'He hasn't got a God. He believes only in his own reason,—and is content to do so, lying there on the very brink of eternity. He is quite content with himself, because he thinks that he has not been selfish. He cares nothing that he has robbed everyone all round. He has no reverence for property and the laws which govern it. He was born only with the life-interest; and he has determined to treat it as though the fee-simple had belonged to him. It is his utter disregard for law,—for what the law has decided, which makes me declare him to have been the wickedest man the world ever produced.'

'It is his disregard for truth which makes you think so.'

'He cares nothing for truth. He scorns it, and laughs at it. And yet about the little things of the world he expects his word to be taken as certainly as that of any other gentleman.'

'I would not take it.'

'Yes, you would, and would be right too. If he would say he'd pay me a hundred pounds tomorrow, or a thousand, I would have his word as soon as any other man's bond. And yet he has utterly got the better of me, and made me believe that a marriage took place, when there was no marriage. I think I'll have a cup of tea.'

'You won't go to sleep, papa?'

'Oh! yes, I shall. When I've been so troubled as that I must have a cup of tea.'

Mr. Grey was often troubled, and as a consequence Dolly was called up for consultation in the middle of the night.

At about one o'clock there came the well-known knock at Dolly's door and the usual invitation. Would she come into her father's room for a few minutes? Then her father trotted back to his bed, and Dolly of course followed him as soon as she had clothed herself decently. 'The fact is, my dear, he wants me to go down to Tretton at once.'

'Why didn't you tell me?'

'I thought I had made up my mind not to go; or I thought rather that I should be able to make up my mind not to go. But it is possible that down there I may have some effect for good.'

'What does he want of you?'

'There is a long question about raising money with which Augustus desires to buy the silence of the creditors.'

'Could he get the money?' asked Dolly.

'Yes, I think he could. The property at present is altogether unembarrassed. To give Mr. Scarborough his due he has never put his name to a scrap of paper. Nor has he had occasion to do so. The Tretton pottery people want more land, or rather more water, and a large sum of money will be forthcoming. But he doesn't see the necessity of giving Mr. Tyrrwhit a penny-piece, or certainly Mr. Hart. He would send them away howling without a scruple. Now Augustus is anxious to settle with them, for some reason which I do not clearly understand. But he wishes to do so without any interference on his father's part. In fact, he and his father have very different ideas as to the property. The squire regards it as his, but Augustus thinks that any day may make it his own. In fact, they are on the very verge of quarrelling.'

Then after a long debate Dolly consented that her father should go down to Tretton, and act if possible the part of peace-maker.

Chapter XVIII

THE CARROLL FAMILY

'AUNT CARROLL is coming to dinner today,' said Dolly the next day with a serious face.

'I know she is. Have a nice dinner for her. I don't think she ever has a nice dinner at home.'

'And the three eldest girls are coming.'

'Three!'

'You asked them yourself on Sunday.'

'Very well. They said their papa would be away on business.' It was understood that Mr. Carroll was never asked to the Manor House.

'Business! There is a club he belongs to where he dines and gets drunk once a month. It's the only thing he does regularly.'

'They must have their dinner, at any rate,' said Mr. Grey. 'I don't think they should suffer because he drinks.' This had been a subject much discussed between them, but on the present occasion Miss Grey would not renew it. She despatched her father in a cab, the cab having been procured because he was supposed to be a quarter of an hour late, and then went to work to order dinner.

It has been said that Miss Grey hated the Carrolls; but she hated the daughters worse than the mother, and of all the people she hated in the world she hated Amelia Carroll the worst. Amelia, the eldest, entertained an idea that she was more of a personage in the world's eyes than her cousin—that she went to more parties, which certainly was true if she went to any—that she wore finer clothes, which was also true, and that she had a lover, whereas Dolly Grey—as

she called her cousin behind her back——had none.
This lover had something to do with horses, and had
only been heard of, had never been seen at the Manor
House. Sophy was a good deal hated also, being a
forward, flirting, tricky girl of seventeen, who had
just left the school at which Uncle John had paid for
her education. Georgina, the third, was still at school
under similar circumstances, and was pardoned her
egregious noisiness and romping propensities under
the score of youth. She was sixteen, and was possessed of terrible vitality. 'I am sure they take after
their father altogether,' Mr. Grey had once said
when the three left the Manor House together.

At half-past six punctually they came. Dolly heard
a great clatter of four people leaving their clogs and
cloaks in the hall, and would not move out of the
unused drawing-room, in which for the moment she
was seated. Betsey had to prepare the dinner-table
downstairs, and would have been sadly discomfited
had she been driven to do it in the presence of three
Carroll girls. For it must be understood that Betsey
had no greater respect for the Carroll girls than her
mistress. 'Well! Aunt Carroll, how does the world
use you?'

'Very badly. You haven't been up to see me for
ten days.'

'I haven't counted; but when I do come I don't
often do any good. How are Minna, and Brenda,
and Potsey?'

'Poor Potsey has got a nasty boil under her
arm.'

'It comes from eating too much toffy,' said Georgina. 'I told her it would.'

'How very nasty you are!' said Miss Carroll. 'Do
leave the child and her ailments alone.'

'Poor papa isn't very well either,' said Sophy, who
was supposed to be her father's pet.

'I hope his state of health will not debar him from
dining with his friends tonight,' said Miss Grey.

'You have always something ill-natured to say about papa,' said Sophy.

'Nothing will ever keep him back when conviviality demands his presence.' This came from his afflicted wife, who, in spite of all his misfortunes, would ever speak with some respect of her husband's employments. 'He wasn't at all in a fit state to go tonight, but he had promised, and that was enough.'

When they had waited three-quarters of an hour Amelia began to complain,—certainly not without reason. 'I wonder why Uncle John always keeps us waiting in this way?'

'Papa has, unfortunately, something to do with his time, which is not altogether his own.' There was not much in these words, but the tone in which they were uttered would have crushed anyone more susceptible than Amelia Carroll. But at that moment the cab arrived, and Dolly went down to meet her father.

'Have they come?' he asked.

'Come!' she answered, taking his gloves and comforter from him, and giving him a kiss as she did so. 'That girl upstairs is nearly famished.'

'I won't be half a moment,' said the repentant father, hastening upstairs to go through the ordinary dressing arrangement.

'I wouldn't hurry for her,' said Dolly; 'but of course you'll hurry. You always do; don't you, papa?' Then they sat down to dinner.

'Well! girls, what is your news?'

'We were out to-day on the Brompton Road,' said the eldest, 'and there came up Prince Chitakov's drag with four roans.'

'Prince Chitakov! I didn't know there was such a prince.'

'Oh! dear yes; with very stiff moustachios, turned up high at the corners, and pink cheeks, and a very sharp, nobby-looking hat, with a light-coloured grey coat, and light gloves. You must know the prince.'

'Upon my word I never heard of him, my dear. What did the prince do?'

'He was tooling his own drag,* and he had a lady with him on the box. I never saw anything more tasty than her dress,—dark red silk with little fluffy fur ornaments all over it. I wonder who she was?'

'Mrs. Chitakov, probably,' said the attorney.

'I don't think the prince is a married man,' said Sophy.

'They never are, for the most part,' said Amelia; 'and she wouldn't be Mrs. Chitakov, Uncle John.'

'Wouldn't she now? What would she be? Can either of you tell me what the wife of a Prince Chitakov would call herself?'

'Princess of Chitakov, of course,' said Sophy. 'It's the Princess of Wales.'

'But it isn't the Princess of Christian, nor yet the Princess of Teck, nor the Princess of England. I don't see why the lady shouldn't be Mrs. Chitakov, if there is such a lady.'

'Papa, don't bamboozle her,' said his daughter.

'But,' continued the attorney, 'why shouldn't the lady have been his wife? Don't married ladies wear little fluffy fur ornaments?'

'I wish, John, you wouldn't talk to the girls in that strain,' said their mother. 'It really isn't becoming.'

'To suggest that the lady was the gentleman's wife?'

'But I was going to say,' continued Amelia, 'that as the prince drove by, he kissed his hand—he did, indeed. And Sophy and I were walking along as demurely as possible. I never was so knocked of a heap in all my life.'

'He did,' said Sophy. 'It's the most impertinent thing I ever heard. If my father had seen it he'd have had the prince off the box of the coach in no time.'

'Then, my dear,' said the attorney, 'I am very glad that your father did not see it.' Poor Dolly, during this conversation about the prince, sat angry and silent, thinking to herself in despair of what extremes of vulgarity even a first cousin of her own could be guilty. That she should be sitting at a table with a girl who could boast that a reprobate foreigner had kissed his hand to her from the box of a fashionable four-horsed coach! For it was in that light that Miss Grey regarded it. 'And did you have any further adventures besides this memorable encounter with the prince?'

'Nothing nearly so interesting,' said Sophy.

'That was hardly to be expected,' said the attorney. 'Jane, will you have a glass of port wine? Girls, you must have a glass of port wine to support you after your disappointment with the prince.'

'We were not disappointed in the least,' said Amelia.

'Pray, pray let the subject drop,' said Dolly.

'That is because the prince did not kiss his hand to you,' said Sophy. Then Miss Grey sank again into silence, crushed beneath this last blow.

In the evening, when the dinner things had been taken away, a matter of business came up, and took the place of the prince and his moustachios. Mrs. Carroll was most anxious to know whether her brother could 'lend' her a small sum of twenty pounds. It came out in conversation that the small sum was needed to satisfy some imperious demand made upon Mr. Carroll by a tailor. 'He must have clothes, you know,' said the poor woman, wailing. 'He doesn't have many, but he must have some.' There had been other appeals on the same subject made not very long since, and to tell the truth, Mr. Grey did require to have the subject argued in fear of the subsequent remarks which would be made to him afterwards by his daughter if he gave the money too easily. The loan had to be arranged in full conclave, as otherwise Mrs. Carroll would have found it difficult to obtain access to her brother's ear. But the one auditor whom she feared was her niece. On the present occasion Miss Grey simply took up her book to show that the subject was one which had no interest for her; but she did undoubtedly listen to all that was said on the subject. 'There was never anything settled about poor Patrick's clothes,' said Mrs. Carroll in a half whisper. She did not care how much her own children heard, and she knew how vain it was to attempt so to speak that Dolly should not hear.

'I dare say something ought to be done at some time,' said Mr. Grey, who knew that he would be told, when the evening was over, that he would give away all his substance to that man if he were asked.

'Papa has not had a new pair of trousers this year,' said Sophy.

'Except those green ones he wore at the races,' said Georgina.

'Hold your tongue, miss,' said her mother. 'That was a pair that I made up for him and sent them to the man to get pressed.'

'When the hundred a year was arranged for all our dresses,' said Amelia, 'not a word was said about papa. Of course, papa is a trouble.'

'I don't see that he is more of a trouble than anyone else,' said Sophy. 'Uncle John would not like not to have any clothes.'

'No, I should not, my dear.'

'And his own income is all given up to the house uses.' Here Sophy touched imprudently on a sore subject. His 'own' income consisted of what had been saved out of his wife's fortune, and was thus named as in opposition to the larger sum paid to Mrs. Carroll by Mr. Grey. There was one hundred and fifty pounds a year coming from settled property, which had been preserved by the lawyer's care, and which was regarded in the family as 'papa's own.'

It certainly is essential for respectability that something should be set apart from a man's income for his wearing apparel; and though the money was, perhaps, improperly so designated, Dolly would not have objected had she not thought that it had already gone to the race-course,—in company with the green trousers. She had her own means of obtaining information as to the Carroll family. It was very necessary that she should do so, if the family was to be kept on its legs at all. 'I don't think any good can come from discussing what my uncle does with the money.' This was Dolly's first speech. 'If he is to have it, let him have it, but let him have as little as possible.'

'I never heard anybody so cross as you always are to papa,' said Sophy.

'Your cousin Dorothy is very fortunate,' said Mrs. Carroll. 'She does not know what it is to want for anything.'

'She never spends anything—on herself,' said her father. 'It is Dolly's only fault that she won't.'

'Because she has it all done for her,' said Amelia.

Dolly had gone back to her book, and disdained to make any further reply. Her father felt that quite enough had been said about it, and was prepared to give the twenty pounds, under the idea that he might be thought to have made a stout fight upon the subject. 'He does want them very badly—for decency's sake,' said the poor wife, thus winding up her plea. Then Mr. Grey got out his cheque-book and wrote the cheque for twenty pounds. But he made it payable, not to Mr., but to Mrs. Carroll.

'I suppose, papa, nothing can be done about Mr. Carroll.' This was said by Dolly as soon as the family had withdrawn.

'In what way "done," my dear?'

'As to settling some further sum for himself.'

'He'd only spend it, my dear.'

'That would be intended,' said Dolly.

'And then he would come back just the same.'

'But in that case he should have nothing more. Though they were to declare that he hadn't a pair of trousers in which to appear at a race-course, he shouldn't have it.'

'My dear,' said Mr. Grey, 'you cannot get rid of the gnats of the world. They will buzz and sting and be a nuisance. Poor Jane suffers worse from this gnat than you or I. Put up with it; and understand in your own mind that when he comes for another twenty pounds he must have it. You needn't tell him, but so it must be.'

'If I had my way,' said Dolly after ten minutes' silence, 'I would punish him. He is an evil thing, and should be made to reap the proper reward. It is not that I wish to avoid my share of the world's burdens; but that justice should be done. I don't know which I hate the worst,—Uncle Carroll or Mr. Scarborough.'

The next day was Sunday, and Dolly was very anxious before breakfast to induce her father to say that he would go to church with her; but he was inclined to be obstinate, and fell back upon his usual excuse, saying that there were Scarborough papers which it would be necessary that he should read before he started for Tretton on the following day. 'Papa, I think it would do you good if you came.'

'Well, yes; I suppose it would. That is the intention; but somehow it fails with me sometimes.'

'Do you think that you hate people when you go to church, as much as when you don't?'

'I am not sure that I hate anybody very much.'

'I do.'

'That seems an argument for your going.'

'But if you don't hate them it is because you won't take the trouble, and that again is not right. If you would come to church you would be better for it all round. You'd hate Uncle Carroll's idleness and abominable self-indulgence worse than you do.'

'I don't love him as it is, my dear.'

'And I should hate him less. I felt last night as

though I could rise from my bed, and go and murder him.'

'Then you certainly ought to go to church.'

'And you had passed him off just as though he were a gnat from which you were to receive as little annoyance as possible, forgetting the influence he must have on those six unfortunate children. Don't you know that you gave her that twenty pounds simply to be rid of a disagreeable subject?'

'I should have given it ever so much sooner, only that you were looking at me.'

'I know you would, you dear, sweet, kind-hearted, but most unchristian father. You must come to church in order that some idea of what Christianity demands of you may make its way into your heart. It is not what the clergyman may say of you, but that your mind will get away for two hours from that other reptile and his concerns.' Then Mr. Grey, with a loud long sigh, allowed his boots, and his gloves, and his church-going hat, and his church-going umbrella to be brought to him. It was, in fact, his aversion to these articles that Dolly had to encounter.

It may be doubted whether the church services of that day did Mr. Grey much good; but they seemed to have had some effect upon his daughter, from the fact that in the afternoon she wrote a letter in kindly words to her aunt. 'Papa is going to Tretton, and I will come up to you on Tuesday. I have got a frock which I will bring with me as a present for Potsey; and I will make her sew on the buttons for herself. Tell Minna I will lend her that book I spoke of. About those boots, I will go with Georgina to the bootmaker.' But as to Amelia and Sophy she could not bring herself to say a good-natured word, so deep in her heart had sunk that sin of which they had been guilty with reference to Prince Chitakov.

On that night she had a long discussion with her father respecting the affairs of the Scarborough family. The discussion was held in the dining-room, and may, therefore, be supposed to have been premeditated. Those at night in Mr. Grey's own bed-room were generally the result of sudden thought. 'I should lay down the law to him,' began Dolly.

'The law is the law,' said her father.

'I don't mean the law in that sense. I should tell him firmly what I advised, and should then make him understand that if he did not follow my advice I must withdraw. If his son is willing to pay these money-lenders what sums they have actually advanced, and if by any effort on his part the money can be raised, let it be done. There seems to be some justice in repaying out of the property that which was lent to the property, when by Mr. Scarborough's own doing the property was supposed to go into the eldest son's hands. Though the eldest son and the money-lenders be spendthrifts and profligates alike, there will in that be something of fairness. Go there prepared with your opinion. But if either father or son will not accept it, then depart, and shake the dust from your feet.'*

'You propose it all, as though it were the easiest thing in the world.'

'Easy or difficult, I would not discuss anything of which the justice may hereafter be disputed.'

What was the result of the consultation on Mr. Grey's mind, he did not declare. But he resolved to take his daughter's advice in all that she said to him.

Chapter XIX

MR. GREY GOES TO TRETTON

MR. GREY went down to Tretton with a great bag of papers. In fact, though he told his daughter that he had to examine them all before he started, and had taken them to Fulham for that purpose, he had not looked at them. And, as another

fact, the bag was not opened till he got home again.
They had been read,—at any rate, what was necessary. He knew his subject. The old squire knew it
well. Mr. Grey was going down to Tretton not to
convey facts or to explain the law, but in order that
he might take the side either of the father or of the
son. Mr. Scarborough had sent for the lawyer to
support his view of the case; and the son had consented to meet him in order that he might the more
easily get the better of his father.

Mr. Grey had of late learned one thing which had
before been dark to him,— had seen one phase of this
complicated farrago of dishonesty which had not
before been visible to him. Augustus suspected his
father of some further treachery. That he should be
angry at having been debarred from his birthright so
long,—debarred from the knowledge of his birthright,—was, Mr. Grey thought, natural. A great
wrong had been done him by his own father, or had
been, at least, intended; and that such a man should
resent it was to have been expected. But of late Mr.
Grey had discovered that it was not in that way that
the son's mind worked. It was not anger but suspicion that he showed; and he used his father's former
treatment of him as a justification for the condemnation implied in his thoughts. There is no knowing
what an old man may do who has already acted as he
had done. It was thus that he expressed himself both
by his words and deeds, and did so openly in his
father's presence. Mr. Grey had not seen them
together, but knew from the letters of both of them
that such was the case. Old Mr. Scarborough scorned
his son's suspicions, and disregarded altogether any
words that might be said as to his own past conduct.
He was willing, or half willing, that Mountjoy's
debts should be, not paid, but settled. But he was
willing to do nothing towards such a step except in
his own way. While the breath was in his body the
property was his, and he chose to be treated as its

only master. If Augustus desired to do anything by 'post-obits,' let him ruin himself after his own fashion. 'It is not very likely that Augustus can raise money by post-obits circumstanced as the property is,' he had written to Mr. Grey with a conveyed sneer and chuckle as to the success of his own villainy. It was as though he had declared that the money-lenders had been too well instructed as to what tricks Mr. Scarborough could play with his property to risk a second venture.

Augustus had in truth been awaiting his father's death with great impatience. It was unreasonable that a man should live who had acted in such a way and who had been so cut about by the doctors. His father's demise had in truth been promised to him, and to all the world. It was an understood thing, in all circles which knew anything, that old Mr. Scarborough could not live another month. It had been understood some time, and was understood at the present moment; and yet Mr. Scarborough went on living,—no doubt as an invalid in the last stage of probable dissolution, but still with the full command of his intellect and mental powers for mischief. Augustus, suspecting him as he did, had begun to fear that he might live too long. His brother had disappeared, and he was the heir. If his father would die,—such had been his first thought,—he could settle with the creditors immediately, before any tidings should be heard of his brother. But tidings had come. His brother had been seen by Mr. Hart at Monte Carlo, and though Mr. Hart had not yet sent home the news to the other creditors, the news had been sent at once to Augustus Scarborough by his own paid attendant upon his brother. Of Mr. Hart's 'little game' he did not yet know the particulars. But he was confident that there was some game.

Augustus by no means gave his mother credit for the disgraceful conduct imputed to her in the story as now told by her surviving husband. It was not that he believed in the honesty of his mother, whom he had never known, and for whose memory he cared little; but that he believed so fully in the dishonesty of his father. His father, when he had thoroughly understood that Mountjoy had enveloped the property in debt, so that nothing but a skeleton would remain when the bonds were paid, had set to work, and by the ingenuity of his brain had resolved to redeem, as far as the Scarboroughs were concerned, their estate from its unfortunate condition. It was so that Augustus believed. This was the theory existing in his mind. That his father should have been so clever, and Mr. Grey so blind, and even Mr. Hart and Mr. Tyrrwhit so easily hoodwinked, was remarkable. But so it was,—or might probably be so. He felt no assurance, but there was ever present to him the feeling of great danger. But the state of things as arranged by his father might be established by himself. If he could get these creditors to give up their bonds while his father's falsehood was still believed, it would be a great thing. He had learned by degrees how small a proportion of the money claimed had in fact been advanced to Mountjoy, and had resolved to confine himself to paying that. That might now probably be accepted with gratitude. The increasing value of the estate might bear that without being crushed. But it should be done at once, while Mountjoy was still absent and before Mr. Tyrrwhit at any rate knew that Mountjoy had not been killed. Then had happened that accidental meeting with Mr. Hart at Monte Carlo. That idiot of a keeper of his had been unable to keep Mountjoy from the gambling-house. But Mr. Hart had as yet told nothing. Mr. Hart was playing some game of his own, in which he would assuredly be foiled. The strong hold which Augustus had was in the great infirmity of his father, and the blindness of Mr. Grey; but it would be well that the thing should be settled. It ought to have been settled already by his father's death

Augustus did feel strongly that the squire ought to complete his work by dying. Were the story, as now told by him, true, he ought certainly to die, so as to make rapid atonement for his wickedness. Were it false, then he ought to go quickly, so that the lie might be effectual. Every day that he continued to live would go far to endanger the discovery. Augustus felt that he must at once have the property in his own hands so as to buy the creditors and obtain security.

Mr. Grey, who was not so blind as Augustus thought him, saw a great deal of this. Augustus suspected him as well as the squire. His mind went backwards and forwards on these suspicions. It was more probable that the squire should have contrived all this with the attorney's assistance than without it. The two, willing it together, might be very powerful. But then Mr. Grey would hardly dare to do it. His father knew that he was dying; but Mr. Grey had no such easy mode of immediate escape if detected. And his father was endowed with a courage as peculiar as it was great. He did not think that Mr. Grey was so brave a man as his father. And then he could trace the payment of no large sum to Mr. Grey,—such as would have been necessary as a bribe in such a case. Augustus suspected Mr. Grey on and off. But Mr. Grey was sure that Augustus suspected his own father. Now of one thing Mr. Grey was certain— Augustus was in truth the rightful heir. The squire had at first contrived to blind him—him, Mr. Grey —partly by his own acuteness, partly through the carelessness of himself and those in his office, partly by the subornation of witnesses who seemed to have been actually prepared for such an event. But there could be no subsequent blinding. Mr. Grey had a well-earned reputation for professional acuteness and honesty. He knew there was no need for such suspicions as those now entertained by the young man; but he knew also that they existed, and he hated the young man for entertaining them.

When he arrived at Tretton Park he first of all saw Mr. Septimus Jones, with whom he was not acquainted.

'Mr. Scarborough will be here directly. He is out somewhere about the stables,' said Mr. Jones, in that tone of voice with which a guest at the house,—a guest for pleasure,—may address sometimes a guest who is a guest on business. In such a case the guest on pleasure cannot be a gentleman, and must suppose that the guest on business is not one either.

Mr. Grey, thinking that the Mr. Scarborough spoken of could not be the squire, put Mr. Jones right. 'It is the elder Mr. Scarborough whom I wish to see. There is quite time enough. No doubt Miss Scarborough will be down presently.'

'You are Mr. Grey, I believe?'

'That is my name.'

'My friend, Augustus Scarborough, is particularly anxious to see you before you go to his father. The old man is in very failing health, you know.'

'I am well acquainted with the state of Mr. Scarborough's health,' said Mr. Grey, 'and will leave it to himself to say when I shall see him. Perhaps to-morrow will be best.' Then he rang the bell; but the servant entered the room at the same moment, and summoned him up to the squire's chamber. Mr. Scarborough also wished to see Mr. Grey before his son, and had been on the alert to watch for his coming.

On the landing he met Miss Scarborough.

'He does not seem to keep up his strength,' said the lady. 'Mr. Merton is living in the house now, and watches him very closely.'

Mr. Merton was a resident young doctor, whom Sir William Brodrick had sent down to see that all medical appliances were at hand, as the sick man might require them. Then Mr. Grey was shown in, and found the squire recumbent on a sofa, with a store of books within his reach, and reading apparatuses of all descriptions, and every appliance which the ingenuity of the skilful can prepare for the relief of the sick and wealthy.

'This is very kind of you, Mr. Grey,' said the squire, speaking in a cheery voice. 'I wanted you to come very much, but I hardly thought that you would take the trouble. Augustus is here, you know.'

'So I have heard from that gentleman downstairs.'

'Mr. Jones? I have never had the pleasure of seeing Mr. Jones. What sort of a gentleman is Mr. Jones to look at?'

'Very much like other gentlemen.'

'I dare say. He has done me the honour to stay a good deal at my house lately. Augustus never comes without him. He is "Fidus Achates,"* I take it, to Augustus. Augustus has never asked whether he can be received. Of course it does not matter. When a man is the eldest son, and, so to say, the only one, he is apt to take liberties with his father's house. I am so sorry that in my position I cannot do the honours, and receive them properly. He is a very estimable and modest young man, I believe?' As Mr. Grey had not come down to Tretton either to be a spy on Mr. Jones, or to answer questions concerning him, he held his tongue. 'Well! Mr. Grey, what do you think about it—eh?' This was a comprehensive question, but Mr. Grey well understood its purport. What did he, Mr. Grey, think of the condition to which the affairs of Tretton had been brought, and those of Mr. Scarborough himself and his two sons? What did he think of Mountjoy, who had disappeared and was still absent? What did he think of Augustus, who was not showing his gratitude in the best way for all that had been done for him? And what did he think of the squire himself, who from his death-bed had so well contrived to have his own way in everything,—to do all manner of illegal things without paying any of the penalties to which illegality is generally subjected? And having asked the question he paused for an answer.

Mr. Grey had had no personal interview with the squire since the time at which it had been declared that Mountjoy was not the heir. Then some very severe words had been spoken. Mr. Grey had first sworn that he did not believe a word of what was said to him, and had refused to deal with the matter at all. If carried out Mr. Scarborough must take it to some other lawyer's offices. There had, since that, been a correspondence as to much of which Mr. Scarborough had been forced to employ an amanuensis. Gradually Mr. Grey had assented, in the first instance on behalf of Mountjoy, and then on behalf of Augustus. But he had done so in the expectation that he should never again see the squire in this world. He, too, had been assured that the man would die, and had felt that it would be better that the management of things should then be in honest hands, such as his own, and in the hands of those who understood them, than be confided to those who did not understand them, and who might probably not be honest. But the squire had not died, and here he was again at Tretton as the squire's guest. 'I think,' said Mr. Grey, 'that the less said about a good deal of it, the better.'

'That, of course, is sweeping condemnation, which however, I expect. Let that be all as though it had been expressed. You don't understand the inner man which rules me,—how it has struggled to free itself from conventionalities. Nor do I quite understand how your inner man has succumbed to them and encouraged them.'

'I have encouraged an obedience to the laws of my country. Men generally find it safer to do so.'

'Exactly; and men like to be safe. Perhaps a condition of danger has had its attractions for me. It is very stupid, but perhaps it is so. But let that go. The rope has been round my own neck and not that of others. Perhaps I have thought of late that if danger should come I could run away from it all, by

the help of the surgeon. They have become so skilful
now that a man has no chance in that way. But what
do you think of Mountjoy and Augustus?'

'I think that Mountjoy has been very ill-used.'

'But I endeavoured to do the best I could for him.'

'And that Augustus has been worse used.'

'But he at any rate has been put right quite in time.
Had he been brought up as the eldest son he might
have done as Mountjoy did.' Then there came a little
gleam of satisfaction across the squire's face as he
felt the sufficiency of his answer. 'But they are
neither of them pleased.'

'You cannot please men by going wrong, even in
their own behalf.'

'I'm not so sure of that. Were you to say that we
cannot please men ever by doing right on their behalf
you would perhaps be nearer the mark. Where do
you think that Mountjoy is?' A rumour had reached
Mr. Grey that Mountjoy had been seen at Monte
Carlo, but it had been only a rumour. The same had
in truth reached Mr. Scarborough, but he chose to
keep his rumour to himself. Indeed, more than a
rumour had reached him.

'I think that he will turn up safely,' said the lawyer.
'I think that if it were made worth his while he would
turn up at once.'

'Is it not better that he should be away?' Mr.
Grey shrugged his shoulders. 'What's the good of
his coming back into a nest of hornets. I have always
thought that he did very well to disappear. Where
is he to live if he came back? Should he come here?'

'Not with his gambling debts unpaid at the club.'

'That might have been settled. Though, indeed,
his gambling was as a tub that had no bottom to it.
There has been nothing for it but to throw him over
altogether. And yet how very much the better he
has been of the two. Poor Mountjoy!'

'Poor Mountjoy!'

'You see, if I hadn't disinherited him I should have

had to go on paying for him till the whole estate would have been squandered even during my lifetime.'

'You speak as though the law had given you the power of disinheriting him.'

'So it did.'

'But not the power of giving him the inheritance.'

'I took that upon myself. There I was stronger than the law. Now I simply and humbly ask the law to come and help me. And the upshot is, that Augustus takes upon himself to lecture me and to feel aggrieved. He is not angry with me for what I did about Mountjoy, but is quarrelling with me because I do not die. I have no idea of dying just to please him. I think it important that I should live just at present.'

'But will you let him have the money to pay these creditors?'

'That is what I want to speak about. If I can see the list of the sums to be paid, and if you can assure yourself that by paying them I shall get back all the post-obit bonds which Mountjoy has given, and that the money can be at once raised upon a joint mortgage, to be executed by me and by Augustus, I will do it. But the first thing must be to know the amount. I will join Augustus in nothing without your consent. He wants to assume the power himself. In fact, the one thing he desires is that I shall go. As long as I remain he shall do nothing except by my co-operation. I will see you and him tomorrow; and now you may go and eat your dinner. I cannot tell you how much obliged I am to you for coming.' And then Mr. Grey left the room, went to his chamber, and in process of time made his way into the drawing-room.

Chapter XX

MR. GREY'S OPINION OF THE
SCARBOROUGH FAMILY

HAD Augustus been really anxious to see Mr.
Grey before Mr. Grey went to his father, he
would probably have managed to do so. He did not
always tell Mr. Jones everything. 'So the fellow has
hurried up to the governor the moment he came into
the house,' he said.

'He's with him now.'

'Of course he is. Never mind. I'll be even with
him in the long run.' Then he greeted the lawyer
with a mock courtesy as soon as he saw him. 'I hope
your journey has done you no harm, Mr. Grey.'

'Not in the least.'

'It's very kind of you, I am sure, to look after
our poor concerns with so much interest. Jones,
don't you think it is time they gave us some dinner?
Mr. Grey, I'm sure, must want his dinner.'

'All in good time,' said the lawyer.

'You shall have your dinner, Mr. Grey. It is the
least we can do for you.'

Mr. Grey felt that in every sound of his voice
there was an insult, and took special notice of every
tone and booked them all down in his memory. After
dinner he asked some unimportant question with
reference to the meeting that was to take place in the
morning, and was at once rebuked. 'I do not know
that we need trouble our friend here with our private
concerns,' he said.

'Not in the least,' said Mr. Grey. 'You have
already been talking about them in my presence and
in his. It is necessary that I should have a list of the
creditors before I can advise your father.'

'I don't see it; but, however, that is for you to
judge. Indeed, I do not know on what points my

father wants your advice. A lawyer generally furnishes such a list.' Then Mr. Grey took up a book, and was soon left alone by the younger men.

In the morning he walked out in the park, so as to have free time for thought. Not a word further had been said between him and Augustus touching their affairs. At breakfast Augustus discussed with his friend the state of the odds respecting some race, and then the characters of certain ladies. No subjects could have been less interesting to Mr. Grey, as Augustus was aware. They breakfasted at ten, and twelve had been named for the meeting. Mr. Grey had an hour or an hour and a half for his walk, in which he could turn over in his mind all these matters of which his thoughts had been full for now many a day.

Of two or three facts he was certain. Augustus was the legitimate heir of his father. Of that he had seen ample documentary evidence. The word of no Scarborough should go for anything with him,—and of that fact he was assured. Whether the squire knew aught of Mountjoy he did not feel sure, but that Augustus did he was quite certain. Who was paying the bills for the scapegrace during his travels he could not say, but he thought it probable that Augustus was finding the money. He, Mountjoy, was kept away so as to be out of the creditors' way. He thought therefore that Augustus was doing this, so that he might the more easily buy up the debts. But why should Augustus go to the expense of buying up the debts, seeing that the money must ultimately come out of his own pocket? Because,—so Mr. Grey thought,—Augustus would not trust his own father. The creditors, if they could get hold of Mountjoy when his father was dead and when the bonds would all become payable, might possibly so unravel the facts as to make it apparent that after all the property was Mountjoy's. This was not Mr. Grey's idea, but was Mr. Grey's idea of the calculation which Augustus was making for his own government. According to Mr. Grey's reading of all the facts of the case, such were the suspicions which Augustus entertained in the matter. Otherwise, why should he be so anxious to take a step which would redound only to the advantage of the creditors? He was quite certain that no money would be paid, at any rate by Augustus, solely with the view of honestly settling their claims.

But there was another subject which troubled his mind excessively as he walked across the park. Why should he soil his hands, or, at any rate, trouble his conscience with an affair so unclean, so perplexed, and so troublesome? Why was he there at Tretton at all to be insulted by a young blackguard such as he believed Augustus Scarborough to be? Augustus Scarborough, he knew, suspected him. But he, in return, suspected Augustus Scarborough. The creditors suspected him. Mountjoy suspected him. The squire did not suspect him, but he suspected the squire. He never could again feel himself to be on comfortable terms of trusting legal friendship with a man who had played such a prank in reference to his marriage as this man had performed. Why, then, should he still be concerned in a matter so distasteful to him? Why should he not wipe his hands of it all and retreat? There was no Act of Parliament compelling him to meddle with this dirt.

Such were his thoughts. But yet he knew that he was compelled. He did feel himself bound to look after interests which he had taken in hand now for many years. It had been his duty,—or the duty of some one belonging to him,—to see into the deceit by which an attempt had been made to rob Augustus Scarborough of his patrimony. It had been his duty, for awhile, to protect Mountjoy, and the creditors who had lent their money to Mountjoy, from what he believed to be a flagitious attempt. Then, as soon as he felt that the flagitious attempt had been made previously, in Mountjoy's favour, it became his duty to protect Augustus, in spite of the strong personal dislike which from the first he had conceived for that young man.

And then he, doubtless, had been attracted by the singularity of all that had been done in the affair, and of all that was likely to be done. He had said to himself that the matter should be made straight, and that he would make it straight. Therefore, during his walk in the park, he resolved that he must persevere.

At twelve o'clock he was ready to be taken up to the sick man's room. When he entered it, under the custody of Miss Scarborough, he found that Augustus was there. The squire was sitting up, with his feet supported, and was apparently in a good humour. 'Well, Mr. Grey,' he said, 'have you settled this matter with Augustus?'

'I have settled nothing.'

'He has not spoken to me about it at all,' said Augustus.

'I told him I wanted a list of the creditors. He said that it was my duty to supply it. That was the extent of our conversation.'

'Which he thought it expedient to have in the presence of my friend, Mr. Jones. Mr. Jones is very well in his way, but he is not acquainted with all my affairs.'

'Your son, Mr. Scarborough, has made no tender to me of any information.'

'Nor, sir, has Mr. Grey sought for any information from me.' During this little dialogue Mr. Scarborough turned his face with a smile from one to the other without a word. 'If Mr. Grey has anything to suggest in the way of advice, let him suggest it,' said Augustus.

'Now, Mr. Grey,' said the squire, with the same smile.

'Till I get further information,' said Mr. Grey, 'I can only limit myself to giving the advice which I offered to you yesterday.'

'Perhaps you will repeat it, so that he may hear it,' said the squire.

'If you get a list of those to whom your son Mountjoy owes money, and an assurance that the moneys named in that list had been from time to time lent by them to him—the actual amount, I mean— then I think that, if you and your son Augustus shall together choose to pay those amounts, you will make the best reparation in your power for the injury you have no doubt done in having contrived that it should be understood that Mountjoy was legitimate.'

'You need not discuss,' said the squire, 'any injuries that I have done. I have done a great many, no doubt.'

'But,' continued the lawyer, 'before any such payment is made, close inquiries should be instituted as to the amounts of money which have absolutely passed.'

'We should certainly be taken in,' said the squire. 'I have great admiration for Mr. Samuel Hart. I do believe that it would be found impossible to extract the truth from Mr. Samuel Hart. If Mr. Samuel Hart does not make money yet out of poor Mountjoy I shall be surprised.'

'The truth may be ascertained,' said Mr. Grey. 'You should get some accountant to examine the cheques.'

'When I remember how easy it was to deceive some really clever men as to the evidence of my marriage,' began Mr. Scarborough—— So the squire began, but then stopped himself with a shrug of his shoulders. Among the really clever men who had been easily deceived Mr. Grey was, if not actually first in importance, foremost at any rate in name.

'The truth may be ascertained,' Mr. Grey repeated, almost with a scowl of anger upon his brow.

'Well, yes; I suppose it may. It will be difficult in opposition to Mr. Samuel Hart.'

'You must satisfy yourselves at any rate. These

men will know that they have no other hope of getting a shilling.'

'It is a little hard to make them believe anything,' said the squire. 'They fancy, you know, that if they could get a hold of Mountjoy, so as to have him in their hands when the breath is out of my body and the bonds are really due,—that then it may be made to turn out that he was really the heir.'

'We know that it is not so,' said Mr. Grey. At this Augustus smiled blandly.

'We know. But is it what we can make Mr. Samuel Hart know? In truth, Mr. Samuel Hart never allows himself to know anything,—except the amount of money which he may have at his bankers. And it will be difficult to convince Mr. Tyrrwhit. Mr. Tyrrwhit is assured that all of us, you and I, and Mountjoy, and Augustus, are in a conspiracy to cheat him and the others.'

'I don't wonder at it,' said Mr. Grey.

'Perhaps not,' continued the squire; 'the circumstances, no doubt, are suspicious. But he will have to find out his mistake. Augustus is very anxious to pay these poor men their money. It is a noble feeling on the part of Augustus; you must admit that, Mr. Grey.' The irony with which this was said was evident in the squire's face and voice. Augustus only quietly laughed. The attorney sat as firm as death. He was not going to argue with such a statement or to laugh at such a joke. 'I suppose it will come to over a hundred thousand pounds.'

'Eighty thousand, I should think,' said Augustus. 'The bonds amount to a great deal more than that,— twice that.'

'It is for him to judge,' said the squire, 'whether he is bound by his honour to pay so large a sum to men whom I do not suppose he loves very well.'

'The estate can bear it,' said Augustus.

'Yes, the estate can bear it,' said the attorney. 'They should be paid what they have expended.

That is my idea. Your son thinks that their silence will be worth the money.'

'What makes you say that?' demanded Augustus.

'Just my own opinion.'

'I look upon it as an insult.'

'Would you be kind enough to explain to us what is your reason for wishing to do this thing?' asked Mr. Grey.

'No, sir; I decline to give any reason. But those which you ascribe to me are insulting.'

'Will you deny them?'

'I will not assent to anything—coming from you, nor will I deny anything. It is altogether out of your place as an attorney to ascribe motives to your clients. Can you raise the money so that it shall be forth-coming at once? That is the question.'

'On your father's authority, backed by your signa-ture, I imagine that I can do so. But I will not answer as a certainty. The best thing would be to sell a portion of the property. If you and your father will join, and Mountjoy also with you, it may be done.'

'What has Mountjoy got to do with it?' asked the father.

'You had better have Mountjoy also. There may be some doubt as to the title. People will think so after the tricks that have been played.' This was said by the lawyer; but the squire only laughed. He always showed some enjoyment of the fun which arose from the effects of his own scheming. The legal world, with its entails, had endeavoured to dispose of his property, but he had shown the legal world that it was not an easy task to dispose of anything in which he was concerned.

'How will you get hold of Mountjoy?' asked Augustus. Then the two older men only looked at each other. Both of them believed that Augustus knew more about his brother than anyone else. 'I think you had better send to Mr. Annesley and ask him.'

'What does Annesley know about him?' asked the squire.

'He was the last person who saw him, at any rate in London.'

'Are you sure of that?' said Mr. Grey.

'I think I may say that I am. I think, at any rate, that I know that there was a violent quarrel between them in the streets, a quarrel in which the two men proceeded to blows, and that Annesley struck him in such a way as to leave him for dead upon the pavement. Then the young man walked away, and Mountjoy has not been heard of, or, at least, has not been seen since. That a man should have struck such a blow, and then, on the spur of the moment, thinking of his own safety, should have left his opponent, I can understand. I should not like to be accused of such treatment myself, but I can understand it. I cannot understand that the man should have been missing altogether, and that then he should have held his tongue.'

'How do you know all this?' asked the attorney.

'It is sufficient that I do know it.'

'I don't believe a word of it,' said the squire.

'Coming from you, of course I must put up with any contradiction,' said Augustus. 'I should not bear it from anyone else,' and he looked at the attorney.

'One has a right to ask for your authority,' said the father.

'I cannot give it. A lady is concerned whose name I shall not mention. But it is of less importance, as his own friends are acquainted with the nature of his conduct. Indeed, it seems odd to see you two gentlemen so ignorant as to the matter which has been a subject of common conversation in most circles. His uncle means to cut him out from the property.'

'Can he too deal with entails?' said the squire.

'He is still in middle life, and he can marry. That is what he intends to do, so much is he disgusted with his nephew. He has already stopped the young

man's allowance, and swears that he shall not have
a shilling of his money if he can help it. The police
for some time were in great doubt whether they
would not arrest him. I think I am justified in saying
that he is a thorough reprobate.'

'You are not at all justified,' said the father.

'I can only express my opinion, and am glad to
say that the world agrees with me.'

'It is sickening, absolutely sickening,' said the
squire, turning to the attorney. 'You would not
believe now——'

But he stopped himself.

'What would not Mr. Grey believe?' asked the
son.

'There is no one knows better than you that after
the row in the street, when Mountjoy was, I believe,
the aggressor, he was again seen by another person.
I hate such deceit and scheming.' Here Augustus
smiled. 'What are you sniggering there at, you
blockhead?'

'Your hatred, sir, at deceit and scheming. The
truth is, that when a man plays a game well, he does
not like to find that he has any equal. Heaven forbid
that I should say that there is rivalry here. You, sir,
are so pre-eminently the first, that no one can touch
you.' Then he laughed long, a low, bitter, inaudible
laugh, during which Mr. Grey sat silent.

'This comes well from you,' said the father.

'Well, sir, you would try your hand upon me. I
have passed over all that you have done on my behalf.
But when you come to abuse me, I cannot quite take
your word as calmly as though there had been no—
shall I say antecedents? Now about this money. Are
we to pay it?'

'I don't care one straw about the money. What
is it to me? I don't owe these creditors anything.'

'Nor do I.'

'Let them rest then, and do the worst they can.
But upon the whole, Mr. Grey,' he added, after a

pause, 'I think we had better pay them. They have endeavoured to be insolent to me, and I have therefore ignored their claim. I have told them to do their worst. If my son here will agree with you in raising the money, and if Mountjoy—as he, too, is necessary—will do so, I too will do what is required of me. If eighty thousand pounds will settle it all, there ought not to be any difficulty. You can inquire what the real amount would be. If they choose to hold to their bonds, nothing will come of it. That's all.'

'Very well, Mr. Scarborough. Then I shall know how to proceed. I understand that Mr. Scarborough, junior, is an assenting party?'

Mr. Scarborough, junior, signified his assent by nodding his head.

'That will do, then, for I think that I have a little exhausted myself.' Then he turned round upon his couch, as though he intended to slumber. Mr. Grey left the room and Augustus followed him; but not a word was spoken between them. Mr. Grey had an early dinner and went up to London by an evening train. What became of Augustus he did not inquire, but simply asked for his dinner and for a conveyance to the train. These were forthcoming, and he returned that night to Fulham.

'Well?' said Dolly, as soon as she had got him his slippers and made him his tea.

'I wish with all my heart I had never seen anyone of the name of Scarborough.'

'That is of course,—but what have you done?'

'The father has been a great knave. He has set the laws of his country at defiance, and should be punished most severely. And Mountjoy Scarborough has proved himself to be unfit to have any money in his hands. A man so reckless is little better than a lunatic. But compared with Augustus they are both estimable, amiable men. The father has ideas of philanthropy, and Mountjoy is simply mad. But

Augustus is as dishonest as either of them, and is odious also all round.' Then at length he explained all that he had learned, and all that he had advised, and at last went to bed combating Dolly's idea that the Scarboroughs ought now to be thrown over altogether.

Chapter XXI

MR. SCARBOROUGH'S THOUGHTS OF HIMSELF

WHEN Mr. Scarborough was left alone he did not go to sleep, as he had pretended, but lay there for an hour, thinking of his position and indulging to the full the feelings of anger which he now entertained towards his second son. He had never, in truth, loved Augustus. Augustus was very like his father in his capacity for organising deceit, for plotting, and so contriving that his own will should be in opposition to the wills of all those around him. But they were thoroughly unlike in the object to be attained. Mr. Scarborough was not a selfish man. Augustus was selfish and nothing else. Mr. Scarborough hated the law,—because it was the law, and endeavoured to put a restraint upon him and others. Augustus liked the law,—unless when in particular points it interfered with his own actions. Mr. Scarborough thought that he could do better than the law. Augustus wished to do worse. Mr. Scarborough never blushed at what he himself attempted, unless he failed, which was not often the case. But he was constantly driven to blush for his son. Augustus blushed for nothing and for nobody. When Mr. Scarborough had declared to the attorney that just praise was due to Augustus for the nobility of the sacrifice he was making, Augustus had understood his father accurately and determined to be revenged, not because of the expression of his father's thoughts, but because he had so expressed himself before the attorney. Mr. Scarborough also thought that he was entitled to his revenge.

When he had been left alone for an hour he rang the bell, which was close to his side, and called for Mr. Merton.

'Where is Mr. Grey?'

'I think he has ordered the waggonette to take him to the station.'

'And where is Augustus?'

'I do not know.'

'And Mr. Jones? I suppose they have not gone to the station. Just feel my pulse, Merton. I am afraid I am very weak.'

Mr. Merton felt his pulse and shook his head. 'There isn't a pulse, so to speak.'

'Oh yes; but it is irregular. If you will exert yourself so violently——'

'That is all very well; but a man has to exert himself sometimes, let the penalty be what it may. When do you think that Sir William will have to come again?' Sir William, when he came, would come with his knife, and his advent was always to be feared.

'It depends very much on yourself, Mr. Scarborough. I don't think he can come very often, but you may make the distances long or short. You should attend to no business.'

'That is absolute rubbish.'

'Nevertheless, it is my duty to say so. Whatever arrangements may be required, they should be made by others. Of course, if you do as you have done this morning I can suggest some little relief. I can give you tonics and increase the amount. But I cannot resist the evil which you yourself do yourself.'

'I understand all about it.'

'You will kill yourself if you go on.'

'I don't mean to go on any farther,—not as I have done to-day; but as to giving up business, that is rubbish. I have got my property to manage, and I

mean to manage it myself as long as I live. Unfortunately there have been accidents which make
the management a little rough at times. I have had
one of the rough moments to-day; but they shall not
be repeated. I give you my word of that. But do
not talk to me about giving up my business. Now
I'll take your tonics, and then would you have the
kindness to ask my sister to come to me?'

Miss Scarborough, who was always in waiting on
her brother, was at once in the room.

'Martha,' he said, 'where is Augustus?'

'I think he has gone out.'

'And where is Mr. Septimus Jones?'

'He is with him, John. The two are always together.'

'You would not mind giving my compliments to
Mr. Jones, and telling him that his bedroom is
wanted?'

'His bedroom wanted! There are lots of bedrooms, and nobody to occupy them.'

'It's a hint that I want him to go; he'd understand that.'

'Would it not be better to tell Augustus?' asked
the lady, doubting much her power to carry out the
instructions given to her.

'He would tell Augustus. It is not, you see, any
objection I have to Mr. Jones. I have not the pleasure
of his acquaintance. He is a most agreeable young
man, I'm sure; but I do not care to entertain an
agreeable young man without having a word to say
on the subject. Augustus does not think it worth his
while even to speak to me about him. Of course,
when I am gone, in a month or so—perhaps a week
or two—he can do as he pleases.'

'Don't, John!'

'But it is so. While I live I am master, at least of
this house. I cannot see Mr. Jones, and I do not wish
to have another quarrel with Augustus. Mr. Merton
says that every time I get angry it gives Sir William

another chance with the knife. I thought that perhaps you could do it.'

Then Miss Scarborough promised that she would do it, and, having her brother's health very much at heart, she did do it. Augustus stood smiling while the message was, in fact, conveyed to him, but he made no answer. When the lady had done, he bobbed his head to signify that he acknowledged the receipt of it, and the lady retired.

'I have got my walking papers,' he said to Septimus Jones ten minutes afterwards.

'I don't know what you mean.'

'Don't you? Then you must be very thick-headed. My father has sent me word that you are to be turned out. Of course he means it for me. He does not wish to give me the power of saying that he sent me away from his house—me, whom he has so long endeavoured to rob—me, to whom he owes so much for taking no steps to punish his fraud. And he knows that I can take none because he is on his deathbed.'

'But you couldn't, could you, if he were—were anywhere else?'

'Couldn't I? That's all you know about it. Understand, however, that I shall start tomorrow morning, and unless you like to remain here on a visit to him, you had better go with me.'

Mr. Jones signified his compliance with the hint, and so Miss Scarborough had done her work.

Mr. Scarborough, when thus left alone, spent his time chiefly in thinking of the condition of his sons. His eldest son, Mountjoy, who had ever been his favourite, whom as a little boy he had spoilt by every means in his power, was a ruined man. His debts had all been paid, except the money due to the moneylenders. But he was not the less a ruined man. Where he was at this moment his father did not know. All the world knew the injustice of which he had been guilty on his boy's behalf, and all the world knew the failure of the endeavour. And now he had

made a great and a successful effort to give back to
his legitimate heir all his property. But in return
the second son only desired his death, and almost
told him so to his face. He had been proud of Augustus as a lad, but he had never loved him as he had
loved Mountjoy. Now he knew that he and Augustus must henceforward be absolutely enemies. Never
for a moment did he think of giving up his power
over the estate, as long as the estate should still be
his. Though it should be but for a month, though it
should be but for a week, he would hold his own.
Such was the nature of the man, and when he swal-
lowed Mr. Merton's tonics, he did so more with the
idea of keeping the property out of his son's hands
than of preserving his own life. According to his
view, he had done much for Augustus, and this was
the return which he received!

And in truth he had done much for Augustus.
For years past it had been his object to leave to his
second son as much as would come to his first. He
had continued to put money by for him, instead of
spending his income on himself. Of this Mr. Grey
had known much, but had said nothing, when he was
speaking those severe words which Mr. Scarborough
had always contrived to receive with laughter. But
he had felt their injustice, though he had himself
ridiculed the idea of law. There had been the two
sons, both born from the same mother, and he had
willed that they should be both rich men, living
among the foremost of their fellow-men, and the
circumstances of the property would have helped him.
The income from year to year went on increasing.
The water-mills of Tretton, and the town of Tretton
had grown and been expanded within his domain,
and the management of the sales, in Mr. Grey's
hands, had been judicious. The revenues were double
now what they had been when Mr. Scarborough first
inherited it. It was all, no doubt, entailed, but for
twenty years he had enjoyed the power of accumula-

ting a sum of money for his second son's sake,—or would have enjoyed it, had not the accumulation been taken from him to pay Mountjoy's debts. It was in vain that he attempted to make Mountjoy responsible for the money. Mountjoy's debts, and irregularities, and gambling went on, till Mr. Scarborough found himself bound to dethrone the illegitimate son, and to place the legitimate in his proper position.

In doing the deed he had not suffered much, though the circumstances which had led to the doing of it had been full of pain. There had been an actual pleasure to him in thus showing himself to be superior to the conventionalities of the world. There was Augustus still ready to occupy the position to which he had in truth been born. And at the moment Mountjoy had gone,—he knew not where. There had been gambling debts which, coming as they did after many others, he had refused to pay. He himself was dying at the moment,—as he thought. It would be better for him to take up with Augustus. Mountjoy he must leave to his fate. For such a son, so reckless, so incurable, so hopeless, it was impossible that anything further should be done. He would at least enjoy the power of leaving those wretched creditors without their money. There would be some triumph, some consolation in that. So he had done, and now his heir turned against him!

It was very bitter to him as he lay thinking of it all. He was a man who was from his constitution and heart capable of making great sacrifices for those he loved. He had a most thorough contempt for the character of an honest man. He did not believe in honesty, but only in mock honesty. And yet he would speak of an honest man with admiration, meaning something altogether different from the honesty of which men ordinarily spoke. The usual honesty of the world was with him all pretence, or, if not, assumed for the sake of the character it would achieve. Mr. Grey he knew to be honest; Mr. Grey's word he knew to be true; but he fancied that Mr. Grey had adopted this absurd mode of living with the view of cheating his neighbours by appearing to be better than others. All virtue and all vice were comprised by him in the words 'good-nature' and 'ill-nature.' All church-going propensities,—and these propensities in his estimate extended very widely,—he scorned from the very bottom of his heart. That one set of words should be deemed more wicked than another, as in regard to swearing, was to him a sign either of hypocrisy, of idolatry, or of feminine weakness of intellect. To women he allowed the privilege of being, in regard to thought, only something better than dogs. When his sister Martha shuddered at some exclamation from his mouth he would say to himself simply that she was a woman, not an idiot or a hypocrite. Of women, old and young, he had been very fond, and in his manner to them very tender; but when a woman rose to a way of thinking akin to his own, she was no longer a woman to his senses. Against such a one his taste revolted. She sank to the level of a man contaminated by petti-coats. And law was hardly less absurd to him than religion. It consisted of a perplexed entanglement of rules got together so that the few might live in comfort at the expense of the many. Robbery, if you could get to the bottom of it, was bad, as was all violence; but taxation was robbery, rent was robbery, prices fixed according to the desire of the seller and not in obedience to justice, were robbery. 'Then you are the greatest of robbers,' his friends would say to him. He would admit it, allowing that in such a state of society he was not prepared to go out and live naked in the streets if he could help it. But he delighted to get the better of the law, and triumphed in his own iniquity, as has been seen by his conduct in reference to his sons.

In this way he lived, and was kind to many people, having a generous and an open hand. But he was a man who could hate with a bitter hatred, and he hated most those suspected by him of mean or dirty conduct. Mr. Grey, who constantly told him to his face that he was a rascal, he did not hate at all. Thinking Mr. Grey to be in some respects idiotic, he respected him, and almost loved him. He thoroughly believed Mr. Grey, thinking him to be an ass for telling so much truth unnecessarily. And he had loved his son Mountjoy in spite of all his iniquities, and had fostered him till it was impossible to foster him any longer. Then he had endeavoured to love Augustus, and did not in the least love him the less because his son told him frequently of the wicked things he had done. He did not object to be told of his wickedness even by his son. But Augustus suspected him of other things than those of which he accused him, and attempted to be sharp with him, and to get the better of him at his own game. And his son laughed at him and scorned him, and regarded him as one who was troublesome only for a time, and who need not be treated with much attention, because he was there only for a time. Therefore he hated Augustus. But Augustus was his heir, and he knew that he must die soon.

But for how long could he live? And what could he yet do before he died? A braver man than Mr. Scarborough never lived,—that is, one who less feared to die. Whether that is true courage may be a question, but it was his, in conjunction with courage of another description. He did not fear to die, nor did he fear to live. But what he did fear was to fail before he died. Not to go out with the conviction that he was vanishing amidst the glory of success, was to him to be wretched at his last moment. And to be wretched at his last moment, or to anticipate that he should be so, was to him,—even so near his last hours,—the acme of misery. How much of life was left to him, so that he might recover something of success? Or was any moment left to him?

He could not sleep, so he rang his bell, and again sent for Mr. Merton. 'I have taken what you told me.'

'So best,' said Mr. Merton. For he did not always feel assured that this strange patient would take what had been ordered.

'And I have tried to sleep.'

'That will come after a while. You would not naturally sleep just after the tonic.'

'And I have been thinking of what you said about business. There is one thing I must do, and then I can remain quiet for a fortnight, unless I should be called upon to disturb my rest by dying.'

'We will hope not.'

'That may go as it pleases,' said the sick man. 'I want you now to write a letter for me to Mr. Grey.' Mr. Merton had undertaken to perform the duties of secretary as well as doctor, and had thought in this way to obtain some authority over his patient for the patient's own good. But he had found already that no authority had come to him. He now sat down at a table close to the bedside, and prepared to write in accordance with Mr. Scarborough's dictation. 'I think that Grey—the lawyer, you know—is a good man.'

'The world, as far as I hear it, says that he is honest.'

'I don't care a straw what the world says. The world says that I am dishonest, but I am not.' Merton could only shrug his shoulders. 'I don't say that because I want you to change your opinion. I don't care what you think. But I tell you a fact. I doubt whether Grey is so absolutely honest as I am, but as things go he is a good man.'

'Certainly.'

'But the world, I suppose, says that my son Augustus is honest.'

'Well, yes; I should suppose so.'

'If you have looked into him and have seen the contrary, I respect your intelligence.'

'I did not mean anything particular.'

'I dare say not, and if so, I mean nothing particular as to your intelligence. He, at any rate, is a scoundrel. Mountjoy,—you know Mountjoy?'

'Never saw him in my life.'

'I don't think he is a scoundrel,—not all round. He has gambled when he has not had money to pay. That is bad. And he has promised when he wanted money, and broken his word as soon as he had got it; which is bad also. And he has thought himself to be a fine fellow because he has been intimate with lords and dukes, which is very bad. He has never cared whether he paid his tailor. I do not mean that he has merely got into debt, which a young man such as he cannot help; but he has not cared whether his breeches were his or another man's. That, too, is bad. Though he has been passionately fond of women, it has only been for himself, not for the women, which is very bad. There is an immense deal to be altered before he can go to heaven.'

'I hope the change may come before it is too late,' said Merton.

'These changes don't come very suddenly, you know. But there is some chance for Mountjoy. I don't think that there is any for Augustus!' Here he paused, but Merton did not feel disposed to make any remark. 'You don't happen to know a young man of the name of Annesley,—Harry Annesley?'

'I have heard his name from your son.'

'From Augustus? Then you didn't hear any good of him, I'm sure. You have heard all the row about poor Mountjoy's disappearance?'

'I heard that he did disappear.'

'After a quarrel with that Annesley.'

'After some quarrel. I did not notice the name at the time.'

'Harry Annesley was the name. Now Augustus says that Harry Annesley was the last person who saw Mountjoy before his disappearance,—the last

who knew him. He implies thereby that Annesley
was the conscious or unconscious cause of his disappearance.'

'Well, yes.'

'Certainly it is so. And as it has been thought by
the police, and by other fools, that Mountjoy was
murdered,—that his disappearance was occasioned
by his death either by murder or suicide, it follows
that Annesley must have had something to do with
it. That is the inference, is it not?'

'I should suppose so,' said Merton.

'That is manifestly the inference which Augustus
draws. To hear him speak to me about it you would
suppose that he suspected Annesley of having killed
Mountjoy.'

'Not that, I hope.'

'Something of the sort. He has intended it to be
believed that Annesley, for his own purposes, had
caused Mountjoy to be made away with. He has
endeavoured to fill the police with that idea. A policeman generally is the biggest fool that London, or
England, or the world produces, and has been selected
on that account. Therefore the police have a beautifully mysterious, but altogether ignorant, suspicion
as to Annesley. That is the doing of Augustus, for
some purpose of his own. Now let me tell you that
Augustus saw Mountjoy after Annesley had seen
him, that he knows this to be the case, and that it was
Augustus who contrived Mountjoy's disappearance.
Now, what do you think of Augustus?' This was a
question which Merton did not find it very easy to
answer. But Mr. Scarborough waited for a reply.
'Eh?' he exclaimed.

'I had rather not give an opinion on a point so
raised.'

'You may. Of course you understand that I intend
you to assert that Augustus is the greatest blackguard you ever knew. If you have anything to say
in his favour you can say it.'

'Only that you may be mistaken. Living down here, you may not know the truth.'

'Just that. But I do know the truth. Augustus is very clever; but there are others as clever as he is. He can pay, but then so can I. That he should want to get Mountjoy out of the way is intelligible. Mountjoy has become disreputable, and had better be out of the way. But why persistently endeavour to throw the blame upon young Annesley? That surprises me,—only I do not care much about it. I hear now for the first time that he has ruined young Annesley, and that does appear to be very horrible. But why does he want to pay eighty thousand pounds to these creditors? That I should wish to do so,— out of a property which must in a very short time become his,—would be intelligible. I may be supposed to have some affection for Mountjoy, and, after all, am not called upon to pay the money out of my own pocket. Do you understand it?'

'Not in the least,' said Merton, who did not indeed very much care about it.

'Nor do I;—only this, that if he could pay these men and deprive them of all power of obtaining further payment, let who would have the property, they at any rate would be quiet. Augustus is now my eldest son. Perhaps he thinks that he might not remain so. If I were out of the way, and these creditors were paid, he thinks that poor Mountjoy wouldn't have a chance. He shall pay this eighty thousand pounds. Mountjoy hasn't a chance as it is; but Augustus shall pay the penalty.'

Then he threw himself back on the bed, and Mr. Merton begged him to spare himself the trouble of the letter for the present. But in a few minutes he was again on his elbow and took some further medicine. 'I'm a great ass,' he said, 'to help Augustus in playing his game. If I were to go off at once he would be the happiest fellow left alive. But come, let us begin.' Then he dictated the letter as follows:

'DEAR MR. GREY,

'I have been thinking much of what passed between us the other day. Augustus seems to be in a great hurry as to paying the creditors, and I do not see why he should not be gratified as the money may now be forthcoming. I presume that the sales, which will be completed before Christmas, will nearly enable us to stop their mouths. I can understand that Mountjoy should be induced to join with me and Augustus, so that in disposing of so large a sum of money the authority of all may be given, both of myself and of the heir, and also of him who a short time since was supposed to be the heir. I think that you may possibly find Mountjoy's address by applying to Augustus, who is always clever in such matters.

'But you will have to be certain that you obtain all the bonds. If you can get Tyrrwhit to help you you will be able to be sure of doing so. The matter to him is one of vital importance, as his sum is so much the largest. Of course he will open his mouth very wide; but when he finds that he can get his principal and nothing more, I think that he will help you.

'I am afraid that I must ask you to put yourself in correspondence with Augustus. That he is an insolent scoundrel I will admit; but we cannot very well complete this affair without him. I fancy that he now feels it to be his interest to get it all done before I die, as the men will be clamorous with their bonds as soon as the breath is out of my body.

'Yours sincerely,

'JOHN SCARBOROUGH.'

'That will do,' he said, when the letter was finished. But when Mr. Merton turned to leave the room Mr. Scarborough retained him. 'Upon the whole I am not dissatisfied with my life,' he said.

'I don't know that you have occasion,' rejoined Mr. Merton. In this he absolutely lied, for according

to his thinking, there was very much in the affairs of
Mr. Scarborough's life which ought to have induced
regret. He knew the whole story of the birth of the
elder son, of the subsequent marriage, of Mr. Scarborough's fraudulent deceit which had lasted so many
years, and of his latter return to the truth so as to
save the property, and to give back to the younger
son all of which for so many years he, his father, had
attempted to rob him. All London had talked of the
affair, and all London had declared that so wicked
and dishonest an old gentleman had never lived.
And now he had returned to the truth simply with
the view of cheating the creditors and keeping the
estate in the family. He was manifestly an old gentleman who ought to be above all others dissatisfied
with his own life; but Mr. Merton, when the assertion was made to him, knew not what other answer
to make.

'I really do not think I have, nor do I know one
to whom Heaven with all its bliss will be more
readily accorded. What have I done for myself?'

'I don't quite know what you have done all your
life.'

'I was born a rich man, and then I married—not
rich as I am now, but with ample means for marrying.'

'After Mr. Mountjoy's birth,' said Merton, who
could not pretend to be ignorant of the circumstance.

'Well, yes. I have my own ideas about marriage
and that kind of thing, which are, perhaps, at variance
with yours.' Whereupon Merton bowed. 'I had the
best wife in the world, who entirely coincided with
me in all that I did. I lived entirely abroad, and
made most liberal allowances to all the agricultural
tenants. I rebuilt all the cottages. Go and look at
them. I let any man shoot his own game till Mountjoy came up in the world and took the shooting into
his own hands. When the people at the pottery
began to build I assisted them in every way in the

world. I offered to keep a school at my own expense, solely on the understanding that what they call dissenters should be allowed to come there. The parson spread abroad a rumour that I was an atheist, and consequently the school was kept for the dissenters only. The School Board*has come and made that all right, though the parson goes on with his rumour. If he understood me as well as I understand him, he would know that he is more of an atheist than I am. I gave my boys the best education, spending on them more than double what is done by men with twice my means. My tastes were all simple and were not specially vicious. I do not know that I have even made anyone unhappy. Then the estate became richer, and Mountjoy grew more and more expensive. I began to find that with all my economies the estate could not keep pace with him, so as to allow me to put by anything for Augustus. Then I had to bethink myself what I had to do to save the estate from those rascals.'

'You took peculiar steps.'

'I am a man who does take peculiar steps. Another would have turned his face to the wall in my state of health, and have allowed two dirty Jews such as Tyrrwhit and Samuel Hart to have revelled in the wealth of Tretton. I am not going to allow them to revel. Tyrrwhit knows me, and Hart will have to know me. They could not keep their hands to themselves till the breath was out of my body. Now I am about to see that each shall have his own shortly, and the estate will still be kept in the family.'

'For Mr. Augustus Scarborough?'

'Yes, alas! yes. But that is not my doing. I do not know that I have cause to be dissatisfied with myself, but I cannot but own that I am unhappy. But I wished you to understand that though a man may break the law, he need not therefore be accounted bad, and though he may have views of his own as to religious matters, he need not be an atheist. I have made efforts on behalf of others, in which I have allowed no outward circumstances to control me. Now I think I do feel sleepy.'

Chapter XXII

HARRY ANNESLEY IS SUMMONED HOME

'JUST now I am triumphant,' Harry Annesley had said to his hostess as he left Mrs. Armitage's house in the Paragon, at Cheltenham. He was absolutely triumphant, throwing his hat up into the air in the abandonment of his joy. For he was not a man to have conceived so well of his own parts as to have flattered himself that the girl must certainly be his. There are at present a number of young men about who think that few girls are worth the winning, but that any girl is to be had, not by asking,—which would be troublesome,—but simply by looking at her. You can see the feeling in their faces. They are for the most part small in stature, well-made little men, who are aware that they have something to be proud of, wearing close-packed shining little hats, by which they seem to add more than a cubit to their stature, men endowed with certain gifts of personal,—dignity I may perhaps call it,—though the word rises somewhat too high. They look as though they would be able to say a clever thing; but their spoken thoughts seldom rise above a small acrid sharpness. They respect no one; above all, not their elders. To such a one his horse comes first, if he have a horse; then a dog; and then a stick; and after that the mistress of his affections. But their fault is not altogether of their own making. It is the girls themselves who spoil them and endure their inanity, because of that assumed look of superiority which to the eyes of the outside world would be a little offensive were it not a little foolish. But they do not marry often. Whether it be that the girls know better at last, or that they themselves do not see sufficiently clearly their future dinners, who can say? They are for the most part younger brothers, and perhaps have discovered the best way of getting out of the world whatever scraps the world can afford them. Harry Annesley's faults were altogether of another kind. In regard to this young woman, the Florence whom he had loved, he had been over-modest. Now his feeling of glory was altogether redundant. Having been told by Florence that she was devoted to him, he walked with his head among the heavens. The first instinct with such a young man as those of whom I have spoken teaches him, the moment he has committed himself, to begin to consider how he can get out of the scrape. It is not much of a scrape, for when an older man comes this way, a man verging towards baldness, with a good professional income, our little friend is forgotten and he is passed by without a word. But Harry had now a conviction,—on that one special night,—that he never would be forgotten and never would forget. He was filled at once with an unwonted pride. All the world was now at his feet, and all the stars were open to him. He had begun to have a glimmering of what it was that Augustus Scarborough intended to do; but the intentions of Augustus Scarborough were now of no moment to him. He was clothed in a panoply of armour which would be true against all weapons. At any rate, on that night and during the next day this feeling remained the same with him.

Then he received a summons from his mother at Buston. His mother pressed him to come at once down to the parsonage. 'Your uncle has been with your father, and has said terrible things about you. As you know, my brother is not very strong-minded, and I should not care so much for what he says were it not that so much is in his hands. I cannot understand what it is all about, but your father says that he does nothing but threaten. He talks of putting the entail on one side. Entails used to be fixed things, I thought; but since what old Mr. Scarborough did, nobody seems to regard them now. But even suppose the entail does remain, what are you to do about the income? Your father thinks you had better come down and have a little talk about the matter.'

This was the first blow received since the moment of his exaltation. Harry knew very well that the entail was fixed and could not be put aside by Mr. Prosper, though Mr. Scarborough might have succeeded with his entail; but yet he was aware that his present income was chiefly dependent on his uncle's good will. To be reduced to live on his fellowship would be very dreadful. And that income, such as it was, depended entirely on his celibacy. And he had too, as he was well aware, engendered habits of idleness during the last two years. The mind of a young man so circumstanced turns always first to the bar and then to literature. At the bar he did not think that there could be any opening for him. In the first place, it was late to begin; and then he was humble enough to believe of himself that he had none of the peculiar gifts necessary for a judge or for an advocate. Perhaps the knowledge that six or seven years of pre-liminary labour would be necessary was a deterrent.

The rewards of literature might be achieved immediately. Such was his idea. But he had another idea,—perhaps as erroneous,—that this career would not become a gentleman who intended to be squire of Buston. He had seen two or three men, decidedly Bohemian in their modes of life, to whom he did not wish to assimilate himself. There was Quaverdale, whom he had known intimately at St. John's, and who was on the press. Quaverdale had quarrelled absolutely with his father, who was also a clergyman, and having been thrown altogether on his own resources, had come out as a writer for The Coming Hour. He made his five or six hundred a year in a

rattling, loose, uncertain sort of fashion, and was,—
so thought Harry Annesley,—the dirtiest man of his
acquaintance. He did not believe in the six hundred
a year, or Quaverdale would certainly have changed
his shirt more frequently, and would sometimes have
had a new pair of trousers. He was very amusing,
very happy, very thoughtless, and as a rule altogether impecunious. Annesley had never known him
without the means of getting a good dinner, but those
means did not rise to the purchase of a new hat.
Putting Quaverdale before him as an example, Annesley could not bring himself to choose literature as a
profession. Thinking of all this when he received his
mother's letter, he assured himself that Florence
would not like professional literature.

He wrote to say that he would be down at Buston
in five days' time. It does not become a son who is
a fellow of a college and the heir to a property to
obey his parents too quickly. But he gave up the
intermediate days to thinking over the condition
which bound him to his uncle, and to discussing his
prospects with Quaverdale, who, as usual, was remaining in town doing the editor's work for The
Coming Hour. 'If he interfered with me I should tell
him to go to bed,' said Quaverdale. The allusion was
of course made to Mr. Prosper.

'I am not on those sort of terms with him.'

'I should make my own terms, and then let him do
his worst. What can he do? If he means to withdraw
his beggarly two hundred and fifty pounds, of course
he'll do it.'

'I suppose I do owe him something, in the way of
respect.'

'Not if he threatens you in regard to money.
What does it come to? That you are to cringe at
his heels for a beggarly allowance which he has been
pleased to bestow upon you without your asking.
"Very well, my dear fellow," I should say to him,
"you can stop it the moment you please. For certain

objects of your own,—that your heir might live in
the world after a certain fashion,—you have bestowed
it. It has been mine since I was a child. If you can
reconcile it to your conscience to discontinue it, do
so." You would find that he would have to think
twice about it.'

'He will stop it, and what am I to do then? Can I
get an opening on any of these papers?' Quaverdale
whistled,—a mode of receiving the overture which
was not pleasing to Annesley. 'I don't suppose that
anything so very superhuman in the way of intellect
is required.' Annesley had got a fellowship, whereas
Quaverdale had done nothing at the university.

'Couldn't you make a pair of shoes? Shoemakers
do get good wages.'

'What do you mean? A fellow never can get you
to be serious for two minutes together.'

'I never was more serious in my life.'

'That I am to make shoes?'

'No, I don't quite think that. I don't suppose you
can make them. You'd have first to learn the trade,
and show that you were an adept.'

'And I must show that I am an adept before I can
write for The Coming Hour.' There was a tone of
sarcasm in this which was not lost on Quaverdale.

'Certainly you must; and that you are a better
adept than I who have got the place or some other
unfortunate who will have to be put out of his berth.
The Coming Hour only requires a certain number.
Of course there are many newspapers in London, and
many magazines and much literary work going. You
may get your share of it, but you have got to begin
by shoving some incompetent fellow out. And in
order to be able to begin you must learn the trade.'

'How did you begin?'

'Just in that way. While you were roaming about
London like a fine gentleman, I began by earning
twenty-four shillings a week.'

'Can I earn twenty-four shillings a week?'

'You won't, because you have already got your fellowship. You had a knack at writing Greek Iambics, and therefore got a fellowship. I picked up at the same time the way of stringing English together. I also soon learned the way to be hungry. I'm not hungry now very often, but I've been through it. My belief is that you wouldn't get along with my editor.'

'That's your idea of being independent.'

'Certainly it is. I do his work and take his pay, and obey his orders. If you think you can do the same, come and try. There's not room here, but there is no doubt room elsewhere. There's the trade to be learned like any other trade; but my belief is that even then you could not do it. We don't want Greek Iambics.'*

Harry turned away disgusted. Quaverdale was like the rest of the world, and thought that a peculiar talent and a peculiar tact were needed for his own business. Harry believed that he was as able to write a leading article at any rate as Quaverdale, and that the Greek Iambics would not stand in his way. But he conceived it to be probable that his habits of cleanliness might do so, and gave up the idea for the present. He thought that his friend should have welcomed him with an open hand into the realms of literature; and, perhaps, it was the case that Quaverdale attributed too much weight to the knack of turning readable paragraphs on any subject at a moment's notice.

But what should he do down at Buston? There were three persons there with whom he had to contend: his father, his mother, and his uncle. With his father he had always been on good terms; but had still been subject to a certain amount of gentle sarcasm. He had got his fellowship and his allowance and had so been lifted above his father's authority. His father thoroughly despised his brother-in-law, and looked down upon him as an absolute ass. But he was reticent, only dropping a word here and there, out of

deference, perhaps, to his wife, and from a feeling
lest his son might be deficient in wise courtesy if he
were encouraged to laugh at his benefactor. He had
said a word or two as to a profession when Harry left
Cambridge; but the word or two had come to nothing.
In those days the uncle had altogether ridiculed the
idea, and the mother, fond of her son, the fellow and
the heir, had altogether opposed the notion. The
rector himself was an idle, good-looking, self-indulgent man,—a man who read a little and understood
what he read, and thought a little and understood
what he thought; but who took no trouble about anything. To go through the world comfortably with a
rather large family and a rather small income, was
the extent of his ambition. In regard to his eldest
son he had begun well. Harry had been educated
free, and had got a fellowship. He had never cost
his father a shilling. And now the eldest of two
grown-up daughters was engaged to be married to
the son of a brewer living in the little town of Buntingford. This also was a piece of good luck which
the rector accepted with a thankful heart. There was
another grown-up girl, also pretty, and then a third
girl not grown up, and the two boys, who were at
present at school at Royston. Thus burdened the
Reverend Mr. Annesley went through the world with
as jaunty a step as was possible, making but little of
his troubles, but anxious to make as much as he could
of his advantages. Of these the position of Harry
was the brightest, if only Harry would be careful to
guard it. It was quite out of the question that he
should find an income for Harry if the squire stopped
the two hundred and fifty pounds per annum which
he at present allowed him.

Then there was Harry's mother, who had already
very frequently discounted the good things which
were to fall to Harry's lot. She was a dear, good,
motherly woman, all whose geese were certainly
counted to be swans. And of all swans Harry was the

whitest; whereas in purity of plumage, Mary, the eldest daughter, who had won the affections of the young Buntingford brewer, was the next. That Harry's allowance should be stopped would be almost as great a misfortune as though Mr. Thoroughbung were to break his neck out hunting with the Parke-ridge[1] hounds—an amusement which, after the manner of brewers, he was much in the habit of following. Mrs. Annesley had lived at Buston all her life, having been born at the Hall. She was an excellent mother of a family, and a good clergyman's wife, being in both respects more painstaking and assiduous than her husband. But she did maintain something of respect for her brother, though in her inmost heart she knew that he was a fool. But to have been born squire of Buston was something, and to have reached the age of fifty unmarried, so as to leave the position of heir open to her own son was more. To such a one a great deal was due; but of that deal Harry was but little disposed to pay any part. He must be talked to, and very seriously talked to, and if possible saved from the sin of offending his easily-offended uncle. A terrible idea had been suggested to her lately by her husband. The entail might be made altogether inoperative by the marriage of her brother. It was a fearful notion, but one which if it entered into her brother's head might possibly be carried out. No one before had ever dreamed of anything so dangerous to the Annesley interests, and Mrs. Annesley now felt that by due submission on the part of the heir it might be avoided.

But the squire himself was the foe whom Harry most feared. He quite understood that he would be required to be submissive, and, even if he were willing, he did not know how to act the part. There was much now that he would endure for the sake of Florence. If Mr. Prosper demanded that after dinner he should sit and hear a sermon, he would sit and

[1] *Sic.* in all editions. Elsewhere 'Puckeridge'.

hear it out. It would be a bore, but might be endured on behalf of the girl whom he loved. But he much feared that the cause of his uncle's displeasure was deeper than that. A rumour had reached him that his uncle had declared his conduct to Mountjoy Scarborough to have been abominable. He had heard no words spoken by his uncle, but threats had reached him through his mother, and also through his uncle's man of business. He certainly would go down to Buston, and carry himself towards his uncle with what outward signs of respect would be possible. But, if his uncle accused him, he could not but tell his uncle that he knew nothing of the matter of which he was talking. Not for all Buston could he admit that he had done anything mean or ignoble. Florence, he was quite sure, would not desire it. Florence would not be Florence were she to desire it. He thought that he could trace the hands,—or rather the tongues,—through which the calumny had made its way down to the Hall. He would at once go to the Hall, and tell his uncle all the facts. He would describe the gross ill-usage to which he had been subjected. No doubt he had left the man sprawling upon the pavement; but there had been no sign that the man had been dangerously hurt; and when two days afterwards the man had vanished, it was clear that he could not have vanished without legs. Had he taken himself off,—as was probable,—then why need Harry trouble himself as to his vanishing? If someone else had helped him in escaping,—as was also probable,—why had not that someone come and told the circumstances when all the enquiries were being made? Why should he have been expected to speak of the circumstances of such an encounter, which could not have been told but to Captain Scarborough's infinite disgrace? And he could not have told of it without naming Florence Mountjoy. His uncle, when he heard the truth, must acknowledge that he had not behaved badly. And yet Harry, as he turned it all in his mind, was uneasy as to his own conduct. He could not quite acquit himself in that he had kept secret all the facts of that midnight encounter in the face of the enquiries which had been made, in that he had falsely assured Augustus Scarborough of his ignorance. And yet he knew that on no consideration would he acknowledge himself to have been wrong.

Chapter XXIII

THE RUMOURS AS TO MR. PROSPER

IT was still October when Harry Annesley went down to Buston, and the Mountjoys had just reached Brussels. Mr. Grey had made his visit to Tretton and had returned to London. Harry went home on an understanding,—on the part of his mother at any rate,—that he should remain there till Christmas. But he felt himself very averse to so long a sojourn. If the Hall and park were open to him he might endure it. He would take down two or three stiff books, which he certainly would never read, and would shoot a few pheasants, and possibly ride one of his future brother-in-law's horses with the hounds. But he feared that there was to be a quarrel by which he would be debarred from the Hall and the park; and he knew too that it would not be well for him to shoot and hunt when his income should have been cut off. It would be necessary that some great step should be taken at once; but then it would be necessary also that Florence should agree to that step. He had a modest lodging in London, but before he started e prepared himself for what must occur by giving notice. 'I don't say as yet that I shall give them up; but I might as well let you know that it's possible.' This he said to Mrs. Brown who kept the lodgings, and who received this intimation as a Mrs. Brown is sure to do. But where should he betake himself when his home at Mrs. Brown's had been lost? He would.

he thought, find it quite impossible to live in absolute idleness at the rectory. Then in an unhappy frame of mind he went down by the train to Stevenage, and was met there by the rectory pony-carriage.

He saw it all in his mother's eye the moment she embraced him. There was some terrible trouble in the wind, and what could it be but his uncle? 'Well, mother, what is it?'

'Oh, Harry, there is such a sad affair up at the Hall.'

'Is my uncle dead?'

'Dead; no!'

'Then why do you look so sad?

> Even such a man, so faint, so spiritless,
> So dull, so dead in look, so woe-begone,
> Drew Priam's curtain in the dead of night.'*

'Oh! Harry, do not laugh. Your uncle says such dreadful things.'

'I don't care much what he says. The question is, —what does he mean to do?'

'He declares that he will cut you off altogether.'

'That is sooner said than done.'

'That is all very well, Harry; but he can do it. Oh, Harry! But come and sit down and talk to me. I told your father to be out so that I might have you alone; and the dear girls are gone into Buntingford.'

'Ah! like them. Thoroughbung will have enough of them.'

'He is our only happiness now.'

'Poor Thoroughbung! I pity him if he has to do happiness for the whole household.'

'Joshua is a most excellent young man. Where we should be without him I do not know.'

The flourishing young brewer was named Joshua, and had been known to Harry for some years, though never as yet known as a brother-in-law.

'I am sure he is; particularly as he has chosen Molly to be his wife. He is just the young man who ought to have a wife.'

'Of course he ought.'

'Because he can keep a family. But now about my uncle. He is to perform this ceremony of cutting me off. Will he turn out to have had a wife and family in former ages? I have no doubt old Scarborough could manage it, but I don't give my uncle credit for so much cleverness.'

'But in future ages,' said the unhappy mother, shaking her head and rubbing her eyes.

'You mean that he is going to have a family?'

'It is all in the hands of Providence,' said the parson's wife.

'Yes, that is true. He is not too old yet to be a second Priam,* and have his curtains drawn the other way. That's his little game, is it?'

'There's a sort of rumour about that it's possible.'

'And who is the lady?'

'You may be sure there will be no lack of a lady if he sets his mind upon it. I was turning it over in my mind, and I thought of Matilda Thoroughbung.'

'Joshua's aunt!'

'Well, she is Joshua's aunt, no doubt. I did just whisper the idea to Joshua, and he says she is fool enough for anything. She has twenty-five thousand pounds of her own, but she lives all by herself.'

'I know where she lives,—just out of Buntingford, as you go to Royston. But she's not alone. Is Uncle Prosper to marry Miss Tickle also?' Miss Tickle was an estimable lady living as companion to Miss Thoroughbung.

'I don't know how they may manage; but it has to be thought of, Harry. We only know that your uncle has been twice to Buntingford.'

'The lady is fifty, at any rate.'

'The lady is barely forty. She gives out that she is thirty-six. And he could settle a jointure on her which would leave the property not worth having.'

'What can I do?'

'Yes, indeed, my dear; what can you do?'

'Why is he going to upset all the arrangements of my life, and his life, after such a fashion as this?'

'That's just what your father says.'

'I suppose he can do it. The law will allow him. But the injustice would be monstrous! I did not ask him to take me by the hand when I was a boy and lead me into this special walk of life. It has been his own doing. How will he look me in the face and tell me that he is going to marry a wife? I should look him in the face and tell him of my wife.'

'But is that settled?'

'Yes, mother; it is settled. Wish me joy for having won the finest lady that ever walked the earth.' His mother blessed him, but said nothing about the finest lady,—who at that moment she believed to be the future bride of Mr. Joshua Thoroughbung. 'And when I shall tell my uncle that it is so, what will he say to me? Will he have the face then to tell me that I am to be cut out of Buston? I doubt whether he will have the courage.'

'He has thought of that, Harry.'

'How thought of it, mother?'

'He has given orders that he is not to see you.'

'Not to see me!'

'So he declares. He has written a long letter to your father, in which he says that he would be spared the agony of an interview.'

'What! is it all done then?'

'Your father got the letter yesterday. It must have taken my poor brother a week to write it.'

'And he tells the whole plan; Matilda Thoroughbung, and the future family?'

'No; he does not say anything about Miss Thoroughbung. He says that he must make other arrangements about the property.'

'He can't make other arrangements; that is, not until the boy is born. It may be a long time first, you know.'

'But the jointure?'

'What does Molly say about it?'

'Molly is mad about it, and so is Joshua. Joshua talks about it just as though he were one of us, and he says that the old people at Buntingford would not hear of it.' The old people spoken of were the father and mother of Joshua, and the half-brother of Miss Matilda Thoroughbung. 'But what can they do?'

'They can do nothing. If Miss Matilda likes Uncle Prosper——'

'Likes, my dear! How young you are! Of course she would like a country house to live in, and the park, and the county society. And she would like somebody to live with besides Miss Tickle.'

'My uncle, for instance.'

'Yes, your uncle.'

'If I had my choice, mother, I should prefer Miss Tickle.'

'Because you are a silly boy. But what are you to do now?'

'In this long letter which he has written to my father, does he give no reason?'

'Your father will show you the letter. Of course he gives reasons. He says that you have done something which you ought not to have done,—about that wretched Mountjoy Scarborough.'

'What does he know about it,—the idiot?'

'Oh, Harry!'

'Well, mother, what better can I say of him? He has taken me as a child and fashioned my life for me; has said that this property should be mine, and has put an income into my hand as though I were an eldest son; has repeatedly declared, when his voice was more potent than mine, that I should follow no profession. He has bound himself to me, telling all the world that I was his heir. And now he casts me out because he has heard some cock-and-bull story, of the truth of which he knows nothing. What better can I say of him than call him an idiot? He must be that or else a heartless knave. And he says that he does not mean to see me,—me with whose life he has thus been empowered to interfere, so as to blast it if not to bless it, and intends to turn me adrift as he might do a dog that did not suit him! And because he knows that he cannot answer me, he declares that he will not see me.'

'It is very hard, Harry.'

'Therefore I call him an idiot in preference to calling him a knave. But I am not going to be dropped out of the running in that way, just in deference to his will. I shall see him. Unless they lock him up in his bedroom I shall compel him to see me!'

'What good would that do, Harry? That would only set him more against you.'

'You don't know his weakness.'

'Oh yes, I do; he is very weak.'

'He will not see me, because he will have to yield when he hears what I have to say for myself. He knows that, and would therefore fain keep away from me. Why should he be stirred to this animosity against me?'

'Why indeed?'

'Because there is someone who wishes to injure me, more strong than he is, and who has got hold of him. Someone has lied behind my back.'

'Who has done this?'

'Ah, that is the question. But I know who has done it, though I will not name him just now. This enemy of mine, knowing him to be weak,—knowing him to be an idiot, has got hold of him and persuaded him. He believes the story which is told to him, and then feels happy in shaking off an incubus. No doubt I have not been very soft with him—nor, indeed, hard. I have kept out of his way, and he is willing to resent it. But he is afraid to face me and tell me that it is so. Here are the girls come back from Bunting-ford. Molly, you blooming young bride, I wish you joy of your brewer.'

'He's none the worse on that account, Master Harry,' said the eldest sister.

'All the better,—very much the better. Where would you be if he was not a brewer? But I congratulate you with all my heart, old girl. I have known him ever so long, and he's one of the best fellows I do know.'

'Thank you, Harry,' and she kissed him.

'I wish Fanny and Kate may even do so well.'

'All in good time,' said Fanny.

'I mean to have a banker,—all to myself,' said Kate.

'I wish you may have half as good a man for your husband,' said Harry.

'And I am to tell you,' continued Molly, who was now in high good humour, 'that there will be always one of his horses for you to ride as long as you remain at home. It is not every brother-in-law that would do as much as that for you.'

'Nor yet every uncle,' said Kate, shaking her head, from which Harry could see that this quarrel with his uncle had been freely discussed in the family circle.

'Uncles are very different,' said the mother; 'uncles can't be expected to do everything as though they were in love.'

'Fancy Uncle Peter in love,' said Kate. Mr. Prosper was called Uncle Peter by the girls, though always in a sort of joke. Then the other two girls shook their heads very gravely, from which Harry learned that the question respecting the choice of Miss Matilda Thoroughbung as a mistress for the Hall had been discussed also before them.

'I am not going to marry all the family,' said Molly.

'Not Miss Matilda, for instance,' said her brother, laughing.

'No, especially not Matilda. Joshua is quite as angry about his aunt as anybody here can be. You'll find that he is more of an Annesley than a Thoroughbung.'

'My dear,' said the mother, 'your husband will, as a matter of course, think most of his own family. And so ought you to do of his family, which will be yours. A married woman should always think most of her husband's family.' In this way the mother told her daughter of her future duties; but behind the mother's back Kate made a grimace, for the benefit of her sister Fanny, showing thereby her conviction that in a matter of blood,—what she called being a gentleman,—a Thoroughbung could not approach an Annesley.

'Mamma does not know it as yet,' Molly said afterwards in privacy to her brother, 'but you may take it for granted that Uncle Peter has been into Buntingford and has made an offer to Aunt Matilda. I could tell it at once, because she looked so sharp at me today. And Joshua says that he is sure it is so by the airs she gives herself.'

'You think she'll have him?'

'Have him? Of course she'll have him. Why shouldn't she? A wretched old maid living with a companion like that would have anyone.'

'She has got a lot of money.'

'She'll take care of her money, let her alone for that. And she'll have his house to live in. And there'll be a jointure. Of course if there were to be children——'

'Oh, bother!'

'Well, perhaps there will not. But it will be just as bad. We don't mean even to visit them; we think it so very wicked. And we shall tell them a bit of our mind as soon as the thing has been publicly declared.'

Chapter XXIV

HARRY ANNESLEY'S MISERY

THE conversation which took place that evening between Harry and his father was more serious in its language, though not more important in its purpose. 'This is bad news, Harry,' said the rector.

'Yes, indeed, sir.'

'Your uncle, no doubt, can do as he pleases.'

'You mean as to the income he has allowed me?'

'As to the income! As to the property itself. It is bad waiting for dead men's shoes.'

'And yet it is what everybody does in this world. No one can say that I have been at all in a hurry to step into my uncle's shoes. It was he that first told you that he should never marry, and as the property had been entailed on me, he undertook to bring me up as his son.'

'So he did.'

'Not a doubt about it, sir. But I had nothing to say to it. As far as I understand, he has been allowing me two hundred and fifty pounds a year for the last dozen years.'

'Ever since you went to the Charterhouse.'

'At that time I could not be expected to have a word to say to it. And it has gone on ever since.'

'Yes, it has gone on ever since.'

'And when I was leaving Cambridge he required that I should not go into a profession.'

'Not exactly that, Harry.'

'It was so that I understood it. He did not wish his heir to be burdened with a profession. He said so to me himself.'

'Yes, just when he was in his pride, because you had got your fellowship. But there was a contract understood, if not made.'

'What contract?' asked Harry with an air of surprise.

'That you should be to him as a son.'

'I never undertook it. I wouldn't have done it at the price,—or for any price. I never felt for him the respect or the love that were due to a father. I did feel both of them, to the full, for my own father. They are a sort of thing which we cannot transfer.'

'They may be shared, Harry,' said the rector, who was flattered.

'No, sir; in this instance that was not possible.'

'You might have sat by while he read a sermon to his sister and nieces. You understood his vanity, and you wounded it, knowing what you were doing. I don't mean to blame you, but it was a misfortune. Now we must look it in the face and see what must be done. Your mother has told you that he has written to me. There is his letter. You will see that he writes with a fixed purpose.' Then he handed to Harry a letter written on a large sheet of paper, the reading of which would be so long that Harry seated himself for the operation.

The letter need not here be repeated at length. It was written with involved sentences, but in very decided language. It said nothing of Harry's want of duty, or not attending to the sermons, or of other deficiencies of a like nature, but based his resolution in regard to stopping the income on his nephew's misconduct—as it appeared to him—in a certain particular case. And unfortunately, though Harry was prepared to deny that his conduct on that occasion had been subject to censure, he could not contradict any of the facts on which Mr. Prosper had founded his opinion. The story was told in reference to Mountjoy Scarborough, but not the whole story. 'I understand that there was a row in the streets late at night, at the end of which young Mr. Scarborough was left as dead under the railings.' 'Left for dead!' exclaimed Harry. 'Who says that he was left for dead? I did not think him to be dead.'

'You had better read it to the end,' said his father,

and Harry read it. The letter went on to describe how Mountjoy Scarborough was missed from his usual haunts, how search was made by the police, how the newspapers were filled with the strange incident, and how Harry had told nothing of what had occurred. 'But beyond this,' the letter went on to say, 'he positively denied, in conversation with the gentleman's brother, that he had anything to do with the gentleman on the night in question. If this be so, he absolutely lied. A man who would lie on such an occasion, knowing himself to have been guilty of having beaten the man in such a way as to have probably caused his death,—for he had left him for dead under the railings in a London street and in the midnight hour,—and would positively assert to the gentleman's brother that he had not seen the gentleman on the night in question, when he had every reason to believe that he had killed him,—a deed which might or might not be murder,—is not fit to be recognised as my heir.' There were other sentences equally long and equally complicated, in all of which Mr. Prosper strove to tell the story with tragic effect, but all of which had reference to the same transaction. He said nothing as to the ultimate destination of the property, nor of his own proposed marriage. Should he have a son, that son would, of course, have the property. Should there be no son, Harry must have it, even though his conduct might have been ever so abominable. To prevent that outrage on society, his marriage,—with its ordinary results,—would be the only step. Of that he need say nothing. But the two hundred and fifty pounds would not be paid after the Christmas quarter, and he must decline for the future the honour of receiving Mr. Henry Annesley at the Hall.

Harry, when he had read it all, began to storm with anger. The man, as he truly observed, had grossly insulted him. Mr. Prosper had called him a liar, and had hinted that he was a murderer. 'You can do nothing to him,' his father said. 'He is your uncle, and you have eaten his bread.'

'I can't call him out and fight him.'

'You must let it alone.'

'I can make my way into the house and see him.'

'I don't think you can do that. You will find it difficult to get beyond the front door, and I would advise you to abandon all such ideas. What can you say to him?'

'It is false!'

'What is false? Though in essence it is false, in words it is true. You did deny that you had seen him.'

'I forget what passed. Augustus Scarborough endeavoured to pump me about his brother, and I did not choose to be pumped. As far as I can ascertain now, it is he that is the liar. He saw his brother after the affair with me.'

'Has he denied it?'

'Practically he denies it by asking me the question. He asked me with the ostensible object of finding out what had become of his brother, when he himself knew what had become of him.'

'But you can't prove it. He positively says that you did deny having seen him on the night in question. I am not speaking of Augustus Scarborough, but of your uncle. What he says is true, and you had better leave him alone. Take other steps for driving the real truth into his brain.'

'What steps can be taken with such a fool?'

'Write your own account of the transaction, so that he shall read it. Let your mother have it. I suppose he will see your mother.'

'And so beg his favour.'

'You need beg for nothing. Or if the marriage comes off——'

'You have heard of the marriage, sir?'

'Yes; I have heard of the marriage. I believe that he contemplates it. Put your statement of what did

occur, and of your motives, into the hands of the
lady's friends. He will be sure to read it.'

'What good will that do?'

'No good, but that of making him ashamed of
himself. You have got to read the world a little more
deeply than you have hitherto done. He thinks that
he is quarrelling with you about the affair in London,
but it is in truth because you have declined to hear
him read the sermons after having taken his money.'

'Then it is he that is the liar rather than I.'

'I, who am a moderate man, would say that neither
is a liar. You did not choose to be pumped, as you
call it, and therefore spoke as you did. According to
the world's ways that was fair enough. He, who is
sore at the little respect you have paid him, takes
any ground of offence rather than that. Being sore
at heart he believes anything. This young Scarborough in some way gets hold of him, and makes
him accept this cock-and-bull story. If you had sat
there punctual all those Sunday evenings, do you
think he would have believed it then?'

'And I have got to pay such a penalty as this?'
The rector could only shrug his shoulders. He was
not disposed to scold his son. It was not the custom
of the house that Harry should be scolded. He was
a fellow of his college and the heir to Buston, and was
therefore considered to be out of the way of scolding.
But the rector felt that his son had made his bed and
must now lie on it, and Harry was aware that this
was his father's feeling.

For two or three days he wandered about the
country very down in the mouth. The natural state
of ovation in which the girls existed was in itself an
injury to him. How could he join them in their ovation,—he who had suffered so much? It seemed to be
heartless that they should smile and rejoice when he,
—the head of the family as he had been taught to
consider himself,—was being so cruelly ill-used. For
a day or two he hated Thoroughbung, though

Thoroughbung was all that was kind to him. He congratulated him with cold congratulations, and afterwards kept out of his way. 'Remember, Harry, that up to Christmas you can always have one of the nags. There's Belladonna and Orange Peel. I think you'd find the mare a little the faster, though perhaps the horse is the bigger jumper.' 'Oh! thank you,' said Harry, and passed on. Now Thoroughbung was fond of his horses, and liked to have them talked about, and he knew that Harry Annesley was treating him badly. But he was a good-humoured fellow, and he bore it without complaint. He did not even say a cross word to Molly. Molly, however, was not so patient. 'You might be a little more gracious when he's doing the best he can for you. It is not every one who will lend you a horse to hunt for two months.' Harry shook his head, and wandered away miserable through the fields, and would not in these days even set his foot upon the soil of the park. 'He was not going to intrude any further,' he said to the rector. 'You can come to church at any rate,' his father said, 'for he certainly will not be there while you are at the Parsonage.' Oh! yes; Harry would go to the church. 'I have yet to understand that Mr. Prosper is the owner of the church, and the path there from the rectory is at any rate open to the public.' For at Buston the church stands on one corner of the park.

This went on for two or three days, during which nothing further was said by the family as to Harry's woes. A letter was sent off to Mrs. Brown, telling her that the lodgings would not be required any longer, and anxious ideas began to crowd themselves on Harry's mind as to his future residence. He thought that he must go back to Cambridge and take his rooms at St. John's, and look for college work. Two fatal years, years of idleness and gaiety, had been passed, but still he thought that it might be possible. What else was there open for him? And then, as he roamed about the fields, his mind naturally ran away to the girl he loved. How would he dare again to look Florence in the face? It was not only the two hundred and fifty pounds per annum that was gone. That would have been a small income on which to marry. And he had never taken the girl's own money into account. He had rather chosen to look forward to the position as squire of Buston, and to take it for granted that it would not be very long before he was called upon to fill the position. He had said not a word to Florence about money, but it was thus that he had regarded the matter. Now the existing squire was going to marry, and the matter could not so be regarded any longer. He saw half-a-dozen little Prospers occupying half-a-dozen little cradles, and a whole suite of nurseries established at the Hall. The name of Prosper would be fixed at Buston, putting it altogether beyond his reach.

In such circumstances would it not be reasonable that Florence should expect him to authorise her to break their engagement? What was he now but the penniless son of a poor clergyman, with nothing on which to depend but a miserable stipend, which must cease were he to marry? He knew that he ought to give her back her troth. And yet, as he thought of doing so, he was indignant with her. Was love to come to this? Was her regard for him to be counted as nothing? What right had he to expect that she should be different from any other girl? Then he was more miserable than ever, as he told himself that such would undoubtedly be her conduct. As he walked across the fields, heavy with the mud of a wet October day, there came down a storm of rain which wet him through. Who does not know the sort of sensation which falls upon a man when he feels that even the elements have turned against him, how he buttons up his coat and bids the clouds open themselves upon his devoted bosom?

> Blow, winds, and crack your cheeks! Rage, blow,
> You cataracts and hurricanes!*

It is thus that a man is apt to address the soft rains of heaven when he is becoming wet through in such a frame of mind; and on the present occasion Harry likened himself to Lear. It was to him as though the steeples were to be drenched, and the cocks drowned when he found himself wet through. In this condition he went back to the house, and so bitter to him were the misfortunes of the world that he would hardly condescend to speak while enduring them. But when he had entered the drawing-room his mother greeted him with a letter. It had come by the day mail, and his mother looked into his face piteously as she gave it to him. The letter was from Brussels, and she could guess from whom it had come. It might be a sweetly soft love-letter; but then it might be neither sweet nor soft in the condition of things in which Harry was now placed. He took it and looked at it, but did not dare to open it on the spur of the moment. Without a word he went up to his room, and then tore it asunder. No doubt, he said to himself, it would allude to his miserable stipend and penniless condition. The letter ran as follows:

'DEAREST HARRY,

'I think it right to write to you, though mamma does not approve of it. I have told her, however, that in the present circumstances I am bound to do so, and that I should implore you not to answer. Though I must write, there must be no correspondence between us. Rumours have been received here very detrimental to your character.' Harry gnashed his teeth as he read this. 'Stories are told about your meeting with Captain Scarborough in London, which I know to be only in part true. Mamma says that because of them I ought to give up my engagement, and my uncle, Sir Magnus, has taken upon himself

to advise me to do so. I have told them both that that
which is said of you is in part untrue; but whether it
be true or whether it be false, I will never give up my
engagement, unless you ask me to do so. They tell
me that as regards your pecuniary prospects you are
ruined. I say that you cannot be ruined as long as
you have my income. It will not be much, but it will,
I should think, be enough.

'And now you can do as you please. You may be
quite sure that I shall be true to you, through ill
report and good report. Nothing that mamma can
say to me will change me, and certainly nothing from
Sir Magnus.

'And now there need not be a word from you if
you mean to be true to me. Indeed, I have promised
that there shall be no word, and I expect you to
keep my promise for me. If you wish to be free of
me, then you must write and say so.

'But you won't wish it, and therefore I am yours,
always, always, always your own   'FLORENCE.'

Harry read the letter standing up in the middle of
the room, and in half a minute he had torn off his wet
coat, and kicked one of his wet boots to the further
corner of the room. Then there was a knock at the
door, and his mother entered.

'Tell me, Harry, what she says.'

He rushed up to his mother all damp and half-
shod as he was, and seized her in his arms. 'Oh,
mother, mother!'

'What is it, dear?'

'Read that, and tell me whether there ever was a
finer human being.' Mrs. Annesley did read it, and
thought her own daughter Molly was just as fine a
creature. Florence was simply doing what any girl
of spirit would do. But she saw that her son was as
jubilant now as he had been downcast, and she was
quite willing to partake of his comfort. 'Not write a
word to her. Ha, ha! I think I see myself at it.'

'But she seems to be in earnest there.'

'In earnest! And so am I in earnest. Would it be possible that a fellow should hold his hand and not write? Yes, my girl; I think that I must write a line. I wonder what she would say if I were not to write?'

'I think she means that you should be silent.'

'She has taken a very odd way of assuming it. I am to keep her promise for her. My darling, my angel, my life! But I cannot do that one thing. Oh, mother, mother! if you only knew how happy I am. What the mischief does it all signify?—Uncle Prosper, Miss Thoroughbung, and the rest of it,—with a girl like that?'

Chapter XXV

HARRY AND HIS UNCLE

HARRY was kissed all round by the girls, and was congratulated warmly on the heavenly excellence of his mistress. They could afford to be generous if he would be good-natured. 'Of course you must write to her,' said Molly, when he came downstairs with dry clothes.

'I should think so, mother.'

'Only she does seem to be so much in earnest about it,' said Mrs. Annesley.

'I think she would rather get just a line to say that he is earnest too,' said Fanny.

'Why should not she like a love-letter as much as anyone else?' said Kate, who had her own ideas. 'Of course she has to tell him about her mamma, but what need he care for that? Of course mamma thinks that Joshua need not write to Molly, but Molly won't mind.'

'I don't think anything of the kind, miss.'

'And besides, Joshua lives in the next parish,' said Fanny, 'and has a horse to ride over on if he has anything to say.'

'At any rate, I shall write,' said Harry, 'even at the risk of making her angry.' And he did write, as follows:

'BUSTON,—October, 188–.

'MY OWN DEAR GIRL,

'It is impossible that I should not send one line in answer. Put yourself in my place, and consult your own feelings. Think that you have had a letter so full of love, so noble, so true, so certain to fill you with joy, and then say whether you would let it pass without a word of acknowledgment. It would be absolutely impossible. It is not very probable that I should ask you to break your engagement, which in the midst of my troubles is the only consolation that I have. But when a man has a rock to stand upon like that, he does not want anything else. As long as a man has the one person necessary to his happiness to believe in him, he can put up with the ill opinion of all the others. You are to me so much that you outweigh all the world.

'I did not choose to have my secret pumped out of me by Augustus Scarborough. I can tell you the whole truth now. Mountjoy Scarborough had told me that he regarded you as affianced to him, and required me to say that I would—drop you. You know now how probable that was. He was drunk on the occasion,—had made himself purposely drunk so as to get over all scruples,—and attacked me with his stick. Then came a scrimmage, in which he was upset. A sober man has always the best of it.' I am afraid that Harry put in that little word sober for a purpose. The opportunity of declaring that he was sober was too good to be lost. 'I went away and left him, certainly not dead, nor apparently much hurt. But if I had told all this to Augustus Scarborough, your name must have come out. Now I should not mind. Now I might tell the truth about you,—with great pride, if occasion required it. But I couldn't do it then. What would the world have said to two

men fighting in the streets about a girl, neither of
whom had a right to fight about her? That was the
reason why I told an untruth;—because I did not
choose to fall into the trap which Augustus Scarborough had laid for me.

'If your mother will understand it all, I do not
think she will object to me on that score. If she does
quarrel with me, she will only be fighting the Scarborough game, in which I am bound to oppose her.
I am afraid the fact is that she prefers the Scarborough game,—not because of my sins but from
auld lang syne.

'But Augustus has got hold of my uncle Prosper,
and has done me a terrible injury. My uncle is a
weak man, and has been predisposed against me from
other circumstances. He thinks that I have neglected
him, and is willing to believe anything against me.
He has stopped my income,—two hundred and fifty
pounds a year,—and is going to revenge himself on
me by marrying a wife. It is too absurd, and the
proposed wife is aunt of the man whom my sister is
going to marry. It makes such a heap of confusion.
Of course, if he becomes the father of a family, I
shall be nowhere. Had I not better take to some
profession? Only what shall I take to? It is almost
too late for the bar. I must see you and talk over it
all.

'You have commanded me not to write, and now
there is a long letter! It is as well to be hung for a
sheep as a lamb. But when a man's character is at
stake, he feels that he must plead for it. You won't
be angry with me because I have not done all that
you told me? It was absolutely necessary that I
should tell you that I did not mean to ask you to
break your engagement, and one word has led to all
the others. There shall be only one other, which
means more than all the rest,—that I am yours,
dearest, with all my heart,

'HARRY ANNESLEY.'

'There!' he said to himself, as he put the letter into the envelope, 'she may think it too long, but I am sure she would not have been pleased had I not written at all.'

That afternoon Joshua was at the rectory, having just trotted over after business hours at the brewery because of some special word which had to be whispered to Molly, and Harry put himself in his way as he went out to get on his horse in the stable-yard. 'Joshua,' he said, 'I know that I owe you an apology.'

'What for?'

'You have been awfully good to me about the horses, and I have been very ungracious.'

'Not at all.'

'But I have. The truth is, I have been made thoroughly miserable by circumstances, and, when that occurs, a man cannot pick himself up all at once. It isn't my uncle that has made me wretched. That is a kind of thing that a man has to put up with, and I think that I can bear it as well as another. But an attack has been made upon me, which has wounded me.'

'I know all about it.'

'I don't mind telling you, as you and Molly are going to hit it off together. There is a girl I love, and they have tried to interfere with her.'

'They haven't succeeded?'

'No, by George! And now I'm as right as a trivet. When it came across me that she might have —might have yielded, you know—it was as though all had been over. I ought not to have suspected her.'

'But she's all right?'

'Indeed she is. I think you'll like her when you see her some day. If you don't, you have the most extraordinary taste I ever knew a man to possess. How about the horse?'

'I have four, you know.'

'What a grand thing it is to be a brewer!'

'And there are two of them will carry you. The other two are not quite up to your weight.'

'You haven't been out yet?'

'Well, no;—not exactly out. The governor is the best fellow in the world, but he draws the line at cub-hunting. He says the business should be the business till November. Upon my word, I think he's right.'

'And how many days a week after that?'

'Well, three regular. I do get an odd day with the Essex sometimes, and the governor winks.'

'The governor hunts himself as often as you.'

'Oh dear, no! three a week does for the governor, and he is beginning to like frosty weather, and to hear with pleasure that one of the old horses isn't as fit as he should be. He's what they call training off. Good-bye, old fellow. Mind you come out on the 7th of November.'

But Harry, though he had been made happy by the letter from Florence, had still a great many troubles on his mind. His first trouble was the having to do something in reference to his uncle. It did not appear to him to be proper to accept his uncle's decision in regard to his income without, at any rate, attempting to see Mr. Prosper. It would be as though he had taken what was done as a matter of course,—as though his uncle could stop the income without leaving him any ground of complaint. Of the intended marriage,—if it were intended,—he would say nothing. His uncle had never promised him in so many words not to marry, and there would be, he thought, something ignoble in his asking his uncle not to do that which he intended to do himself without even consulting his uncle about it. As he turned it all over in his mind he began to ask himself why his uncle should be asked to do anything for him, whereas he had never done anything for his uncle. He had been told that he was the heir, not to the uncle, but to Buston, and had gradually been taught to look upon Buston as his right,—as though he had a certain indefeasible property in the acres. He now began to perceive that there was no such thing. A tacit contract had been made on his behalf, and he had declined to accept his share of the contract. But he had been debarred from following any profession by his uncle's promised allowance. He did not think that he could complain to his uncle about the proposed marriage; but he did think that he could ask a question or two as to the income.

Without saying a word to any of his own family he walked across the park, and presented himself at the front door of Buston Hall. In doing so he would not go upon the grass. He had told his father that he would not enter the park, and therefore kept himself to the road. And he had dressed himself with some little care, as a man does when he feels that he is going forth on some mission of importance. Had he intended to call on old Mr. Thoroughbung there would have been no such care. And he rang at the front door, instead of entering the house by any of the numerous side inlets with which he was well acquainted. The butler understood the ring, and put on his company coat when he answered the bell.

'Is my uncle at home, Matthew?' he said.

'Mr. Prosper, Mr. Harry? Well, no; I can't say that he just is;' and the old man groaned, and wheezed, and looked unhappy.

'He is not often out at this time.' Matthew groaned again, and wheezed more deeply, and looked unhappier. 'I suppose you mean to say that he has given orders that I am not to be admitted.' To this the butler made no answer, but only looked woefully into the young man's face. 'What is the meaning of it all, Matthew?'

'Oh! Mr. Harry, you shouldn't ask me as is merely a servant.'

Harry felt the truth of this rebuke, but was not going to put up with it.

'That's all my eye, Matthew; you know all about it as well as anyone. It is so. He does not want to see me.'

'I don't think he does, Mr. Harry.'

'And why not? You know the whole of my family story as well as my father does, or my uncle. Why does he shut his doors against me, and send me word that he does not want to see me?'

'Well, Mr. Harry, I'm not just able to say why he does it,—and you the heir. But if I was asked I should make answer that it has come along of them sermons.' Then Matthew looked very serious, and scratched his head.

'I suppose so.'

'That was it, Mr. Harry. We, none of us, were very fond of the sermons.'

'I dare say not.'

'We in the kitchen. But we was bound to have them, or we should have lost our places.'

'And now I must lose my place.' The butler said nothing, but his face assented. 'A little hard, isn't it, Matthew? But I wish to say a few words to my uncle,—not to express any regret about the sermons, but to ask what it is that he intends to do.' Here Matthew shook his head very slowly. 'He has given positive orders that I shall not be admitted?'

'It must be over my dead body, Mr. Harry;' and he stood in the way with the door in his hand, as though intending to sacrifice himself should he be called upon to do so by the nature of the circumstances. Harry, however, did not put him to the test; but, bidding him good-bye with some little joke as to his fidelity, made his way back to the parsonage.

That night before he went to bed he wrote a letter to his uncle, as to which he said not a word to either his father, or mother, or sisters. He thought that the letter was a good letter, and would have been proud to show it; but he feared that either his father or his mother would advise him not to send it, and he was ashamed to read it to Molly. He therefore sent the letter across the park the next morning by the gardener.

The letter was as follows:

'MY DEAR UNCLE,

'My father has shown me your letter to him, and, of course, I feel it incumbent on me to take some notice of it. Not wishing to trouble you with a letter I called this morning, but I was told by Matthew that you would not see me. As you have expressed yourself to my father very severely as to my conduct, I am sure you will agree with me that I ought not to let the matter pass by without making my own defence.

'You say that there was a row in the streets between Mountjoy Scarborough and myself in which he was "left for dead." When I left him I did not think he had been much hurt, nor have I had reason to think so since. He had attacked me, and I had simply defended myself. He had come upon me by surprise; and, when I had shaken him off, I went away. Then in a day or two he had disappeared. Had he been killed, or much hurt, the world would have heard of it; but the world simply heard that he had disappeared, which could hardly have been the case had he been much hurt.

'Then you say that I denied in conversation with Augustus Scarborough that I had seen his brother on the night in question. I did deny it. Augustus Scarborough, who was evidently well acquainted with the whole transaction, and who had, I believe, assisted his brother in disappearing, wished to learn from me what I had done, and to hide what he had done. He wished to saddle me with the disgrace of his brother's departure, and I did not choose to fall into his trap. At the moment of his asking me he knew that his brother was safe. I think that the word "lie," as used by you, is very severe for such an occurrence. A man is not generally held to be bound to tell everything respecting himself to the first person that shall ask him. If you will ask any man who knows the world, —my father for instance,—I think you will be told that such conduct was not faulty.

'But it is at any rate necessary that I should ask you what you intend to do in reference to my future life. I am told that you intend to stop the income which I have hitherto received. Will this be considerate on your part?' (In his first copy of the letter Harry had asked whether it would be 'fair,' and had then changed the word for one that was milder.) 'When I took my degree you yourself said that it would not be necessary that I should go into any profession, because you would allow me an income, and would then provide for me. I took your advice, in opposition to my father's, because it seemed then that I was to depend on you rather than on him. You cannot deny that I shall have been treated hardly if I now be turned loose upon the world.

'I shall be happy to come and see you if you shall wish it, so as to save you the trouble of writing to me. Your affectionate nephew,

'HENRY ANNESLEY.'

Harry might have been sure that his uncle would not see him,—probably was sure when he added the last paragraph. Mr. Prosper enjoyed greatly two things: the mysticism of being invisible, and the opportunity of writing a letter. Mr. Prosper had not a large correspondence, but it was laborious, and, as he thought, effective. He believed that he did know how to write a letter, and he went about it with a will. It was not probable that he would make himself common by seeing his nephew on such an occasion, or that he would omit the opportunity of spending an entire morning with pen and ink. The result was very short, but to his idea it was satisfactory.

'Sir,' he began. He considered this matter very deeply; but as the entire future of his own life was concerned in it, he felt that it became him to be both grave and severe.

'I have received your letter and have read it with attention. I observe that you admit that you told Mr. Augustus Scarborough a deliberate untruth. This is what the plain-speaking world, when it wishes to be understood as using the unadorned English language, which is always the language I prefer myself, calls a lie;—a LIE! I do not choose that this humble property shall fall at my death in the hands of A LIAR. Therefore I shall take steps to prevent it,—which may or may not be successful.

'As such steps, whatever may be their result, are to be taken, the income—intended to prepare you for another alternative, which may possibly not now be forthcoming—will naturally now be no longer allowed.

'I am, sir, your obedient servant,
'PETER PROSPER.'

The first effect of the letter was to produce laughter at the rectory. Harry could not but show it to his father, and in an hour or two it became known to his mother and sister, and, under an oath of secrecy, to Joshua Thoroughbung. It could not be matter of laughter when the future hopes of Miss Matilda Thoroughbung were taken into consideration.

'I declare I don't know what you are all laughing about,' said Kate, 'except that Uncle Peter does use such comical phrases.' But Mrs. Annesley, though the most good-hearted woman in the world, was almost angry. 'I don't know what you all see to laugh at in it. Peter has in his hands the power of making or marring Harry's future.'

'But he hasn't,' said Harry.

'Or he mayn't have,' said the rector.

'It's all in the hands of the Almighty,' said Mrs. Annesley, who felt herself bound to retire from the room and to take her daughter with her.

But, when they were alone, both the father and his son were very angry. 'I have done with him for ever,' said Harry. 'Let what come what may, I will never see him or speak to him again. A "lie," and "liar"! He has written those words in that way so as to salve his own conscience for the injustice he is doing. He knows that I am not a liar. He cannot understand what a liar means, or he would know that he is one himself.'

'A man seldom has such knowledge as that.'

'Is it not so when he stigmatises me in this way merely as an excuse to himself? He wants to be rid of me,—probably because I did not sit and hear him read the sermons. Let that pass. I may have been wrong in that, and he may be justified, but because of that he cannot believe really that I have been a liar,—a liar in such a determined way as to make me unfit to be his heir.'

'He is a fool, Harry. That is the worst of him.'

'I don't think it is the worst.'

'You cannot have worse. It is dreadful to have to depend on a fool,—to have to trust to a man who cannot tell wrong from right. Your uncle intends to be a good man. If it were brought home to him that he were doing a wrong he would not do it. He would not rob; he would not steal; he must not commit murder, and the rest of it. But he is a fool, and he does not know when he is doing these things.'

'I will wash my hands of him.'

'Yes; and he will wash his hands of you. You do not know him as I do. He has taken it into his silly head that you are the chief of sinners because you said what was not true to that man, who seems really to be the sinner, and nothing will eradicate the idea. He will go and marry that woman because he thinks that in that way he can best carry his purpose, and then he will repent at leisure. I used to tell you that you had better listen to the sermons.'

'And now I must pay for it.'

'Well! my boy, it is no good crying for spilt milk. As I was saying just now there is nothing worse than a fool.'

Chapter XXVI

MARMADUKE LODGE

ON the seventh of next month two things occurred each of great importance. Hunting commenced in the Puckeridge country, and Harry with that famous mare Belladonna was there. And Squire Prosper was driven in his carriage into Buntingford, and made his offer with all due formality to Miss Thoroughbung. The whole household, including Matthew, and the cook, and the coachman, and the boy, and the two housemaids, knew what he was going to do. It would be difficult to say how they knew, because he was a man who had never told anything. He was the last man in England who, on such a matter, would have made a confidant of his butler. He never spoke to a servant about matters unconnected with their service. He considered that to do so would be altogether against his dignity. Nevertheless, when he ordered his carriage, which he did not do very frequently at this time of the year, when the horses were wanted on the farm,—and of which he gave twenty-four hours' notice to all the persons concerned; and when early in the morning he ordered that his Sunday suit should be prepared for wearing, and when his aspect grew more and more serious as the hours drew nigh,—it was well understood by them all that he was going to make the offer that day.

He was both proud and fearful as to the thing to be done,—proud that he, the squire of Buston, should be called on to take so important a step; proud by anticipation of his feelings, as he would return home a jolly thriving wooer,—and yet a little fearful lest he might not succeed. Were he to fail, the failure would be horrible to him. He knew that every man and woman about the place would know all about it. Among the secrets of the family there was a story, never now mentioned, of his having done the same thing once before. He was then a young man, about twenty-five, and he had come forth to lay himself and Buston at the feet of a baronet's daughter who lived some twenty-five miles off. She was very beautiful, and was said to have a fitting dower; but he had come back,—and had shut himself up in the house for a week afterwards. To no human ears had he ever since spoken of his interview with Miss Courteney. The doings of that day had been wrapped in impenetrable darkness. But all Buston and the neighbouring parishes had known that Miss Courteney had refused him. Since that day he had never gone forth again on such a mission.

There were those who said of him that his love had been so deep and enduring that he had never got the better of it. Miss Courteney had been married to a much grander lover, and had been taken off to splendid circles. But he had never mentioned her name. That story of his abiding love was thoroughly believed by his sister, who used to tell it of him to his credit when at the rectory the rector would declare him to be a fool. But the rector used to say that he was dumb from pride, or that he could not bear to have it known that he had failed at anything. At any rate he had never again attempted love, and had formally declared to his sister that, as he did not intend to marry, Harry should be regarded as his son. Then at last had come the fellowship, and he had been proud of his heir, thinking that in some way he had won the fellowship himself, as he had paid the bills. But now all was altered, and he was to go forth to his wooing again.

There had been a rumour about the country that he was already accepted; but such was not the case. He had never even asked. He had fluttered about Buntingford, thinking of it; but he had never put the question. To his thinking it would not have been becoming to do so without some ceremony. Buston was not to be made away with during the turnings of a quadrille or as a part of an ordinary conversation. It was not probable, nay, it was impossible, that he should mention the subject to anyone; but still he must visibly prepare for it, and I think that he was aware that the world around him knew what he was about.

And the Thoroughbungs knew, and Miss Matilda Thoroughbung knew well. All Buntingford knew. In those old days in which he had sought the hand of the baronet's daughter, the baronet's daughter and the baronet's wife, and the baronet himself, had known what was coming, though Mr. Prosper thought that the secret dwelt alone in his own bosom. Nor did he dream now that Harry and Harry's father, and Harry's mother and sisters, had all laughed at the conspicuous gravity of his threat. It was the general feeling on the subject which made the rumour current that the deed had been done. But when he came downstairs with one new grey kid-glove on, and the other dangling in his hand, nothing had been done.

'Drive to Buntingford,' said the squire.

'Yes, sir,' said Matthew, the door of the carriage in his hand.

'To Marmaduke Lodge.'

'Yes, sir.' Then Matthew told the coachman, who had heard the instructions very plainly, and knew them before he had heard them. The squire threw himself back in the carriage, and applied himself to wondering how he should do the deed. He had, in truth, barely studied the words; but not at all the manner of delivering them. With his bare hand up to his eyes so that he might hold the glove unsoiled in the other, he devoted his intellect to the task; nor did he withdraw his hand till the carriage turned in at the gate. The drive up to the door of Marmaduke Lodge was very short, and he had barely time to arrange his waistcoat and his whiskers before the carriage stood still. He was soon told that Miss Thoroughbung was at home, and within a moment he found himself absolutely standing on the carpet in her presence.

Report had dealt unkindly with Miss Thoroughbung in the matter of her age. Report always does deal unkindly with unmarried young women who have ceased to be girls. There is an idea that they will wish to make themselves out to be younger than they are, and therefore report makes them older. She had been called forty-five and even fifty. Her exact age at this moment was forty-two; and as Mr. Prosper was only fifty there was no discrepancy in the marriage. He would have been young-looking for his age, but for an air of ancient dandyism which had grown upon him. He was somewhat dry, too, and skinny, with high cheek-bones and large dull eyes. But he was clean, and grave, and orderly,—a man promising well to a lady on the look-out for a husband. Miss Thoroughbung was fat, fair, and forty to the letter, and she had a just measure of her own good looks, of which she was not unconscious. But she was specially conscious of twenty-five thousand pounds, the possession of which had hitherto stood in the way of her search after a husband. It was said commonly about Buntingford that she looked too high, seeing that she was only a Thoroughbung and had no more than twenty-five thousand pounds.

But Miss Tickle was in the room, and might have been said to be in the way, were it not that a little temporary relief was felt by Mr. Prosper to be a comfort. Miss Tickle was at any rate twenty years older than Miss Thoroughbung, and was of all slaves at the same time the humblest and the most irritating.

She never asked for anything, but was always paint-ing the picture of her own deserts. 'I hope I have the pleasure of seeing Miss Tickle quite well,' said the squire, as soon as he had paid his first compliments to the lady of his love.

'Thank you, Mr. Prosper; pretty well. My anxiety is all for Matilda.' Matilda had been Matilda to her since she had been a little girl, and Miss Tickle was not going now to drop the advantage which the old intimacy gave her.

'I trust there is no cause for it.'

'Well, I'm not so sure. She coughed a little last night, and would not eat her supper. We always do have a little supper. A despatched crab it was; and when she would not eat it I knew there was something wrong.'

'Nonsense! What a fuss you make! Well, Mr. Prosper, have you seen your nephew yet?'

'No, Miss Thoroughbung; nor do I intend to see him. The young man has disgraced himself.'

'Dear, dear; how sad!'

'Young men do disgrace themselves, I fear, very often,' said Miss Tickle.

'We won't talk about it, if you please, because it is a family affair.'

'Oh no,' said Miss Thoroughbung.

'At least, not as yet. It may be,—but never mind; I would not wish to be premature in anything.'

'I am always telling Matilda so. She is so im-pulsive. But as you may have matters of business, Mr. Prosper, on which to speak to Miss Thorough-bung, I will retire.'

'It is very thoughtful on your part, Miss Tickle.'

Then Miss Tickle retired, from which it may be surmised that the probable circumstances of the inter-view had been already discussed between the ladies. Mr. Prosper drew a long breath, and sighed audibly, as soon as he was alone with the object of his affec-tions. He wondered whether men were ever bright and jolly in such circumstances. He sighed again, and then he began: 'Miss Thoroughbung!'

'Mr. Prosper!'

All the prepared words had flown from his memory. He could not even bethink himself how he ought to begin. And, unfortunately, so much must depend upon manner! But the property was unembarrassed, and Miss Thoroughbung thought it probable that she might be allowed to do what she would with her own money. She had turned it all over to the right and to the left, and she was quite minded to accept him. With this view she had told Miss Tickle to leave the room, and she now felt that she was bound to give the gentleman what help might be in her power. 'Oh, Miss Thoroughbung!' he said.

'Mr. Prosper, you and I are such good friends, that—that—that——'

'Yes, indeed. You can have no more true friend than I am. Not even Miss Tickle.'

'Oh, bother Miss Tickle! Miss Tickle is very well.'

'Exactly so. Miss Tickle is very well; a most estimable person.'

'We'll leave her alone just at present.'

'Yes, certainly. We had better leave her alone in our present conversation. Not but what I have a strong regard for her.' Mr. Prosper had surely not thought of the opening he might be giving as to a future career for Miss Tickle by such an assertion.

'So have I for the matter of that, but we'll drop her just now.' Then she paused, but he paused also. 'You have come over today probably in order that you might congratulate them at the brewery on the marriage with one of your family.' Then Mr. Prosper frowned; but she did not care for his frowning. 'It will not be a bad match for the young lady, as Joshua is fairly steady, and the brewery is worth money.'

'I could have wished him a better brother-in-law,'

said the lover, who was taken away from the consideration of his love by the allusion to the Annesleys.
He had thought of all that, and in the dearth of fitting
objects of affection had resolved to endure the drawback of the connection. But it had for a while weighed
very seriously with him, so that had the twenty-five
thousand pounds been twenty thousand pounds, he
might have taken himself to Miss Puffle, who lived
near Saffron Walden, and who would own Smickham
Manor when her father died. The property was said
to be involved, and Miss Puffle was certainly forty-
eight. As an heir was the great desideratum, he had
resolved that Matilda Thoroughbung should be the
lady in spite of the evils attending the new connection. He did feel that in throwing over Harry he
would have to abandon all the Annesleys, and to
draw a line between himself with Miss Thoroughbung and the whole family of the Thoroughbungs
generally.

'You mustn't be too bitter against poor Molly,'
said Miss Thoroughbung.

Mr. Prosper did not like to be called bitter, and in
spite of the importance of the occasion, could not but
show that he did not like it. 'I don't think that we
need talk about it.'

'Oh! dear no. Kate and Miss Tickle need neither
be talked about.' Mr. Prosper disliked all familiarity,
and especially that of being laughed at, but Miss
Thoroughbung did laugh. So he drew himself up,
and dangled his glove more slowly than before.
'Then you were not going on to congratulate them
at the brewery?'

'Certainly not.'

'I did not know.'

'My purpose carries me no farther than Marmaduke Lodge. I have no desire to see anyone today
besides Miss Thoroughbung.'

'That is a compliment.'

Then his memory suddenly brought back to him

one of his composed sentences. 'In beholding Miss Thoroughbung I behold her on whom I hope I may depend for all the future happiness of my life.' He did feel that it had come in the right place. It had been intended to be said immediately after her acceptance of him. But it did very well where it was. It expressed, as he assured himself, the feelings of his heart, and must draw from her some declaration of hers.

'Goodness gracious me, Mr. Prosper.'

This sort of coyness was to have been expected, and he therefore continued with another portion of his prepared words, which now came glibly enough to him. But it was a previous portion. It was all the same to Miss Thoroughbung, as it declared plainly the gentleman's intention. 'If I can induce you to listen to me favourably, I shall say of myself that I am the happiest gentleman in Hertfordshire.'

'Oh, Mr. Prosper!'

'My purpose is to lay at your feet my hand, my heart, and the lands of Buston.' Here he was again going backwards, but it did not matter much now in what sequence the words were said. The offer had been thoroughly completed and was thoroughly understood.

'A lady, Mr. Prosper, has to think of these things,' said Miss Thoroughbung.

'Of course I would not wish to hurry you prematurely to any declaration of your affections.'

'But there are other considerations, Mr. Prosper. You know about my property?'

'Nothing particularly. It has not been a matter of consideration with me.' This he said with some slight air of offence. He was a gentleman, whereas Miss Thoroughbung was hardly a lady. Matter of consideration her money of course had been. How should he not consider it? But he was aware that he ought not to rush on that subject, but should leave it to the arrangement of lawyers, expressing his own views through her own lawyer. To her it was the thing of most importance, and she had no feelings which induced her to be silent on a matter so near to her. She rushed.

'But it has to be considered, Mr. Prosper. It is all my own, and comes to very nearly one thousand a year. I think it is nine hundred and seventy-two pounds six shillings and eightpence. Of course when there is so much money it would have to be tied up somehow.' Mr. Prosper was undoubtedly disgusted, and if he could have receded at this moment would have transferred his affections to Miss Puffle. 'Of course you understand that.'

She had not accepted him as yet, nor said a word of her regard for him. All that went, it seemed, as a matter of no importance whatever. He had been standing for the last few minutes, and now he remained standing and looking at her. They were both silent, so that he was obliged to speak. 'I understand that between a lady and gentleman so circumstanced there should be a settlement.'

'Just so.'

'I also have some property,' said Mr. Prosper with a touch of pride in his tone.

'Of course you have. Goodness gracious me! why else would you come? You have got Buston, which I suppose is two thousand a year. At any rate it has that name. But it isn't your own?'

'Not my own?'

'Well, no. You couldn't leave it to your widow, so that she might give it to anyone she pleased when you were gone.' Here the gentleman frowned very darkly, and thought that after all Miss Puffle would be the woman for him. 'All that has to be considered, and it makes Buston not exactly your own. If I were to have a daughter she wouldn't have it.'

'No, not a daughter,' said Mr. Prosper, still wondering at the thorough knowledge of the business in hand displayed by the lady.

'Oh! if it were to be a son, that would be all right, and then my money would go to the younger children, divided equally between boys and girls.' Mr. Prosper shook his head as he found himself suddenly provided with so plentiful and thriving a family. 'That, I suppose, would be the way of the settlement, together with a certain income out of Buston set apart for my use. It ought to be considered that I should have to provide a house to live in. This belongs to my brother, and I pay him forty pounds a year for it. It should be something better than this.'

'My dear Miss Thoroughbung, the lawyer would do all that.' There did come upon him an idea that she, with her aptitude for business, would not be altogether a bad helpmate.

'The lawyers are very well; but in a transaction of this kind there is nothing like the principals understanding each other. Young women are always robbed when their money is left altogether to the gentlemen.'

'Robbed!'

'Don't suppose I mean you, Mr. Prosper; and the robbery I mean is not considered disgraceful at all. The gentlemen I mean are the fathers and the brothers, and the uncles and the lawyers. And they intend to do right after the custom of their fathers and uncles. But woman's rights are coming up.'

'I hate woman's rights.'

'Nevertheless they are coming up. A young woman doesn't get taken in as she used to do. I don't mean any offence, you know.' This was said in reply to Mr. Prosper's repeated frown. 'Since woman's rights have come up a young woman is better able to fight her own battle.'

Mr. Prosper was willing to admit that Miss Thoroughbung was fair, but she was fat also, and at least forty. There was hardly need that she should refer so often to her own unprotected youth. 'I should like

to have the spending of my own income, Mr. Prosper;
—that's a fact.'

'Oh, indeed!'

'Yes, I should. I shouldn't care to have to go to
my husband if I wanted to buy a pair of stockings.'

'An allowance, I should say.'

'And what should be my own income.'

'Nothing to go to the house?'

'Oh, yes! There might be certain things which
I might agree to pay for. A pair of ponies I should
like.'

'I always keep a carriage and a pair of horses.' ,

'But the ponies would be my look-out. I shouldn't
mind paying for my own maid, and the champagne,
and my clothes, of course, and the fishmonger's bill.
There would be Miss Tickle, too. You said you
would like Miss Tickle. I should have to pay for her.
That would be about enough, I think.'

Mr. Prosper was thoroughly disgusted; but when
he left Marmaduke Lodge he had not said a word as
to withdrawing from his offer. She declared that she
would put her terms into writing and give them to
her lawyer, who would communicate with Mr. Grey.
Mr. Prosper was surprised to find that she knew the
name of his lawyer, who was in truth our old friend.
And then, while he was still hesitating, she astounded
—nay, shocked him—by her mode of ending the con-
ference. She got up, and throwing her arms round
his neck, kissed him most affectionately. After that
there was no retreating for Mr. Prosper, no immediate mode of retreat, at all events. He could only
back out of the room, and get into his carriage, and
be carried home as quickly as possible.

Chapter XXVII

THE PROPOSAL

IT had never happened to him before. The first thought that came upon Mr. Prosper, when he got into his carriage, was that it had never occurred to him before. He did not reflect that he had not put himself in the way of it; but now the strangeness of the sensation overwhelmed him. He inquired of himself whether it was pleasant, but he found himself compelled to answer the question with a negative. It should have come from him, but not yet; not yet, probably for some weeks. But it had been done, and by the doing of it she had sealed him utterly as her own. There was no getting out of it now. He did feel that he ought not to attempt to get out of it after what had taken place. He was not sure but that the lady had planned it all with that purpose; but he was sure that a strong foundation had been laid for a breach of promise case if he were to attempt to escape. What might not a jury do against him, giving damages out of the acres of Buston Hall? And then Miss Thoroughbung would go over to the other Thoroughbungs and to the Annesleys, and his condition would become intolerable. In some moments as he was driven home he was not sure but that it had all been got up as a plot against him by the Annesleys.

When he got out of his carriage Matthew knew that things had gone badly with his master. But he could not conjecture in what way. The matter had been fully debated in the kitchen, and it had been there decided that Miss Thoroughbung was certainly to be brought home as the future mistress of Buston. The step to be taken by their master was not popular in the Buston kitchen. It had been there considered that Master Harry was to be the future master, and, by some perversity of intellect they had all thought that this would occur soon. Matthew was much older than the squire, who was hardly to be called a sickly man, and yet Matthew had made up his mind that Mr. Harry was to reign over him as squire of Buston. When, therefore, the tidings came that Miss Thoroughbung was to be brought to Buston as the mistress, there had been some slight symptoms of rebellion. 'They didn't want any 'Tilda Thoroughbung there.' They had their own idea of a lady and gentleman, which, as in all such cases, was perfectly correct. They knew the squire to be a fool, but they believed him to be a gentleman. They heard that Miss Thoroughbung was a clever woman, but they did not believe her to be a lady. Matthew had said a few words to the cook as to a public-house at Stevenage. She had told him not to be an old fool, and that he would lose his money, but she had thought of the public-house. There had been a mutinous feeling. Matthew helped his master out of the carriage, and then came a revulsion. That 'froth of a beer-barrel,' as Matthew had dared to call her, had absolutely refused his master.

Mr. Prosper went into the house very meditative, and sad at heart. It was a matter almost of regret to him that it had not been as Matthew supposed. But he was caught and bound and must make the best of it. He thought of all the particulars of her proposed mode of living, and recapitulated them to himself. A pair of ponies, her own maid, champagne, the fishmonger's bill, and Miss Tickle. Miss Puffle would certainly not have required such expensive luxuries. Champagne and the fish would require company for their final consumption. The ponies assumed a tone of being quite opposed to that which he had contemplated. He questioned with himself whether he would like Miss Tickle as a perpetual inmate. He had, in sheer civility, expressed a liking for Miss Tickle; but what need could there be to a married woman of a Miss Tickle? And then he thought of the education of the five or six children which she had almost promised him! He had suggested to himself simply an heir—just one heir—so that the nefarious Harry might be cut out. He already saw that he would not be enriched to the extent of a shilling by the lady's income. Then there would be all the trouble and the disgrace of a separate purse. He felt that there would be disgrace in having the fish and the champagne which were consumed in his own house paid for by his wife without reference to him. What if the lady had a partiality for champagne? He knew nothing about it, and would know nothing about it, except when he saw it in her heightened colour. Despatched crabs for supper! He always went to bed at ten, and had a tumbler of barley-water brought to him,— a glass of barley-water with just a squeeze of lemon-juice.

He saw ruin before him. No doubt she was a good manager, but she would be a good manager for herself. Would it not be better for him to stand the action for breach of promise, and betake himself to Miss Puffle? But Miss Puffle was fifty, and there could be no doubt that the lady ought to be younger than the gentleman. He was much distressed in mind. If he broke off with Miss Thoroughbung, ought he to do so at once, before she had had time to put the matter into the hands of the lawyer? And on what plea should he do it? Before he went to bed that night he did draw out a portion of a letter, which, however, was never sent.

'MY DEAR MISS THOROUGHBUNG,

'In the views which we both promulgated this morning I fear that there was some essential misunderstanding as to the mode of life which had occurred to both of us. You, as was natural at your age, and with all your charms, have not been slow to anticipate a coming period of unchequered delights. Your allusion to a pony-carriage, and other incidental allusions,'—he did not think it well to mention more particularly the fish and champagne—'have made clear the sort of future life which you have pictured to yourself. Heaven forbid that I should take upon myself to find fault with anything so pleasant and so innocent! But my prospects of life are different, and in seeking the honour of an alliance with you I was looking for a quiet companion in my declining years, and it might be also for a mother to a possible future son. When you honoured me with an unmistakable sign of your affection on my going, I was just about to explain all this. You must excuse me if my mouth was then stopped by the mutual ardour of our feeling. I was about to say——' But he had found it difficult to explain what he had been about to say, and on the next morning when the time for writing had come, he heard news which detained him for the day, and then the opportunity was gone.

On the following morning when Matthew appeared at his bedside with his cup of tea at nine o'clock, tidings were brought him. He took in the Bunting-ford Gazette, which came twice a week, and as Matthew laid it, opened and unread, in its accustomed place, he gave the information, which he had no doubt gotten from the paper. 'You haven't heard it, sir, I suppose, as yet?'

'Heard what?'

'About Miss Puffle.'

'What about Miss Puffle? I haven't heard a word. What about Miss Puffle?' He had been thinking that moment of Miss Puffle,—of how she would be superior to Miss Thoroughbung in many ways. So that he sat up in his bed, holding the untasted tea in his hand.

'She's gone off with young Farmer Tazlehurst.'

'Miss Puffle gone off, and with her father's tenant's son!'

'Yes, indeed, sir. She and her father have been quarrelling for the last ten years, and now she's off.

She was always riding and roystering about the country with them dogs and them men; and now she's gone.'

'Oh, Heavens!' exclaimed the squire, thinking of his own escape.

'Yes, indeed, sir. There's no knowing what any of them is up to. Unless they gets married afore they're thirty, or thirty-five at most, they're most sure to get such ideas into their head as no one can mostly approve.' This had been intended by Matthew as a word of caution to his master, but had really the opposite effect. He resolved at the moment that the latter should not be said of Miss Thoroughbung.

And he turned Matthew out of the room with a flea in his ear. 'How dare you to speak in that way of your betters? Mr. Puffle, the lady's father, has for many years been my friend. I am not saying anything of the lady, nor saying that she has done right. Of course, downstairs, in the servants'-hall, you can say what you please; but up here, in my presence, you should not speak in such language of a lady behind whose chair you may be called upon to wait.'

'Very well, sir; I won't no more,' said Matthew, retiring with mock humility. But he had shot his bolt, and he supposed successfully. He did not know what had taken place between his master and Miss Thoroughbung; but he did think that his speech might assist in preventing a repetition of the offer.

Miss Puffle gone off with the tenant's son! The news made matrimony doubly dangerous to him, and yet robbed him of the chief reason by which he was to have been driven to send her a letter. He could not, at any rate, now fall back upon Miss Puffle. And he thought that nothing would have induced Miss Thoroughbung to go off with one of the carters from the brewery. Whatever faults she might have they did not lie in that direction. Champagne and ponies were, as faults, less deleterious.

Miss Puffle gone off with young Tazlehurst; a

lady of fifty with a young man of twenty-five! And she the reputed heiress of Smickham Manor! It was a comfort to him as he remembered that Smickham Manor had been bought no longer ago than by the father of the present owner. The Prospers had been at Buston ever since the time of George the First. You cannot make a silk purse out of a sow's ear. He had been ever assuring himself of that fact, which was now more of a fact than ever. And fifty years old! It was quite shocking. With a steady middle-aged man like himself, and with the approval of her family, marriage might have been thought of. But with this harum-scarum young tenant's son, who was in no respect a gentleman, whose only thought was of galloping over hedges and ditches, such an idea showed a state of mind which,—well,—absolutely disgusted him. Mr. Prosper, because he had grown old himself, could not endure to think that others, at his age, should retain a smack of their youth. There are ladies, besides Miss Puffle, who like to ride across the country with a young man before them, or perhaps following; and never think much of their fifty years.

But the news certainly brought to him a great change of feeling,—so that the letter to which he had devoted the preceding afternoon was put back into the letter-case, and was never finished. And his mind immediately recurred to Miss Thoroughbung, and he bethought himself that the objection which he felt was, perhaps, in part frivolous. At any rate she was a better woman than Miss Puffle. She certainly would run after no farmer's son. Though she might be fond of champagne, it was, he thought, chiefly for other people. Though she was ambitious of ponies, the ambition might be checked. At any rate she could pay for her own ponies, whereas Mr. Puffle was a very hale old man of seventy. Puffle, he told himself, had married young, and might live for the next ten years, or twenty. To Mr. Prosper, whose imagination did not fly far afield, the world afforded at present but two ladies. These were Miss Puffle and Miss Thoroughbung, and as Miss Puffle had fallen out of the running, there seemed to be a walk over for Miss Thoroughbung.

He did think, during the two or three days which passed without any further step on his part,—he did think how it might be were he to remain unmarried. As regarded his own comfort, he was greatly tempted. Life would remain so easy to him! But then duty demanded of him that he should marry, and he was a man who, in honest sober talk, thought much of his duty. He was absurdly credulous, and as obstinate as a mule. But he did wish to do what was right. He had been convinced that Harry Annesley was a false knave, and had been made to swear an oath that Harry should not be his heir. Harry had been draped in the blackest colours, and to each daub of black something darker had been added by his uncle's memory of those neglected sermons. It was now his first duty in life to beget an heir, and for that purpose a wife must be had.

Putting aside the ponies and the champagne,—and the despatched crab, the sound of which, as coming to him from Miss Tickle's mouth, was uglier than the other sounds,—he still thought that Miss Thoroughbung would answer his purpose. From her side there would not be the making of a silk purse; but then 'the boy' would be his boy as well as hers, and would probably take more after the father. He passed much of these days with the Peerage*in his hand, and satisfied himself that the best blood had been maintained frequently by second-rate marriages. Health was a great thing. Health in the mother was everything. Who could be more healthy than Miss Thoroughbung? Then he thought of that warm embrace. Perhaps, after all, it was right that she should embrace him after what he had said to her.

Three days only had passed by, and he was still

thinking what ought to be his next step, when there
came to him a letter from Messrs. Soames and Simpson, attorneys in Buntingford. He had heard of
Messrs. Soames and Simpson, had been familiar with
their names for the last twenty years, but had never
dreamed that his own private affairs should become
a matter of consultation in their office. Messrs. Grey
and Barry, of Lincoln's Inn, were his lawyers, who
were quite gentlemen. He knew nothing against
Messrs. Soames and Simpson, but he thought that
their work consisted generally in the recovery of
local debts. Messrs. Soames and Simpson now wrote
to him with full details as to his future life. Their
client, Miss Thoroughbung, had communicated to
them his offer of marriage. They were acquainted
with all the lady's circumstances, and she had asked
them for their advice. They had proposed to her that
the use of her own income should be by deed left to
herself. Some proportion of it should go into the
house, and might be made matter of agreement.
They suggested that an annuity of a thousand pounds
a year, in shape of dower, should be secured to their
client in the event of her outliving Mr. Prosper. The
estate, should, of course, be settled on the eldest child.
The mother's property should be equally divided
among the other children. Buston Hall should be
the residence of the widow till the eldest son should
be twenty-four, after which Mr. Prosper would no
doubt feel that their client would have to provide a
home for herself. Messrs. Soames and Simpson did
not think that there was anything in this to which
Mr. Prosper would object, and if this were so, they
would immediately prepare the settlement. 'That
woman didn't say against it, after all,' said Matthew
to himself as he gave the letter from the lawyers to
his master.

The letter made Mr. Prosper very angry. It did,
in truth, contain nothing more than a repetition of
the very terms which the lady had herself suggested;

but coming to him through these local lawyers, it was doubly distasteful. What was he to do? He felt it to be out of the question to accede at once. Indeed, he had a strong repugnance to putting himself into communication with the Buntingford lawyers. Had the matter been other than it was, he would have gone to the rector for advice. The rector generally advised him. But that was out of the question now. He had seen his sister once since his visit to Buntingford, but had said nothing to her about it. Indeed, he had been anything but communicative, so that Mrs. Annesley had been forced to leave him with a feeling almost of offence. There was no help to be had in that quarter, and he could only write to Mr. Grey, and ask that gentleman to assist him in his difficulties.

He did write to Mr. Grey, begging for his immediate attention. 'There is that fool Prosper going to marry a brewer's daughter down at Buntingford,' said Mr. Grey to his daughter.

'He's sixty years old.'

'No, my love. He looks it, but he's only fifty. A man at fifty is supposed to be young enough to marry. There's a nephew who has been brought up as his heir; that's the hard part of it. And the nephew is mixed up in some way with the Scarboroughs.'

'Is it he who is to marry that young lady?'

'I think it is. And now there's some devil's play going on. I've got nothing to do with it.'

'But you will have?'

'Not a turn. Mr. Prosper can marry if he likes it. They have sent him most abominable proposals as to the lady's money; and as to her jointure, I must stop that if I can, though I suppose he is not such a fool as to give way.'

'Is he soft?'

'Well, not exactly. He likes his own money. But he's a gentleman, and wants nothing but what is or ought to be his own.'

'There are but few like that now.'

'It's true of him. But then he does not know what is his own, or what ought to be. He's almost the biggest fool I have ever known, and will do an injustice to that boy simply from ignorance.' Then he drafted his letter to Mr. Prosper, and gave it to Dolly to read. 'That's what I shall propose. The clerk can put it into proper language. He must offer less than he means to give.'

'Is that honest, father?'

'It's honest on my part, knowing the people with whom I have to deal. If I were to lay down the strict minimum which he should grant, he would add other things which would cause him to act not in accordance with my advice. I have to make allowance for his folly,—a sort of windage*which is not dishonest. Had he referred her lawyers to me, I could have been as hard and honest as you please.' All of which did not quite satisfy Dolly's strict ideas of integrity.

But the terms proposed were that the lady's means should be divided so that one half should go to herself for her own personal expenses, and the other half to her husband for the use of the house; that the lady should put up with a jointure of two hundred and fifty pounds, which ought to suffice when joined to her own property, and that the settlement among the children should be as recommended by Messrs. Soames and Simpson.

'And if there are not any children, papa?'

'Then each will receive his or her own property.'

'Because it may be so.'

'Certainly, my dear; very probably.'

Chapter XXVIII

MR. HARKAWAY

WHEN the first Monday in November came Harry was still living at the rectory. Indeed, what other home had he in which to live? Other friends had become shy of him besides his uncle. He had been accustomed to receive many invitations. Young men, who are the heirs to properties, and are supposed to be rich because they are idle, do get themselves asked about, here and there—and think a great deal of themselves in consequence. 'There's young Jones. He is fairly good-looking, but hasn't a word to say for himself. He will do to pair off with Miss Smith, who'll talk for a dozen. He can't hit a haystack, but he's none the worse for that. We haven't got too many pheasants. He'll be sure to come when you ask him—and he'll be sure to go.' So Jones is asked, and considers himself to be the most popular man in London. I will not say that Harry's invitations had been of exactly that description; but he too had considered himself to be popular, and now greatly felt the withdrawal of such marks of friendship. He had received one 'put off,'—from the Ingoldsbys of Kent. Early in June, he had promised to be there in November. The youngest Miss Ingoldsby was very pretty, and he, no doubt, had been gracious. She knew that he had meant nothing,— could have meant nothing. But he might come to mean something, and had been most pressingly asked. In September there came a letter to him to say that the room intended for him at Ingoldsby had been burnt down. Mrs. Ingoldsby was so extremely sorry,—and so were the 'girls!' Harry could trace it all up. The Ingoldsbys knew the Greens, and Mrs. Green was sister to Septimus Jones, who was absolutely the slave—the slave, as Harry said, repeating the word to himself, with emphasis—of Augustus Scarborough. He was very unhappy, not that he cared in the least for Miss Ingoldsby, but that he began to be conscious that he was to be dropped.

He was to be taken up, on the other hand, by Joshua Thoroughbung. Alas! alas! though he smiled and resolved to accept his brother-in-law with a good heart, this did not in the least salve the wound. His own county was to him less than other counties, and his own neighbourhood less than other neighbourhoods. Buntingford was full of Thoroughbungs, the best people in the world, but not quite up to what he believed to be his mark. Mr. Prosper himself was the stupidest ass! At Welwyn, people smelt of the City. At Stevenage, the parson's set began. Baldock was a 'caput mortuum'*of dulness. Royston was alive only on market days. Of his own father's house, and even of his mother and sisters, he entertained ideas that savoured a little of depreciation. But, to redeem him from this fault,—a fault which would have led to the absolute ruin of his character had it not been redeemed and at last cured,—there was a consciousness of his own vanity and weakness. 'My father is worth a dozen of them, and my mother and sisters two dozen,' he would say of the Ingoldsbys when he went to bed in the room which was to be burned down in preparation for his exile. And he believed it. They were honest; they were unselfish; they were unpretending. His sister Molly was not above owning that her young brewer was all the world to her; a fine honest bouncing girl, who said her prayers with a meaning, thanked the Lord for giving her Joshua, and laughed so loud that you could hear her out of the rectory garden half across the park. Harry knew that they were good, did in his heart know that where the parsons begin the good things were likely to begin also.

He was in this state of mind, the hand of good pulling one way and the devil's pride the other, when

young Thoroughbung called for him one morning to
carry him on to Cumberlow Green. Cumberlow
Green was a popular meet in that county, where
meets have not much to make them popular except
the good-humour of those who form the hunt. It is
not a county either pleasant or easy to ride over, and
a Puckeridge fox is surely the most ill-mannered of
foxes. But the Puckeridge men are gracious to
strangers, and fairly so among themselves. It is
more than can be said of Leicestershire, where sportsmen ride in brilliant boots and breeches, but with
their noses turned supernaturally into the air. 'Come
along; we've four miles to do, and only twenty
minutes to do it in. Holloa, Molly, how d'ye do?
Come up on to the step and give us a kiss.'

'Go away,' said Molly, rushing back into the
house. 'Did you ever hear anything like his impudence?'

'Why shouldn't you?' said Kate. 'All the world
knows it.' Then the gig, with the two sportsmen,
was driven on. 'Don't you think he looks handsome
in his pink coat?' whispered Molly afterwards to her
elder sister. 'Only think; I have never seen him in
a red coat since he was my own. Last April, when
the hunting was over he hadn't spoken out; and this
is the first day he has worn pink this year.'

Harry, when he reached the meet, looked about
him to watch how he was received. There are not
many more painful things in life than when an honest
gallant young fellow has to look about him in such
a frame of mind. It might have been worse had he
deserved to be dropped, some one will say. Not at
all. A different condition of mind exists then, and a
struggle is made to overcome the judgment of men
which is not in itself painful. It is part of the natural
battle of life, which does not hurt one at all,—unless,
indeed, the man hate himself for that which has
brought upon him the hatred of others. Repentance
is always an agony,—and should be so. Without the

agony there can be no repentance. But even then it is
hardly so sharp as that feeling of injustice which
accompanies the unmeaning look, and dumb faces,
and pretended indifference of those who have condemned.

When Harry descended from the gig he found
himself close to old Mr. Harkaway, the master of the
hounds. Mr. Harkaway was a gentleman who had
been master of these hounds for more than forty
years, and had given as much satisfaction as the
county could produce. His hounds, which were his
hobby, were perfect. His horses were good enough
for the Hertfordshire lanes and Hertfordshire hedges.
His object was not so much to run a fox as to kill him
in obedience to certain rules of the game. Ever so
many hindrances have been created to bar the killing
a fox,—as for instance that you shouldn't knock him
on the head with a brickbat,—all of which had to Mr.
Harkaway the force of a religion. The laws of hunting are so many, that most men who hunt cannot
know them all. But no law had ever been written, or
had become a law by the strength of tradition, which
he did not know. To break them was to him treason.
When a young man broke them he pitied the young
man's ignorance, and endeavoured to instruct him
after some rough fashion. When an old man broke
them, he regarded him as a fool who should stay at
home, or as a traitor, who should be dealt with as
such. And with such men he could deal very hardly.
Forty years of reigning had taught him to believe
himself to be omnipotent, and he was so in his own
hunt. He was a man who had never much affected
social habits. The company of one or two brother
sportsmen to drink a glass of port wine with him and
then to go early to bed, was the most of it. He had a
small library, but not a book ever came off the shelf
unless it referred to farriers or the 'Res Venatica.' *
He was unmarried. The time which other men gave
to their wives and families he bestowed upon his

hounds. To his stables he never went, looking on
a horse as a necessary adjunct to hunting, expensive, disagreeable, and prone to get you into danger.
When anyone flattered him about his horse he would
only grunt, and turn his head on one side. No one
in these latter years had seen him jump any fence.
But yet he was always with his hounds, and when
anyone said a kind word as to their doings, that he
would take as a compliment. It was they who were
there to do the work of the day, which horses and
men could only look at. He was a sincere, honest,
taciturn, and withal, affectionate man, who could on
an occasion be very angry with those who offended
him. He knew well what he could do, and never
attempted that which was beyond his power. 'How
are you, Mr. Harkaway?' said Harry.

'How are you, Mr. Annesley; how are you?' said
the master, with all the grace of which he was
capable. But Harry caught a tone in his voice which
he thought implied displeasure. And Mr. Harkaway
had in truth heard the story,—how Harry had been
discarded at Buston, because he had knocked the man
down in the streets at night-time, and had then gone
away. After that Mr. Harkaway toddled off, and
Harry sat and frowned with embittered heart.

'Well, Malt-and-hops, and how are you?' This
came from a fast young banker who lived in the
neighbourhood, and who thus intended to show his
familiarity with the brewer; but when he saw Annesley, he turned round and rode away. 'Scaly trick
that fellow played the other day. He knocked a
fellow down, and when he thought that he was dead,
he lied about it like old boots.' All of which made
itself intelligible to Harry. He told himself that he
had always hated that banker.

'Why do you let such a fellow as that call you
Malt-and-hops?' he said to Joshua.

'What, young Florin? He's a very good fellow,
and doesn't mean anything.'

'A vulgar cad, I should say.'

Then he rode on in silence till he was addressed by an old gentleman of the county who had known his father for the last thirty years. The old gentleman had had nothing about him to recommend him either to Harry's hatred or love, till he spoke; and after that Harry hated him.

'How d'you do, Mr. Annesley?' said the old gentleman, and then rode on.

Harry knew that the old man had condemned him as the others had done, or he would never have called him Mr. Annesley. He felt that he was 'blown upon' in his own county as well as by the Ingoldsbys down in Kent.

They had but a moderate day's sport, going a considerable distance in search of it, till an incident arose which gave quite an interest to the field generally, and nearly brought Joshua Thoroughbung into a scrape. They were drawing a covert which was undoubtedly the property of their own hunt,—or rather just going to draw it,—when all of a sudden they became aware that every hound in the pack was hunting. Mr. Harkaway at once sprang from his usual cold apathetic manner into full action. But they who knew him well could see that it was not the excitement of joy. He was in an instant full of life, but it was not the life of successful enterprise. He was perturbed and unhappy, and his huntsman, Dillon,— a silent, cunning, not very popular man, who would obey his master in everything,—began to move about rapidly, and to be at his wits' end. The younger men prepared themselves for a run, one of those short decisive spurts which come at the spur of the moment, and in which a man, if he is not quite awake to the demands of the moment, is very apt to be left behind. But the old stagers had their eyes on Mr. Harkaway, and knew that there was something amiss. Then there appeared another field of hunters, first one man leading them, then others following, and after them the first ruck, and then the crowd. It was apparent to all who knew anything that two packs had joined. These were the Hitchiners, as the rival sportsmen would call them, and this was the Hitchin Hunt, with Mr. Fairlawn their master. Mr. Fairlawn was also an old man, popular no doubt in his own county, but by no means beloved by Mr. Harkaway. Mr. Harkaway used to declare how Mr. Fairlawn had behaved very badly about certain common coverts about thirty years ago, when the matter had to be referred to a committee of masters. No one in these modern days knew aught of the quarrel, or cared. The men of the two hunts were very good friends, unless they met under the joint eyes of the two masters, and then they were supposed to be bound to hate each other. Now the two packs were mixed together, and there was only one fox between them.

The fox did not trouble them long. He could hardly have saved himself from one pack, but very soon escaped from the fangs of the two. Each hound knew that his neighbour hound was a stranger, and in scrutinising the singularity of the occurrence, lost all the power of hunting. In ten minutes there were nearly forty couples of hounds running hither and thither, with two huntsmen and four whips swearing at them with strange voices, and two old gentlemen giving orders each in opposition to the other. Then each pack was got together, almost on the same ground, and it was necessary that something should be done. Mr. Harkaway waited to see whether Mr. Fairlawn would ride away quickly to his own country. He would not have spoken to Mr. Fairlawn if he could have helped it. Mr. Fairlawn was some miles away from his country. He must have given up the day for lost had he simply gone away. But there was another covert a mile off, and he thought that one of his hounds had 'shown a line,'—or said that he thought so. Now, it is well known that you may follow a hunted fox through whatever country he may

take you to, if only your hounds are hunting him con-
tinuously. And one hound for that purpose is as good
as thirty, and if a hound can only 'show a line' he is
held to be hunting. Mr. Fairlawn was quite sure that
one of his hounds had been showing a line and had
been whipped off it by one of Mr. Harkaway's men.
The man swore that he had only been collecting his
own hounds. On this plea Mr. Fairlawn demanded
to take his whole pack into Greasegate Wood,—the
very covert that Mr. Harkaway had been about to
draw. 'I'm d—— if you do!' said Mr. Harkaway,
standing, whip in hand, in the middle of the road, so
as to prevent the enemy's huntsman passing by with
his hounds. It was afterwards declared that Mr.
Harkaway had not been heard to curse and swear for
the last fifteen years. 'I'm d—— if I don't!' said Mr.
Fairlawn, riding up to him. Mr. Harkaway was ten
years the older man, and looked as though he had
much less of fighting power. But no one saw him
quail or give an inch. Those who watched his face
declared his lips were white with rage and quivered
with passion.

   To tell the words which passed between them
after that would require Homer's pathos and Homer's
imagination.* The two old men scowled and scolded
at each other and, had Mr. Fairlawn attempted to
pass, Mr. Harkaway would certainly have struck him
with his whip. And behind their master a crowd of
the Puckeridge men collected themselves, foremost
among whom was Joshua Thoroughbung. 'Take 'em
round to the covert by Winnipeg Lane,' said Mr.
Fairlawn to his huntsman. The man prepared to
take his pack round by Winnipeg Lane, which would
have added a mile to the distance. But the huntsman
when he had got a little to the left, was soon seen
scurrying across the country in the direction of the
covert, with a dozen others at his heels, and the
hounds following him. But old Mr. Harkaway had
seen it too, and having possession of the road, gal-

loped along it at such a pace that no one could pass
him. All the field declared that they had regarded it
as impossible that their master should move so fast.
And Dillon, and the whips, and Thoroughbung, and
Harry Annesley, with half-a-dozen others, kept pace
with him. They would not sit there and see their
master outmanœuvred by any lack of readiness on
their part. They got to the covert first, and there,
with their whips drawn, were ready to receive the
second pack. Then one hound went in without an
order; but for their own hounds they did not care.
They might find a fox and go after him, and nobody
would follow them. The business here at the covert-
side was more important and more attractive.

Then it was that Mr. Thoroughbung nearly fell
into danger. As to the other hounds, Mr. Fairlawn's
hounds, doing any harm in the covert, or doing any
good for themselves or their owners, that was out
of the question. The rival pack was already there,
with their noses up in the air, and thinking of anything but a fox; and this other pack, the Hitchiners,
were just as wild. But it was the object of Mr. Fairlawn's body-guard to say that they had drawn the
covert in the teeth of Mr. Harkaway, and to achieve
this one of the whips thought that he could ride
through the Puckeridge men, taking a couple of
hounds with him. That would suffice for triumph.

But to prevent such triumph on the part of the
enemy Joshua Thoroughbung was prepared to sacrifice himself. He rode right at the whip, with his own
whip raised, and would undoubtedly have ridden
over him had not the whip tried to turn his horse
sharp round, stumbled, and fallen in the struggle, and
had not Thoroughbung, with his horse, fallen over
him.

It will be the case that a slight danger or injury
in one direction will often stop a course of action
calculated to create greater dangers and worse injuries. So it was in this case. When Dick, the Hitchin

whip, went down, and Thoroughbung, with his horse, was over him,—two men and two horses struggling together on the ground,—all desire to carry on the fight was over. The huntsman came up, and at last Mr. Fairlawn also, and considered it to be their duty to pick up Dick, whose breath was knocked out of him by the weight of Joshua Thoroughbung, and the Puckeridge side felt it to be necessary to give their aid to the valiant brewer. There was then no more attempt to draw the covert. Each general in gloomy silence took off his forces, and each afterwards deemed that the victory was his. Dick swore, when brought to himself, that one of his hounds had gone in, whereas Squire 'Arkaway 'had swore most 'orrid oaths that no 'Itchiner 'ound should ever live to put his nose in. One of 'is 'ounds 'ad, and Squire 'Arkaway would have to be——' Well, Dick declared that he would not say what would happen to Mr. Harkaway.

Chapter XXIX

RIDING HOME

THE two old gentlemen rode away, each in his own direction, in gloomy silence. Not a word was said by either of them, even to one of his own followers. It was nearly twenty miles to Mr. Harkaway's house, and along the entire twenty miles he rode silent. 'He's in an awful passion,' said Thoroughbung; 'he can't speak from anger.' But, to tell the truth, Mr. Harkaway was ashamed of himself. He was an old gentleman, between seventy and eighty, who was supposed to go out for his amusement, and had allowed himself to be betrayed into most unseemly language. What though the hound had not 'shown a line?' Was it necessary that he, at his time of life, should fight on the road for the maintenance of a trifling right of sport? But yet there came upon

him from time to time a sense of the deep injury done
to him. That man, Fairlawn, that blackguard, that
creature of all others the furthest removed from a
gentleman, had declared that he in his, Mr. Harkaway's teeth, he would draw his, Mr. Harkaway's
covert! Then he would urge on his old horse, and
gnash his teeth; and then, again, he would be
ashamed. 'Tantæne animis cœlestibus iræ?'*

But Thoroughbung rode home high in spirits, very
proud, and conscious of having done good work. He
was always anxious to stand well with the hunt
generally, and was aware that he had now distinguished himself. Harry Annesley was on one side
of him, and on the other rode Mr. Florin, the banker.
'He's an abominable liar,' said Thoroughbung, 'a
wicked wretched liar!' He was alluding to the
Hitchiners' whip, whom in his wrath he had nearly
sent to another world. 'He says that one of his
hounds got into the covert, but I was there and saw
it all. Not a nose was over the little bank which runs
between the field and the covert.'

'You must have seen a hound if he had been there,'
said the banker.

'I was as cool as a cucumber, and could count the
hounds he had with him. There were three of them.
A big black-spotted bitch was leading, the one that I
nearly fell upon. When the man went down the
hound stopped, not knowing what was expected of
him. How should he? The man would have been
in the covert, but, by George! I managed to stop
him.'

'What did you mean to do when you rode at him
so furiously?' asked Harry.

'Not let him get in there. That was my resolute
purpose. I suppose I should have knocked him off
his horse with my whip.'

'But suppose he had knocked you off your horse?'
suggested the banker.

'There is no knowing how that might have been.

I never calculated those chances. When a man wants to do a thing like that he generally does it.'

'And you did it?' said Harry.

'Yes; I think I did. I dare say his bones are sore. I know mine are. But I don't care for that in the least. When this day comes to be talked about, as I dare say it will be for many a long year, no one will be able to say that the Hitchiners got into that covert.' Thoroughbung, with the genuine modesty of an Englishman, would not say that he had achieved by his own prowess all this glory for the Puckeridge Hunt; but he felt it down to the very end of his nails. Had he not been there that whip would have got into the wood, and a very different tale would then have been told in those coming years to which his mind was running away with happy thoughts. He had ridden the aggressors down; he had stopped the first intrusive hound. But though he continued to talk of the subject, he did not boast in so many words that he had done it. His 'veni, vidi, vici'* was confined to his own bosom.

As they rode home together there came to be a little crowd of men round Thoroughbung, giving him the praises that were his due. But one by one they fell off from Annesley's side of the road. He soon felt that no one addressed a word to him. He was, probably, too prone to encourage them in this. It was he that fell away, and courted loneliness, and then in his heart accused them. There was no doubt something of truth in his accusations; but another man less sensitive might have lived it down. He did more than meet their coldness half way, and then complained to himself of the bitterness of the world. 'They are like the beasts of the field,' he said, 'who when another beast has been wounded, turn upon him and rend him to death.' His future brother-in-law, the best-natured fellow that ever was born, rode on thoughtlessly, and left Harry alone for three or four miles, while he received the pleasant plaudits

of his companions. In Joshua's heart was that tale
of the whip's discomfiture. He did not see that
Molly's brother was alone as soon as he would have
done but for his own glory. 'He is the same as the
others,' said Harry to himself. 'Because that man
has told a falsehood of me, and has had the wit to
surround it with circumstances, he thinks it becomes
him to ride away and cut me.' Then he asked himself
some foolish questions as to himself and as to Joshua
Thoroughbung, which he did not answer as he should
have done, had he remembered that he was then
riding Thoroughbung's horse, and that his sister was
to become Thoroughbung's wife.

After half-an-hour of triumphant ovation, Joshua
remembered his brother-in-law, and did fall back so
as to pick him up. 'What's the matter, Harry? Why
don't you come on and join us?'

'I'm sick of hearing of that infernal squabble.'

'Well; as to a squabble, Mr. Harkaway behaved
quite right. If a hunt is to be kept up, the right of
entering coverts must be preserved for the hunt they
belong to. There was no line shown. You must
remember that there isn't a doubt about that. The
hounds were all astray when we joined them. It's a
great question whether they brought their fox into
that first covert. There are they who think that
Bodkin was just riding across the Puckeridge country
in search of a fox.' Bodkin was Mr. Fairlawn's
huntsman. 'If you admit that kind of thing, where
will you be? As a hunting county, just nowhere.
Then as a sportsman, where are you? It is necessary
to put down such gross fraud. My own impression
is that Mr. Fairlawn should be turned out from being
master. I own I feel very strongly about it. But
then I always have been fond of hunting.'

'Just so,' said Harry sulkily, who was not in the
least interested as to the matter on which Joshua was
so eloquent.

Then Mr. Proctor rode by, the gentleman who in

the early part of the day had disgusted Harry by
calling him 'Mister.' 'Now, Mr. Proctor,' continued Joshua, 'I appeal to you whether Mr. Harkaway was not quite right? If you won't stick up for
your rights in a hunting county——' But Mr.
Proctor rode on, wishing them good-night, very
discourteously declining to hear the remainder of the
brewer's arguments. 'He's in a hurry, I suppose,'
said Joshua.

'You'd better follow him. You'll find that he'll
listen to you then.'

'I don't want him to listen to me particularly.'

'I thought you did.' Then for half a mile the two
men rode on in silence.

'What's the matter with you, Harry?' said Joshua.
'I can see there's something up that riles you. I
know you're a Fellow of your college, and have
other things to think of besides the vagaries of a fox.'

'The Fellow of a college!' said Harry, who, had
he been in a good humour, would have thought much
more of being along with a lot of fox hunters than of
any college honours.

'Well, yes; I suppose it is a great thing to be a
Fellow of a college. I never could have been one if
I had mugged for ever.'

'My being a Fellow of a college won't do me
much good. Did you see that old man Proctor go
by just now?'

'Oh yes, he never likes to be out after a certain
hour.'

'And did you see Florin, and Mr. Harkaway, and
a lot of others? You yourself have been going on
ahead for the last hour without speaking to me.'

'How do you mean, without speaking to you?'
said Joshua, turning sharp round.

Then Harry Annesley reflected that he was doing
an injustice to his future brother-in-law. 'Perhaps I
have done you wrong,' he said.

'You have.'

'I beg your pardon. I believe you are as honest and true a fellow as there is in Hertfordshire; but for those others——'

'You think it is about Mountjoy Scarborough, then?' asked Joshua.

'I do. That infernal fool, Peter Prosper, has chosen to publish to the world that he has dropped me because of something that he has heard of that occurrence. A wretched lie has been told with a purpose by Mountjoy Scarborough's brother, and my uncle has taken it into his wise head to believe it. The truth is, I have not been as respectful to him as he thinks I ought, and now he resents my neglect in this fashion. He is going to marry your aunt in order that he may have a lot of children, and cut me out. In order to justify himself, he has told these lies about me, and you see the consequence. Not a man in the county is willing to speak to me.'

'I really think a great deal of it's fancy.'

'You go and ask Mr. Harkaway. He's honest, and he'll tell you. Ask this new cousin of yours, Mr. Prosper.'

'I don't know that they are going to make a match of it, after all.'

'Ask my own father. Only think of it,—that a puling, puking idiot like that, from a mere freak, should be able to do a man such a mischief! He can rob me of my income, which he himself has brought me up to expect. That he can do by a stroke of his pen. He can threaten to have sons like Priam.* All that is within his own bosom. But to justify himself to the world at large, he picks up a scandalous story from a man like Augustus Scarborough, and immediately not a man in the county will speak to me. I say that that is enough to break a man's heart,—not the injury done, which a man should bear, but the injustice of the doing. Who wants his beggarly allowance? He can do as he likes about his own money. I shall never ask him for his money. But that he should tell such a lie as this about the county is more than a man can endure.'

'What was it that did happen?' asked Joshua.

'The man met me in the street when he was drunk, and he struck at me, and was insolent. Of course I knocked him down. Who wouldn't have done the same? Then his brother found him somewhere, or got hold of him, and sent him out of the country, and says that I had held my tongue when I left him in the street. Of course I held my tongue. What was Mountjoy to me? Then Augustus has asked me sly questions, and accuses me of lying because I did not choose to tell him everything. It all comes out of that.'

Here they had reached the Rectory, and Harry, after seeing that the horses were properly supplied with gruel, took himself and his ill-humour upstairs to his own chamber. But Joshua had a word or two to say to one of the inmates of the Rectory. He felt that it would be improper to ride his horse home without giving time to the animal to drink his gruel, and therefore made his way into the little breakfast-parlour, where Molly had a cup of tea and buttered toast ready for him. He of course told her first of the grand occurrence of the day,—how the two packs of hounds had mixed themselves together, how violently the two masters had fallen out and had nearly flogged each other, how Mr. Harkaway had sworn horribly, —who had never been heard to swear before,—how a final attempt had been made to seize a second covert, and how, at last, it had come to pass that he had distinguished himself. 'Do you mean to say that you absolutely rode over the unfortunate man?' asked Molly.

'I did. Not that the man had the worst of it,—or very much the worse. There we were both down, and the two horses, all in a heap together.'

'Oh, Joshua, suppose you had been kicked!'

'In that case I should have been—kicked.'

'But a kick from an infuriated horse!'

'There wasn't much infuriation about him. The man had ridden all that out of the beast.'

'You are sure to laugh at me, Joshua, because I think what terrible things might have happened to you. Why do you go putting yourself so forward in every danger now that you have got somebody else to depend upon you and to care for you? It's very, very wrong.'

'Somebody had to do it, Molly. It was most important, in the interests of hunting generally, that those hounds should not have been allowed to get into that covert. I don't think that outsiders ever understand how essential it is to maintain your rights. It isn't as though it were an individual. The whole county may depend upon it.'

'Why shouldn't it be some man who hasn't got a young woman to look after?' said Molly, half laughing and half crying.

'It's the man who first gets there who ought to do it,' said Joshua. 'A man can't stop to remember whether he has got a young woman or not.'

'I don't think you ever want to remember.' Then that little quarrel was brought to the usual end with the usual blandishments, and Joshua went on to discuss with her that other source of trouble, her brother's fall. 'Harry is awfully cut up,' said the brewer.

'You mean these affairs about his uncle.'

'Yes. It isn't only the money he feels, or the property, but people look askew at him. You ought all of you to be very kind to him.'

'I am sure we are.'

'There is something in it to vex him. That stupid old fool, your uncle——; I beg your pardon, you know, for speaking of him in that way.'

'He is a stupid old fool.'

'Is behaving very badly. I don't know whether he shouldn't be treated as I did that fellow up at the covert.'

'Ride over him?'

'Something of that kind. Of course Harry is sore about it, and when a man is sore he frets at a thing like that more than he ought to do. As for that aunt of mine at Buntingford, there seems to be some hitch in it. I should have said she'd have married The Old Gentleman* had he asked her.'

'Don't talk like that, Joshua.'

'But there is some screw loose. Simpson came up to my father about it yesterday, and the governor let enough of the cat out of the bag to make me know that the thing is not going as straight as she wishes.'

'He has offered, then?'

'I am sure he has asked her.'

'And your aunt will accept him?' asked Molly.

'There's probably some difference about money. It's all done with the intention of injuring poor Harry. If he were my own brother I could not be more unhappy about him. And as to Aunt Matilda, she's a fool. They are two fools together. If they choose to marry we can't hinder them. But there is some screw loose, and if the two young lovers don't know their own minds things may come right at last.' Then, with some further blandishments, the prosperous brewer walked away.

Chapter XXX

PERSECUTION

IN the meantime Florence Mountjoy was not passing her time pleasantly at Brussels. Various troubles there attended her. All her friends around her were opposed to her marriage with Harry Annesley. Harry Annesley had become a very unsavoury word in the mouths of Sir Magnus and the British Embassy generally. Mrs. Mountjoy told her grief to her brother-in-law, who thoroughly took her part, as did also, very strongly, Lady Mountjoy. It got to be generally understood that Harry was a *mauvais sujet*. Such was the name that was attached to him, and the belief so conveyed was thoroughly entertained by them all. Sir Magnus had written to friends in London, and the friends in London bore out the reports that were so conveyed. The story of the midnight quarrel was told in a manner very prejudicial to poor Harry, and both Sir Magnus and his wife saw the necessity of preserving their niece from anything so evil as such a marriage. But Florence was very firm, and was considered to be very obstinate. To her mother she was obstinate but affectionate. To Sir Magnus she was obstinate, and in some degree respectful. But to Lady Mountjoy she was neither affectionate nor respectful. She took a great dislike to Lady Mountjoy, who endeavoured to domineer, and who, by the assistance of the two others, was, in fact, tyrannical. It was her opinion that the girl should be compelled to abandon the man, and Mrs. Mountjoy found herself constrained to follow this advice. She did love her daughter, who was her only child. The main interest of her life was centred in her daughter. Her only remaining ambition rested on her daughter's marriage. She had long revelled in the anticipation of being the mother-in-law of the owner of Tretton Park. She had been very proud of her daughter's beauty. Then had come the first blow, when Harry Annesley had come to Montpellier Place and had been welcomed by Florence. Mrs. Mountjoy had seen it all along before Florence had been aware of it. And the first coming of Harry had been long before the absolute disgrace of Captain Scarborough,—at any rate before the tidings of that disgrace had reached Cheltenham. Mrs. Mountjoy had been still able to dream of Tretton Park, after the Jews had got their fingers on it,—even after the Jews had been forced to relinquish their hold. It can hardly be said that up to this very time Mrs. Mountjoy had lost all hope in her nephew, thinking that as the property had been entailed some portion of it must ultimately belong to him. She had heard that Augustus was to have it, and her desires had vacillated between the two. Then Harry had positively declared himself, and Augustus had given her to understand how wretched, how mean, how wicked had been Harry's conduct. And he fully explained to her that Harry would be penniless. She had indeed been aware that Buston, quite a trifling thing compared to Tretton, was to belong to him. But entails were nothing nowadays. It was part of the Radical abomination* to which England was being subjected. Not even Buston was now to belong to Harry Annesley. The small income which he had received from his uncle was stopped. He was reduced to live upon his Fellowship,—which would be stopped also if he married. She even despised him because he was the Fellow of a college. She had looked for a husband for her daughter so much higher than any college could produce. It was not from any lack of motherly love that she was opposed to Florence, or from any innate cruelty that she handed her daughter over to the tender mercies of Lady Mountjoy.

And since she had been at Brussels there had come up further hopes. Another mode had shown itself of escaping Harry Annesley, who was of all catastrophes the most dreaded and hated. Mr. Anderson, the second secretary of Legation, he whose business it was to ride about the boulevard with Sir Magnus, had now declared himself in form. 'Never saw a fellow so bowled over,' Sir Magnus had declared, by which he had intended to signify that Mr. Anderson was now truly in love. 'I've seen him spooney a dozen times,' Sir Magnus had said confidentially to his sister-in-law, 'but he has never gone to this length. He has asked a lot of girls to have him, but he has always been off it again before the week was over. He has written to his mother now.' And Mr. Anderson showed his love by very unmistakable signs. Sir Magnus, too, and Lady Mountjoy, were evidently on the same side as Mr. Anderson. Sir Magnus thought there was no longer any good in waiting for his nephew, the captain, and of that other nephew, Augustus, he did not entertain any very high idea. Sir Magnus had corresponded lately with Augustus, and was certainly not on his side. But he so painted Mr. Anderson's prospects in life, as did also Lady Mountjoy, as to make it appear that if Florence could put up with young Anderson she would do very well with herself.

'He's sure to be a baronet some of these days, you know,' said Sir Magnus.

'I don't think that would go very far with Florence,' said her mother.

'But it ought. Look about in the world and you'll see that it does go a long way. He'd be the fifth baronet.'

'But his elder brother is alive.'

'The queerest fellow you ever saw in your born days, and his life is not worth a year's purchase. He's got some infernal disease,—nostalgia, or what d'ye call it?—which never leaves him a moment's peace; and then he drinks nothing but milk. Sure to go off; —cock-sure.'

'I shouldn't like Florence to count upon that.'

'And then Hugh Anderson, the fellow here, is very well off as it is. He has four hundred pounds here, and another five hundred pounds of his own. Florence has, or will have, four hundred pounds of her own. I should call them deuced rich. I should, indeed, as beginners. She could have her pair of ponies here, and what more would she want?'

These arguments did go very far with Mrs. Mountjoy, the further because in her estimation Sir Magnus was a great man. He was the greatest Englishman at any rate in Brussels, and where should she go for advice but to an Englishman? And she did not know that Sir Magnus had succeeded in borrowing a considerable sum of money from his second secretary of Legation.

'Leave her to me for a little,—just leave her to me,' said Lady Mountjoy.

'I would not say anything hard to her,' said the mother, pleading for her naughty child.

'Not too hard, but she must be made to understand. You see there have been misfortunes. As for Mountjoy Scarborough, he's past hoping for.'

'You think so?'

'Altogether. When a man has disappeared there's an end of him. There was Lord Baltiboy's younger son disappeared, and he turned out to be a Zouave corporal in a French regiment. They did get him out, of course, but then he went preaching in America. You may take it for granted that when a man has absolutely vanished from the clubs, he'll never be any good again as a marrying man.'

'But there's his brother, who, they say, is to have the property.'

'A very cold-blooded sort of young man, who doesn't care a straw for his own family.' He had received very sternly the overtures for a loan from Sir Magnus. 'And he, as I understand, has never declared himself in Florence's favour. You can't count upon Augustus Scarborough.'

'Not just count upon him.'

'Whereas there's young Anderson, who is the most gentlemanlike young man I know, all ready. It will have been such a turn of luck your coming here and catching him up.'

'I don't know that it can be called a turn of luck. Florence has a very nice fortune of her own.'

'And she wants to give it to this penniless reprobate. It is just one of those cases in which you must deal roundly with a girl. She has to be frightened, and that's about the truth of it.'

After this, Lady Mountjoy did succeed in getting

Florence alone with herself into her morning-room. When her mother told her that her aunt wished to see her, she answered first that she had no special wish to see her aunt. Her mother declared that in her aunt's house she was bound to go when her aunt sent for her. To this Florence demurred. She was, she thought, her aunt's guest, but by no means at her aunt's disposal. But at last she obeyed her mother. She had resolved that she would obey her mother in all things but one, and therefore she went one morning to her aunt's chamber.

But as she went she was, in the first instance, caught by her uncle, and taken by him into a little private sanctum behind his official room. 'My dear,' he said, 'just come in here for two minutes.'

'I am on my way up to my aunt.'

'I know it, my dear. Lady Mountjoy has been talking it all over with me. Upon my word you can't do anything better than take young Anderson.'

'I can't do that, Uncle Magnus.'

'Why not? There's poor Mountjoy Scarborough, he has gone astray.'

'There is no question of my cousin.'

'And Augustus is no better.'

'There is no question of Augustus either.'

'As to that other chap, he isn't any good;—he isn't indeed.'

'You mean Mr. Annesley.'

'Yes; Harry Annesley as you call him. He hasn't got a shilling to bless himself with, or wouldn't have if he was to marry you.'

'But I have got something.'

'Not enough for both of you, I'm afraid. That uncle of his has disinherited him.'

'His uncle can't disinherit him.'

'He's quite young enough to marry and have a family, and then Annesley will be disinherited. He has stopped his allowance anyway, and you mustn't think of him. He did something uncommonly unhandsome the other day, though I don't quite know what.'

'He did nothing unhandsome, Uncle Magnus.'

'Of course a young lady will stand up for her lover, but you will really have to drop him. I'm not a hard sort of man, but this was something that the world will not stand. When he thought the man had been murdered he didn't say anything about it for fear they should tax him with it. And then he swore he had never seen him. It was something of that sort.'

'He never feared that anyone would suspect him.'

'And now young Anderson has proposed. I should not have spoken else, but it's my duty to tell you about young Anderson. He's a gentleman all round.'

'So is Mr. Annesley.'

'And Anderson has got into no trouble at all. He does his duty here uncommonly well. I never had less trouble with any young fellow than I have had with him. No licking him into shape,—or next to none; and he has a very nice private income. You together would have plenty, and could live here till you had settled on apartments. A pair of ponies would be just the thing for you to drive about and support the British interests. You think of it, my dear; and you'll find that I'm right.' Then Florence escaped from that room and went up to receive the much more severe lecture which she was to have from her aunt.

'Come in, my dear,' said Lady Mountjoy in her most austere voice. She had a voice which could assume austerity when she knew her power to be in the ascendant. As Florence entered the room Miss Abbott left it by a door on the other side. 'Take that chair, Florence. I want to have a few minutes' conversation with you.' Then Florence sat down. 'When a young lady is thinking of being married a great many things have to be taken into consideration.' This seemed to be so much a matter of fact that Florence did not feel it necessary to make any reply. 'Of course I am aware you are thinking of being married.'

'Oh! yes,' said Florence.

'But to whom?'

'To Harry Annesley,' said Florence, intending to imply that all the world knew that.

'I hope not; I hope not. Indeed I may say that it is quite out of the question. In the first place he is a beggar.'

'He has begged from none,' said Florence.

'He is what the world calls a beggar, when a young man without a penny thinks of being married.'

'I'm not a beggar, and what I've got will be his.'

'My dear, you're talking about what you don't understand. A young lady cannot give her money away in that manner. It will not be allowed. Neither your mother, nor Sir Magnus, nor will I permit it.' Here Florence restrained herself, but drew herself up in her chair as though prepared to speak out her mind if she should be driven. Lady Mountjoy would not permit it! She thought that she would feel herself quite able to tell Lady Mountjoy that she had neither power nor influence in the matter, but she determined to be silent a little longer. 'In the first place a gentleman who is a gentleman never attempts to marry a lady for her money.'

'But when a lady has the money she can express herself much more clearly than she could otherwise.'

'I don't quite understand what you mean by that, my dear.'

'When Mr. Annesley proposed to me he was the acknowledged heir to his uncle's property.'

'A trumpery affair at the best of it.'

'It would have sufficed for me. Then I accepted him.'

'That goes for nothing from a lady. Of course your acceptance was contingent on circumstances.'

'It was so,—on my regard. Having accepted him, and as my regard remains just as warm as ever, I

certainly shall not go back because of anything his
uncle may do. I only say this to explain that he was
quite justified in his offer. It was not for my small
fortune that he came to me.'

'I am not so sure of that.'

'But if my money can be of any use to him he's
quite welcome to it. Sir Magnus spoke to me about
a pair of ponies. I'd rather have him than a pair of
ponies.'

'I'm coming to that just now. Here is Mr.
Anderson.'

'Oh! yes; he's here.'

There was certainly a touch of impatience in the
tone in which this was uttered. It was as though she
had said that Mr. Anderson had so contrived that
she could have no doubt whatever about his continued
presence. Mr. Anderson had made himself so conspicuous as to be visible to her constantly. Lady
Mountjoy, who intended at present to sing Mr.
Anderson's praises, felt this to be impertinent.

'I don't know what you mean by that. Mr. Anderson has behaved himself quite like a gentleman, and
you ought to be very proud of any token you may
receive of his regard and affection.'

'But I'm not bound to return it.'

'You are bound to think of it when those who are
responsible for your actions tell you to do so.'

'Mamma, you mean?'

'I mean your uncle, Sir Magnus Mountjoy.' She
did not quite dare to say that she had meant herself.
'I suppose you will admit that Sir Magnus is a com-
petent judge of young men's characters?'

'He may be a judge of Mr. Anderson, because Mr.
Anderson is his clerk.'

There was something of an intention to depreciate
in the word 'clerk.' Florence had not thought much
of Mr. Anderson's worth, nor, as far as she had seen
them, of the duties generally performed at the British
Embassy. She was ignorant of the peculiar little

niceties and intricacies which required the residence at Brussels of a gentleman with all the tact possessed by Sir Magnus. She did not know that while the mere international work of the office might be safely intrusted to Mr. Blow and Mr. Bunderdown, all those little niceties, that smiling and that frowning, that taking off of hats and only half taking them off, that genial easy manner and that still hauteur, formed the peculiar branch of Sir Magnus himself,—and, under Sir Magnus, of Mr. Anderson. She did not understand that even to that pair of ponies which was promised to her, were to be attached certain important functions which she was to control as the deputy of the great man's deputy. And now she had called the great man's deputy a clerk!

'Mr. Anderson is no such thing,' said Lady Mountjoy.

'His young man, then—or private secretary, only somebody else is that.'

'You are very impertinent and very ungrateful. Mr. Anderson is second secretary of Legation. There is no officer attached to our establishment of more importance. I believe you say it on purpose to anger me. And then you compare this gentleman to Mr. Annesley, a man to whom no one will speak.'

'I will speak to him.' Had Harry heard her say that, he ought to have been a happy man in spite of his trouble.

'You! What good can you do him?'

Florence nodded her head, almost imperceptibly, but still there was a nod, signifying more than she could possibly say. She thought that she could do him a world of good if she were near him, and some good too though she were far away. If she were with him she could hang on to his arm,—or perhaps at some future time round his neck,—and tell him that she would be true to him though all others might turn away. And she could be just as true where she was, though she could not comfort him by telling him so with her own words. Then it was that she resolved upon writing that letter. He should already have what little comfort she might administer in his absence. 'Now listen to me, Florence. He is a thorough reprobate.'

'I will not hear him so called. He is no reprobate.'

'He has behaved in such a way that all England is crying out about him. He has done that which will never allow any gentleman to speak to him again.'

'Then there will be more need that a lady should do so. But it is not true.'

'You put your knowledge of character against that of Sir Magnus.'

'Sir Magnus does not know the gentleman; I do. What's the good of talking of it, aunt? Harry Annesley has my word, and nothing on earth shall induce me to go back from it. Even were he what you say I would be true to him.'

'You would?'

'Certainly I would. I could not willingly begin to love a man whom I knew to be base; but when I had loved him I would not turn because of his baseness. I couldn't do it. It would be a great,—a terrible misfortune; but it would have to be borne. But here——. I know all the story to which you allude.'

'I know it too.'

'I am quite sure that the baseness has not been on his part. In defence of my name he has been silent. He might have spoken out, if he had known all the truth then. I was as much his own then as I am now. One of these days I suppose I shall be more so.'

'You mean to marry him then?'

'Most certainly I do; or I will never be married. And as he is poor now, and I must have my own money when I am twenty-four, I suppose I shall have to wait till then.'

'Will your mother's word go for nothing with you?'

'Poor mamma! I do believe that mamma is very

unhappy because she makes me unhappy. What may take place between me and mamma I am not bound, I think, to tell you. We shall be away soon, and I shall be left to mamma alone.'

And mamma would be left alone to her daughter, Lady Mountjoy thought. The visit must be prolonged so that at last Mr. Anderson might be enabled to prevail.

The visit had been originally intended for a month, but it was now prolonged indefinitely. After that conversation between Lady Mountjoy and her niece two or three things happened, all bearing upon our story. Florence at once wrote her letter. If things were going badly in England with Harry Annesley, Harry should at any rate have the comfort of knowing what were her feelings,—if there might be comfort to him in that. 'Perhaps after all he won't mind what I may say,' she thought to herself; but only pretended to think it, and at once flatly contradicted her own 'perhaps.' Then she told him most emphatically not to reply. It was very important that she should write. He was to receive her letter, and there must be an end of it. She was quite sure that he would understand her. He would not subject her to the trouble of having to tell her own people that she was maintaining a correspondence, for it would amount to that. But still when the time came for the answer she had counted it up to the hour. And when Sir Magnus sent for her and handed to her the letter,— having discussed that question with her mother,—she fully expected it, and felt properly grateful to her uncle. She wanted a little comfort too, and when she had read the letter she knew that she had received it.

There had been a few words spoken between the two elder ladies after the interview between Florence and Lady Mountjoy. 'She is a most self-willed young woman,' said Lady Mountjoy.

'Of course she loves her lover,' said Mrs. Mountjoy, desirous of making some excuse for her own daughter. The girl was very troublesome, but was not the less her daughter. 'I don't know any of them that don't, who are worth anything.'

'If you regard it in that light, Sarah, she'll get the better of you. If she marries him she will be lost; that is the way you have got to look at it. It is her future happiness you must think of,—and respectability. She is a headstrong young woman, and has to be treated accordingly.'

'What would you do?'

'I would be very severe.'

'But what am I to do? I can't beat her; I can't lock her up in a room.'

'Then you mean to give it up?'

'No, I don't; you shouldn't be so cross to me,' said poor Mrs. Mountjoy. When it had reached this the two ladies had become intimate. 'I don't mean to give it up at all; but what am I to do?'

'Remain here for the next month, and,—and worry her; let Mr. Anderson have his chance with her. When she finds that everything will smile with her if she accepts him, and that her life will be made a burden to her if she still sticks to her Harry Annesley, she'll come round if she be like other girls. Of course a girl can't be made to marry a man; but there are ways and means.' By this Lady Mountjoy meant that the utmost cruelty should be used which would be compatible with a good breakfast, dinner, and bedroom. Now Mrs. Mountjoy knew herself to be incapable of this, and knew also, or thought that she knew, that it would not be efficacious.

'You stay here,—up to Christmas if you like it,' said Sir Magnus to his sister-in-law. 'She can't but see Anderson every day, and that goes a long way. She of course puts on a resolute air as well as she can. They all know how to do that. Do you be resolute in return. The deuce is in it if we can't have our way with her among us. When you talk of ill-usage, nobody wants you to put her in chains. There are different ways of killing a cat. You get friends to write to you from England about young Annesley, and I'll do the same,—the truth, of course, I mean.'

'Nothing can be worse than the truth,' said Mrs. Mountjoy, shaking her head sorrowfully.

'Just so,' said Sir Magnus, who was not at all sorrowful to hear so bad an account of the favoured suitor. 'Then we'll read her the letters. She can't help hearing them. Just the true facts, you know. That's fair; nobody can call that cruel. And then, when she breaks down and comes to our call, we'll all be as soft as mother's milk to her. I shall see her going about the boulevards with a pair of ponies yet.' Mrs. Mountjoy felt that when Sir Magnus spoke of Florence coming to his call, he did not know her daughter. But she had nothing better to do than to obey Sir Magnus. Therefore she resolved to stay at Brussels for another period of six weeks, and told Florence that she had so resolved. Just at present Brussels and Cheltenham would be all the same to Florence.

'It will be a dreadful bore having them so long,' said poor Lady Mountjoy piteously to her husband. For in the presence of Sir Magnus she was by no means the valiant woman that she was with some of her friends.

'You find everything a bore. What's the trouble?'

'What am I to do with them?'

'Take 'em about in the carriage. Lord bless my soul! what have you got a carriage for?'

'Then, with Miss Abbott, there's never room for any one else.'

'Leave Miss Abbott at home, then. What's the good of talking to me about Miss Abbott? I suppose it doesn't matter to you who my brother's daughter marries?' Lady Mountjoy did not think that it did matter much; but she declared that she had already evinced the most tender solicitude. 'Then stick to it.

The girl doesn't want to go out every day. Leave her alone, where Anderson can get at her.'

'He's always out riding with you.'

'No, he's not; not always. And leave Miss Abbott at home. Then there'll be room for two others. Don't make difficulties. Anderson will expect that I shall do something for him, of course.'

'Because of the money,' said Lady Mountjoy, whispering.

'And I've got to do something for her too.' Now there was a spice of honesty about Sir Magnus. He knew that as he could not at once pay back these sums, he was bound to make it up in some other way. The debts would be left the same. But that would remain with Providence.

Then came Harry's letter, and there was a deep consultation. It was known to have come from Harry by the Buntingford postmark. Mrs. Mountjoy proposed to consult Lady Mountjoy, but to that Sir Magnus would not agree. 'She'd take her skin off her if she could now that she's angered,' said the lady's husband, who, no doubt, knew the lady well. 'Of course she'll learn that the letter has been written, and then she'll throw it in our teeth. She wouldn't believe that it had gone astray in coming here. We should give her a sort of a whip-hand over us.' So it was decided that Florence should have her letter.

Chapter XXXI

FLORENCE'S REQUEST

THUS it was arranged that Florence should be left in Mr. Anderson's way. Mr. Anderson, as Sir Magnus had said, was not always out riding. There were moments in which even he was off duty. And Sir Magnus contrived to ride a little earlier than usual so that he should get back while the carriage

was still out on its rounds. Lady Mountjoy certainly
did her duty, taking Mrs. Mountjoy with her daily,
and generally Miss Abbott, so that Florence was, as
it were, left to the mercies of Mr. Anderson. She
could of course shut herself up in her bedroom, but
things had not as yet become so bad as that. Mr.
Anderson had not made himself terrible to her. She
did not in truth fear Mr. Anderson at all, who was
courteous in his manner and complimentary in his
language; and she came at this time to the conclusion
that if Mr. Anderson continued his pursuit of her she
would tell him the exact truth of the case. As a
gentleman, and as a young man, she thought that
he would sympathise with her. The one enemy
whom she did dread was Lady Mountjoy. She too
had felt that her aunt could 'take her skin off her,' as
Sir Magnus had said. She had not heard the words,
but she knew that it was so, and her dislike to Lady
Mountjoy was in proportion. It cannot be said that
she was afraid. She did not intend to leave her skin
in her aunt's hands. For every inch of skin taken she
resolved to have an inch in return. She was not acquainted with the expressive mode of language which
Sir Magnus had adopted, but she was prepared for
all such attacks. For Sir Magnus himself, since he
had given up the letter to her, she did feel some
regard.

Behind the British Minister's house, which, though
entitled to no such name, was generally called the
Embassy, there was a large garden which, though not
much used by Sir Magnus or Lady Mountjoy, was
regarded as a valuable adjunct to the establishment.
Here Florence betook herself for exercise, and here
Mr. Anderson, having put off the muddy marks of his
riding, found her one afternoon. It must be under-
·stood that no young man was ever more in earnest
than Mr. Anderson. He too, looking through the
glass which had been prepared for him by Sir Magnus,
thought that he saw in the not very far distant future

a Mrs. Hugh Anderson driving a pair of grey ponies along the boulevard, and he was much pleased with the sight. It reached to the top of his ambition. Florence was to his eyes really the sort of girl whom a man in his position ought to marry. A Secretary of Legation in a small foreign capital cannot do with a dowdy wife, as may a clerk, for instance, in the Foreign Office. A Secretary of Legation,—the second secretary he told himself,—was bound, if he married at all, to have a pretty and *distinguée* wife. He knew all about those intricacies which had fallen in a peculiar way into his own hand. Mr. Blow might have married a South Sea Islander, and would have been none the worse as regarded his official duties. Mr. Blow did not want the services of a wife in discovering and reporting all the secrets of the Belgian iron trade. There was no intricacy in that, no nicety. There was much of what, in his lighter moments, Mr. Anderson called 'sweat.' He did not pretend to much capacity for such duties; but in his own peculiar walk he thought that he was great. But it was very fatiguing, and he was sure that a wife was necessary to him. There were little niceties which none but a wife could perform. He had a great esteem for Sir Magnus. Sir Magnus was well thought of by all the court, and by the foreign minister at Brussels. But Lady Mountjoy was of really no use. The beginning and the end of it all with her was to show herself in a carriage. It was incumbent upon him, Anderson, to marry.

He was loving enough, and very susceptible. He was too susceptible, and he knew his own fault, and he was always on guard against it,—as behoved a young man with such duties as his. He was always falling in love, and then using his diplomatic skill in avoiding the consequences. He had found out that though one girl had looked so well under wax-light she did not endure the wear and tear of the day. Another could not be always graceful, or, though she could talk well enough during a waltz, she had nothing to say for herself at three o'clock in the morning. And he was driven to calculate that he would be wrong to marry a girl without a shilling. 'It is a kind of thing that a man cannot afford to do unless he's sure of his position,' he had said on such an occasion to Montgomery Arbuthnot, alluding especially to his brother's state of health. When Mr. Anderson spoke of not being sure of his position, he was always considered to allude to his brother's health. In this way he had nearly got his little boat on to the rocks more than once, and had given some trouble to Sir Magnus. But now he was quite sure. 'It's all there all round,' he had said to Arbuthnot more than once. Arbuthnot said that it was there—'all round, all round.' Waxlight and daylight made no difference to her. She was always graceful. 'Nobody with an eye in his head can doubt that,' said Anderson. 'I should think not, by Jove!' replied Arbuthnot. 'And for talking, —you never catch her out; never.' 'I never did, certainly,' said Arbuthnot, who, as third secretary, was obedient and kind-hearted. 'And then look at her money. Of course, a fellow wants something to help him on. My position is so uncertain that I cannot do without it.' 'Of course not.' 'Now with some girls it's so deuced hard to find out. You hear that a girl has got money, but when the time comes, it depends on the life of a father who doesn't think of dying,—damme, doesn't think of it.' 'Those fellows never do,' said Arbuthnot. 'But here, you see, I know all about it. When she's twenty-four,—only twenty-four,—she'll have ten thousand pounds of her own. I hate a mercenary fellow.' 'Oh, yes; that's beastly.' 'Nobody can say that of me. Circumstanced as I am, I want something to help to keep the pot boiling. She has got it,—quite as much as I want,—quite, and I know all about it without the slightest doubt in the world.' For the small loan of fifteen hundred pounds, Sir Magnus paid the full value of the interest and deficient security. 'Sir Magnus tells me that if I'll only stick to her I shall be sure to win. There's some fellow in England has just touched her heart,—just touched it, you know.' 'I understand,' said Arbuthnot, looking very wise. 'He is not a fellow of very much account,' said Anderson; 'one of those handsome fellows without conduct and without courage.' 'I've known lots of 'em,' said Arbuthnot. 'His name is Annesley,' said Anderson. 'I never saw him in my life, but that's what Sir Magnus says. He has done something awfully disreputable. I don't quite understand what it is, but it's something which ought to make him unfit to be her husband. Nobody knows the world better than Sir Magnus, and he says that it is so.' 'Nobody does know the world better than Sir Magnus,' said Arbuthnot. And so that conversation was brought to an end.

One day soon after this he caught her walking in the garden. Her mother and Miss Abbott were still out with Lady Mountjoy in the carriage, and Sir Magnus had retired after the fatigue of his ride to sleep for half-an-hour before dinner. 'All alone, Miss Mountjoy,' he said.

'Yes, all alone, Mr. Anderson. I'm never in better company.'

'So I think; but then if I were here you wouldn't be all alone; would you?'

'Not if you were with me.'

'That's what I mean. But yet two people may be alone, as regards the world at large; mayn't they?'

'I don't understand the nicety of language well enough to say. We used to have a question among us when we were children whether a wild-beast could howl in an empty cavern. It's the same sort of thing.'

'Why shouldn't he?'

'Because the cavern would not be empty if the wild-beast were in it. Did you ever see a girl bang an egg against a wall in a stocking, and then look awfully surprised because she had smashed it?'

'I don't understand the joke.'

'She had been told she couldn't break an egg in an empty stocking. Then she was made to look in, and there was the broken egg for her pains. I don't know what made me tell you that story.'

'It's a very good story. I'll get Miss Abbott to do it to-night. She believes everything.'

'And everybody? Then she's a happy woman.'

'I wish you'd believe everybody.'

'So I do; nearly everybody. There are some inveterate liars whom nobody can believe.'

'I hope I am not regarded as one.'

'You! Certainly not! If anybody were to speak of you as such behind your back no one would take your part more loyally than I. But nobody would.'

'That's something at any rate. Then you do believe that I love you?'

'I believe that you think so.'

'And that I don't know my own heart?'

'That's very common, Mr. Anderson. I wasn't quite sure of my own heart twelve months ago, but I know it now.' He felt that his hopes ran very low when this was said. She had never before spoken to him of his rival, nor had he to her. He knew,—or fancied that he knew,—that 'her heart had been touched,' as he had said to Arbuthnot. But the 'touch' must have been very deep if she felt herself constrained to speak to him on the subject. It had been his desire to pass over Mr. Annesley and never to hear the name mentioned between them. 'You were speaking of your own heart.'

'Well, I was, no doubt. It is a silly thing to talk of, I dare say.'

'I'm going to tell you of my heart, and I hope you won't think it silly. I do so because I believe you to be a gentleman, and a man of honour.' He blushed at the words and the tone in which they were spoken,—but his heart fell still lower. 'Mr. Anderson, I am engaged.' Here she paused a moment, but

he had nothing to say. 'I am engaged to marry a
gentleman whom I love with all my heart, and all my
strength, and all my body. I love him so that nothing
can ever separate me from him, or at least from the
thoughts of him. As regards all the interests of life,
I feel as though I were already his wife. If I ever
marry any man I swear to you that it will be him.'
Then Mr. Anderson felt that all hope had utterly
departed from him. She had said that she believed
him to be a man of truth. He certainly believed her
to be a truth-speaking woman. He asked himself,
and he found it to be quite impossible to doubt her
word on this subject. 'Now I will go on and tell you
my troubles. My mother disapproves of the man.
Sir Magnus has taken upon himself to disapprove,
and Lady Mountjoy disapproves especially. I don't
care two straws about Sir Magnus and Lady Mountjoy. As to Lady Mountjoy, it is simply an impertinence on her part, interfering with me.' There was
something in her face as she said this, which made
Mr. Anderson feel that if he could only succeed in
having her and the pair of ponies, he would be a
prouder man than the ambassador at Paris. But he
knew that it was hopeless. 'As to my mother, that
is indeed a sorrow. She has been to me the dearest
mother, putting her only hopes of happiness in me.
No mother was ever more devoted to a child, and of
all children I should be the most ungrateful were I
to turn against her. But from my early years she has
wished me to marry a man whom I could not bring
myself to love. You have heard of Captain Scarborough?'

'The man who disappeared?'

'He was, and is, my first cousin.'

'He is in some way connected with Sir Magnus.'

'Through mamma. Mamma is aunt to Captain
Scarborough, and she married the brother of Sir
Magnus. Well, he has disappeared and been dis-
inherited. I cannot explain all about it, for I don't

understand it; but he has come to great trouble. It was not on that account that I would not marry him. It was partly because I did not like him, and partly because of Harry Annesley. I will tell you everything, because I want you to know my story. But my mother has disliked Mr. Annesley because she has thought he has interfered with my cousin.'

'I understand all that.'

'And she has been taught to think that Mr. Annesley has behaved very badly. I cannot quite explain it, because there is a brother of Captain Scarborough who has interfered. I never loved Captain Scarborough, but that man I hate. He has spread those stories. Captain Scarborough has disappeared, but before he went he thought it well to revenge himself on Mr. Annesley. He attacked him in the street late at night, and endeavoured to beat him.'

'But why?'

'Why, indeed! That such a trumpery cause as a girl's love should operate with such a man!'

'I can understand it;—oh! yes, I can understand it.'

'I believe he was tipsy, and he had been gambling and had lost all his money;—more than all his money. He was a ruined man, and reckless and wretched. I can forgive him, and so does Harry. But in the struggle Harry got the best of it, and left him there in the street. No weapons had been used, except that Captain Scarborough had a stick. There was no reason to suppose him hurt, nor was he much hurt. He had behaved very badly, and Harry left him. Had he gone for a policeman he could only have given him in charge. The man was not hurt, and seems to have walked away.'

'The papers were full of it.'

'Yes; the papers were full of it, because he was missing. I don't know yet what became of him, but I have my suspicions.'

'They say he has been seen at Monaco.'

'Very likely. But I have nothing to do with that. Though he was my cousin, I am touched nearer in another place. Young Mr. Scarborough, who I suspect knows all about his brother, took upon himself to cross-question Mr. Annesley. Mr. Annesley did not care to tell anything of that struggle in the streets, and denied that he had seen him. In truth, he did not want to have my name mentioned. My belief is that Augustus Scarborough knew exactly what had taken place when he asked the question. It was he who really was false. But he is now the heir to Tretton and a great man in his way, and in order to injure Harry Annesley he has spread abroad the story which they all tell here.'

'But why?'

'He does; that is all I know. But I will not be a hypocrite. He chose to wish that I should not marry Harry Annesley. I cannot tell you further than that. But he has persuaded mamma, and has told everyone. He shall never persuade me.'

'Everybody seems to believe him,' said Mr. Anderson, not as intending to say that he believed him now; but that he had done so.

'Of course they do. He has simply ruined Harry. He, too, has been disinherited now. I don't know how they do these things, but it has been done. His uncle has been turned against him, and his whole income has been taken from him. But they will never persuade me. Nor, if they did, would I be untrue to him. It is a grand thing for a girl to have a perfect faith in the man she has to marry;—as I have. I know my man, and will as soon disbelieve in heaven as in him. But were he what they say he is, he would still have to become my husband. I should be broken-hearted, but I should still be true. Thank God, though,— thank God,—he has done nothing and will do nothing to make me ashamed of him. Now you know my story.'

'Yes;—now I know it.' The tears came very near the poor man's eyes as he answered.

'And what will you do for me?'

'What shall I do?'

'Yes; what will you do? I have told you all my story, believing you to be a fine-tempered gentleman. You have entertained a fancy which has been encouraged by Sir Magnus. Will you promise me not to speak to me of it again? Will you relieve me of so much of my trouble? Will you,—will you?' Then, when he turned away, she followed him, and put both her hands upon his arm. 'Will you do that little thing for me?'

'A little thing!'

'Is it not a little thing;—when I am so bound to that other man that nothing can move me? Whether it be little or whether it be much, will you not do it?' She still held him by the arm, but his face was turned from her so that she could not see it. The tears, absolute tears, were running down his cheeks. What did it behove him as a man to do? Was he to believe her vows now and grant her request, and was she then to give herself to some third person and forget Harry Annesley altogether? How would it be with him then? A faint heart never won a fair lady. All is fair in love and war. You cannot catch cherries by holding your mouth open. A great amount of wisdom such as this came to him at the spur of the moment. But there was her hand upon his arm, and he could not elude her request. 'Will you not do it for me?' she asked again.

'I will,' he said, still keeping his face turned away.

'I knew it,—I knew you would. You are high-minded and honest, and cannot be cruel to a poor girl. And if in time to come, when I am Harry Annesley's wife, we shall chance to meet each other,—as we will,—he shall thank you.'

'I shall not want that. What will his thanks do

for me? You do not think that I shall be silent to oblige him?' Then he walked forth from out of the garden, and she had never seen his tears. But she knew well that he was weeping, and she sympathised with him.

Chapter XXXII

MR. ANDERSON IS ILL

WHEN they all went down to dinner that day, it became known that Mr. Anderson did not intend to dine with them. 'He's got a headache!' said Sir Magnus. 'He says he's got a headache. I never knew such a thing in my life before.' It was quite clear that Sir Magnus did not think that his lieutenant ought to have such a headache as would prevent his coming to dinner, and that he did not quite believe in the headache. There was a dinner ready, a very good dinner, which it was his business to provide. He always did provide it, and took a great deal of trouble to see that it was good. 'There isn't a table so well kept in all Brussels,' he used to boast. But when he had done his share, he expected that Anderson and Arbuthnot should do theirs,— especially Anderson. There had been sometimes a few words,—not quite a quarrel but nearly so,—on the subject of dining out. Sir Magnus only dined out with royalty, cabinet ministers, and other diplomats. Even then he rarely got a good dinner,—what he called a good dinner. He often took Anderson with him. He was the *doyen* among the diplomats in Brussels, and a little indulgence was shown to him. Therefore he thought that Anderson should be as true to him as was he to Anderson. It was not for Anderson's sake, indeed, who felt the bondage to be irksome. And Sir Magnus knew that his subordinate sometimes groaned in spirit. But a good dinner is a good dinner,—especially the best dinner in Brussels, and Sir Magnus felt that something ought to be given in return. He had not that perfect faith in mankind which is the surest evidence of a simple mind. Ideas crowded upon him. Had Anderson a snug little dinner-party, just two or three friends in his own room, Sir Magnus would not have been very angry. He was rarely very angry. But he should like to show his cleverness by finding it out. Anderson had been quite well when he was out riding, and he did not remember him ever before to have had a headache. 'Is he very bad, Arbuthnot?'

'I haven't seen him, sir, since he was riding.'

'Who has seen him?'

'He was in the garden with me,' said Florence boldly.

'I suppose that did not give him a headache.'

'Not that I perceived.'

'It is very singular that he should have a headache just when dinner is ready,' continued Sir Magnus.

'You had better leave the young man alone,' said Lady Mountjoy.

Anyone who knew the ways of living at the British Embassy would be sure that after this Sir Magnus would not leave the young man alone. His nature was not simple. It seemed to him again that there might be a little dinner party, and that Lady Mountjoy knew all about it. 'Richard,' he said to the butler, 'go into Mr. Anderson's room and see if he is very bad.' Richard came back, and whispered to the great man that Mr. Anderson was not in his room. 'This is very remarkable. A bad headache, and not in his room! Where is he? I insist on knowing where Mr. Anderson is.'

'You had better leave him alone,' said Lady Mountjoy.

'Leave a man alone because he's ill. He might die.'

'Shall I go and see?' said Arbuthnot.

'I wish you would, and bring him in here,—if he's well enough to show. I don't approve of a young man's going without his dinner. There's nothing so bad.'

'He'll be sure to get something, Sir Magnus,' said Lady Mountjoy. But Sir Magnus insisted that Mr. Arbuthnot should go and look after his friend.

It was now November, and at eight o'clock was quite dark, but the weather was fine, and something of the mildness of autumn remained. Arbuthnot was not long in discovering that Mr. Anderson was again walking in the garden. He had left Florence there and had gone to the house, but had found himself to be utterly desolate and miserable. She had exacted from him a promise which was not compatible with any kind of happiness to which he could now look forward. In the first place all Brussels knew that he had been in love with Florence Mountjoy. He thought that all Brussels knew it. And they knew that he had been in earnest in this love. He did believe that all Brussels had given him credit for so much. And now they would know that he had suddenly ceased to make love. It might be that this should be attributed to gallantry on his part,—that it should be considered that the lady had been deserted. But he was conscious that he was not so good a hypocrite as not to show that he was broken-hearted. He was quite sure that it would be seen that he had got the worst of it. But when he asked himself questions as to his own condition he told himself that there was suffering in store for him more heavy to bear than these. There could be no ponies, with Florence driving them, and a boy in his own livery behind, seen upon the boulevards. That vision was gone, and for ever. And then came upon him an idea that the absence of the girl from other portions of his life might touch him more nearly. He did feel something like actual love. And the more she had told him of her devotion to Harry Annesley, the more strongly he had felt the value of that devotion. Why should this man have it and not he? He had not been disinherited. He had not been knocked about in a street quarrel. He had not been driven to tell a lie as to his having not seen a man when he had in truth knocked him down. He had quite agreed with Florence that Harry was justified in the lie. But there was nothing in it to make the girl love him the better for it. And then, looking forward, he could perceive the possibility of an event, which, if it should occur, would cover him with confusion and disgrace. If after all Florence were to take, not Harry Annesley, but somebody else? How foolish, how credulous, how vain would he have been then to have made the promise! Girls did such things every day. He had promised, and he thought that he must keep his promise; but she would be bound by no promise! As he thought of it he reflected that he might even yet exact such a promise from her.

But when the dinner-time came he really was sick with love,—or sick with disappointment. He felt that he could not eat his dinner under the battery of the raillery which was always coming from Sir Magnus, and therefore he had told the servants that as the evening progressed he would have something to eat in his own room. And then he went out to wander in the dusk beneath the trees in the garden. Here he was encountered by Mr. Arbuthnot with his dress boots and white cravat. 'What the mischief are you doing here, old fellow?'

'I'm not very well. I have an awfully bilious headache.'

'Sir Magnus is kicking up a deuce of a row because you're not there.'

'Sir Magnus be blowed. How am I to be there if I've got a bilious headache? I'm not dressed. I could not have dressed myself for a five-pound note.'

'Couldn't you now? Shall I go back and tell him

that? But you must have something to eat. I don't know what's up, but Sir Magnus is in a taking.'

'He's always in a taking. I sometimes think he's the biggest fool out.'

'And there's the place kept vacant next to Miss Mountjoy. Grascour wanted to sit there, but her ladyship wouldn't let him. And I sat next Miss Abbott because I didn't want to be in your way.'

'Tell Grascour to go and sit there,—or you may do so. It's all nothing to me.' This he said in the bitterness of his heart, by no means intending to tell his secret, but unable to keep it within his own bosom.

'What's the matter, Anderson?' asked the other piteously.

'I am clean broken-hearted. I don't mind telling you. I know you're a good fellow, and I'll tell you everything. It's all over.'

'All over,—with Miss Mountjoy?' Then Anderson began to tell the whole story; but before he had got half through, or a quarter through, another message came from Sir Magnus. 'Sir Magnus is becoming very angry indeed,' whispered the butler. 'He says that Mr. Arbuthnot is to go back.'

'I'd better go or I shall catch it.'

'What's up with him, Richard?' asked Anderson.

'Well, if you ask me, Mr. Anderson, I think he's —a suspecting of something.'

'What does he suspect?'

'I think he's a thinking that perhaps you are having a jolly time of it.' Richard had known his master many years, and could almost read his inmost thoughts. 'I don't say as it is so, but that's what I am thinking.'

'You tell him I ain't. You tell him I've a bad bilious headache, and that the air in the garden does it good. You tell him that I mean to have something to eat upstairs when my head is better;—and do you mind and let me have it, and a bottle of claret.'

With this the butler went back, and so did Arbuthnot, after asking one other question. 'I'm so sorry it isn't all serene with Miss Mountjoy?'

'It isn't then. Don't mind now, but it isn't serene. Don't say a word about her; but she has done me. I think I shall get leave of absence and go away for two months. You'll have to do all the riding, old fellow. I shall go—— But I don't know where I shall go. You return to them now, and tell them I've such a bilious headache I don't know which way to turn myself.'

Arbuthnot went back and found Sir Magnus quarrelling grievously with the butler. 'I don't think he's doing anything as he shouldn't,' the butler whispered, having seen into his master's mind.

'What do you mean by that?'

'Do let the matter drop,' said Lady Mountjoy, who had also seen into her husband's mind, and saw, moreover, that the butler had done so. 'A young man's dinner isn't worth all this bother.'

'I won't let the matter drop. What does he mean when he says that he isn't doing anything that he shouldn't? I've never said anything about what he was doing.'

'He isn't dressed, Sir Magnus. He finds himself a little better now, and means to have something upstairs.' Then there came an awful silence, during which the dinner was eaten. Sir Magnus knew nothing of the truth, simply suspecting the headache to be a myth. Lady Mountjoy, with a woman's quickness, thought that there had been some words between Florence and her late lover, and, as she disliked Florence, was inclined to throw all the blame upon her. A word had been said to Mrs. Mountjoy. 'I don't think he'll trouble me any more, mamma,'— which Mrs. Mountjoy did not quite understand, but which she connected with the young man's absence. But Florence understood it all, and liked Mr. Anderson the better. Could it really be that for love of her he would lose his dinner? Could it be that he was so grievously afflicted at the loss of a girl's heart? There he was, walking out in the dark and the cold, half-famished, all because she loved Harry Annesley so well that there could be no chance for him! Girls believe so little in the truth of the love of men that any sign of its reality touches them to the core. Poor Hugh Anderson! A tear came into her eye as she thought that he was wandering there in the dark, and all for the love of her. The rest of the dinner passed away in silence, and Sir Magnus hardly became cordial and communicative with M. Grascour, even under the influence of his wine.

On the next morning just before lunch Florence was waylaid by Mr. Anderson as she was passing along one of the passages in the back part of the house. 'Miss Mountjoy,' he said, 'I want to ask from your great goodness the indulgence of a few words.'

'Certainly.'

'Could you come into the garden?'

'If you will give me time to go and change my boots and get a shawl. We ladies are not ready to go out always as are you gentlemen.'

'Anywhere will do. Come in here;' and he led the way into a small parlour which was not often used.

'I was so sorry to hear last night that you were unwell, Mr. Anderson.'

'I was not very well certainly after what I had heard before dinner.' He did not tell her that he so far recovered as to be able to drink a bottle of claret, and to smoke a couple of cigars in his bedroom. 'Of course you remember what took place yesterday.'

'Remember! oh! yes. I shall not readily forget it.'

'I made you a promise.'

'You did;—very kindly.'

'And I mean to keep it.'

'I'm sure you do;—because you're a gentleman.'

'I don't think I ought to have made it.'

'Oh! Mr. Anderson!'

'I don't think I ought. See what I am giving up.'

'Nothing!—except the privilege of troubling me.'

'But if it should be something else? Do not be angry with me,—but, loving you as I do, of course my mind is full of it. I have promised, and must be dumb.'

'And I shall be spared great vexation.'

'But suppose I were to hear that in six months' time you had married someone else!'

'Mr. Annesley, you mean. Not in six months.'

'Somebody else. Not Mr. Annesley.'

'There is nobody else.'

'But there might be.'

'It is impossible. After all that I told you, do not you understand?'

'But if there were?' The poor man as he made the suggestion looked very piteous. 'If there were, I think you should promise me I shall be that somebody else. That would be no more than fair.'

She paused a moment to think, frowning the while. 'Certainly not!'

'Certainly not?'

'I can make no such promise, nor should you ask it. I am to promise that under certain circumstances I would become your wife, when I know that under no circumstances I would do so.'

'Under no circumstances?'

'Under none. What would you have me say, Mr. Anderson? Supposing yourself engaged to marry a girl——'

'I wish I were,—to you.'

'To a girl who loved you, and whom you loved.'

'There's no doubt about my loving her.'

'You can follow my meaning, and I wish that you would do so. What would you think if you were to hear that she had promised to marry someone else in the event of your deserting her? It is out of the question. I mean to be the wife of Harry Annesley. Say that it is not to be so, and you will simply destroy me. Of one thing I may be sure,—that I will marry him or nobody. You promised me, not because your promise was necessary for that, but to spare me from trouble till that time shall come. And I am grateful —very grateful.' Then she left him,—suffering from another headache.

'Was there anything said between you and Mr. Anderson yesterday?' her aunt inquired that afternoon.

'Why do you ask?'

'Because it is necessary that I should know.'

'I do not see the necessity. Mr. Anderson has at any rate your permission to say what he likes to me, but I am not on that account bound to tell you all that he does say. But I will tell you. He has promised to trouble me no further. I told him that I was engaged to Mr. Annesley, and he, like a gentleman, has assured me that he will desist.'

'Just because you asked him?'

'Yes, aunt; just because I asked him.'

'He will not be bound by such a promise for a moment. It is a thing not to be heard of. If that kind of thing is to go on, any young lady will be entitled to ask any young gentleman not to say a word of marriage, just at her request.'

'Some of the young ladies would not care for that, perhaps.'

'Don't be impertinent.'

'I should not, for one, aunt; only that I am already engaged.'

'And of course the young ladies would be bound to make such requests,—which would go for nothing at all. I never heard of anything so monstrous. You are not only to have the liberty of refusing, but are to be allowed to bind a gentleman not to ask!'

'He has promised.'

'Pshaw! It means nothing.'

'It is between him and me. I asked him because I wished to save myself from being troubled.'

'As for that other man, my dear, it is quite out of the question. From all that I hear it is on the cards that he may be arrested and put into prison. I am quite sure that at any rate he deserves it. The letters which Sir Magnus gets about him are fearful. The things that he has done—; well; penal servitude for life would be the proper punishment. And it will come upon him sooner or later. I never knew a man of that kind escape. And you now to come and tell us that you intend to be his wife!'

'I do,' said Florence, bobbing her head.

'And what your uncle says to you has no effect?'

'Not the least in the world; nor what my aunt says. I believe that neither the one nor the other know what they are talking about. You have been defaming a gentleman of the highest character, a Fellow of a college, a fine-hearted, noble, high-spirited man, simply because,—because,—because ——' Then she burst into tears and rushed out of the room; but she did not break down before she had looked at her aunt, and spoken to her aunt with a fierce indignation which had altogether served to silence Lady Mountjoy for the moment.

Chapter XXXIII

MR. BARRY

'GOOD-BYE, sir. You ought not to be angry with me. I am sure it will be better for us both to remain as we are.' This was said by Miss Dorothy Grey, as a gentleman departed from her and made his way out of the front door at the Fulham Manor House. Miss Grey had received an offer of marriage, and had declined it. The offer had been made by a worthy man, he being no other than her father's partner, Mr. Barry.

It may be remembered that, on discussing the affairs of the firm with her father, Dolly Grey had been accustomed to call this partner 'the Devil.' It was not that she had thought this partner to be specially devilish; nor was he so. It had ever been Miss Grey's object to have the affairs of the firm managed with an integrity which among lawyers might be called Quixotic. Her father she had dubbed 'Reason,' and herself 'Conscience;' but in calling Mr. Barry 'the Devil,' she had not intended to signify any defalcation from honesty more than ordinary in lawyers' offices. She did, in fact, like Mr. Barry. He would occasionally come out and dine with her father. He was courteous and respectful, and performed his duties with diligence. He spent nobody's money but his own, and not all of that; nor did he look upon the world as a place to which men were sent that they might play. He was nearly forty years old, was clean, a little bald, and healthy in all his ways. There was nothing of a devil about him,—except that his conscience was not peculiarly attentive to abstract honesty and abstract virtue. There must, according to him, be always a little 'give and take' in the world; but in the pursuit of his profession he gave a great deal more than he took. He thought himself to be an honest practitioner, and yet in all domestic professional conferences with her father Mr. Barry had always been Miss Grey's 'Devil.'

The possibility of such a request, as had been now made, had been already discussed between Dolly and her father. Dolly had said that the idea was absurd. Mr. Grey had not seen the absurdity. There had been nothing more common, he had said, than that a young partner should marry an old partner's daughter. 'It's not put into the partnership deed?' Dolly had rejoined. But Dolly had never believed that the time would come. Now it had come.

Mr. Barry had as yet possessed no more than a fourth of the business. He had come in without any capital, and had been contented with a fourth. He now suggested to Dolly that on their marriage the business should be equally divided. And he had named the house in which they would live. There was a pleasant genteel residence on the other side of the water,—at Putney. Miss Grey had suggested that the business might be divided in a manner that would be less burdensome to Mr. Barry. As for the house,—she could not leave her father. Upon the whole she had thought that it would be better for both of them that they should remain as they were. By that Miss Grey had not intended to signify that Mr. Barry was to remain single, but that he would have to do so in reference to Miss Grey.

When he was gone Dolly Grey spent the remainder of the afternoon in contemplating what would have been her condition had she agreed to join her lot to that of Mr. Barry, and she came to the conclusion that it would have been simply unendurable. There was nothing of romance in her nature; but as she looked at matrimony with all its blisses, —and Mr. Barry among them,—she told herself that death would be preferable. 'I know myself,' she said. 'I should come to hate him with a miserable hatred. And then I should hate myself for having done him so great an evil.' And as she continued thinking, she assured herself that there was but one man with whom she could live, and that that man was her father. And then other questions presented themselves to her; which were not so easily answered. What would become of her when he should go? He was now sixty-six, and she was only thirty-two. He was healthy for his age, but would complain of his work. She knew that he must in course of nature go much the first. Ten years he might live, while she might probably be called upon to endure for thirty more. 'I shall have to do it all alone,' she said; 'all alone;— without a companion, without one soul to whom I can open my own. But if I were to marry Mr. Barry,'

she continued, 'I should at once be encumbered with
a soul to whom I could not open my own. I suppose
I shall be enabled to live through it as do others.'
Then she began to prepare for her father's coming.
As long as he did remain with her she would make
the most of him.

'Papa,' she said as she took him by the hand as
he entered the house, and led him into the dining-
room. 'Who do you think has been here?'

'Mr. Barry.'

'Then he has told you?'

'Not a word;—not even that he was coming. But
I saw him as he left the chambers, and he had on a
bright hat and a new coat.'

'And he thought that those could move me.'

'I have not known that he has wanted to move
you. You asked me to guess, and I have guessed
right, it seems.'

'Yes; you have guessed right.'

'And why did he come?'

'Only to ask me to be his wife.'

'And what did you say to him, Dolly?'

'What did I say to the Devil?' She still held him
by the hand, and now she laughed lightly as she
looked into his face. 'Cannot you guess what I said
to him?'

'I am sorry for it;—that's all.'

'Sorry for it? Oh, papa, do not say that you are
sorry. Do you want to lose me?'

'I do not want to think that for my own selfish
purposes I have retained you. So he has asked you?'

'Yes; he has asked me.'

'And you have answered him positively!'

'Most positively.'

'And for my sake?'

'No, papa; I have not said that. I was joking when
I asked whether you wished to lose me. Of course
you do not want to lose me.' Then she wound her
arm round him, and put up her face to be kissed. 'But

now come and dress yourself, as you call it. The dinner is late. We will talk about it again after dinner.'

But immediately after dinner the conversation went away to Mr. Scarborough and the Scarborough matters. 'I am to see Augustus, and he is to tell me something about Mountjoy and his affairs. They say that Mountjoy is now in Paris. The money can be given to them now, if he will consent and will sign the deed releasing the property. But the men have not all as yet agreed to accept the simple sums which they advanced. That fellow Hart stands out and says that he would sooner lose it all.'

'Then he will lose it all,' said Dolly.

'But the squire will consent to pay nothing unless they all agree. Augustus is talking about his excessive generosity.'

'It is generous on his part,' said Dolly.

'He sees his own advantage, though I cannot quite understand where. He tells Tyrrwhit that as there is so great an increase to the property he is willing, for the sake of the good name of the family, to pay all that has been in truth advanced; but he is most anxious to do it now, while his father is alive. I think he fears that there will be law-suits, and that they may succeed. I doubt whether he thanks his father.'

'But why should his father lie for his sake since they are on such bad terms?'

'Because his father was on worse terms with Mountjoy when he told the lie. That is what I think Augustus thinks. But his father told no lie at that time; and cannot now go back to falsehood. My belief is that if he were confident that such is the fact he would not surrender a shilling to pay these men their moneys. He may stop a law-suit,—which is like enough, though they could only lose it. And if Mountjoy should turn out to be the heir,—which is impossible, —he will be able to turn round and say that by his efforts he had saved so much of the property.'

'My head becomes so bewildered,' said Dolly, 'that I can hardly understand it yet.'

'I think I understand it; but I can only guess at his mind. But he has got Tyrrwhit to accept forty thousand pounds, which is the sum he in truth advanced. The stake is too great for the man to lose it without ruin. He can get it back now, and save himself. But Hart is the more determined blackguard. He, with two others, has a claim for thirty-five thousand pounds, for which he has given but ten thousand pounds in hard cash, and he thinks that he may get some profit out of Tyrrwhit's money, and holds out.'

'For how much?'

'For the entire debt, he tells me; but I know that he is trying to deal with Tyrrwhit. Tyrrwhit would pay him five thousand, I think, so as to secure the immediate payment of his own money. Then there are a host of others who are contented to take what they have advanced, but not contented if Hart is to have more. There are other men in the background who advanced the money. All the rascaldom of London is let loose upon me. But Hart is the one man who holds his head the highest.'

'But if they will accept no terms they will get nothing,' said Dolly. 'If once they attempt to go to law all will be lost.'

'There are wheels within wheels. When the old man dies Mountjoy himself will probably put in a claim to the entire estate, and will get some lawyer to take up the case for him.'

'You would not?'

'Certainly not,—because I know that Augustus is the eldest legitimate son. As far as I can make it out Augustus is at present allowing Mountjoy the money on which he lives. His father does not. But the old man must know that Augustus does, though he pretends to be ignorant.'

'But why is Hart to get money out of Tyrrwhit?'

'To secure the payment of the remainder. Mr. Tyrrwhit would be very glad to get his forty thousand pounds back—would pay five thousand pounds to get the forty back. But nothing will be paid unless they all agree to join in freeing the property. Therefore Hart, who is the sharpest rascal of the lot, stands out for some share of his contemplated plunder.'

'And you must be joined in such an arrangement?'

'Not at all. I cannot help surmising what is to be done. In dealing with the funds of the property I go to the men, and say to them so much, and so much, and so much you have actually lost. Agree among yourselves to accept that, and it shall be paid to you. That is honest?'

'I do not know.'

'But I do. Every shilling that the son of my client has had from them my client is ready to pay. There is some hitch among them, and I make my surmises. But I have no dealings with them. It is for them to come to me now.' Dolly only shook her head. 'You cannot touch pitch and not be defiled.' That was what Dolly said, but she said it to herself. And then she went on and declared to herself still further that Mr. Barry was pitch. She knew that Mr. Barry had seen Hart, and had seen Tyrrwhit, and had been bargaining with them. She excused her father because he was her father; but according to her thinking there should have been no dealings with such men as these, except at the end of a pair of tongs.

'And now, Dolly,' said her father, after a long pause, 'tell me about Mr. Barry.'

'There is nothing more to be told.'

'Not of what you said to him, but of the reasons which have made you so determined. Would it not be better for you to be married?'

'If I could choose my husband.'

'Whom would you choose?'

'You.'

'That is nonsense. I am your father.'

'You know what I mean. There is no one else

among my circle of acquaintances with whom I should care to live. There is no one else with whom I should care to do more than die. When I look at it all round it seems to be absolutely impossible that I should on a sudden entertain habits of the closest intimacy with such a one as Mr. Barry. What should I say to him when he went forth in the morning? How should I welcome him when he came back at night? What would be our breakfast, and what would be our dinner? Think what are yours and mine;—all the little solicitudes; all the free abuse; all the certainty of an affection which has grown through so many years; all the absolute assurance on the part of each that the one does really know the inner soul of the other.'

'It would come.'

'With Mr. Barry? That is your idea of my soul, with which you have been in communion for so many years? In the first place you think that I am a person likely to be able to transfer myself suddenly to the first man that comes in my way?'

'Gradually you might do so,—at any rate so as to make life possible. You will be all alone. Think what it will be to have to live all alone.'

'I have thought. I do know that it would be well that you should be able to take me with you.'

'But I cannot.'

'No. There is the hardship. You must leave me, and I must be alone. That is what we have to expect. But for your sake, and for mine, we may be left while we can be left. What would you be without me? Think of that.'

'I should bear it.'

'You couldn't. You'd break your heart and die. And if you can imagine my living there, and pouring out Mr. Barry's tea for him, you must imagine also what I should have to say to myself about you: "He will die, of course. But then he has come to that sort of age, at which it doesn't much signify." Then I should go on with Mr. Barry's tea. He'd come to kiss me when he went away, and I—should plunge a knife into him.'

'Dolly!'

'Or into myself, which would be more likely. Fancy that man calling me Dolly.' Then she got up and stood behind his chair, and put her arms round his neck. 'Would you like to kiss him? Or any man, for the matter of that? There is no one else to whom my fancy strays, but I think that I should murder them all,—or commit suicide. In the first place I should want my husband to be a gentleman. There are not a great many gentlemen about.'

'You are fastidious.'

'Come now, be honest. Is our Mr. Barry a gentleman?' Then there was a pause, during which she waited for a reply. 'I will have an answer. I have a right to demand an answer to that question, since you have proposed the man to me as a husband.'

'Nay, I have not proposed him.'

'You have expressed a regret that I have not accepted him. Is he a gentleman?'

'Well,—yes; I think he is.'

'Mind; we are sworn, and you are bound to speak the truth. What right has he to be a gentleman? Who was his father and who was his mother? Of what kind were his nursery belongings? He has become an attorney, and so have you. But has there been anyone to whisper to him among his teachings that in that profession, as in all others, there should be a sense of high honour to guide him? He must not cheat, or do anything to cause him to be struck off the rolls; but is it not with him what his client wants and not what honour demands? And in the daily intercourse of life would he satisfy what you call my fastidiousness?'

'Nothing on earth will ever do that.'

'You do. I agree with you that nothing else on earth ever will. The man who might, won't come. Not that I can imagine such a man, because I know that I am spoiled. Of course there are gentlemen, though not a great many. But he mustn't be ugly, and he mustn't be good-looking. He mustn't seem to be old, and certainly he mustn't seem to be young. I should not like a man to wear old clothes, but he mustn't wear new. He must be well read, but never show it. He must work hard, but he must come home to dinner at the proper time.' Here she laughed, and gently shook her head. 'He must never talk about his business at night. Though dear, dear, darling old father, he shall do that if he will talk like you. And then, which is the hardest thing of all, I must have known him intimately for at any rate ten years. As for Mr. Barry, I never should know him intimately, though I were married to him for ten years.'

'And it has all been my doing?'

'Just so. You have made the bed and you must lie on it. It hasn't been a bad bed.'

'Not for me! Heaven knows it has not been bad for me.'

'Nor for me, as things go;—only that there will come an arousing before we shall be ready to get up together. Your time will probably be the first. I can better afford to lose you than you to lose me.'

'God send that it shall be so.'

'It is nature,' she said. 'It is to be expected, and will on that account be the less grievous because it has been expected. I shall have to devote myself to those Carroll children. I sometimes think that the work of the world should not be made pleasant to us. What profit will it be to me to have done my duty by you? I think there will be some profit if I am good to my cousins.'

'At any rate, you won't have Mr. Barry?' said the father.

'Not if I know it,' said the daughter; 'and you, I think, are a wicked old man to suggest it.' Then she bade him good-night and went to bed, for they had been talking now till near twelve.

But Mr. Barry, when he had gone home, told himself that he had progressed in his love-suit quite as far as he had expected on the first opportunity. He went over the bridge and looked at the genteel house, and resolved as to certain little changes which should be made. That one room should look here, and the nursery should look there. The walk to the railway would only take five minutes, and there would be five minutes again from the Temple Station in London. He thought it would do very well for domestic felicity. And as for a fortune, half of the business would not be bad. And then the whole business would follow, and he in his turn would be enabled to let some young fellow in who should do the greater part of the work and take the smaller part of the pay,—as had been the case with himself.

But it had not occurred to him that the young lady had meant what she said when she refused him. It was the ordinary way with young ladies. Of course he had expected no enthusiasm of love; nor had he wanted it. He would wait for three weeks, and then he would go to Fulham again.

Chapter XXXIV

MR. JUNIPER

THOUGH there was an air of badinage, almost of tomfoolery, about Dolly when she spoke of her matrimonial prospects to her father,—as when she said that she would 'stick a knife' into Mr. Barry,— still there was a seriousness in all she said which was more than grave. She was pathetic and melancholy. She knew that there was nothing before her but to stay with her father, and then to devote herself to her cousins, from whom she was aware that she recoiled almost with hatred. And she knew that it would be a good thing to be married,—if only the right man would come. The right man would have to bear with her father, and live in the same house with him to the end. The right man must be a '*preux chevalier sans peur et sans reproche*.'* The right man must be strong-minded and masterful, and must have a will of his own; but he must be strong-minded always for good. And where was she to find such a man as this, she who was only an attorney's daughter, plain too, and with many eccentricities? She was not intended to marry, and consequently the only man who came in her way was her father's partner,—for whom, in regard to a share in the business, she might be desirable.

Devotion to the Carroll cousins was manifestly her duty. The two eldest girls she absolutely did hate,—and their father. To hate the father, because he was vicious beyond cure, might be very well; but she could not hate the girls without being aware that she was guilty of a grievous sin. Every taste possessed by them was antagonistic to her. Their amusements, their literature, their clothes, their manners,—especially in regard to men,—their gestures and colour, were distasteful to her. 'They hide their dirt with a thin veneer of cheap finery,' said Dolly to her father. He had replied by telling her that she was nasty. 'No; but, unfortunately, I cannot but see nastiness.' Dolly herself was clean to fastidiousness. Take off her coarse frock, and there the well-dressed lady began. 'Look at the heels of Sophie's boots. Give her a push, and she'd fall off her pins as though they were stilts. They're always asking to have a shoemaker's bill paid, and yet they won't wear stout boots.' 'I'll pay the man,' she said to Amelia one day, 'if you'll promise to wear what I'll buy you for the next six months.' But Amelia had only turned up her nose. These were the relatives to whom it would become her duty to devote her life!

The next morning she started off to call in Bolsover Terrace with an intention, not to begin her duty, but to make a struggle at the adequate performance of it. She took with her some article of clothing intended for one of the younger children, but which the child herself was to complete. But when she entered the parlour, she was astounded at finding that Mr. Carroll was there. It was nearly twelve o'clock, and at that time Mr. Carroll never was there. He was either in bed, or at Tattersall's, or —— Dolly did not care where. She had long since made up her mind that there must be a permanent quarrel between herself and her uncle, and her desire was generally respected. Now, unfortunately, he was present, and with him were his wife and two elder daughters. To be devoted, thought Dolly to herself, to such a family as this,—and without anybody else in the world to care for! She gave her aunt a kiss, and touched the girls' hands, and made a very distant bow to Mr. Carroll. Then she began about the parcel in her hands, and having given her instructions, was about to depart.

But her aunt stopped her. 'I think you ought to know, Dorothea.'

'Certainly,' said Mr. Carroll. 'It is quite right that your cousin should know.'

'If you think it proper, I'm sure I can't object,' said Amelia.

'She won't approve, I'm sure,' said Sophie.

'Her young man has come forward and spoken,' said Mr. Carroll.

'And quite in a proper spirit,' said Amelia.

'Of course,' said Mrs. Carroll, 'we are not to expect too much. Though we are respectable, in birth and all that, we are poor. Mr. Carroll has got nothing to give her.'

'I've been the most unfortunate man in the world,' said Mr. Carroll.

'We won't talk about that now,' continued Mrs. Carroll. 'Here we are without anything.'

'You have decent blood,' said Dolly; 'at any rate, on one side;'—for she did not believe in the Carrolls.

'On both, on both,' said Mr. Carroll, rising up, and putting his hand upon his heart. 'I can boast of royal blood among my ancestors.'

'But here we are without anything,' said Mrs. Carroll again. 'Mr. Juniper is a most respectable man.'

'He has been attached to some of the leading racing establishments in the kingdom,' said Mr. Carroll. Dolly had heard of Mr. Juniper as a trainer, though she did not accurately know what a trainer meant.

'He is almost as great a man as the owner, for the matter of that,' said Amelia, standing up for her lover.

'He is not to say young; perhaps forty,' said Mrs. Carroll, 'and he has a very decent house of his own at Newmarket.' Dolly immediately began to think whether this might be for the better or for the worse. Newmarket was a long way off, and the girl would be taken away. And it might be a good thing to dispose of one of such a string of daughters, even to Mr. Juniper. Of course there would be the disagreeable nature of the connection. But, as Dolly had once said to her father, their share of the world's burdens had to be borne, and this was one of them. Her first cousin must marry the trainer. She, who had spoken so enthusiastically about gentlemen, must put up with it. She knew that Mr. Juniper was but a small man in his own line, but she would never disown him by word of mouth. He should be her cousin Juniper. But she did hope that she might not be called upon to see him frequently. After all, he might be much more respectable than Mr. Carroll.

'I am glad he has a house of his own,' said Dolly.

'It's a much better house than Fulham Manor,' said Amelia.

Dolly was angered, not at the comparison between the houses, but at the ingratitude and insolence of the girl. 'Very well,' said she, addressing herself to her aunt; 'if her parents are contented, of course it is not for me or for papa to be discontented. The thing to think of is the honesty of the man and his industry;— not the excellence of the house.'

'But you seemed to think that we were to live in a pigsty,' said Amelia.

'Mr. Juniper stands very high on the turf,' said Mr. Carroll. 'Mr. Leadbit's horses have always run straight, and Mousetrap won the Two-year-old Trial Stakes last spring, giving two pounds to Box-and-Cox. A good-looking, tall fellow. You remember seeing him here once last summer.' This was addressed to Miss Grey; but Miss Grey had made up her mind never to exchange a word with Mr. Carroll.

'When is it to be, my dear?' said Miss Grey, turning to the ladies, but intending to address herself to Amelia. She had already made up her mind to forgive the girl for her insolence about the house. If the girl was to be taken away there was so much the more reason for forgiving her that and other things.

'Oh! I thought you did not mean to speak to me at all,' said Amelia. 'I supposed the cut was to be extended from papa to me.'

'Amelia, how can you be so silly?' said the mother.

'If you think that I am going to put up with that kind of thing, you're mistaken,' said Amelia. She had got not only a lover but a husband in prospect, and was much superior to her cousin,—who had neither one nor the other, as far as she was aware. 'Mr. Juniper, with an excellent house and a plentiful income, is quite good enough for me, though he hasn't got any regal ancestors.' She did not intend to laugh at her father, but was aware that something had been said about ancestors by her cousin. 'A gentleman who has the management of horses is almost the same as owning them.'

'But when is it to be?' again asked Dolly.

'That depends a little upon my brother,' said Mrs.

Carroll, in a voice hardly above a whisper. 'Mr. Juniper has spoken about a day.'

'Then it will depend chiefly on himself and the young lady, I suppose.'

'Well, Dorothea, there are money difficulties. There's no denying it.'

'I wish I could shower gold into her lap,' said Mr. Carroll;—'only for the accursed conventionalities of the world.'

'Bother papa,' said Sophia.

'It will be the last of it as far as I am concerned,' said Amelia.

'Mr. Juniper has said something about a few hundred pounds,' said Mrs. Carroll. 'It isn't much that he wants.'

Then Miss Grey spoke in a severe tone. 'You must speak to my father about that.'

'I am not to have your good word, I suppose,' said Amelia. Human flesh and blood could not but remember all that had been done, and always with her consent. 'Five hundred pounds is not a great deal for portioning off a girl when that is to be the last that she is ever to have.' One of six nieces whose father and mother were maintained, and that without the slightest claim! It was so that Dorothy argued; but her arguments were kept to her own bosom. 'But I must trust to my dear uncle. I see that I am not to have a word from you.'

The matter was now becoming serious. Here was the eldest girl, one of six daughters, putting in her claim for five hundred pounds portion. This would amount to three thousand pounds for the lot, and, as the process of marrying them went on, they would all have to be maintained as at present. What with their school expenses and their clothes, the necessary funds for the Carroll family amounted to six hundred pounds a year. That was the regular allowance, and there were others whenever Mr. Carroll wanted a pair of trousers. And Dolly's acerbation was aroused by a belief on her part that the money asked for trousers took him generally to race-courses. And now five hundred pounds was boldly demanded so as to induce a groom to make one of the girls his wife! She almost regretted that in former years she had promised to assist her father in befriending the Carroll relations. 'Perhaps, Dorothea, you won't mind stepping into my bedroom with me, just for a moment.' This was said by Mrs. Carroll, and Dolly most unwillingly followed her aunt upstairs.

'Of course I know all that you've got to say,' began Mrs. Carroll.

'Then, aunt, why bring me in here?'

'Because I wish to explain things a little. Don't be ill-natured, Dorothea.'

'I won't if I can help it.'

'I know your nature, how good it is.' Here Dorothy shook her head. 'Only think of me and of my sufferings! I haven't come to this without suffering.' Then the poor woman began to cry.

'I feel for you through it all; I do,' said Dolly.

'That poor man! To have to be always with him, and always doing my best to keep him out of mischief.'

'A man who will do nothing else must do harm.'

'Of course he must. But what can he do now? And the children! I can see. Of course I know that they are not all that they ought to be. But with six of them, and nobody but myself, how can I do it all? And they are his children as well as mine.' Dolly's heart was filled with pity as she heard this, which she knew to be so true! 'In answering you they have uppish bad ways. They don't like to submit to one so near their own age.'

'Not a word that has come from the mouth of one of them addressed to myself has ever done them any harm with my father. That is what you mean.'

'No;—but with yourself.'

'I do not take anger,—against them,—out of the room with me.'

'Now about Mr. Juniper?'

'The question is one much too big for me. Am I to tell my father?'

'I was thinking,—that if you would do so!'

'I cannot tell him that he ought to find five hundred pounds for Mr. Juniper.'

'Perhaps four would do.'

'Nor can I ask him to drive a bargain.'

'How much would he give her,—to be married?'

'Why should he give her anything? He feeds her and gives her clothes. It is only fit that the truth should be explained to you. Girls so circumstanced, when they are clothed and fed by their own fathers, must be married without fortunes or must remain unmarried. As Sophie, and Georgina, and Minna, and Brenda come up, the same requests will be made.'

'Poor Potsey!' said the mother. For Potsey was a plain girl.

'If this be done for Amelia, must it not be done for all of them? Papa is not a rich man, but he has been very generous. Is it fair to ask him for five hundred pounds to give to—Mr. Juniper?'

'A gentleman nowadays does not like not to get something.'

'Then a gentleman must go where something is to be got. The truth has to be told, Aunt Carroll. My father is willing enough to do what he can for you and the girls, but I do not think that he will give five hundred pounds to Mr. Juniper.'

'It is once for all. Four hundred pounds perhaps would do.'

'I do not think that he can make a bargain,—nor that he will pay any sum to Mr. Juniper.'

'To get one of them off would be so much! What is to become of them? To have one married would be the way for others. Oh! Dorothy, if you would only think of my condition! I know your papa will do what you tell him.'

Dolly felt that her father would be more likely to

do it if she were not to interfere at all. But she could not say that. She did feel the request to be altogether unreasonable. She struggled to avert from her own mind all feeling of dislike for the girl, and to look at it as she might have done if Amelia had been her special friend.

'Aunt Carroll,' she said, 'you had better go up to London and see my father there,—in his chambers. You will catch him if you go at once.'

'Alone?'

'Yes, alone. Tell him about the girl's marriage, and let him judge what he ought to do.'

'Could not you come with me?'

'No. You don't understand. I have to think of his money. He can say what he will do with his own.'

'He will never give it without coming to you.'

'He never will if he does come to me. You may prevail with him. A man may throw away his own money as he pleases. I cannot tell him that he ought to do it. You may say that you have told me, and that I have sent you to him. And tell him, let him do what he will, that I shall find no fault with him. If you can understand me and him you will know that I can do nothing for you beyond that.' Then Dolly took her leave, and went home.

The mother, turning it all over in her mind, did understand something of her niece, and went off to London as quick as the omnibus could take her. There she did see her brother, and he came back in consequence to dinner a little earlier than usual. 'Why did you send my sister to me?' were the first words which he said to Dolly.

'Because it was your business, and not mine.'

'How dare you separate my business and yours? What do you think I have done?'

'Given the young lady five hundred pounds down the nail.'

'Worse than that.'

'Worse?'

'Much worse. But why did you send my sister to my chambers?'

'But what have you done, papa? You don't mean that you have given the shark more than he demands?'

'I don't know that he's a shark. Why shouldn't the man want five hundred pounds with his wife? Mr. Barry would want much more with you, and would be entitled to ask for much more.'

'You are my father.'

'Yes;—but those poor girls have been taught to look upon me almost as their father.'

'But what have you done?'

'I have promised them each three hundred and fifty pounds on their wedding-day,—three hundred pounds to go to their husbands, and fifty pounds for wedding expenses,—on condition that they marry with my approval. I shall not be so hard to please for them as for you.'

'And you have approved of Mr. Juniper?'

'I have already set on foot inquiries down at Newmarket; and I have made an exception in favour of Mr. Juniper. He is to have four hundred and fifty pounds. Jane only asked for four hundred pounds to begin with. You are not to find fault with me.'

'No;—that is part of the bargain. I wonder whether my aunt knew what a thoroughly good-natured thing I did. We must have no more puddings now, and you must come down by the omnibus.'

'It is not quite so bad as that, Dolly.'

'When one has given away one's money extravagantly one ought to be made to feel the pinch one's self. But dear, dear, darling old man, why shouldn't you give away your money as you please? I don't want it. I am not in the least afraid but what there will be plenty for me. But when the girl talks about her five hundred pounds so glibly, as though she had a right to expect it, and spoke of this jockey with such inward pride of heart——'

'A girl ought to be proud of her husband.'

'Your niece ought not to be proud of marrying a groom. But she angered me, and so did my aunt,— though I pitied her. Then I reflected that they could get nothing from me in my anger,—not even a promise of a good word. So I sent her to you. It was, at any rate, the best thing I could do for them.' Mr. Grey thought that it was.

Chapter XXXV

MR. BARRY AND MR. JUNIPER

THE joy in Bolsover Terrace was intense when Mrs. Carroll returned home. 'We are all to have three hundred and fifty pound fortunes when we get husbands,' said Georgina, anticipating at once the pleasures of matrimony.

'I am to have four hundred and fifty,' said Amelia. 'I do think he might have made it five hundred pounds. If I had it to give away I never would show the cloven hoof about the last fifty pounds.'

'But he's only to have four hundred pounds,' said Sophia. 'Your things are to be bought with the other fifty pounds.'

'I never can do it for fifty pounds,' said Amelia. 'I did not expect that I was to find my own trousseau out of my own fortune.'

'Girls, how can you be so ungrateful?' said their mother.

'I'm not ungrateful, mamma,' said Potsey. 'I shall be very much obliged when I get my three hundred and fifty pounds. How long will it be?'

'You've got to find the young man first, Potsey. I don't think you'll ever do that,' said Georgina, who was rather proud of her own good looks.

This took place on the evening of the day on which Mrs. Carroll had gone to London, where Mr. Carroll was about attending to some of those duties of

conviviality in the performance of which he was so
indefatigable. On the following morning at twelve
o'clock he was still in bed. It was a well-known fact
in the family that on such an occasion he would lie in
bed, and that before twelve o'clock he would have
managed to extract from his wife's little hoardings at
any rate two bottles of soda-water and two glasses of
alcoholic mixture which was generally called brandy.
'I'll have a gin and potash, Sophie,' he had said on
this occasion with reference to the second dose, 'and
do make haste. I wish you'd go yourself, because
that girl always drinks some of the spirits.'

'What!—go to the gin-shop?'

'It's a most respectable publican's,—just round
the corner.'

'Indeed, I shall do nothing of the kind. You've
no feeling about your daughters at all.' But Sophie
went on her errand, and in order to protect her
father's small modicum of 'sperrits' she slipped on
her cloak and walked out so as to be able to watch
the girl. Still I think that the maiden managed to get
a sip as she left the bar. The father in the meantime,
with his head upon his hands, was ruminating on the
'cocked up way which girls have who can't do a turn
for their father.'

But with the gin and potash, and with Sophie, Mr.
Juniper made his appearance. He was a well-featured,
tall man, but he looked the stable and he smelt of it.
His clothes, no doubt, were decent, but they were
made by some tailor who must surely work for horsey
men and no others. There is a class of men who
always choose to show by their outward appearance
that they belong to horses, and they succeed. Mr.
Juniper was one of them. Though good-looking he
was anything but young, verging by appearance on
fifty years. 'So he has been at it again, Miss Sophie,'
said Juniper. Sophie, who did not like being detected in the performance of her filial duties, led the
way in silence into the house, and disappeared up-

stairs with the gin and potash. Mr. Juniper turned into the parlour, where was Mrs. Carroll, with the other girls. She was still angry, as angry as she could be, with her husband, who on being informed that morning of what his wife had done had called her brother 'a beastly, stingy old beau,' because he had cut Amelia off with four hundred and fifty instead of five hundred pounds. Mr. Carroll probably knew that Mr. Juniper would not take his daughter without the entirety of the sum stipulated, and would allow no portion of it to be expended on wedding dresses.

'Oh, Dick, is this you?' said Amelia. 'I suppose you've come for your news.' Mr. Juniper's Christian-name was Richard. On this occasion he showed no affectionate desire to embrace his betrothed.

'Yes, it's me,' he said, and then gave his hand all round, first to Mrs. Carroll and then to the girls.

'I've seen Mr. Grey,' said Mrs. Carroll. But Dick Juniper held his tongue and sat down and twiddled his hat.

'Where have you come from?' asked Georgina.

'From the Brompton Road. I come down on a 'bus.'

'You've come from Tattersall's, young man,' said Amelia.

'Then I just didn't.' But to tell the truth he had come from Tattersall's, and it might be difficult to follow up the workings of his mind and find out why he had told the lie. Of course it was known that when in London much of his business was done at Tatter-sall's. But the horsey man is generally on the alert to take care that no secret of his trade escapes from him unawares. And it may be that he was thus pre-pared for a gratuitous lie.

'Uncle's gone a deal further than ever I expected,' said Amelia.

'He's been most generous to all the girls,' said Mrs. Carroll, moved nearly to tears.

Mr. Juniper did not care very much about 'all the

girls,' thinking that the uncle's affection at the present moment should be shown to the one girl who had found a husband, and thinking also that if the husband was to be secured, the proper way of doing so would be by liberality to him. Amelia had said that her uncle had gone further than she expected. Mr. Juniper concluded from this that he had not gone as far as he had been asked, and boldly resolved, at the spur of the moment, to stand by his demand. 'Five hundred pound ain't much,' he said.

'Dick, don't make a beast of yourself,' said Amelia. Upon this Dick only smiled.

He continually twiddled his hat for three or four minutes, and then rose up straight. 'I suppose,' said he, 'I had better go upstairs and talk to the old man. I see'd Miss Sophie taking a pick-up to him; so I suppose he'll be able to talk.'

'Why shouldn't he talk?' said Mrs. Carroll. But she quite understood what Mr. Juniper's words were intended to imply.

'It don't always follow,' said Juniper as he walked out of the room.

'Now there'll be a row in the house; you see if there isn't,' said Amelia. But Mrs. Carroll expressed her opinion that the man must be the most ungrateful of creatures if he kicked up a row on the present occasion. 'I don't know so much about that, mamma,' said Amelia.

Mr. Juniper walked upstairs with heavy, slow steps, and knocked at the door of the marital chamber. There are men who can't walk upstairs as though to do so were an affair of ordinary life. They perform the task as though they walked upstairs once in three years. It is to be presumed that such men always sleep on the ground floor, though where they find their bedrooms it is hard to say. Mr. Juniper was admitted by Sophie, who stepped out as he went in. 'Well! old fellow; B. and S., and plenty of it. That's the ticket, eh?'

'I did have a little headache this morning. I think it was the cigars.'

'Very like;—and the stuff as washed 'em down. You haven't got any more of the same, have you?'

'I'm uncommonly sorry,' said the sick man, rising up on his elbow in the bed, 'but I'm afraid there is not. To tell the truth, I had the deuce of a job to get this from the old woman.'

'It don't matter,' said the impassive Mr. Juniper; 'only I have been down among the 'orses at the yard till my throat is full of dust. So your lady has been and seen her brother.'

'Yes; she's done that.'

'Well.'

'He ain't altogether a bad 'un;—isn't old Grey. Of course he's an attorney.'

'I never think much of them chaps.'

'There's good and bad, Juniper. No doubt my brother-in-law has made a little money.'

'A pot of it;—if all they say's true.'

'But all they say isn't true. All they say never is true.'

'I suppose he's got something.'

'Yes, he's got something.'

'And how is it to be?'

'He's given the girl four hundred pounds on the nail,'—upon this Mr. Juniper turned up his nose,— 'and fifty pounds for her wedding-clothes.'

'He'd better let me have that.'

'Girls think so much of it.' Mr. Juniper only shook his head. 'And, upon my word, it's more than she had a right to expect.'

'It ain't what she had a right to expect, but I,'— here Mr. Carroll shook his head,—'I said five hundred pounds out, and I means to hold by it. That's about it. If he wants to get the girl married, why— he must open his pocket. It isn't very much that I'm asking. I'm that sort of fellow, that if I didn't want it, I'd take her without a shilling.'

'But you are that sort of fellow that always does want it.'

'I wants it now. It's better to speak out,—ain't it? I must have the five hundred pounds before I put my neck into the noose, and there must be no paring off for petticoats and pelisses.'

'And Mr. Grey says that he must make inquiries into character,' said Carroll.

'Into what?'

'Into character. He isn't going to give his money without knowing something about the man.'

'I'm all straight at Newmarket. I ain't going to stand any inquiries into me, you know. I can stand inquiries better than some people. He's got a partner named Barry;—ain't he?'

'There is such a gentleman. I don't know much about the business ways of my respected brother-in-law. Mr. Barry is, I believe, a good sort of man.'

'It's he as is acting for Captain Scarborough.'

'Is it now? It may be, for anything I know.'

Then there came a long conversation, during which Mr. Juniper told some details of his former life, and expressed himself very freely upon certain points. It appeared that in the event of Mr. Scarborough having died, as was expected in the course of the early summer, and of Captain Scarborough succeeding to the property in the accustomed manner, Mr. Juniper would have been one of those who would have come forward with a small claim upon the estate. He had lent, he said, a certain sum of money to help the captain in his embarrassment, and expected to get it back again. Now, inquiries had latterly been made very disagreeable in their nature to Mr. Juniper; but Mr. Juniper, seeing how the land lay,—to use his own phrase,—consented only to accept so much as he had advanced. 'It don't make much difference to me,' he had said. 'Let me have the three hundred and fifty pounds which the captain got in hard money.' Then the inquiries were made by Mr. Barry,—that very

Mr. Barry to whom the subsequent inquiries were committed,—and Mr. Barry could not satisfy himself as to the three hundred and fifty pounds which the captain was said to have got in hard money. There had been words spoken which seemed, to Mr. Juniper, to make it very inexpedient, and we may say very unfair, that these further inquiries into his character as a husband should be intrusted to the same person. He regarded Mr. Barry as an enemy to the human race, from whom, in the general confusion of things, no plunder was to be extracted. Mr. Barry had asked for the cheque by which the three hundred and fifty pounds had been paid to Captain Scarborough in hard cash. There had been no cheque, Mr. Juniper had said. Such a small sum as that had been paid in notes at Newmarket. He said that he could not, or rather that he would not, produce any evidence as to the money. Mr. Barry had suggested that even so small a sum as three hundred and fifty pounds could not have come and could not have gone without leaving some trace. Mr. Juniper very indignantly had referred to an acknowledgment on a bill-stamp for six hundred pounds which he had filled in, and which the captain had undoubtedly signed. 'It's not worth the paper it's written on,' Mr. Barry had said.

'We'll see about that,' said Mr. Juniper. 'As soon as the breath is out of the old squire's body, we'll see whether his son is to repudiate his debts in that way. Ain't that the captain's signature?' and he slapped the bill with his hand.

The old ceremony was gone through of explaining that the captain had no right to a shilling of the property. It had become an old ceremony now. 'Mr. Augustus Scarborough is going to pay out of his own good-will only those sums of the advance of which he has indisputable testimony.'

'Ain't he my testimony of this?' said Mr. Juniper. 'This bill is for six hundred pounds.'

'In course it is.'

'Why don't you say you advanced him five hundred and fifty pounds instead of three hundred and fifty pounds?'

'Because I didn't.'

'Why do you say three hundred and fifty pounds instead of one hundred and fifty pounds?'

'Because I did.'

'Then we have only your bare word. We are not going to pay any one a shilling on such testimony.' Then Mr. Juniper had sworn an awful oath that he would have every man bearing the name of Scarborough hanged. But Mr. Barry's firm did not care much for any law proceedings which might be taken by Mr. Juniper alone. No law proceedings would be taken. The sum to be regained would not be worth the while of any lawyer to insure the hopeless expense of fighting such a battle. It would be shown in court on Mr. Barry's side, that the existing owner of the estate, out of his own generosity, had repaid all sums of money as to which evidence existed that they had been advanced to the unfortunate illegitimate captain. They would appear with clean hands; but poor Mr. Juniper would receive the sympathy of none. Of this Mr. Juniper had by degrees become aware, and was already looking on his claim on the Scarborough property as lost. And now, on this other little affair of his, on this matrimonial venture, it was very hard that inquiries as to his character should be referred to the same Mr. Barry.

'I'm d—— if I stand it,' he said, thumping his fist down on Mr. Carroll's bed, on which he was sitting.

'It isn't any of my doing. I'm on the square with you.'

'I don't know so much about that.'

'What have I done? Didn't I send her to the girl's uncle, and didn't she get from him a very liberal promise?'

'Promises! Why didn't he stump up the rhino?

What's the good of promises? There's as much ado about a beggarly five hundred pounds as though it were fifty thousand pounds. Inquiries! Of course he knew very well what that meant. It's a most ungentlemanlike thing for one gentleman to take upon himself to make inquiries about another. He is not the girl's father. What right has he to make inquiries?'

'I didn't put it into his head,' said Carroll, almost sobbing.

'He must be a low-bred pettifogging lawyer.'

'He is a lawyer,' said Carroll, on whose mind the memory of the great benefit he had received had made some impression. 'I have admitted that.'

'Psha!'

'But I don't think he's pettifogging; not Mr. Grey. Four hundred pounds down, with fifty pounds for dress, and the same or most the same to all the girls, isn't pettifogging. If you ever comes to have a family, Juniper——'

'I ain't in the way.'

'But when you are, and there comes six of 'em, you won't find an uncle pettifogging when he speaks out like Mr. Grey.'

The conversation was carried on for some time further, and then Mr. Juniper left the house without again visiting the ladies. His last word was that if inquiries were made into him, they might all go to— Bath! If the money were forthcoming, they would know where to find him,—but it must be five hundred pounds 'square,' with no parings made from it on behalf of petticoats and pelisses. With this last word, Mr. Juniper stamped down the stairs and out of the house.

'He's a brute after all,' said Sophie.

'No; he isn't. What do you know about brutes? Of course a gentleman has to make the best fight he can for his money.' This was what Amelia said at the moment; but in the seclusion of her own room she wept bitterly. 'Why didn't he come in to see me and just give me one word? I hadn't done anything amiss. It wasn't my fault if Uncle John is stingy.'

'And he isn't so very stingy after all,' said Sophie.

'Of course papa hasn't got anything, and wouldn't have anything, though you were to pour golden rivers into his lap.'

'There are worse than papa,' said Sophie.

'But he knows all that, and that our uncle isn't any more than an uncle. And why should he be so particular just about a hundred pounds? I do think gentlemen are the meanest creatures when they are looking after money. Ladies ain't half so bad. He'd no business to expect five hundred pounds all out.'

This was very melancholy, and the house was kept in a state of silent sorrow for four or five days, till the result of the inquiries had come. Then there was weeping and gnashing of teeth. Mr. Barry came to Bolsover Terrace to communicate the result of the inquiry, and was shut up for half-an-hour with poor Mrs. Carroll. He was afraid that he could not recommend the match. 'Oh, I'm sorry for that,—very sorry,' said Mrs. Carroll. 'The young lady will be—disappointed.' And her handkerchief went up to her eyes. Then there was silence for awhile, till she asked why an opinion so strongly condemnatory had been expressed.

'The gentleman, ma'am,—is not what a gentleman should be. You may take my word for that. I must ask you not to repeat what I say of him.'

'Oh! dear no.'

'But perhaps the least said the soonest mended. He is not what a gentleman should be.'

'You mean a—fine gentleman.'

'He is not what a man should be. I cannot say more than that. It would not be for the young lady's happiness that she should select such a partner for her life.'

'She is very much attached to him.'

'I am sorry that it should be so. But it will be better that she should—live it down. At any rate I am bound to communicate to you Mr. Grey's decision. Though he does not at all mean to withhold his bounty in regard to any other proposed marriage, he cannot bring himself to pay money to Mr. Juniper.'

'Nothing at all?' asked Mrs. Carroll.

'He will make no payment that will go into the pocket of Mr. Juniper.'

Then Mr. Barry went, and there was weeping and wailing in the house in Bolsover Terrace. So cruel an uncle as Mr. Grey had never been heard of in history, or even in romance. 'I know it's that old cat, Dolly,' said Amelia. 'Because she hasn't managed to get a husband for herself, she doesn't want anyone else to get one.'

'My poor child,' said Mr. Carroll, in a maudlin condition, 'I pity thee from the bottom of my heart.'

'I wish that Mr. Barry may be made to marry a hideous old maid past forty,' said Georgina.

'I shouldn't care what they said, but would take him straight off,' said Sophie.

Upon this Mrs. Carroll shook her head. 'I don't suppose that he is quite all that he ought to be.'

'Who is, I should like to know?' said Amelia.

'But my brother has to give his money according to his judgment.' As she said this the poor woman thought of those other five who in process of time might become claimants. But here the whole family attacked her, and almost drove her to confess that her brother was a stingy old curmudgeon.

Chapter XXXVI

GURNEY AND MALCOLMSON'S

IN Red Lion Square, on the first floor of a house which partakes of the general dinginess of the neighbourhood, there are two rooms which bear on the outside door the well-sounding names of Gurney and Malcolmson; and on the front door to the street are the names of Gurney and Malcolmson, showing that the business transacted by Messrs. Gurney and Malcolmson outweighs in importance any others conducted in the same house. In the first room, which is the smaller of the two occupied, sits usually a lad, who passes most of his time in making up and directing circulars, so that a stranger might be led to suppose that the business of Gurney and Malcolmson was of an extended nature. But on the occasion to which we are about to allude the door of the premises was closed and the boy was kept on the alert, posting, or perhaps delivering, the circulars which were continually issued. This was the place of business affected by Mr. Tyrrwhit, or at any rate one of the firm. Who were Gurney and Malcolmson it is not necessary that our chronicle should tell. No Gurney or no Malcolmson was then visible, and though a part of the business of the firm in which it is to be supposed that Gurney and Malcolmson were engaged, was greatly discussed, their name on the occasion was never mentioned.

A meeting had been called, at which the presiding genius was Mr. Tyrrwhit. You might almost be led to believe that, from the manner in which he made himself at home, Mr. Tyrrwhit was Gurney and Malcolmson. But there was another there who seemed to be almost as much at home as Mr. Tyrrwhit, and this was Mr. Samuel Hart, whom we last saw when he had unexpectedly made himself known to his friend the captain at Monaco. He had a good deal to say for himself, and as he sat during the meeting with his hat on, it is presumed that he was not in awe of his companions. Mr. Juniper also was there. He took a seat at one corner of the table, and did not say much. There was also a man who, in speaking of himself and his own affairs, always called himself Evans and Crooke. And there was one Spicer, who sat silent for the most part, and looked very fierce. In all matters, however, he appeared to agree with Mr. Tyrrwhit. He is specially named, as his interest in the matter discussed was large. There were three or four others, whose affairs were of less moment, though to them they were of intense interest. These gentlemen assembled were they who had advanced money to Captain Scarborough, and this was the meeting of the captain's creditors, at which they were to decide whether they would give up their bonds on payment of the sums they had actually advanced, or whether they would stand out till the old squire's death and then go to law with the owner of the estate.

At the moment at which we may be presumed to be introduced, Mr. Tyrrwhit had explained the matter in a nervous hesitating manner, but still in words sufficiently clear. 'There's the money down now if you like to take it, and I'm for taking it.' These were the words with which Mr. Tyrrwhit completed his address.

'Circumstances is different,' said the man with his hat on.

'I don't know much about that, Mr. Hart,' said Tyrrwhit.

'Circumstances is different. I can't 'elp whether you know it or not.'

'How different?'

'They is different;—and that's all about it. It'll perhaps shuit you and them other shentlemen to take a pershentage.'

'It won't suit Evans and Crooke,' said the man who represented that firm.

'But perhaps Messrs. Evans and Crooke may be willing to save so much of their property,' said Mr. Tyrrwhit.

'They'd like to have what's due to 'em.'

'We should all like that,' said Spicer; and he gnashed his teeth and shook his head.

'But we can't get it all,' said Tyrrwhit.

'Speak for yourself, Mr. Tyrrwhit,' said Hart. 'I think I can get mine. This is the most almighty abandoned swindle I ever met in all my born days.' The whole meeting, except Mr. Tyrrwhit, received this assertion with loudly expressed applause. 'Such a blackguard, dirty thieving job never was up before in my time. I don't know 'ow to talk of it in language as a man isn't ashamed to commit himself to. It's downright robbery.'

'I say so too,' said Evans and Crooke.

'By George!' continued Mr. Hart, 'we come forward to 'elp a shentleman in his trouble and to wait for our moneys till the father is dead, and then when 'e's 'ad our moneys the father turns round and says that 'is own son is a ——! Oh! it's too shocking! I 'aven't slept since I 'eard it,—not a regular night's rest. Now it's my belief the captain 'as no 'and in it.'

Here Mr. Juniper scratched his head and looked doubtful, and one or two of the other silent gentlemen scratched their heads. Messrs. Evans and Crooke scratched his head. 'It's a matter on which I would not like to give an opinion one way or the other,' said Tyrrwhit.

'No more wouldn't I,' said Spicer.

'Let every man speak as he finds,' continued Hart. 'That's my belief. I don't mind giving up a little of my claim, just a thousand or so, for ready cash. The old sinner ought to be dead and can't last long. My belief is that when 'e's gone I'm so circumstanced I shall get the whole. Whether or no, I've gone in for 'elping the captain with all my savings, and I mean to stick to them.'

'And lose everything,' said Tyrrwhit.

'Why don't we go and lug the old sinner into prison?' said Evans and Crooke.

'Certainly, that's the game,' said Juniper,—and there was another loud acclamation of applause from the entire room.

'Gentlemen, you don't know what you're talking about; you don't indeed,' said Tyrrwhit.

'I don't believe as we do,' said Spicer.

'You can't touch the old gentleman. He owes you nothing, nor have you a scratch of his pen. How are you to lug an old gentleman to prison when he's lying there cut up by the doctors almost to nothing? I don't know that anybody can touch him. The captain perhaps might if the present story be false, and the younger son if the other be true. And then they'd have to prove it. Mr. Grey says that no one can touch him.'

'He's in the swim as bad as any of 'em,' said Evans and Crooke.

'Of course he is,' said Hart. 'But let everybody speak for himself. I've gone in to earn a 'eavy stake honestly.'

'That's all right,' said Evans and Crooke.

'And I mean to 'ave it or nothing. Now, Mr. Tyrrwhit, you know a piece of my mind. It's a biggish lot of money.'

'We know what your claim is.'

'But no man knows what the captain got, and I don't mean 'em to know.'

'About fifteen thousand,' came in a whisper from someone in the room.

'That's a lie,' said Mr. Hart,—'so there's no getting out of that. If the shentleman will mind 'is own concerns I'll mind mine. Nobody knows,— barring the captain, and he like enough has forgot,—and nobody's going to know. What's written on these eight bits of paper everybody may know;' and he pulled out of a large case or purse, which he carried in his breast coat-pocket, a fat sheaf of bills. 'There are five thou' written on each of them, and for five thou' on each of them I means to stand out, 'it or miss. If any shentleman chooses to talk to me about ready money I'll take two thou' off. I like ready money as well as another.'

'We can all say the same as that, Mr. Hart,' said Tyrrwhit.

'No doubt. And if you think you can get it, I advise you to stick to it. If you thought you could get it, you would say the same. But I should like to get that old man's 'ead between my fistes. Wouldn't I punch it! Thief! scoundrel! 'orrid old man! It ain't for myself that I'm speaking now, because I'm a going to get it. It's for humanity at large. This kind of thing wiolates one's best feelings.'

' 'Ear; 'ear; 'ear,' said one of the silent gentlemen.

'Them's the sentiments of Evans and Crooke,' said the representative of the firm.

'They're all our sentiments in course,' said Spicer; 'but what's the use?'

'Not a ha'p'orth,' said Mr. Tyrrwhit.

'Asking your pardon, Mr. Tyrrwhit,' said Mr. Hart, 'but as this is a meeting of creditors who 'ave a largish lot of money to deal with, I don't think they ought to part without expressing their opinions in the way of British commerce. I say crucifying 'd be too good for him.'

'You can't get at him to crucify him.'

'There's no knowing about that,' said Mr. Hart.

'And now,' said Mr. Tyrrwhit, drawing out his watch, 'I expect Mr. Augustus Scarborough to call upon us.'

'You can crucify him,' said Evans and Crooke.

'It is the old man, and neither of the sons as have done it,' said Hart.

'Mr. Scarborough,' continued Tyrrwhit, 'will be

here, and will expect to learn whether we have accepted his offer. He will be accompanied by Mr. Barry. If one rejects all reject.'

'Not at all,' said Hart.

'He will not consent to pay anything unless he can make a clean hit of it. He is about to sacrifice a very large sum of money.'

'Sacrifice!' said Juniper.

'Yes; sacrifice a very large sum of money. His father cannot pay it without his consent. The father may die any day, and then the money will belong altogether to the son. You have, none of you, any claim upon him. It is likely he may think you will have a claim on the estate,—not trusting his own father.'

'I wouldn't trust him, not 'alf as far as I could see him, though he was twice my father.' This again came from Mr. Hart.

'I want to explain to these gentlemen how the matter stands.'

'They understand,' said Hart.

'I'm for securing my own money. It's very hard, —after all the risk. I quite agree with Mr. Hart in what he says about the squire. Such a piece of premeditated dishonesty for robbing gentlemen of their property I never before heard. It's awful!'

' 'Orrid old man,' said Mr. Hart.

'Just so. But half a loaf is better than no bread. Now here is a list, prepared in Mr. Grey's chambers.'

' 'E's another, nigh as 'orrid.'

'On this list we're all down, with the sums he says we advanced. Are we to take them? If so we must sign our names, each to his own figure.' Then he passed the list down the table.

The men there assembled all crowded to look at the list, and among others Mr. Juniper. He showed his anxiety by the eager way in which he nearly annihilated Messrs. Evans and Crooke, by leaning over him as he struggled to read the paper. 'Your name ain't down at all,' said Evans and Crooke. Then a tremendous oath, very bitter and very wicked, came from the mouth of Mr. Juniper, most unbefitting a young man engaged to marry a young lady. 'I tell you it isn't here,' said Evans and Crooke, trying to extricate himself.

'I shall know how to right myself,' said Juniper, with another oath. And he then walked out of the room.

'The captain, when he was drunk one night, got a couple of ponies from him. It wasn't a couple all out. And Juniper made him write his name for five hundred pounds. It was thought then that the squire 'd have been dead next day, and Juniper 'd 've got a good thing.'

'I 'ate them ways,' said Mr. Hart. 'I never deal with a shentleman if he's, to say—drunk. Of course it comes in my way, but I never does.'

Now there was heard a sound of steps on the stairs, and Mr. Tyrrwhit rose from his chair so as to perform the duty of master of the ceremonies to the gentlemen who were expected. Augustus Scarborough entered the room followed by Mr. Barry. They were received with considerable respect, and seated on two chairs at Mr. Tyrrwhit's right hand. 'Gentlemen, you most of you know these two gentlemen. They are Mr. Augustus Scarborough and Mr. Barry, junior partner in the firm of Messrs. Grey and Barry.'

'We knows 'em,' said Hart.

'My client has made a proposition to you,' said Mr. Barry. 'If you will give up your bonds against his brother, which are not worth the paper they are written on——'

'Gammon,' said Mr. Hart.

'I will sign cheques paying to you the sums of money written on that list. But you must all agree to accept such sums in liquidation in full. I see you have not signed the paper yet. No time is to be lost.

In fact you must sign it now, or my client will withdraw from his offer.'

'Withdraw, will 'e?' said Hart. 'Suppose we withdraw? 'O does your client think is the honestest man in this 'ere swim?'

Mr. Barry seemed somewhat abashed by this question. 'It isn't necessary to go into that, Mr. Hart,' said he.

Mr. Hart laughed long and loud, and all the gentlemen laughed. There was something to them extremely jocose in their occupying as it were the other side of the question, and appearing as the honest, injured party. They enjoyed it thoroughly, and Mr. Hart was disposed to make the most of it. 'No, it ain't necessary; is it? There ain't no question of honesty to be asked in this 'ere business. We quite understand that.'

Then up and spoke Augustus Scarborough. He rose on his legs, and the very fact of his doing so, quieted for a time the exuberant mirth of the party. 'Gentlemen, Mr. Hart speaks to you of honesty. I am not going to boast of my own. I am here to consent to the expenditure of a very large sum of money, for which I am to get nothing, and which, if not paid to you, will all go into my own pocket. Unless you believed that, you wouldn't be here to meet me.'

'We don't believe nothing,' said Hart.

'Mr. Hart, you should let Mr. Scarborough speak,' said Tyrrwhit.

'Vell; let 'im speak. Vat's the odds?'

'I do not wish to delay you,—nor to delay myself,' continued Augustus. 'I can go,—and will go; at once. But I shall not come back. There is no good discussing this matter any longer.'

'Oh no;—not the least. Ve don't like discussion; do ve, captain?' said Mr. Hart. 'But you ain't the captain; is you?'

'As there seems to be no intention of signing that document, I shall go,' said Augustus. Then Mr.

Tyrrwhit took the paper, and signed it on the first line with his own name at full length. He wrote his name to a very serious sum of money, but it was less than half what he and others had expected to receive when the sum was lent. Had that been realised there would have been no further need for the formalities of Gurney and Malcolmson, and that young lad must have found other work to do than the posting of circulars. The whole matter, however, had been much considered, and he signed the document. Mr. Hart's name came next, but he passed it on. 'I ain't made up my mind yet. Maybe I shall have to call on Mr. Barry. I ain't just consulted my partner.' Then the document went down to Mr. Spicer, who signed it, grinning horribly; as did also Evans and Crooke and all the others. They did believe that was the only way in which they could get back the money they had advanced. It was a great misfortune; a serious blow. But in this way there was something short of ruin. They knew that Scarborough was about to pay the money so that he might escape a law-suit which might go against him; but then they also wished to avoid the necessity of bringing the law-suit. Looking at the matter all round we may say that the lawyers were the persons most aggrieved by what was done that morning. They all signed it as they sat there,—except Mr. Hart, who passed it on, and still wore his hat.

'You won't agree, Mr. Hart?' said Tyrrwhit.

'Not yet I von't,' said Hart, 'I ain't thought it out. I ain't in the same boat with the rest. I'm not afraid of my money. I shall get that all right.'

'Then I may as well go,' said Augustus.

'Don't be in a hurry, Mr. Scarborough,' said Tyrrwhit. 'Things of this kind can't be done just in a moment.' But Augustus explained that they must be done in a very few moments, if they were to be done at all. It was not his intention to sit there in Gurney and Malcolmson's office discussing the matter with Mr. Hart. Notice of his intention had been given, and they might take his money or leave it.

'Just so, captain,' said Mr. Hart. 'Only I believe you ain't the captain. Where's the captain now? I see him last at Monte Carlo, and he had won a pot of money. He was looking uncommon well after his little accident in the streets with young Annesley.'

Mr. Tyrrwhit contrived to get all the others out of the room, he remaining there with Hart and Augustus Scarborough and Mr. Barry. And then Hart did sign the document with altered figures;—only that so much was added on to the sum which he agreed to accept, and a similar deduction made from that to which Mr. Tyrrwhit's name was signed. But this was not done without renewed expostulation from the latter gentleman. It was very hard, he said, that all the sacrifice should be made by him. He would be ruined, utterly ruined by the transaction. But he did sign for the altered sum, and Mr. Hart also signed the paper. 'Now, Mr. Barry, as the matter is completed, I think I will withdraw,' said Augustus.

'It's five thousand pounds clean gone out of my pocket,' said Hart, 'and I vas as sure of it as ever I vas in my life. There vas no better money than the captain's. Vell, vell! This vorld's a queer place.' So saying, he followed Augustus and Mr. Barry out of the room, and left Mr. Tyrrwhit alone in his misery.

Chapter XXXVII

VICTORIA STREET

LOUNGING in an armchair in a small but luxuriously furnished room in Victoria Street sat Captain Mountjoy Scarborough, and opposite to him, equally comfortably placed as far as externals were concerned, but without any of that lounging look which the captain affected, sat his brother. It was nearly eight o'clock, and the sound of the dinner plates could be heard through the open doors from the next room. It was evident, or at any rate was the fact, that Augustus found his brother's presence a bore, and as evident that the captain intended to disregard the dissatisfaction evinced by the owner of the chambers. 'Do shut the door, Mountjoy,' said the younger. 'I don't suppose we want the servant to hear everything that we say.'

'He's welcome for me,' said Mountjoy, without moving. Then Augustus got up and banged the door. 'Don't be angry because I sometimes forget that I am no longer considered to be your elder brother,' said Mountjoy.

'Bother about elder brother. I suppose you can shut a door.'

'A man is sometimes compelled by circumstances to think whether he can or not. I'd 've shut the door for you readily enough the other day. I don't know that I can now. Ain't we going to have some dinner? It's eight o'clock.'

'I suppose they'll get dinner for you,—I'm not going to dine here.' The two men were both dressed, and after this they remained silent for the next five minutes. Then the servant came in and said that dinner was ready.

All this happened in December. It must be explained that the captain had come to London at his brother's instance, and was there, in his rooms, at his invitation. Indeed, we may say that he had come at his brother's command. Augustus had during the last few months taken upon himself to direct the captain's movements, and though he had not always been obeyed, still, upon the whole, his purposes had been carried out as well as he could expect. He had offered to supply the money necessary for the captain's tour, and had absolutely sent a servant to accompany the traveller. When the traveller had won money at Monaco he had been unruly, but this had not happened very often. When we last saw him he had expressed his intention to Mr. Hart of making a return journey to the Caucasian provinces. But he got no further than Genoa on his way to the Caucasus, and then, when he found that Mr. Hart was not at his back, he turned round and went back to Monte Carlo. Monte Carlo, of all places on the world's surface, had now charms for him. There was no longer a club open to him, either in London or Paris, at which he could win or lose one hundred pounds. At Monte Carlo he could still do so readily; and, to do so, need not sink down into any peculiarly low depth of social gathering. At Monte Carlo the *ennui* of the day was made to disappear. At Monte Carlo he could lie in bed till eleven and then play till dinner time. At Monte Carlo there was always someone who would drink a glass of wine with him without inquiring too closely as to his antecedents. He had begun by winning a large sum of money. He had got some sums from his brother, and when at last he was summoned home he was penniless. Had his pocket been still full of money it may be doubted whether he would have come, although he understood perfectly the importance of the matter on which he had been recalled.

He had been sent for in order that he might receive from Mr. Grey a clear statement of what it was intended to do in reference to the payment of money to the creditors. Mr. Grey had, in the first place, endeavoured to assure him that his co-operation was in no respect made necessary by the true circumstances of the case, but in order to satisfy the doubts of certain persons. The money to be paid was the joint property of his father and his brother;—of his father, as far as the use of it for his life was concerned, and of his brother as to its continued and perpetual enjoyment. They were willing to pay so much for the redemption of the bonds given by him, the captain. As far as these bonds were concerned the captain would thus be a free man. There could be no doubt that nothing but benefit was intended for him,—as though he were himself the heir. 'Though as to that I have no hesitation in telling you that you will at your father's death have no right to a shilling of the property.' The captain had said that he was quite willing, and had signed the deed. He was glad that these bonds should be recovered so cheaply. But as to the property,—and here he spoke with much spirit to Mr. Grey,—it was his purpose at his father's death to endeavour to regain his position. He would never believe, he said, that his mother was—— Then he turned away, and, in spite of all that had come and gone, Mr. Grey respected him.

But he had signed the deed, and the necessity for his presence was over. What should his brother do with him now? He could not keep him concealed, —or not concealed,—in his rooms. But something must be done. Some mode of living must be invented for him. Abroad! Augustus said to himself, —and to Septimus Jones who was his confidential friend,—that Mountjoy must live 'abroad.'

'Oh, yes; he must go abroad. There's no doubt about that. It's the only place for him.' So spoke Septimus Jones, who, though confidential friend, was not admitted to the post of confidential adviser. Augustus liked to have a depositary for his resolutions, but would admit no advice. And Septimus Jones had become so much his creature that he had to obey him in all things.

We are apt to think that a man may be disposed of by being made to go abroad; or, if he is absolutely penniless and useless, by being sent to the Colonies,—that he may there become a shepherd and drink himself out of the world. To kill the man, so that he may be no longer a nuisance, is perhaps the

chief object in both cases. But it was not easy to get
the captain to go abroad, unless, indeed he was sent
back to Monte Carlo. Some Monte Carlo, such as
a club might be with stakes practically unlimited,
was the first desire of his heart. But behind that or
together with it, was an anxious longing to remain
near Tretton and 'see it out,' as he called it, when
his father should die. His father must die very
shortly, and he would like 'to see it out,' as he
told Mr. Grey; and, with this wish, there was a
longing also for the company of Florence Mountjoy.
He used to tell himself, in those moments of sad
thoughts,—thoughts serious as well as sad which
will come even to a gambler,—that if he could have
Tretton and Florence Mountjoy he would never
touch another card. And there was present to him
an assurance that his aunt, Mrs. Mountjoy, would
still be on his side. If he could talk over his circumstances with Mrs. Mountjoy, he thought that he
might be encouraged to recover his position as an
English gentleman. His debts at the club had
already been paid, and he had met on the sly a
former friend who had given him some hope that
he might be readmitted. But at the present moment
his mind turned to Brussels. He had learned that
Florence and her mother were at the Embassy there,
and, though he hesitated still, he desired to go. But
this was not the 'abroad' contemplated by Augustus.
Augustus did not think it well that his father's
bastard son, who had been turned out of a London
club for not paying his card debts, and had then
disappeared in a mysterious way for six months,
should show himself at the British Embassy, and
there claim admittance and relationship. Nor was
he anxious that his brother should see Florence
Mountjoy. He had suggested a prolonged tour in
South America, which he had declared to be the most
interesting country in the world. 'I think I had
rather go to Brussels,' Mountjoy had answered

gallantly, keeping his seat in the armchair and picking his teeth the while. This occurred on the evening before that on which we found them just now. On the morning of that day Mountjoy had had his interview with Mr. Grey.

Augustus had declared that he intended to dine out. This he had said in disgust at his brother's behaviour. No doubt he could get his dinner at ten minutes' notice. He had not been expelled from his club. But he had ordered the dinner on that day with a view to eat it himself, and in effect he carried out his purpose. The captain got up, thinking to go alone when the dinner was announced, but expressed himself gratified when his brother said that he 'had changed his mind.' 'You made yourself such an ass about shutting the door that I resolved to leave you to yourself. But come along.' And he accompanied the captain into the other room.

A very pretty little dinner was prepared,—quite such as one loving friend might give to another when means are sufficient,—such a dinner as the heir of Tretton might have given to his younger brother. The champagne was excellent, and the bottle of Léoville. Mountjoy partook of all the good things with much gusto, thinking all the while that he ought to have been giving the dinner to his younger brother. When that conversation had sprung up about going to Brussels or South America, Mountjoy had suggested a loan. 'I'll pay your fare to Rio, and give you an order on a banker there.' Mountjoy had replied that that would not at all suit his purpose. Then Augustus had felt that it would be almost better to send his brother even to Brussels than to keep him concealed in London. He had been there now for three or four days, and, even in respect of his maintenance, had become a burden. The pretty little dinners had to be found every day, and were eaten by the captain alone, when left alone, without an attempt at an apology on his part. Augustus had begun with some intention of exhibiting his mode of life. He would let his brother know what it was to be the heir of Tretton. No doubt he did assume all the outward glitter of his position, expecting to fill his brother's heart with envy. But Mountjoy had seen and understood it all, and remembering the days, not long removed, when he had been the heir, he bethought himself that he had never shown off before his brother. And he was determined to express no gratitude or thankfulness. He would go on eating the little dinners, exactly as though they had been furnished by himself. It certainly was dull. There was no occupation for him, and in the matter of pocket-money he was lamentably ill supplied. But he was gradually becoming used to face the streets again, and had already entered the shops of one or two of his old tradesmen. He had had quite a confidential conversation with his bootmaker, and had ordered three or four new pairs of boots. Nobody could tell how the question of the property would be decided till his father should have died. His father had treated him most cruelly, and he would only wait for his death. He could assure the bootmaker that when that time came he should look for his rights. He knew that there was a suspicion abroad that he was in a conspiracy with his father and brother to cheat his creditors. No such thing. He himself was cheated. He pledged himself to the bootmaker that, to the best of his belief, his father was robbing him, and that he would undoubtedly assert his right to the Tretton property as soon as the breath should be out of his father's body. The truth of what he told the bootmaker he certainly did believe. There was some little garnishing added to his tale, which, perhaps, under the circumstances, was to be forgiven. The blow had come upon him so suddenly, he said, that he was not able even to pay his card account, and had left town in dismay at the mine which had been exploded under his feet. The boot-maker believed him so far that he undertook to supply his orders.

When the dinner had been eaten, the two brothers lit their cigars and drew to the fire. 'There must unfortunately come an end to this, you know,' said Augustus.

'I certainly can't stand it much longer,' said Mountjoy.

'You, at any rate, have had the best of it. I have endeavoured to make my little crib comfortable for you.'

'The grub is good, and the wine. There's no doubt about that. Somebody says somewhere that nobody can live upon bread alone.* That includes the whole menu, I suppose.'

'What do you suggest to do with yourself?'

'You said, go abroad.'

'So I did,—to Rio.'

'Rio is a long way off;—somewhere across the equator, isn't it?'

'I believe it is.'

'I think we'd better have it out clearly between us, Augustus. It won't suit me to be at Rio Janeiro when our father dies.'

'What difference will his death make to you?'

'A father's death generally does make a difference to his eldest son,—particularly if there is any property concerned.'

'You mean to say that you intend to dispute the circumstances of your birth?'

'Dispute them! Do you think that I will allow such a thing to be said of my mother without disputing it? Do you suppose that I will give up my claim to one of the finest properties in England without disputing it?'

'Then I had better stop the payment of that money, and let the gentlemen know that you mean to raise the question on their behalf.'

'That's your affair. The arrangement is a very good one for me; but you made it.'

'You know very well that your present threat means nothing. Ask Mr. Grey. You can trust him.'

'But I can't trust him. After having been so wickedly deceived by my own father, I can trust no one. Why did not Mr. Grey find it out before, if it be true? I give you my word, Augustus, the lawyers will have to fight it out before you will be allowed to take possession.'

'And yet you do not scruple to come and live here at my cost.'

'Not in the least. At whose cost can I live with less scruple than at yours? You, at any rate, have not robbed our mother of her good name as my father has done. The only one of the family with whom I could not stay is the governor. I could not sit at the table with a man who has so disgraced himself.'

'Upon my word I am very much obliged to you for the honour you do me.'

'That's my feeling. The chance of the game and his villainy have given you for the moment the possession of the good things. They are all mine by rights.'

'Cards have had nothing to do with it?'

'Yes;—they have. But they have had nothing to do with my being the eldest legitimate son of my father. The cards have been against me, but they have not affected my mother. Then there came the blow from the governor; and where was I to look for my bread but to you? I suppose if the truth be known you get the money from the governor.'

'Of course I do. But not for your maintenance.'

'On what does he suppose that I have been living since last June? It mayn't be in the bond, but I suppose he has made allowance for my maintenance. Do you mean to say that I am not to have bread and cheese out of Tretton?'

'If I were to turn you out of these rooms you'd find it very difficult to get it.'

'I don't think you'll do that.'

'I'm not so sure.'

'You're meditating it, are you? I shouldn't go just at present, because I have not got a sovereign in the world. I was going to speak to you about money. You must let me have some.'

'Upon my word, I like your impudence.'

'What the devil am I to do? The governor has asked me to go down to Tretton, and I can't go without a five-pound note in my pocket.'

'The governor has asked you to Tretton?'

'Why not? I got a letter from him this morning.' Then Augustus asked to see the letter, but Mountjoy refused to show it. From this there arose angry words, and Augustus told his brother that he did not believe him. 'Not believe me? You do believe me! You know that what I say is the truth. He has asked me with all his usual soft-soap. But I have refused to go. I told him that I could not go to the house of one who had injured my mother so seriously.'

All that Mountjoy said as to the proposed visit to Tretton was true. The squire had written to him without mentioning the name of Augustus, and had told him that, for the present, Tretton would be the best home for him. 'I will do what I can to make you happy; but you will not see a card,' the squire had said. It was not the want of cards which prevented Mountjoy; but a feeling on his part that for the future there could be nothing but war between him and his father. It was out of the question that he should accept his father's hospitality without telling him of his intention; and he did not know his father well enough to feel that such a declaration would not affect him at all. He had therefore declined.

Then Harry Annesley's name was mentioned. 'I think I've done for that fellow,' said Augustus.

'What have you done?'

'I've cooked his goose. In the first place his uncle has stopped his allowance, and in the second place the old fellow is going to marry a wife. At any rate he has quarrelled with Master Harry *à outrance*. Master Harry has gone back to the parental parsonage, and is there eating the bread of affliction and drinking the waters of poverty. Flossy Mountjoy may marry him if she pleases. A girl may marry a man now without leave from anybody. But if she does, my dear cousin will have nothing to eat.'

'And you have done this?'

'Alone I did it, boy.'

'Then it's an infernal shame. What harm had he ever done you? For me I had some ground of quarrel with him; but for you there was none.'

'I have my own quarrel with him also.'

'I have quarrelled with him,—with a cause. I do not care if I quarrel with him again. He shall never marry Florence Mountjoy if I can help it. But to rob a fellow of his property I think a very shabby thing.' Then Augustus got up and walked out of the chambers into the street, and Mountjoy soon followed him.

'I must make him understand that he must leave this at once,' said Augustus to himself, 'and if necessary I must order the supplies to be cut off.'

Chapter XXXVIII

THE SCARBOROUGH CORRESPONDENCE

IT was as Mountjoy had said. The squire had written to him a letter, inviting him to Tretton, and telling him that it would be the best home for him till death should have put Tretton into other hands. Mountjoy had thought the matter over, sitting in the easy-chair in his brother's room, and had at last declined the invitation. As his letter was emblematic of the man, it may be as well to give it to the reader:

'MY DEAR FATHER,

'I don't think it will suit me to go down to Tretton at present. I don't mind the cards, and I don't doubt that you would make it better than this place. But, to tell the truth, I don't believe a word of what you have told to the world about my mother, and some of these days I mean to have it out with Augustus. I shall not sit quietly by and see Tretton taken out of my mouth. Therefore I think I had better not go to Tretton.—Yours truly,

'MOUNTJOY SCARBOROUGH.'

This had not at all surprised the father, and had not in the least angered him. He rather liked his son for standing up for his mother, and was by no means offended at the expression of his son's incredulity. But what was there in the prospect of a future lawsuit to prevent his son coming to Tretton? There need be no word spoken as to the property. Tretton would be infinitely more comfortable than those rooms in Victoria Street; and he was aware that the hospitality of Victoria Street would not be given in an ungrudging spirit. 'I shouldn't like it,' said the old squire to himself as he lay quiet on his sofa. 'I shouldn't like at all to be the humble guest of Augustus. Augustus would certainly say a nasty word or two.'

The old man knew his younger son well, and he had known, too, the character of his elder son; but he had not calculated enough on the change which must have been made by such a revelation as he, his father, had made to him. Mountjoy had felt that all the world was against him, and that, as best he might, he would make use of all the world,—excepting only his father, who of all the world was the falsest and the most cruel. As for his brother, he would bleed his brother to the very last drop without any compunction. Every bottle of champagne that came into the house was, to Mountjoy's thinking, his own, bought with his money, and therefore fit to be enjoyed by him. But as for his father,— he doubted whether he could remain with his father without flying at his throat.

The old man decidedly preferred his elder son of the two. He had found that Augustus could not bear success, and had first come to dislike him, and then to hate him. What had he not done for Augustus? And with what a return! No doubt Augustus had, till the spring of this present year, been kept in the background; but no injury had come to him from that. His father, of his own good will, with infinite labour and successful ingenuity, had struggled to put him back in the place which had been taken from him. Augustus might, not unnaturally, have expressed himself as angry. He had not done so, but had made himself persistently disagreeable, and had continued to show that he was waiting impatiently for his father's death. It had come to pass that at their last meeting he had hardly scrupled to tell his father that the world would be no world for him till his father had left it. This was the reward which the old man received for having struggled to provide handsomely and luxuriously for his son! He still made his son a sufficient allowance befitting the heir of a man of large property; but he had resolved never to see him again. It was true that he almost hated him, and thoroughly despised him.

But since the departure and mysterious disappearance of his eldest son, his regard for the sinner had returned. He had become apparently a hopeless gambler. His debts had been paid and repaid. At last the squire had learned that Mountjoy owed so much on post-obits, that the further payment of them was an impossibility. There was no way of saving him. To save the property he must undo the doings of his early youth, and prove that the elder son was illegitimate. He had still kept the proofs, and he did it. To the great disgust of Mr. Grey, to the dismay of the creditors, to the incredulous wonder of Augustus, and almost to the annihilation of Mountjoy himself, he had done it. But there had been nothing in Mountjoy's conduct which had in truth wounded him. Mountjoy's vices had been dangerous, destructive, absurdly foolish, but not, to his father, a shame. He ridiculed gambling as a source of excitement. No man could win much without dishonest practices; and fraud at cards would certainly be detected. But he did not on that account hate cards. There was no reason why Mountjoy should not become to him as pleasant a companion as ever for the few days that might be left to him, if only he would come. But, when asked, he refused to come. When the squire received the letter above given, he was not in the least angry with his son, but simply determined, if possible, that he should be brought to Tretton. Mountjoy's debts would now be paid, and something, if possible, should be done for him. He was so angry with Augustus that he would, if possible, revoke his last decision,—but that, alas! would be impossible.

Sir William Brodrick had, when he last saw him, expressed some hope,—not of his recovery, which was by all admitted to be impossible,—but of his continuance in the land of the living for another three months, or perhaps six, as Sir William had finally suggested, opening out as he himself seemed to think indefinite hope. 'The most wonderful constitution, Mr. Scarborough, I ever saw in my life. I've never known a dog even so cut about, and yet bear it.' Mr. Scarborough bowed and smiled, and accepted the compliment. He would have taken the hat off his head, had it been his practice to wear a hat in his sitting-room. Mr. Merton had gone farther. Of course he did not mean, he said, to set up his opinion against Sir William's, but if Mr. Scarborough would live strictly by rule, Mr. Merton did not see why either three months or six should be the end of it. Mr. Scarborough had replied that he could not undertake to live precisely by rule; and Mr. Merton had shaken his head. But from that time forth Mr. Scarborough did endeavour to obey the injunctions given to him. He had something worth doing in the six months now offered to him.

He had heard lately very much of the story of Harry Annesley, and had expressed great anger at the ill-usage to which that young man had been subjected. It had come to his ears that it was intended that Harry should lose the property he had expected, and that he had already lost his immediate income. This had come to him through Mr. Merton, between whom and Augustus Scarborough there was no close friendship. And the squire understood that Florence Mountjoy had been the cause of Harry's misfortune. He himself recognised it as a fact that his son Mountjoy was unfit to marry any young lady. Starvation would assuredly stare such young lady in the face. But not the less was he acerbated and disgusted at the idea that Augustus should endeavour to take the young lady to himself. 'What!' he had exclaimed to Mr. Merton; 'he wants both the property and the girl. There is nothing on earth that he does not want. The greater the impropriety in his craving, the stronger the craving.' Then he picked up by degrees all the details of the midnight feud between Harry and Mountjoy, and set himself to work to undermine Augustus. But he had steadily carried out the plan for settling with the creditors; and, with the aid of Mr. Grey, had, as he thought, already concluded that business. Conjunction with Augustus had been necessary, but that had been obtained.

It is not too much to say that, at the present moment of his life, the idea of doing some injury to Augustus was the one object which exercised Mr. Scarborough's mind. Since he had fallen into business relations with his younger son, he had become convinced that a more detestable young man did not exist. The reader will perhaps agree with Mr. Scarborough, but it can hardly be hoped that he should entertain the opinion as strongly. Augustus was now the recognised eldest legitimate son of the squire; and as the property was entailed, it must no doubt belong to him. But the squire was turning in his mind all means of depriving that condition as far as was possible of its glory. When he had first heard of the injury that had been done to Harry Annesley, he thought that he would leave to our hero all the furniture, all the gems, all the books, all the wine, all the cattle which were accumulated at Tretton. Augustus should have the bare acres, and still barer house, but nothing else. In thinking of this he had been actuated by a conviction that it would be useless for him to leave them to Mountjoy. Whatever might be left to Mountjoy, would in fact be left to the creditors; and therefore Harry Annesley with his injuries had been felt to be a proper recipient, not of the squire's bounty, but of the results of his hatred for his son.

To run counter to the law! That had ever been the chief object of the squire's ambition. To arrange everything so that it should be seen that he had set all laws at defiance! That had been his great pride. He had done so notably, and with astonishing astuteness, in reference to his wife and two sons. But now there had come up a condition of things in which he could again show his cleverness. Augustus had been most anxious to get up all the post-obit bonds which the creditors held, feeling,—as his father well understood,—that he would thus prevent them from making any further inquiry when the squire should have died. Why should they stir in the matter by going to law, when there would be nothing to be gained? Those bonds had now been redeemed, and were in the possession of Mr. Grey. They had been bought up nominally by himself, and must be given to him. Mr. Grey, at any rate, would have the proof that they had been satisfied. They could not be used again to gratify any spite that Augustus might entertain. The captain, therefore, could now enjoy any property which might be left to him. Of course, it would all go to the gaming-table. It might even yet be better to leave it to Harry Annesley. But blood was thicker than water,—though it were but the blood of a bastard. He would do a good turn for Harry in another way. All the furniture, and all the gems, and all the money, should again be the future property of Mountjoy.

But in order that this might be effected before he died, he must not let the grass grow under his feet. He thought of the promised three months, with a possible extension to six, as suggested by Sir William. 'Sir William says three months,' he said to Mr. Merton, speaking in the easiest way of the possibility of his living.

'He said six.'

'Ah! that is if I do what I'm told. But I shall not exactly do that. Three or six would be all the same, only for a little bit of business I want to get through. Sir William's orders would include the abandonment of my business.'

'The less done the better. Then I do not see why Sir William should limit you to six months.'

'I think that three will nearly suffice.'

'A man does not want to die, I suppose,' said Merton.

'There are various ways of looking at that question,' replied the squire. 'Many men desire the prolongation of life as a lengthened period of enjoyment. There is, perhaps, something of that feeling with me; but when you see how far I am crippled and curtailed, how my enjoyments are confined to breathing the air, to eating and drinking, and to the occasional reading of a few pages, you must admit that there cannot be much of that. A conversation with you is the best of it. Some want to live for the sake of their wives and children. In the ordinary acceptation of the words, that is all over with me. Many desire to live because they fear to die. There is nothing of that in me, I can assure you. I am not afraid to meet my Creator. But there are those who wish for life that their purposes of love, or stronger purposes of hatred, may be accomplished. I am among the number. But, on that account, I only wish it till those purposes have been completed. I think I'll go to sleep for an hour; but there are a couple of letters I want you to write before post-time.' Then Mr. Scarborough turned himself round, and thought of the letters he was to write. Mr. Merton went out, and as he wandered about the park in the dirt and slush of December, tried to make up his mind whether he most admired his patron's philosophy or condemned his general lack of principle.

At the proper hour he appeared again, and found Mr. Scarborough quite alert. 'I don't know whether I shall have the three months unless I behave better,' he said. 'I have been thinking about those letters, and very nearly made an attempt to write them. There are things about a son which a father doesn't wish to communicate to anyone.' Merton only shook his head. 'I'm not a bit afraid of you, nor do I care for your knowing what I have to say. But there are words which it would be difficult even to write, and almost impossible to dictate.' But he did make the attempt, though he did not find himself able to say all that he had intended. The first letter was to the lawyer.

'MY DEAR MR. GREY,

'You will be surprised at my writing to summon you once again to my bedside. I think there was some kind of a promise made that the request should not be repeated; but the circumstances are of such a nature, that I do not well know how to avoid it. However, if you refuse to come, I will give you my instructions. It is my purpose to make another will, and to leave everything that I am capable of leaving to my son Mountjoy. You are aware that he is now free from debt, and capable of enjoying any property that he may possess. As circumstances are at present he would on my death be absolutely penniless, and Heaven help the man who should find himself dependent on the mercy of Augustus Scarborough.

'What I possess would be the balance at the bank, the house in town, and everything contained in and about Tretton, as to which I should wish that the will should be very explicit in making it understood that every conceivable item of property is to belong to Mountjoy. I know the strength of an entail, and not for worlds would I venture to meddle with anything so holy.' There came a grin of satisfaction over his face as he uttered these words, and his scribe was utterly unable to keep from laughing. 'But as Augustus must have the acres, let him have them bare.'

'Underscore that word, if you please;' and the word was underscored. 'If I had time I would have every tree about the place cut down.'

'I don't think you could under the entail,' said Merton.

'I would use up every stick in building the farmers' barns and mending the farmers' gates, and I would cover an acre just in front of the house with a huge conservatory. I respect the law, my boy, and they would find it difficult to prove that I had gone beyond it. But there is no time for that kind of finished revenge.'

Then he went on with the letter. 'You will understand what I mean. I wish to divide my property so that Mountjoy may have everything that is not strictly entailed. You will of course say that it will all go to the gambling-table. It may go to the devil, so that Augustus does not have it. But it need not go to the gambling-table. If you would consent to come down to me once more we might possibly devise some scheme for saving it. But whether we can do so or not, it is my request that my last will may be prepared in accordance with these instructions.—Very faithfully yours,

'JOHN SCARBOROUGH.'

'And now for the other,' said Mr. Scarborough.

'Had you not better rest a bit?' asked Merton.

'No; this is a kind of work at which a man does not want to rest. He is carried on by his own solicitudes and his own eagerness. This will be very short, and when it is done, then perhaps I may sleep.'

The second letter was as follows:

'MY DEAR MOUNTJOY,

'I think you are foolish in allowing yourself to be prevented from coming here by a sentiment. But in truth, independently of the pleasure I should derive from your company, I wish you to be here on a matter of business which is of some importance to yourself. I am about to make a new will, and although I am bound to pay every respect to the entail, and would not for worlds do anything in opposition to the law, still I may be enabled to do something for your benefit. Your brother has kindly interfered for the payment of your creditors, and as all the outstanding bonds have been redeemed, you would now, by his generosity, be enabled to enjoy any property which might be left to you. There are a few tables and chairs at my disposal, and a gem or two, and some odd volumes which perhaps you might like to possess. I have written to Mr. Grey on the subject, and I would wish you to see him. This you might do whether you come here or not. But I do not the less wish that you should come.—Your affectionate father,

'JOHN SCARBOROUGH.'

'I think that the odd volumes will fetch him. He was always fond of literature.'

'I suppose it means the entire library,' replied Merton.

'And he likes tables and chairs. I think he will come and look after the tables and chairs.'

'Why not beds and washhand-stands,' said Mr. Merton.

'Well, yes; he may have the beds and the wash-hand-stands. Mountjoy is not a fool, and will understand very well what I mean. I wonder whether I could scrape the paper off the drawing-room walls, and leave the scraps to his brother, without interfering with the entail. But now I am tired and will rest.'

But he did not even then go to rest, but lay still scheming, scheming, scheming about the property. There was now another letter to be written, for the writing of which he would not again summon Mr. Merton. He was half-ashamed to do so, and at last sent for his sister. 'Martha,' said he, 'I want you to write a letter for me.'

'Mr. Merton has been writing letters for you all the morning.'

'That's just the reason why you should write one now. I am still in some slight degree afraid of his authority, but I am not at all afraid of yours.'

'You ought to be quiet, John; indeed you ought.'

'And in order that I may be quiet, you must write this letter. It's nothing particular or I should not have asked you to do it. It's only an invitation.'

'An invitation to ask somebody here?'

'Yes; to ask somebody to come here. I don't know whether he'll come.'

'Do I know him?'

'I hope you may, if he comes. He's a very good-looking young man, if that is anything.'

'Don't talk nonsense, John.'

'But I believe he's engaged to another young lady,

with whom I must beg you not to interfere. You
remember Florence?'

'Florence Mountjoy? Of course I remember my
own niece.'

'The young man is engaged to her.'

'She was intended for poor Mountjoy.'

'Poor Mountjoy has put himself beyond all possibility of a wife.'

'Poor Mountjoy!' and the soft-hearted aunt almost
shed tears.

'But we haven't to do with Mountjoy now. Sit
down there and begin. "Dear Mr. Annesley———" '

'Oh! It's Mr. Annesley; is it?'

'Yes, it is. Mr. Annesley is the handsome young
man. Have you any objection?'

'Only people do say———'

'What do they say?'

'Of course I don't know; only I have heard———'

'That he is a scoundrel?'

'Scoundrel is very strong,' said the old lady,
shocked.

'A villain, a liar, a thief, and all the rest of it.
That's what you have heard. And I'll tell you who
has been your informant. Either first or second-
hand, it has come to you from Mr. Augustus Scarborough. Now we'll begin again. "Dear Mr.
Annesley———" ' The old lady paused a moment, and
then, setting herself firmly to the task, commenced
and finished her letter as follows:

'Dear Mr. Annesley,

'You spent a few days here on one occasion, and
I want to renew the pleasure which your visit gave
me. Will you extend your kindness so far as to come
to Tretton for any time you may please to name beyond two or three days? I am sorry to say that
your friend Augustus Scarborough cannot be here to
meet you. My other son, Mountjoy, may be here.
If you wish to escape him, I will endeavour so to fix

the time when I shall have heard from you. But I think there need be no ill-blood there. Neither of you did anything of which you are, probably, ashamed; though as an old man I am bound to express my disapproval.'

'Surely he must be ashamed,' said Miss Scarborough.

'Never you mind. Believe me, you know nothing about it.' The he went on with his letter. 'But it is not merely for the pleasure of your society that I ask you. I have a word to say to you which may be important.—Yours faithfully,

'JOHN SCARBOROUGH.'

Chapter XXXIX

HOW THE LETTERS WERE RECEIVED

WE must now describe the feelings of Mr. Scarborough's correspondents as they received his letters. When Mr. Grey began to read that which was addressed to him, he declared that on no consideration would he go down to Tretton. But when he came to inquire within himself as to his objection, he found that it lay chiefly in his great dislike to Augustus Scarborough. For poor Mountjoy, as he called him, he entertained a feeling of deep pity,—and pity we know is akin to love. And for the squire he in his heart felt but little of that profound dislike which he was aware such conduct as the squire's ought to have generated. 'He is the greatest rascal that I ever knew,' he said again and again, both to Dolly and to Mr. Barry. But yet he did not regard him as an honest man regards a rascal, and was angry with himself in consequence. He knew that there remained with him even some spark of love for Mr. Scarborough, which to himself was inexplicable. From the moment in which he had first admitted the fact that Augustus Scarborough was the true heir-at-law, he had been most determined in taking care that that heirship should be established. It must be known to all men that Mountjoy was not the eldest son of his father, as the law required him to be for the inheritance of the property, and that Augustus was the eldest son; but in arranging that these truths should be notorious, it had come to pass that he had learned to hate Augustus with an intensity that had redounded to the advantage both of Mountjoy and their father. It must be so. Augustus must become Augustus Scarborough, Esquire, of Tretton,—but the worse luck for Tretton and all connected with it. And Mr. Grey did resolve that, when that day should come, all relation between himself and Tretton should cease.

It had never occurred to him that by redeeming the post-obit bonds Mountjoy would become capable of owning and enjoying any property that might be left to him. With Tretton, all the belongings of Tretton, in the old-fashioned way would of course go to the heir. The belongings of Tretton, which were personal property, would in themselves amount to wealth for a younger son. That which Mr. Scarborough would in this way be able to bequeath, might probably be worth thirty thousand pounds. Out of the proceeds of the real property the debts had been paid. And because Augustus had consented so to pay them, he was now to be mulcted of those loose belongings which gave its charm to Tretton! Because Augustus had paid Mountjoy's debts, Mountjoy was to be enabled to rob Augustus! There was a wickedness in this redolent of the old squire. But it was a wickedness in arranging which Mr. Grey hesitated to participate. As he thought of it, however, he could not but feel what a very clever man he had for a client.

'It will all go to the gambling-table, of course,' he said that night to Dolly.

'It is no affair of ours.'

'No. But when a lawyer is consulted, he has to think of the prudent or imprudent disposition of property.'

'Mr. Scarborough hasn't consulted you, papa.'

'I must look at it as though he had. He tells me what he intends to do, and I am bound to give him my advice. I cannot advise him to bestow all these things on Augustus, whom I regard as a long way the worst of the family.'

'You need not care about that.'

'And here again,' continued Mr. Grey, 'comes up the question, What is it that duty demands? Augustus is the eldest son, and is entitled to what the law allots him; but Mountjoy was brought up as the eldest son, and is certainly entitled to what provision the father can make him.'

'You cannot provide for such a gambler.'

'I don't know that that comes within my duty. It is not my fault that Mountjoy is a gambler, any more than it is my fault that Augustus is a beast. Gambler and beast, there they are. And, moreover, nothing will turn the squire from his purpose. I am only a tool in his hands,—a trowel for the laying of his mortar and bricks. Of course I must draw his will, and shall do it with some pleasure, because it will dispossess Augustus.'

Then Mr. Grey went to bed, as did also Dolly; but she was not at all surprised at being summoned to his couch after she had been an hour in her own bed.

'I think I shall go down to Tretton,' said Mr. Grey.

'You declared that you would never go there again.'

'So I did; but I did not know then how much I might come to hate Augustus Scarborough.'

'Would you go to Tretton merely to injure him?' said his daughter.

'I have been thinking about that,' said Mr. Grey. 'I don't know that I would go simply to do him an injury; but I think that I would go to see that justice is properly done.'

'That can be arranged without your going to Tretton.'

'By putting our heads together, I think we can contrive that the deed shall be more effectually performed. What we must attempt to do is to save this property from going to the gambling-table. There is only one way that occurs to me.'

'What is that?'

'It must be left to his wife.'

'He hasn't a wife.'

'It must be left to some woman whom he will consent to marry. There are three objects:—to keep it from Augustus; to give the enjoyment of it to Mountjoy; and to prevent Mountjoy from gambling with it. The only thing I can see is a wife.'

'There is a girl he wants to marry,' said Dolly.

'But she doesn't want to marry him, and I doubt whether he can be got to marry anyone else. There is still a peck of difficulties.'

'Oh, papa, I wish you would wash your hands of the Scarboroughs.'

'I must go to Tretton first,' said he; 'and now, my dear, you are doing no good by sitting up here and talking to me.' Then, with a smile, Dolly took herself off to her own chamber.

Mountjoy, when he got his letter, was sitting over a late breakfast in Victoria Street. It was near twelve o'clock, and he was enjoying the delicious luxury of having his breakfast to eat, with a cigar after it, and nothing else that he need do. But the fruition of all these comforts was somewhat marred by the knowledge that he had no such dinner to expect. He must go out and look for a dinner among the eating-houses. The next morning would bring him no breakfast, and if he were to remain longer in

Victoria Street he must do so in direct opposition
to the owner of the establishment. He had that
morning received notice to quit, and had been told
that the following breakfast would be the last meal
served to him. 'Let it be good of its kind,' Mountjoy
had said.

'I believe you care for nothing but eating and
drinking.'

'There's little else that you can do for me.' And
so they parted.

Mountjoy had taken the precaution of having his
letters addressed to the house of the friendly bootmaker; and now, as he was slowly pouring out his
first cup of coffee, and thinking how nearly it must
be his last, his father's letter was brought to him.
The letter had been delayed one day, as he himself
had omitted to call for it. It was necessarily a sad
time for him. He was a man who fought hard against
melancholy, taking it as a primary rule of life, that,
for such a one as he had become, the pleasures of the
immediate moment should suffice. If one day, or,
better still, one night of excitement was in store for
him, the next day should be regarded as the unlimited future, for which no man can be responsible.
But such philosophy will too frequently be insuffi-
cient for the stoutest hearts. Mountjoy's heart
would occasionally almost give way, and then his
thoughts would be dreary enough. Hunger, absolute hunger, without the assured expectation of food,
had never yet come upon him; but in order to put a
stop to its cravings, if he should find it troublesome
to bear, he had already provided himself with pistol
and bullets.

And now, with his cup of coffee before him,
aromatic, creamy, and hot, with a filleted sole rolled
up before him on a little dish, three or four plover's
eggs, on which to finish, lying by, and, on the distance of the table, a chasse of brandy, of which he
already knew well the virtues, he got his father's

letter. He did not at first open it, disliking all
thoughts as to his father. Then gradually he tore
the envelope, and was slow in understanding the full
meaning of the last lines. He did not at once perceive the irony of 'his brother's kindly interference,'
and of the 'generosity' which had enabled him,
Mountjoy, to be a recipient of property. But his
father purposed to do something for his benefit.
Gradually it dawned upon him that his father could
only do that something effectually, because of his
brother's dealings with the creditors.

Then the chairs and tables, and the gem or two,
and the odd volumes, one by one, made themselves
intelligible. That a father should write so to one
son, and should so write of another, was marvellous.
But then his father was a marvellous man, whose
character he was only beginning to understand.
His father, he told himself, had fortunately taken it
into his head to hate Augustus, and intended, in
consequence, to strip Tretton and the property
generally of all their outside personal belongings.

Yes;—he thought that, with such an object before him, he would certainly go and see Mr. Grey.
And if Mr. Grey should so advise him he would go
down to Tretton. On such business as this he would
consent to see his father. He did not think that just
at present he need have recourse to his pistol for
his devices. He could not on the very day go to
Tretton, as it would be necessary that he should
write to his father first. His brother would probably extend his hospitality for a couple of days when
he should hear of the proposed journey, and, if not,
would lend him money for his present purposes, or
under existing circumstances he might probably be
able to borrow it from Mr. Grey. With a heart
elevated to almost absolute bliss he ate his breakfast, and drank his chasse, and smoked his cigar, and
then rose slowly that he might proceed to Mr.
Grey's chambers. But at this moment Augustus

came in. He had only breakfasted at his own club, much less comfortably than he would have done at home, in order that he might not sit at table with his brother. He had now returned so that he might see to Mountjoy's departure.

'After all, Augustus, I am going down to Tretton,' said the elder brother as he folded up his father's letter.

'What arguments has the old man used now?' Mountjoy did not think it well to tell his brother the exact nature of the arguments used, and therefore put the letter into his pocket.

'He wishes to say something to me about property,' said Mountjoy.

Then some idea of the old squire's scheme fell with a crushing weight of anticipated sorrow on Augustus. In a moment it all occurred to him, what his father might do, what injuries he might inflict; and,—saddest of all feelings,—there came the immediate reflection that it had all been rendered possible by his own doings. With the conviction that so much might be left away from him, there came also a further feeling that after all there was a chance that his father had invented the story of his brother's illegitimacy, that Mountjoy was now free from debt, and that Tretton with all its belongings might now go back to him. That his father would do it if it were possible he did not doubt. From week to week he had waited impatiently for his father's demise, and had expected little or none of that mental activity which his father had exercised. 'What a fool he had been!' he said to himself, sitting opposite to Mountjoy, who in the vacancy of the moment had lighted another cigar;—'what an ass!' Had he played his cards better, had he comforted and flattered and cosseted the old man, Mountjoy might have gone his own way to the dogs. Now, at the best, Tretton would come to him stripped of everything; and,—at the worst,—no Tretton would come to him at all. 'Well, what are you going to do?' he said roughly.

'I think I shall probably go down and just see the governor.'

'All your feelings about your mother, then, are blown to the wind.'

'My feelings about your mother are not blown to the winds at all; but to speak of her to you would be wasting breath.'

'I hadn't the pleasure of knowing her,' said Augustus. 'And I am not aware that she did me any great kindness in bringing me into the world. Do you go to Tretton this afternoon?'

'Probably not.'

'Or tomorrow?'

'Possibly tomorrow,' said Mountjoy.

'Because I shall find it convenient to have your room.'

'Today, of course, I cannot stir. Tomorrow morning I should at any rate like to have my breakfast.' Here he paused for a reply, but none came from his brother. 'I must have some money to go down to Tretton with; I suppose you can lend it me just for the present.'

'Not a shilling,' said Augustus in thorough ill-humour.

'I shall be able to pay you very shortly.'

'Not a shilling. The return I have had from you for all that I have done, is not of a nature to make me do more.'

'If I had ever thought that you had expended a sovereign except for the object of furthering some plot of your own, I should have been grateful. As it is I do not know that we owe very much to each other.' Then he left the room, and, getting into a cab, went away to Lincoln's Inn.

Harry Annesley received Mr. Scarborough's letter down at Buston, and was much surprised by it. He had not spent the winter hitherto very pleasantly.

His uncle he had never seen, though he had heard from day to day sundry stories of his wooing. He had soon given up his hunting, feeling himself ashamed, in his present nameless position, to ride Joshua Thoroughbung's horses. He had taken to hard reading, but the hard reading had failed, and he had been given up to the miseries of his position. The hard reading had been continued for a fortnight or three weeks, during which he had at any rate respected himself; but in an evil hour he had allowed it to escape from him, and now was again miserable. Then the invitation from Tretton had been received. 'I have got a letter. It's from Mr. Scarborough of Tretton.'

'What does Mr. Scarborough say?'

'He wants me to go down there.'

'Do you know Mr. Scarborough? I believe you have altogether quarrelled with his son.'

'Oh yes; I have quarrelled with Augustus, and have had an encounter with Mountjoy not on the most friendly terms. But the father and Mountjoy seem to be reconciled. You can see his letter. I at any rate shall go there.' To this Mr. Annesley senior had no objection to make.

Chapter XL

VISITORS AT TRETTON

IT so happened that the three visitors who had been asked to Tretton all agreed to go on the same day. There was, indeed, no reason why Harry should delay his visit, and much why the other two should expedite theirs. Mr. Grey knew that the thing, if done at all, should be done at once: and Mountjoy, as he had agreed to accept his father's offer, could not put himself too quickly under the shelter of his father's roof. 'You can have twenty pounds,'

Mr. Grey had said when the subject of the money was mooted. 'Will that suffice?' Mountjoy had said that it would suffice amply, and then, returning to his brother's rooms, had waited there with what patience he possessed till he sallied forth to The Continental to get the best dinner which that restaurant could afford him. He was beginning to feel that his life was very sad in London, and to look forward to the glades of Tretton with some anticipation of rural delight.

He went down by the same train as Mr. Grey;— 'a great grind,' as Mountjoy called it, when Mr. Grey proposed a departure at ten o'clock. Harry followed, so as to reach Tretton only in time for dinner. 'If I may venture to advise you,' said Mr. Grey in the train, 'I should do in this matter whatever my father asked me.' Hereupon Mountjoy frowned. 'He is anxious to make some provision for you.'

'I am not grateful to my father, if you mean that.'

'It is hard to say whether you should be grateful. But, from the first, he has done the best he could for you, according to his lights.'

'You believe all this about my mother?'

'I do.'

'I don't. That's the difference. And I don't think that Augustus believes it.'

'The story is undoubtedly true.'

'You must excuse me if I will not accept it.'

'At any rate you had parted with your share in the property.'

'My share was the whole.'

'After your father's death,' said Mr. Grey; 'and that was gone.'

'We needn't discuss the property. What is it that he expects me to do now?'

'Simply to be kind in your manner to him, and to agree to what he says about the personal property.

It is his intention, as far as I understand, to leave you everything.'

'He is very kind.'

'I think he is.'

'Only that it would all have been mine if he had not cheated me of my birthright.'

'Or Mr. Tyrrwhit's, and Mr. Hart's, and Mr. Spicer's.'

'Mr. Tyrrwhit, and Mr. Hart, and Mr. Spicer could not have robbed me of my name. Let them have done what they would with their bonds, I should have been at any rate Scarborough of Tretton. My belief is that I need not blush for my mother. He has made it appear that I should do so. I can't forgive him because he gives me the chairs and tables.'

'They will be worth thirty thousand pounds,' said Mr. Grey.

'I can't forgive him.'

The cloud sat very black upon Mountjoy Scarborough's face as he said this, and the blacker it sat the more Mr. Grey liked him. If something could be done to redeem from ruin a young man who so felt about his mother,—who so felt about his mother, simply because she had been his mother,— it would be a good thing to do. Augustus had entertained no such feeling. He had said to Mr. Grey, as he had said also to his brother, that 'he had not known the lady.' When the facts as to the distribution of the property had been made known to him, he had cared nothing for the injury done by the story to his mother's name. The story was too true. Mr. Grey knew that it was true; but he could not on that account do other than feel an intense desire to confer some benefit on Mountjoy Scarborough. He put his hand out affectionately, and laid it on the other man's knee. 'Your father has not long to live, Captain Scarborough.'

'I suppose not.'

'And he is at present anxious to make what reparation is in his power. What he can leave you will produce, let us say, fifteen hundred a year. Without a will from him you would have to live on your brother's bounty.'

'By Heaven, no!' said Mountjoy, thinking of the pistol and the bullets.

'I see nothing else.'

'I see, but I cannot explain.'

'Do you not think that fifteen hundred a year would be better than nothing,—with a wife, let us say?' said Mr. Grey, beginning to introduce the one argument on which he believed so much must depend.

'With a wife?'

'Yes; with a wife.'

'With what wife? A wife may be very well, but a wife must depend on who it is. Is there anyone that you mean?'

'Not exactly any particular person,' said the lawyer lamely.

'Pshaw! What do I want with a wife? Do you mean to say that my father has told you that he intends to clog his legacy with the burden of a wife? I would not accept it with such a burden, unless I could choose the wife myself. To tell the truth, there is a girl——'

'Your cousin?'

'Yes; my cousin. When I was well-to-do in the world I was taught to believe that I could have her. If she will be mine, Mr. Grey, I will renounce gambling altogether. If my father can manage that, I will forgive him,—or will endeavour to do so. The property which he can leave me shall be settled altogether upon her. I will endeavour to reform myself, and so to live that no misfortune shall come upon her. If that is what you mean, say so.'

'Well; not quite that.'

'To no other marriage will I agree. That has

been the dream of my life through all those moments
of hot excitement and assured despair which I have
endured. Her mother has always told me that it
should be so, and she herself in former days did not
deny it. Now you know it all. If my father wishes
to see me married, Florence Mountjoy must be my
wife.' Then he sank back on his seat, and nothing
more was said between them till they had reached
Tretton.

The father and son had not met each other since
the day on which the former had told the latter the
story of his birth. Since then Mountjoy had disappeared from the world, and for a few days his
father thought that he had been murdered. But now
they met as they might have done had they seen each
other a week ago. 'Well, Mountjoy, how are you?'
And 'How are you, sir?' Such were the greetings
between them. And no others were spoken. In a
few minutes the son was allowed to go and look
after the rural joys he had anticipated, and the lawyer
was left closeted with the squire.

Mr. Grey soon explained his proposition. Let
the property be left to trustees, who should realise
from it what money it should fetch, and keep the
money in their own hands, paying Mountjoy the
income. 'There could,' he said, 'be nothing better
done, unless Mountjoy would agree to marry. He
is attached, it seems, to his cousin,' said Mr. Grey,
'and he is unwilling at present to marry anyone else.'

'He can't marry her,' said the squire.

'I do not know the circumstances.'

'He can't marry her. She is engaged to the young
man who will be here just now. I told you,—did I
not?—that Harry Annesley is coming here. My son
knows that he will be here to-day.'

'Everybody knows the story of Mr. Annesley
and the captain.'

'They are to sit down to dinner together, and I
trust they may not quarrel. The lady of whom you

are speaking is engaged to young Annesley, and
Mountjoy's suit in that direction is hopeless.'

'Hopeless, you think?'

'Utterly hopeless. Your plan of providing him
with a wife would be very good if it were feasible.
I should be very glad to see him settled. But if he
will marry no one but Florence Mountjoy he must
remain unmarried. Augustus has had his hand in
that business, and don't let us dabble in it.' Then
the squire gave the lawyer full instructions as to
the will which was to be made. Mr. Grey and Mr.
Bullfist were to be named as trustees, with instructions to sell everything which it would be in the
squire's legal power to bequeath. The books, the
gems, the furniture, both at Tretton and in London,
the plate, the stock, the farm-produce, the pictures
on the walls, and the wine in the cellars, were all
named. He endeavoured to persuade Mr. Grey to
consent to a cutting of the timber, so that the value
of it might be taken out of the pocket of the younger
brother and put into that of the elder. But to this
Mr. Grey would not assent. 'There would be an
air of persecution about it,' he said, 'and it mustn't
be done.' But to the general stripping of Tretton
for the benefit of Mountjoy he gave a cordial
agreement.

'I am not quite sure that I have done with Augustus as yet,' said the squire. 'I had made up my mind
not to be put out by trifles; not to be vexed at a
little. My treatment of my children has been such,
that though I have ever intended to do them good,
I must have seemed to each at different periods to
have injured him. I have not therefore expected
much from them. But I have received less than
nothing from Augustus. It is possible that he may
hear from me again.' To this Mr. Grey said nothing,
but he had taken his instructions about the drawing
of the will.

Harry came down by the train in time for dinner.

On the journey down he had been perplexed in his
mind, thinking of various things. He did not quite
understand why Mr. Scarborough had sent for him.
His former intimacy had been with Augustus, and
though there had been some cordiality of friendship
shown by the old man to the son's companion, it
had amounted to no more than might be expected
from one who was notably good-natured. A great
injury had been done to Harry, and he supposed
that his visit must have some reference to that
injury. He had been told in so many words that,
come when he might, he would not find Augustus
at Tretton. From this and from other signs he
almost saw that there existed a quarrel between the
squire and his son. Therefore he felt that something
was to be said as to the state of his affairs at Buston.

But if, as the train drew near to Tretton, he was
anxious as to his meeting with the squire, he was
much more so as to the captain. The reader will
remember all the circumstances under which they
two had last seen each other. Harry had been
furiously attacked by Mountjoy and had then left
him sprawling,—dead as some folks had said on the
following day,—under the rail. His only crime had
been that he was drunk. If the disinherited one
would give him his hand and let bygones be bygones,
he would do the same. He felt no personal animosity.
But there was a difficulty.

As he was driven up to the door in a cab belonging
to the squire, there was Mountjoy standing before
the house. He too had thought of the difficulties, and
had made up his mind that it would not do for him to
meet his late foe without some few words intended
for the making of peace. 'I hope you are well, Mr.
Annesley,' he said, offering his hand as the other got
out of the cab. 'It may be as well that I should
apologise at once for my conduct. I was at that
moment considerably distressed, as you may have
heard. I had been declared to be penniless, and to

be nobody. The news had a little unmanned me, and I was beside myself.'

'I quite understand it;—quite understand it,' said Annesley, giving his hand. 'I am very glad to see you back again, and in your father's house.' Then Mountjoy turned on his heel, and went through the hall, leaving Harry to the care of the butler. The captain thought that he had done enough, and that the affair in the street might now be regarded as a dream. Harry was taken up to shake hands with the old man, and in due time came down to dinner, where he met Mr. Grey and the young doctor. They were all very civil to him, and, upon the whole, he spent a pleasant evening. On the next day about noon the squire sent for him. He had been told at breakfast that it was the squire's intention to see him in the middle of the day, and he had been unable therefore to join Mountjoy's shooting-party.

'Sit down, Mr. Annesley,' said the old man. 'You were surprised, no doubt when you got my invitation?'

'Well, yes; perhaps so; but I thought it very kind.'

'I meant to be kind. But still, it requires some explanation. You see, I am such an old cripple that I cannot give invitations like anybody else. Now you are here I must not eat and drink with you, and in order to say a few words to you, I am obliged to keep you in the house till the doctor tells me that I am strong enough to talk.'

'I am glad to find you so much better than when I was here before.'

'I don't know much about that. There will never be a "much better" in my case. The people about me talk with the utmost unconcern of whether I can live one month or possibly two. Anything beyond that is quite out of the question.' The squire took a pride in making the worst of his case, so that the people to whom he talked should marvel the more at his vitality. 'But we won't mind my health now. It is true, I fear, that you have quarrelled with your uncle.'

'It is quite true that he has quarrelled with me.'

'I am afraid that that is more important. He means, if he can, to cut you out of the entail.'

'He does not mean that I shall have the property if he can prevent it.'

'I don't think very much of entails myself,' said the squire. 'If a man has a property he should be able to leave it as he pleases; or,—or else he doesn't have it.'

'That is what the law intends, I suppose,' said Harry.

'Just so; but the law is such an old woman that she never knows how to express herself to any purpose. I haven't allowed the law to bind me. I dare say you know the story.'

'About your two sons,—and the property? I think all the world knows the story.'

'I suppose it has been talked about a little,' said the squire with a chuckle. 'My object has been to prevent the law from handing over my property to the fraudulent claims which my son's creditors were enabled to make;—and I have succeeded fairly well. On that head I have nothing to regret. Now your uncle is going to take other means.'

'Yes; he is going to take means which are at any rate lawful.'

'But which will be tedious, and may not, perhaps, succeed. He is intending to have an heir of his own.'

'That I believe is his purpose,' said Harry.

'There is no reason why he shouldn't;—but he mayn't, you know.'

'He is not married yet.'

'No;—he is not married yet. And then he has also stopped the allowance he used to make you.' Harry nodded assent. 'Now all this is a great shame.'

'I think so.'

'The poor gentleman has been awfully bamboozled.'

'He is not so very old,' said Harry. 'I don't think he is more than fifty.'

'But he is an old goose. You'll excuse me, I know. Augustus Scarborough got him up to London, and filled him full of lies.'

'I am aware of it.'

'And so am I aware of it. He has told him stories as to your conduct with Mountjoy, which, added to some youthful indiscretions of your own——'

'It was simply because I didn't like to hear him read sermons.'

'That was an indiscretion, as he had the power in his hands to do you an injury. Most men have got some little bit of pet tyranny in their hearts. I have had none.' To this Harry could only bow. 'I let my two boys do as they pleased, only wishing that they should lead happy lives. I never made them listen to sermons or even to lectures. Probably I was wrong. Had I tyrannised over them, they would not have tyrannised over me as they have done. Now I'll tell you what it is that I propose to do. I will write to your uncle, or will get Mr. Merton to write for me, and will explain to him as well as I can, the depth, and the blackness, and the cruelty,—the unfathomable heathen cruelty, together with the falsehoods, the premeditated lies, and the general rascality on all subjects,—of my son Augustus. I will explain to him that of all men I know, he is the least trustworthy. I will explain to him that, if led in a matter of importance by Augustus Scarborough, he will be surely led astray. And I think that between us,—between Merton and me that is,—we can concoct a letter that shall be efficacious. But I will get Mountjoy also to go and see him, and explain to him out of his own mouth what in truth occurred that night when he and you fell out in the streets. Mr. Prosper must be a more vindictive man than I take him to be in regard to sermons if he will hold out after that.' Then Mr. Scarborough allowed him to go out, and if possible find the shooters somewhere about the park.

Chapter XLI

MOUNTJOY SCARBOROUGH GOES TO BUSTON

MR. GREY returned to London after staying but one night, having received fresh instructions as to the will. The will was to be prepared at once, and Mr. Barry was to bring it down for execution. 'Shall I not inform Augustus?' asked Mr. Grey.

But this did not suit with Mr. Scarborough's views of revenge. 'I think not. I would do by him whatever honesty requires; but I have never told him that I mean to leave him anything. Of course he knows that he is to have the estate. He is revelling in the future poverty of poor Mountjoy. He turned him out of his house just now because Mountjoy would not obey him by going to——Brazil. He would turn him out of his house if he could because I won't at once go——to the devil. He is something over-masterful, is Master Augustus, and a rub or two will do him good. I'd rather you wouldn't tell him, if you please.' Then Mr. Grey departed without making any promise; but he determined that he would be guided by the squire's wishes. Augustus Scarborough was not of nature to excite very warmly the charity of any man.

Harry remained for two or three days' shooting with Mountjoy, and once or twice he saw the squire again. 'Merton and I have managed to concoct that letter,' said the squire. 'I'm afraid your uncle will find it rather long. Is he impatient of long letters?'

'He likes long sermons.'

'If anybody will listen to his reading. I think you have a deal to answer for yourself, when you could not make so small a sacrifice to the man to whom you were to owe everything. But he ought to look for a wife in consequence of that crime, and not falsely allege another. If, as I fear, he finds the wife plan troublesome, our letter may perhaps move him, and Mountjoy is to go down and open his eyes. Mountjoy hasn't made any difficulty about it.'

'I shall be greatly distressed——' Harry began.

'Not at all. He must go. I like to have my own way in these little matters. He owes you as much reparation as that, and we shall be able to see what members of the Scarborough family you would trust the most.'

Harry, during the two days, shot some hares in company with Mountjoy, but not a word more was said about the adventure in London. Nor was the name of Florence Mountjoy ever mentioned between the two suitors. 'I'm going to Buston, you know,' Mountjoy said once.

'So your father told me.'

'What sort of a fellow shall I find your uncle?'

'He's a gentleman, but not very wise.' No more was said between them on that head, but Mountjoy spoke at great length about his own brother and his father's will.

'My father is the most singular man you ever came across.'

'I think he is.'

'I am not going to say a good word for him. I wouldn't let him think that I had said a good word for him. In order to save the property he has maligned my mother, and has cheated me and the creditors most horribly;—most infernally. That's my conviction, though Grey thinks otherwise. I can't forgive him,—and won't, and he knows it. But after that he is going to do the best thing he can for me. And he has begun by making me a

decent allowance again as his son. But I'm to have
that only as long as I remain here at Tretton. Of
course I have been fond of cards.'

'I suppose so.'

'Not a doubt of it. But I haven't touched a card
now for a month nearly. And then he is going to
leave me what property he has to leave. And he and
my brother have paid off those Jews among them.
I'm not a bit obliged to my brother. He's got some
game of his own which I don't quite clearly see, and
my father is doing this for me simply to spite my
brother. He'd cut down every tree upon the place if
Grey would allow it. And yet to give Augustus the
property my father has done this gross injustice.'

'I suppose the money-lenders would have had the
best of it had he not.'

'That's true. They would have had it all. They
had measured every yard of it, and had got my name
down for the full value. Now they're paid.'

'That's a comfort.'

'Nothing's a comfort. I know that they're right,
and that if I got the money into my own hand it
would be gone to-morrow. I should be off to Monte
Carlo like a shot; and of course it would go after
the other. There is but one thing would redeem
me.'

'What's that?'

'Never mind. We won't talk of it.' Then he
was silent, but Harry Annesley knew very well that
he had alluded to Florence Mountjoy.

Then Harry went, and Mountjoy was left to the
companionship of Mr. Merton, and such pleasure as
he could find in a daily visit to his father. He was at
any rate courteous in his manner to the old man,
and abstained from those irritating speeches which
Augustus had always chosen to make. He had on
one occasion during this visit told his father what
he thought about him; but this the squire had taken
quite as a compliment.

'I believe, you know, that you've done a monstrous injustice to everybody concerned.'

'I rather like doing what you call injustices.'

'You have set the law at defiance.'

'Well; yes; I think I have done that.'

'According to my belief it's all untrue.'

'You mean about your mother. I like you for that; I do indeed. I like you for sticking up for your poor mother. Well, now you shall have fifty pounds a month; say twelve pounds ten a week as long as you remain at Tretton, and you may have whom you like here as long as they bring no cards with them. And if you want to hunt, there are horses; and if they ain't good enough, you can get others. But if you go away from Tretton there's an end of it. It will all be stopped the next day.'

Nevertheless he did make arrangements by which Mountjoy should proceed to Buston stopping two nights as he went in London. 'There isn't a club he can enter,' said the squire, comforting himself, 'nor a Jew that will lend him a five-pound note.'

Mountjoy had told the truth when he had said that nothing was a comfort. Though it seemed to his father and to the people around him at Tretton that he had everything that a man could want, he had in fact nothing,—nothing that could satisfy him. In the first place he was quite alive to the misery of that decision given by the world against him, which had been of such comfort to his father. Not a club in London would admit him. He had been proclaimed a defaulter after such a fashion that all his clubs had sent to him for some explanation, and as he had given none, and had not answered their letters, his name had been crossed out in the books of them all. He knew himself to be a man disgraced, and when he had fled from London he had gone under the conviction that he would certainly never return. There were the pistol and bullet as his last assured resource; but a certain amount of good fortune had

awaited him,—enough to save him from having recourse to their aid. His brother had supplied him
with small sums of money, and from time to time a
morsel of good luck had enabled him to gamble, not
to his heart's content, but in some manner so as to
make his life bearable. But now, he was back in
his own country, and he could gamble not at all,
and hardly even see those old companions with whom
he had lived. It was not only for the card-tables
that he sighed, but for the companions of the card-
table. And though he knew that he had been
scratched out from the lists of all clubs as a dishonest
man, he knew also, or thought that he knew, that
he had been as honest as the best of those companions. As long as he could by any possibility
raise money he had paid it away, and by no false
trick had he ever endeavoured to get it back again.
Had a little time been allowed him all would have
been paid;—and all had been paid. He knew that
by the rules of such institutions time could not be
granted; but still he did not feel himself to have been
a dishonest man. Yet he had been so disgraced that
he could hardly venture to walk about the streets of
London in the daylight. And then there came upon
him, when he found himself alone at Tretton, an
irrepressible desire for gambling. It was as though
his throat were parched with an implacable thirst.
He walked about ever meditating certain fortunate
turns of the cards, and when he had worked himself
up to some realisation of his old excitement, he
would remember that it was all a vain and empty
bubble. He had money in his pocket, and could rush
up to London if he would, and if he did so he could
no doubt find some coarse hell at which he could
stake it till it would be all gone; but the gates of
the A—— and the B—— and the C—— would be
closed against him. And he would then be driven
to feel that he had indeed fallen into the nethermost
pit. Were he once to play at such places as his mind

painted to him he could never play at any other. And yet when the day drew nigh on which he was to go to London on his way to Buston, he did bethink himself where these places were to be found. His throat was parched, and the thirst upon him was extreme. Cards were the weapons he had used. He had played écarté, piquet, whist, and baccarat, with an occasional night at some foolish game such as cribbage or vingt-et-un. Though he had always lost, he had always played with men who had played honestly. There is much that is in truth dishonest even in honest play. A man who can keep himself sober after dinner, plays with one who flusters himself with drink. The man with a trained memory plays with him who cannot remember a card. The cool man plays with the impetuous;—the man who can hold his tongue, with him who cannot but talk; the man whose practised face will tell no secrets, with him who loses a point every rubber by his uncontrolled grimaces. And then there is the man who knows the game, and plays with him who knows it not at all! Of course, the cool, the collected, the thoughtful, the practised, they who have given up their whole souls to the study of cards, will play at a great advantage, which in their calculations they do not fail to recognise. See the man standing by and watching the table, and laying all the bets he can on A and B as against C and D, and, however ignorant you may be, you will soon become sure that A and B know the game, whereas C and D are simply infants. That is all fair and acknowledged; but looking at it from a distance, as you lie under your apple-trees in your orchard, far from the shout of 'Two by honours,' you will come to doubt the honesty of making your income after such a fashion.

Such as it is, Mountjoy sighed for it bitterly;— sighed for it, but could not see where it was to be found. He had a gentleman's horror of those resorts in gin shops, or kept by the disciples of gin shops, where he would surely be robbed,—which did not appal him,—but robbed in bad company. Thinking of all this he went up to London late in the afternoon, and spent an uncomfortable evening in town. It was absolutely innocent as regarded the doings of the night itself, but was terrible to him. There was a slow drizzling rain, but not the less after dinner at his hotel he started off to wander through the streets. With his great-coat and his umbrella he was almost hidden, and as he passed through Pall Mall, up St. James's Street and along Piccadilly, he could pause and look in at the accustomed door. He saw men entering whom he knew, and knew that within five minutes they could be seated at their tables. 'I had an awfully heavy time of it last night,' one said to another as he went up the steps; and Mountjoy, as he heard the words, envied the speaker. Then he passed back and went again a tour of all the clubs. What had he done that he, like a poor Peri, should be unable to enter the gates of all these Paradises?* He had now in his pocket fifty pounds. Could he have been made absolutely certain that he would have lost it, he would have gone into any Paradise, and have staked his money with that certainty. At last, having turned up Waterloo Place, he saw a man standing in the doorway of one of these palaces, and he was aware at once that the man had seen him. He was a man of such a nature that it would be impossible that he should have seen a worse. He was a small, dry, good-looking little fellow, with a carefully preserved moustache, and a head from the top of which age was beginning to move the hair. He lived by cards, and lived well. He was called Captain Vignolles, but it was only known of him that he was a professional gambler. He probably never cheated. Men who play at the clubs scarcely ever cheat. There are so many with whom they play sharp enough to discover them, and with the discovered gambler all in this world is over.

Captain Vignolles never cheated; but he found that an obedience to those little rules which I have named above stood him well in lieu of cheating. He was not known to have any particular income, but he was known to live on the best of everything as far as club-life was concerned.

He immediately followed Mountjoy down into the street and greeted him. 'Captain Scarborough, as I am a living man!'

'Well, Vignolles; how are you?'

'And so you have come back once more to the land of the living. I was awfully sorry for you, and think that they treated you uncommon harshly. As you've paid your money, of course they'll let you in again.' In answer to this, Mountjoy had very little to say; but the interview ended by his accepting an invitation from Captain Vignolles to supper for the following evening. If Captain Scarborough would come at eleven o'clock Captain Vignolles would ask a few fellows to meet him, and they would have,— just a little rubber of whist. Mountjoy knew well the nature of the man who asked him, and understood perfectly what would be the result. But there thrilled through his bosom as he accepted the invitation a sense of joy which he could himself hardly understand.

On the following morning Mountjoy was up for him very early, and, taking a return ticket, went down to Buston. He had written to Mr. Prosper, sending his compliments, and saying that he would do himself the honour of calling at a certain hour.

At the hour named he drove up at Buston Hall in a fly from Buntingford Station, and was told by Matthew, the old butler, that his master was at home. If Captain Mountjoy would step into the drawing-room, Mr. Prosper should be informed. Mountjoy did as he was bidden, and after half-an-hour he was joined by Mr. Prosper. 'You have received a letter from my father,' he began by saying.

'A very long letter,' said the squire of Buston.

'I dare say; I did not see it, and have, in fact, very little to say as to its contents. I do not know indeed what they were.'

'The letter refers to my nephew, Mr. Henry Annesley.'

'I suppose so. What I have to say refers to Mr. Henry Annesley also.'

'You are kind; very kind.'

'I don't know about that; but I have come altogether at my father's instance, and I think indeed that in fairness I ought to tell you the truth as to what took place between me and your nephew.'

'You are very good; but your father has already given me his account,—and I suppose yours.'

'I don't know what my father may have done, but I think that you ought to desire to hear from my lips an account of the transaction. An untrue account has been told to you.'

'I have heard it all from your own brother.'

'An untrue account has been told to you. I attacked your nephew.'

'What made you do that?' asked the squire.

'That has nothing to do with it; but I did.'

'I understood all that before.'

'But you didn't understand that Mr. Annesley behaved perfectly well in all that occurred.'

'Did he tell a lie about it afterwards?'

'My brother no doubt lured him on to make an untrue statement.'

'A lie!'

'You may call it so if you will. If you think that Augustus was to have it all his own way, I disagree with you altogether. In point of fact, your nephew behaved through the whole of that matter as well as a man could do. Practically, he told no lie at all. He did just what a man ought to do, and anything that you have heard to the contrary is calumnious and false. As I am told that you have been led by my brother's statement to disinherit your nephew——'

'I have done nothing of the kind.'

'I am very glad to hear it. He has not at any rate deserved it; and I have felt it to be my duty to come and tell you.'

Then Mountjoy retired, not without hospitality having been coldly offered by Mr. Prosper, and went back to Buntingford and to London. Now at last would come, he said to himself through the whole of the afternoon, now at last would come a repetition of those joys for which his very soul had sighed so eagerly.

Chapter XLII

CAPTAIN VIGNOLLES ENTERTAINS HIS FRIENDS

MOUNTJOY, when he reached Captain Vignolles's rooms, was received apparently with great indifference. 'I didn't feel at all sure you would come. But there is a bit of supper if you like to stay. I saw Moody this morning, and he said he would look in if he was passing this way. Now sit down and tell me what you have been doing since you disappeared in that remarkable manner.' This was not at all what Mountjoy had expected, but he could only sit down and say that he had done nothing in particular. Of all clubmen Captain Vignolles would be the worst with whom to play alone during the entire evening. And Mountjoy remembered now that he had never been inside four walls with Vignolles except at a club. Vignolles regarded him simply as a piece of prey whom chance had thrown up on the shore. And Moody, who would no doubt show himself before long, was another bird of the same covey, though less rapacious. Mountjoy put his hand up to his breast-pocket, and knew that the fifty pounds was there, but he knew also that it would soon be gone. Even to him it seemed to be expedient to get up and at once to go. What delight would there be to him in playing piquet with such a face opposite to him as that of Captain Vignolles, or with such a one as that of old Moody? There could be none of the brilliance of the room, no pleasant hum of the voices of companions, no sense of his own equality with others. There would be none to sympathise with him when he cursed his ill-luck; there would be no chance of contending with an innocent who would be as reckless as was he himself. He looked round. The room was gloomy and uncomfortable. Captain Vignolles watched him, and was afraid that his prey was about to escape. 'Won't you light a cigar?' Mountjoy took the cigar, and then felt that he could not go quite at once. 'I suppose you went to Monaco?'

'I was there for a short time.'

'Monaco isn't bad. Though there is of course the pull which the tables have against you. But it's a grand thing to think that skill can be of no avail. I often think that I ought to play nothing but rouge-et-noir.'

'You!'

'Yes; I. I don't deny that I'm the luckiest fellow going. But I never can remember cards. Of course I know my trade. Every fellow knows his trade, and I'm up pretty nearly in all that the books tell you.'

'That's a great deal.'

'Not when you come to play with men who know what play is. Look at Grossengrannel. I'd sooner bet on him than any man in London. Grossengrannel never forgets a card. I'll bet a hundred pounds that he knows the best card in every suit throughout an entire day's play. That's his secret. He gives his mind to it,—which I can't. Hang it! I'm always thinking of something quite different, of what I'm going to eat, or that sort of thing. Grossengrannel is always looking at the cards, and he wins the odd rubber out of every eleven by his attention. Shall we have a game of piquet?'

Now on the moment, in spite of all that he had felt during the entire day, in the teeth of all his longings, in opposition to all his thirst, Mountjoy for a minute or two did think that he could rise and go. His father was about to put him on his legs again, —if only he would abstain. But Vignolles had the card-table open, with clean packs and chairs at the corners, before he could decide. 'What is it to be? Twos on the game, I suppose.' But Mountjoy would not play piquet. He named écarté,* and asked that it might be only ten shillings a game. It was many months now since he had played a game of écarté. 'Oh, hang it!' said Vignolles still holding the pack in his hands. When thus appealed to, Mountjoy relented, and agreed that a pound should be staked on each game. When they had played seven games Vignolles had won but one pound, and expressed an opinion that that kind of thing wouldn't suit them at all. 'Schoolgirls would do better,' he said. Then Mountjoy pushed back his chair as though to go; when the door opened and Major Moody entered the room. 'Now we'll have a rubber at dummy,' said Captain Vignolles.

Major Moody was a grey-headed old man of about sixty, who played his cards with great attention, and never spoke a word,—either then or at any other period of his life. He was the most taciturn of men, and was known not at all to any of his companions. It was rumoured of him that he had a wife at home, whom he kept in moderate comfort on his winnings. It seemed to be the sole desire of his heart to play with reckless, foolish young men, who up to a certain point did not care what they lost. He was popular, as being always ready to oblige everyone, and, as was frequently said of him, was the very soul of honour. He certainly got no amusement from the play, working at it very hard,— and very constantly. No one ever saw him anywhere but at the club. At eight o'clock he went home to dinner, let us hope to the wife of his bosom, and at eleven he returned, and remained as long as there were men to play with. A tedious and unsatisfactory life he had, and it would have been well for him could his friends have procured on his behoof the comparative ease of a stool in a counting-house. But, as no such Elysium*was open to him, the major went on accepting the smaller profits and the harder work of club life. In what regiment he had been a major no one knew or cared to inquire. He had been received as Major Moody for twenty years or more, and twenty years is surely time enough to settle a man's claim to a majority without reference to the Army List.*

'How are you, Major Moody?' said Mountjoy.

'Not much to boast of. I hope you're pretty well, Captain Scarborough.' Beyond that there was no word of salutation, and no reference to Mountjoy's wonderful absence.

'What's it to be? twos and tens?' said Captain Vignolles, arranging the cards and the chairs.

'Not for me,' said Mountjoy, who seemed to have been enveloped by a most unusual prudence.

'What! are you afraid;—you who used to fear neither man nor devil?'

'There is so much in not being accustomed to it,' said Mountjoy. 'I haven't played a game of whist since I don't know when.'

'Twos and tens is heavy against dummy,' said Major Moody.

'I'll take dummy if you like it,' said Vignolles. Moody only looked at him.

'We'll each have our own dummy, of course,' said Mountjoy.

'Just as you please,' said Vignolles. 'I'm host here, and of course will give way to anything you may propose. What's it to be, Scarborough?'

'Pounds and fives. I shan't play higher than that.' There came across Mountjoy's mind as he stated the stakes for which he consented to play a remembrance that in the old days he had always been called Captain Scarborough by this man who now left out the captain. Of course, he had fallen since that,—fallen very low. He ought to feel obliged to any man who had in the old days been a member of the same club with him, who would now greet him with the familiarity of his unadorned name. But the remembrance of the old sounds came back upon his ear, and the consciousness that before his father's treatment of him he had been known to the world at large as Captain Scarborough of Tretton.

'Well, well; pounds and fives,' said Vignolles. 'It's better than pottering away at écarté at a pound a game. Of course a man could win something if the games were to run all one way. But where they alternate so quickly it amounts to nothing. You've got the first dummy, Scarborough. Where will you sit? Which cards will you take? I do believe that at whist everything depends upon the cards;—or else on the hinges. I've known eleven rubbers running to follow the hinges. People laugh at me because I believe in luck. I speak as I find it; that's all. You've turned up an honour already. When a man begins with an honour he'll always go on with honours. That's my observation. I know you're pretty good at this game, Moody, so I'll leave it to you to arrange the play, and will follow up as well as I can. You lead up to the weak, of course.' This was not said till the card was out of his partner's hand. 'But when your adversary has got ace, king, queen in his own hand there is no weak. Well, we've saved that, and it's as much as we can expect. If I'd begun by leading a trump it would have been all over with us. Won't you light a cigar, Moody?'

'I never smoke at cards.'

'That's all very well for the club, but you might relax a little here. Scarborough will take another cigar.' But even Mountjoy was too prudent. He did not take the cigar, but he did win the rubber. 'You're in for a good thing tonight. I feel as certain of it as though the money were in your pocket.'

Mountjoy, though he would not smoke, did drink. What would they have? asked Vignolles. There was champagne, and whisky, and brandy. He was afraid there was no other wine. He opened a bottle of champagne, and Mountjoy took the tumbler that was filled for him. He always drank whisky and water himself. So he said, and filled for himself a glass in which he poured a very small allowance of alcohol. Major Moody asked for barley-water. As there was none, he contented himself with sipping Apollinaris.*

A close record of the events of that evening would make but a tedious tale for readers. Mountjoy of course lost his fifty pounds. Alas! he lost much more than his fifty pounds. The old spirit soon came upon him, and the remembrance of what his father was to do for him passed away from him, and all thoughts of his adversaries,—who and what they were. The major pertinaciously refused to increase his stakes, and, worse again, refused to play for anything but ready money. 'It's a kind of thing I never do. You may think me very odd, but it's a kind of thing I never do.' It was the longest speech he made through the entire evening. Vignolles reminded him that he did in fact play on credit at the club. 'The committee look to that,' he murmured, and shook his head. Then Vignolles offered again to take the dummy, so that there should be no necessity for Moody and Scarborough to play against each other, and offered to give one point every other rubber as the price to be paid for the advantage. But Moody, whose success for the night was assured by the thirty pounds which he had in his pocket, would come to no terms. 'You mean to say you're going to break us up,' said Vignolles. 'That'll be hard on Scarborough.'

'I'll go on for money,' said the immovable major.
'I suppose you won't have it out with me at
double dummy,' said Vignolles to his victim. 'But
double dummy is a terrible grind at this time of
night.' And he pushed all the cards up together,
so as to show that the amusement for the night was
over. He too saw the difficulty which Moody so
pertinaciously avoided. He had been told wondrous
things of the old squire's intentions towards his
eldest son, but he had been told them only by that
eldest son himself. No doubt he could go on winning.
Unless in the teeth of a most obstinate run of cards,
he would be sure to win against Scarborough's
apparent forgetfulness of all rules and ignorance of
the peculiarities of the game he was playing. But he
would more probably obtain payment of the two
hundred and thirty pounds now due to him,—that or
nearly that,—than of a larger sum. He already had
in his possession the other twenty pounds which poor
Mountjoy had brought with him. So he let the
victim go. Moody went first, and Vignolles then
demanded the performance of a small ceremony.
'Just put your name to that,' said Vignolles. It
was a written promise to pay Captain Vignolles the
exact sum of two hundred and twenty-seven pounds
on or before that day week. 'You'll be punctual;
won't you?'

'Of course I'll be punctual,' said Mountjoy,
scowling.

'Well, yes; no doubt. But there have been mistakes.'

'I tell you, you'll be paid. Why the devil did you
win it of me if you doubt it?'

'I saw you just roaming about, and I meant to be
good-natured.'

'You knew as well as any man what chances
you should run, and when to hold your hand. If
you tell me about mistakes, I shall make it personal.'

'I didn't say anything, Scarborough, that ought to be taken up in that way.'

'Hang your Scarborough! When one gentleman talks to another about mistakes he means something.' Then he smashed down his hat upon his head and left the room.

Vignolles emptied the bottle of champagne, in which one glass was left, and sat himself down with the document in his hand. 'Just the same fellow!' he said to himself; 'overbearing, reckless, pig-headed, and a bully. He'd lose the Bank of England if he had it. But then he don't pay! He hasn't a scruple about that! If I lose I have to pay. By Jove, yes! Never didn't pay a shilling I lost in my life! It's deuced hard when a fellow is on the square like that to make two ends meet when he comes across defaulters. Those fellows should be hung. They're the very scum of the earth. Talk of welchers! They're worse than any welcher. Welcher is a thing you needn't have to do with if you're careful. But when a fellow turns round upon you as a de-faulter at cards, there is no getting rid of him. Where the play is all straightforward and honourable, a defaulter when he shows himself ought to be well-nigh murdered.'

Such were Captain Vignolles's plaints to himself, as he sat there looking at the suspicious document which Mountjoy had left in his hands. To him it was a fact that he had been cruelly used in having such a bit of paper thrust upon him instead of being paid by a cheque which on the morning would be honoured. And as he thought of his own career; his ready-money payments; his obedience to certain rules of the game,—rules, I mean, against cheating; —as he thought of his hands, which in his own estima-tion were beautifully clean; his diligence in his pro-fession, which to him was honourable; his hard work; his late hours; his devotion to a task which was often tedious; his many periods of heartrending loss,

which when they occurred would drive him nearly
mad; his small customary gains; his inability to put
by anything for old age; of the narrow edge by
which he himself was occasionally divided from
defalcation, he spoke to himself of himself as of an
honest hard-working professional man upon whom
the world was peculiarly hard.

But Major Moody went home to his wife quite
content with the thirty pounds which he had won.

Chapter XLIII

MR. PROSPER IS VISITED BY HIS LAWYERS

MR. PROSPER had not been in good spirits at
the time at which Mountjoy Scarborough had
visited him. He had received, some time previously,
a letter from Mr. Grey, as described in a previous
chapter, and had also known exactly what proposal
had been made by Mr. Grey to Messrs. Soames and
Simpson. An equal division of the lady's income,
one half to go to the lady herself, and the other half
to Mr. Prosper, with an annuity of two hundred and
fifty pounds out of the estate for the lady if Mr.
Prosper should die first,—these were the terms
which had been offered to Miss Thoroughbung
with the object of inducing her to become the wife
of Mr. Prosper. But to these terms Miss Thoroughbung had declined to accede, and had gone about
the arrangement of her money-matters in a most
precise and business-like manner. A third of her
income she would give up since Mr. Prosper desired
it, but more than that she 'would owe it to herself
and her friends to decline to abandon.' The payment
for the fish and the champagne must be omitted from
any agreement on her part. As to the ponies, and
their harness, and the pony-carriage, she would
supply them. The ponies and the carriage would

be indispensable to her happiness. But the maintenance of the ponies must be left to Mr. Prosper.
As for the dower, she could not consent to accept
less than four hundred,—or five hundred if no house
was to be provided. She thought that seven hundred
and fifty would be little enough if there were no
children, as in that case there was no heir for whom
Mr. Prosper was especially anxious. But as there
probably would be children, Miss Thoroughbung
thought that this was a matter to which Mr. Prosper
would not give much consideration. Throughout it
all she maintained a beautiful equanimity, and made
two or three efforts to induce Mr. Prosper to repeat
his visit to Marmaduke Lodge. She herself wrote
to him, saying that she thought it odd that, considering their near alliance, he should not come and
see her. Once she said that she had heard that he was
ill, and offered to go to Buston Hall to visit him.

All this was extremely distressing to a gentleman
of Mr. Prosper's delicate feelings. As to the proposals in regard to money, the letters from Soames
and Simpson to Grey and Barry, all of which came
down to Buston Hall, seemed to be innumerable.
With Soames and Simpson Mr. Prosper declined to
have any personal communication. But every letter
from the Buntingford attorneys was accompanied by
a further letter from the London attorneys, till the
correspondence became insupportable. Mr. Prosper
was not strong enough to stick firmly to his guns as
planted for him by Messrs. Grey and Barry. He did
give way in some matters, and hence arose renewed
letters which nearly drove him mad. Messrs. Soames
and Simpson's client was willing to accept four hundred pounds as the amount of the dower, without
reference to the house, and to this Mr. Prosper
yielded. He did not much care about any heir as yet
unborn, and felt by no means so certain in regard to
children as did the lady. But he fought hard about
the ponies. He could not undertake that his wife

should have ponies. That must be left to him as master of the house. He thought that a pair of carriage-horses for her use would be sufficient. He had always kept a carriage, and intended to do so. She might bring her ponies if she pleased, but if he thought well to part with them he would sell them. He found himself getting deeper and deeper into the quagmire, till he began to doubt whether he should be able to extricate himself unmarried if he were anxious to do so. And all the while there came affectionate little notes from Miss Thoroughbung asking after his health, and recommending him what to take, till he entertained serious thoughts of going to Cairo for the remainder of the winter.

Then Mr. Barry came down to see him after Mountjoy had made his visit. It was now January, and the bargaining about the marriage had gone on for more than two months. The letter which he had received from the squire of Tretton had moved him; but he had told himself that the property was his own, and that he had a right to enjoy it as he liked best. Whatever might have been Harry's faults in regard to that midnight affair, it had certainly been true that he had declined to hear the sermons. Mr. Prosper did not exactly mention the sermons to himself, but there was present to him a feeling that his heir had been wilfully disobedient, and the sermons no doubt had been the cause. When he had read the old squire's letter he did not as yet wish to forgive his nephew. He was becoming very tired of his courtship, but in his estimation the wife would be better than the nephew. Though he had been much put out by the precocity of that embrace, there was nevertheless a sweetness about it which lingered on his lips. Then Mountjoy had come down, and he had answered Mountjoy very stoutly. 'A lie!' he had exclaimed. 'Did he tell a lie?' he asked, as though all must be over with a young man who had once allowed himself to depart from the rigid truth.

Mountjoy had made what excuse he could, but Mr.
Prosper had been very stern.

On the very day after Mountjoy's coming Mr.
Barry came. His visit had been arranged, and Mr.
Prosper was with great care prepared to encounter
him. He was wrapped in his best dressing-gown,
and Matthew had shaved him with the greatest care.
The girls over at the parsonage declared that their
uncle had sent into Buntingford for a special pot of
pomatum.* The story was told to Joe Thoroughbung
in order that it might be passed on to his aunt, and
no doubt it did travel as it was intended. But Miss
Thoroughbung cared nothing for the pomatum with
which the lawyer from London was to be received.
It would be very hard to laugh her out of her lover
while the title-deeds to Buston held good. But Mr.
Prosper had felt that it would be necessary to look
his best, so that his marriage might be justified in the
eyes of the lawyer.

Mr. Barry was shown into the book-room at
Buston, in which Mr. Prosper was seated ready to
receive him. The two gentlemen had never before
met each other, and Mr. Prosper did no doubt assume
something of the manner of an aristocratic owner of
land. He would not have done so had Mr. Grey
come in his partner's place. But there was a humility
about Mr. Barry on an occasion such as the present,
which justified a little pride on the part of the client.
'I am sorry to give you the trouble to come down,
Mr. Barry,' he said. 'I hope the servant has shown
you your room.'

'I shall be back in London to-day, Mr. Prosper,
thank you. I must see these lawyers here, and when
I have received your final instructions I will return
to Buntingford.' Then Mr. Prosper pressed him
much to stay. He had quite expected, he said, that
Mr. Barry would have done him the pleasure of remaining at any rate one night at Buston. But Mr.
Barry settled the question by saying that he had not

brought a dress-coat. Mr. Prosper did not care to sit down to dinner with guests who did not bring their dress-coats. 'And now,' continued Mr. Barry, 'what final instructions are we to give to Soames and Simpson?'

'I don't think much of Messrs. Soames and Simpson.'

'I believe they have the name of being honest practitioners.'

'I dare say; I do not in the least doubt it. But they are people to whom I am not at all desirous of intrusting my own private affairs. Messrs. Soames and Simpson have not, I think, a large county business. I had no idea that Miss Thoroughbung would have put this affair into their hands.'

'Just so, Mr. Prosper. But I suppose it was necessary for her to employ somebody. There has been a good deal of correspondence.'

'Indeed there has, Mr. Barry.'

'It has not been our fault, Mr. Prosper. Now what we have got to decide is this;—what are the final terms which you mean to propose? I think, sir, the time has come when some final terms should be suggested.'

'Just so. Final terms—must be what you call— the very last. That is, when they have once been offered, you must—must——'

'Just stick to them, Mr. Prosper.'

'Exactly, Mr. Barry. That is what I intend. There is nothing I dislike so much as this haggling about money,—especially with a lady. Miss Thoroughbung is a lady for whom I have the highest possible esteem.'

'That's of course.'

'For whom, I repeat, I have the highest possible esteem. But she has friends who have their own ideas as to money. The brewery in Buntingford belongs to them, and they are very worthy people. I should explain to you, Mr. Barry, as you are my confidential adviser, that were I about to form a matrimonial alliance in the heyday of my youth, I should probably not have thought of connecting myself with the Thoroughbungs. As I have said before they are most respectable people. But they do not exactly belong to that class in which I should under those circumstances have looked for a wife. I might probably have ventured to ask for the hand of the daughter of some county family. But years have slipped by me, and now wishing in middle life to procure for myself the comfort of wedded happiness, I have looked about, and have found no one more likely to give it me than Miss Thoroughbung. Her temper is excellent, and her person pleasing.' Mr. Prosper, as he said this, thought of the kiss which had been bestowed upon him. 'Her wit is vivacious, and I think that upon the whole she will be desirable as a companion. She will not come to this house empty-handed; but of her pecuniary affairs you already know so much that I need perhaps tell you nothing further. But though I am exceedingly desirous to make this lady my wife, and am, I may say, warmly attached to her, there are certain points which I cannot sacrifice. Now about the ponies——'

'I think I understand about the ponies. She may bring them on trial.'

'I'm not to be bound to keep any ponies at all. There are a pair of carriage horses which must suffice. On second thoughts she had better not bring the ponies.' This decision had at last come from some little doubt on his mind as to whether he was treating Harry justly.

'And four hundred pounds is the sum fixed on for her jointure.'

'She is to have her own money for her own life,' said Mr. Prosper.

'That's a matter of course.'

'Don't you think that under these circumstances, four hundred will be quite enough?'

'Quite enough if you ask me. But we must decide.'

'Four hundred it shall be.'

'And she is to have two-thirds of her own money for her own expenses during your life?' asked Mr. Barry.

'I don't see why she should want six hundred a year for herself; I don't indeed. I am afraid it will only lead to extravagance!' Mr. Barry assumed a look of despair. 'Of course, as I have said so, I will not go back from my word. She shall have two-thirds. But about the ponies my mind is quite made up. There shall be no ponies at Buston. I hope you understand that, Mr. Barry.' Mr. Barry said that he did understand it well; and then folding up his papers prepared to go, congratulating himself that he would not have to pass a long evening at Buston Hall.

But before he went, and when he had already put on his great-coat in the hall, Mr. Prosper called him back to ask him one further question. And for that purpose he shut the door carefully, and uttered his words in a whisper. Did Mr. Barry know anything of the life and recent adventures of Mr. Henry Annesley? Mr. Barry knew nothing; but he thought that his partner, Mr. Grey, knew something. He had heard Mr. Grey mention the name of Mr. Henry Annesley. Then as he stood there enveloped in his great-coat, with his horse standing in the cold, Mr. Prosper told him much of the story of Harry Annesley, and asked him to induce Mr. Grey to write and tell him what he thought of Harry's conduct.

Chapter XLIV

MR. PROSPER'S TROUBLES

AS Mr. Prosper sank into his armchair after the fatigue of the interview with his lawyer, he reflected that when all was considered Harry Annesley was an ungrateful pig,—it was thus he called him,—and that Miss Thoroughbung had many attractions. Miss Thoroughbung had probably done well to kiss him,—though the enterprise had not been without its peculiar dangers. He often thought of it when alone, and, as distance lent enchantment to the view, he longed to have the experiment repeated. Perhaps she had been right. And it would be a good thing, certainly, to have dear little children of his own. Miss Thoroughbung felt very certain on the subject, and it would be foolish for him to doubt. Then he thought of the difference between a pretty fair-haired little boy and that ungrateful pig, Harry Annesley. He told himself that he was very fond of children. The girls over at the parsonage would not have said so, but they probably did not know his character.

When Harry had come back with his fellowship, his uncle had for a few weeks been very proud of him, —had declared that he should never be called upon to earn his bread, and had allowed him two hundred and fifty pounds a year to begin with. But no return had been made to this favour. Harry had walked in and out of the Hall as though it had already belonged to him,—as many a father delights to see his eldest son doing. But the uncle in this instance had not taken any delight in seeing it. An uncle is different from a father,—an uncle who has never had a child of his own. He wanted deference, what he would have called respect; while Harry was at first prepared to give him a familiar affection based on equality,—on an equality in money matters and worldly interests, though I fear that Harry allowed to be seen his own intellectual superiority. Mr. Prosper, though an ignorant man, and by no means clever, was not such a fool as not to see all this. Then had come the persistent refusal to hear the sermons, and Mr. Prosper had sorrowfully declared to himself that his heir was not the young man that he should have been. He did not then think of marrying, nor did he stop the allowance; but he did feel that his heir was not what he should have been. But then the terrible disgrace of that night in London had occurred, and his eyes had been altogether opened by that excellent young man, Mr. Augustus Scarborough; then he began to look about him. Then dim ideas of the charms and immediate wealth of Miss Thoroughbung flitted before his eyes, and he told himself again and again of the prospects and undoubted good birth of Miss Puffle. Miss Puffle had disgraced herself, and therefore he had thrown Buston Hall at the feet of Miss Thoroughbung.

But now he had heard stories about that 'excellent young man, Augustus Scarborough,' which had shaken his faith. He had been able to exclaim indignantly that Harry Annesley had told a lie. 'A lie!' He had been surprised to find that a young man who had lived so much in the fashionable world as Captain Scarborough had cared nothing of this. And as Miss Thoroughbung became more and more exacting in regard to money, he thought, himself, less and less of the lie. It might be well that Harry should ultimately have the property, though he should never again be taken into favour, and there should be no further question of the allowance. As Miss Thoroughbung reiterated her demands for the ponies, he began to feel that the acres of Buston would not be disgraced for ever by the telling of that lie. But the sermons remained, and he would never willingly again see his nephew. As he turned all this in his mind, the idea of spending what was left of the winter at Cairo returned to him. He would go to Cairo for the winter, and to the Italian lakes for the spring, and to Switzerland for the summer. Then he might return to Cairo. At the present moment Buston Hall and the neighbourhood of Buntingford had few charms for him. He was afraid that Miss Thoroughbung would not give way about the ponies; and against the ponies he was resolved.

He was sitting in this state with a map before him, and with the squire's letter upon the map, when Matthew, the butler, opened the door and announced a visitor. As soon as Mr. Barry had gone he had supported nature by a mutton-chop and a glass of sherry, and the *débris* were now lying on the side-table. His first idea was to bid Matthew at once remove the glass and the bone, and the unfinished potato, and the crust of bread. To be taken with such remnants by any visitor would be bad, but by this visitor would be dreadful. Lunch should be eaten in the dining-room, where chop-bones and dirty glasses would be in their place. But here in his book-room they would be disgraceful. But then as Matthew was hurriedly collecting the two plates and the salt-cellar, his master began to doubt whether this visitor should be received at all. It was no other than Miss Thoroughbung.

Mr. Prosper, in order to excuse his slackness in calling on the lady, had let it be known that he was not quite well, and Miss Thoroughbung had responded to this move by offering her services as nurse to her lover. He had then written to herself that though he had been a little unwell, 'suffering from a cold in the chest, to which at this inclement season of the year he was peculiarly liable,' he was not in need of anything beyond a little personal attention, and would not trouble her for those services, for the offer of which he was bound to be peculiarly grateful. Thus he had thought to keep Miss

Thoroughbung at a distance. But here she was, with those hated ponies at his very door. 'Matthew,' he said, making a confidant in the distress of the moment, of his butler, 'I don't think I can see her.'

'You must, sir; indeed you must.'

'Must?'

'Well; yes; I'm afraid so. Considering all things; the materrimonial prospects and the rest of it, I think you must, sir.'

'She hasn't a right to come here, you know,—as yet.' It will be understood that Mr. Prosper was considerably discomposed when he spoke with such familiar confidence to his servants. 'She needn't come in here at any rate.'

'In the drawing-room, if I might be allowed to suggest, sir.'

'Show Miss Thoroughbung into the drawing-room,' said he with all his dignity. Then Matthew retired, and the squire of Buston felt that five minutes might be allowed to collect himself. And the mutton-chop bone need not be removed.

When the five minutes were over, with slow steps he walked across the intervening billiard-room, and slowly opened the drawing-room door. Would she rush into his arms, and kiss him again, as he entered? He sincerely hoped that there would be no such attempt; but if there were, he was sternly resolved to repudiate it. There should be nothing of the kind till she had clearly declared, and had put it under writing by herself and her lawyers, that she would consent to come to Buston without the ponies. But there was no such attempt.

'How do you do, Mr. Prosper?' she said in a loud voice, standing up in the middle of the room. 'Why don't you ever come and see me? I take it very ill of you; and so does Miss Tickle. There is no one more partial to you than Miss Tickle. We were talking of you only last night over a despatched crab that we had for supper.' Did they have despatched crabs for supper every night? thought Mr. Prosper to himself. It was certainly a strong reason against his marriage. 'I told her that you had a cold in your head.'

'In my chest,' said Mr. Prosper meekly.

' "Bother colds," said Miss Tickle. "When people are keeping company together they ought to see each other." Those were Miss Tickle's very words.'

That it should be said of him, Mr. Prosper, of Buston, that he was 'keeping company' with any woman! He almost resolved, on the spur of the moment, that under no circumstances could he now marry Miss Thoroughbung. But unfortunately his offer had been made, and the terms of the settlement, as suggested by himself, placed in the hands of his lawyer. If Miss Thoroughbung chose to hold him to his offer, he must marry her. It was not that he feared an action for breach of promise, but that, as a gentleman, it would behove him to be true to his word. He need not, however, marry Miss Tickle. He had offered no terms in respect to Miss Tickle. With great presence of mind, he resolved at once that Miss Tickle should never find a permanent resting-place for her foot at Buston Hall. 'I am extremely indebted to Miss Tickle,' said he.

'Why haven't you come over just to have a little chat in a friendly way? It's all because of those stupid lawyers, I suppose. What need you and I care for the lawyers? They can do their work without troubling us, except that they will be sure to send in their bills fast enough.'

'I have had Mr. Barry, from the firm of Messrs. Grey and Barry, of Lincoln's Inn, with me this morning.'

'I know you have. I saw the little man at Soames and Simpson's, and drove out here immediately, after five minutes' conversation. Now, Mr. Prosper, you must let me have those ponies.'

That was the very thing which he was determined not to do. The ponies grew in imagination, and became enormous horses capable of consuming any amount of oats. Mr. Prosper was not of a stingy nature, but he had already perceived that his escape, if it were effected, must be made good by means of those ponies. A steady old pair of carriage horses had been kept by him, and by his father before him, and he was not going to be driven out of the old family ways by a brewer's daughter. And he had but that morning instructed his lawyer to stand out against the ponies. He felt that this was the moment for firmness. Now, this instant, he must be staunch, or he would be saddled with this woman,—and with Miss Tickle,—for the whole of his life. She had left him no time for consideration, but had come upon him as soon almost as the words spoken to the lawyer had been out his mouth. But he would be firm. Miss Thoroughbung opened out instantly about the ponies, and he at once resolved that he would be firm. But was it not very indelicate on her part to come to him and to press him in this manner? He began to hope that she also would be firm about the ponies, and that in this way the separation might be effected. At the present moment he stood dumb. Silence would not in this case be considered as giving consent. 'Now, like a good man, do say that I shall have the ponies,' she continued. 'I can keep 'em out of my own money, you know, if that's all.' He perceived at once that the offer amounted to a certain yielding on her part, but he was no longer anxious that she should give way. 'Do 'ee now say yes, like a dear old boy.' She came closer to him, and took hold of his arm, as though she were going to perform that other ceremony. But he was fully aware of the danger. If there came to be kissing between them it would be impossible for him to go back afterwards, in such a manner but that the blame of the kiss should rest with him. When he should desire to be 'off,' he could not plead

that the kissing had been all her doing. A man in
Mr. Prosper's position has difficulties among which
he must be very wary. And then the ridicule of the
world is so strong a weapon, and is always worst on
the side of the women. He gave a little start, but he
did not at once shake her off. 'What's the objection
to the ponies, dear?'

'Two pair of horses! It's more than we ought
to keep.' He should not have said 'we.' He felt,
when it was too late, that he should not have said
'we.'

'They arn't horses.'

'It's the same as far as the stables are concerned.'

'But there's room enough, Lord bless you! I've
been in to look. I can assure you that Dr. Stubbs
says they are required for my health. You ask him
else. It's just what I'm up to,—is driving. I've
only taken to them lately, and I cannot bring myself
to give 'em up. Do 'ee, love. You're not going to
throw over your own Matilda for a couple of little
beasts like that!'

Every word that came out of her mouth was an
offence. But he could not tell her so; nor could he
reject her on that score. He should have thought
beforehand what kind of words might probably come
out of her mouth. Was her name Matilda? Of
course he knew the fact. Had anyone asked him he
could have said, with two minutes' consideration,
that her name was Matilda. But it had never become
familiar to his ears, and now she spoke of it as though
he had called her Matilda since their earliest youth.
And to be called 'Love!' It might be very nice when
he had first called her 'Love' a dozen times. But now
it sounded extravagant,—and almost indelicate.
And he was about to throw her over for a couple of
little beasts. He felt that that was his intention, and
he blushed because it was so. He was a true gentleman, who would not willingly depart from his word.
If he must go on with the ponies, he must. But he

had never yet yielded about the ponies. He felt now that they were his only hope. But as the difficulties of his position pressed upon him, the sweat stood out upon his brow. She saw it all and understood it all, and deliberately determined to take advantage of his weakness. 'I don't think that there is anything else astray between us. We've settled about the jointure;—four hundred a year. It's too little, Soames and Simpson say; but I'm soft and in love, you know.' Here she leered at him, and he began to hate her. 'You oughtn't to want a third of my income, you know. But you're to be lord and master, and you must have your own way. All that's settled.'

'There is Miss Tickle,' he said in a voice that was almost cadaverous.

'Miss Tickle is of course to come. You said that from the very first moment when you made the offer.'

'Never!'

'Oh, Peter! how can you say so?' He shrank visibly from the sound of his own Christian-name. But she determined to persevere. The time must come when she should call him Peter, and why not commence the practice now at once? Lovers always do call each other Peter and Matilda. She wasn't going to stand any nonsense, and if he intended to marry her, and use a large proportion of her fortune, Peter he should be to her. 'You did, Peter. You know you told me how much attached you were to her.'

'I didn't say anything about her coming with you.'

'Oh, Peter! how can you be so cruel? Do you mean to say that you will deprive me of the friend of my youth?'

'At any rate, there shall never be a pony come into my yard.' He knew when he made this assertion that he was abandoning his objection to Miss Tickle. She had called him cruel, and his conscience told him that if he received Miss Thoroughbung and refused admission to Miss Tickle, he would be cruel. Miss

Tickle, for aught that he knew, might have been the friend of her youth. At any rate, they had been constant companions for many years. Therefore, as he had another solid ground on which to stand, he could afford to yield as to Miss Tickle. But as he did so, he remembered that Miss Tickle had accused him of 'keeping company,' and he declared to himself that it would be impossible to live in the same house with her.

'But Miss Tickle may come,' said Miss Thoroughbung. Was the solid ground, the rock, as he believed it to be, of the ponies, about to sink beneath his feet? 'Say that Miss Tickle may come. I should be nothing without Miss Tickle. You cannot be so hardhearted as that.'

'I don't see what is the good of talking about Miss Tickle till we have come to some settlement about the ponies. You say that you must have the ponies. To tell you the truth, Miss Thoroughbung, I don't like any such word as "must." And a good many things have occurred to me.'

'What kind of things, deary?'

'I think you are inclined to be—gay.'

'Me,—gay!'

'While I am sober, and perhaps a little grave in my manners of life. I am thinking only of domestic happiness, while your mind is intent upon social circles. I fear that you would look for your bliss abroad.'

'In France or Germany?'

'When I say abroad, I mean out of your own house. There is perhaps some discrepancy of taste of which I ought earlier to have taken cognisance.'

'Nothing of the kind,' said Miss Thoroughbung. 'I am quite content to live at home, and do not want to go abroad, either to France, nor yet to any other English county. I should never ask for anything, unless it be for a single month in London.'

Here was a ground upon which he perhaps could

make his ground. 'Quite impossible,' said Mr. Prosper.

'Or for a fortnight,' said Miss Thoroughbung.

'I never go up to London except on business.'

'But I might go alone, you know—with Miss Tickle. I shouldn't want to drag you away. I have always been in the habit of having a few weeks in London about the Exhibition time.'

'I shouldn't wish to be left by my wife.'

'Of course we could manage all that. We're not to settle every little thing beforehand, and put it into the deeds. A precious sum we should have to pay the lawyers.'

'It's as well we should understand each other.'

'I think it pretty nearly is all settled that has to go into the deeds. I thought I'd just run over after seeing Mr. Barry, and give the final touch. If you'll give way, dear, about Miss Tickle and the ponies, I'll yield in everything else. Nothing surely can be fairer than that.'

He knew that he was playing the hypocrite, and he knew also that it did not become him as a gentleman to be false to a woman. He was aware that from minute to minute, and almost from word to word, he was becoming ever more and more averse to this match which he had proposed to himself. And he knew that in honesty he ought to tell her that it was so. It was not honest in him to endeavour to get rid of her by a side blow, as it were. And yet this was the attempt which he had hitherto been making. But how was he to tell her the truth? Even Mr. Barry had not understood the state of his mind. Indeed his mind had altered since he had seen Mr. Barry. He had heard within the last half hour many words spoken by Miss Thoroughbung, which proved that she was altogether unfit to be his wife. It was a dreadful misfortune that he should have rushed into such peril; but was he not bound as a gentleman to tell her the truth? 'Say that I shall have Jemima

Tickle?' The added horrors of the Christian-name operated upon him with additional force. Was he to be doomed to have the word Jemima holloed about his rooms and staircases for the rest of his life? And she had given up the ponies, and was taking her stand upon Miss Tickle, as to whom at last he would be bound to give way. He could see now that he should have demanded her whole income, and have allowed her little or no jointure. That would have been grasping, monstrous, altogether impracticable; but it would not have been ungentlemanlike. This chaffering about little things was altogether at variance with his tastes; and it would be futile. He must summon courage to tell her that he no longer wished for the match; but he could not do it on this morning. Then,—for that morning,—some benign god preserved him.

Matthew came into the room and whispered into his ear that a gentleman wished to see him. 'What gentleman?' Matthew again whispered that it was his brother-in-law. 'Show him in,' said Mr. Prosper with a sudden courage. He had not seen Mr. Annesley since the day of his actual quarrel with Harry. 'I shall have the ponies,' said Miss Thoroughbung during the moment that was allowed to her.

'We are interrupted now. I am afraid that the rest of this interview must be postponed.' It should never be renewed, though he might have to leave the country for ever. Of that he gave himself assurance. Then the parson was shown into the room.

The constrained introduction was very painful to Mr. Prosper, but was not at all disagreeable to the lady. 'Mr. Annesley knows me very well. We are quite old friends. Joe is going to marry his eldest girl. I hope Molly is quite well.' The rector said that Molly was quite well. When he had come away from home just now he had left Joe at the parsonage. 'You'll find him there a deal oftener

than at the brewery,' said Miss Thoroughbung.
'You know what we're going to do, Mr. Annesley.
There are no fools like old fools.' A thunder-black
cloud came across Mr. Prosper's face. That this
woman should dare to call him an old fool! 'We
were discussing a few of our future arrangements.
We've arranged everything about money in the
most amicable manner, and now there is merely a
question of a pair of ponies.'

'We need not trouble Mr. Annesley about that,
I think.'

'And Miss Tickle! I'm sure the rector will agree
with me that old friends like me and Miss Tickle
ought not to be separated. And it isn't as though
there was any dislike between them, because he has
already said that he finds Miss Tickle charming.'

'Damn Miss Tickle!' he said;—whereupon the
rector looked astonished, and Miss Thoroughbung
jumped a foot from off the ground. 'I beg the lady's
pardon,' said Mr. Prosper piteously, 'and yours,
Miss Thoroughbung;—and yours, Mr. Annesley.'
It was as though a new revelation of character had
been given. No one, except Matthew, had ever
heard the squire of Buston swear. And with Matthew
the cursings had been by no means frequent, and had
been addressed generally to some article of his
clothing or to some morsel of food prepared with less
than the usual care. But now the oath had been
directed against a female, and the chosen friend of his
betrothed. And it had been uttered in the presence
of a clergyman, his brother-in-law, and the rector of
his parish. Mr. Prosper felt that he was disgraced
for ever. Could he have overheard them laughing
over his ebullition in the rectory drawing-room half
an hour afterwards, and almost praising his violence,
some part of the pain might have been removed. As
it was he felt at the time that he was disgraced for ever.

'We will return to the subject when next we
meet,' said Miss Thoroughbung.

'I am very sorry that I should so far have forgotten myself,' said Mr. Prosper, 'but——'

'It does not signify;—not as far as I am concerned;' and she made a little motion to the clergyman, half bow and half curtsy. Mr. Annesley bowed in
return, as though declaring that neither did it signify
very much as far as he was concerned. Then she left
the room, and Matthew handed her into the carriage,
when she took the ponies in hand with quite as much
composure as though her friend had not been sworn at.

'Upon my word, sir,' said Prosper, as soon as the
door was shut, 'I beg your pardon. But I was so
moved by certain things which have occurred that I
was carried much beyond my usual habits.'

'Don't mention it.'

'It is peculiarly distressing to me, that I should
have been induced to forget myself in the presence of
a clergyman of the parish and my brother-in-law.
But I must beg you to forget it.'

'Oh certainly. I will tell you now why I have
come over.'

'I can assure you that such is not my habit,'
continued Mr. Prosper, who was thinking much more
of the unaccustomed oath which he had sworn, than
of his brother-in-law's visit, strange as it was. 'No
one as a rule is more guarded in his expressions than
I am. How it should have come to pass that I was so
stirred I can hardly tell. But Miss Thoroughbung
had said certain words which had moved me very
much.' She had called him 'Peter,' and 'deary,' and
had spoken of him as 'keeping company' with
her. All these disgusting terms of endearment, he
could not repeat to his brother-in-law; but felt it
necessary to allude to them.

'I trust that you may be happy with her, when she
is your wife.'

'I can't say. I really don't know. It's a very
important step to take at my age; and I am not quite
sure that I should be doing wisely.'

'It's not too late,' said Mr. Annesley.

'I don't know. I can't quite say.' Then Mr. Prosper drew himself up, remembering that it would not become him to discuss the matter of his marriage with the father of his heir.

'I have come over here,' said Mr. Annesley, 'to say a few words about Harry.' Mr. Prosper again drew himself up. 'Of course you're aware that Harry is at present living with us.' Here Mr. Prosper bowed. 'Of course, in his altered circumstances, it will not do that he shall be idle, and yet he does not like to take a final step without letting you know what it is.' Here Mr. Prosper bowed twice. 'There is a gentleman of fortune going out to the United States on a mission which will probably occupy him for four or five years. I am not exactly warranted in mentioning his name; but he has taken in hand a political project of much importance.' Again Mr. Prosper bowed. 'Now, he has offered to Harry the place of private secretary, on condition that Harry will undertake to stay the entire term. He is to have a salary of three hundred a year, and his travelling expenses will of course be paid for him. If he goes, poor boy, he will in all probability remain in his new home and become a citizen of the United States. Under these circumstances, I have thought it best to step up and tell you in a friendly manner what his plans are.' Then he had told his tale, and Mr. Prosper again bowed.

The rector had been very crafty. There was no doubt about the wealthy gentleman with the American project, and the salary had been offered. But in other respects there had been some little exaggeration. It was well known to the rector that Mr. Prosper regarded America and all her institutions with a religious hatred. An American was to him an ignorant, impudent, foul-mouthed, fraudulent creature, to have any acquaintance with whom was a disgrace. Could he have had his way, he would have

reconstituted the United States as British Colonies
at a moment's notice. Were he to die without having begotten another heir, Buston must become the
property of Harry Annesley; and it would be dreadful to him to think that Buston should be owned by
an American citizen. 'The salary offered is too good
to be abandoned,' said Mr. Annesley when he saw
the effect which his story had produced.

'Everything is going against me,' exclaimed Mr.
Prosper.

'Well; I will not talk about that. I did not come
here to discuss Harry or his sins;—nor, for the
matter of that, his virtues. But I felt it would be
improper to let him go upon his journey without
communicating with you.' So saying he took his
departure and walked back to the rectory.

Chapter XLV

A DETERMINED YOUNG LADY

WHEN this offer had been made to Harry
Annesley he found it to be absolutely necessary that he should write a further letter to Florence.
He was quite aware that he had been forbidden to
write. He had written one letter since that order had
been given to him, and no reply had come to him.
He had not expected a reply; but still her silence had
been grievous to him. It might be that she was
angry with him, really angry. But let that be as it
might, he could not go to America, and be absent for
so long a period, without telling her. She and her
mother were still at Brussels when January came.
Mrs. Mountjoy had gone there, as he had understood, for a month, and was still at the embassy when
three months had passed. 'I think I shall stay here
the winter,' Mrs. Mountjoy had said to Sir Magnus,
'but we will take lodgings. I see that very nice

sets of apartments are to be let.' But Sir Magnus would not hear of this. He said, and said truly, that the ministerial house was large; and at last he declared the honest truth. His sister-in-law had been very kind to him about money, and had said not a word on that troubled subject since her arrival. Mrs. Mountjoy, with that delicacy which still belongs to some English ladies, would have suffered extreme poverty rather than have spoken on such a matter. In truth she suffered nothing, and hardly thought about it. But Sir Magnus was grateful, and told her that if she went to look for lodgings he should go to the lodgings and say that they were not wanted. Therefore Mrs. Mountjoy remained where she was, entertaining a feeling of increased good-will towards Sir Magnus.

Life went on rather sadly with Florence. Anderson was as good as his word. He pleaded his own cause no further, telling both Sir Magnus and Lady Mountjoy of the pledge he had made. He did in fact tell two or three other persons, regarding himself as a martyr to chivalry. All this time he went about his business looking very wretched. But though he did not speak for himself, he could not hinder others from speaking for him. Sir Magnus took occasion to say a word on the subject once daily to his niece. Her mother was constant in her attacks. But Lady Mountjoy was the severest of the three, and was accounted by Florence as her bitterest enemy. The words which passed between them were not the most affectionate in the world. Lady Mountjoy would call her 'miss,' to which Florence would reply by addressing her aunt as 'my lady.' 'Why do you call me my lady? It isn't usual in common conversation.' 'Why do you call me miss? If you cease to call me miss, I'll cease to call you my lady.' But no reverence was paid by the girl to the wife of the British Minister. It was this that Lady Mountjoy specially felt,—as she explained to her companion, Miss Abbott. Then another cause for trouble sprang up during the winter, of which mention must be made further on. The result was that Florence was instant with her mother to take her back to England.

We will return, however, to Harry Annesley, and give the letter, verbatim, which he wrote to Florence:

'DEAR FLORENCE,

'I wonder whether you ever think of me, or ever remember that I exist. I know you do. I cannot have been forgotten like that. And you yourself are the truest girl that ever owned to loving a man. But there comes a chill across my heart when I think how long it is since I wrote to you, and that I have not had a line even to acknowledge my letter. You bade me not to write, and you have not even forgiven me for disobeying your order. I cannot but get stupid ideas into my mind, which one word from you would dissipate.

'Now, however, I must write again, order or no order. Between a man and a woman, circumstanced as you and I, things will arise which make it incumbent on one or the other to write. It is absolutely necessary that you should now know what are my intentions, and understand the reasons which have actuated me. I have found myself left in a most unfortunate condition by my uncle's folly. He is going on with a stupid marriage for the purpose of disinheriting me, and has in the meantime stopped the allowance which he had made me since I left college. Of course I have no absolute claim on him. But I cannot understand how he can reconcile himself to do so, when he himself prevented my going to the Bar, saying that it would be unnecessary.

'But so it is, and I am driven to look about for myself. It is very hard at my time of life to find an opening in any profession. I think I told you before that I had ideas of going to Cambridge and endeavouring to get pupils, trusting to my fellowship rather than to my acquirements. But this I have always looked upon with great dislike, and would only have taken to it if nothing else was to be had. Now there has come forward an old college acquaintance, a man who is three or four years my senior, who has offered to take me to America as his private secretary. He proposes to remain there for three years. I of course shall not bind myself to stay as long; but I may not improbably do so. He is to pay my expenses and to give me a salary of three hundred a year. This will perhaps lead to nothing else; but will for the present be better than nothing. I am to start in just a month from the present time.

'Now you know it all, except that the man's name is Sir William Crook. He is a decent sort of fellow, and has got a wife who is to go with him. He is the hardest working man I know, but between you and me he will never set the Thames on fire. If the Thames is to be illumined at all, I rather think that I shall be expected to do it.

'Now, my own one, what am I to say about you, and of myself, as your husband that is to be? Will you wait, at any rate, for three years, with the conviction that the three years will too probably end in your having to wait again?

'I do feel that in my altered position I ought to give you back your troth, and tell you that things shall be as they used to be before that happy night at Mrs. Armitage's party. I do not know but that it is clearly my duty. I almost think that it is. But I am sure of this,—that it is the one thing in the world that I cannot do. I don't think that a man ought to be asked to tear himself altogether in pieces, because someone else has ill-treated him. At any rate I cannot. If you say that it must be so, you shall say it. I don't suppose it will kill me, but it will go a long way.

'In writing so far I have not said a word of love, because, as far as I understand you, that is a subject on which you expect me to be silent. When you order me not to write, I suppose you intend that I am to write no love-letter. This, therefore, you will take simply as a matter of business, and as such, I suppose, you will acknowledge it. In this way I shall at any rate see your handwriting.—Yours affectionately,

'HARRY ANNESLEY.'

Harry, when he wrote this letter, considered that it had been cold, calm, and philosophical. He could not go to America for three years without telling her of his purpose; nor could he mention that purpose, as he thought, in any language less glowing. But Florence, when she received it, did not regard it in the same light. To her thinking the letter was full of love, and of love expressed in the warmest possible language. 'Sir William Crook!' she said to herself. 'What can he want of Harry in America for three years? I am sure he is a stupid man. Will I wait? Of course I will wait. What are three years? And why should I not wait? But for the matter of that——' Then thoughts came into her mind which even to herself she could not express in words. Sir William Crook had got a wife, and why should not Harry take a wife also? She did not see why a private secretary should not be a married man; and as for money there would be plenty for such a style of life as they would live. She could not exactly propose this, but she thought that if she were to see Harry just for one short interview before he started, that he might probably then propose it himself.

'Things be as they used to be,' she exclaimed to herself. 'Never! Things cannot be as they used to be. I know what is his duty. It is his duty not to think of anything of the kind. Remember that he exists,' she said, turning back to the earlier words of the letter. 'That of course is his joke. I wonder whether he knows that every moment of my life is devoted to him. Of course I bade him not to write. But I can tell him now, that I have never gone to bed without his letter beneath my pillow.' This and much more of the same kind was uttered in soliloquys, but need not be repeated at length to the reader.

But she had to think what steps she must first take. She must tell her mother of Harry's intention. She had never for an instant allowed her mother to think that her affection had dwindled, or her purpose failed her. She was engaged to marry Harry Annesley, and marry him some day she would. That her mother should be sure of that, was the immediate purpose of her life. And in carrying out that purpose she must acquaint her mother with the news which this letter had brought to her. 'Mamma, I have got something to tell you.'

'Well, my dear.'

'Harry Annesley is going to America.' There was something pleasing to Mrs. Mountjoy in the sound of these words. If Harry Annesley went to America, he might be drowned, or it might more probably be that he would never come back. America was, to her imagination, a long way off. Lovers did not go to America, except with the intention of deserting their lady-loves. Such were her ideas. She felt at the moment that Florence would be more easily approached in reference either to her cousin Mountjoy or to Mr. Anderson. Another lover had sprung up too in Brussels of whom a word shall be said by-and-by. If her Harry, the pernicious Harry, should have taken himself to America, the chances of all these three gentlemen would be improved. Any one of them would now be accepted by Mrs. Mountjoy as a bar, fatal to Harry Annesley. Mountjoy was again the favourite with her. She had heard that he had returned to Tretton, and was living amicably with his father. She knew even of the income allotted to him for the present,—of the six hundred pounds a year, and had told Florence that as a preliminary income it was more than double that two hundred and fifty pounds which had been taken away from Harry,—taken away never to be restored. There was not much in this argument, but still she thought it well to use it. The captain was living with his father, and she did not believe a word about the entail having been done away with. It was certain that Harry's uncle had quarrelled with him, and she did understand that a baby at Buston would altogether rob Harry of his chance. And then, look at the difference in the properties! It was thus that she argued the matter. But in truth her word had been pledged to Mountjoy Scarborough, and Mountjoy Scarborough had ever been a favourite with her. Though she could talk about the money, it was not the money that touched her feelings. 'Well;—he may go to America. It is a dreadful destiny for a young man, but in his case it may be the best thing that he can do.'

'Of course he intends to come back again.'

'That is as it may be.'

'I do not understand what you mean by a dreadful destiny, mamma. I don't see that it is a destiny at all. He is getting a very good offer for a year or two, and thinks it best to take it. I might go with him for that matter.'

A thunderbolt had fallen at Mrs. Mountjoy's feet! Florence go with him to America! Among all the trials which had come upon her with reference to this young man there had been nothing so bad as this proposal. Go with him! The young man was to start in a month! Then she began to think whether it would be within her power to stop her daughter. What would all the world be to her with one daughter, and she in America married to Harry Annesley? Her quarrel with Florence was not at all as was the quarrel of Lady Mountjoy. Lady Mountjoy would be glad to get rid of the girl, whom she thought to be impertinent and believed to be false. But to her mother Florence was the very apple of her eye. It was because she thought that Mountjoy Scarborough was a grand fellow, and because she thought all manner of evil of Harry Annesley, that she wished Florence to marry her cousin, and to separate herself for ever from the other. When she had heard that Harry was to go to America she had rejoiced,—as though he was to be transported to Botany Bay. Her ideas were old-fashioned. But when it was hinted that Florence was to go with him she nearly fell to the ground.

Florence certainly had behaved badly in making the suggestion. She had not intended to make it; had not in truth thought of it. But when her mother talked of Harry's destiny, as though some terrible evil had come upon him,—as though she were speaking of a poor wretch condemned to be hanged when all chances of a reprieve were over,—then her spirit rose within her. She had not meant to say that she was going. Harry had never asked her to go. 'If you talk of his destiny I am quite prepared to share it with him.' That was her meaning. But her mother already saw her only child in the hands of those American savages. She threw herself on to a sofa, buried her face in her hands, and burst into tears.

'I don't say that I am going, mamma.'

'My darling, my dearest, my child.'

'Only that there is no reason why I shouldn't, except that it would not suit him. At least I suppose it would not.'

'Has he said so?'

'He has said nothing about it.'

'Thank Heaven for that! He does not intend to rob me of my child.'

'But, mamma, I am to be his wife.'

'No, no, no!'

'It is that that I want to make you understand. You know nothing of his character; nothing.'

'I do know that he told a base falsehood.'

'Nothing of the kind! I will not admit it. It is of no use going into that again, but there was nothing base about it. He has got an appointment in the United States, and is going out to do the work. He has not asked me to go with him. The two things would probably not be compatible.' Here Mrs. Mountjoy rose from the sofa and embraced her child, as though liberated from her deepest grief. 'But, mamma, you must remember this,—that I have given him my word, and will never be induced to abandon it.' Here her mother threw up her hands and again began to weep. 'Either to-day or to-morrow, or ten years hence,—if he will wait as long I will,—we shall be married. As far as I can see we need not wait ten years, or perhaps more than one or two. My money will suffice for us.'

'He proposes to live upon you?'

'He proposes nothing of the kind. He is going to America because he will not propose it. Nor am I proposing it,—just at present.'

'At any rate, I am glad of that.'

'And now, mamma, you must take me back home as soon as possible.'

'When he has started.'

'No, mamma. I must be there before he starts. I cannot let him go without seeing him. If I am to remain here, here he must come.'

'Your uncle would never receive him.'

'I should receive him.'

This was dreadful;—this flying into actual disobedience. Whatever did she mean? Where was she to receive him? 'How could you receive a young man in opposition to the wishes, and indeed to the commands, of all your friends?'

'I'm not going to be at all shame-faced about it, mamma. I am the woman he has selected to be his

wife, and he is the man I have selected to be my
husband. If he were coming, I should go to my
uncle and ask to have him received.'

'Think of your aunt.'

'Yes; I do think of her. My aunt would make
herself very disagreeable. Upon the whole, mamma,
I think it would be best that you should take me back
to England. There is this M. Grascour here, who is
a great trouble, and you may be sure of this, that I
intend to see Harry Annesley before he starts for
America.'

So the interview was ended; but Mrs. Mountjoy
was left greatly in doubt as to what she might best
do. She felt sure that were Annesley to come to
Brussels, Florence would see him,—would see him
in spite of all her uncle and aunt, and Mr. Anderson, and M. Grascour could do to prevent it. That
reprobate young man would force his way into the
embassy, or Florence would force her way out. In
either case there would be a terrible scene. But if
she were to take Florence back to Cheltenham, interviews to any extent would be arranged for at the
house of Mrs. Armitage. As she thought of all this,
the idea came across her, that when a young girl is
determined to be married nothing can prevent it.

Florence in the meantime wrote an immediate
answer to her lover, as follows:

'DEAR HARRY,

'Of course you were entitled to write when there
was something to be said which it was necessary
that I should know. When you have simply to say
that you love me, I know that well enough without
any further telling.

'Go to America for three years! It is very very
serious. But of course you must know best, and I
shall not attempt to interfere. What are three years
to you and me? If we were rich people, of course
we should not wait; but as we are poor, of course we

must act as do other people who are poor. I have about four hundred a year; and it is for you to say how far that may be sufficient. If you think so, you will not find that I shall want more.

'But there is one thing necessary before you start. I must see you. There is no reason on earth for our remaining here,—except that mamma has not made up her mind. If she will consent to go back before you start, it will be best so. Otherwise you must take the trouble to come here,—where I am afraid you will not be received as a welcome guest. I have told mamma that if I cannot see you here in a manner that is becoming, I shall go out, and meet you in the streets, in a manner that is unbecoming.

'Your affectionate—wife that is to be,

'FLORENCE MOUNTJOY.'

This letter she took to her mother, and read aloud to her in her own room. Mrs. Mountjoy could only implore that it might not be sent; but prevailed not at all.

'There is not a word in it about love,' said Florence. 'It is simply a matter of business, and as such I must send it. I do not suppose my uncle will go to the length of attempting to lock me up. He would, I think, find it difficult to do so.' There was a look in Florence's face as she said this which altogether silenced her mother. She did not think that Sir Magnus would consent to lock Florence up, and she did think that were he to attempt to do so, he would find the task very difficult.

Chapter XLVI

MONSIEUR GRASCOUR

M. GRASCOUR was a Belgian about forty years old, who looked as though he were no more than thirty, except that his hair was in patches

beginning to be a little gray. He was in the government service of his country, well educated, and
thoroughly a gentleman. As is the case with many
Belgians, he would have been taken to be an Englishman were his country not known. He had dressed
himself in English mirrors, living mostly with the
English. He spoke English so well that he would
only be known to be a foreigner by the correctness
of his language. He was a man of singularly good
temper, and there was running, through all that he
did, somewhat of a chivalric spirit which came from
study rather than nature. He had looked into things
and seen whether they were good, or at any rate
popular, and endeavoured to grasp hard to make his
own whatever he found to be so. He was hitherto
unmarried, and was regarded generally by his
friends as a non-marrying man. But Florence Mountjoy was powerful over him, and he set to work
to make her his wife.

He was intimate at the house of Sir Magnus, and
saw, no doubt, that Anderson was doing the same
thing. But he saw also that Anderson did not succeed. He had told himself from the first that if
Anderson did succeed, he would not wish to do so.
The girl who would be satisfied with Anderson
would hardly content him. He remained therefore
quiet till he saw that Anderson had failed. The
young man at once took to an altered mode of life
which was sufficiently marked. He went, like Sir
Proteus, ungartered.* Everything about him had of
late 'demonstrated a careless desolation.'* All this
M. Grascour observed, and, when he saw it, he felt
that his own time had come.

He took occasion at first to wait upon Lady
Mountjoy. He believed that to be the proper way of
going to work. He was very intimate with the
Mountjoys, and was aware that his circumstances
were known to them. There was no reason, on the
score of money, why he should not marry the niece

of Sir Magnus. He had already shown some attention to Florence, which, though it had excited no
suspicion in her mind, had been seen and understood
by her aunt. And it had been understood also by
Mr. Anderson. 'That accursed Belgian! If, after
all, she should take up with him! I shall tell her
a bit of my mind if anything of that kind should
occur.'

'My niece, M. Grascour!'

'Yes, my lady.' M. Grascour had not quite got
over the way of calling Lady Mountjoy 'my lady.'
'It is presumption, I know.'

'Not at all.'

'I have not spoken to her. Nor would I do so till
I had first addressed myself to you or to her mother.
May I speak to Mrs. Mountjoy?'

'Oh! certainly. I do not in the least know what
the young lady's ideas are. She has been much
admired here and elsewhere, and that may have
turned her head.'

'I think not.'

'You may be the better judge, M. Grascour.'

'I think that Miss Mountjoy's head has not been
turned by any admiration. She does not appear to
be a young lady whose head would easily be turned.
It is her heart of which I am thinking.'

The interview ended by Lady Mountjoy passing
the Belgian lover on to Mrs. Mountjoy.

'Florence!' said Mrs. Mountjoy.

'Yes, Mrs. Mountjoy;—I have the great honour
of asking your permission. I am well known to Sir
Magnus and Lady Mountjoy, and they can tell
what are my circumstances. I am forty years of
age.'

'Oh yes; everything is, I am sure, quite as it
should be. But my daughter thinks about these
things for herself.' Then there was a pause, and
M. Grascour was about to leave the room, having
obtained the permission he desired, when Mrs.

Mountjoy thought it well to acquaint him with something of her daughter's condition. 'I ought to tell you that my daughter has been engaged.'

'Indeed!'

'Yes;—and I hardly know how to explain the circumstances. I should say that she had been promised to her cousin, Captain Scarborough; but to this she will not give her assent. She has since met a gentleman, Mr. Annesley, for whom she professes an attachment. Neither can I, nor can her uncle and aunt, hear of Mr. Annesley as a husband for Florence. She is therefore at present disengaged. If you can gain her affections, you have my leave.' With this permission M. Grascour departed, professing himself to be contented.

He did not see Florence for two or three days, no doubt leaving the matter to be discussed with her by her mother and her aunt. To him it was quite indifferent what might be the fate of Captain Scarborough, or of Mr. Annesley, or indeed of Mr. Anderson. And to tell the truth he was not under any violent fear or hope as to his own fate. He admired Miss Mountjoy, and thought it would be well to secure for a wife such a girl with such a fortune as would belong to her. But he did not intend to go 'ungartered,' nor yet to assume an air of 'desolation.' If she would come to him, it would be well; if she would not,—why, it would still be well. The only outward difference made by his love was that he brushed his clothes and his hair a little more carefully, and had his boots brought to a higher state of polish than was usual.

Her mother spoke to her first. 'My dear, M. Grascour is a most excellent man.'

'I am sure he is, mamma.'

'And he is a great friend to your uncle and Lady Mountjoy.'

'Why do you say this, mamma? What can it matter to me?'

'My dear, M. Grascour wishes you to—to—to become his wife.'

'Oh! mamma, why didn't you tell him that it is impossible?'

'How was I to know, my dear?'

'Mamma, I am engaged to marry Harry Annesley, and no word shall ever turn me from that purpose, unless it be spoken by himself. The crier may say that all round the town if he wishes. You must know that it is so. What can be the use of sending M. Grascour or any other gentleman to me? It is only giving me pain and him too. I wish, mamma, you could be got to understand this.' But Mrs. Mountjoy could not altogether be got as yet to understand the obstinacy of her daughter's character.

There was one point on which Florence received information from these two suitors who had come to her at Brussels. They were both favoured, one after the other, by her mother; and would not have been so favoured had her mother absolutely believed in Captain Mountjoy. It seemed to her as though her mother would be willing that she should marry anyone, so long as it was not Harry Annesley. 'It is a pity that there should be such a difference,' she said to herself. 'But we will see what firmness can do.'

Then Lady Mountjoy spoke to her. 'You have heard of M. Grascour, my dear?'

'Yes; I have heard of him, aunt.'

'He intends to do you the honour of asking you to be his wife.'

'So mamma tells me.'

'I have only to say that he is a man most highly esteemed here. He is well known at the court; and is at the royal parties. Should you become his wife you would have all the society of Brussels at your feet.'

'All the society of Brussels would do no good.'

'Perhaps not.'

'Nor the court and the royal parties.'

'If you choose to be impertinent when I tell you what are his advantages and conditions in life, I cannot help it.'

'I do not mean to be impertinent.'

'What you say about the royal parties and the court is intended for impertinence, knowing as you do know your uncle's position.'

'Not at all. You know my position. I am engaged to marry another man, and cannot therefore marry M. Grascour. Why should he be sent to me, except that you won't believe me when I tell you that I am engaged?' Then she marched out of the room, and considered within her own bosom what answer she would give to this new Belgian suitor.

She was made perfectly aware when the Belgian suitor was about to arrive. On the day but one after the interview with her aunt, she was left alone when the other ladies went out, and suspected that even the footman knew what was to happen, when M. Grascour was shown into the drawing-room. There was a simple mode of dealing with the matter on his part,—very different from that state of agitation into which Harry had been thrown when he had made his proposition. She was quite prepared to admit that M. Grascour's plan might be the wisest. But Harry's manner had been full of real love, and had charmed her. M. Grascour was not in the least flustered, whereas poor Harry had been hardly able to speak his mind. But it had not mattered much whether Harry spoke his mind or not; whereas all the eloquence in the world could have done no good for M. Grascour. Florence had known that Harry did love her, whereas of M. Grascour she only knew that he wanted to make her his wife.

'Miss Mountjoy,' he said, 'I am charmed to find you here. Allow me to add that I am charmed to find you alone.' Florence, who knew all about it, only bowed. She had to go through it, and thought that she would be able to do so with equanimity. 'I do not know whether your aunt or your mother have done me the honour of mentioning my name to you.'

'They have both spoken to me.'

'I thought it best that they should have the opportunity of doing so. In our country these things are arranged chiefly by the lady's friends. With your people I know it is different. Perhaps it is much better that it should be so in a matter in which the heart has to be concerned.'

'It would come to the same thing with me. I must decide for myself.'

'I am sure of it. May I venture to feel a hope that ultimately that decision may not go against me?' M. Grascour as he said this did throw some look of passion into his face. 'But I have spoken nothing as yet of my own feelings.'

'It is unnecessary.'

This might be taken in either one of two senses; but the gentleman was not sufficiently vain to think that the lady had intended to signify to him that she would accept his love as a thing of which she could have no doubt. 'Ah! Miss Mountjoy,' he continued, 'if you would allow me to say that since you have been at Brussels not a day has passed in which mingled love and respect have not grown within my bosom. I have sat by and watched while my excellent young friend Mr. Anderson has endeavoured to express his feelings. I have said to myself that I would bide my time. If you could give yourself to him,—why then the aspiration would be quenched within my own breast. But you have not done so; though, as I am aware, he has been assisted by my friend Sir Magnus. I have seen and have heard and have said to myself at last,—now, too, my turn may come. I have loved much, but I have been very patient. Can it be that my turn should have come at last?' Though he had spoken of Mr. Anderson he had not thought it expedient to say a word either of Captain Scarborough or of Mr. Annesley. He

knew quite as much of them as he did of Mr.
Anderson. He was clever, and had put together with
absolute correctness what Mrs. Mountjoy had told
him; with other little facts which had reached his ears.

'M. Grascour, I suppose I am very much obliged
to you. I ought to be.' Here he bowed his head.
'But my only way of being grateful is to tell you
the truth.' Again he bowed his head. 'I am in
love with another man. That's the truth.' Here he
shook his head with the smallest possible shake, as
though deprecating her love, but not doing so with
any harshness. 'I am engaged to marry him, too.'
There was another shake of the head somewhat more
powerful. 'And I intend to marry him.' This she
said with much bold assurance. 'All my old friends
know that it is so, and ought not to have sent you
to me. I have given a promise to Harry Annesley,
and Harry Annesley alone can make me depart from
it.' This she said in a low voice, but almost with
violence, because there had come another shake of
the head in reply to her assurance that she meant
to marry Annesley. 'And though he were to make
me depart from it;—which he never will do,—I
should be just the same as regards anybody else.
Can't you understand that when a girl has given
herself heart and soul to a man, she won't change?'

'Girls do change,—sometimes.'

'You may know them; I don't;—not girls that
are worth anything.'

'But when all your friends are hostile?'

'What can they do? They can't make me marry
another person. They may hinder my happiness; but
they can't hand me over like a parcel of goods to
anyone else. Do you mean to say that you would
accept such a parcel of goods?'

'Oh yes;—such a parcel!'

'You would accept a girl who would come to you
telling you that she loved another man? I don't
believe it of you.'

'I should know that my tenderness would beget tenderness in you.'

'It wouldn't do anything of the kind. It would be all horror,—horror. I should kill myself,—or else you,—or perhaps both.'

'Is your aversion so strong?'

'No; not at all; not at present. I like you very much. I do indeed. I'd do anything for you,—in the way of friendship. I believe you to be a real gentleman.'

'But you would kill me!'

'You make me talk of a condition of things which is quite, quite impossible. When I say that I like you, I am talking of the present condition of things. I have not the least desire to kill you, or myself, or anybody. I want to be taken back to England, and there to be allowed to marry Mr. Henry Annesley. That's what I want. But I intend to remain engaged to him. That's my purpose. And no man and no woman shall stir me from it.' He smiled and again shook his head, and she began to doubt whether she did like him so much. 'Now I've told you all about myself,' she said, rising to her feet. 'You may believe me or not, as you please; but as I have believed you, I have told you all.' Then she walked out of the room.

M. Grascour, as soon as he was alone, left the room and the house, and, making his way into the Park, walked round it twice, turning in his mind his success and his want of success. For in truth he was not at all dispirited by what had occurred. With her other Belgian lover,—that is, with Mr. Anderson,—Florence had at any rate succeeded in making the truth appear to be the truth. He did believe that she had taken such a fancy to that 'fellow, Harry Annesley,' that there would be no overcoming it. He had got a glimpse into the firmness of her character which was denied to M. Grascour. M. Grascour, as he walked up and down the shady paths of the park, told himself that such events as this so-called love on the part of Florence were very common in the lives of English young ladies. 'They are the best in the world,' he said to himself, 'and they make the most charming wives. But their education is such that there is no preventing these accidents.' The passion displayed in the young lady's words he attributed solely to her power of expression. One girl would use language such as had been hers, and such a girl would be clever, eloquent, and brave; another girl would hum and haw with half a 'yes' and a quarter of a 'no,' and would mean just the same thing. He did not doubt but that she had engaged herself to Harry Annesley; nor did he doubt that she had been brought to Brussels to break off that engagement;—and he thought it most probable that her friends would prevail. Under these circumstances, why should he despair;—or why, rather, as he was a man not given to despair, should he not think that there was for him a reasonable chance of success? He must show himself to be devoted, true, and not easily repressed. She had used, he did not doubt, the same sort of language in silencing Anderson. Mr. Anderson had accepted her words; but he knew too well the value of words coming from a young lady's mouth to take them at their true meaning. He had at this interview affected a certain amount of intimacy with Florence of which he thought that he appreciated the value. She had told him that she would kill him,—of course in joke; and a joke from a girl on such an occasion was worth much. No Belgian girl would have joked. But then he was anxious to marry Florence because Florence was English. Therefore when he went back to his own home, he directed that the system of the high polish should be continued with his boots.

'I don't suppose he will come again,' Florence had said to her mother, misunderstanding the character of her latest lover quite as widely as he misunderstood hers. But M. Grascour, though he did not absolutely renew his offer at once, gave it to be understood that he did not at all withdraw from the contest. He obtained permission from Lady Mountjoy to be constantly at the Embassy; and succeeded even in obtaining a promise of support from Sir Magnus. 'You're quite up a tree,' Sir Magnus had said to his Secretary of Legation. 'It's clear she won't look at you.'

'I have pledged myself to abstain,' said poor Anderson in a tone which seemed to confess that all chance was over with him.

'I suppose she must marry someone, and I don't see why Grascour should not have as good a chance as another.' Anderson had stalked away brooding over the injustice of his position, and declaring to himself that this Belgian should never be allowed to marry Florence Mountjoy in peace.

But M. Grascour continued his intentions; and this it was which had induced Florence to tell her mother that the Belgian was 'a great trouble,' which ought to be avoided by a return to England.

Chapter XLVII

FLORENCE BIDS FAREWELL TO HER LOVERS

'MAMMA, had you not better take me back to Cheltenham at once?'

'Has that unfortunate young man written to you?'

'Yes. The young man whom you call unfortunate has written. Of course I cannot agree to have him so called. And to tell the truth I don't think he is so very unfortunate. He has got a girl who really loves him, and that I think is a step to happiness.'

Every word of this was said by Florence as though with the purpose of provoking her mother; and so did Mrs. Mountjoy feel it. But behind this purpose there was that other fixed resolution to get Harry at last accepted as her husband, and perhaps the means taken were the best. Mrs. Mountjoy was already beginning to feel that there would be nothing for her but to give up the battle, and to open her motherly arms to Harry Annesley. Sir Magnus had told her that M. Grascour would probably prevail. M. Grascour was said to be exactly the man likely to be effective with such a girl as Florence. That had been the last opinion expressed by Sir Magnus. But Mrs. Mountjoy had found no comfort in it. Florence was going to have her own way. Her mother knew that it was so, and was very unhappy. But she was still anxious to continue a weak, ineffective battle. 'It was very impertinent of him writing,' she said.

'When he was going to America for years! Dear mamma, do put yourself in my place. How was it possible that he should not write?'

'A young man has no business to come and insinuate himself into a family in that way. And then, when he knows he is not welcome, to open a correspondence!'

'But, mamma, he knows that he is welcome. If he had gone to America without writing to me—— Oh, it would have been impossible! I should have gone after him!'

'No—no—never!'

'I am quite in earnest, mamma. But it is no good talking about what could not have taken place.'

'We ought to have prevented you from receiving or sending letters.' Here Mrs. Mountjoy touched on a subject on which the practice of the English world has been much altered during the last thirty or forty years,—perhaps we may say fifty or sixty years. Fifty years ago young ladies were certainly not allowed to receive letters as they chose, and to write them, and to demand that this practice should be

carried on without any supervision from their elder
friends. It is now usually the case that they do so.
A young lady, before she falls into a correspondence
with a young man, is expected to let it be understood that she does so. But she does not expect that
his letters, either coming or going, shall be subject
to any espial, and she generally feels that the option
of obeying or disobeying the instructions given to
her rests with herself. Practically the use of the post-
office is in her own hands. And as this spirit of self-
conduct has grown up, the morals and habits of our
young ladies have certainly not deteriorated. In
America they carry latch-keys, and walk about with
young gentlemen as young gentlemen walk about
with each other. In America the young ladies are as
well-behaved as with us,—as well-behaved as they
are in some continental countries in which they are
still watched close till they are given up as brides to
husbands with whom they have had no means of becoming acquainted. Whether the latch-key system,
or that of free correspondence, may not rob the
flowers of some of that delicate aroma which we used
to appreciate, may be a question; but then it is also
a question whether there does not come something in
place of it which in the long run is found to be more
valuable. Florence, when this remark was made as
to her own power of sending and receiving letters,
remained silent, but looked very firm. She thought
that it would have been difficult to silence her after
this fashion. 'Sir Magnus could have done it at any
rate, if I had not been able.'

'Sir Magnus could have done nothing, I think,
which would not have been within your power. But
it is useless talking of this. Will you not take me
back to England, so as to prevent the necessity of
Harry coming here?'

'Why should he come?'

'Because, mamma, I intend to see my future
husband before he goes from me for so great a

distance, and for so long a time. Don't you feel any
pity for me, mamma?'

'Do you feel pity for me?'

'Because one day you wish me to marry my
cousin Scarborough, and the next Mr. Anderson, and
then the next M. Grascour? How can I pity you for
that? It is all done because you have taken it in your
head to think ill of one whom I believe to be especially
worthy. You began by disliking him because he
interfered with your plans about Mountjoy. I never
would have married my cousin Mountjoy. He is not
to my taste, and he is a gambler. But you have
thought that you could do what you liked with me.'

'It has always been for your own happiness.'

'But I must be the judge of that. How could I
be happy with any of these men, seeing that I do not
care for them in the least? It would be utterly impossible for me to have myself married to either of
them. To Harry Annesley I have given myself
altogether; but you, because you are my mother, are
able to keep us apart. Do you not pity me for the
sorrow and trouble which I must suffer?'

'I suppose a mother always pities the sufferings
of a child.'

'And removes them when she can do so. But
now, mamma, is he to come here, or will you take me
back to England?'

This was a question which Mrs. Mountjoy found
it very difficult to answer. On the spur of the moment
she could not answer it, as it would be necessary that
she should first consult Sir Magnus. Could Sir
Magnus undertake to confine her daughter within
the precincts of the Embassy, and to exclude the lover
during such time as Harry Annesley might remain in
Brussels? As she thought of the matter in her own
room, she conceived that there would be great difficulty in the matter. All the world of Brussels would
become aware of what was going on. The young
lady would endeavour to get out, and could only be

constrained by the co-operation of the servants; and the young gentleman in his endeavours to get in could only be prevented by the assistance of the police. Dim ideas presented themselves to her mind of further travel. But wherever she went there would be a post-office, and she was aware that the young man could pursue her much quicker than she could fly. How good it would be that in such an emergency she might have the privilege of locking her daughter up in some convent! And yet it must be a Protestant convent, as all things savouring of the Roman Catholic religion were abhorrent to her. Altogether, as she thought of her own condition and that of her daughter, she felt that the world was sadly out of joint.

'Coming here, is he?' said Sir Magnus. 'Then he will just have to go back again, as wise as he came.'

'But can you shut your doors against him?'

'Shut my doors! Of course I can. He'll never be able to get his nose in here if once an order has been given for his exclusion. Who's Mr. Annesley? I don't suppose he knows an Englishman in Brussels.'

'But she will go out to meet him.'

'What! in the streets?' said Sir Magnus in horror.

'I fear she would.'

'By George! She must be a stiff-necked one if she'll do that.' Then Mrs. Mountjoy with tears in her eyes began to explain with very many epithets that her daughter was the best girl in all the world. She was entirely worthy of confidence. Those who knew her were aware that no better-behaved young woman could exist. She was very conscientious, religious, and high-principled. 'But she'll go out in the streets and walk with a young man when all her friends tell her not. Is that her idea of religion?' Then Mrs. Mountjoy, with some touch of anger in the tone of her voice, said that she would return to England, and carry her daughter with her. 'What the deuce can I do, Sarah, when the young lady is so unruly? I can give orders to have him shut out, and can take care that they are obeyed. But I cannot give orders to have her shut in. I should be making her a prisoner, and everybody would talk about it. In that matter you must give her the orders;—only you say that she would not comply with them.'

On the following day Mrs. Mountjoy informed her daughter that they would go back to Cheltenham. She did not name an immediate day, because it would be well, she thought, to stave off the evil hour. Nor did she name a distant day, because were she to do so the terrible evil of Harry Annesley's arrival in Brussels would not be prevented. At first she wished to name no day, thinking that it would be a good thing to cross Harry on the road. But here Florence was too strong for her, and at last a day was fixed. In a week's time they would take their departure, and go home by slow stages. With this arrangement Florence expressed herself well pleased, and of course made Harry acquainted with the probable time of their arrival.

M. Grascour, when he heard that the day had been suddenly fixed for the departure of Mrs. Mountjoy and her daughter, not unnaturally conceived that he himself was the cause of the ladies' departure. Nor did he on that account resign all hope. The young lady's mother was certainly on his side, and he thought it quite possible that, were he to appear in England, he might be successful. But when he had heard of her coming departure, of course it was necessary that he should say some special farewell. He dined one evening at the British Embassy, and took an opportunity during the evening of finding himself alone with Florence. 'And so, Miss Florence,' he said, 'you and your estimable mamma are about to return to England?'

'We have been here a very long time, and are going home at last.'

'It seems to me but the other day when you came,' said M. Grascour, with all a lover's eagerness.

'It was in autumn, and the weather was quite mild and soft. Now we are in the middle of January.'

'I suppose so. But still the time has gone only too rapidly. But the heart can hardly take account of days and weeks.' As this was decided lover's talk, and was made in terms which even a young lady cannot pretend to misunderstand, Florence was obliged to answer it in some manner equally direct. And now she was angry with him. She had informed him that she was in love with another man. In doing so she had done much more than the necessity of the case demanded, and had told him, as the best way of silencing him, that which she might have been expected to keep as her own secret. And yet here he was talking to her about his heart. She made him no immediate answer, but frowned at him and looked stern. It was clear to her intelligence that he had no right to talk to her about his heart after the information she had given him. 'I hope, Miss Mountjoy, that I may look forward to the pleasure of seeing you when I go over to England.'

'But we don't live in London, or near it. We live down in the country,—at Cheltenham.'

'Distance would be nothing.'

This was very bad and must be stopped, thought Florence. 'I suppose I shall be married by that time. I don't know where we may live, but I shall be very happy to see you if you call.'

She had here made a bold assertion, and one which M. Grascour did not at all believe. He was speaking of a visit which he might make perhaps in a month or six weeks, and the young lady told him that he would find her married! And yet, as he knew very well, her mother and her uncle and her aunt were all opposed to this marriage. And she spoke of it without a blush, without any reticence! Young ladies were much emancipated, but he did not think that they generally carried their emancipation so far as this. 'I hope not that,' he said.

'I don't know why you should be so ill-natured as to hope it. The fact is, M. Grascour, you don't believe what I told you the other day. Perhaps as a young lady I ought not to have alluded to it, but I do so in order to set the matter at rest altogether. Of course I can't tell when you may come. If you come quite at once I shall not be married.'

'No;—not married.'

'But I shall be as much engaged as it is possible for a girl to be. I have given my word, and nothing will make me false to it. I don't suppose you will come on my account.'

'Solely on your account.'

'Then stay at home. I am quite in earnest;—and now I must say good-bye.'

She departed, and left him seated alone on the sofa. He at first told himself that she was unfeminine. There was a hard way with her of talking about herself, which he almost pronounced to be unladylike. An unmarried girl should, he thought, under no circumstances speak of the gentleman to whom her affections had been given as Miss Mountjoy spoke of Mr. Annesley. But nevertheless he would sooner possess her as his own wife than any other girl he had ever met. Something of the real passion of unsatisfied love made him feel chill at his heart. Who was this Harry Annesley for whom she professed so warm a feeling? Her mother declared Harry Annesley to be a scapegrace, and something of the story of a discreditable midnight street quarrel between him and the young lady's cousin had reached his ears. He did not suppose it to be possible that the young lady could actually get married without her mother's co-operation, and therefore he thought that he still would go to England. In one respect he was altogether untouched. If he could ultimately succeed in marrying the young lady, she would not be a bit

the worse as his wife because she had been attached
to Harry Annesley. That was a kind of folly which a
girl could very quickly get over when she had not
been allowed to have her own way. Therefore upon
the whole he thought that he would go to England.

But the parting with Anderson had also to be
endured and must necessarily be more difficult. She
owed him a debt for having abstained, and she could
not go without paying the debt by some expression
of gratitude. That she would have done so had he
kept aloof was a matter of course; but equally a matter
of course was it that he would not keep aloof. 'I
shall want to see you for just five minutes tomorrow
morning before you take your departure,' he said in
a lugubrious voice during her last evening.

He had kept his promise to the very letter, moon-
ing about in his desolate manner very conspicuously.
The desolation had been notorious, and very painful
to Florence;—but the promise had been kept, and
she was grateful. 'Oh! certainly; if you wish it,' she
said.

'I do wish it.' Then he made an appointment,
and she promised to keep it.

It was in the ball-room, a huge chamber, very
convenient for its intended purpose and always
handsome at night time; but looking as desolate in
the morning as did poor Anderson himself. He was
stalking up and down the long room when she entered
it, and being at the further end stalked up to her
and addressed her with words which he had chosen
for the purpose. 'Miss Mountjoy,' he said, 'you
found me here a happy, light-hearted young man.'

'I hope I leave you, soon to be the same in spite
of this little accident.'

He did not say that he was a blighted being,
because the word had, he thought, become ridiculous;
but he would have used it had he dared, as expressing
most accurately his condition.

'A cloud has passed over me, and its darkness

will never be effaced. It has certainly been your doing.'

'Oh! Mr. Anderson, what can I say?'

'I have loved before,—but never like this.'

'And so you will again.'

'Never! When I declare that, I expect my word to be respected.' He paused for an answer, but what could she say? She did not at all respect his word on such a subject, but she did respect his conduct. 'Yes; I call upon you to believe me when I say that for me all that is over. But it can be nothing to you.'

'It will be very much to me.'

'I shall go on in the same disconsolate miserable way. I suppose I shall stay here, because I shall be as well here as anywhere else. I might move to Lisbon; but what good would that do me? Your image would follow me to whatever capital I might direct my steps. But there is one thing you can do.' Here he brightened up, putting on quite an altered face.

'I will do anything, Mr. Anderson,—in my power.'

'If—if—if you should change.'

'I shall never change,' she said with an angry look.

'If you should change, I think you should remember the promise you exacted and the fidelity with which it has been kept.'

'I do remember it.'

'And then I should be allowed to come again and have my chance. Wherever I may be, at the court of the Shah of Persia or at the Chinese capital, I will instantly come. I promised you when you asked me. Will you not now promise me?'

'I cannot promise anything—so impossible.'

'It will bind you to nothing but to let me know that Mr. Henry Annesley has gone his way.' But she had to explain to him that it was impossible she should make any promise founded on the idea that

Mr. Henry Annesley should ever go any way in which she would not accompany him. With that he had to be as well satisfied as the circumstances of the case would admit, and he left her with an assurance not intended to be quite audible that he was and ever should be a blighted individual.

When the carriage was at the door Sir Magnus came down into the hall full of smiles and good-humour, but at that moment Lady Mountjoy was saying a last word of farewell to her relatives in her own chamber. 'Good-bye, my dear; I hope you will get well through all your troubles.' This was addressed to Mrs. Mountjoy. 'And as for you, my dear,' she said, turning to Florence, 'if you would only contrive to be a little less stiff-necked, I think the world would go easier with you.'

'I think my stiff neck, aunt, as you call it, is what I have chiefly to depend upon; I mean in reference to other advice than mamma's. Good-bye, aunt.'

'Good-bye, Florence.' And the two parted, hating each other as only female enemies can hate. But Florence, when she was in the carriage, threw herself on to her mother's neck and kissed her.

Chapter XLVIII

MR. PROSPER CHANGES HIS MIND

WHEN Florence with her mother reached Chel-tenham, she found a letter lying for her which surprised her much. The letter was from Harry, and seemed to have been written in better spirits than he had lately displayed. But it was very short.

'DEAREST FLORENCE,

'When can I come down? It is absolutely neces-sary that I should see you. All my plans are likely

to be changed in the most extraordinary manner.
—Yours affectionately,

'H. A.

'Nobody can say that this is a love-letter.'

Florence, of course, showed the letter to her
mother, who was much frightened by its contents.
'What am I to say to him when he comes?' she
exclaimed.

'If you will be so very, very good as to see him,
you must not say anything unkind.'

'Unkind! How can I say anything else than what
you would call unkind? I disapprove of him altogether. And he is coming here with the express
object of taking you away from me.'

'Oh! no;—not at once.'

'But at some day,—which I trust may be very
distant. How can I speak to him kindly when I feel
that he is my enemy?' But the matter was at last
set at rest by a promise from Florence, that she
would not marry her lover in less than three years
without her mother's express consent. Three years
was a long time, was Mrs. Mountjoy's thought, and
many things might occur within that term. Harry,
of whom she thought all manner of unnatural things,
might probably in that time have proved himself to
be utterly unworthy. And Mountjoy Scarborough
might again have come forward in the light of the
world. She had heard of late that Mountjoy had been
received once more into his father's full favour. And
the old man had become so enormously rich through
the building of mills which had been going on at
Tretton, that, as Mrs. Mountjoy thought, he would
be able to make any number of elder sons. On the
subject of entail her ideas were misty; but she felt
sure that Mountjoy Scarborough would even yet
become a rich man. That Florence should be made
to change on that account she did not expect. But she
did think that when she should have learned that

Harry was a murderer, or a midnight thief, or a
wicked conspirator, she would give him up. Therefore she agreed to receive him with not actually
expressed hostility, when he should call at Montpellier Place.

But now in the proper telling of our story we
must go back to Harry Annesley himself. It will be
remembered that his father had called upon Mr.
Prosper, to inform him of Harry's projected journey
to America; that Mountjoy Scarborough had also
called at Buston Hall; and that previous to these
two visits old Mr. Scarborough had himself written
a long letter, giving a detailed account of the conflict
which had taken place in the London streets. These
three events had operated strongly on Mr. Prosper's
mind; but not so strongly as the conduct of Miss
Thoroughbung and Messrs. Soames and Simpson.
It had been made evident to him from the joint
usage which he had received from these persons
that he was simply 'made use of' with the object of
obtaining from him the best possible establishment
for the lady in question. After that interview, at
which the lady, having obtained in way of jointure
much more than was due to her, demanded also for
Miss Tickle a life-long home, and for herself a pair
of ponies, he received a further letter from the
lawyers. This offended him greatly. Nothing on
earth should induce him to write a line to Messrs.
Soames and Simpson. Nor did he see his way to
writing again to Messrs. Grey and Barry about such
trifles as those contained in the letter from the Buntingford lawyers. Trifles to him they were not; but
trifles they must become if put into a letter addressed
to a London firm. 'Our client is anxious to know
specifically that she is to be allowed to bring Miss
Tickle with her when she removes to Buston Hall.
Her happiness depends greatly on the company of
Miss Tickle, to which she has been used now for
many years. Our client wishes to be assured also

that she shall be allowed to keep a pair of ponies in
addition to the carriage-horses which will be maintained, no doubt, chiefly for your own purposes.'
These were the demands as made by Messrs. Soames
and Simpson, and felt by Mr. Prosper to be altogether impossible. He recollected the passionate
explosion of wrath to which the name of Miss Tickle
had already brought him in the presence of the clergyman of his parish. He would endure no further disgrace on behalf of Miss Tickle. Miss Tickle should
never be an inmate of his house, and as for the ponies,
no pony should ever be stabled in his stalls. A pony
was an animal which of its very nature was objectionable to him. There was a want of dignity in a
pony to which Buston Hall should never be subjected.
'And also,' he said to himself at last, 'there is a lack
of dignity about Miss Thoroughbung herself which
would do me an irreparable injury.'

But how should he make known his decision to the
lady herself, and how should he escape from the marriage in such a manner as to leave no stain on his
character as a gentleman? If he could have offered
her a sum of money, he would have done so at once:
but that he thought would not be gentlemanlike, and
would be a confession on his own part that he had
behaved wrongly.

At last he determined to take no notice of the lawyers' letter, and himself to write to Miss Thoroughbung, telling her that the objects which they proposed
to themselves by marriage were not compatible; and
that therefore their matrimonial intentions must be
allowed to subside. He thought it well over, and felt
assured that very much of the success of such a
measure must depend upon the wording of the letter.
There need be no immediate haste. Miss Thoroughbung would not come to Buston again quite at once
to disturb him by a further visit. Before she would
come, he would have flown to Italy. The letter must
be courteous, and somewhat tender; but it must be

absolutely decisive. There must be no loop-hole left by which she could again entangle him; no crevice by which she could creep into Buston! The letter should be a work of time. He would give himself a week or ten days for composing it. And then when it should have been sent, he would be off to Italy.

But before he could allow himself to go upon his travels, he must settle the question about his nephew, which now lay heavy upon his conscience. He did feel that he had ill-treated the young man. He had been so told in very strong language by Mr. Scarborough of Tretton, and Mr. Scarborough of Tretton was a man of very large property, and much talked about in the world. Very wonderful things were said about Mr. Scarborough, but they all tended to make Mr. Prosper believe that he was a man of distinction. And he had also heard lately about Mr. Scarborough's younger son,—or, indeed, his only son, according to the new way of speaking of him,— tidings which were not much in that young man's favour. It was from Augustus Scarborough that he had heard those evil stories about his own nephew. Therefore his belief was shaken; and it was by no means clear to him that there could be any other heir for their property. Miss Thoroughbung had proved herself to be altogether unfit for the high honour he had intended her. Miss Puffle had gone off with Farmer Tazlehurst's son. Mr. Prosper did not think that he had energy enough to look for a third lady who might be fit at all points to become his wife. And now another evil had been added to all these. His nephew had declared his purpose of emigrating to the United States, and becoming an American. It might be true that he should be driven to do so by absolute want. He, Mr. Prosper, had stopped his allowance, and had done so after deterring him from following any profession by which he might have earned his bread. He had looked into the law, and, as far as he could understand it, Buston must become the property of his nephew, even though his nephew should become an American citizen. His conscience pricked him sorely as he thought of the evil which might thus accrue, and of the disgrace which would be attached to his own name. He therefore wrote the following letter to his nephew, and sent it across to the parsonage, done up in a large envelope, and sealed carefully with the Buston arms. And on the corner of the envelope, 'Peter Prosper' was written very legibly.

'MY DEAR NEPHEW, HENRY ANNESLEY,

'Under existing circumstances you will, I think, be surprised at a letter written in my handwriting; but facts have arisen which make it expedient that I should address you.

'You are about, I am informed, to proceed to the United States, a country against which I acknowledge I entertain a serious antipathy. They are not a gentlemanlike people, and I am given to understand that they are generally dishonest in their dealings. Their President is a low person, and all their ideas of government are pettifogging. Their ladies, I am told, are very vulgar, though I have never had the pleasure of knowing one of them. They are an irreligious nation, and have no respect for the established Church of England and her bishops. I should be very sorry that my heir should go among them.

'With reference to my stopping the income which I have hitherto allowed you, it was a step I took upon the best advice, nor can I allow it to be thought that there is any legal claim upon me for a continuance of the payment. But I am willing for the present to continue it on the full understanding that you at once give up your American project.

'But there is a subject on which it is essentially necessary that I should receive from you as my heir a full and complete explanation. Under what circumstances did you beat Captain Scarborough in the streets late on the night of the 3rd of June last? And how did it come to pass that you left him bleeding, speechless, and motionless on that occasion?

'As I am about to continue the payment of the sum hitherto allowed, I think it only fitting that I should receive this explanation under your own hand.

'I am your affectionate uncle,
                    'PETER PROSPER.'

'P.S.—A rumour may probably have reached you of a projected alliance between me and a young lady belonging to a family with which your sister is about to connect herself. It is right that I should tell you that there is no truth in this report.'

This letter, which was much easier to write than the one intended for Miss Thoroughbung, was unfortunately sent off a little before the completion of the other. A day's interval had been intended. But the missive to Miss Thoroughbung was, under the press of difficulties, delayed longer than was intended.

There was, we grieve to say, much of joy, but more of laughter at the rectory when this letter was received. As usual, Joe Thoroughbung was there, and it was found impossible to keep the letter from him. The postscript burst upon them all as a surprise, and was welcomed by no one with more vociferous joy than by the lady's nephew. 'So there is an end for ever to the hope that a child of the Buntingford Brewery should sit upon the throne of the Prospers.' It was thus that Joe expressed himself.

'Why shouldn't he have sat there?' said Polly. 'A Thoroughbung is as good as a Prosper any day.' But this was not said in the presence of Mrs. Annesley, who on that subject entertained views very different from her daughter.

'I wonder what his idea is of the Church of England!' said Mr. Annesley. 'Does he think that the

Archbishop of Canterbury is supreme in all religious matters in America?'

'How on earth he knows that the women are all vulgar when he has never seen one of them is a mystery!' said Harry.

'And that they are dishonest in all their dealings!' said Joe. 'I suppose he got that out of some of the Radical newspapers.' For Joe, after the manner of brewers, was a staunch Tory.

'And their President, too, is vulgar as well as the ladies!' said Mr. Annesley. 'And this is the opinion of an educated Englishman, who is not ashamed to own that he entertains serious antipathies against a whole nation.'

But at the parsonage they soon returned to a more serious consideration of the matter. Did Uncle Prosper intend to forgive the sinner altogether? And was he coerced into doing so by a conviction that he had been told lies, or by the uncommon difficulties which presented themselves to him in reference to another heir? At any rate it was agreed to by them all that Harry must meet his uncle half way, and write the 'full and complete explanation' as desired. 'Bleeding, speechless, and motionless!' said Harry. 'I can't deny that he was bleeding; he certainly was speechless; and for a few moments he may have been motionless. What am I to say?' But the letter was not a difficult one to write, and was sent across on the same day to the Hall. There Mr. Prosper gave up a day to its consideration; a day which would have been much better devoted to applying the final touch to his own letter to Miss Thoroughbung. And he found at last that his nephew's letter required no rejoinder.

But Harry had much to do. It was first necessary that he should see his friend, and explain to him that causes over which he had no control forbade him to go to America. 'Of course, you know, I can't fly in my uncle's face. I was going because he intended to disinherit me; but he finds that more troublesome than letting me alone, and therefore I must remain. You see what he says about the Americans.' The gentleman, whose opinion about our friends on the other side of the Atlantic was very different from Mr. Prosper's, fell into a long argument on the subject. But he was obliged at last to give up his companion.

Then came the necessity of explaining the change in all his plans to Florence Mountjoy, and with this view he wrote the short letter given at the beginning of the chapter, following it down in person to Cheltenham. 'Mamma, Harry is here,' said Florence to her mother.

'Well, my dear! I did not bring him.'

'But what am I to say to him?'

'How can I tell? Why do you ask me?'

'Of course he must come and see me,' said Florence. 'He has sent a note to say that he will be here in ten minutes.'

'Oh dear! oh dear!' exclaimed Mrs. Mountjoy.

'Do you mean to be present, mamma? That is what I want to know.' But that was the question which at the moment Mrs. Mountjoy could not answer. She had pledged herself not to be unkind on condition that no marriage should take place for three years. But she could not begin by being kind, as otherwise she would immediately have been pressed to abandon that very condition. 'Perhaps, mamma, it would be less painful if you would not see him.'

'But he is not to make repeated visits.'

'No; not at present; I think not.'

'He must come only once,' said Mrs. Mountjoy firmly. 'He was to have come because he was going to America. But now he has changed all his plans. It isn't fair, Florence.'

'What can I do? I cannot send him to America because you thought that he was to go there. I thought so too; and so did he. I don't know what has changed him; but it wasn't likely that he'd write and say he wouldn't come because he had altered his plans. Of course he wants to see me;—and so do I want to see him,—very much. Here he is!'

There was a ring at the bell, and Mrs. Mountjoy was driven to resolve what she would do at the moment. 'You mustn't be above a quarter of an hour. I won't have you together for above a quarter of an hour,—or twenty minutes at the furthest.' So saying, Mrs. Mountjoy escaped from the room, and within a minute or two Florence found herself in Harry Annesley's arms.

The twenty minutes had become forty before Harry had thought of stirring, although he had been admonished fully a dozen times that he must at that moment take his departure. Then the maid knocked at the door, and brought word 'that missus wanted to see Miss Florence in her bedroom.'

'Now, Harry, you must go. You really shall go, —or I will. I am very, very happy to hear what you have told me.'

'But three years!'

'Unless mamma will agree.'

'It is quite out of the question. I never heard anything so absurd.'

'Then you must get mamma to consent. I have promised her for three years, and you ought to know that I will keep my word. Harry, I always keep my word; do I not? If she will consent, I will. Now, sir, I really must go.' Then there was a little form of farewell which need not be especially explained, and Florence went upstairs to her mother.

Chapter XLIX

CAPTAIN VIGNOLLES GETS HIS MONEY

WHEN we last left Captain Scarborough, he had just lost an additional sum of two hundred and twenty-seven pounds to Captain Vignolles, which he was not able to pay, besides the sum of fifty pounds which he had received the day before, as the first instalment of his new allowance. This was but a bad beginning of the new life he was expected to lead under the renewed fortunes which his father was preparing for him. He had given his promissory note for the money at a week's date, and had been extremely angry with Captain Vignolles because that gentleman had, under the circumstances, been a little anxious about it. It certainly was not singular that he should have been so, as Captain Scarborough had been turned out of more than one club in consequence of his inability to pay his card debts. As he went home to his lodgings, with Captain Vignolles's champagne in his head, he felt very much as he had done that night when he attacked Harry Annesley. But he met no one whom he could consider as an enemy, and therefore got himself to bed, and slept off the fumes of the drink.

On that day he was to return to Tretton; but, when he woke, he felt that before he did so he must endeavour to make some arrangements for paying the amount due at the end of the week. He had already borrowed twenty pounds from Mr. Grey, and had intended to repay him out of the sum which his father had given him. But that sum now was gone, and he was again nearly penniless. In this emergency there was nothing left to him but again to go to Mr. Grey.

As he was shown up the stairs to the lawyer's room, he did feel thoroughly ashamed of himself.

Mr. Grey knew all the circumstances of his career, and it would be necessary now to tell him of this last adventure. He did tell himself, as he dragged himself up the stairs, that for such a one as he was there could be no redemption. 'It would be better that I should go back,' he said, 'and throw myself from the Monument.'* But yet he felt that if Florence Mount-joy could still be his, there might yet be a hope that things would go well with him.

Mr. Grey began by expressing surprise at seeing Captain Scarborough in town. 'Oh yes! I have come up. It does not matter why, because, as usual, I have put my foot in it. It was at my father's bidding; but that does not matter.'

'How have you put your foot in it?' said the attorney. There was one way in which the captain was always 'putting' both his 'feet in it;' but, since he had been turned out of his clubs, Mr. Grey did not think that that way was open to him.

'The old story.'

'Do you mean that you have been gambling again?'

'Yes;—I met a friend last night, and he asked me to his rooms.'

'And he had the cards ready?'

'Of course he had. What else would anyone have ready for me?'

'And he won back that remnant of the twenty pounds which you borrowed from me, and therefore you want another.' Hereupon the captain shook his head. 'What is it then that you do want?'

'Such a man as I met,' said the captain, 'would not be content with the remnant of twenty pounds. I had received fifty from my father, and had intended to call here and pay you.'

'That has all gone too.'

'Yes; indeed. And in addition to that I have given him a note for two hundred and twenty-seven pounds, which I must take up in a week's time.

Otherwise I must disappear again;—and this time for ever.'

'It is a bottomless gulf,' said the attorney. Captain Scarborough sat silent, with something almost approaching to a smile on his mouth; but his heart within him certainly was not smiling. 'A bottomless gulf,' repeated the attorney. Upon this the captain frowned. 'What is it that you wish me to do for you? I have no money of your father's in my hands, nor could I give it you if I had it.'

'I suppose not. I must go back to him and tell him that it is so.' Then it was the lawyer's turn to be silent; and he remained thinking of it all, till Captain Scarborough rose from his seat, and prepared to go. 'I won't trouble you any more, Mr. Grey,' he said.

'Sit down,' said Mr. Grey. But the captain still remained standing. 'Sit down. Of course I can take out my cheque-book and write a cheque for this sum of money. Nothing would be so easy, and if I could succeed in explaining it to your father during his lifetime, he, no doubt, would repay me. And, for the sake of auld lang syne, I should not be unhappy about my money whether he did so or not. But would it be wise? On your own account would it be wise?'

'I cannot say that anything done for me would be wise;—unless you could cut my throat.'

'And yet there is no one whose future life might be easier. Your father, the circumstances of whose life are the most singular I ever knew,——'

'I shall never believe all this about my mother, you know.'

'Never mind that now. We will pass that by for the present. He has disinherited you.'

'That will be a question some day for the lawyers, —should I live.'

'But circumstances have so gone with him that he is enabled to leave you another fortune. He is very angry with your brother, in which anger I sympathise. He will strip Tretton as bare as the palm of my hand for your sake. You have always been his favourite, and so, in spite of all things, you are still. They tell me he cannot last for six months longer.'

'Heaven knows I do not wish him to die.'

'But he thinks that your brother does. He feels that Augustus begrudges him a few months' longer life, and he is angry. If he could again make you his heir, now that the debts are all paid, he would do so.' Here the captain shook his head. 'But as it is, he will leave you enough for all the needs of even luxurious life. Here is his will, which I am going to send down to him for final execution this very day. My senior clerk will take it, and you will meet him there. That will give you ample for life. But what is the use of it all, if you can lose it in one night or in one month among a pack of scoundrels?'

'If they be scoundrels, I am one of them.'

'You lose your money. You are their dupe. To the best of my belief you have never won. The dupes lose, and the scoundrels win. It must be so.'

'You know nothing about it, Mr. Grey.'

'This man who had your money last;—does he not live on it as a profession? Why should he win always, and you lose?'

'It is my luck.'

'Luck! There is no such thing as luck. Toss up, right hand against left for an hour together, and the result will be the same. If not for an hour, then do it for six hours. Take the average, and your cards will be the same as another man's.'

'Another man has his skill,' said Mountjoy.

'And uses it against the unskilled to earn his daily bread. That is the same as cheating. But what is the use of all this? You must have thought of it all before.'

'Yes; indeed.'

'And thinking of it, you are determined to persevere. You are impetuous, not thoughtless, with your brain clouded with drink, and for the mere excitement of the thing you are determined to risk all in a contest for which there is no chance for you; and by which you acknowledge you will be driven to self-destruction, as the only natural end.'

'I fear it is so,' said the captain.

'How much shall I draw it for?' said the attorney, taking out his cheque-book. 'And to whom shall I make it payable? I suppose I may date it to-day, so that the swindler who gets it may think that there is plenty more behind for him to get.'

'Do you mean that you are going to lend it me?'

'Oh! yes.'

'And how do you mean to get it again?'

'I must wait I suppose till you have won it back among your friends. If you will tell me that you do not intend to look for it in that fashion, then I shall have no doubt as to your making me a legitimate payment in a very short time. Two hundred and twenty pounds won't ruin you, unless you are determined to ruin yourself.' Mr. Grey the meanwhile went on writing the cheque. 'Here is provided for you a large sum of money,' and he laid his hand upon the will, 'out of which you will be able to pay me without the slightest difficulty. It is for you to say whether you will or not.'

'I will.'

'You need not say it in that fashion. That's easy. You must say it at some moment when the itch of play is on you; when there shall be no one by to hear; when the resolution, if held, shall have some meaning in it. Then say,—there is that money which I had from old Grey. I am bound to pay it. But if I go in there I know what will be the result. The very coin that should go into his coffers will become a part of the prey on which those harpies will feed. There's the cheque for the two hundred and twenty-seven pounds. I have drawn it exact, so that you may send the identical bit of paper to your friend. He will suppose that I am some money-lender who has

engaged to supply your needs while your recovered
fortune lasts. Tell your father he shall have the will
tomorrow. I don't suppose I can send Smith with it
to-day.'

Then it became necessary that Scarborough should
go; but it would be becoming that he should first
utter some words of thanks. 'I think you will get
it back, Mr. Grey.'

'I dare say.'

'I think you will. It may be that the having to pay
you will keep me for a while from the gambling-table.'

'You don't look for more than that?'

'I am an unfortunate man, Mr. Grey. There is
one thing that would cure me, but that one thing is
beyond my reach.'

'Some woman?'

'Well;—it is a woman. I think I could keep my
money for the sake of her comfort. But never mind.
Good-bye, Mr. Grey, I think I shall remember what
you have done for me.' Then he went and sent the
identical cheque to Captain Vignolles, with the
shortest and most uncourteous epistle.

'DEAR SIR,

'I send you your money. Send back the note.—
Yours,

'M. SCARBOROUGH'

'I hardly expected this,' said the captain to himself as he pocketed the cheque; 'at any rate not so
soon. Nothing venture nothing have. That Moody
is a slow coach, and will never do anything. I thought
there'd be a little money about with him for a time.'
Then the captain turned over in his mind that night's
good work with the self-satisfied air of an industrious
professional worker.

But Mr. Grey was not so well satisfied with himself; and determined for a while to say nothing to
Dolly of the two hundred and twenty-seven pounds
which he had undoubtedly risked by the loan. But

his mind misgave him before he went to sleep, and he felt that he could not be comfortable till he had made a clean breast of it. During the evening Dolly had been talking to him of all the troubles of all the Carrolls;—how Amelia would hardly speak to her father or her mother because of her injured lover, and was absolutely insolent to her, Dolly, whenever they met; how Sophia had declared that promises ought to be kept, and that Amelia should be got rid of; and how Mrs. Carroll had told her in confidence that Carroll *père* had come home the night before drunker than usual, and had behaved most abominably. But Mr. Grey had attended very little to all this, having his mind preoccupied with the secret of the money which he had lent.

Therefore Dolly did not put out her candle, and arrayed herself for bed in the costume with which she was wont to make her nocturnal visits. She had perceived that her father had something on his mind which it would be necessary that he should tell. She was soon summoned, and having seated herself on the bed, began the conversation. 'I knew you would want me to-night.'

'Why so?'

'Because you've got something to tell. It's about Mr. Barry.'

'No, indeed.'

'That's well. Just at this moment I seem to care about Mr. Barry more than any other trouble. But I fear that he has forgotten me altogether,—which is not complimentary.'

'Mr. Barry will turn up all in proper time,' said her father. 'I have got nothing to say about Mr. Barry just at present, so if you are love-lorn you had better go to bed.'

'Very well. When I am love-lorn, I will. Now what have you got to tell me?'

'I have lent a man a large sum of money;—two hundred and twenty-seven pounds!'

'You are always lending people large sums of money.'

'I generally get it back again.'

'From Mr. Carroll, for instance,—when he borrows it for a pair of breeches and spends it in gin-and-water.'

'I never lent him a shilling. He is a burr,* and has to be pacified not by loans but gifts. It is too late now for me to prevent the brother-in-lawship of poor Carroll.'

'Who has got this money?'

'A professed gambler, who never wins anything and constantly loses more than he is able to pay. Yet I do think this man will pay me some day.'

'It is Captain Scarborough,' said Dolly. 'Seeing that his father is a very rich man indeed, and as far as I can understand gives you a great deal more trouble than he is worth, I don't see why you should lend a large sum of money to his son.'

'Simply because he wanted it.'

'Oh dear; oh dear!'

'He wanted it very much. He had gone away a ruined man because of his gambling, and now when he had come back and was to be put upon his legs again, I could not see him again ruined for the need of such a sum. It was very foolish.'

'Perhaps a little rash, papa.'

'But now I have told you; and so there may be an end of it. But I'll tell you what, Dolly; I'll bet you a new straw hat he pays me within a month of his father's death.' Then Dolly was allowed to escape and betake herself to her bed.

On that same day Mountjoy Scarborough went down to Tretton, and was at once closeted with his father. Mr. Scarborough had questions to ask about Mr. Prosper, and was anxious to know how his son had succeeded in his mission. But the conversation was soon turned from Mr. Prosper to Captain Vignolles and Mr. Grey. Mountjoy had determined, as soon as he had got the cheque from Mr. Grey, to say nothing about it to his father. He had told Mr. Grey in order that he need not tell his father,—if the money were forthcoming. But he had not been five minutes in his father's room before he rushed to the subject. 'You got among those birds of prey again,' said his father.

'There was only one bird,—or at least two. A big bird and a small one.'

'And you lost how much?' Then the captain told the precise sum. 'And Grey has lent it you?' The captain nodded his head. 'Then you must ride into Tretton and catch the mail to-night with a cheque to repay him. That you should have been able in so short a time to have found a man willing to fleece you! I suppose it's hopeless?'

'I cannot tell.'

'Altogether hopeless.'

'What am I to say, sir? If I make a promise it will go for nothing.'

'For absolutely nothing.'

'Then what would be the use of my promising?'

'You are quite logical, and look upon the matter in altogether a proper light. As you have ruined yourself so often, and done your best to ruin those that belong to you, what hope can there be? About this money that I have left you, I do not know that anything farther can be said, unless I leave it all to a hospital. It is better that you should have it and throw it away among the gamblers, than that it should fall into the hands of Augustus. Besides, the demand is moderate. No doubt it is only a beginning, but we will see.'

Then he got out his cheque-book, and made Mountjoy himself write the cheque, including the two sums which had been borrowed. And he dictated the letter to Mr. Grey.

'MY DEAR GREY,

'I return the money which Mountjoy has had from

you,—two hundred and twenty-seven pounds, and twenty. That, I think, is right. You are the most foolish man I know with your money. To have given it to such a scapegrace as my son Mountjoy! But you are the sweetest and finest gentleman I ever came across. You have got your money now, which is a great deal more than you can have expected or ought to have obtained. However, on this occasion you have been in great luck.

'Yours faithfully,
'JOHN SCARBOROUGH.'

This letter his son himself was forced to write, though it dealt altogether with his own delinquencies; and yet, as he told himself, he was not sorry to write it, as it would declare to Mr. Grey that he had himself acknowledged at once his own sin. The only further punishment which his father exacted was that his son should himself ride into Tretton and post the letter before he ate his dinner.

'I've got my money,' said Mr. Grey, waving the cheque as he went into his dressing-room with Dolly at his heels.

'Who has paid it?'

'Old Scarborough; and he made Mountjoy write the letter himself, calling me an old fool for lending it. I don't think I was such a fool at all. However, I've got my money, and you may pay the bet and not say anything more about it.'

Chapter L

THE LAST OF MISS THOROUGHBUNG

MR. PROSPER, with that kind of energy which was distinctively his own, had sent off his letter to Harry Annesley, with his postscript in it about his blighted matrimonial prospects, a letter easy to be written, before he had completed his grand epistle to

Miss Thoroughbung. The epistle to Miss Thoroughbung was one requiring great consideration. It had
to be studied in every word, and re-written again and
again with the profoundest care. He was afraid that
he might commit himself by an epithet. He dreaded
even an adverb too much. He found that a full stop
expressed his feelings too violently, and wrote the
letter again, for the fifth time, because of the big
initial which followed the full stop. The consequence
of all this long delay was that Miss Thoroughbung
had heard the news, through the brewery, before it
reached her in its legitimate course. Mr. Prosper had
written his postscript by accident, and, in writing it,
had forgotten the intercourse between his brother-in-
law's house and the Buntingford people. He had
known well of the proposed marriage; but he was a
man who could not think of two things at the same
time, and thus had committed the blunder.

Perhaps it was better for him as it was; and the
blow came to him with a rapidity which created less
of suffering than might have followed the slower
mode of proceeding which he had intended. He was
actually making the fifth copy of the letter, rendered
necessary by that violent full stop, when Matthew
came to him and announced that Miss Thoroughbung
was in the drawing-room. 'In the house!' ejaculated
Mr. Prosper.

'She would come into the hall; and then where
was I to put her?'

'Matthew Pike, you will not do for my service.'
This had been said about once every three months
throughout the long course of years in which Matthew
had lived with his master.

'Very well, sir. I am to take it for a month's warn-
ing, of course.' Matthew understood well enough
that this was merely an expression of his master's
displeasure, and, being anxious for his master's welfare, knew that it was decorous that some decision
should be come to at once as to Miss Thoroughbung,

and that time should not be lost in his own little personal quarrel. 'She is waiting, you know, sir; and she looks uncommon irascible. There is the other lady left outside in the carriage.'

'Miss Tickle! Don't let her in, whatever you do. She is the worst. Oh, dear; oh, dear! Where are my coat and waistcoat; and my braces? And I haven't brushed my hair. And these slippers won't do. What business has she to come at this time of day, without saying a word to anybody?' Then Matthew went to work, and got his master into decent apparel, with as little delay as possible. 'After all,' said Mr. Prosper, 'I don't think I'll see her. Why should I see her?'

'She knows you are at home, sir.'

'Why does she know I'm at home? That's your fault. She oughtn't to know anything about it. Oh, dear; oh, dear; oh, dear!' These last ejaculations arose from his having just then remembered the nature of his postscript to Harry Annesley; and the engagement of Joe Thoroughbung to his niece. He made up his mind at the moment,—or thought that he had made up his mind,—that Harry Annesley should not have a shilling as long as he lived. 'I am quite out of breath. I cannot see her yet. Go and offer the lady cake and wine: and tell her that you had found me very much indisposed. I think you will have to tell her that I am not well enough to receive her to-day.'

'Get it over, sir, and have done with it.'

'It's all very well to say have done with it! I shall never have done with it. Because you have let her in to-day, she'll think that she can come always. Good Lord! There she is on the stairs! Pick up my slippers.' Then the door was opened, and Miss Thoroughbung herself entered the room. It was an upstairs chamber, known as Mr. Prosper's own; and from it was the door into his bedroom. How Miss Thoroughbung had learned her way to it he never could guess. But she had come up the stairs, as though she had been acquainted with all the intricacies of the house from her childhood.

'Mr. Prosper,' she said, 'I hope I see you quite well this morning;—and that I have not disturbed you at your toilet.' That she had done so was evident, from the fact that Matthew, with the dressing-gown and slippers, was seen disappearing into the bedroom.

'I am not very well, thank you,' said Mr. Prosper, rising from his chair, and offering her his hand, with the coldest possible salutation.

'I am sorry for that,—very. I hope it is not your indisposition which has prevented you from coming to see me. I have been expecting you every day since Soames wrote his last letter. But it's no use pretending any longer. Oh, Peter, Peter!' This use of his Christian-name struck him absolutely dumb,—so that he was unable to utter a syllable. He should, first of all, have told her that any excuse she had before for calling him by his Christian-name, was now at an end. But there was no opening for speech such as that. 'Well,' she continued, 'have you got nothing to say to me? You can write flippant letters to other people, and turn me into ridicule glibly enough.'

'I have never done so.'

'Did you not write to Joe Thoroughbung, and tell him you had given up all thoughts of having me?'

'Joe!' he exclaimed. His very surprise did not permit him to go further, at the moment, than this utterance of the young man's Christian-name.

'Yes, Joe;—Joe Thoroughbung, my nephew, and yours that is to be. Did you not write and tell him that everything was over?'

'I never wrote to young Mr. Thoroughbung in my life. I should not have dreamed of such a correspondence on such a subject.'

'Well, he says you did. Or, if you didn't write to Joe himself, you wrote to somebody.'

'I may have written to somebody, certainly.'

'And told them that you didn't mean to have anything further to say to me?' That traitor Harry had now committed a sin worse than knocking a man down in the middle of the night, and leaving him bleeding, speechless, and motionless; worse than telling a lie about it; worse even than declining to listen to sermons read by his uncle. Harry had committed such a sin that no shilling of allowance should evermore to paid to him. Even at this moment there went through Mr. Prosper's brain an idea that there might be some unmarried female in England besides Miss Puffle and Miss Thoroughbung. 'Peter Prosper, why don't you answer like a man, and tell me the honest truth?' He had never before been called Peter Prosper in his whole life.

'Perhaps you had better let me make a communication by letter,' he said. At that very moment the all but completed epistle was lying on the table before him, where even her eyes might reach it. In the flurry of the moment he covered it up.

'Perhaps that is the letter which has taken you so long to write,' she said.

'It is the letter.'

'Then hand it me over, and save yourself the penny stamp.' In his confusion he gave her the letter, and threw himself down on the sofa while she read it. 'You have been very careful in choosing your language, Mr. Prosper. "It will be expedient that I should make known to you the entire truth." Certainly, Mr. Prosper, certainly. The entire truth is the best thing,—next to entire beer,* my brother would say.' 'The horrid vulgar woman!' Mr. Prosper ejaculated to himself. ' "There seems to have been a complete misunderstanding with regard to that amiable lady, Miss Tickle." No misunderstanding at all. You said you liked her, and I supposed you did. And when I had been living for twenty years with a female companion who hasn't sixpence in the world to buy a rag with, but what she gets from me, was it to be expected that I should turn her out for any man?'

'An annuity might have been arranged, Miss Thoroughbung.'

'Bother an annuity! That's all you think about feelings! Was she to go and live alone and desolate, because you wanted someone to nurse you? And then those wretched ponies. I tell you, Peter Prosper, that let me marry whom I will, I mean to drive a pair of ponies, and am able to do so out of my own money. Ponies indeed! It's an excuse. Your heart has failed you. You've come to know a woman of spirit, and now you're afraid that she'll be too much for you. I shall keep this letter, though it has not been sent.'

'You can do as you please about that, Miss Thoroughbung.'

'Oh yes; of course I shall keep it, and shall give it to Messrs. Soames and Simpson. They are most gentlemanlike men, and will be shocked at such conduct as this from the squire of Buston. The letter will be published in the newspapers, of course. It will be very painful to me, no doubt; but I shall owe it to my sex to punish you. When all the county are talking of your conduct to a lady, and saying that no man could have done it, let alone no gentleman, then you will feel it. Miss Tickle! And a pair of ponies! You expected to get my money and nothing to give for it. Oh, you mean man!'

She must have been aware that every word she spoke was a dagger. There was a careful analysis of his peculiar character displayed in every word of reproach which she uttered. Nothing could have wounded him more than the comparison between himself and Soames and Simpson. They were gentlemen! 'The vulgarest men in all Buntingford!' he declared to himself, and always ready for any sharp practice. Whereas he was no man, Miss Thoroughbung had said; a mean creature, altogether unworthy to be regarded as a gentleman. He knew himself to be

Mr. Prosper of Buston Hall, with centuries of Prospers for his ancestors; whereas Soames was the son of a tax-gatherer; and Simpson had come down from London, as a clerk from a solicitor's office in the City. And yet it was true that people would talk of him as did Miss Thoroughbung! His cruelty would be in every lady's mouth. And then his stinginess about the ponies would be the gossip of the county for twelve months. And, as he found out what Miss Thoroughbung was, the disgrace of even having wished to marry her loomed terribly large before him.

But there was a twinkle of jest in the lady's eyes all the while, which he did not perceive, and which, had he perceived it, he could not have understood. Her anger was but simulated wrath. She, too, had thought that it might be well, under circumstances, if she were to marry Mr. Prosper; but had quite understood that those circumstances might not be forthcoming. 'I don't think it will do at all, my dear,' she had said to Miss Tickle. 'Of course an old bachelor like that won't want to have you.'

'I beg you won't think of me for a moment,' Miss Tickle had answered with solemnity.

'Bother! Why can't you tell the truth? I'm not going to throw you over, and of course you'd be just nowhere if I did. I shan't break my heart for Mr. Prosper. I know I should be an old fool if I were to marry him; and he is more of an old fool for wanting to marry me. But I did think he wouldn't cut up so rough about the ponies.' And then, when no answer came to the last letter from Soames and Simpson, and the tidings reached her, round from the brewery, that Mr. Prosper intended to be off, she was not in the least surprised. But the information, she thought, had come to her in an unworthy manner. So she determined to punish the gentleman, and went out to Buston Hall and called him Peter Prosper. We may doubt, however, whether she had ever realised how terribly her scourges would wale him.

'And to think that you would let it come round to me in that way, through the young people,—writing about it just as a joke.'

'I never wrote about it like a joke,' said Mr. Prosper, almost crying.

'I remember now. It was to your nephew; and of course everybody at the Rectory saw it. Of course they were all laughing at you.' There was one thing now written in the book of fates, and sealed as certainly as the crack of doom. No shilling of allowance should ever be paid to Harry Annesley. He would go abroad. He said so to himself as he thought of this, and said also that, if he could find a healthy young woman anywhere, he would marry her, sacrificing every idea of his own happiness to his desire of revenge upon his nephew. This, however, was only the passionate feeling of the moment. Matrimony had become altogether so distasteful to him, since he had become intimately acquainted with Miss Thoroughbung, as to make any release in that manner quite impossible to him. 'Do you propose to make me any amends?' asked Miss Thoroughbung.

'Money?' said he.

'Yes; money! Why shouldn't you pay me money? I should like to keep three ponies, and to have Miss Tickle's sister to come and live with me.'

'I do not know whether you are in earnest, Miss Thoroughbung.'

'Quite in earnest, Peter Prosper. But perhaps I had better leave that matter in the hands of Soames and Simpson. Very gentlemanlike men, and they'll be sure to let you know how much you ought to pay. Ten thousand pounds wouldn't be too much, considering the distress to my wounded feelings.' Here Miss Thoroughbung put her handkerchief up to her eyes.

There was nothing that he could say. Whether she were laughing at him, as he thought to be most probable, or whether there was some grain of truth in the demand which she made, he found it equally impossible to make any reply. There was nothing that he could say; nor could he absolutely turn her out of the room. But after ten minutes' further continuation of these amenities, during which it did at last come home to his brain that she was merely laughing at him, he began to think that he might possibly escape, and leave her there in possession of his chamber.

'If you will excuse me, Miss Thoroughbung, I will retire,' he said, rising from the sofa.

'Regularly chaffed out of your own den,' she said, laughing.

'I do not like this interchange of wit on subjects that are so serious.'

'Interchange! There is very little interchange, according to my idea. You haven't said anything witty. What an idea of interchange the man has.'

'At any rate I will escape from your rudeness.'

'Now, Peter Prosper, before you go let me ask you one question. Which of the two has been the rudest to the other? You have come and asked me to marry you, and have evidently wished to back out of it from the moment in which you found that I had ideas of my own about money. And now you call me rude, because I have my little revenge. I have called you Peter Prosper, and you can't stand it. You haven't spirit enough to call me Matty Thoroughbung in reply. But good-bye, Mr. Prosper, —for I never will call you Peter again. As to what I said to you about money, that, of course, is all bosh. I'll pay Soames's bill, and will never trouble you. There's your letter, which, however, would be of no use because it is not signed. A very stupid letter it is. If you want to write naturally you should never copy a letter. Good-bye, Mr. Prosper,—Peter that never shall be.' Then she got up and walked out of the room.

Mr. Prosper, when he was left alone, remained

for a while nearly paralysed. That he should have ever entertained the idea of making that woman his wife! Such was his first thought. Then he reflected that he had, in truth, escaped from her more easily than he had hoped, and that she had certainly displayed some good qualities, in spite of her vulgarity and impudence. She did not, at any rate, intend to trouble him any further. He would never again hear himself called Peter by that terribly loud voice. But his anger became very fierce against the whole family at the Rectory. They had ventured to laugh at him, and he could understand that, in their eyes, he had become very ridiculous. He could see it all,—the manner in which they had made fun at him, and had been jocose over his intended marriage. He certainly had not intended to be funny in their eyes. But while he had been exercising the duty of a stern master over them, and had been aware of his own extreme generosity in his efforts to forgive his nephew, that very nephew had been laughing at him, in conjunction with the nephew of her whom he had intended to make his wife! Not a shilling, again, should ever be allowed to Harry Annesley. If it could be so arranged, by any change of circumstances, he might even yet become the father of a family of his own.

Chapter LI

MR. PROSPER IS TAKEN ILL

WHEN Harry Annesley returned from Cheltenham, which he did about the beginning of February, he was a very happy man. It may be said, indeed, that within his own heart he was more exalted than is fitting for a man mortal,—for a human creature who may be cut off from his joys tomorrow, or may have the very source of his joy turned into sorrow. He walked like a god, not showing it by his outward gesture, not declaring that it was so by any assumed grace or arrogant carriage of himself; but knowing within himself that that had happened down at Cheltenham which had all but divested him of humanity, and made a star of him. To no one else had it been given to have such feelings, such an assurance of heavenly bliss, together with the certainty that, under any circumstances, it must be altogether his own, for ever and ever. It was thus he thought of himself and what had happened to him. He had succeeded in getting himself kissed by a young woman.

Harry Annesley was in truth very proud of Florence, and altogether believed in her. He thought the better of himself because Florence loved him;—not with the vulgar self-applause of a man, who fancies himself to be a lady-killer, and therefore a grand sort of fellow; but as conceiving himself to be something better than he had hitherto believed simply because he had won the heart of this one special girl. During that half-hour at Cheltenham she had so talked to him, had managed in her own pretty way so to express herself, as to make him understand that of all that there was of her he was the only lord and master. 'May God do so to me, and more also, if to the end I do not treat her, not only with all affection, but also with all delicacy of observance.' It was thus that he spoke to himself of her, as he walked away from the door of Mrs. Mountjoy's house in Cheltenham.

From thence he went back to Buston, and entered his father's house with all that halo of happiness shining round his heart. He did not say much about it, but his mother and his sisters felt that he was altered; and he understood their feelings when his mother said to him, after a day or two, that 'it was a great shame' that they none of them knew his Florence.

'But you will have to know her,—well.'

'That's of course; but it's a thousand pities that we should not be able to talk of her to you as of one whom we know already.' Then he felt that they had, among them, acknowledged her to be such as she was.

There came to the rectory some tidings of the meeting which had taken place at the Hall between his uncle and Miss Thoroughbung. It was Joe who brought to them the first account; and then further particulars leaked out among the servants of the two houses. Matthew was very discreet; but even Matthew must have spoken a word or two. In the first place there came the news that Mr. Prosper's anger against his nephew was hotter than ever. 'Mr. Harry must have put his foot in it somehow.' That had been Matthew's assurance, made with much sorrow to the housekeeper, or head-servant, at the rectory. And then Joe had declared that all the misfortunes which had attended Mr. Prosper's courtship had been attributed to Harry's evil influences. At first this could not be but a matter of joke. Joe's stories as he told them were full of ridicule; and had no doubt come to him from Miss Thoroughbung, either directly or through some of the ladies at Buntingford. 'It does seem that your aunt has been too many for him.' This had been said by Molly, and had been uttered in the presence both of Joe Thoroughbung and of Harry.

'Why, yes,' said Joe. 'She has had him under the thong altogether; and has not found it difficult to flog him when she had got him by the hind leg.' This idea had occurred to Joe from his remembrance of a peccant hound in the grasp of a tyrant whip. 'It seems that he offered her money.'

'I should hardly think that,' said Harry, standing up for his uncle.

'She says so; and says that she declared that ten thousand pounds would be the very lowest sum. Of course she was laughing at him.'

'Uncle Prosper doesn't like to be laughed at,' said Molly.

'And she did not spare him,' said Joe. And then she had by heart the whole story, how she had called him Peter, and how angry he had been at the appellation.

'Nobody calls him Peter except my mother,' said Harry.

'I should not dream of calling him Uncle Peter,' said Molly. 'Do you mean to say that Miss Thoroughbung called him Peter? Where could she have got the courage?' To this Joe replied that he believed his aunt had courage for anything under the sun. 'I don't think that she ought to have called him Peter,' continued Molly. 'Of course after that there couldn't be a marriage.'

'I don't quite see why not,' said Joe. 'I call you Molly, and I expect you to marry me.'

'And I call you Joe, and I expect you to marry me; but we ain't quite the same.'

'The squire of Buston,' said Joe, 'considers himself squire of Buston. I suppose that the old Queen of Heaven didn't call Jupiter Jove* till they had been married at any rate some centuries.'

'Well done, Joe!' said Harry.

'He'll become fellow of a college yet,' said Molly.

'If you'll let me alone I will,' said Joe. 'But only conceive the kind of scene there must have been at the house up there, when Aunt Matty had forced her way in among your uncle's slippers and dressing-gowns. I'd have given a five-pound note to have seen and heard it.'

'I'd have given two if it had never occurred. He had written me a letter which I had taken as a pardon in full for all my offences. He had assured me that he had no intention of marrying, and had offered to give me back my old allowance. Now I am told that he has quarrelled with me again altogether, because of some light word as to me and my concerns spoken by this vivacious old aunt of yours. I wish your vivacious old aunt had remained at Buntingford.'

'And we had wished that your vivacious old uncle had remained at Buston when he came love-making to Marmaduke Lodge.'

'He was an old fool; and, among ourselves, always has been,' said Molly, who on the occasion thought it incumbent upon her to take the Thoroughbung rather than the Prosper side of the quarrel.

But, in truth, this renewed quarrel between the Hall and the rectory was likely to prove extremely deleterious to Harry Annesley's interests. For his welfare depended not solely on the fact that he was at present heir presumptive to his uncle, nor yet on the small allowance of two hundred and fifty pounds made to him by his uncle, and capable of being withdrawn at any moment; but also on the fact, supposed to be known to all the world,—which was known to all the world before the affair in the streets with Mountjoy Scarborough,—that Harry was his uncle's heir. His position had been that of eldest son, and indeed that of only child to a man of acres and squire of a parish. He had been made to hope that this might be restored to him, and at this moment absolutely had in his pocket the cheque for sixty-two pounds ten which had been sent to him by his uncle's agent in payment of the quarter's income which had been stopped. But he also had a further letter written on the next day, telling him that he was not to expect any repetition of the payment. Under these circumstances, what should he do?

Two or three things occurred to him. But he resolved at last to keep the cheque without cashing it for some weeks, and then to write to his uncle when the fury of his wrath might be supposed to have passed by, offering to restore it. His uncle was undoubtedly a very silly man; but he was not one who could acknowledge to himself that he had done an unjust act without suffering for it. At the present

moment, while his wrath was hot, there would be no
sense of contrition. His ears would still tingle with
the sound of the laughter of which he had supposed
himself to have been the subject at the rectory. But
that sound in a few weeks might die away, and some
feeling of the propriety of justice would come back
upon the poor man's mind. Such was the state of
things upon which Harry resolved to wait for a few
weeks.

But in the meantime tidings came across from the
Hall that Mr. Prosper was ill. He had remained in
the house for two or three days after Miss Thoroughbung's visit. This had given rise to no especial remarks, because it was well known that Mr. Prosper
was a man whose feelings were often too many for
him. When he was annoyed it would be long before
he would get the better of the annoyance; and during
such periods he would remain silent and alone. There
could be no question that Miss Thoroughbung had
annoyed him most excessively. And Matthew had
been aware that it would be better that he should
abstain from all questions. He would take the daily
newspaper in to his master, and ask for orders as to
the daily dinner, and that would be all. Mr. Prosper,
when in a fairly good humour, would see the cook
every morning, and would discuss with her the propriety of either roasting or boiling the fowl, and the
expediency either of the pudding or the pie. His
idiosyncrasies were well known, and the cook might
always have her own way by recommending the contrary to that which she wanted, because it was a point
of honour with Mr. Prosper not to be led by his servants. But during these days he simply said, 'Let
me have dinner, and do not trouble me.' This went
on for a day or two without exciting much comment
at the rectory. But when it went on beyond a day or
two it was surmised that Mr. Prosper was ill.

At the end of a week he had not been seen outside the house, and then alarm began to be felt. The

rumour had got abroad that he intended to go to
Italy, and it was expected that he would start. But
no sign came of his intended movements. Not a
word more had been said to Matthew on the subject.
He had been ordered to admit no visitor into the house
at all, unless it were someone from the firm of Grey
and Barry. From the moment in which he had got
rid of Miss Thoroughbung he had been subject to
some dread lest she should return. Or if not she
herself, she might, he thought, send Soames and
Simpson or some denizen from the brewery. And he
was conscious that not only all Buston but all Buntingford was aware of what he had attempted to do.
Everyone whom he chanced to meet would, as he
thought, be talking of him, and therefore he feared
to be seen by the eye of man, woman, or child. There
was a self-consciousness about him which altogether
overpowered him. That cook with whom he used to
have the arguments about the boiled chicken was
now an enemy, a domestic enemy, because he was
sure that she talked about his projected marriage in
the kitchen. He would not see his coachman or his
groom, because some tidings would have reached
them about that pair of ponies. Consequently he
shut himself up altogether, and the disease became
worse with him because of his seclusion.

And now from day to day, or, it may be more
properly said, from hour to hour, news came across
to the rectory of the poor squire's health. Matthew,
to whom alone was given free intercourse with his
master, became very gloomy. Mr. Prosper was no
doubt gloomy and the feeling was contagious. 'I
think he's going off his head; that's what I do think,'
he said in confidential intercourse with the cook.
That conversation resulted in Matthew's walking
across to the rectory, and asking advice from the
rector; and in the rector paying a visit to the Hall.
He had again consulted with his wife, and she had
recommended him to endeavour to see her brother.

'Of course, what we hear about his anger only comes from Joe, or through the servants. If he is angry what will it matter?'

'Not in the least to me,' said the rector, 'only I would not willingly trouble him.'

'I would go,' said the rector's wife, 'only I know he would require me to agree with him about Harry. That, of course, I cannot do.'

Then the rector walked across to the Hall, and sent up word by Matthew that he was there, and that he would be glad to see Mr. Prosper, if Mr. Prosper were disengaged. But Matthew after an interval of a quarter of an hour came back with merely a note. 'I am not very well, and an interview at the present moment would only be depressing. But I would be glad to see my sister if she would come across tomorrow at twelve o'clock. I think it would be well that I should see someone, and she is now the nearest.—P.P.' Then there arose a great discussion at the rectory, as to what this note indicated. 'She is now the nearest!' He might have so written had the doctor who attended him told him that death was imminent. Of course she was the nearest. What did the 'now' mean? Was it not intended to signify that Harry had been his heir, and therefore the nearest; but that now he had been repudiated? But it was, of course, resolved that Mrs. Annesley should go to the Hall, at the hour indicated, on the morrow.

'Oh, yes; I'm up here; where else should I be,—unless you expected to find me in my bed?' It was thus that he answered his sister's first enquiry as to his condition.

'In bed; oh, no! Why should anyone expect to find you in bed, Peter?'

'Never call me by that name again,' he said, rising from his chair, and standing erect, with one arm stretched out. She called him Peter, simply because it had been her custom so to do, during the period of nearly fifty years in which they had lived in the same parish as brother and sister. She could, therefore, only stare at him, and his tragic humour, as he stood there before her. 'Though, of course, it is madness on my part to object to it! My godfather and godmother christened me Peter, and our father was Peter before me, and his father, too, was Peter Prosper. But that woman has made the name sound abominable in my ears.'

'Miss Thoroughbung, you mean?'

'She came here, and so be-Petered me in my own house,—nay, up in this very room,—that I hardly knew whether I was on my head or my heels.'

'I would not mind what she said. They all know that she is a little flighty.'

'Nobody told me so. Why couldn't you let me know that she was flighty beforehand? I thought she was a person whom it would have done to marry.'

'If you will only think of it, Peter——' Here he shuddered visibly. 'I beg your pardon; I will not call you so again. But it is unreasonable to blame us for not telling you about Miss Thoroughbung.'

'Of course it is. I am unreasonable; I know it.'

'Let us hope that it is all over now.'

'Cart-ropes wouldn't drag me up to the hymeneal altar;—at least not with that woman.'

'You have sent for me, Peter,—I beg pardon. I was so glad when you sent. I would have come before, only I was afraid that you would be annoyed. Is there anything that we can do for you?'

'Nothing at all that you can do,—I fear.'

'Somebody told us that you were thinking of going abroad.' Here he shook his head. 'I think it was Harry.' Here he shook his head again and frowned. 'Had you not some idea of going abroad?'

'That is all gone,' he said solemnly.

'It would have enabled you to get over this disappointment without feeling it so acutely.'

'I do feel it; but not exactly the disappointment. There I think I have been saved from a misfortune which would certainly have driven me mad. That woman's voice daily in my ear could have had no other effect. I have at any rate been saved from that.'

'What is it then that troubles you?'

'Everybody knows that I intended it. All the county has heard of it. But yet was not my purpose a good one? Why should not a gentleman marry if he wants to leave his estate to his own son?'

'Of course he must marry before he can do that.'

'Where was I to get a young lady,—just outside of my own class? There was Miss Puffle. I did think of her. But just at the moment she went off with young Tazlehurst. That was another misfortune. Why should Miss Puffle have descended so low just before I had thought of her? And I couldn't marry quite a young girl. How could I expect such a one to live here with me at Buston where it is rather dull? When I looked about there was nobody except that horrid Miss Thoroughbung. You just look about and tell me if there was anyone else. Of course my circle is circumscribed. I have been very careful whom I have admitted to my intimacy, and the result is that I know almost nobody. I may say that I was driven to ask Miss Thoroughbung.'

'But why marry at all unless you're fond of somebody to be attached to?'

'Ah!'

'Why marry at all? I say. I ask the question knowing very well why you intended to do it.'

'Then why do you ask?' he said angrily.

'Because it is so difficult to talk of Harry to you. Of course I cannot help feeling that you have injured him.'

'It is he that has injured me. It is he that has brought me to this condition. Don't you know that you've all been laughing at me down at the rectory since the affair of that terrible woman?' While he paused for an answer to his question, Mrs. Annesley sat silent. 'You know it is true. He and that man whom Molly means to marry, and the other girls, and their father and you, have all been laughing at me.'

'I have never laughed.'

'But the others?' And again he waited for a reply. But the no reply which came did as well as any other answer. There was the fact that he had been ridiculed by the very young man whom it was intended that he should support by his liberality. It was impossible to tell him that a man who had made himself so absurd must expect to be laughed at by his juniors. There was running through his mind an idea that very much was due to him from Harry; but there was also an idea that something too was due from him. There was present, even to him, a noble feeling that he should bear all the ignominy with which he was treated, and still be generous. But he had sworn to himself, and had sworn to Matthew, that he would never forgive his nephew. 'Of course you all wish me to be out of the way?'

'Why do you say that?'

'Because it is true. How happy you would all be if I were dead, and Harry were living here in my place.'

'Do you think so?'

'Yes, I do. Of course you would all go into mourning, and there would be some grimace of sorrow among you for a few weeks, but the sorrow would soon be turned into joy. I shall not last long, and then his time will come. There! you may tell him that his allowance shall be continued in spite of all his laughing. It was for that purpose that I sent for you. And now you know it you can go and leave me.' Then Mrs. Annesley did go, and rejoiced them all up at the rectory by these latest tidings from the Hall. But now the feeling was, how could they show their gratitude and kindness to poor Uncle Prosper?

Chapter LII

MR. BARRY AGAIN

'MR. BARRY has given me to understand that he means to come down tomorrow.' This was said by Mr. Grey to his daughter.

'What does he want to come here for?'

'I suppose you know why he wants to come here?' Then the father was silent, and for some time Dolly remained silent also. 'He is coming to ask you to consent to be his wife.'

'Why do you let him come, papa?'

'I cannot hinder him. That in the first place. And then I don't want to prevent his coming.'

'Oh, papa!'

'I do not want to prevent his coming. And I do not wish you now at this instant to pledge yourself to anything.'

'I cannot but pledge myself.'

'You can at any rate remain silent while I speak to you.' There was a solemnity in his manner which almost awed her, so that she could only come nearer to him and sit close to him, holding his hand in hers. 'I wish you to hear what I have got to say to you, and to make no answer till you shall make it tomorrow to him, after having fully considered the whole matter. In the first place he is an honest and good man, and certainly will not ill-treat you.'

'Is that so much?'

'It is a great deal as men go. It would be a great deal to me to be sure that I had left you in the hands of one, who is, of his nature, tender and affectionate.'

'That is something; but not enough.'

'And then he is a careful man, who will certainly screen you from all want; and he is prudent, walking about the world with his eyes open,—much wider than your father has ever done.' Here she only pressed his hand. 'There is nothing to be said against him, except that something which you spotted at once when you said that he was not a gentleman. According to your ideas, and to mine, he is not quite a gentleman; but we are both fastidious.'

'We must pay the penalty of our tastes in that respect.'

'You are paying the penalty now by your present doubts. But it is not yet too late for you to get the better of it. Though I have acknowledged that he is not quite a gentleman, he is by no means the reverse. You are quite a lady.'

'I hope so.'

'But you are not particularly good-looking.'

'Papa, you are not complimentary.'

'My dear, I do not intend to be so. To me your face, such as it is, is the sweetest thing on earth to look upon.'

'Oh, papa; dear papa!' and she threw her arms round his neck and kissed him.

'But having lived so long with me you have acquired my habits and thoughts, and have learned to disregard utterly your outward appearance.'

'I would be decent and clean and womanly.'

'That is not enough to attract the eyes of men in general. But he has seen deeper than most men do.'

'Into the value of the business, you mean,' said she.

'No, Dolly; I will not have that. That is ill-natured, and as I believe altogether untrue. I think of Mr. Barry that he would not marry any girl for sake of the business, unless he loved her.'

'That is nonsense, papa. How can Mr. Barry love me? Did he and I ever have five minutes of free conversation together?'

'Unless he meant to love would be nearer the mark; and knew that he could do so. You will be quite safe in his hands.'

'Safe, papa!'

'So much for yourself; and now I must say a few words as to myself. You are not bound to marry him, or anyone else, to do me a good turn; but I think you are bound to remember what my feelings would be if on my death-bed I were leaving you quite alone in the world. As far as money is concerned, you would have enough for all your wants; but that is all that you would have. You have become so thoroughly my friend, that you have hardly another real friend in the world.'

'That is my disposition.'

'Yes; but I must guard against the ill effects of that disposition. I know that if some man came the way whom you could in truth love, you would make the sweetest wife that ever a man possessed.'

'Oh, papa, how you talk! No such man will come the way and there's an end of it.'

'Mr. Barry has come the way. And as things go is deserving of your regard. My advice to you is to accept him. Now you will have twenty-four hours to think of that advice, and to think of your own future condition. How will life go with you if you should be left living in this house, all alone?'

'Why do you speak as though we were to be parted tomorrow?'

'Tomorrow or next day,' he said very solemnly. 'The day will surely come before long. Mr. Barry may not be all that your fancy has imagined.'

'Decidedly not.'

'But he has those good qualities which your reason should appreciate. Think it over, my darling. And now we will say nothing more about Mr. Barry till he shall have been here and pleaded his own cause.' Then there was not another word said on the subject between them, and on the next morning Mr. Grey went away to his chambers as usual.

Though she had strenuously opposed her father through the whole of the conversation above given, still as it had gone on, she had resolved to do as he

would have her;—not indeed, that is, to marry this
suitor, but to turn him over in her mind yet once
again, and find out whether it would be possible that
she should do so. She had dismissed him on that
former occasion, and had not since given a thought
to him, except as to a nuisance of which she had so far
rid herself. Now the nuisance had come again, and
she was to endeavour to ascertain how far she could
accustom herself to its perpetual presence, without
incurring perpetual misery. But it has to be acknowledged that she did not begin the enquiry in a fair
frame of mind. She declared to herself that she would
think about it all the night and all the morning without a prejudice, so that she might be able to accept
him if she found it possible. But at the same time,
there was present to her a high, black, stone wall,
at one side of which stood she herself while Mr.
Barry was on the other. That there should be any
clambering over that wall by either of them she felt
to be quite impossible, though at the same time she
acknowledged that a miracle might occur by which
the wall would be removed.

So she began her thinking, and used all her father's
arguments. Mr. Barry was honest and good, and
would not ill-treat her. She knew nothing about him,
but would take all that for granted as though it were
gospel,—because her father had said so. And then
it was to her a fact that she was by no means good-
looking,—the meaning of which was that no other
man would probably want her. Then she remembered her father's words, 'To me your face is the
sweetest thing on earth to look upon.' This she
did believe. Her plainness did not come against her
there. Why should she rob her father of the one
thing which to him was sweet in the world? And to
her, her father was the one noble human being whom
she had ever known. Why should she rob herself of
his daily presence? Then she told herself,—as she
had told him,—that she had never had five minutes'

free conversation with Mr. Barry in her life. That
certainly was no reason why free conversation should
not be commenced. But then she did not believe that
free conversation was within the capacity of Mr.
Barry. It would never come, though she might be
married to him for twenty years. He too might perhaps talk about his business; but there would be none
of those considerations as to radical good or evil
which made the nucleus of all such conversations
with her father. There would be a flatness about it
all which would make any such interchange of words
impossible. It would be as though she had been
married to a log of wood, or rather a beast of the
field, as regarded all sentiment. How much money
would be coming to him? Now her father had never
told her how much money was coming to him. There
had been no allusion to that branch of the subject.

And then there came other thoughts as to that
interior life which it would be her destiny to lead with
Mr. Barry. Then came a black cloud upon her face
as she sat thinking of it. 'Never,' at last she said,
'never, never. He is very foolish not to know that
it is impossible.' The 'he' of whom she then spoke
was her father and not Mr. Barry. 'If I have to be
left alone, I shall not be the first. Others have been
left alone before me. I shall at any rate be left
alone.' Then the wall became higher and more
black than ever. And there was no coming of that
miracle by which it was to be removed. It was
clearer to her than ever that neither of them could
climb it. 'And after all,' she said to herself, 'to
know that your husband is not a gentleman! Ought
that not to be enough? Of course a woman has to
pay for her fastidiousness. Like other luxuries, it is
costly. But then, like other luxuries, it cannot be
laid aside.' So before that morning was gone she
had made up her mind steadily that Mr. Barry should
never be her lord and master.

How could she best make him understand that it was so,—so that she might be quickly rid of him? When the first hour of thinking was done after breakfast, it was that which filled her mind. She was sure that he would not take an answer easily and go. He would have been prepared by her father to persevere, —not by his absolute words, but by his mode of speaking. Her father would have given him to understand that she was still in doubt; and, therefore, might possibly be talked over. She must teach him at once, as well as she could, that such was not her character, and that she had come to a resolution which left him no chance. And she was guilty of one weakness which was almost unworthy of her. When the time came she changed her dress, and put on an old shabby frock, with which she was wont to call upon the Carrolls. Her best dresses were all kept for her father,—and, perhaps, accounted for that opinion, that to his eyes, her face was the sweetest thing on earth to look upon. As she sat there waiting for Mr. Barry, she certainly did look ten years older than her age.

In truth, both Mr. Grey and Dolly had been somewhat mistaken in their reading of Mr. Barry's character. There was more of intellect and merit in him than he had obtained credit for from either of them. He did care very much for the income of the business, and, perhaps, his first idea in looking for Dolly's hand had been the probability that he would thus obtain the whole of that income for himself. But, while wanting money, he wanted also some of the good things which ought to accompany it. A superior intellect,—an intellect slightly superior to his own, of which he did not think meanly, a power of conversation, which he might imitate, and that fineness of thought which, he flattered himself, he might be able to achieve while living with the daughter of a gentleman,—these were the treasures which Mr. Barry hoped to gain by his marriage with Dorothy

Grey. And there had been something in her personal appearance which, to his eyes, had not been distasteful. He did not think her face the sweetest thing in the world to look at, as her father had done; but he saw in it the index of that intellect which he had desired to obtain for himself. As for her dress, that, of course, should all be altered. He imagined that he could easily become so far master of his wife as to make her wear fine clothes without difficulty. But then, he did not know Dolly Grey.

He had studied deeply his manner of attacking her. He would be very humble at first, but after a while his humility should be discontinued, whether she accepted or rejected him. He knew well that it did not become a husband to be humble; and as regarded a lover he thought that humility was merely the outside gloss of love-making. He had been humble enough on the former occasion, and would begin now in the same strain. But, after a while, he would stir himself, and assume the manner of a man. 'Miss Grey,' he said, as soon as they were alone, 'you see that I have been as good as my word, and have come again.' He had already observed her old frock and her mode of dressing up her hair, and had guessed the truth.

'I knew that you were to come, Mr. Barry.'

'Your father has told you so.'

'Yes.'

'And he has spoken a good word in my favour?'

'Yes; he has.'

'Which I trust will be effective.'

'Not at all. He knows that it is the only subject on which I cannot take his advice. I would burn my hand off for my father; but I cannot afford to give it to anyone at his instance. It must be exclusively my own,—unless someone should come very different from those who are likely to ask for it.'

There was something Mr. Barry thought of offence in this, but he could not altogether throw off his humility as yet. 'I quite admit the value of the treasure,' he said.

'There need not be any nonsense between us, Mr. Barry. It has no special value to anyone,—except to myself. But to myself I mean to keep it. At my father's instance I had thought over the proposition you have made me much more seriously than I had thought it possible that I should do.'

'That is not flattering,' he said.

'There is no need for flattery either on the one side or on the other. You had better take that as established. You have done me the honour of wishing for certain reasons that I should be your wife.'

'The common reason,—that I love you.'

'But I am not able to return the feeling, and do not therefore wish that you should be my husband. That sounds to be uncivil.'

'Rather.'

'But I say it in order to make you understand the exact truth. A woman cannot love a man because she feels for him even the most profound respect. She will often do so when there is neither respect or esteem. My father has so spoken of you to me, that I do esteem you; but that has no effect in touching my heart, therefore I cannot become your wife.'

Now, as Mr. Barry thought, had come the time in which he must assert himself. 'Miss Grey,' he said, 'you have probably a long life before you.'

'Long or short it can make no difference.'

'If I understood you aright, you are one who lives very much to yourself.'

'To myself and my father.'

'He is growing in years.'

'So am I for the matter of that. We are all growing in years.'

'Have you looked out for yourself and thought what manner of home yours will be when he shall have been dead and buried?' He paused, but she remained silent, and assumed a special cast of countenance, as though she might say a word if he pressed her, which it would be disagreeable for him to hear. 'When he has gone will you not be very solitary without a husband?'

'No doubt I shall.'

'Had you not better accept one when one comes your way who is not, as he tells you, quite unworthy of you?'

'In spite of such worth solitude would be preferable.'

'You certainly have a knack, Miss Grey, of making the most unpalatable assertions.'

'I will make another more unpalatable. Solitude I could bear,—and death; but not such a marriage. You force me to tell you the whole truth because half a truth will not suffice.'

'I have endeavoured to be at any rate civil to you,' he said.

'And I have endeavoured to save you what trouble I could by being straightforward.' Still he paused, sitting in his chair uneasily, but looking as though he had no intention of going. 'If you will only take me at my word and have done with it!' Still he did not move. 'I suppose there are young ladies who like this kind of thing; but I have become old enough to hate it. I have had very little experience of it, but it is odious to me. I can conceive nothing more disagreeable than to have to sit still and hear a gentleman declare that he wants to make me his wife, when I am quite sure that I do not intend to make him my husband.'

'Then, Miss Grey,' he said, rising from his chair suddenly, 'I shall bid you adieu.'

'Good-bye, Mr. Barry.'

'Good-bye, Miss Grey. Farewell.' And so he went.

'Oh, papa, we have had such a scene!' she said the moment she felt herself alone with her father.

'You have not accepted him?'

'Accepted him! Oh, dear, no! I am sure at this moment he is only thinking how he would cut my throat if he could get hold of me.'

'You must have offended him then very greatly.'

'Oh, mortally! I said everything I possibly could to offend him. But then he would have been here still had I not done so. There was no other way to get rid of him,—or indeed to make him believe that I was in earnest.'

'I am sorry that you should have been so ungracious.'

'Of course I am ungracious. But how can you stand bandying compliments with a man when it is your object to make him know the very truth that is in you? It was your fault, papa. You ought to have understood how very impossible it is that I should marry Mr. Barry.'

Chapter LIII

THE BEGINNING OF THE LAST PLOT

WHEN Mr. Scarborough had written the cheque and sent it to Mr. Grey, he did not utter another word on the subject of gambling. 'Let us make another beginning,' he said, as he told his son to make out another cheque for sixty pounds as his first instalment of the allowance.

'I do not like to take it,' said the son.

'I don't think you need be scrupulous now with me.' That was early in the morning, at their first interview, about ten o'clock. Later on in the day Mr. Scarborough saw his son again, and on this occasion kept him in the room for some time. 'I don't suppose I shall last much longer now,' he said.

'Your voice is as strong as I ever heard it.'

'But unfortunately my body does not keep pace

with my voice. From what Merton says, I don't suppose that there is above a month left.'

'I don't see why Merton is to know.'

'Merton is a good fellow, and if you can do anything for him, do it for my sake.'

'I will.' Then he added, after a pause, 'If things go on as we expect, Augustus can do more for him than I. Why don't you leave him a sum of money?'

Then Miss Scarborough came into the room and hovered about her brother, and fed him, and entreated him to be silent; but when she had gone he went back to the subject. 'I will tell you why, Mountjoy. I have not wished to load my will with other considerations, so that it might be seen that solicitude for you has been in my last moments my only thought. Of course I have done you a deep injury.'

'I think you have.'

'And because you tell me so, I like you all the better. As for Augustus—— But I will not burden my spirit now at the last with uttering curses against my own son.'

'He is not worth it.'

'No; he is not worth it. What a fool he has been not to have understood me better! Now you are not half as clever a fellow as he is.'

'I dare say not.'

'You never read a book, I suppose?'

'I don't pretend to read them, which he does.'

'I don't know anything about that;—but he has been utterly unable to read me. I have poured out my money with open hands for both of you.'

'That is true, sir, certainly, as regards me.'

'And have thought nothing of it. Till it was quite hopeless with you I went on, and would have gone on. As things were then, I was bound to do something to save the property.'

'These poor devils have put themselves out of the running now,' said Mountjoy.

'Yes; Augustus with his suspicions has enabled

us to do that. After all he was quite right with his suspicions.'

'What do you mean by that, sir?'

'Well;—it was natural enough that he should not trust me. I think, too, that perhaps he saw a screw loose where old Grey did not. But he was such an ass, that he could not bring himself to keep on good terms with me for the few months that were left. And then he brought that brute Jones down here, without saying a word to me as to asking my leave. And here he used to remain, hardly ever coming to see me; but waiting for my death from day to day. He is a cold-blooded selfish brute. He certainly takes after neither his father nor his mother. But he will find yet, perhaps, that I am even with him before all is over.'

'I shall try it on with him, sir. I have told you so from the beginning; and now if I have this money it will give me the means of doing so. You ought to know for what purpose I shall use it.'

'That is all settled,' said the father. 'The document properly completed has gone back with the clerk. Were I to die this minute you would find that everything inside the house is your own;—and everything outside except the bare acres. There is a lot of plate with the banker which I have not wanted of late years. And there are a lot of trinkets too;—things which I used to fancy, though I have not cared so much about them lately. And there are a few pictures which are worth money. But the books are the most valuable;—only you do not care for them.'

'I shall not have a house to put them in.'

'There is no saying. What an idiot, what a fool, what a blind unthinking ass Augustus has been!'

'Do you regret it, sir,—that he should not have them and the house too?'

'I regret that my son should have been such a fool! I did not expect that he should love me. I did not even want him to be kind to me. Had he remained away and been silent, that would have been sufficient. But he came here to enjoy himself, as he looked about the park which he thought to be his own, and insulted me because I would not die at once and leave him in possession. And then he was fool enough to make way for you again, and did not perceive that by getting rid of your creditors, he once again put you into a position to be his rival. I don't know whether I hate him most for the hardness of his heart, or despise him for the slowness of his intellect.'

During the time that these words had been spoken, Miss Scarborough had once or twice come into the room, and besought her brother to take some refreshment which she offered him, and then give himself up to rest. But he had refused to be guided by her till he had come to a point in the conversation at which he had found himself thoroughly exhausted. Now she came for the third time, and that period had arrived, so that Mountjoy was told to go about his business, and shoot birds, or hunt foxes in accordance with his natural proclivities. It was then three o'clock on a gloomy December afternoon, and was too late for the shooting of birds; and as for the hunting of foxes the hounds were not in the neighbourhood. So he resolved to go through the house, and look at all those properties which were so soon to become his own. And he at once strolled into the library. This was a long gloomy room which contained perhaps ten thousand volumes, the greater number of which had, in the days of Mountjoy's early youth, been brought together by his own father. And they had been bound in the bindings of modern times, so that the shelves were bright, although the room itself was gloomy. He took out book after book, and told himself with something of sadness in his heart that they were all 'caviare' to him. Then he reminded himself that he was not yet thirty years of age, and that there was surely time enough left for him to make them his companions. He took one at random, and found it to be a volume of Clarendon's History of the Rebellion.* He pitched upon a sentence in which he counted that there were sixteen lines, and when he began to read it, it became to him utterly confused and unintelligible. So he put it back and went to another portion of the room and took down Wither's Hallelujah.* And of this he could make neither head nor tail. He was informed by a heading in the book itself that a piece of poetry was to be sung 'as the ten commandments.' He could not do that, and put the book back again, and declared to himself that further search would be useless. He looked round the room and tried to price the books, and told himself that three or four days at the club might see an end of it all. Then he wandered on into the state drawing-room, an apartment which he had not entered for years, and found that all the furniture was carefully covered. Of what use could it all be to him? unless that it too might be sent to the melting-pot and brought into some short-lived use at the club.

But as he was about to leave the room, he stood for a moment on the rug before the fire-place and looked into the huge mirror which stood there. If the walls might be his, as well as the garnishing of them, and if Florence Mountjoy could come and reign there, then he fancied that they all might be put to a better purpose than that of which he had thought. In earlier days, two or three years ago, at a time which now seemed to him to be very distant, he had regarded Florence as his own, and as such had demanded her hand. In the pride of his birth and position and fashion, he had had no thought of her feelings, and had been imperious. He told himself that it had been so, with much self-condemnation. At any rate he had learned during those months of solitary wandering the power of condemning himself. And now he told himself that if she would yet come he might still learn to sing that song of the old fashioned poet 'as the ten commandments.' At any rate he would endeavour to sing it, as she bade him. He went on through all the bedrooms, remembering, but hardly more than remembering them, as he entered them. 'Oh, Florence! my Florence!' he said, as he passed on. He had done it all for himself, brought down upon his own head this infinite ruin; and for what? He had scarcely ever won, and Tretton was gone from him for ever. But still there might yet be a chance,—if he could abstain from gambling.

And then, when it was dusk within the house, he went out, and passed through the stables, and roamed about the gardens till the evening had altogether set in, and black night had come upon him. Two years ago he had known that he was the heir to it all, though even then that habit was so strong upon him he had felt that his tenure of it would be but slight. But he had then always to tell himself that when his marriage had taken place a great change would be effected. His marriage had not taken place, and the next fatal year had fallen upon him. As long as the inheritance of the estate was certainly his, he could assuredly raise money,—at a certain cost. It was well known that the property was rising in value, and the money had always been forthcoming,—at a tremendous sacrifice. He had excused to himself his recklessness on the ground of his delayed marriage; but still always treating her on the few occasions on which they had met with an imperiousness which had been natural to him. Then the final crash had come, and the estate was as good as gone. But the crash, which had been in truth final, had come afterwards, almost as soon as his father had learned what was to be the fate of Tretton, and he had found himself to be a bastard with a dishonoured mother,—just a nobody in the eyes of the world. And he learned at the same time that Harry Annesley was the lover whom Florence Mountjoy really loved. What had followed has been told already,—perhaps too often.

But at this moment as he stood in the gloom of the night, below the porch in the front of the house, swinging his stick at the top of the big steps, an acknowledgment of contrition was very heavy upon him. Though he was prepared to go to law the moment that Augustus put himself forward as the eldest son, he did recognise how long-suffering his father had been, and how much had been done for him in order if possible to preserve him. And he knew, whatever might be the result of his law-suit, that his father's only purpose had been to save the property for one of them. As it was, legacies which might be valued at perhaps thirty thousand pounds would be his. He would expend it all on the law-suit,—if he could find lawyers to undertake his suit. His anger too against his brother was quite as hot as was that of his father. When he had been obliterated and obliged to vanish, from the joint effects of his violence in the streets, and his inability to pay his gambling debts at the club, he had in an evil moment submitted himself to Augustus. And from that hour Augustus had become to him the most cruel of tyrants. And this tyranny had come to an end with his absolute banishment from his brother's house. Though he had been subdued to obedience in the lowest moment of his fall, he was not the man who could bear such tyranny well. 'I can forgive my father,' he said, 'but Augustus I will never forgive.' Then he went into the house, and in a short time was sitting at dinner with Merton, the young doctor and secretary. Miss Scarborough seldom came to table at that hour, but remained in a room upstairs, close to her brother, so that she might be within call should she be wanted. 'Upon the whole, Merton,' he said, 'what do you think of my father?' The doctor shrugged his shoulders. 'Will he live or will he die?'

'He will die, certainly.'

'Do not joke with me. But I know you would not joke on such a subject. And my question did not merely go to the state of his health. What do you think of him as a man generally? Do you call him an honest man?'

'How am I to answer you?'

'Just the truth.'

'If you will have an answer, I do not consider him an honest man. All this story about your brother is true or is not true. In neither case can one look upon him as honest.'

'Just so.'

'But I think that he has within him a capacity for love, and an unselfishness, which almost atones for his dishonesty. And there is about him a strange dislike to conventionality and to law which is so interesting as to make up the balance. I have always regarded your father as a most excellent man; but thoroughly dishonest. He would rob any-one,—but always to eke out his own gifts to other people. He has therefore to my eyes been most romantic.'

'And as to his health?'

'Ah! as to that I cannot answer so decidedly. He will do nothing because I tell him.'

'Do you mean that you could prolong his life?'

'Certainly I think that I could. He has exerted himself this morning; whereas I have advised him not to exert himself. He could have given himself the same counsel, and would certainly live longer by obeying it than the reverse. As there is no diffi-culty in the matter, there need be no conceit on my part in saying that so far my advice might be of service to him.'

'How long will he live?'

'Who can say? Sir William Brodrick, when that fearful operation was performed in London, thought that a month would see the end of it. That is eight months ago, and he has more vitality now than he had then. For myself I do not think that he can live another month.'

Later on in the evening, Mountjoy Scarborough began again. 'The governor thinks that you have behaved uncommonly well to him.'

'I am paid for it all.'

'But he has not left you anything by his will.'

'I have certainly expected nothing; and there could be no reason why he should.'

'He has entertained an idea of late that he wishes to make what reparation may be possible to me. And, therefore, as he says, he does not choose to burden his will with legacies. There is some provision made for my aunt, who, however, has her own fortune. He has told me to look after you.'

'It will be quite unnecessary,' said Mr. Merton.

'If you choose to cut up rough you can do so. I would propose that we should fix upon some sum which shall be yours at his death;—just as though he had left it to you. Indeed he shall fix the sum himself.' Merton of course said that nothing of the kind would be necessary. But with this understanding Mountjoy Scarborough went that night to bed.

Early on the following morning his father again sent for him. 'Mountjoy,' he said, 'I have thought much about it, and I have changed my mind.'

'About your will?'

'No, not about my will at all. That shall remain as it is. I do not think I should have strength to make another will; nor do I wish to do so.'

'You mean about Merton.'

'I don't mean about Merton at all. Give him five hundred pounds, and he ought to be satisfied. This is a matter of more importance than Mr. Merton;—or even than my will.'

'What is it?' said Mountjoy in a tone of much surprise.

'I do not think I can tell you now. But it is right that you should know that Merton wrote by my instructions to Mr. Grey early this morning, and has implored him to come to Tretton once again. There!

I cannot say more than that now.' Then he turned round on his couch as was his custom, and was unassailable.

Chapter LIV

RUMMELSBURG

MR. SCARBOROUGH had again sent for Mr. Grey, but a couple of weeks passed before he came. At first he refused to come, saying that he would send his clerk down if any work were wanted such as the clerk might do. And the clerk did come and was very useful. But Mr. Scarborough persevered, using arguments which Mr. Grey found himself unable at last to resist. He was dying, and there would soon be an end of it. That was his strongest argument. Then it was alleged that a lawyer of experience was certainly needed, and that Mr. Scarborough could not very well put his affairs into the hands of a stranger. And old friendship was brought up. And then, at last, the squire alleged that there were other secrets to be divulged respecting his family, of which Mr. Scarborough thought that Mr. Grey would approve. What could be the 'other secrets'? But it ended in Mr. Grey assenting to go, in opposition to his daughter's advice. 'I would have nothing more to do with him or his secrets,' Dolly had said.

'You do not know him.'

'I know as much about him as a woman can know of a man she doesn't know; and all from yourself. You have said over and over again that he is a "rascal".'

'Not a rascal. I don't think I said he was a rascal.'

'I believe you used that very word.'

'Then I unsay it. A rascal has something mean about him. Juniper's a rascal.'

'He cares nothing for his word.'

'Nothing at all,—when the law is concerned.'

'And he has defamed his own wife.'

'That was done many years ago.'

'For a fixed purpose, and not from passion,' Dolly continued. 'He is a thoroughly bad man. You have made his will for him, and now I would leave him.' After that Mr. Grey declined for a second time to go. But at last he was persuaded.

On the evening of his arrival he dined with Mountjoy and Merton, and on that occasion Miss Scarborough joined them. Of course there was much surmise as to the cause for this further visit. Merton declared that, as he had acted as the sick man's private secretary, he was bound to keep his secret as far as he knew it. He only surmised what he believed to be the truth, but of that he could say nothing. Miss Scarborough was altogether in the dark. She, and she alone, spoke of her brother with respect, but in that she knew nothing.

'I cannot tell what it is,' said Mountjoy; 'but I suspect it to be something intended for my benefit and for the utter ruin of Augustus.' Miss Scarborough had now retired. 'If it could be possible, I should think that he intended to declare that all he had said before was false.' To this, however, Mr. Grey would not listen. He was very stout in denying the possibility of any reversion of the decision to which they had all come. Augustus was undoubtedly by law his father's eldest son. He had seen with his own eyes copies of the registry of the marriage, which Mr. Barry had gone across the Continent to make. And in that book his wife had signed her maiden name according to the custom of the country. This had been done in the presence of the clergyman and of a gentleman,—a German, then residing on the spot, who had himself been examined, and had stated that the wedding, as a wedding, had been regular in all respects. He was since dead, but the clergyman who had married them was still alive. Within twelve

months of that time Mr. Scarborough and his bride
had arrived in England, and Augustus had been born.
'Nothing but the most indisputable evidence would
have sufficed to prove a fact by which you were so
cruelly wronged,' he said, addressing himself to
Mountjoy. 'And when your father told me that no
wrong could be done to you, as the property was
hopelessly in the hands of the Jews, I told him that
for all purposes of the law, the Jews were as dear to
me as you were. I do say that nothing but the most
certain facts would have convinced me. Such facts,
when made certain, are immovable. If your father
has any plot for robbing Augustus, he will find me as
staunch a friend to Augustus as ever I have been to
you.' When he had so spoken they separated for the
night, and his words had been so strong that they
had altogether affected Mountjoy. If such were his
father's intention, it must be by some further plot
that he endeavoured to carry it out; and in his father's
plots he would put no trust whatever.

And yet he declared his own purpose as he discussed the matter late into the night with Merton.
'I cannot trust Grey at all, nor my father either,
because I do not believe, as Grey believes, this story
of the marriage. My father is so clever, and so resolute in his purpose to set aside all control over the
property as arranged by law, that to my mind it has
all been contrived by himself. Either Mr. Barry has
been squared, or the German parson, or the foreign
gentleman, or more probably all of them. Mr. Grey
himself may have been squared for all I know;—
though he is the kindest-hearted gentleman I ever
came across. Anything shall be more probable to me
than that I am not my father's eldest son.' To all
this Mr. Merton said very little, though no doubt he
had his own ideas.

The next morning the three gentlemen, with Mr.
Grey's clerk, sat down to breakfast solemn and silent.
The clerk had been especially entreated to say no-

thing of what he had learned, and was therefore not
questioned by his master. But in truth he had learned
but little, having spent his time in the sorting and
copying of letters which, though they all bore upon
the subject in hand, told nothing of the real tale.
Further surmises were useless now, as, at eleven
o'clock, Mr. Grey and Mr. Merton were to go up
together to the squire's room. The clerk was to
remain within call, but there would be no need of
Mountjoy. 'I suppose I may as well go to bed,' said
he, 'or up to London, or anywhere.' Mr. Grey very
sententiously advised him at any rate not to go up
to London.

The hour came, and Mr. Grey, with Merton and
the clerk, disappeared upstairs. They were summoned by Miss Scarborough, who seemed to feel
heavily the awful solemnity of the occasion. 'I am
sure he is going to do something very dreadful this
time,' she whispered to Mr. Grey, who seemed himself to be a little awestruck, and did not answer her.

At two o'clock they all met again at lunch, and
Mr. Grey was silent, and in truth very unhappy.
Merton and the clerk were also silent,—as was Miss
Scarborough, silent as death. She indeed knew
nothing, but the other three knew as much as Mr.
Scarborough could or would tell them. Mountjoy
was there also, and in the middle of the meal broke
out violently: 'Why the mischief among you don't
you tell me what it is that my father has said to you?'

'Because I do not believe a word of his story,' said
Mr. Grey.

'Oh, Mr. Grey!' ejaculated Miss Scarborough.

'I do not believe a word of his story,' repeated
Mr. Grey. 'Your father's intelligence is so high,
and his principles so low, that there is no scheme
which he does not think that he cannot carry out
against the established laws of his country. His
present tale is a made-up fable.'

'What do you say, Merton?' asked Mountjoy.

'It looks to me to be true,' said Merton, 'but I am no lawyer.'

'Why don't you tell me what it is?' said Mountjoy.

'I cannot tell you,' said Grey, 'though he commissioned me to do so. Greenwood there will tell you.' Greenwood was the name of the clerk. 'But I advise you to take him with you to your own room. And Mr. Merton would, I am sure, go with you. As for me, it would be impossible that I should do credit in the telling of it to a story of which I do not believe a single word.'

'Am I not to know?' asked Miss Scarborough plaintively.

'Your nephew will tell you,' said Mr. Grey, 'or Mr. Merton;—or Mr. Greenwood can do so if he has permission from Mr. Scarborough. I would rather tell no one. It is to me incredible.' With that he got up and walked away.

'Now, then, Merton,' said Mountjoy, rising from his chair.

'Upon my word I hardly know what to do,' said Merton.

'You must come and tell me this wonderful tale. I suppose that in some way it does affect my interests?'

'It affects your interests very much.'

'Then I think I may say that I certainly shall believe it. My father at present would not wish to do me an injury. It must be told, so come along. Mr. Greenwood had better come also.' Then he left the room, and the two men followed him. They went away to the smoking-room, leaving Mr. Grey with Miss Scarborough.

'Am I to know nothing about it?' said Miss Scarborough.

'Not from me, Miss Scarborough. You can understand that I cannot tell you a story which will require at every word that I should explain my thorough disbelief in your brother. I have been very angry with him, and he has been more energetic than can have been good for him.'

'Oh me, you will have killed him among you!'

'It has been his own doing. You, however, had better go to him. I must return to town this evening.'

'You will stay for dinner?'

'No; I cannot stay for dinner. I cannot sit down with Mountjoy—who has done nothing in the least wrong—because I feel myself to be altogether opposed to his interests. I would rather be out of the house.' So saying, he did leave the house, and went back to London by train that afternoon.

The meeting that morning, which had been very stormy, cannot be given word by word. From the moment in which the squire had declared his purpose, the lawyer had expressed his disbelief in all that was said to him. This Mr. Scarborough had at first taken very kindly, but Mr. Grey clung to his purpose with a pertinacity which had at last beaten down the squire's ill-humour, and had called for the interference of Mr. Merton. 'How can I be quiet,' the squire had said, 'when he tells me that everything I say is a lie?'

'It is a lie!' said Mr. Grey, who had lost all control of himself.

'You should not say that, Mr. Grey,' said Merton.

'He should spare a man on his death-bed, who is endeavouring to do his duty by his children,' said the man who thus declared himself to be dying.

'I will go away,' said Mr. Grey rising. 'He has forced me to come here against my will, and has known,—must have known,—that I should tell him what I thought. Even though a man be dying, a man cannot accept what he says on a matter of business such as this unless he believe him. I must tell him that I believe him or that I do not. I disbelieve the whole story, and will not act upon it as though I believed it. ' But even after this the meeting was continued, Mr. Grey consenting to sit there and to hear what was said to the end.

The purport of Mr. Scarborough's story will probably have been understood by our readers. It was Mr. Scarborough's present intention to make it understood that the scheme intended for the disinheritance of Mountjoy had been false from the beginning to the end, and had been arranged, not for the injury of Mountjoy, but for the salvation of the estate from the hands of the Jews. Mountjoy would have lost nothing, as the property would have gone entirely to the Jews had Mr. Scarborough then died, and Mountjoy been taken as his legitimate heir. He was not anxious, he had declared, to say anything on the present occasion in defence of his conduct in that respect. He would soon be gone, and he would leave men to judge him who might do so the more honestly when they should have found that he had succeeded in paying even the Jews in full the moneys which they had actually advanced. But now things were again changed, and he was bound to go back to the correct order of things.

'No!' shouted Mr. Grey.

'To the correct order of things,' he went on. Mountjoy Scarborough was, he declared, undoubtedly legitimate. And then he made Merton and the clerk bring forth all the papers,—as though he had never brought forth any papers to prove the other statement to Mr. Grey. And he did expect Mr. Grey to believe them. Mr. Grey simply put them all back, metaphorically, with his hand. There had been two marriages, absolutely prepared with the intent of enabling him at some future time to upset the law altogether, if it should seem good to him to do so.

'And your wife!' shouted Mr. Grey.

'Dear woman! She would have done anything that I told her;—unless I had told her to do what was absolutely wrong.'

'Not wrong!'

'Well;—you know what I mean. She was the purest and the best of women.' Then he went on with his tale. There had been two marriages, and he now brought forth all the evidence of the former marriage. It had taken place in a remote town, a village, in the northern part of Prussia, whither she had been taken by her mother to join him. The two ladies had both been since long dead. He had been laid up at the little Prussian town under the plea of a bad leg. He did not scruple to say now that the bad leg had been pretence, and a portion of his scheme. The law, he thought, in endeavouring to make arrangements for his property,—the property which should have been his own,—had sinned so greatly as to drive a wise man to much scheming. He had begun scheming early in the business. But for his bad leg the old lady would not have brought her daughter to be married at so out-of-the-way a place as Rummelsburg* in Pomerania. He had travelled about and found Rummelsburg peculiarly fitted for his enterprise. There was a most civil old Lutheran clergyman there, to whom he had made himself peculiarly acceptable. He had now certified copies of the registry at Rummelsburg, which left no loop-hole for doubt. But he had felt that probably no inquiry would have been made about what had been done thirty years ago at Rummelsburg, had he himself desired to be silent on the subject. 'There will be no difficulty,' he said, 'in making the Rummelsburg marriage known to all the world.'

'I think there will,—very great difficulty,' Mr. Grey had said.

'Not the least. But when I had to be married in the light of day, after Mountjoy's birth, at Nice in Italy, then there was the difficulty. It had to be done in the light of day; and that little traveller with his nurse were with us. Nice was in Italy then,* and some contrivance was, I assure you, necessary. But it was done, and I have always had with me the double sets of certificates. As things have turned up, I have had to keep Mr. Grey altogether in the dark as regards Rummelsburg. It was very difficult; but I have succeeded.'

That Mr. Grey should have been almost driven to madness by such an outrage as this was a matter of course. But he preferred to believe that Rummelsburg and not Nice was the myth. 'How did your wife travel with you during the whole of that year?' he had asked.

'As Mrs. Scarborough, no doubt. But we had been very little in society, and the world at large seemed willing to believe almost anything of me that was wrong. However, there's the Rummelsburg marriage, and if you send to Rummelsburg you'll find that it's all right; a little white church in a corner, with a crooked spire. The old clergyman is, no doubt, dead, but I should imagine that they would keep their registers.' Then he explained how he had travelled about the world with the two sets of certificates, and had made the second public when his object had been to convert Augustus into his eldest son. Many people then had been found who had remembered something of the marriage at Nice, and remembered to have remembered something at the time of having been in possession of some secret as to the lady. But Rummelsburg had been kept quite in the dark. Now it was necessary that a strong light should be thrown on the absolute legality of the Rummelsburg marriage.

He declared that he had more than once made up his mind to destroy those Rummelsburg documents, but had always been deterred by the reflection that when they were once gone, they could not be brought back again. 'I had always intended,' he had said, 'to burn the papers the last thing before my death. But as I learned Augustus's character, I made quite certain by causing them to be sealed up in a parcel addressed to him, so that, if I had died by accident, they might have fallen into proper hands. But I see now the wickedness of my project, and, therefore, I give them over to Mr. Grey.' So saying he tendered the parcel to the attorney.

Mr. Grey, of course, refused to take, or even to touch the Rummelsburg parcel. He then prepared to leave the room, declaring it would be his duty to act on the part of Augustus, should Augustus be pleased to accept his services. But Mr. Scarborough, almost with tears, implored him to change his purpose. 'Why should you set two brothers by the ears?' At this Mr. Grey only shook his head incredulously. 'And why ruin the property without an object?'

'The property will come to ruin.'

'Not if you will take the matter up in the proper spirit. But if you determine to drive one brother to hostility against the other, and promote unnecessary litigation, of course the lawyers will get it all.' Then Mr. Grey left the room, boiling with anger, in that he, with his legal knowledge and determination to do right, had been so utterly thrown aside, while Mr. Scarborough sank exhausted by the efforts he had gone through.

Chapter LV

MR. GREY'S REMORSE

MR. GREY'S feeling as he returned home was chiefly one of self-reproach,—so that, though he persisted in not believing the story which had been told to him, he did in truth believe it. He believed at any rate in Mr. Scarborough. Mr. Scarborough had determined that the property should go hither and thither according to his will, without reference to the established laws of the land, and had carried and would carry his purpose. His object had been to save his estate from the hands of those harpies, the money-lenders, and as far as he was concerned he would have saved it. He had, in fact, forced the money-lenders to lend their money without interest and without security, and then to consent to accept their principal when it was offered to them. No one could say but that the deed when done was a good deed. But this man in doing it had driven his coach and horses through all the laws,—which were to Mr. Grey as Holy Writ; and in thus driving his coach and horses he had forced Mr. Grey to sit upon the box and hold the reins. Mr. Grey had thought himself to be a clever man,—at least a well-instructed man, but Mr. Scarborough had turned him round his finger, this way and that way, just as he had pleased.

Mr. Grey when in his rage he had given the lie to Mr. Scarborough had, no doubt, spoken as he had believed at that moment. To him the new story must have sounded like a lie, as he had been driven to accept the veritable lie as real truth. He had looked into all the circumstances of the marriage at Nice, and had accepted it. He had sent his partner over and had picked up many incidental confirmations. That there had been a marriage at Nice between Mr. Scarborough and the mother of Augustus was certain. He had traced back Mr. Scarborough's movements before the marriage, and could not learn where the lady had joined him who afterwards became his wife. But it had become manifest to him that she had travelled with him, bearing his name. But in Vienna Mr. Barry had learned that Mr. Scarborough had called the lady by her maiden name. He might have learned that he had done so very often at other places; but it had all been done in preparation for the plot in hand,—as had scores of other little tricks which have not cropped up to the surface in this narrative. Mr. Scarborough's whole life had been passed in arranging tricks for the defeat of the law. And it had been his great glory

so to arrange them as to make it impossible that the
law should touch him. Mountjoy had declared that
he had been defrauded. The creditors swore with
many oaths that they had been horribly cheated by
this man. Augustus no doubt would so swear very
loudly. No man could swear more loudly than did
Mr. Grey as he left the squire's chamber after this
last revelation. But there was no one who could
punish him. The money-lenders had no writing
under his hand. Had Mountjoy been begotten without a marriage ceremony, it would have been very
wicked, but the vengeance of the law would not have
reached him. If you deceive your attorney with false
facts he cannot bring you before the magistrates.
Augustus had been the most injured of all; but a son,
though he may bring an action against his father for
bigamy, cannot summon him before any tribunal
because he has married his mother twice over. These
were Mr. Scarborough's death-bed triumphs; but
they were very sore upon Mr. Grey.

On his journey back to town, as he turned the
facts over more coolly in his mind, he began to fear
that he saw a glimmer of the truth. Before he
reached London he almost thought that Mountjoy
would be the heir. He had not brought a scrap of
paper away with him, having absolutely refused to
touch the documents offered to him. He certainly
would not be employed again either by Mr. Scarborough or on behalf of his estate or his executors.
He had threatened that he would take up the cudgels
on behalf of Augustus, and had felt at the moment
that he was bound to do so, because, as he had then
thought, Augustus had the right cause. But as that
idea crumbled away from him, Augustus and his
affairs became more and more distasteful to him.
After all, it ought to be wished that Mountjoy should
become the elder son,—even Mountjoy, the incurable
gambler. It was terrible to Mr. Grey that the old
fixed arrangement should be unfixed, and certainly

there was nothing in the character of Augustus to reconcile him to such a change.

But he was a very unhappy man when he put himself into a cab to be carried down to Fulham. How much better would it have been for him had he taken his daughter's advice and persistently refused in making this last journey to Tretton! He would have to acknowledge to his daughter that Mr. Scarborough had altogether got the better of him, and his unhappiness would consist in the bitterness of that acknowledgment. But when he reached the Manor House his daughter met him with news of her own which for the moment kept his news in abeyance. 'Oh, papa,' she said, 'I am so glad you've come.' He had sent her a telegram to say that he was coming. 'Just when I got your message I was frightened out of my life. Who do you think was here with me?'

'How am I to think, my dear?'

'Mr. Juniper.'

'Who on earth is Mr. Juniper?' he asked. 'Oh, I remember; Amelia's lover.'

'Do you mean to say you forgot Mr. Juniper? I never shall forget him. What a horrid man he is.'

'I never saw Mr. Juniper in my life. What did he want of you?'

'He says you have ruined him utterly. He came here about two o'clock, and found me at work in the garden. He made his way in through the open gate, and would not be sent back though one of the girls told him that there was nobody at home. He had seen me, and I could not turn him out of course.'

'What did he say to you? Was he impudent?'

'He did not insult me if you mean that, but he was impudent in not going away, and I could not get rid of him for an hour. He says that you have doubly ruined him.'

'As how?'

'You would not let Amelia have the fortune that

you promised her, and I think his object now was to get the fortune without the girl. And he said also that he had lent five hundred pounds to your Captain Scarborough.'

'He is not my Captain Scarborough.'

'And that when you were settling the captain's debts, his was the only one you would not pay in full.'

'He is a rogue;—an arrant rogue.'

'But he says that he's got the captain's name to the five hundred pounds; and he means to get it some of these days now that the captain and his father are friends again. The long and the short of it is that he wants five hundred pounds by hook or by crook, and that he thinks you ought to let him have it.'

'He'll get it, or the greater part of it. There's no doubt he'll get it if he has got the captain's name. If I remember right the captain did sign a note for him to that amount. And he'll get the money if he has stuck to it.'

'Do you mean that Captain Scarborough would pay all his debts?'

'He will have to pay that one, because it was not included in the schedule. What do you think has turned up now?'

'Some other scheme?'

'It is all scheming;—base false scheming, to have been concerned with which will be a disgrace to my name for ever!'

'Oh, papa!'

'Yes; for ever. He has told me now, that Mountjoy is his true, legitimate, eldest son. He declares that that story which I have believed for the last eight months has been altogether false and made out of his own brain to suit his own purposes. In order to enable him to defraud these money-lenders he used a plot which he had concocted long since, and boldly declared Augustus to be his heir. He made me believe it, and because I believed it even those greedy grasping men, who would not have given up a tithe of their prey to save the whole family, even they believed it too. Now, at the very point of death, he comes forward with perfect coolness, and tells me that the whole story was a plot made out of his own head.'

'Do you believe him now?'

'I became very wroth, and said that it was a lie. I did think that it was a lie. I did flatter myself that in a matter concerning my own business, and in which I was bound to look after the welfare of others, he could not so have deceived me. But I find myself as a child—as a baby in his hands.'

'Then you do believe him now?'

'I am afraid so. I will never see him again if it be possible for me to avoid him. He has treated me as no one should have treated his enemy; let alone a faithful friend. He must have scoffed and scorned at me merely because I had faith in his word. Who could have thought of a man laying his plots so deeply,—arranging for twenty years past the frauds which he has now executed! For thirty years or nearly his mind has been busy on these schemes, and on others, no doubt, which he has not thought it necessary to execute, and has used me in them simply as a machine. It is impossible that I should forgive him.'

'And what will be the end of it?' she asked.

'Who can say? But this is clear. He has utterly destroyed my character as a lawyer.'

'No; nothing of the kind.'

'And it will be well if he have not done so as a man. Do you think that when people hear that these changes have been made with my assistance they will stop to unravel it all, and to see that I have been only a fool, and not a knave? Can I explain under what stress of entreaty I went down there on this last occasion?'

'Papa, you were quite right to go. He was your old friend, and he was dying.'

Even for this he was grateful. 'Who will judge me as you do; you who persuaded me that I should not have gone? See how the world will use my name. He has made me a party to each of his frauds. He disinherited Mountjoy, and he forced me to believe the evidence he brought. Then, when Mountjoy was nobody, he half paid the creditors by means of my assistance.'

'They got all they were entitled to get.'

'No. Till the law had decided against them they were entitled to their bonds. But they, ruffians though they are, had advanced so much hard money; and I was anxious that they should get their hard money back again. But unless Mountjoy had been illegitimate,—so as to be capable of inheriting nothing,—they would have been cheated;—and they have been cheated. Will it be possible that I should make them or make others think that I have had nothing to do with it? And Augustus, who will be open-mouthed; what will he say against me? In every turn and double of the man's crafty mind I shall be supposed to have turned and doubled with him. I do not mind telling the truth about myself to you.'

'I should hope not.'

'The light that has guided me through my professional life has been a love of the law. As far as my small powers have gone I have wished to preserve it intact. I am sure that the law and justice may be made to run on all-fours. I have been so proud of my country as to make that the rule of my life. The chance has brought me into the position of having for a client a man the passion of whose life has been the very reverse. Who would not say that for any attorney to have such a man as Mr. Scarborough of Tretton for his client, was not a feather in his cap? But I have found him to be not only fraudulent but too clever for me. In opposition to myself he has carried me into his paths.'

'He has never induced you to do anything that was wrong.'

' *"Nil conscire sibi."** That ought to be enough for a simple man. But it is not enough for me. It cannot be enough for a man who intends to act as an attorney for others. Others must know it as well as I myself. You know it. But can I remain an attorney for you only? There are some of whom just the other thing is known; but then they look for work of the other kind. I have never put up a shop-board for sharp practice. After this the sharpest kind of practice will be all that I shall seem to be fit for. It isn't the money. I can retire with enough for your wants and mine. If I could retire amidst the good words of men I should be happy. But even if I retire men will say that I have filled my pockets with plunder from Tretton.'

'That will never be said.'

'Were I to publish an account of the whole affair, —which I am bound in honour not to do,—explaining it all from beginning to end, people would only say that I was endeavouring to lay the whole weight of the guilt upon my confederate who was dead. Why did he pick me out for such usage—me who have been so true to him?'

There was something almost weak, almost feminine in the tone of Mr. Grey's complaints. But to Dolly they were neither feminine nor weak. To her, her father's grief was true and well-founded; but for herself in her own heart there was some joy to be drawn from it. How would it have been with her if the sharp practice had been his, and the success? What would have been her state of mind had she known her father to have conceived these base tricks? Or what would have been her condition had her father been of such a kind as to have taught her that the doing of such tricks should be indifferent to her?

To have been high above them all,—for him and for her,—was not that everything? And was she not sure that the truth would come to light at last? And if not here would not the truth come to light elsewhere where light would be of more avail than here? Such was the consolation with which Dolly consoled herself.

On the next two days Mr. Grey went to his chambers and returned without any new word as to Mr. Scarborough and his affairs. One day he did bring back some tidings as to Juniper. 'Juniper has got into some row about a horse,' he said, 'and is, I fear, in prison. All the same, he'll get his five hundred pounds; and if he knew that fact it would help him.'

'I can't tell him, papa. I don't know where he lives.'

'Perhaps Carroll could do so.'

'I never speak to Mr. Carroll; and I would not willingly mention Juniper's name to my aunt or to either of the girls. It will be better to let Juniper go on in his row.'

'With all my heart,' said Mr. Grey. And then there was an end of that.

On the next morning, the fourth after his return from Tretton, Mr. Grey received a letter from Mountjoy Scarborough. 'He was sure,' he said, 'that Mr. Grey would be sorry to hear that his father had been very weak since Mr. Grey had gone, and unable even to see him (Mountjoy) for more than two or three minutes at a time. He was afraid that all would soon be over; but he and everybody around the squire had been surprised to find how cheerful and high-spirited he was. It seems,' wrote Mountjoy, 'as though he had nothing to regret either as regards this world or the next. He has no remorse, and certainly no fear. Nothing, I think, could make him angry, unless the word "repentance" were mentioned to him. To me and to his sister he is unwontedly affectionate, but Augustus's name has not crossed his lips since you left the house.' Then he went on to the matter as to which his letter had been written. 'What am I to do when all is over with him? It is natural that I should come to you for advice. I will promise nothing about myself, but I trust that I may not return to the gambling-table. If I have this property to manage, I may be able to remain down here without going up to London. But shall I have the property to manage? And what steps am I to take with the view of getting it? Of course I shall have to encounter opposition, but I do not think that you will be one of those to oppose me. I presume that I shall be left here in possession, and that they say is nine points of the law. In the usual way I ought, I presume, simply to do nothing, but merely to take possession. The double story about the two marriages ought to count for nothing. And I should be as though no such plot had ever been hatched. But they have been hatched, and other people know of them. The creditors I presume can do nothing. You have all the bonds in your possession. They may curse and swear, but will, I imagine, have no power. I doubt whether they have a morsel of ground on which to raise a law-suit; for whether I or Augustus be the eldest son, their claims have been satisfied in full. But I presume that Augustus will not sit quiet. What ought I to do in regard to him? As matters stand at present, he will not get a shilling piece. I fear my father is too ill to make another will. But at any rate he will make none in favour of Augustus. Pray tell me what I ought to do. And tell me whether you can send anyone down to assist me when my father shall have gone.'

'I will meddle no farther with anything in which the name of Scarborough is concerned.' Such had been Mr. Grey's first assertion when he received Mountjoy's letter. He would write to him, and tell him that after what had passed there could be nothing of business transacted between him and his father's estate. Nor was he in the position to give any advice on the subjects mooted. He would wash his hands of it altogether. But, as he went home, he thought over the matter, and told himself that it would be impossible for him thus to repudiate the name. He would undertake no law-suit either on behalf of Augustus or of Mountjoy. But he must answer Mountjoy's letter, and tender him some advice.

During the long hours of the subsequent night he discussed the whole matter with his daughter. And the upshot of his discussion was this,—that he would withdraw his name from the business, and leave Mr. Barry to manage it. Mr. Barry might then act for either party as he pleased.

Chapter LVI

SCARBOROUGH'S REVENGE

ALL these things were not done at Tretton altogether unknown to Augustus Scarborough. Tidings as to the will reached him, and then he first perceived the injury he had done himself in lending his assistance to the payment of the creditors. Had his brother been utterly bankrupt, so that the Jews might have seized any money that might have come to him, his father would have left no will in his favour. All that was now intelligible to Augustus. The idea that his father should strip the house of every stick of furniture, and the estate of every chattel upon it, had not occurred to him before the thing was done. He had thought that his father was indifferent to all personal offence, and therefore he had been offensive. He found out his mistake, and therefore was angry with himself. But he still thought that he had been right in regard to the creditors. Had the creditors been left in the possession of their unpaid bonds they would have offered terrible impediments to the taking possession of the property. He had been right then, he thought. The fact was that his father had lived too long. However, the property would be left to him, Augustus, and he must make up his mind to buy the other things from Mountjoy. He at any rate would have to provide the funds out of which Mountjoy must live, and he would take care that he did not buy the chattels twice over. It was thus he consoled himself till rumours of something worse reached his ears.

How the rumours reached him it would be difficult to say. There were probably some among the servants who got an inkling of what the squire was doing when Mr. Grey again came down. Or Miss Scarborough had some confidential friend. Or Mr. Grey's clerk may have been indiscreet. The tidings in some unformed state did reach Augustus and astounded him. His belief in his father's story as to his brother's illegitimacy had been unfixed and doubtful. Latterly it had verged towards more thorough belief as the creditors had taken their money—less than a third of what would have been theirs had the power remained with them of recovering their full debt. The creditors had thus proved their belief, and they were a people not likely to believe such a statement without some foundation. But at any rate he had conceived it to be impossible that his own father should go back from his first story, and again make himself out to be doubly a liar and doubly a knave.

But if it were so what should he do? Was it not the case that in such event he would be altogether ruined, a penniless adventurer with his profession absolutely gone from him? What little money he had got together had been expended on behalf of Mountjoy—a sprat thrown out to catch a whale. Everything according to the present tidings had been left to Mountjoy. He had only half known his father, who had turned against him with virulence, because of his unkindness. Who could have expected that a man in such a condition should have lived so long, and have been capable of a will so powerful? He had not dreamt of a hatred so inveterate as his father's for him.

He received news also from Tretton, that his father was not now expected by anyone to live long. 'It may be a week, the doctors say, and it is hardly possible that he should remain alive for another month.' Such was the news which reached him from his own emissary at Tretton. What had he better do in the emergency of the moment?

There was only one possibly effective step that he could take. He might, of course, remain tranquil, and accept what chance might give him, when his father should have died. But he might at once go down to Tretton and demand an interview with the dying man. He did not think that his father even on his death-bed would refuse to see him. His father's pluck was indomitable, and he thought that he could depend on his own pluck. At any rate he resolved that he would immediately go to Tretton and take his chance. He reached the house about the middle of the day, and at once sent his name up to his father. Miss Scarborough was sitting by her brother's bed-side, and from time to time was reading to him a few words. 'Augustus!' he said, as soon as the servant had left the room. 'What does Augustus want with me? The last time he saw me he bade me die out of hand if I wished to retrieve the injury I had done him.'

'Do not think of that now, John,' his sister said.

'As God is my Judge, I will think of it to the last moment. Words such as those, spoken by a son to his father, demand a little thought. Were I to tell you that I did not think of them, would you not know that I was a hypocrite?'

'You need not speak of them, John.'

'Not unless he came here to harass my last

moments. I strove to do very much for him;—you know with what return. Mountjoy has been, at any rate, honest and straightforward; and, considering all things, not lacking in respect. I shall, at any rate, have some pleasure in letting Augustus know the state of my mind.'

'What shall I say to him?' his sister asked.

'Tell him that he had better go back to London. I have tried them both, as few sons can be tried by their father, and I know them now. Tell him, with my compliments, that it will be better for him not to see me. There can be nothing pleasant said between us. I have no communication to make to him which could in the least interest him.'

But before night came the squire had been talked over, and had agreed to see his son. 'The interview will be easy enough for me,' he had said, 'but I cannot imagine what he will get from it. But let him come as he will.'

Augustus spent much of the intervening time in discussing the matter with his aunt. But not a word on the subject was spoken by him to Mountjoy, whom he met at dinner, and with whom he spent the evening in company with Mr. Merton. The two hours after dinner were melancholy enough. The three adjourned to the smoking-room, and sat there almost without conversation. A few words were said about the hunting, but Mountjoy had not hunted this winter. There were a few also of greater interest about the shooting. The shooting was of course still the property of the old man, and, in the early months, had without many words spoken become as it were an appanage of the condition of life to which Augustus aspired; but of late Mountjoy had assumed the command. 'You found plenty of pheasants here, I suppose,' Augustus remarked.

'Well, yes; not too many. I didn't trouble myself much about it. When I saw a pheasant I shot it. I've been a little troubled in spirit, you know.'

'Gambling again, I heard.'

'That didn't trouble me much. Merton can tell you that we've had a sick house.'

'Yes, indeed,' said Merton. 'It hasn't seemed to be a time in which a man would think very much of his pheasants.'

'I don't know why,' said Augustus, who was determined not to put up with the rebuke implied in the doctor's words. After that there was nothing more said between them till they all went to their separate apartments.

'Don't contradict him,' his aunt said to him the next morning, 'and if he reprimands you, acknowledge that you have been wrong.'

'That's hard, when I haven't been wrong.'

'But so much depends upon it; and he is so stern. Of course, I wish well for both of you. There is plenty enough;—plenty; if only you could agree together.'

'But the injustice of his treatment. Is it true that he now declares Mountjoy to be the eldest son?'

'I believe so. I do not know, but I believe it.'

'Think of what his conduct has been to me. And then you tell me that I am to own that I have been wrong! In what have I been wrong?'

'He is your father, and I suppose you have said hard words to him.'

'Did I rebuke him because he had fraudulently kept me for so many years in the position of a younger son? Did I not forgive him that iniquity?'

'But he says you are a younger son.'

'This last move,' he said, with great passion, 'has only been made in an attempt to punish me, because I would not tell him that I was under a world of obligations to him for simply declaring the truth as to my birth. We cannot both be his eldest son.'

'No, certainly not both.'

'At last he declared that I was his heir. If I did say hard words to him, were they not justified?'

'Not to your father,' said Miss Scarborough, shaking her head.

'That is your idea? How was I to abstain? Think what had been done to me. Through my whole life he had deceived me, and had attempted to rob me.'

'But he says that he had intended to get the property for you.'

'To get it! It was mine. According to what he said it was my own. He had robbed me to give it to Mountjoy. Now he intends to rob me again in order that Mountjoy may have it. He will leave such a kettle of fish behind him, with all his manœuvring, that neither of us will be the better of Tretton.'

Then he went to the squire. In spite of what had passed between him and his aunt he had thought deeply of his conduct to his father in the past, and of the manner in which he would now carry himself. He was aware that he had behaved—not badly, for that he esteemed nothing—but most unwisely. When he had found himself to be the heir to Tretton he had fancied himself to be almost the possessor, and had acted on the instincts which in such a case would have been natural to him. To have pardoned the man because he was his father, and then to have treated him with insolent disdain, as some dying old man, almost entirely beneath his notice, was what he felt the nature of the circumstances demanded. And whether the story was true or false it would have been the same. He had come at last to believe it to be true, and had therefore been the more resolute; but, whether it were true or false, the old man had struck his blow, and must abide by it. Till the moment came in which he had received that communication from Tretton, the idea had never occurred to him that another disposition of the property might still be within his father's power. But he had little known the old man's power, or the fertility of his resources, or the extent of his malice. 'After what you have done you should cease to stay and disturb

us,' he had once said, when his father had jokingly
alluded to his own death. He had at once repented,
and had felt that such a speech had been iniquitous
as coming from a son. But his father had, at the
moment, expressed no deep animosity. Some sarcastic words had fallen from him of which Augustus
had not understood the bitterness. But he had
remembered it since, and was now not so much
surprised at his father's wish to injure him as at
his power.

But could he have any such power? Mr. Grey, he
knew, was on his side, and Mr. Grey was a thorough
lawyer. All the world was on his side, all the world
having been instructed to think and to believe that
Mr. Scarborough had not been married till after
Mountjoy was born. All the world had been much
surprised, and would be unwilling to encounter
another blow. Should he go into his father's room
altogether penitent, or should he hold up his head
and justify himself?

One thing was brought home to him, by thinking,
as a matter of which he might be convinced. No
penitence could now avail him anything. He had at
any rate by this time looked sufficiently into his
father's character to be sure that he would not forgive such an offence as had been his. Any vice, any
extravagance, almost any personal neglect, would
have been pardoned. 'I have so brought him up,'
the father would have said, 'and the fault must be
counted as my own.' But this son had deliberately
expressed a wish for his father's death, and had
expressed it in his father's presence. He had shown
not only neglect, which may arise at a distance, and
may not be absolutely intentional; but these words
had been said with the purpose of wounding, and
were, and would be, unpardonable. Augustus, as he
went along the corridor to his father's room, determined that he would at any rate not be penitent.

'Well, sir, how do you find yourself?' he said,

walking in briskly, and putting out his hand to his father. The old man languidly gave his hand, but only smiled. 'I hear of you, though not from you, and they tell me that you have not been quite so strong of late.'

'I shall soon cease to stay and trouble you,' said the squire, with affected weakness, in a voice hardly above a whisper, using the very words which Augustus had spoken.

'There have been some moments between us, sir, which have been, unfortunately, unpleasant.'

'And yet I have done so much to make them pleasant to you! I should have thought that the offer of all Tretton would have gone for much with you!'

Augustus was again taken in. There was a piteous whine about his father's voice which once more deceived him. He did not dream of the depth of the old man's anger. He did not imagine that at such a moment it could boil over with such ferocity; nor was he altogether aware of the catlike quietude with which he could pave the way for his last spring. Mountjoy, by far the least gifted of the two, had gained the truer insight to his father's character.

'You had done much, or rather, as I supposed, circumstances had done much.'

'Circumstances!'

'The facts, I mean, as to Mountjoy's birth and my own.'

'I have not always left myself to be governed by actual circumstances.'

'If there was any omission on my part of an expression of proper feeling, I regret it.'

'I don't know that there was. What is proper feeling? There was no hypocrisy, at any rate.'

'You sometimes are a little bitter, sir.'

'I hope you won't find it so when I'm gone.'

'I don't know what I said that has angered you; but I may have been driven to say what I did not feel.'

'Certainly not to me.'

'I'm not here to beg pardon for any special fault, as I do not quite know of what I am accused.'

'Of nothing. There is no accusation at all.'

'Nor what the punishment is to be. I have learned that you have left to Mountjoy all the furniture in the house.'

'Yes, poor boy! When I found that you had turned him out.'

'I never turned him out,—not till your house was open to receive him.'

'You would not have wished him to go into the poor-house.'

'I did the very best for him. I kept him going when there was no one else to give him a shilling.'

'He must have had a bitter time,' said the father. 'I hope it may have done him good.'

'I think I behaved to him just as an elder brother should have done. He was not particularly grateful, but that was not my fault.'

'Still I thought it best to leave him the old sticks about the place. As he was to have the property, it was better that he should have the sticks.' As he said this he managed to turn himself round and look his son full in the face. Such a look as it was! There was the gleam of victory, and the glory of triumph, and the venom of malice. 'You wouldn't have them separated, would you?'

'I have heard of some further trick of this kind.'

'Just the ordinary way in which things ought to be allowed to run. Mr. Grey, who is a very good man, persuaded me. No man ought to interfere with the law. An attempt in that direction led to evil. Mountjoy is the eldest son, you know.'

'I know nothing of the kind.'

'Oh, dear, no! there is no question at all as to the date of my marriage with your mother. We were married in quite a straightforward way at Rummelsburg. When I wanted to save the property from

those harpies, I was surprised to find how easily I
managed it. Grey was a little soft there; an excellent
man, but too credulous for a lawyer.'

'I do not believe a word of it.'

'You'll find it all go as naturally as possible when
I have ceased to stay and be troublesome. But one
thing I must say in your favour.'

'What do you mean?'

'I never could have managed it all unless you had
consented to that payment of the creditors. Indeed,
I must say that was chiefly your own doing. When
you first suggested it, I saw what a fine thing you
were contriving for your brother. I should think,
after that, of leaving it all, so that you need not find
out the truth when I am dead. I do think I had so
managed it that you would have had the property.
Mountjoy, who has some foolish feeling about his
mother, and who is obstinate as a pig, would have
fought it out; but I had so contrived that you would
have had it. I had sealed up every document
referring to the Rummelsburg marriage, and had
addressed them all to you. I couldn't have made it
safer, could I?'

'I don't know what you mean.'

'You would have been enabled to destroy every
scrap of the evidence which will be wanted to prove
your brother's legitimacy. Had I burned the papers
I could not have put them more beyond poor Mountjoy's reach. Now they are quite safe, in Mr. Grey's
office; his clerk took them away with him. I would
not leave them here with Mountjoy because,—well,
—you might come, and he might be murdered.'
Now Mr. Scarborough had had his revenge.

'You think you have done your duty,' said
Augustus.

'I do not care two straws about doing my duty,
young man.' Here Mr. Scarborough raised himself
in part, and spoke in that strong voice which was
supposed to be so deleterious to him. 'Or rather, in

seeking my duty, I look beyond the conventionalities
of the world. I think that you have behaved damn-
ably, and that I have punished you. Because of
Mountjoy's weakness, because he had been knocked
off his legs, I endeavoured to put you upon yours.
You at once turned upon me, when you thought the
deed was done, and bade me go—and bury myself.
You were a little too quick in your desire to become
the owner of Tretton Park at once. I have stayed
long enough to give some further trouble. You will
not say, after this, that I am *non compos,** and unable
to make a will. You will find that, under mine, not
one penny piece, not one scrap of property, will
become yours. Mountjoy will take care of you, I do
not doubt. He must hate you, but will recognise
you as his brother. I am not so soft-hearted, and
will not recognise you as my son. Now you may go
away.' So saying, he turned himself round to the
wall, and refused to be induced to utter another word.
Augustus began to speak, but when he had commenced his second sentence, the old man rung his
bell. 'Mary,' said he to his sister, 'will you have the
goodness to get Augustus to go away? I am very
weak, and if he remains he will be the death of me.
He can't get anything by killing me at once; it is too
late for that.'

Then Augustus did leave the room, and before
the night came had left Tretton also. He presumed
there was nothing for him to do there. One word he
did say to Mountjoy: 'You will understand, Mountjoy, that, when our father is dead, Tretton will not
become your property.'

'I shall understand nothing of the kind,' said
Mountjoy, 'but I suppose Mr. Grey will tell me
what I am to do.'

Chapter LVII

MR. PROSPER SHOWS HIS GOOD NATURE

WHILE these things were going on at Tretton, and while Mr. Scarborough was making all arrangements for the adequate disposition of his property,—in doing which he had happily come to the conclusion that there was no necessity for interfering with what the law had settled,—Mr. Prosper was lying very ill at Buston, and was endeavouring on his sick bed to reconcile himself to what the entail had done for him. There could be no other heir to him, but Harry Annesley. As he thought of the unmarried ladies of his acquaintance, he found that there was no one who would have done for him but Miss Puffle and Matilda Thoroughbung. All others were too young or too old, or chiefly penniless. Miss Puffle would have been the exact thing,—only for that intruding farmer's son.

As he lay there alone in his bedroom his mind used to wander a little, and he would send for Matthew, his butler, and hold confidential discussions with him. 'I never did think, sir, that Miss Thoroughbung was exactly the lady,' said Matthew.

'Why not?'

'Well, sir! There is a saying—— But you'll excuse me.'

'Go on, Matthew.'

'There is a saying as how you can't make a silk purse out of a sow's ear.'

'I've heard that.'

'Just so, sir. Now, Miss Thoroughbung is a very nice lady.'

'I don't think she's a nice lady at all.'

'But—— Of course it's not becoming in me to speak against my betters, and as a menial servant I never would.'

'Go on, Matthew.'

'Miss Thoroughbung is——'

'Go on, Matthew.'

'Well. She is a sow's ear. Ain't she, now? The servants here never would have looked upon her as a silk purse.'

'Wouldn't they?'

'Never. She has a way with her, just as though she didn't care for silk purses. And it's my mind, sir, that she don't. She wishes however to be uppermost, and if she had come here she'd have said so.'

'That can never be. Thank God; that can never be!'

'Oh no! Brewers is brewers, and must be. There's Mr. Joe—— He's very well, no doubt.'

'I haven't the pleasure of his acquaintance.'

'Him as is to marry Miss Molly. But Miss Molly ain't the head of the family;—is she, sir?' Here the squire shook his head. 'You're the head of the family, sir.'

'I suppose so.'

'And is—— I might make so bold as to speak.'

'Go on, Matthew.'

'Miss Thoroughbung would be a little out of place at Buston Hall. Now as to Miss Puffle——'

'Miss Puffle is a lady,—or was.'

'No doubt, sir. The Puffles is not quite equal to the Prospers, as I can hear. But the Puffles is ladies, —and gentlemen. The servants below all give it up to them that they're real gentlefolk. But——'

'Well!'

'She demeaned herself terribly with young Tazle-hurst. They all said as there were more where that came from.'

'What should they mean by that?'

'She'd indulge in low 'abits,—such as never would have been put up with at Buston Hall. A-cursing and a-swearing——'

'Miss Puffle!'

'Not herself! I don't say that; but it's like enough if you 'ad heard all. But them as lets others do it almost does it themselves. And them as lets others drink sperrits o' mornings come nigh to having a dram down their own throats.'

'Oh laws!' exclaimed Mr. Prosper, thinking of the escape he had had.

'You wouldn't have liked it, sir, if there had been a bottle of gin in the bedroom.' Here Mr. Prosper hid his face among the bedclothes. 'It ain't all that comes silk out of the skein that does to make a purse of.'

There were difficulties in the pursuit of matrimony of which Mr. Prosper had not thought. His imagination at once pictured to himself a bride with a bottle of gin under her pillow, and he went on shivering till Matthew almost thought that he had been attacked by an ague fit.

'I shall give it up, at any rate,' he said after a pause.

'Of course you're a young man, sir.'

'No, I'm not.'

'That is, not exactly young.'

'You're an old fool to tell such lies.'

'Of course I'm an old fool; but I endeavour to be veracious. I never didn't take a shilling as were yours, nor a shilling's worth, all the years I have known you, Mr. Prosper.'

'What has that to do with it? I'm not a young man.'

'What am I to say, sir? Shall I say as you are middle-aged?'

'The truth is, Matthew, I'm worn out.'

'Then I wouldn't think of taking a wife.'

'Troubles have been too heavy for me to bear. I don't think I was intended to bear trouble.'

'Man is born to trouble as the sparks fly upward,' said Matthew.

'I suppose so. But one man's luck is harder than

another's. They've been too many for me, and I feel
that I'm sinking under them. It's no good my thinking of marrying now.'

'That's what I was coming to when you said I
was an old fool. Of course I am an old fool.'

'Do have done with it. Mr. Harry hasn't been
exactly what he ought to have been to me.'

'He's a very comely young gentleman.'

'What has comely to do with it?'

'Them as is plain-featured is more likely to stay
at home and be quiet. You couldn't expect one as is
so handsome to stay at Buston and hear sermons.'

'I don't expect him to be knocking men about in
the streets at midnight.'

'It ain't that, sir.'

'I say it is that.'

'Very well, sir. Only we've all heard downstairs
as Mr. Harry wasn't him as struck the first blow. It
was all about a young lady.'

'I know what it was about.'

'A young lady as is a young lady.' This was felt
to the quick by Mr. Prosper, in regard to the gin-
drinking Miss Puffle and the brewer-bred Miss
Thoroughbung; but as he was beginning to think
that the continuation of the family of the Prospers
must depend on the marriage which Harry might
make, he passed over the slur upon himself for the
sake of the praise given to the future mother of the
Prospers. 'And when a young gentleman has set his
heart on a young lady he's not going to be braggy-
doshoed out of it.'

'Captain Scarborough knew her first.'

'First come, first served, isn't always the way with
lovers. Mr. Harry was the conquering hero. *"Weni;
widi; wici."'*

'Halloa, Matthew!'

'Them's the words as they say a young gentleman
ought to use when he's got the better of a young
lady's affections; and I dare say they're the very

words as put the captain into such a towering passion. I can understand how it happened, just as if I saw it.'

'But he went away,—and left him bleeding and speechless.'

'He'd knocked his *weni, widi, wici* out of him, I guess. I think, Mr. Prosper, you should forgive him.' Mr. Prosper had thought so too, but had hardly known how to express himself after his second burst of anger. But he was at the present ill and weak, and was anxious to have someone near to him who should be more like a silk purse than his butler, Matthew. 'Suppose you was to send for him, sir.'

'He wouldn't come.'

'Let him alone for coming. They tell me, sir——'

'Who tells you?'

'Why, sir, the servants now at the rectory. Of course, sir, where two families is so near connected, the servants are just as near. It's no more than natural. They tell me now that since you were so kind about the allowance, their talk of you is all changed.' Then the squire's anger was heated hot again. Their talk had all been against him till he had opened his hand in regard to the allowance. And now when there was something again to be got they could be civil. There was none of that love of him for himself for which an old man is always hankering, for which the sick man breaks his heart; but which the old and sick find it so difficult to get from the young and healthy. It is in nature that the old man should keep the purse in his own pocket, or otherwise he will have so little to attract. He is weak, querulous, ugly to look at, apt to be greedy, cross, and untidy. Though he himself can love, what is his love to anyone? Duty demands that one shall smooth his pillow, and someone does smooth it,—as a duty. But the old man feels the difference, and remembers the time when there was one who was anxious to share it. Mr. Prosper was not in years an

old man, and had not as yet passed that time of life
at which many a man is regarded by his children as
the best of their playfellows. But he was weak
in body, self-conscious, and jealous in spirit. He
had the heart to lay out for himself a generous line
of conduct, but not the purpose to stick to it steadily.
His nephew had ever been a trouble to him, because
he had expected from his nephew a kind of worship
to which he had felt that he was entitled as the head
of the family. All good things were to come from
him, and therefore good things should be given to
him. Harry had told himself that his uncle was not
his father, and that it had not been his fault that he
was his uncle's heir. He had not asked his uncle for
an allowance. He had grown up with the feeling that
Buston Hall was to be his own, and had not regarded
his uncle as the donor. His father, with his large
family, had never exacted much,—had wanted no
special attention from him. And if not his father,
then why his uncle? But his inattention, his absence
of gratitude for peculiar gifts, had sunk deep into Mr.
Prosper's bosom. Hence had come Miss Thoroughbung as his last resource, and Miss Thoroughbung
had—called him Peter. Hence his mind had wandered to Miss Puffle, and Miss Puffle had gone off
with the farmer's son, and, as he was now informed,
had taken to drinking gin. Therefore he turned his
face to the wall and prepared himself to die.

On the next day he sent for Matthew again.
Matthew first came to him always in the morning,
but on that occasion very little conversation ever
took place. In the middle of the day he had a bowl
of soup brought to him, and by that time had managed
to drag himself out of bed, and to clothe himself in
his dressing-gown, and to seat himself in his armchair. Then when the soup had been slowly eaten he
would ring his bell, and the conversation would
begin. 'I have been thinking over what I was saying
yesterday, Matthew.' Matthew simply assented; but

he knew in his heart that his master had been thinking over what he himself had said.

'Is Mr. Harry at the rectory?'

'Oh yes! He's there now. He wouldn't stir from the rectory till he hears that you are better.'

'Why shouldn't he stir? Does he mean to say that I'm going to die? Perhaps I am. I'm very weak, but he doesn't know it.'

Matthew felt that he had made a blunder, and that he must get out of it as well as he could. 'It isn't that he is thinking anything of that, but you are confined to your room, sir. Of course he knows that.'

'I never told him.'

'He's most particular in his inquiries,—from day to day.'

'Does he come here?'

'He don't venture on that, because he knows as how you wouldn't wish it.'

'Why shouldn't I wish it? It'd be the most natural thing in the world.'

'But there has been—a little—I'm quite sure Mr. Harry don't wish to intrude. If you'd let me give it to be understood that you'd like him to call, he'd be over here in a jiffy.' Then, very slowly, Mr. Prosper did give it to be understood that he would take it as a compliment if his nephew would walk across the park and ask after him. He was most particular as to the mode in which this embassy should be conducted. Harry was not to be made to think that he was to come rushing into the house after his old fashion. 'Halloa, uncle, aren't you well? Hope you'll be better when I come back! Have got to be off by the next train.' Then he used to fly away and not be heard of again for a week! And yet the message was to be conveyed with an alluring courtesy that might be attractive, and might indicate that no hostility was intended. But it was not to be a positive message; but one which would signify what might possibly take place. If it should happen that

Mr. Harry was walking in this direction, it might also happen that his uncle would be pleased to see him. There was no better ambassador at hand than Matthew, and therefore Matthew was commissioned to arrange matters. 'If you can get at Mrs. Weeks and do it through his mother,' suggested Mr. Prosper. Then Matthew winked and departed on his errand.

In about two hours there was a ring at the back door, of which Mr. Prosper knew well the sound. Miss Thoroughbung had not been there very often, but he had learned to distinguish her ring or her servant's. In old days, not so very far removed, Harry had never been accustomed to ring at all. But yet his uncle knew that it was he, and not the doctor, who might probably come,—or Mr. Soames, of whose coming he lived in hourly dread. 'You can show him up,' he said to Matthew, opening the door with great exertion, and attempting to speak to the servant down the stairs. Harry at any rate was shown up, and in two minutes' time was standing over his uncle's sick chair. 'I have not been quite well just lately,' he said in answer to the inquiries made.

'We are very sorry to hear that, sir.'

'I suppose you've heard it before.'

'We did hear that you were a little out of sorts.'

'Out of sorts! I don't know what you call out of sorts. I have not been out of this room for well nigh a month. My sister came to see me one day, and that's the last Christian I've seen.'

'My mother would be over daily if she fancied you'd like it.'

'She has her own duties, and I don't want to be troublesome.'

'The truth is, Uncle Prosper, that we have all felt that we have been in your black books; and as we have not thought that we deserved it, there has been a little coolness.'

'I told your mother that I was willing to forgive you.'

'Forgive me what? A fellow does not care to be forgiven when he has done nothing. But if you'll only say that bygones shall be bygones quite past I'll take it so.' He could not give up his position as head of the family so easily,—an injured head of the family. And yet he was anxious that bygones should be bygones,—if only the young man would not be so jaunty, as he stood there by his armchair. 'Just say the word and the girls shall come up and see you as they used to do.' Mr. Prosper thought at the moment that one of the girls was going to marry Joe Thoroughbung, and that he would not wish to see her. 'As for myself, if I've been in any way negligent, I can only say that I did not intend it. I do not like to say more, because it would seem as though I were asking you for money.'

'I don't know why you shouldn't ask me.'

'A man doesn't like to do that. But I'd tell you of everything if you'd only let me.'

'What is there to tell?' said Uncle Prosper, knowing well that the love story would be communicated to him.

'I've got myself engaged to marry a young woman.'

'A young woman!'

'Yes;—she's a young woman of course. But she's a young lady as well. You know her name. It is Florence Mountjoy.'

'That is the young lady that I've heard of. Was there not some other gentleman attached to her?'

'There was;—her cousin, Mountjoy Scarborough.'

'His father wrote to me.'

'His father is the meanest fellow I ever met.'

'And he himself came to me,—down here. They were fighting your battle for you.'

'I'm much obliged to them. For I have even interfered with him about the lady.'

Then Harry had to repeat his *veni, vidi, vici* after his own fashion. 'Of course I interfered with him. How is a fellow to help himself. We both of us were spooning on the same girl, and of course she had to decide it.'

'And she decided for you.'

'I fancy she did. At any rate I decided for her, and I mean to have her.'

Then Mr. Prosper was, for him, very gracious in his congratulations, saying all manner of good things of Miss Mountjoy. 'I think you'd like her, Uncle Prosper.' Mr. Prosper did not doubt but that he would 'appease the solicitor.' He also had heard of Miss Mountjoy, and what he had heard had been much to the 'young lady's credit.' Then he asked a few questions as to the time fixed for the marriage. Here Harry was obliged to own that there were difficulties. Miss Mountjoy had promised not to marry for three years without her mother's consent. 'Three years!' said Mr. Prosper. 'Then I shall be dead and buried.' Harry did not tell his uncle that in that case the difficulty might probably vanish, as the same decree of fate which had robbed him of his poor uncle would have made him owner of Buston. In such case as that Mrs. Mountjoy might probably give way.

'But why is the young lady to be kept from marriage for three years? Does she wish it?'

Harry said that he did not exactly think that Miss Mountjoy, on her own behalf, did wish for so prolonged a separation. 'The fact is, sir, that Mrs. Mountjoy is not my best friend. This nephew of hers, Mountjoy Scarborough, has always been her favourite.'

'But he's a man that always loses his money at cards.'

'He's to have all Tretton now, it seems.'

'And what does the young lady say?'

'All Tretton won't move her. I'm not a bit afraid. I've got her word and that's enough for me. How

it is that her mother should think it possible,—
that's what I do not know.'

'The three years are quite fixed.'

'I don't quite say that altogether.'

'But a young lady who will be true to you will be
true to her mother also.' Harry shook his head. He
was quite willing to guarantee Florence's truth as to
her promise to him, but he did not think that her
promise to her mother need be put on the same
footing. 'I shall be very glad if you can arrange it
any other way. Three years is a long time.'

'Quite absurd, you know,' said Harry with energy.

'What made her fix on three years?'

'I don't know how they did it between them.
Mrs. Mountjoy perhaps thought that it might give
time to her nephew. Ten years would be the same
as far as he is concerned. Florence is a girl who,
when she says that she loves a man, means it. For
you don't suppose I intend to remain three years?'

'What do you intend to do?'

'One has to wait a little and see.' Then there was
a long pause, during which Harry stood twiddling
his fingers. He had nothing further to suggest, but
he thought that his uncle might say something.
'Shall I come again tomorrow, Uncle Prosper?' he said.

'I have got a plan,' said Uncle Prosper.

'What is it, uncle?'

'I don't know that it can lead to anything. It's
of no use of course if the young lady will wait the
three years.'

'I don't think she's at all anxious,' said Harry.

'You might marry almost at once.'

'That's what I should like.'

'And come and live here.'

'In this house?'

'Why not? I'm nobody. You'd soon find that I
am nobody.'

'That's nonsense, Uncle Prosper. Of course
you're everybody in your own house.'

'You might endure it for six months in the year.'

Harry thought of the sermons, but resolved at once to face them boldly. 'I am only thinking how generous you are.'

'It's what I mean. I don't know the young lady, and perhaps she mightn't like living with an old gentleman. In regard to the other six months, I'll raise the two hundred and fifty pounds to five hundred pounds. If she thinks well of it, she should come here first and let me see her. She and her mother might both come.' Then there was a pause. 'I should not know how to bear it,—I should not indeed. But let them both come.'

After some further delay this was at last decided on. Harry went away supremely happy and very grateful, and Mr. Prosper was left to meditate on the terrible step he had taken.

Chapter LVIII

MR. SCARBOROUGH'S DEATH

IT is a melancholy fact that Mr. Barry, when he heard the last story from Tretton, began to think that his partner was not so 'wide-awake' as he had hitherto always regarded him. As time runs on, such a result generally takes place in all close connections between the old and the young. Ten years ago Mr. Barry had looked up to Mr. Grey with a trustful respect. Words which fell from Mr. Grey were certainly words of truth, but they were, in Mr. Barry's then estimation, words of wisdom also. Gradually an altered feeling had grown up; and Mr. Barry, though he did not doubt the truth, thought less about it. But he did doubt the wisdom constantly. The wisdom practised under Mr. Barry's vice-management was not quite the same as Mr. Grey's. And Mr. Barry had come to understand that though it might be well to tell the truth on occasions, it was folly to suppose that anyone else would do so. He had always thought that Mr. Grey had gone a little too fast in believing squire Scarborough's first story. 'But you've been to Nice yourself, and discovered that it is true,' Mr. Grey would say. Mr. Barry would shake his head and declare that in having to deal with a man of such varied intellect as Mr. Scarborough, there was no coming at the bottom of a story.

But there had then been no question of any alterations in the mode of conducting the business of the firm. Mr. Grey had been, of course, the partner by whose judgment any question of importance must ultimately be decided; and, though Mr. Barry had been sent to Nice, the Scarborough property was especially in Mr. Grey's branch. He had been loud in declaring the iniquity of his client, but had altogether made up his mind that the iniquity had been practised; and all the clerks in the office had gone with him, trusting to his great character for sober sagacity. And Mr. Grey was not a man who would easily be put out of his high position. The respect generally felt for him was too high; and he carried himself before his partner and clerks too powerfully to lose at once his prestige. But Mr. Barry, when he heard the new story, looked at his own favourite clerk and almost winked an eye; and when he came to discuss the matter with Mr. Grey, he declined even to pretend to be led at once by Mr. Grey's opinion. 'A gentleman who has been so very clever on one occasion may be very clever on another.' That had been his argument. Mr. Grey's reply had simply been to the effect that you cannot twice catch an old bird with chaff. Mr. Barry seemed, however, to think, in discussing the matter with the favourite clerk, that the older the bird became the more often he could be caught with chaff.

Mr. Grey in these days was very unhappy,—not

made so simply by the iniquity of his client, but by the insight which he got into his partner's aptitude for business. He began to have his doubts about Mr. Barry. Mr. Barry was tending towards sharp practice. Mr. Barry was beginning to love his clients, —not with a proper attorney's affection, as his children, but as sheep to be shorn. With Mr. Grey the bills had gone out and had been paid no doubt, and the money had in some shape found its way into Mr. Grey's pockets. But he had never looked at the two things together. Mr. Barry seemed to be thinking of the wool as every client came, or was dismissed. Mr. Grey, as he thought of these things, began to fancy that his own style of business was becoming antiquated. He had said good words of Mr. Barry to his daughter, but just at this period his faith both in himself and in his partner began to fail. His partner was becoming too strong for him, and he felt that he was failing. Things were changed; and he did not love his business as he used to do. He had fancies, and he knew that he had fancies, and that fancies were not good for an attorney. When he saw what was in Mr. Barry's mind as to this new story from Tretton, he became convinced that Dolly was right. Dolly was not fit, he thought, to be Mr. Barry's wife. She might have been the wife of such another as himself, had the partner been such another. But it was not probable that any partner should have been such as he was. 'Old times are changed,' he said to himself; 'old manners gone.' Then he determined that he would put his house in order, and leave the firm. A man cannot leave his work for ever without some touch of melancholy.

But it was necessary that someone should go to Rummelsburg and find what could be learned there. Mr. Grey had sworn that he would have nothing to do with the new story, as soon as the new story had been told to him; but it soon became apparent to him that he must have to do with it. As soon as the

breath should be out of the old squire's body, someone must take possession of Tretton, and Mountjoy
would be left in the house. In accordance with Mr.
Grey's theory, Augustus would be the proper possessor. Augustus no doubt would go down and claim
the ownership,—unless the matter could be decided
to the satisfaction of them both beforehand. Mr.
Grey thought that there was little hope of such
satisfaction; but it would of course be for him or his
firm to see what could be done. 'That I should ever
have got such a piece of business,' he said to himself.
But it was at last settled among them that Mr. Barry
should go to Rummelsburg. He had made the inquiry at Nice, and he would go on with it at Rummelsburg. Mr. Barry started, with Mr. Quaverdale,
of St. John's, the gentleman whom Harry Annesley
had consulted as to the practicability of his earning
money by writing for the press. Mr. Quaverdale
was supposed to be a German scholar, and therefore
had his expenses paid for him, with some bonus for
his time.

A conversation between Mr. Barry and Mr.
Quaverdale, which took place on their way home,
shall be given, as it will be best to describe the result
of their inquiry. This inquiry had been conducted
by Mr. Barry's intelligence, but had owed so much to
Mr. Quaverdale's extensive knowledge of languages,
that the two gentlemen may be said, as they came
home, to be equally well instructed in the affairs
of Mr. Scarborough's property.

'He has been too many for the governor,' said
Barry. Mr. Barry's governor was Mr. Grey.

'It seems to me that Mr. Scarborough is a gentleman who is apt to be too many for most men.'

'The sharpest fellow I ever came across, either in
the way of a cheat or in any other walk of life. If
he wanted anyone else to have the property, he'd
come out with something to show that the entail
itself was all moonshine.'

'But when he married again at Nice, he couldn't
have quarrelled with his eldest son already. The
child was not above four or five months old.' This
came from Quaverdale.

'It's my impression,' said Barry, 'that it was then
his intention to divide the property, and that this was
done as a kind of protest against primogeniture.
Then he found that that would fail,—that if he came
to explain the whole matter to his sons, they would
not consent to be guided by him, and to accept a
division. From what I have seen of both of them,
they are bad to guide after that fashion. Then
Mountjoy got frightfully into the hands of the
money-lenders, and in order to do them it became
necessary that the whole property should go to
Augustus.'

'They must look upon him as a nice sort of old
man,' said Quaverdale.

'Rather! But they have never got at him to speak
a bit of their mind to him. And then how clever he
was in getting round his own younger son. The
property got into such a condition that there was
money enough to pay the Jews the money they had
really lent. Augustus, who was never quite sure of
his father, thought it would be best to disarm them;
and he consented to pay them, getting back all their
bonds. But he was very uncivil to the squire,—told
him that the sooner he died the better, or something
of that sort;—and then the squire immediately turned
round and sprang this Rummelsburg marriage upon
us, and has left every stick about the place to Mountjoy. It must all go to Mountjoy,—every acre, every
horse, every bed, and every book.'

'And these, in twelve months' time, will have been
divided among the card-players of the metropolis,'
said Quaverdale.

'We've got nothing to do with that. If ever a man
did have a lesson he has had it. If he chose to take it,
no man would ever have been saved in so miraculous

a manner. But there can be no doubt that John Scarborough and Ada Sneyd were married at Rummelsburg, and that it will be found to be impossible to unmarry them.'

'Old Mrs. Sneyd, the lady's mother, was then present,' said Quaverdale.

'Not a doubt about it,—and that Fritz Deutchmann was present at the marriage. I almost think that we ought to have brought him away with us. It would have cost a couple of hundred pounds, but the estate can bear that. We can have him by sending for him if we should want it.' Then, after many more words on the same subject and to the same effect, Mr. Barry went on to give his own private opinions. 'In fact, the only blemish in old Scarborough's plans was this;—that the Rummelsburg marriage was sure to come out sooner or later.'

'Do you think so? Fritz Deutchmann is the only one of the party alive, and it's not probable that he would ever have heard of Tretton.'

'These things always do come out. But it does not signify now. And the world will know how godless and reprobate old Scarborough has been; but that will not interfere with Mountjoy's legitimacy. And the world has pretty well understood already that the old man has cared nothing for God or man. It was bad enough according to the other story that he should have kept Augustus so long in the dark, and determined to give it all to a bastard by means of a plot and a fraud. The world has got used to that. The world will simply be amused by this other turn. And as the world generally is not very fond of Augustus Scarborough, and entertains a sort of good-natured pity for Mountjoy, the first marriage will be easily accepted.'

'There'll be a law-suit, I suppose,' said Quaverdale.

'I don't see that they'll have a leg to stand on. When the old man dies the property will be exactly as it would have been. This latter intended fraud in

favour of Augustus will be understood as having
been old Scarborough's farce. The Jews are the party
who have really suffered.'

'And Augustus?'

'He will have lost nothing to which he was by law
entitled. His father might of course make what will
he pleased. If Augustus was uncivil to his father,
his father could of course alter his will. The world
would see all that. But the world will be inclined to
say that these poor money-lenders have been awfully
swindled.'

'The world won't pity them.'

'I'm not so sure. It's a hard case to get hold of
a lot of men and force them to lend you a hundred
thousand pounds without security and without interest. That's what has been done in this case.'

'They'll have no means of recovering anything.'

'Not a shilling. The wonder is that they should
have got the hundred thousand pounds. They never
would have had it unless the squire had wished to
pave the way back for Mountjoy. And then he made
Augustus do it for him! In my mind he has been so
clever that he ought to be forgiven all his rascality.
There had been, too, no punishment for him, and no
probability of punishment. He has done nothing for
which the law can touch him. He has proposed to
cheat people, but before he would have cheated them
he might be dead. The money-lenders will have
been swindled awfully, but they have never had any
ground of tangible complaint against him. "Who
are you?" he has said, "I don't know you." They
alleged that they had lent their money to his eldest
son. "That's as you thought," he replied. "I ain't
bound to come and tell you all the family arrangements about my marriage!" If you look at it all
round it was uncommonly well done.'

When Mr. Barry got back he found that it was
generally admitted at the Chambers that the business
had been well done. Everybody was prepared to

allow that Mr. Scarborough had not left a screw loose in the arrangement,—though he was this moment on his death-bed, and had been under surgical tortures and operations, and, in fact, slowly dying during the whole period that he had been thus busy. Everyone concerned in the matter seemed to admire Mr. Scarborough; except Mr. Grey, whose anger, either with himself or his client, became the stronger, the louder grew the admiration of the world.

A couple of barristers very learned in the law were consulted, and they gave it as their opinion that from the evidence as shown to them there could be no doubt but that Mountjoy was legitimate. There was no reason in the least for doubting it, but for that strange episode which had occurred when, in order to get the better of the law, Mr. Scarborough had declared that at the time of Mountjoy's birth he had not been married. They went on to declare that on the squire's death the Rummelsburg marriage must of course have been discovered, and had given it as their opinion that the squire had never dreamed of doing so great an injustice either to his elder or his younger son. He had simply denied, as they thought, to cheat the money-lenders, and had cheated them beautifully. That Mr. Tyrrwhit should have been so very soft was a marvel to them; but it only showed how very foolish a sharp man of the world might be when he encountered one sharper.

And Augustus, through an attorney acting on his own behalf, consulted two other barristers,—whose joint opinion was not forthcoming quite at once, but may have to be stated. Augustus was declared by them to have received at his father's hands a most irreparable injury, to such an extent that an action for damages would in their opinion lie. He had by accepting his father's first story altered the whole course of his life, abandoned his profession, and even paid large sums of money out of his own pocket for the maintenance of his elder brother. A jury would

probably award him some very considerable sum,—
if a jury could get hold of his father while still living.
No doubt the furniture and other property would
remain, and might be held to be liable for the present
owner's laches.* But these two learned lawyers did
not think that an action could be taken with any
probability of success against the eldest son, with
reference to his tables and chairs, when the Tretton
estates should have become his. As these learned
lawyers had learned that old Mr. Scarborough was at
this moment almost *in articulo mortis*,* would it not
be better that Augustus should apply to his elder
brother to make him such compensation as the peculiarities of the case would demand? But as this
opinion did not reach Augustus till his father was
dead, the first alternative proposed was of no use.

'I suppose, sir, we had better communicate with
Mr. Scarborough,' Mr. Barry said to his partner, on
his return.

'Not in my name,' Mr. Grey replied; 'I've put
Mr. Scarborough in such a state that he is not
allowed to see any business letter. Sir William
Brodrick is there now.' But communications were
made both to Mountjoy and to Augustus. There was
nothing for Mountjoy to do; his case was in Mr.
Barry's hands, nor could he take any steps till something should be done to oust him from Tretton.
Augustus, however, immediately went to work and
employed his counsel, learned in the law.

'You will do something, I suppose, for poor Gus?'
the old man said to his son one morning. It was the
last morning on which he was destined to awake in
the world, and he had been told by Sir William and
by Mr. Merton that it would probably be so. But
death to him had no terror. Life to him, for many
weeks past, had been so laden with pain as to make
him look forward to a release from it with hope. But
the business of life had pressed so hard upon him as
to make him feel that he could not tell what had been

accomplished. The adjustment of such a property as
Tretton required, he thought, his presence, and, till
it had been adjusted, he clung to life with a pertinacity which had seemed to be oppressive. Now
Mountjoy's debts had been paid, and Mountjoy
could be left a bit happier. Having achieved so much,
he was delighted to think that he might. But there
had come latterly a claim upon him equally strong,—
that he should wreak his vengeance upon Augustus.
Had Augustus abused him for keeping him in the
dark so long, he would have borne it patiently. He
had expected as much. But his son had ridiculed him,
laughed at him, made nothing of him, and had at last
told him to die out of the way. He would, at any
rate, do something before he died.

He had had his revenge, very bitter of its kind.
Augustus should be made to feel that he had not been
ridiculous,—not to be laughed at in his last days. He
had ruined his son, inevitably ruined him, and was
about to leave him penniless upon the earth. But
now, in his last moments, in his very last, there came
upon him some feeling of pity, and, in speaking of
his son, he once more called him 'Gus.'

'I don't know how it will all be, sir; but if the
property is to be mine——'

'It will be yours; it must be yours.'

'Then I will do anything for him that he will
accept.'

'Do not let him starve, or have to earn his
bread.'

'Say what you wish, sir, and it shall be done, as
far as I can do it.'

'Make an offer to him of some income, and settle
it on him. Do it at once.' The old man, as he said
this, was thinking probably of the great danger that
all Tretton might before long have been made to
vanish. 'And Mountjoy——'

'Sir.'

'You have gambled surely enough for amusement.

With such a property as this in your hands, gambling becomes very serious.'

They were the last words,—the last intelligible words,—which the old man spoke. He died with his left hand on his son's neck, and Merton and his sister by his side. It was a death-bed not without its lesson, not without a certain charm in the eyes of some fancied beholder. Those who were there seemed to love him well, and should do so.

He had contrived in spite of his great faults to create a respect in the minds of those around him which is itself a great element of love. But there was something in his manner which told of love for others. He was one who could hate to distraction, and on whom no bonds of blood would operate to mitigate his hatred. He would persevere to injure with a terrible persistency. But yet in every phase of his life he had been actuated by love for others. He had never been selfish, thinking always of others rather than of himself. Supremely indifferent he had been to the opinion of the world around him, but he had never run counter to his own conscience. For the conventionalities of the law he entertained a supreme contempt, but he did wish so to arrange matters with which he was himself concerned as to do what justice demanded. Whether he succeeded in the last year of his life the reader may judge. But certainly the three persons who were assembled around his death-bed did respect him, and had been made to love him by what he had done.

Merton wrote the next morning to his friend Henry Annesley respecting the scene. 'The poor old boy has gone at last, and in spite of all his faults I feel as though I had lost an old friend. To me he has been most kind, and did I not know of all his sins I should say that he had been always loyal and always charitable. Mr. Grey condemns him, and all the world must condemn him. One cannot make an apology for him without being ready to throw all truth and all morality to the dogs. But if you can imagine for yourself a state of things in which neither truth nor morality shall be thought essential, then old Mr. Scarborough would be your hero. He was the bravest man I ever knew. He was ready to look all opposition in the face, and prepared to bear it down. And whatever he did he did with the view of accomplishing what he thought to be right for other people. Between him and his God I cannot judge, but he believed in an Almighty One, and certainly went forth to meet Him without a fear in his heart.'

Chapter LIX

JOE THOROUGHBUNG'S WEDDING

WHILE some men die others are marrying. While the funeral dirge was pealing sadly at Tretton, the joyful marriage bells were ringing both at Buntingford and Buston. Joe Thoroughbung, dressed all in his best, was about to carry off Molly Annesley to Rome previous to settling down to a comfortable life of hunting and brewing in his native town. Miss Thoroughbung sent her compliments to Mrs. Annesley. Would her brother be there? She thought it probable that Mr. Prosper would not be glad to see her. She longed to substitute 'Peter' for Mr. Prosper, but abstained. In such case she would deny herself the pleasure of 'seeing Joe turned off.' Then there was an embassy sent to the Hall. The two younger girls went with the object of inviting Uncle Prosper,—but with a desire at their hearts that Uncle Prosper might not come. 'I presume the family at Buntingford will be represented,' Uncle Prosper had asked. 'Somebody will come, I suppose,' said Fanny. Then Uncle Prosper had sent down a pretty jewelled ring, and said that he would remain in his room. His health hardly permitted of his being

present with advantage. So it was decided that Miss
Thoroughbung should come, and everyone felt that
she would be the troubling spirit, if not at the ceremony—at the banquet which would be given afterwards.

Miss Thoroughbung was not the only obstacle,
had the whole been known. Young Soames, the son
of the attorney with whom Mr. Prosper had found it
so evil a thing to have to deal, was to act as Joe's
best man. Mr. Prosper learned this probably from
Matthew, but he never spoke of it to the family. It
was a sad disgrace in his eyes that any Soames should
have been so far mixed up with the Prosper blood.
Young Algy Soames was in himself a very nice sort
of young fellow, who liked a day's hunting when he
could be spared out of his father's office, and whose
worst fault it was that he wore loud cravats. But he
was an abomination to Mr. Prosper,—who had never
seen him. As it was, he carried himself very mildly
on this occasion.

'It's a pity we're not to have two marriages at the
same time,' said Mr. Crabtree, a clerical wag from
the next parish. 'Don't you think so, Mrs. Annesley?'
Mrs. Annesley was standing close by, as was also
Miss Thoroughbung, but she made no answer to the
appeal. People who understood anything knew that
Mrs. Annesley would not be gratified by such an
allusion. But Mr. Crabtree was a man who understood nothing.

'The old birds never pair so readily as the young
ones,' said Miss Thoroughbung.

'Old! Who talks of being old?' said Mr. Crabtree. 'My friend Prosper is quite a boy. There's a
good time coming, and I hope you'll give way yet,
Miss Thoroughbung.'

Then they were all marshalled on their way to
church. It is quite out of my power to describe the
bride's dress,—or those of the bridesmaids. They
were the bride's sisters, and two of his sisters. An

attempt had been made to induce Florence Mountjoy to come down, but it had been unsuccessful. Things had gone so far now at Cheltenham that Mrs. Mountjoy had been driven to acknowledge that, if Florence held to her project for three years, she should be allowed to marry Harry Annesley. But she had accompanied this permission by many absurd restrictions. Florence was not to see him at any rate during the first year. But she was to see Mountjoy Scarborough if he came to Cheltenham. Florence declared this to be impossible, but as the Buston marriage took place just at this moment, she could not have her way in everything. Joe drove up to the church with Algy Soames, it not having been thought discreet that he should enter the parsonage on that morning, though he had been there nearly every day through the winter. 'I declare here he is,' said Miss Thoroughbung, very loudly. 'I never thought he'd have the courage at the last moment.'

'I wonder how a certain gentleman would have felt when it came to his last moment,' said Mr. Crabtree.

Mrs. Annesley took to weeping bitterly, which seemed to be unnecessary, as she had done nothing but congratulate herself since the match had first been made, and had rejoiced greatly that one of her numerous brood should have 'put into such a haven of rest.'

'My dear Mrs. Annesley,' said Mrs. Crabtree, consoling her in that she would not be far removed from her child, 'you can almost see the brewery chimneys from the church tower.' Those who knew the two ladies well were aware that there was some little slur intended by the allusion to brewery chimneys. Mrs. Crabtree's girl had married the third son of Sir Reginald Rattlepate. The Rattlepates were not rich, and the third son was not inclined to earn his bread.

'Thank God, yes!' said Mrs. Annesley through

her tears. 'Whenever I shall see them I shall know that there's an income coming out with the smoke.'

The boys were home from school for the occasion. 'Molly, there's Joe coming after you,' said the elder.

'If he gives you a kiss now you needn't pretend to mind,' said the other.

'My darling,—my own one, that so soon will be my own no longer,' said the father, as he made his way into the vestry to put on his surplice.

'Dear papa!' It was the only word the bride said as she walked in at the church door and prepared to make her way up the nave at the head of her little bevy. They were all very bright as they stood there before the altar, but the brightest spot among them was Algy Soames's blue necktie. Joe for the moment was much depressed, and thought nothing of the last run in which he had distinguished himself;—but nevertheless he held up his head well as a man and a brewer.

'Dont'ee take on so,' Miss Thoroughbung said to Mrs. Annesley at the last moment. 'He'll give her plenty to eat and to drink and will never do her a morsel of harm.' Joe overheard this, and wished that his aunt was back in her bed at Marmaduke Lodge.

Then the marriage was over, and they all trooped into the vestry to sign the book. 'You can't get out of that now,' said Mrs. Crabtree to Joe.

'I don't want. I have got the fairest girl in these parts for my wife, and as I believe the best young woman.' This he said with a spirit for which Mrs. Crabtree had not given him credit, and Algy Soames heard him and admired his friend beneath his blue necktie. And one of the girls heard it, and cried tears of joy as she told her sister afterwards in the bedroom. 'Oh, what a darling he is!' Molly had said amidst her own sobbing. Joe stood an inch higher among them all because of that word.

Then came the breakfast, that dullest, saddest, hour of all. To feed heavily about twelve in the morning is always a nuisance,—a nuisance so abominable that it should be avoided under any other circumstances than a wedding in your own family. But that wedding-breakfast, when it does come, is the worst of all feeding. The smart dresses and bare shoulders seen there by daylight, the handing people in and out among the seats, the very nature of the food, made up of chicken and sweets and flummery, the profusion of champagne, not sometimes of the very best on such an occasion;—and then the speeches! They fall generally to the lot of some middle-aged gentlemen, who seem always to have been selected for their incapacity! But there is a worse trouble yet remaining,—in the unnatural repletion which the sight even of so much food produces, and the fact that your dinner for that day is destroyed utterly and for ever.

Mr. Crabtree and the two fathers made the speeches, over and beyond that which was made by Joe himself. Joe's father was not eloquent. He brewed, no doubt, good beer, without a taste in it beyond malt and hops. No man in the county brewed better beer. But he couldn't make a speech. He got up, dressed in a big white waistcoat, and a face as red as his son's hunting-coat, and said that he hoped his boy would make a good husband. All he could say was that being a lover had not helped to make him a good brewer. Perhaps when Molly Annesley was brought nearer to Buntingford, Joe mightn't spend so much of his time in going to and fro. Perhaps Mr. Joe might not demand so much of her attention. This was the great point he made, and it was received well by all but the bride, who whispered to Joe that if he thought that he was to be among the brewing tubs from morning to night he'd find he was mistaken. Mr. Annesley threw a word or two of feeling into his speech, as is usual with the father of the young lady, but nobody seemed to care much for that. Mr. Crabtree was facetious with the ordinary wedding jests,—as might have been expected, seeing that he had been present at every wedding in the county for the last twenty years. The elderly ladies laughed good-humouredly, and Mrs. Crabtree was heard to say that the whole affair would have been very tame but that Mr. Crabtree had 'carried it all off.' But in truth, when Joe got up the fun of the day had commenced, for Miss Thoroughbung, though she kept her chair, was able to utter as many words as her nephew. 'I'm sure I'm very much obliged to you for what you've all been saying.'

'So you ought, sir, for you have heard more good of yourself than you'll ever hear again.'

'Then I'm the more obliged to you. What my people have said about my being so long upon the road——'

'That's only just what you have told them at the brewery. Nobody knows where you have been.'

'Molly can tell you all about that.'

'I can't tell them anything,' Molly said in a whisper.

'But it comes only once in a man's lifetime,' continued Joe; 'and I dare say if we knew all about the governor when he was of my age, which I don't remember, he was as spooney as anyone.'

'I only saw him once for six months before he was married,' said Mrs. Thoroughbung in a funereal voice.

'He's made up for it since,' said Miss Thoroughbung.

'I'm sure I'm very proud to have got such a young lady to have come and joined her lot with mine,' continued Joe; 'and nobody can think more about his wife's family than I do.'

'And all Buston,' said the aunt.

'Yes, and all Buston.'

'I'm sure we're all sorry that the bride's uncle, from Buston Hall, has not been able to come here to-day. You ought to say that, Joe.'

'Yes, I do say it. I'm very sorry that Mr. Prosper isn't able to be here.'

'Perhaps Miss Thoroughbung can tell us something about him,' said Mr. Crabtree.

'Me! I know nothing special. When I saw him last he was in good health. I did nothing to him to make him keep his bed. Mrs. Crabtree seems to think that I have got your uncle in my keeping. Molly, I beg to say that I'm not responsible.'

It must be allowed that amidst such free conversation it was difficult for Joe to shine as an orator. But as he had no such ambition perhaps the interruptions only served him. But Miss Thoroughbung's witticism did throw a certain damp over the wedding breakfast. It was perhaps to have been expected that the lady should take her revenge for the injury done to her. It was the only revenge that she did take. She had been ill-used, she thought, and yet she had not put Mr. Prosper to a shilling of expense. And there was present to her a feeling that the uncle had at the last moment been debarred from complying with her small requests in favour of Miss Tickle and the ponies on behalf of the young man who was now sitting opposite to her, and that the good things coming from Buston Hall were to be made to flow in the way of the Annesleys generally rather than in her way. She did not regret them very much, and it was not in her nature to be bitter; but still all those little touches about Mr. Prosper were pleasant to her, and were, of course, unpleasant to the Annesleys. Then, it will be said, she should not have come to partake of a breakfast in Mr. Annesley's dining-room. That is a matter of taste, and perhaps Miss Thoroughbung's taste was not altogether refined.

Joe's speech came to an end, and with it his aunt's remarks. But as she left the room she said a few words to Mr. Annesley. 'Don't suppose that I am angry;—not in the least; certainly not with you or Harry. I'd do him a good turn tomorrow if I could; —and so for the matter of that I would to his uncle. But you can't expect but what a woman should have her feelings and express them.' Mr. Annesley, on the other hand, thought it strange that a woman in such a position should express her feelings.

Then at last came the departure. Molly was taken up into her mother's room and cried over for the last time. 'I know that I'm an old fool.'

'Oh, mamma; now, dearest mamma!'

'A good husband is the greatest blessing that God can send a girl, and I do think that he is good and sterling.'

'He is, mamma, he is. I know he is.'

'And when that woman talks about brewery chimneys, I know what a comfort it is that there should be chimneys, and that they should be near. Brewery chimneys are better than a do-nothing scamp that can't earn a meal for himself or his children. And when I see Joe with his pink coat on going to the meet, I thank God that my Molly has got a lad that can work hard, and ride his own horses, and go out hunting with the best of them.'

'Oh! mamma, I do like to see him then. He is handsome.'

'I would not have anything altered. But,— but,—— Oh, my child, you are going away.'

'As Mrs. Crabtree says, I shan't be far.'

'No, no! But you won't be all mine. The time will come when you'll think of your girls in the same way. You haven't done a thing that I haven't seen and known and pondered over; you haven't worn a skirt but what it has been dear to me; you haven't uttered a prayer but what I have heard it as it went up to God's throne. I hope he says his prayers.'

'I'm sure he does,' said Molly, with confidence more or less well founded.

'Now go, and leave me here. I'm such an old stupid that I can't help crying; and if that woman was to say anything more to me about the chimneys I should give her a bit of my mind.'

Then Molly went down with her travelling hat on, looking twice prettier than she had done during the whole of the morning ceremonies. It is, I suppose, on the bridegroom's behalf that the bride is put forth in all her best looks just as she is about to become, for the first time, exclusively his own. Molly on the present occasion was very pretty, and Joe was very proud. It was not the least of his pride that he, feeling himself to be not quite as yet removed from the 'Bung' to the 'Thorough,' had married into a family by which his ascent might be matured.

And then, as they went, came the normal shower of rice, to be picked up in the course of the next hour by the vicarage fowls, and not by the London beggars,* and the air was darkened by a storm of old shoes. In London, white satin slippers are the fashion. But Buston and Buntingford combined could not afford enough of such missiles; and, from the hands of the boys, black shoes, and boots too, were thrown freely. 'There go my best pair,' said one of the boys, as the chariot was driven off, 'and I don't mean to let them lie there.' Then the boots were recovered and taken up to the bedroom.

Now that Molly was gone, Harry's affairs became paramount at Buston. After all, Harry was of superior importance to Molly, though those chimneys at Buntingford could probably give a better income than the acres belonging to the park. But Harry was to be the future Prosper of the county, to assume at some future time the family name; and there was undoubtedly present to them all at the parsonage a feeling that Harry Annesley Prosper would loom in future years a bigger squire than the parish had ever known before. He had got a fellowship, which no Prosper had ever done; and he had the look and tone of a man who had lived in London, which had never belonged to the Prospers generally. And he was to bring a wife, with a good fortune, and one of whom a reputation for many charms had preceded her. And Harry, having been somewhat under a cloud for the last six months, was now emerging from it brighter than ever. Even Uncle Prosper could not do without him. That terrible Miss Thoroughbung had thrown a gloom over Buston Hall, which could only be removed, as the squire himself had felt, by the coming of the natural heir. Harry was indispensable, and was no longer felt by anyone to be a burden.

It was now the end of March. Old Mr. Scarborough was dead and buried, and Mountjoy was living at Tretton. Nothing had been heard of his coming up to London. No rushing to the card-tables had been announced. That there were to be some terribly internecine law contests between him and Augustus had been declared in many circles, but of this nothing was known at the Buston Rectory. Harry had been one day at Cheltenham, and had been allowed to spend the best part of an hour with his sweetheart; but this permission had been given on the understanding that he was not to come again, and now for a month he had abstained. Then had come his uncle's offer, that generous offer under which Harry was to bring his wife to Buston Hall, and live there during half the year; and to receive an increased allowance for his maintenance during the other half. As he thought of his ways and means he fancied that they would be almost rich. She would have four hundred a year, and he as much; and an established home would be provided for them. Of all these good things he had written to Florence, but had not yet seen her since the offer had been made. Her answer had not been as propitious as it might be, and it was absolutely necessary that he should go down to Cheltenham and settle things. The three years had in his imagination been easily reduced to one, which was still as he thought an impossible time for waiting. By degrees it came down to six months in his imagination, and now to three, resulting in an idea that they might be easily married early in June, so as to have the whole of the summer before them for their wedding tour. 'Mother,' he said, 'I shall be off tomorrow.'

'To Cheltenham?'

'Yes, to Cheltenham. What is the good of waiting. I think a girl may be too obedient to her mother.'

'It is a fine feeling, which you will be glad to remember that she possessed.'

'Supposing that you had declared that Molly shouldn't have married Joe Thoroughbung?'

'Molly has got a father,' said Mrs. Annesley.

'Suppose she had none.'

'I cannot suppose anything so horrible.'

'As if you and he had joined together to forbid Molly.'

'But we didn't.'

'I think a girl may carry it too far,' said Harry. 'Mrs. Mountjoy has committed herself to Mountjoy Scarborough, and will not go back from her word. He has again come back to the fore, and out of a ruined man has appeared as the rich proprietor of the town of Tretton. Of course the mother hangs on to him still.'

'You don't think Florence will change?'

'Not in the least. I'm not a bit afraid of Mountjoy Scarborough, and all his property. But I can see that she may be subjected to much annoyance from which I ought to extricate her.'

'What can you do, Harry?'

'Go and tell her so. Make her understand that she should put herself into my hands at once, and that I could protect her.'

'Take her away from her mother by force!' said Mrs. Annesley, with horror.

'If she were once married her mother would think no more about it. I don't believe that Mrs. Mountjoy has any special dislike to me. She thinks of her own nephew, and as long as Florence is Florence Mountjoy there will be for her the chance. I know that he has no chance; and I don't think that I ought to leave her there to be bullied for some endless period of time. Think of three years;—of dooming a girl to live three years without ever seeing her lover! There is an absurdity about it which is revolting. I shall go down tomorrow and see if I cannot put a stop to it.' To this the mother could make no objection, though she could express no approval of a project under which Florence was to be made to marry without her mother's consent.

Chapter LX

MR. SCARBOROUGH IS BURIED

WHEN Mr. Scarborough died, and when he had been buried, his son Mountjoy was left alone at Tretton, living in a very desolate manner. Till the day of the funeral, Merton, the doctor, had remained with him, and his aunt, Miss Scarborough. But when the old squire had been laid in his grave they both departed. Miss Scarborough was afraid of her nephew, and could not look forward to living comfortably at the big house; and Dr. Merton had the general work of his life to call him away. 'You might as well stay for another week,' Mountjoy had said to him. But Merton had felt that he could not remain at Tretton without some especial duty, and he too went his way.

The funeral had been very strange. Augustus had refused to come and stand at his father's grave. 'Considering all things, I had rather decline,' he had written to Mountjoy. Other guests, none were invited, except the tenants. They came in a body, for the squire had been noted among them as a liberal landlord. But a crowd of tenants does not in any way make up that look of family sorrow which is expected at the funeral of such a man as Mr. Scarborough. Mountjoy was there, and stood through the ceremony speechless, and almost sullen. He went down to the church behind the body with Merton, and then walked away from the ground without having uttered a syllable. But during the ceremony he had seen that which had caused him to be sullen. Mr. Samuel Hart had been there, and Mr. Tyrrwhit. And there was a man whom he called to his mind as connected with the names of Evans and Crooke, and Mr. Spicer, and Mr. Richard Juniper. He knew them all as they stood there round the grave, not in decorous funereal array, but as strangers who had strayed into the cemetery. He could not but feel, as he looked at them and they at him, that they had come to look after their interest,—their heavy interest on the money which had been fraudulently repaid to them. He knew that they had parted with their bonds. But he knew also that almost all that was now his would have been theirs, had they not been cheated into believing that he, Mountjoy Scarborough, was not, and never would be, Scarborough of Tretton Park. They said nothing as they stood there, and did not in any way interrupt the ceremony; but they looked at Mountjoy as they were standing, and their looks disconcerted him terribly.

He had declared that he would walk back to the house, which was not above two miles distant from the graveyard, and therefore when the funeral was over there was no carriage to take him. But he knew that the men would dog his steps as he walked. He had only just got within the precincts of the park when he saw them all. But Mr. Tyrrwhit was by himself, and came up to him. 'What are you going to do, Captain Scarborough,' he said, 'as to our claims?'

'You have no claims of which I am aware,' he said roughly.

'Oh, yes! Captain Scarborough; we have claims certainly. You've come up to the front lately with a deal of luck; I don't begrudge it, for one; but I have claims,—I and those other gentlemen; we have claims. You'll have to admit that.'

'Send in the documents. Mr. Barry is acting as my lawyer; he is Mr. Grey's partner, and is now taking the leading share in the business.'

'I know Mr. Barry well; a very sharp gentleman is Mr. Barry.'

'I cannot enter into conversation with yourself at such a time as this.'

'We are sorry to trouble you; but then our interests are so pressing. What do you mean to do, Captain Scarborough? That's the question.'

'Yes; with the estate,' said Mr. Samuel Hart, coming up and joining them. Of the lot of men, Mr. Samuel Hart was the most distasteful to Mountjoy. He had last seen his Jew persecutor at Monaco, and had then, as he thought, been grossly insulted by him. 'What are you hafter, captain?' To this Mountjoy made no answer, but Hart, walking a step or two in advance, turned upon his heels and looked at the park around him. 'Tidy sort of place, ain't it, Tyrrwhit, for a gentleman to hang his 'at up, when we were told he was a bastard, not worth a shilling?'

'I have nothing to do with all that,' said Mountjoy; 'you and Mr. Tyrrwhit held my acceptances for certain sums of money. They have, I believe, been paid in full.'

'No, they ain't; they ain't been paid in full at all; you knows they ain't.' As he said this, Mr. Hart walked on in front, and stood in the pathway, facing Mountjoy. 'How can you 'ave the cheek to say we've been paid in full? You know it ain't true.'

'Evans and Crooke haven't been paid, so far,' said a voice from behind.

'More ain't Spicer,' said another voice.

'Captain Scarborough, I haven't been paid in full,' said Mr. Juniper, advancing to the front. 'You don't mean to tell me that my five hundred pounds have been paid in full. You've ruined me, Captain Scarborough. I was to have been married to a young lady with a large fortune,—your Mr. Grey's niece,—and it has been broken off altogether, because of your bad treatment. Do you mean to assert that I have been paid in full?'

'If you have got any document, take it to Mr. Barry.'

'No, I won't; I won't take it to any lawyer. I'll take it right in before the Court, and expose you. My name is Juniper, and I've never parted with a morsel of paper that has your name to it.'

'Then, no doubt, you'll get your money,' said the captain.

'I thought, gentlemen, you were to allow me to be the spokesman on this occasion,' said Mr. Tyrrwhit. 'We certainly cannot do any good if we attack the captain all at once. Now, Captain Scarborough, we don't want to be uncivil.'

'Uncivil be blowed!' said Mr. Hart; 'I want to get my money, and mean to 'ave it. I agreed as you was to speak, Mr. Tyrrwhit; but I means to be spoken up for; and if no one else can do it, I can do it myself. Is we to have any settlement made to us, or is we to go to law?'

'I can only refer you to Mr. Barry,' said Mountjoy, walking on very rapidly. He thought that when he reached the house he might be able to enter in and leave them out, and he thought also that, if he kept them on the trot, he would thus prevent them from attacking him with many words. Evans and Crooke were already lagging behind, and Mr. Spicer was giving signs of being hard pressed. Even Hart, who was younger than the others, was fat and short, and already showed that he would have to halt if he made many speeches.

'Barry be d——d!' exclaimed Hart.

'You see how it is, Captain Scarborough,' said Tyrrwhit; 'your father, as has just been laid to rest in hopes of a happy resurrection, was a very peculiar gentleman.'

'The most hinfernal swindler I ever 'eard tell of,' said Hart.

'I don't wish to say a word disrespectful,' continued Tyrrwhit, 'but he had his own notions. He said as you was illegitimate,—didn't he now?'

'I can only refer you to Mr. Barry,' said Mountjoy.

'And he said that Mr. Augustus was to have it all; and he proved his words. Didn't he now? And then he made out that, if so, our deeds weren't worth the paper they were written on. Isn't it all true what I'm saying? And then when we'd taken what small sums of money he chose to offer us, just to save ourselves from ruin, then he comes up and says you are the heir, as legitimate as anybody else, and are to have all the property. And he proves that too! What are we to think about it?'

There was nothing left for Mountjoy Scarborough but to make the pace as good as possible. Mr. Hart tried once and again to stop their progress by standing in the captain's path, but could only do this sufficiently at each stoppage to enable him to express his horror with various interjections. 'Oh laws! that such a liar as 'e should ever be buried.'

'You can't do anything by being disrespectful, Mr. Hart,' said Tyrrwhit.

'What—is it—he means—to do?' ejaculated Spicer.

'Mr. Spicer,' said Mountjoy, 'I mean to leave it all in the hands of Mr. Barry; and if you will believe me, no good can be done by any of you by hunting me across the park.'

'Hare you a bastard, or haren't you?' ejaculated Hart.

'No, Mr. Hart, I am not.'

'Then pay us what you h'owes us. You h'ain't h'agoing to say as you don't h'owe us.'

'Mr. Tyrrwhit,' said the captain, 'it is of no use my answering Mr. Hart because he is angry.'

'H'angry! By George! I h'am angry! I'd like to pull that h'old sinner's bones h'out of the ground!'

'But to you I can say that Mr. Barry will be better able to tell you than I am what can be done by me to defend my property.'

'Captain Scarborough,' said Mr. Tyrrwhit mildly, 'we had your name, you know. We did have your name.'

'And my father bought the bonds back.'

'Oh laws! And he calls himself a shentleman!'

'I have nothing further to say to you now, gentlemen, and can only refer you to Mr. Barry.' The path on which they were walking had then brought them to the corner of a garden wall, through which a door opened into the garden. Luckily, at the moment, it occurred to Mountjoy that there was a bolt on the other side of the gate; and he entered in quickly and bolted the door. Mr. Tyrrwhit was left on the other side, and was joined by his companions as quickly as their failing breath enabled them to do so. ''Ere's a go,' said Mr. Hart, striking the door violently with the handle of his stick.

'He had nothing for it but to leave us when we attacked him altogether,' said Mr. Tyrrwhit. 'If you had left it to me he would have told us what he intended to do. You, Mr. Hart, had not so much cause to be angry as you had received a considerable sum for interest.' Then Mr. Hart turned upon Mr. Tyrrwhit, and abused him all the way back to their inn. But it was pleasant to see how these commercial gentlemen, all engaged in the natural course of trade, expressed their violent indignation, not so much as to

their personal losses, but at the commercial dishonesty generally of which the Scarboroughs, father
and son, had been and were about to be guilty.

Mountjoy, when he reached the house of which he
was now the only occupant besides the servants,
stood for an hour in the dining-room with his back
towards the fire, thinking of his position. He had
many things of which to think. In the first place there
were these pseudo-creditors who had just attacked
him in his own park with much acrimony. He endeavoured to comfort himself by telling himself that
they were certainly pseudo-creditors, to whom he
did not in fact owe a penny. Mr. Barry could deal
with them. But then his conscience reminded him
that they had in truth been cheated,—cheated by his
father for his benefit. For every pound which they
had received they would have claimed three or four.
They would no doubt have cheated him. But how
was he now to measure the extent of his father's
fraud against that of his creditors? And though it
would have been right in him to resist the villany of
these Jews, he felt that it was not fit that he should
escape from their fangs altogether by his father's
deceit. He had not become so dead to honour but that
noblesse oblige did still live within his bosom. And yet
there was nothing that he could do to absolve his
bosom. The income of the estate was nearly clear,
the money brought in by the late sales having all but
sufficed to give these gentlemen that which his father
had chosen to pay them. But was he sure of that
income? He had just now asserted boldly that he
was the legitimate heir to the property. But did he
know that he was so? Could he believe his father?
Had not Mr. Grey asserted that he would not accept
this later evidence? Was he not sure that Augustus
intended to proceed against him; and was he not
aware that nothing could be called his own till that
law-suit should have been decided? If that should
be given against him, then these harpies would have

been treated only too well; then there would be no question at any rate by him as to what *noblesse oblige* might require of him! He could take no immediate step in regard to them, and therefore for the moment drove that trouble from his mind.

But what should he do with himself as to his future life? To be persecuted and abused by these wretched men, as had this morning been his fate, would be intolerable. Could he shut himself up from Mr. Samuel Hart and still live in England? And then could he face the clubs,—if the clubs would be kind enough to re-elect him? And then there came a dark frown across his brow, as he bethought himself that even at this moment his heart was longing to be once more among the cards. Could he not escape to Monaco, and there be happy among the gambling-tables? Mr. Hart would surely not follow him there, and he would be free from the surveillance of that double blackguard, his brother's servant and his father's spy.

But, after all, as he declared to himself, did it not altogether turn on the final answer which he might get from Florence Mountjoy? Could Florence be brought to accede to his wishes, he thought that he might still live happily, respectably, and in such a manner that his name might go down to posterity not altogether blasted. If Florence would consent to live at Tretton, then could he remain there. He thought it over as he stood there with his back to the fire, and he told himself that with Florence the first year would be possible, and that after the first year the struggle would cease to be a struggle. He knew himself—he declared, and he made all manner of excuses for his former vicious life, basing them all on the hardness of her treatment of him. He did not know himself, and such assurances were vain. But buoyed up by such assurances, he resolved that his future fate must be in her hands, and that her word alone could suffice either to destroy him or to save him.

Thinking thus of his future life, he resolved that he would go at once to Cheltenham, and throw himself, and what of Tretton belonged to him, at the girl's feet. Nor could he endure himself to rest another night at Tretton till he had done so. He started at once, and got late to Gloucester, where he slept, and on the next morning, at eleven o'clock, was at Cheltenham, out on his way to Montpellier Terrace. He at once asked for Florence, but circumstances so arranged themselves that he first found himself closeted with her mother. Mrs. Mountjoy was delighted and yet shocked to see him. 'My poor brother!' she said; 'and he was buried only yesterday!' Such explanation as Mountjoy could give was given. He soon made the whole tenor of his thoughts intelligible to her. 'Yes; Tretton was his; at least he supposed so. As to his future life he could say nothing. It must depend on Florence. He thought that if she would promise to become at once his wife, there would be no more gambling. He had felt it to be incumbent on him to come and tell her so.'

Mrs. Mountjoy, frightened by the thorough blackness of his apparel, and by the sternness of his manner, had not a word to say to him in opposition. 'Be gentle with her,' she said, as she led the way to the room in which Florence was found. 'Your cousin has come to see you,' she said; 'has come immediately after the funeral. I hope you will be gracious to him.' Then she closed the door, and the two were alone together.

'Florence,' he said.

'Mountjoy! We hardly expected you here so soon.'

'Where the heart strays, the body is apt to follow. I could speak to no one, I could do nothing, I could hope and pray for nothing till I had seen you.'

'You cannot depend on me like that,' she answered.

'I do depend on you most entirely. No human being can depend more thoroughly on another. It is not my fortune that I have come to offer you or simply my love; but in very truth my soul.'

'Mountjoy, that is wicked.'

'Then wicked let it be. It is true. Tretton by singular circumstances is all my own, free of debt. At any rate I and others believe it to be so.'

'Tretton being all your own can make no difference.'

'I told you that I had not come to offer you my fortune.' And he almost scowled at her as he spoke. 'You know what my career has hitherto been; though you do not perhaps know what has driven me to it. Shall I go back, and live after the same fashion, and let Tretton go to the dogs? It will be so unless you take me and Tretton into your hands.'

'It cannot be.'

'Oh, Florence! think of it before you pronounce my doom.'

'It cannot be. I love you well as my cousin, and for your sake I love Tretton also. I would suffer much to save you, if any suffering on my part would be of avail. But it cannot be in that fashion.' Then he scowled again at her. 'Mountjoy, you frighten me by your hard looks, but though you were to kill me you cannot change me. I am the promised wife of Harry Annesley. And for his honour I must bid you plead this cause no more.' Then just at this moment there was a ring at the bell and a knock at the door, each of them somewhat impetuous, and Florence Mountjoy, jumping up with a start, knew that Harry Annesley was there.

Chapter LXI

HARRY ANNESLEY IS ACCEPTED

SHE knew that Harry Annesley was at the door. He had written to say that he must come again, though he had fixed no day for his coming. She had

been delighted to think that he should come, though
she had, after her fashion, scolded him for the
promised visit. But, though his comings had not
been frequent, she recognised already the sounds of
his advent. When a girl really loves her lover, the
very atmosphere tells of his whereabouts. She was
expecting him with almost breathless expectation
when her cousin Mountjoy was brought to her; and
so was her mother, who had been told that Harry
Annesley had business on which he intended to call.
But now the two foes must meet in her presence.
That was the idea which first came upon her. She was
sure that Harry would behave well. Why should not
a favoured lover on such occasions always behave
well? But how would Mountjoy conduct himself,
when brought face to face with his rival? As Florence
thought of it, she remembered that, when last they
met, the quarrel between them had been outrageous.
And Mountjoy had been the sinner, while Harry had
been made to bear the punishment of the sin.

Harry, when he was told that Miss Mountjoy was
at home, had at once walked in and opened for himself the door of the front room downstairs. There he
found Florence and Mountjoy Scarborough. Mrs.
Mountjoy was still upstairs in her bedroom, and was
palpitating with fear, as she thought of the anger
of the two combative lovers. To her belief, Harry
was, of the two, the most like to a roaring lion,
because she had heard of him that he had roared so
dreadfully on that former occasion. But she did
not instantly go down, detained in her bedroom
by the eagerness of her fear, and by the necessity
of resolving how she would behave when she got
there.

Harry, when he entered, stood a moment at the
door, and then, hurrying across the room, offered
Scarborough his hand. 'I have been so sorry,' he
said, 'to hear of your loss; but your father's health
was such that you could not have expected that his

life should be prolonged.' Mountjoy muttered something, but his mutterings, as Florence had observed,
were made in courtesy. And the two men had taken
each other by the hand; after that they could hardly
fly at each other's throats in her presence. Then
Harry crossed to Florence and took her hand. 'I
never get a line from you,' he said, laughing, 'but
what you scold me. I think I escape better when I
am present; so here I am.'

'You always make wicked propositions, and of
course I scold you. A girl has to go on scolding till
she's married, and then it's her turn to get it.'

'No wonder, then, that you talk of three years so
glibly; I want to be able to scold you.'

All this was going on in Mountjoy's presence,
while he stood by, silent, black, and scowling. His
position was very difficult,—that of hearing the billing and cooing of these lovers. But theirs also was
not too easy, which made the billing and cooing
necessary in his presence. Each had to seem to be
natural, but the billing and cooing were in truth
affected. Had he not been there, would they not have
been in each other's arms? and would not she have
made him the proudest man in England, by a loving
kiss? 'I was asking Miss Mountjoy, when you came
in, to be my wife.' This Scarborough said with a
loud voice, looking Harry full in the face.

'It cannot be,' said Florence; 'I told you that, for
his honour,' and she laid her hand on Harry's arm,
'I could listen to no such request.'

'The request has to be made again,' he said.

'It will be made in vain,' said Harry.

'So no doubt you think,' said Captain Scarborough.

'You can ask herself,' said Harry.

'Of course it will be made in vain,' said Florence.
'Does he think that a girl in such a matter as that
of loving a man can be turned here and there at a
moment's notice, that she can say yes and no alter-
nately to two men? It is impossible. Harry Annesley

has chosen me, and I am infinitely happy in his choice.' Here Harry made an attempt to get his arm round her waist, in which, however, she prevented him, seeing the angry passion rising in her cousin's eyes. 'He is to be my husband, I hope. I have told him that I love him,—and I tell you so also. He has my promise, and I cannot take it back without perjury to him, and ruin,—absolute ruin to myself. All my happiness in this world depends on him. He is to me my own, one absolute master, to whom I have given myself altogether, as far as this world goes. Even were he to reject me I could not give myself to another.'

'My Florence! my darling!' Harry exclaimed.

'After having told you so much can you ask your cousin to be untrue to her word, and to her heart,—and to become your wife when her heart is utterly within his keeping? Mountjoy, it is impossible.'

'What of me then?' he said.

'Rouse yourself and love some other girl, and marry her, and so do well with yourself and with your property.'

'You talk of your heart,' he said, 'and you bid me use my own after such fashion as that.'

'A man's heart can be changed, but not a woman's. His love is but one thing among many.'

'It is the one thing,' said Harry. Then the door opened, and Mrs. Mountjoy entered the room.

'Oh dear! oh dear!' she said, 'you both of you here together.'

'Yes; we are both here together,' said Harry.

There was an unfortunate smile on his face as he said so, which made Mountjoy Scarborough very angry. The two men were both handsome, two as handsome men as you shall see on a summer's day. Mountjoy was dark-visaged, with coal-black whiskers and moustaches, with sparkling angry eyes, and every feature of his face well cut and finely formed. But there was absent from him all look of contentment or satisfaction. Harry was light-haired, with long silken beard, and bright eyes, but there was usually present to his face a look of infinite joy, which was comfortable to all beholders. If not strong, as was the other man's, it was happy and eloquent of good temper. But in one thing they were alike,—neither of them counted aught on his good looks. Mountjoy had attempted to domineer by his bad temper, and had failed; but Harry, without any attempt at domineering, always doubting of himself till he had been assured of success by her lips, had succeeded. Now he was very proud of his success; but he was proud of her, and not of himself.

'You come in here and boast of what you have done, in my presence,' said Mountjoy Scarborough.

'How can I not seem to boast when she tells me that she loves me?' said Harry.

'For God's sake do not quarrel here,' said Mrs. Mountjoy.

'They shall not quarrel at all,' said Florence. 'There is no cause for quarrelling. When a girl has given herself away there should be an end of it. No man who knows that she has done so should speak to her again in the way of love. I will leave you now; but Harry,—you must come again, in order that I may tell you that you must not have it all your own way,—just as you please, sir.' Then she gave him her hand, and passing on at once to Mountjoy, tendered her hand to him also. 'You are my cousin, and the head now of my mother's family. I would fain know that you would say a kind word to me, and bid me "God speed."'

He looked at her, but did not take her hand. 'I cannot do it,' he said. 'I cannot bid you "God speed." You have ruined me, trampled upon me, destroyed me. I am not angry with him,' and he pointed across the room to Harry Annesley; 'nor with you; but only with myself.' Then, without speaking a word to his aunt, he marched out of the room, and left the house, closing the front door after him with a loud noise, which testified to his anger.

'He has gone,' said Mrs. Mountjoy, with a tone of deep tragedy.

'It is better so,' said Florence.

'A man must take his chance in such warfare as this,' said Harry. 'There is something about Mountjoy Scarborough that, after all, I like. I do not love Augustus, but with certain faults Mountjoy is a good fellow.'

'He is the head of our family,' said Mrs. Mountjoy, 'and is the owner of Tretton.'

'That has nothing to do with it,' said Florence.

'It has much to do with it,' said her mother, 'though you would never listen to me. I had set my heart upon it, but you have determined to thwart me. And yet there was a time when you preferred him to everyone else.'

'Never,' said Florence with energy.

'Yes; you did;—before Mr. Annesley here came in the way.'

'It was before I came at any rate,' said Harry.

'I was young, and I did not wish to be disobedient. But I never loved him, and I never told him so. Now it is out of the question.'

'He will never come back again,' said Mrs. Mountjoy mournfully.

'I should be very glad to see him back when I and Florence are man and wife. I don't care how soon we should see him.'

'No; he will never come back,' said Florence; 'not as he came to-day. That trouble is at last over. mamma.'

'And my trouble is going to begin.'

'Why should there be any trouble? Harry will not give you trouble;—will you, Harry?'

'Never, I trust,' said Harry.

'He cannot understand,' said Mrs. Mountjoy; 'he knows nothing of the desire and ambition of my life.

I had promised him my child, and my word to him is now broken.'

'He will have known, mamma, that you could not promise for me. Now go, Harry, because we are flurried. May I not ask him to come here tonight and to drink tea with us?' This she said, addressing her mother in a tone of sweetest entreaty. To this Mrs. Mountjoy unwillingly yielded, and then Harry also took his departure.

Florence was aware that she had gained much by the interview of the morning. Even to her it began to appear unnecessary that she should keep Harry waiting three years. She had spoken of postponing the time of her servitude and of preserving for herself the masterdom of her own condition. But in that respect the truth of her own desires was well understood by them all. She was anxious enough to submit to her new master, and now she felt that the time was coming. Her mother had yielded so much, and Mountjoy had yielded. Harry was saying to himself at this very moment that Mountjoy had thrown up the sponge. She, too, was declaring the same thing for her own comfort in less sporting phraseology; and, what was much more to her, her mother had nearly thrown up the sponge also. In the worst days of her troubles any suitor had made himself welcome to her mother who would rescue her child from the fangs of that roaring lion, Harry Annesley. Mr. Anderson had been received with open arms, and even M. Grascour. Mrs. Mountjoy had then got it into her head that of all lions which were about in those days Harry roared the loudest. His sins in regard to leaving poor Mountjoy speechless and motionless on the pavement had filled her with horror. But Florence now felt that all that had come to an end. Not only had Mountjoy gone away, but no mention would probably be ever again made of Anderson or Grascour. When Florence was preparing herself for tea that evening she sang a little song to herself as to the coming of the conquering hero. 'A man must take his chance in such warfare as this,' she said, repeating to herself her lover's words.

'You can't expect me to be very bright,' her mother said to her before Harry came.

There was a sign of yielding in this also; but Florence in her happiness did not wish to make her mother miserable. 'Why not be bright, mamma? Don't you know that Harry is good?'

'No. How am I to know anything about him? He may be utterly penniless.'

'But his uncle has offered to let us live in the house and to give us an income. Mr. Prosper has abandoned all idea of getting married.'

'He can be married any day. And why do you want to live in another man's house when you may live in your own? Tretton is ready for you; the finest mansion in the whole county.' Here Mrs. Mountjoy exaggerated a little, but some exaggeration may be allowed to a lady in her circumstances.

'Mamma, you know that I cannot live at Tretton.'

'It is the house in which I was born.'

'How can that signify? When such things happen they are used as additional grounds for satisfaction. But I cannot marry your nephew because you were born in a certain house. And all that is over now, you know that Mountjoy will not come back again.'

'He would,' exclaims the mother, as though with new hopes.

'Oh, mamma! how can you talk like that? I mean to marry Harry Annesley. You know that I do. Why not make your own girl happy by accepting him?' Then Mrs. Mountjoy left the room and went to her own chamber and cried there, not bitterly, I think, but copiously. Her girl would be the wife of the squire of Buston, who, after all, was not a bad sort of fellow. At any rate he would not gamble. There had always been that terrible drawback. And he was a fellow of his college, in which she would look for and probably would find some compensation as to Tretton. When, therefore, she came down to tea, she was able to receive Harry, not with joy, but at least without rebuke.

Conversation was at first somewhat flat between the two. If the old lady could have been induced to remain upstairs, Harry felt that the evening would have been much more satisfactory. But as it was, he found himself enabled to make some progress. He at once began to address Florence as his undoubted future spouse, very slyly using words adapted for that purpose; and she, without any outburst of her intention,—as she had made when discussing the matter with her cousin,—answered him in the same spirit, and by degrees came so to talk as though the matter were entirely settled. And then, at last, that future day was absolutely brought on the tapis*as though now to be named.

'Three years!' ejaculated Mrs. Mountjoy, as though not even yet surrendering her last hope.

Florence, from the nature of the circumstances, received this in silence. Had it been ten years she might have expostulated. But a young lady's bashfulness was bound to appear satisfied with an assurance of marriage within three years. But it was otherwise with Harry. 'Good G——, Mrs. Mountjoy, we shall all be dead,' he cried out.

Mrs. Mountjoy showed by her countenance that she was extremely shocked. 'Oh, Harry!' said Florence, 'none of us, I hope, will be dead in three years.'

'I shall be a great deal too old to be married, if I am left alive. Three months you mean. It will be just the proper time of year, which does go for something. And three months is always supposed to be long enough to allow a girl to get her new frocks.'

'You know nothing about it, Harry,' said Florence. And so the matter was discussed,—in such a manner that when Harry took his departure that evening he

was half inclined to sing a song of himself about the
conquering hero. 'Dear mamma,' said Florence,
kissing her mother with all the warm clinging affection of former years. It was very pleasant, but still
Mrs. Mountjoy went to her room with a sad heart.

When there she sat for a while over the fire, and
then drew out her desk. She had been beaten,—
absolutely beaten, and it was necessary that she
should own so much in writing to one person. So
she wrote her letter, which was as follows:

'DEAR MOUNTJOY,

'After all it cannot be as I would have had it. As
they say, "Man proposes, but God disposes." I
would have given her to you now, and would even
yet have trusted that you would have treated her well,
had it not been that Mr. Annesley has gained such a
hold upon her affections. She is wilful, as you are,
and I cannot bend her. It has been the longing of
my heart that you two should live together at Tretton. But such longings are, I think, wicked, and are
seldom realised.

'I write now just this one line to tell you that it
is all settled. I have not been strong enough to prevent such a settling. He talks of three months. But
what does it matter? Three months or three years
will be the same to you, and nearly the same to me.

'Your affectionate aunt,

'SARAH MOUNTJOY.'

'P.S.—May I as your loving aunt add one word of
passionate entreaty? All Tretton is yours now, and
the honour of Tretton is within your keeping. Do
not go back to those wretched tables!'

Mountjoy Scarborough when he received this
letter cannot be said to have been made unhappy by
it, because he had already known all his unhappiness.
But he turned it in his mind as though to think what
would now be the best course of life open to him.
And he did think that he had better go back to those

tables against which his aunt had warned him, and there remain till he had made the acres of Tretton utterly disappear. There was nothing for him which seemed to be better. And here at home in England even that would at present be impossible to him. He could not enter the clubs, and elsewhere Samuel Hart would be ever at his heels. And there was his brother with his law-suit,—though on that matter a compromise had already been offered to him. Augustus had proposed to him by his lawyer to share Tretton. He would never share Tretton. His brother should have an income secured to him, but he would keep Tretton in his own hands,—as long as the gambling-tables would allow him.

He was in truth a wretched man, as on that night he did make up his mind, and ringing his bell called his servant out of his bed to bid him prepare everything for a sudden start. He would leave Tretton on the following day, or on the day after, and intended at once to go abroad. 'He is off for that place nigh to Italy where they have the gambling-tables,' said the butler on the following morning to the valet who declared his master's intentions.

'I shouldn't wonder, Mr. Stokes,' said the valet. 'I'm told it's a beauteous country, and I should like to see a little of that sort of life myself.' Alas, alas! Within a week from that time Captain Scarborough might have been seen seated in the Monte Carlo room without any friendly Samuel Hart to stand over him and guard him.

Chapter LXII

THE LAST OF MR. GREY

'I HAVE put in my last appearance at the old chamber in Lincoln's Inn Fields,' said Mr. Grey, on arriving home one day early in June.

'Papa, you don't mean it,' said Dolly.

'I do. Why not one day as well as another? I have made up my mind that it is to be so. I have been thinking of it for the last six weeks. It is done now.'

'But you have not told me.'

'Well, yes; I have told you all that was necessary. It has come now a little sudden; that is all.'

'You will never go back again?'

'Well; I may look in. Mr. Barry will be lord and master.'

'At any rate he won't be my lord and master,' said Dolly, showing by the tone of her voice that the matter had been again discussed by them since the last conversation which was recorded, and had been settled to her father's satisfaction.

'No;—you at least will be left to me. But the fact is, I cannot have any further dealings with the affairs of Mr. Scarborough. The old man who is dead was too many for me. Though I call him old, he was ever so much younger than I am. Barry says he was the best lawyer he ever knew. As things go now a man has to be accounted a fool if he attempts to run straight. Barry does not tell me that I have been a fool, but he clearly thinks so.'

'Do you care what Mr. Barry thinks or says?'

'Yes, I do,—in regard to the professional position which I hold. He is confident that Mountjoy Scarborough is his father's eldest legitimate son, and he believes that the old squire simply was anxious to supersede him to get some cheap arrangement made as to the debts.'

'I suppose that was the case, before.'

'But what am I to think of such a man? Mr. Barry speaks of him almost with affection. How am I to get on with such a man as Mr. Barry?'

'He himself is honest.'

'Well; yes, I believe so. But he does not hate the absolute utter roguery of our own client. And

U 2

that is not quite all. When the story of the Rummels-burg marriage was told I did not believe one word of it, and I said so most strongly. I did not at first believe the story that there had been no such marriage, and I swore to Mr. Scarborough that I would pro-tect Mountjoy and Mountjoy's creditors against any such scheme as that which was intended. Then I was convinced. All the details of the Nice marriage were laid before me. It was manifest that the lady had sub-mitted to be married in a public manner and with all regular forms, while she had a baby as it were in her arms. And I got all the dates. Taking that marriage for granted, Mountjoy was clearly illegitimate, and I was driven so to confess. Then I took up arms on behalf of Augustus. Augustus was a thoroughly bad fellow,—a bully and a tyrant; but he was the eldest son. Then came the question of paying the debts. I thought it a very good thing that the debts should be paid in the proposed fashion. The men were all to get the money they had actually lent, and no better arrangement seemed to be probable. I helped in that, feeling that it was all right. But it was a swindle that I was made to assist in. Of course it was a swindle, if the Rummelsburg marriage be true, and all these creditors think that I have been a party to it. Then I swore that I wouldn't believe the Rummelsburg marriage. But Barry and the rest of them only shake their heads and laugh, and I am told that Mr. Scar-borough was the best lawyer among us!'

'What does it matter? How can that hurt you?' asked Dolly.

'It does hurt me. That is the truth. I have been at my business long enough. Another system has grown up which does not suit me. I feel that they all can put their fingers in my eyes. It may be that I am a fool, and that my idea of honesty is a mistake.'

'No!' shouted Dolly.

'I heard of a rich American the other day who had been poor, and was asked how he had suddenly become so well off. "I found a partner," said the American, "and we went into business together. He had the capital and I had the experience. We just made a change. He has the experience now and I have the capital." When I knew that story I went to strip his coat off the wretch's back; but Mr. Barry would give him a fine fur cloak as a mark of respect. When I find that clever rascals are respectable, I think it is time that I should give up work altogether.'

Thus it was that Mr. Grey left the house of Grey and Barry, driven to premâture retirement by the vices, or rather frauds, of old Mr. Scarborough. When Augustus went to work, which he did immediately on his father's death, to wrest the property from the hands of his brother,—or what part of the property might be possible,—Mr. Grey absolutely declined to have anything to do with the case. Mr. Barry explained how impossible it was that the house, even for its own sake, should absolutely secede from all consideration of the question. Mountjoy had been left in possession, and according to all the evidence now before them was the true owner. Of course he would want a lawyer, and, as Mr. Barry said, would be very well able to pay for what he wanted. It was necessary that the firm should protect themselves against the vindictiveness of Mr. Tyrrwhit and Samuel Hart. Should the firm fail to do so, it would leave itself open to all manner of evil calumnies. The firm had been so long employed on behalf of the Scarboroughs that now, when the old squire was dead, it could not afford to relinquish the business till this final great question had been settled. It was necessary, as Mr. Barry said, that they should see it out, Mr. Barry taking a much more leading part in these discussions than had been his wont. Consequently Mr. Grey had told him that he might do it himself, —and Mr. Barry had been quite contented. Mr. Barry, in talking the matter over with one of the clerks, whom he afterwards took into partnership,

expressed his opinion that 'poor old Grey was altogether off the hooks.' 'Old Grey' had always been
Mr. Grey when spoken of by Mr. Barry till that day,
and the clerk, remarking this, left Mr. Grey's bell
unanswered for three or four minutes. Mr. Grey,
though he was quite willing to shelve himself, understood it all, and knocked them about in the chambers
that afternoon with unwonted severity. He said
nothing about it when he came home that evening;
but the next day was the last on which he took his
accustomed chair.

'What will you do with yourself, papa?' Dolly
said to him the next morning.

'Do with myself?'

'What employment will you take in hand? One
has to think of that, and to live accordingly. If you
would like to turn farmer, we must live in the
country.'

'Certainly I shall not do that. I need not absolutely throw away what money I have saved.'

'Or if you were fond of shooting or hunting?'

'You know very well I never shot a bird and
hardly ever crossed a horse in my life.'

'But you are fond of gardening.'

'Haven't I got garden enough here?'

'Quite enough if you think so; but will there be
occupation sufficient in that to find you employment
for all your life.'

'I shall read.'

'It seems to me,' she said, 'that reading becomes
wearisome as an only pursuit, unless you've made
yourself accustomed to it.'

'Shan't I have as much employment as you?'

'A woman is so different! Darning will get
through an unlimited number of hours. A new set of
underclothing will occupy me for a fortnight. Turning the big girls' dresses over there into frocks for
the little girls is sufficient to keep my mind in employment for a month. Then I have the maidservants

to look after and to guard against their lovers. I have the dinners to provide, and to see that the cook does not give the fragments to the policeman. I have been brought up to do these things, and habit has made them usual occupations to me. I never envied you when you had to encounter all Mr. Scarborough's vagaries; but I knew that they sufficed to give you something to do.'

'They have sufficed,' said he, 'to leave me without anything that I can do.'

'You must not allow yourself to be so left. You must find out some employment.' Then they sat silent for a time, while Mr. Grey occupied himself with some of the numerous papers which it would be necessary that he should hand over to Mr. Barry. 'And now,' said Dolly, 'Mr. Carroll will have gone out, and I will go over to the Terrace. I have to see them every day, and Mr. Carroll has the decency to take himself off to some billiard-table so as to make room for me.'

'What are they doing about that man?' said Mr. Grey.

'About the lover? Mr. Juniper has I fancy made himself extremely disagreeable, not satisfying himself with abusing you and me; but poor aunt as well, and all the girls. He has I fancy got some money of his own.'

'He has had money paid to him by Captain Scarborough; but that I should fancy would rather make him in a good humour than the reverse.'

'He is only in a good humour, I take it, when he has something to get. However, I must be off now, or the legitimate period of Uncle Carroll's absence will be over.'

Mr. Grey, when he was left alone, at once gave up the manipulation of his papers, and throwing himself back into his chair, began to think of that future life of which he had talked so easily to his daughter. What should he do with himself? He believed that he could manage with his books for two hours a day; but even of that he was not sure. He much doubted whether for many years past the time devoted to reading in his own house had amounted to one hour a day. He thought that he could employ himself in the garden for two hours; but that would fail him when there should be hail, or fierce sunshine, or frost, or snow, or rain. Eating and drinking would be much to him; but he could not but look forward to self-reproach if eating and drinking were to be the joy of his life. Then he thought of Dolly's life,—how much purer, and better, and nobler it had been than his own. She talked in a slighting, careless tone of her usual day's work, but how much of her time had been occupied in doing the tasks of others? He knew well that she disliked the Carrolls. She would speak of her own dislike of them as of her great sin, of which it was necessary that she should repent in sackcloth and ashes. But yet how she worked for the family! turning old dresses into new frocks, as though the girls who had worn them, and the children who were to wear them, had been to her her dearest friends. Every day she went across to the house intent upon doing good offices; and this was the repentance in sackcloth and ashes which she exacted from herself. Could not he do as she did? He could not darn Minnie's and Brenda's stockings, but he might do something to make those children more worthy of their cousin's care. He could not associate with his brother-in-law, because he was sure that Mr. Carroll would not endure his society; but he might labour to do something for the reform even of this abominable man. Before Dolly had come back to him he had resolved that he could only redeem his life from the stagnation with which it was threatened by working for others, now that the work of his own life had come to a close. 'Well, Dolly,' he said, as soon as she had entered the room, 'have you heard anything more about Mr. Juniper?'

'Have you been here ever since, papa?'

'Yes, indeed; I used to sit at chambers for six or seven hours at a stretch, almost without getting out of my chair.'

'And are you still employed about those awful papers?'

'I have not looked at them since you left the room.'

'Then you must have been asleep.'

'No, indeed; I have not been asleep. You left me too much to think of to enable me to sleep. What am I to do with myself besides eating and drinking, so that I shall not sleep always, on this side of the grave?'

'There are twenty things, papa,—thirty, fifty, for a man so minded as you are.' This she said trying to comfort him.

'I must endeavour to find one or two of the fifty.' Then he went back to his papers, and really worked hard on that day.

On the following morning, early, he went across to Bolsover Terrace, to begin his task of reproving the Carroll family, without saying a word to Dolly indicative of his purpose. He found that the task would be difficult, and as he went he considered within his mind how best it might be accomplished. He had put a prayerbook in his pocket, without giving it much thought; but before he knocked at the door he had assured himself that the prayerbook would not be of avail. He would not know how to begin to use it, and felt that it would be ridiculed. He must leave that to Dolly or to the clergyman. He could talk to the girls; but they would not care about the affairs of the firm; and, in truth, he did not know what they would care about. With Dolly he could hold sweet converse as long as she would remain with him. But he had been present at the bringing up of Dolly, and did think that gifts had been given to Dolly which had not fallen to the lot of the Carroll girls. 'They all want to be married,' he said to himself, 'and that at any rate is a legitimate desire.'

With this he knocked at the door, and when it was opened by Sophia, he found an old gentleman with black cotton gloves and a doubtful white cravat just preparing for his departure. There was Amelia, then giving him his hat and looking as pure and proper as though she had never been winked at by Prince Chitakov. Then the mother came through from the parlour into the passage. 'Oh, John!—how very kind of you to come. Mr. Matterson, pray let me introduce you to my brother, Mr. Grey. John, this is the Rev. Mr. Matterson, a clergyman who is a very intimate friend of Amelia.'

'Me! ma! Why me in particular?'

'Well, my dear, because it is so. I suppose it is so because Mr. Matterson likes you the best.'

'Laws, ma; what nonsense.' Mr. Matterson appeared to be a very shy gentleman, and only anxious to escape from the hall door. But Mr. Grey remembered that in former days, before the coming of Mr. Juniper upon the scene, he had heard of a clerical admirer. He had been told that the gentleman's name was Matterson, that he was not very young nor very rich, that he had five or six children, and that he could afford to marry if the wife could bring with her about one hundred pounds a year. He had not then thought much of Mr. Matterson, and no direct appeal had been made to him. After that Mr. Juniper had come forward, and then Mr. Juniper had been altogether abolished. But it occurred to Mr. Grey, that Mr. Matterson was at any rate better than Mr. Juniper; that he was by profession a gentleman, and that here might be a beginning of those good deeds by which he was anxious to make the evening of his days bearable to himself.

'I am delighted to make Mr. Matterson's acquaintance,' he said, as that old gentleman scrambled out of the door.

Then his sister took him by the arm and led him
at once into the parlour. 'You might as well come
and hear what I have to say, Amelia.' So the daughter
followed them in. 'He is the most praiseworthy
gentleman you ever knew, John,' began Mrs. Carroll.

'A clergyman, I think.'

'Oh, yes! he is in orders,—in priest's orders,' said
Mrs. Carroll, meaning to make the most of Mr.
Matterson. 'He has a church over at Putney.'

'I am glad of that,' said Mr. Grey.

'Yes, indeed; though it isn't very good, because
it's only a curate's one hundred and fifty pounds! Yes!
he does have one hundred and fifty pounds, and something out of the surplice fees.'

'Another one hundred pounds I believe it is,' said
Amelia.

'Not quite so much as that, my dear, but it is
something.'

'He is a widower with children, I believe,' said
Mr. Grey.

'There are children,—five of them; the prettiest
little dears one ever saw. The eldest is just about
thirteen.' This was a fib, because Mrs. Carroll knew
that the eldest boy was sixteen; but what did it
signify? 'Amelia is so warmly attached to them.'

'It's a settled thing then?'

'We do hope so. It cannot be said to be quite
settled because there are always money difficulties.
Poor Mr. Matterson must have some increase to his
income before he can afford it.'

'Ah! yes.'

'You did say something, uncle, about five hundred
pounds,' said Amelia.

'Four hundred and fifty, my dear,' said Mr. Grey.

'Oh, I had forgotten. I did say that I hoped there
would be five hundred.'

'There shall be five hundred,' said Mr. Grey,
remembering that now had come the time for doing
to one of the Carroll family the good things of which

he had thought to himself. 'As Mr. Matterson is a clergyman of whom I have heard nothing but good, it shall be five hundred.' He had in truth heard nothing either good or bad respecting Mr. Matterson.

Then he asked Amelia to take a walk with him as he went home, reflecting that now had come the time in which a little wholesome conversation might have its effect. And an idea entered his head that in his old age an acquaintance with a neighbouring clergyman might be salutary to himself. So Amelia got her bonnet and walked home with him.

'Is he an eloquent preacher, my dear?' But Amelia had never heard him preach. 'I suppose there will be plenty for you to do in your new home.'

'I don't mean to be put upon, if you mean that, uncle.'

'But five children!'

'There is a servant who looks after them. Of course I shall have to see to Mr. Matterson's own things, but I have told him that I cannot slave for them all. The three eldest have to be sent somewhere; that has been agreed upon. He has got an unmarried sister who can quite afford to do as much as that.' Then she explained her reasons for the marriage. 'Papa is getting to be quite unbearable, and Sophy spoils him in everything.'

Poor Mr. Grey, when his niece turned and went back home, thought that, as far as the girl was concerned, or her future household, there would be very little room for employment for him. Mr. Matterson wanted an upper servant who, instead of demanding wages, would bring a little money with her, and he could not but feel that the poor clergyman would find that he had taken into his house a bad and expensive upper servant.

'Never mind, papa,' said Dolly, 'we will go on and persevere, and, if we intend to do good, good will certainly come of it.'

Chapter LXIII

THE LAST OF AUGUSTUS SCARBOROUGH

WHEN old Mr. Scarborough was dead, and had been for a while buried, Augustus made his application in form to Messrs. Grey and Barry. He had made it through his own attorney, and had now received Mr. Barry's answer, through the same attorney. The nature of the application had been in this wise: That Mr. Augustus Scarborough had been put into the position of the eldest son; that he did not himself in the least doubt that such was his true position; that close enquiry had been made at the time, and that the lawyers, including Mr. Grey and Mr. Barry, had assented to the statements as then made by old Mr. Scarborough; that he himself had then gone to work to pay his brother's debts, for the honour of the family, and had paid them, partly out of his own immediate pocket, and partly out of the estate, which was the same as his own property; that during his brother's 'abeyance' he had assisted in his maintenance, and, on his brother's return, had taken him to his own home; that then his father had died, and that this incredible new story had been told. Mr. Augustus Scarborough was in no way desirous of animadverting on his father's memory, but was forced to repeat his belief that he was his father's eldest son; and was, in fact, at that moment the legitimate owner of Tretton, in accordance with the existing contract. He did not wish to dispute his father's will, though his father's mental and bodily condition, at the time of the making of the will, might, perhaps, enable him to do so with success. The will might be allowed to pass as valid, but the rights of primogeniture must be held sacred.

Nevertheless, having his mother's memory in great honour, he felt himself ill-inclined to drag the family history before the public. For his mother's sake he was open to a compromise. He would advise that the whole property,—that which would pass under the entail, and that which was intended to be left by will,—should be valued, and that the total should then be divided between them. If his brother chose to take the family mansion, it should be so. Augustus Scarborough had no desire to set himself over his brother. But if this offer were not accepted, he must at once go to law, and prove that their Nice marriage had been, in fact, the one marriage by which his father and mother had been joined together. There was another proviso added to this offer: as the valuation and division of the property must take time, an income at the rate of two hundred pounds a month should be allowed to Augustus till such time as it should be completed. Such was the offer which Augustus had authorised his attorney to make.

There was some delay in getting Mountjoy to consent to a reply. Before the offer had reached Mr. Barry, he was already at Monte Carlo, with that ready money his father had left behind him. At every venture that he made,—at least at every loss which he incurred,—he told himself that it was altogether the doing of Florence Mountjoy. But he returned to England, and consented to a reply. He was the eldest son, and meant to support that position, both on his mother's behalf and on his own. As to his father's will, made in his favour, he felt sure that his brother would not have the hardihood to dispute it. A man's bodily sufferings were no impediment to his making a will; of mental incapacity he had never heard his father accused till the accusation had now been made by his own son. He was, however, well aware that it would not be preferred. As to what his brother had done for himself, it was hardly worth his while to answer such an allegation. His memory carried him but little further back than the day on which his brother turned him out of his rooms.

There were, however, many reasons,—and this was put in at the suggestion of Mr. Barry,—why he would not wish that his brother should be left penniless. If his brother would be willing to withdraw altogether from any law-suit, and would lend his cooperation to a speedy arrangement of the family matters, a thousand a year, or twenty-five thousand pounds, should be made over to him, as a younger brother's portion. To this offer it would be necessary that a speedy reply should be given, and, under such circumstances, no temporary income need be supplied.

It was early in June when Augustus was sitting in his luxurious lodgings in Victoria Street, contemplating this reply. His own lawyer had advised him to accept the offer, but he had declared to himself a dozen times since his father's death, that in this matter of the property he would either make a spoon or spoil a horn.* And the lawyer was no friend of his own,—was a man who knew nothing of the facts of the case beyond what were told him, and nothing of the working of his client's mind. Augustus had looked to him only for the law in the matter, and the lawyer had declared the law to be against his client. 'All that your father said about the Nice marriage will go for nothing. It will be shown that he had an object.'

'But there certainly was such a marriage.'

'No doubt there was some ceremony,—performed with an object. A second marriage cannot invalidate the first, though it may itself be altogether invalidated. The Rummelsburg marriage is, and will be, an established fact, and of the Rummelsburg marriage your brother was no doubt the issue. Accept the offer of an income. Of course we can come to terms as to the amount; and from your brother's character it is probable enough that he may increase it.' Such had been his lawyer's advice, and Augustus was sitting there in his lodging thinking of it.

He was not a happy man as he sat there. In the

first place he owed a little money, and the debt had come upon him chiefly from his lavish expenditure in maintaining Mountjoy and Mountjoy's servant upon their travels. At that time he had thought that by lavish expenditure he might make Tretton certainly his own. He had not known his brother's character, and had thought that by such means he could keep him down,—with his head well under water. His brother might drink,—take to drinking regularly at Monte Carlo or some such place,—and might so die. Or he would surely gamble himself into further and utter ruin. At any rate he would be well out of the way, and Augustus in his pride had been glad to feel that he had his brother well under his thumb. Then the debt had been paid,—with the object of saving the estate from litigation on the part of the creditors. That had been his one great mistake. And he had not known his father,—or his father's guile, or his father's strength. Why had not his father died at once? as all the world had assured him would be the case. Looking back, he could remember that the idea of paying the creditors had at first come from his father,—simply as a vague idea! Oh, what a crafty rascal his father had been! And then he had allowed himself, in his pride, to insult his father, and had spoken of his father's coming death as a thing that was desirable! From that moment his father had plotted his ruin. He could see it all now.

He was still minded to make the spoon; but he found,—he found that he should spoil the horn. Had there been anyone to assist him he would still have persevered. He thought that he could have persevered with a lawyer who would really have taken up his case with interest. If Mountjoy could be made to drink,—so as to die! He was still next in the entail; and he was his brother's heir should his brother die without a will. But so he would be if he took the twenty-five thousand pounds. But to accept so poor a modicum would go frightfully against the grain with him. He seemed to think that by taking the allowance he would bring back his brother to all the long-lived decencies of life. He would have to surrender altogether that feeling of conscious superiority which had been so much to him. 'D—— the fellow!' he exclaimed to himself. 'I should not wonder if he were in that fellow's pay.' The first 'fellow' here was the lawyer, and the second was his brother.

When he had sat there alone for half an hour he could not make up his mind. When all his debts were paid he would not have much above twenty-five thousand pounds. His father had absolutely extracted five thousand pounds from him towards paying his brother's debts! The money had been wanted immediately. Together with the sum coming from the new purchasers, father and son must each subscribe five thousand pounds to pay those Jews. So it had been represented to him, and he had borrowed the money to carry out his object. Had ever anyone been so swindled, so cruelly treated? This might probably be explained, and the five thousand pounds might be added to the twenty-five thousand pounds. But the explanation would be necessary, and all his pride would rebel against it. On that night when by chance he had come across his brother, bleeding and still half drunk as he was about to enter his lodging, how completely under his thumb he had been! And now he was offering him of his bounty this wretched pittance! Then with half-muttered curses he execrated the names of his father, his brother, of Grey, and of Barry, and of his own lawyer.

At that moment the door was opened, and his bosom friend, Septimus Jones, entered the room. At any rate this friend was the nearest he had to his bosom. He was a man without friends in the true sense. There was no one who knew the innermost wishes of his heart, the secret desires of his soul.

There are thus so many who can divulge to none those secret wishes! And how can such a one have a friend who can advise him as to what he shall do? Scarcely can the honest man have such a friend, because it is so difficult for him to find a man who will believe in him! Augustus had no desire for such a friend, but he did desire someone who would do his bidding as though he were such a friend. He wanted a friend who would listen to his words, and act as though they were the truth. Mr. Septimus Jones was the man he had chosen, but he did not in the least believe in Mr. Septimus Jones himself. 'What does that man say?' asked Septimus Jones. The man was the lawyer, of whom Augustus was now thinking, at this very moment, all manner of evil.

'D—— him!' said Augustus.

'With all my heart. But what does he say? As you are to pay him for what he says, it is worth while listening to it.'

There was a tone in the voice of Septimus Jones which declared at once some diminution of his usual respect. So it sounded, at least, to Augustus. He was no longer the assured heir of Tretton, and in this way he was to be told of the failure of his golden hopes. It would be odd, he thought, if he could not still hold his dominion over Septimus Jones. 'I am not at all sure that I shall listen to him or to you either.'

'As for that, you can do as you like.'

'Of course I can do as I like.' Then he remembered that he must still use the man as a messenger, if in no other capacity. 'Of course he wants to compromise it. A lawyer always proposes a compromise. He cannot be beat that way, and it is safe for him.'

'You had agreed to that.'

'But what are the terms to be? That is the question. I made my offer: half and half. Nothing fairer can be imagined,—unless, indeed, I choose to stand out for the whole property.'

'But what does your brother say?'

He could not use his friend even as a messenger without telling him something of the truth. 'When I think of it, of this injustice, I can hardly hold myself. He proposes to give me twenty-five thousand pounds.'

'Twenty-five thousand pounds! For everything?'

'Everything; yes. What the devil do you suppose I mean? Now just listen to me.' Then he told his tale as he thought that it ought to be told. He recapitulated all the money he had spent on his brother's behalf, and all that he chose to say that he had spent. He painted in glowing colours the position in which he would have been put by the Nice marriage. He was both angry and pathetic about the creditors. And he tore his hair almost with vexation at the treatment to which he was subjected.

'I think I'd take the twenty-five thousand pounds,' said Jones.

'Never. I'd rather starve first.'

'That's about what you'll have to do if all that you tell me is true.' There was again that tone of disappearing subjection. 'I'll be shot if I wouldn't take the money.' Then there was a pause. 'Couldn't you do that and go to law with him afterwards? That was what your father would have done.' Yes. But Augustus had to acknowledge that he was not as clever as his father.

At last he gave Jones a commission. Jones was to see his brother and explain to him that before any question could be raised as to the amount to be paid under the compromise, a sum of ten thousand pounds must be handed to Augustus, to reimburse him for money out of pocket. Then Jones was to say, as out of his own head, that he thought that Augustus might probably accept fifty thousand pounds, in lieu of twenty-five thousand pounds. That would still leave the bulk of the property to Mountjoy, although Mountjoy must be aware of the great difficulties which would be thrown in his way by his father's conduct. But Jones had to come back the next day with an intimation that Mountjoy had again gone abroad, leaving full authority with Mr. Barry.

Jones was sent to Mr. Barry, but without effect. Mr. Barry would discuss the matter with the lawyer, or, if Augustus was so pleased, with himself; but he was sure that no good would be done by any conversation with Mr. Jones. A month went on. Two months went by; and nothing came of it. 'It is no use your coming here, Mr. Scarborough,' at last Mr. Barry said to him with but scant courtesy. 'We are perfectly sure of our ground. There is not a penny due to you,—not a penny. If you will sign certain documents, which I would advise you to do in the presence of your own lawyer, there will be twenty-five thousand pounds for you. You must excuse me if I say that I cannot see you again on the subject,— unless you accept your brother's liberality.'

At this time Augustus was very short of money, and, as is always the case, those to whom he owed aught became pressing as his readiness to pay them gradually receded. But to be so spoken to by a lawyer,—he, Scarborough of Tretton as he had all but been,—to be so addressed by a man whom he had regarded as old Grey's clerk, was bitter indeed. He had been so exalted by that Nice marriage, had been so lifted high in the world, that he was now absolutely prostrate. He quarrelled with his lawyer, and he quarrelled also with Septimus Jones. There was no one with whom he could discuss the matter, or rather no one who would discuss it with him on his terms. So, at last, he accepted the money, and went daily into the city, in order that he might turn it into more. What became of him in the city it is hardly the province of this chronicle to tell.

Chapter LXIV

THE LAST OF FLORENCE MOUNTJOY

NOW at last in this chapter has to be told the fate of Florence Mountjoy,—as far as it can be told in these volumes. It was, at any rate, her peculiarity to attach to herself, by bonds which could not easily be severed, those who had once thought that they might be able to win her love. An attempt has been made to show how firm and determined were the affections of Harry Annesley, and how absolutely he trusted in her word when once it had been given to him. He had seemed to think that, when she had even nodded to him in answer to his assertion that he desired her to be his wife, all his trouble as regarded her heart had been off his mind. There might be infinite trouble as to time,—as to ten years, three years, or even one year; trouble in inducing her to promise that she would become his wife in opposition to her mother; but he had felt sure that she never would be the wife of anyone else. How he had at last succeeded in mitigating the opposition of her mother, so as to make the three years, or even the one year, appear to himself an altogether impossible delay, the reader knows. How he at last contrived to have his own way altogether, so that, as Florence told him, she was merely a ball in his hand, the reader will have to know very shortly. But not a shade of doubt had ever clouded Harry's mind as to his eventual success, since she had nodded to him at Mrs. Armitage's ball. Though this girl's love had been so grand a thing to have achieved, he was quite sure from that moment that it would be his for ever.

With Mountjoy Scarborough there had never come such a moment,—and never could; yet he had been very confident, so that he had lived on the assurance that such a moment would come. And the self-deportment natural to her had been such that he had shown his assurance. He never would have succeeded; but he should not the less love her sincerely. And when the time came for him to think what he should do with himself, those few days after his father's death, he turned to her as his one prospect of salvation. If his cousin Florence would be good to him, all might yet be well. He had come by that time to lose his assurance. He had recognised Harry Annesley as his enemy,—as has been told often enough in these pages. Harry was to him a hateful stumbling-block. And he had not been quite as sure of her fidelity to another as Harry had been sure of it to himself. Tretton might prevail. Trettons do so often prevail. And the girl's mother was all on his side. So he had gone to Cheltenham, true as the needle to the pole, to try his luck yet once again. He had gone to Cheltenham,—and there he found Harry Annesley. All hopes for him were then over, and he started at once for Monaco; or, as he himself told himself,—for the devil.

Among the lovers of Florence some memory may attach itself to poor Hugh Anderson. He too had been absolutely true to Florence. From the hour in which he had first conceived the idea that she would make him happy as his wife, it had gone on growing upon him with all the weight of love. He did not quite understand why he should have loved her so dearly,—but thus it was. Such a Mrs. Hugh Anderson, with a pair of horses on the boulevards, was to his imagination the most lovely sight which could be painted. Then Florence took the mode of disabusing him which has been told, and Hugh Anderson gave the required promise. Alas;—in what an unfortunate moment had he done so! Such was his own thought. For though he was sure of his own attachment to her, he could not mount high enough to be as sure of hers to somebody else. It was a 'sort of thing a man oughtn't to have been asked to promise,' he said to the third secretary. And having so determined he made up his mind to follow her to England and to try his fortune once again.

Florence had just wished Harry good-bye for the day,—or rather for the week. She cared nothing now, in the way of protestations of affection. 'Come, Harry;—there now;—don't be so unreasonable. Am not I just as impatient as you are? This day fortnight you will be back. And then!'

'Then there will be some peace; won't there? But mind you write every day.' And so Harry was whisked away, as triumphant a man as ever left Cheltenham by the London train. On the following morning Hugh Anderson reached Cheltenham and appeared in Montpellier Place.

'My daughter is at home certainly,' said Mrs. Mountjoy. There was something in the tone which made the young man at once assure himself that he had better go back to Brussels. He had even been a favourite with Mrs. Mountjoy. In his days of love-making poor Mountjoy had been absent, declared no longer to have a chance of Tretton, and Harry had been—the very evil one himself. Mrs. Mountjoy had been assured by the Brussels Mountjoys that with the view of getting well rid of the evil one, she had better take poor Anderson to her bosom. She had opened her bosom accordingly,—but with very poor results. And now he had come to look after what result there might be. Mrs. Mountjoy felt that he had better go back to Brussels.

'Could I not see her?' asked Anderson.

'Well, yes; you could see her.'

'Mrs. Mountjoy, I'll tell you everything,—just as though you were my own mother. I have loved your daughter,—oh, I don't know how it is! If she'd be my wife for two years, I don't think I'd mind dying afterwards.'

'Oh, Mr. Anderson!'

'I wouldn't. I never heard of a case where a girl had got such a hold of a man as she has of me.'

'You don't mean to say that she has behaved badly.'

'Oh, no! She couldn't behave badly. It isn't in her. But she can bowl a fellow over in the most— well, most desperate manner. As for me, I'm not worth my salt since I first saw her. When I go to ride with the governor I haven't a word to say to him.' But this ended in Mrs. Mountjoy going and promising that she would send Florence down in her place. She knew that it would be in vain; but to a young man who had behaved so well as Mr. Anderson so much could not be refused. 'Here I am again,' he said, very much like Punch in the pantomime.*

'Oh, Mr. Anderson! how do you do?'

A lover who is anxious to prevail with a lady should always hold up his head. Where is the writer of novels, or of human nature, who does not know as much as that? And yet the man who is in love, truly in love, never does hold up his head very high. It is the man who is not in love who does so. Nevertheless it does sometimes happen that the true lover obtains his reward. In this case it was not observed to be so. But now Mr. Anderson was sure of his fate, so that there was no encouragement to him to make any attempt at holding up his head. 'I have come once more to see you,' he said.

'I am sure it gives mamma so much pleasure.'

'Mrs. Mountjoy is very kind. But it hasn't been for her. The truth is I couldn't settle down in this world without having another interview.'

'What am I to say, Mr. Anderson?'

'I'll just tell you how it all is. You know what my prospects are.' She did not quite remember but she bowed to him. 'You must know because I told you. There is nothing I kept concealed.' Again she bowed. 'There can be no possible family reason for my going to Kamtschatka.'

'Kamtschatka!'

'Yes, indeed. The F. O.——' The F. O. always meant the Foreign Office. 'The F. O. wants a young man on whom it can thoroughly depend to go to Kamtschatka. The allowances are handsome enough, but the allowances are nothing to me.'

'Why should you go?'

'It is for you to decide. Yes, you can detain me. If I go to that bleak and barren desert it will merely be to court exile from that quarter of the globe in which you and I would have to live together and not separate. That I cannot stand. In Kamtschatka—— Well, there is no knowing what may happen to me then.'

'But I'm engaged to be married to Mr. Annesley.'

'You told me something of that before.'

'But it's all fixed. Mamma will tell you. It's to be this day fortnight. If you'd only stay and come as one of my friends.' Surely such a proposition as this is the unkindest that any young lady can make. But we believe that it is made not unfrequently. In the present case it received no reply.

Mr. Anderson took up his hat and rushed to the door. Then he returned for a moment. 'God bless you, Miss Mountjoy,' he said. 'In spite of the cruelty of that suggestion I must bid God bless you.' And then he was gone.

About a week afterwards, M. Grascour appeared upon the scene with precisely the same intention. He, too, retained in his memory a most vivid recollection of the young lady and her charms. He had heard that Captain Scarborough had inherited Tretton, and had been informed that it was not probable that Miss Florence Mountjoy would marry her cousin. He was somewhat confused in his ideas, and thought that, were he now to reappear on the scene, there might still be a chance for him. There was no lover more unlike Mr. Anderson than M. Grascour. Not even for Florence Mountjoy, not even to own her, would he go to Kamtschatka; and were he not to see her he would simply go back to Brussels. And yet he loved her as well as he knew how to love any-one, and, would she have become his wife, would have treated her admirably. He had looked at it all round, and could see no reason why he should not marry her. Like a persevering man, he persevered; but as he did so no glimmering of an idea of Kamtschatka disturbed him.

But from this further trouble Mrs. Mountjoy was able to save her daughter. M. Grascour made his way into Mrs. Mountjoy's presence, and there declared his purpose. He had been sent over on some question connected with the literature of commerce, and had ventured to take the opportunity of coming down to Cheltenham. He hoped that the truth of his affection would be evinced by the journey. Mrs. Mountjoy had observed, while he was making his little speech, how extremely well brushed was his hat. She had observed, also, that poor Mr. Ander-son's hat was in such a condition as almost to make her try to smooth it down for him. 'If you make objection to my hat, you should brush it yourself,' she had heard Harry say to Florence, and Florence had taken the hat, and had brushed it with fond linger-ing touches.

'M. Grascour, I can assure you that she is really engaged,' Mrs. Mountjoy had said. M. Grascour bowed and sighed. 'She is to be married this day week.'

'Indeed!'

'To Mr. Harry Annesley.'

'Oh—h—h! I remember the gentleman's name. I had thought——'

'Well, yes; there were objections, but they have luckily disappeared.' Though Mrs. Mountjoy was only as yet happy in a melancholy manner, rejoicing with but bated joy at her girl's joys, she was too loyal to say a word now against Harry Annesley.

'I should not have troubled you, but——'

'I am sure of that, M. Grascour; and we are both of us grateful to you for your good opinion. I know very well how high is the honour which you are doing Florence; and she will quite understand it. But you see the thing is fixed; it's only a week.' Florence was said, at the moment, to be not at home, though she was upstairs, looking at four dozen new pocket-handkerchiefs which had just come from the pocket-handkerchief merchant, with the letters F. A. upon them. She had much more pleasure in looking at them than she would have had in listening to the congratulations of M. Grascour.

'He's a very good man, no doubt, mamma; a deal better, perhaps, than Harry.' That, however, was not her true opinion. 'But one can't marry all the good men.'

There was almost more trouble taken down at Buston about Harry's marriage than his sister's, though Harry was to be married at Cheltenham; and only his father, and one of his sisters as a brides-maid, were to go down to assist upon the occasion. His father was to marry them. And his mother had at last consented to postpone the joy of seeing Florence till she was brought home from her travels, a bride three months old. Nevertheless, a great fuss was made, especially at Buston Hall. Mr. Prosper had become comparatively light in heart since the duty of providing a wife for Buston and a future mother for Buston heirs had been taken off his shoulders and thrown upon those of his nephew. The more he looked back upon the days of his own courtship the more did his own deliverance appear to him to be almost the work of Heaven. Where would he have been had Miss Thoroughbung made good her footing in Buston Hall? He used to shut his eyes and gently raise his left hand towards the skies as he told himself that this evil thing had passed by him. But it had passed by, and it was expected that there should be a lunch of some sort at Buston, and as, with all his diligent inquiry, he had heard nothing but good of Florence, she should be received with as hearty a welcome as he could give her. There was one point which troubled him more than all others. He was determined to refurnish the drawing-room and also the bedroom in which Florence was destined to sleep. He told his sister in his most solemn manner that he had at last made up his mind thoroughly. The thing should be done. She understood how great a thing it was for him to do. 'The two centre rooms!' he said with an almost tragic air. Then he sent for her the next day and told her that, on further consideration he had determined to add in the dressing-room.

The whole parish felt the effect. It was not so much that the parish was struck by the expenditure proposed, because the squire was known to be a man who had not for years spent all his income, but that he had given way so far on behalf of a nephew whom he had lately been so anxious to disinherit. Rumour had already reached Buntingford of what the squire had intended to do on the receipt of his own wife,— rumours which had of course since faded away into nothing. It had been positively notified to Buntingford that there should be really a new carpet and new curtains in the drawing-room. Miss Thorough-bung had been known to have declared at the brewery that the whole thing should be done before she had been there twelve months.

'He shall go the whole hog,' she had said. And there had been a little bet about it between her and her brother, who entertained an idea that Mr. Prosper was an obstinate man. And Joe had brought tidings of the bet to the parsonage,—so that there had been much commotion on the subject. When the best room had been included, and then the dressing-room, even Matthew had been alarmed. 'It'll come to as much as five hundred pounds!' he had whispered to

Mrs. Annesley. Matthew seemed to think that it was quite time that there should be somebody to control his master. 'Why, ma'am, it's only the other day, because I can remember it myself, when that loo-table came into the house new!' Matthew had been in the place over twenty years. When Mrs. Annesley reminded him that fashions were changed, and that other kinds of table were required, he only shook his head.

But there was a question more vital than that of expense. How was the new furniture to be chosen? The first idea was that Florence should be invited to spend a week at her future home, and go up and down to London with either Mrs. Annesley or her brother, and select the furniture herself. But there were reasons against this. Mr. Prosper would like to surprise her by the munificence of what he did. And the suggestion of one day was sure to wane before the stronger lights of the next. Mr. Prosper, though he intended to be munificent, was still a little afraid that it should be thrown away as a thing of course,— or that it should appear to have been Harry's work. That would be manifestly unjust. 'I think I had better do it myself,' he said to his sister.

'Perhaps I could help you, Peter.' He shuddered; but it was at the memory of the sound of the word 'Peter,' as it had been blurted out for his express annoyance by Miss Thoroughbung. 'I wouldn't mind going up to London with you.' He shook his head, demanding still more time for deliberation. Were he to accept his sister's offer he would be bound by his acceptance. 'It's the last drawing-room carpet I shall ever buy,' he said to himself, with true melancholy, as he walked back home across the park.

Then there had been the other grand question of the journey or not down to Cheltenham. In a good-natured way Harry had told him that the wedding would be no wedding without his presence. That had moved him considerably. It was very desirable that the wedding should be more than a merely legal wedding. The world ought to be made aware that the heir to Buston had been married in the presence of the squire of Buston. But the journey was a tremendous difficulty. If he could have gone from Buston direct to Cheltenham it would have been comparatively easy. But he must pass through London, and to do this must travel the whole way between the Northern and Western railway-stations. And the trains would not fit. He studied his Bradshaw* for an entire morning, and found that they would not fit. 'Where am I to spend the hour and a quarter?' he asked his sister mournfully. 'And there would be four journeys, going and coming;—four separate journeys!' And these would be irrespective of numerous carriages and cabs. It was absolutely impossible that he should be present in the flesh on that happy day at Cheltenham. He was left at home for three months, July, August, and September, in which to buy the furniture,—which, however, was at last procured by Mr. Annesley.

The marriage, as far as the wedding was concerned, was not nearly as good fun as that of Joe and Molly. There was no Mr. Crabtree there, and no Miss Thoroughbung. And Mrs. Mountjoy, though she meant to do it all as well as it could be done, was still joyous only with bated joy. Some tinge of melancholy still clung to her. She had for so many years thought of her nephew as the husband destined for her girl, that she could not be as yet demonstrative in her appreciation of Harry Annesley. 'I have no doubt we shall come to be true friends, Mr. Annesley,' she had said to him.

'Don't call me Mr. Annesley.'

'No, I won't, when you come back again and I am used to you. But at present there—there is a something.'

'A regret, perhaps.'

'Well, not quite a regret. I am an old-fashioned

person and I can't change my manners all at once.
You know what it was that I used to hope.'

'Oh yes! But Florence was very stupid and would
have a different opinion.'

'Of course I am happy now. Her happiness is all
the world to me. And things have undergone a
change.'

'That's true. Mr. Prosper has made over the
marrying business to me, and I mean to go through
it like a man. Only you must call me Harry.' This
she promised to do, and did in the seclusion of her
room give him a kiss. But still her joy was not loud,
and the hilarity of her guests was moderated. Mrs.
Armitage did her best, and the bridesmaids' dresses
were pretty,—which is all that is required of a brides-
maid. Then, at last, the father's carriage came, and
they were carried away to Gloucester, where they
were committed to the untender, commonplace, but
much more comfortable mercies of the railway-
carriage. There we will part with them, and encounter them again but for a few moments as after a
long day's ramble they made their way back to a solitary but comfortable hotel among the Bernese Alps.
Florence was on a pony, which Harry had insisted
on hiring for her, though Florence had declared
herself able to walk the whole way. It had been
very hot, and she was probably glad of the pony.
They had both alpenstocks* in their hands, and on
the pommel of her saddle hung the light jacket with
which he had started, and which had not been so
light but that he had been glad to ease himself of the
weight. The guide was lagging behind, and they
two were close together. 'Well, old girl!' he said,
'and now what do you think of it all?'

'I'm not so very much older than I was when
you took me, pet.'

'Oh, yes, you are. Half of your life has gone;
you have settled down into the cares and duties of
married life, none of which had been so much as

thought of when I took you.'

'Not thought of! They have been on my mind ever since that night at Mrs. Armitage's.'

'Only in a romantic and therefore untrue sort of manner. Since that time you have always thought of me with a white choker and dress boots.'

'Don't flatter yourself; I never looked at your boots.'

'You knew that they were the boots and the clothes of a man making love, didn't you? I don't care personally very much about my own boots. I never shall care about another pair. But I should care about them. Anything that might give me the slightest assistance!'

'Nothing was wanted; it had all been done, Harry.'

'My pet! But still a pair of highlows heavy with nails would not have been efficacious then. I should think I love him, you might have said to yourself, but he is such an awkward fellow.'

'It had gone much beyond that at Mrs. Armitage's'.

'But now you have to take my highlows* as part of your duty.'

'And you?'

'When a man loves a woman he falls in love with everything belonging to her. You don't wear highlows. Everything you possess as specially your own has to administer to my sense of love and beauty.'

'I wish, I wish it might be so.'

'There is no danger about that at all. But I have to come before you on an occasion such as this as a kind of navvy.* And you must accept me.' She glanced around furtively to see whether their guide was looking, but the guide had gone back out of sight. For, sitting on her pony, she had her arm around his neck and kissed him. 'And then there is ever so much more,' he continued. 'I don't think I snore.'

'Indeed, no! There isn't a sound comes from you. I sometimes look to see if I think you are alive.'

'But if I do, you'll have to put up with it. That would be one of your duties as a wife. You never could have thought of that when I had those dress boots on.'

'Of course I didn't. How can you talk such rubbish?'

'I don't know whether it is rubbish. Those are the kind of things that must fall upon a woman so heavily. Suppose I were to beat you.'

'Beat me!'

'Yes,—hit you over the head with this stick?'

'I am sure you would not do that.'

'So am I. But suppose I were to. Your mother used to tell of my leaving that poor man bloody and speechless. What if I were to carry out my usual habits as then shown. Take care, my darling, or that brute'll throw you.' This he said as the pony stumbled over a stone.

'Almost as unlikely as you are. One has to risk dangers in the world, but one makes the risk as little as possible. I know they won't give me a pony that will tumble down. And I know that I've told you to look to see that they don't. You chose the pony, but I had to choose you. I don't know very much about ponies, but I do know something about a lover;—and I know that I have got one that will suit me.'

EXPLANATORY NOTES

1 *Albany*: a building off Piccadilly originally designed for the Duke of York and converted into bachelor apartments in 1804.

2 *delf-works*: a factory for the making of delf, originally a kind of glazed earthenware made at Delf, or Delft, in Holland and imported into England, where it was later imitated.

entail: the settlement on a landed estate of a fixed rule of descent, so that no single possessor has the right to bequeath it.

cornet: the officer who carried the colours in a troop of cavalry.

3 *post-obits*: abbreviated form of the latin *post obitum*, after decease, and short for '*post obit* bonds', which were given as security for a sum of money to be paid on the death of a named person.

9 *Amalekites*: an ancient tribe mentioned frequently in the Old Testament as enemies of the Israelites.

11 *quidnuncs*: inquisitive people.

14 *Machiavellian*: Niccolò Machiavelli, in his work *Del Principe*, advocated expediency in statecraft.

16 *Apollo*: sun-god of the Greeks and Romans.

22 *Charterhouse*: an English public school.

26 *Junior United Service Club*: junior branch of the United Service Club, founded in 1815 by army officers as the General Military Club and renamed in 1816 when it was joined by the Navy Club. The building in Charles Street was the first clubhouse to be built in London.

30 *Scotland Yard*: in 1829 Peel's Metropolitan Police Act set up a commissioner of police with headquarters at Scotland Yard.

Lincoln's Inn: one of the Inns of Court, where Trollope's father, a Chancery barrister, had chambers.

33 *God tempers the wind to the shorn lamb*: Laurence Sterne, *Sentimental Journey* (1768; Penguin edition, 1967, p. 139).

37 *see into a millstone*: wonderfully sharp-sighted.

39 *Temple*: two of the Inns of Court, the Inner and Middle Temple, stand on the site once occupied by the Templars, an ancient military and religious order devoted to the protection of the Holy Sepulchre.

44 *story of Esau and of Jacob*: Esau was tricked out of his father's blessing by his younger brother, Jacob, at the instigation of their mother, Rebekah. See Genesis 27.

47 *policeman in plain clothes*: the CID was established in 1842.

49 *Land League*: an association of Irish tenant farmers, which called itself 'The Irish National Land League', organized by Charles Stewart Parnell in 1879 and suppressed by the Government in 1881. Its aims were the reduction of rents and ultimately the removal of the landlord system.

54 *Hyperion's curls . . . to threaten and command*: Hamlet, III. iv. 56–7.

61 *Kamschatka*: Kamchatka, a large peninsula in the east of the USSR.

66 *mechanics*: manual labourers, with the secondary meaning of 'lower orders'.

67 *see how a Christian could die?*: see Edward Young, *Conjectures on Original Composition* (1759, p. 102). Joseph Addison's dying words to his stepson, Lord Warwick, were: 'See in what peace a Christian can die.'

75 *fly*: a light, one-horse carriage, usually for hire.

79 *a hole in his own coat*: a moral weakness (current slang).

88 *minister plenipotentiary*: a minister below the level of ambassador, but invested with full representative power.

89 *English residents at Brussels*: Trollope had firsthand experience of the English in Brussels, having spent six weeks there as a classics teacher at an English school in the summer of 1834.

93 *gambling-house at Monte Carlo*: the casino opened in 1861. Roulette and *trente-et-quarante* were the chief games played.

 rouge et noir: a French card-game. Its name comes from the colours marked on the layout. Its other name, *trente-et-quarante*, derives from the fact that the winning point always lies between these numbers.

94 *pieces*: the term popularly applied to English gold sovereigns.

 napoleons: gold twenty-franc pieces issued by Napoleon I.

 Madame Blanc: the wife of the first proprietor of the casino at Monte Carlo, François Blanc of Homburg.

 Che va piano va sano: 'who goes softly goes safely'.

95 *music-room*: the casino had a magnificent theatre and was renowned for its concerts.

Philharmonic: the Philharmonic Society (now the Royal Philharmonic Society) founded in 1813 for professional musicians, although membership has always been open to the public. The concert programmes regularly included two symphonies, two overtures, and a concerto.

St James's Hall: situated in Regent Street and possessing excellent acoustics, it was London's principal concert hall and the home of the famous 'Popular Concerts' until 1898.

96 *linkboy*: a boy employed to carry a link, or torch to light people along the street.

'*all that mortal remains*': more usually, 'the remains'.

97 *august sovereign*: Charles III of Monaco, who granted a charter permitting a company to build the casino. In 1866, five years after it was opened, the prince declared the district around it to be Monte Carlo.

99 *chained Chance to his chariot-wheel*: see Ralph Waldo Emerson, *Essays, First Series: Self-Reliance* (Dent, 1924, p. 56). Emerson advises the reader to refrain from gambling with Fortune, and continues: 'In the Will work and acquire, and thou hast chained the wheel of Chance, and shall always drag her after thee.'

104 *Montpellier Place*: although Trollope knew Cheltenham well, this address is fictitious.

105 *like Patience . . . smiling at grief*: *Twelfth Night*, II. iv. 113–14.

112 *Paragon*: see note to p. 104.

127 *Secretary of Legation*: chief administrator in the suite of a diplomatic minister.

free-trader: a political economist who supported the free trade movement, which developed from concern about import duties into a coherent philosophy of commercial liberalism, and included such figures as Cobden, Bright, Peel, and Gladstone.

129 *up to the time of day*: the most fashionable way of doing something (current slang).

Styria: a province of SE Austria, which became a duchy in the 17th and 18th centuries (German: Steiermark).

130 *spilikins*: 'a game played with a heap of slips or small rods of wood, bone, or the like, the object being to pull off each by means of a hook without disturbing the rest' (*OED*).

backgammon: a game for two played on a board with counters.

cotillon: cotillion, a late 18th- and 19th-century French court dance which was also popular in England.

Gother School: so far as I am aware, this school is fictitious.

131 *Bird of Paradise*: these birds, which occur in the New Guinea highlands and nearby islands, are noted for their brilliant plumage.

146 '*whips and scorns*': *Hamlet*, III. i. 70.

149 *slouch hat*: a hat or bonnet which droops, partly concealing the face.

150 *Speaker*: the member chosen by the House of Commons to preside over its debates.

153 '*Stare super vias antiquas*': 'to stand in the old-established ways'. See Jeremiah 6: 16.

161 *comforter*: a long woollen scarf.

drag: a private coach with seating like a stage-coach, usually drawn by four horses.

162 *tooling his own drag*: driving his own coach (current slang).

168 *depart, and shake the dust from your feet*: Matthew 10: 14: 'When ye depart out of that house or city, shake off the dust of your feet.'

174 "*Fidus Achates*": 'Faithful Achates', Virgil, *Aeneid*, VI. 158. Achates was the loyal companion of the wanderer, Aeneas.

202 *School Board*: Forster's Education Act of 1870 introduced free elementary education in schools provided by the state and administered by school boards.

208 *Greek Iambics*: Greek verse.

213 *Even such a man . . . in the dead of night*: 2 *Henry IV*, I. i. 70.

214 *Priam*: the last king of Troy. According to Homer, he had many sons and daughters.

227 *Blow, winds . . . and hurricanes!*: *King Lear*, III. ii. 1–2.

257 *Peerage*: Burke's *Peerage and Baronetage* was first published in 1826.

260 *windage*: allowance made for deflection caused by the wind, particularly in shooting.

262 '*caput mortuum*': 'dead head', or worthless residue.

264 '*Res Venatica*': 'pursuit of hunting'.

268 *Homer's pathos and Homer's imagination*: Trollope is referring to the great single combat between Achilles and Hector, the Greek and Trojan champions, in Homer's *Iliad*, XXII. 250–366.

271 '*Tantæne animis cœlestibus iræ?*': 'Is there such wrath in heavenly minds?', Virgil, *Aeneid*, I. 11.

272 *veni, vidi, vici*: 'I came, I saw, I conquered.' Seneca, *Suasoriae*, ii. 19. Julius Caesar is recorded as having said this when he defeated Pharnaces at Zela, in Pontus, a kingdom of Asia Minor.

275 *sons like Priam*: see note to p. 214.

278 *The Old Gentleman*: the Devil.

280 *Radical abomination*: radicalism had opposed the Lords, the electoral system, and the landed interest, and because it also sought the disestablishment of the Church, was regarded by many as a godless movement.

322 '*preux chevalier sans peur et sans reproche*': 'gallant knight without fear and without reproach', a description of the 16th-century Chevalier Bayard.

338 *rhino*: money (current slang).

358 *nobody can live upon bread alone*: Matthew 4: 4: 'Man shall not live by bread alone, but by every word that proceedeth out of the mouth of God.' See also Deuteronomy 8: 3.

397 *poor Peri . . . Paradises?*: see Thomas Moore, 'Paradise and the Peri', in *Lalla Rookh* (1817, p. 87): 'One morn a Peri at the gate / Of Eden stood, disconsolate.'

402 *écarté*: a card-game for two people invariably played for a stake.

dummy: a game played with an imaginary player, whose 'hand' is managed by one of the participants.

403 *Elysium*: the paradise in Greek mythology to which were sent heroes on whom the gods conferred immortality.

Army List: official list of all the commissioned officers of the army.

405 *Apollinaris*: a mineral water produced at Apollinarisburg near Bonn in Germany.

411 *pomatum*: an ointment made with the pulp of apples, used on the hair with powder as a cosmetic aid.

440 *like Sir Proteus, ungartered*: see *Two Gentlemen of Verona*, II. i. 65.

`demonstrated a careless desolation`: see *As You like It*, III. ii. 373–4.

470 *Monument*: a Doric column designed by Sir Christopher Wren and built in the City of London to commemorate the Great Fire of 1666.

476 *He is a burr*: see *Measure for Measure*, I. iii. 189.

482 *entire beer*: a term applied from about 1722 to a dark-brown malt liquor.

490 *Queen of Heaven . . . Jove*: Jupiter, or Jove, was the supreme god of the Roman pantheon and protector of the city and state. His consort, Juno, became the goddess and symbol of the Roman matron.

511 *History of the Rebellion*: Edward Hyde, Earl of Clarendon, published *The History of the Rebellion and Civil Wars in England* in 1702–4. Trollope may have had in mind B. Bandinel's seven-volume edition of 1849.

Hallelujah: the poet George Wither published this devotional work in 1641. Trollope may have been familiar with the Library of Old Authors edition of 1856, or the more recent 1879 edition.

523 *Rummelsburg*: now in Poland and renamed Miastko.

Nice was in Italy then: Nice and Savoy were annexed by Napoleon III in 1860.

532 *"Nil conscire sibi"*: 'to have a crime on one's conscience', Horace, *Epistles*, I. i. 61.

545 *non compos*: more fully *non compos mentis*: 'not of sound mind'.

565 *laches*: negligence in performing a legal obligation.

in articulo mortis: 'at the point of death'.

576 *London beggars*: begging was still a problem in London in the late 1870s. Vagrants came into the city for charity during the winter and were concentrated in the fashionable West End.

596 *brought on the tapis*: brought on to the tablecloth: i.e. under discussion.

611 *make a spoon or spoil a horn*: either succeed or fail. The phrase first appears in Scott's *Rob Roy*.

620 *like Punch in the pantomime*: Punchinello, the grotesque principal character in the puppet-show, Punch and Judy; also a living performer.

626 *Bradshaw*: George Bradshaw's *Railway Guide* first appeared in 1839.

627 *alpenstocks*: long staffs tipped with iron, first used in climbing the Alps, but now in general use in mountain-climbing.

628 *highlows*: laced boots reaching up over the ankle.

navvy: abbreviated form of navigator; a labourer employed in the construction of various kinds of earthworks.